— THE COMPLETE —

WESTERN STORIES

STORIES

★ ★ ★ OF ★ ★ ★

ELMORE

LEONARD

Also by Elmore Leonard

Mr. Paradise

When the Women Come Out to Dance

Tishomingo Blues

Pagan Babies

Be Cool

The Tonto Woman & Other Western Stories

Cuba Libre

Out of Sight

Riding the Rap

Pronto

Rum Punch

Maximum Bob

Get Shorty

Killshot

Freaky Deaky

Touch

Bandits

Glitz

LaBrava

Stick

Cat Chaser

Split Images

City Primeval

Gold Coast

Gunsights

The Switch

The Hunted

Unknown Man No. 89

Swag

Fifty-two Pickup

Mr. Majestyk

Forty Lashes Less One

Valdez Is Coming

The Moonshine War

The Big Bounce

Hombre

Last Stand at Saber River

Escape from Five Shadows

The Law at Randado

The Bounty Hunters

WILLIAM MORROW

An Imprint of HarperCollins*Publishers*

THE COMPLETE
WESTERN
STORIES
OF
ELMORE
LEONARD

Grateful acknowledgment is made to the following:

Saturday Evening Post covers © SEPS: Licensed by Curtis Publishing Co., Indianapolis, IN. All rights reserved. www.curtispublishing.com

The covers from *Argosy, Dime Western, Fifteen Western Tales, Ten Story Western,* and *Western Story* magazines and their distinctive logos and respective composite cover designs are trademarks and are reproduced here with permission: TM and copyright © 2004 Argosy Communications, Inc. All Rights Reserved.

FIRST EDITION

Designed by Betty Lew

Map designed by Jane S. Kim

Collection Editor, Gregg Sutter

Printed on acid-free paper

Library of Congress Cataloging-in-Publication Data

Leonard, Elmore, 1925–
    The complete Western stories of Elmore Leonard.—1st ed.
        p.   cm.
    ISBN 0-06-072425-0 (alk. paper)
      1. Western stories.   I. Title.

PS3562.E55A6 2004
    813'.54—dc22   2004055969

04 05 06 07 08 WBC/RRD 10 9 8 7 6 5 4 3 2 1

★ CONTENTS ★

Map   *ix*

A Conversation with Elmore Leonard   *xi*

1   Trail of the Apache   *1*

2   Apache Medicine   *37*

3   You Never See Apaches . . .   *51*

4   Red Hell Hits Canyon Diablo   *67*

5   The Colonel's Lady   *89*

6   Law of the Hunted Ones   *103*

7   Cavalry Boots   *135*

8   Under the Friar's Ledge   *149*

9   The Rustlers   *163*

10   Three-Ten to Yuma   *179*

11   The Big Hunt   *195*

12   Long Night   *209*

13   The Boy Who Smiled   *223*

14   The Hard Way   *237*

15   The Last Shot   *249*

16   Blood Money   *263*

17   Trouble at Rindo's Station   *279*

18   Saint with a Six-Gun   *309*

19   The Captives   *323*

20   No Man's Guns   *357*

21   The Rancher's Lady   *371*

22   Jugged   *385*

23   Moment of Vengeance   *399*

24   Man with the Iron Arm   *415*

25   The Longest Day of His Life   *431*

26   The Nagual   *459*

27   The Kid   *473*

28   Only Good Ones   *489*

29   The Tonto Woman   *503*

30   "Hurrah for Captain Early!"   *517*

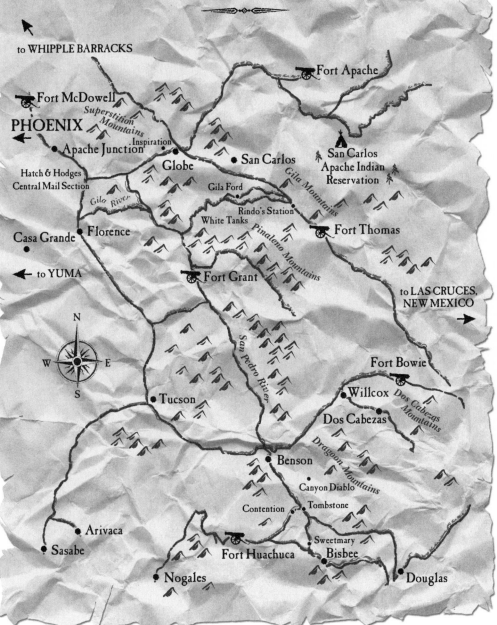

ARIZONA TERRITORY 1880s

to WHIPPLE BARRACKS

Fort Apache

Fort McDowell

PHOENIX

Superstition Mountains

Apache Junction · Inspiration

Hatch & Hodges Central Mail Section

Globe

San Carlos

San Carlos Apache Indian Reservation

Gila Mountains

Gila River

Gila Ford

Rindo's Station

White Tanks

Pinaleno Mountains

Fort Thomas

Casa Grande · Florence

to YUMA

Fort Grant

to LAS CRUCES, NEW MEXICO

N
W E
S

San Pedro River

Fort Bowie

Willcox

Dos Cabezas

Dos Cabezas Mountains

Tucson

Benson

Dragoon Mountains

Canyon Diablo

Contention · Tombstone

Arivaca

Sasabe

Sweetmary

Fort Huachuca · Bisbee

Nogales

Douglas

★ A CONVERSATION ★ WITH ELMORE LEONARD

ELMORE JOHN LEONARD, Jr., started his life of writing in the fifth grade, when as a student at Blessed Sacrament Grade School in Detroit, he was inspired by a *Detroit Times* serialization of *All Quiet on the Western Front,* wrote a play, and staged it at school, the classroom desks serving as no man's land. He did not write again until his college years at the University of Detroit, where he majored in English. He wrote a few experimental short stories while spending most of his free time reading and going to the movies. "I was discovering who I liked to read," he said. "I wasn't reading for story, I was reading for style."

Sometime shortly after college Elmore decided he wanted to be a writer. "I looked for a genre where I could learn how to write and be selling at the same time," he recalls. "I chose Westerns because I liked Western movies. From the time I was a kid I liked them. Movies like *The Plainsman* with Gary Cooper in 1936 up through *My Darling Clementine* and *Red River* in the late forties."

There was a surge of interest in Western stories in the early fifties, Elmore notes, "from *Saturday Evening Post* and *Colliers* down through *Argosy, Adventure, Blue Book,* and probably at least a dozen pulp magazines, the better ones like *Dime Western* and *Zane Grey Magazine* paying two cents a word."

His first attempt at writing a Western was not a success. "I wrote about a gunsmith that made a certain kind of gun. I have no idea now what the story was about when I sent it to a pulp magazine and it was rejected. I decided I'd better do some research. I read *On the Border with Crook, The Truth about Geronimo, The Look of the West,* and *Western Words,* and I subscribed to *Arizona Highways.* It had stories about guns—I insisted on authentic guns in my stories—stagecoach lines, specific looks at different little facets of the West, plus all the four-color shots that I could use for my descriptions, things I could put in and sound like I knew what I was talking about."

He distilled all this valuable detail into a ledger book, which became a constant reference for his story writing throughout the decade.

Properly armed with a sense of the West, he wrote his first Western, *Tizwin,* the Apache name for corn beer. It didn't sell immediately. "The editor at *Argosy* passed it on to one of their pulp magazines at Popular Publications," Elmore remembers, "and they bought it." And changed the title to "Red Hell Hits Canyon Diablo." "The *Argosy* editor said, 'If you have anything else about this period, we'd like to read it.' So I sat down and wrote 'Trail of the Apache,' which was the first one that was published."

A growing family and a full-time job as a copywriter on the Chevrolet account at Campbell-Ewald Advertising in Detroit did not give Elmore a lot of time to write.

"I realized that I was going to have to get up at five in the morning if I wanted to write fiction. It took a while, the alarm would go off and I'd roll over. Finally I started to get up and go into the living room and sit at the coffee table with a yellow pad and try to write two pages. I made a rule that I had to get something down on paper before I could put the water on for the coffee. *Know where you're going and then put the water on.* That seemed to work because I did it for most of the fifties."

He'd also get a little writing done at the agency. "I'd put my arm in the drawer and have the tablet in there and I'd just start writing and if somebody came in I'd stop writing and close the drawer."

Elmore began to focus on a particular area of the West for his stories. "I liked Arizona and New Mexico," he said. "I didn't care that much for the High Plains Indians, I liked the Apaches because of their reputation as raiders and the way they dressed, with a headband and high moccasins up to their knees. I also liked their involvement with things Mexican and their use of Spanish names and words."

The Complete Western Stories begins with Elmore's first five shorts: Apache and cavalry stories set in Arizona in the 1870s and '80s.

"I was disappointed by rejections from the better-paying magazines, *The Saturday Evening Post* and *Colliers*," Elmore says. "They felt my stories were too relentless and lacked lighter moments or comic relief. But I continued to write what pleased me while trying to improve my style."

The next direction for Elmore's writing was obvious: write a Western novel. The result was *The Bounty Hunters* (1953), the prototype for many an Elmore Leonard Western. Take the most dangerous Apache, the wisest scout, and the greediest outlaw, put them all together in the desert sun, and see who wins.

As he spun out novels and short stories from five to seven in the morning, Hollywood came calling and bought a *Dime Western* story, "Three-Ten to Yuma," and from *Argosy*, "The Captives," filmed as *The Tall T*. Elmore was excited but in both cases "saw how easily Hollywood could screw up a simple story." Both films, released in 1957, are now regarded as minor classics.

Elmore reached his goal as a Western writer in April of 1956, when *The Saturday Evening Post* published his story "Moment of Vengeance."

In less than five years he had entered the pantheon of Western writers. But the Western was on its way out. "Television killed the Western," Elmore says. "The pulps were mostly gone by then too, the market was drying up."

In 1960, Elmore took his profit sharing from Campbell-Ewald—$11,500—with the intention of becoming a full-time writer. He had put his ten years in. "The money would have lasted six months, and in that time I could write a book and sell it." Instead, the family bought a house and he wrote freelance advertising copy and educational films to pay the bills until the movie version of his novel *Hombre* was bought by a studio in 1966, and he finally had the money to write his first non-Western novel, *The Big Bounce*.

But he wasn't through with the Westerns by any means. He had yet to write what many consider to be his masterpiece.

Just before his five-year fiction-writing hiatus, in 1961, he wrote a story for *Roundup*, a Western Writers of America anthology, called "Only Good Ones," the story of Bob Valdez, soon to be the classic

Elmore Leonard hero who is misjudged by the antagonist, "the bad guys realizing too late they'll be lucky to get out of this alive."

Six years later, in search of an idea for a novel he could sell to the movies, Elmore picked up "Only Good Ones" and, in seven weeks, expanded it into *Valdez Is Coming* (1970) which was brought to the big screen with Burt Lancaster three years later.

"Look what I got away with," Elmore says. "In the final scene of *Valdez* there is no shootout, not even in the film version. Writing this one I found that I could loosen up, concentrate on bringing the characters to life with recognizable traits, and ignore some of the conventions found in most Western stories."

The Complete Western Stories of Elmore Leonard charts the evolution of Elmore's style and particular sound from the very beginning of his writing career. In five years, between 1951 and 1956, he wrote twenty-seven of the thirty stories in this volume. He carved out his turf in the Arizona and New Mexico Territories, from Bisbee to Contention, from Yuma Territorial Prison to the Jicarilla Apache Subagency in Puerco, creating dozens of memorable characters: good, bad, and really bad. (Those are the ones we like the most.)

Elmore Leonard wrote a total of eight Western novels before, during, and after his *Complete Western Stories*; he even wrote a few Western stories contained herein, after he began writing contemporary crime novels ("The Tonto Woman" and " 'Hurrah for Captain Early!' ").

Over time, the suffocating heat and alkali dust of the Arizona desert gave way to the mean streets of Detroit and the subtropical weirdness of South Florida. But Elmore will be the first to tell you, they're all derived from what he learned writing *these* Western stories; he just changed the setting and the century.

—GREGG SUTTER, LOS ANGELES, 2004

Thanks to Joel Lyczak for providing the original magazine covers gracing the endpapers of this volume. Also for supplying and hunting down copies of missing stories.

— THE COMPLETE —

WESTERN STORIES

OF

★ ★ ★ ★ ★ ★

ELMORE LEONARD

1

Trail of the Apache

Original title: Apache Agent
Argosy, December 1951

UNDER THE THATCHED roof ramada that ran the length of the agency office, Travisin slouched in a canvas-backed chair, his boots propped against one of the support posts. His gaze took in the sun-beaten, gray adobe buildings, all one-story structures, that rimmed the vacant quadrangle. It was a glaring, depressing scene of sun on rock, without a single shade tree or graceful feature to redeem the squat ugliness. There was not a living soul in sight. Earlier that morning, his White Mountain Apache charges had received their two-weeks' supply of beef and flour. By now they were milling about the cook fires in front of their wickiups, eating up a two-weeks' ration in two days. Most of the Indians had built their wickiups three miles farther up the Gila, where the flat, dry land began to buckle into rock-strewn hills. There the thin, sparse Gila cottonwoods grew taller and closer together and the mesquite and prickly pear thicker. And there was the small game that sustained them when their government rations were consumed.

At the agency, Travisin lived alone. By actual count there were forty-two Coyotero Apache scouts along with the interpreter, Barney Fry, and his wife, a Tonto woman, but as the officers at Fort Thomas looked at it, he was living alone. There is no question that to most young Eastern gentlemen on frontier station, such an alien means of existence would have meant nothing more than a very slow way to die, with boredom reading the services. But, of course, they were not Travisin.

✯ ✯ ✯

FROM WHIPPLE BARRACKS, through San Carlos and on down to Fort Huachuca, it went without argument that Eric Travisin was the best Apache campaigner in Arizona Territory. There was a time, of course, when this belief was not shared by all and the question would pop up often, along the trail, in the barracks at Fort Thomas, or in a Globe barroom. Barney Fry's name would always come up then—though most discounted him for his one-quarter Apache blood. But that was a time in the past when Eric Travisin was still new; before the sweltering sand-rock Apache country had burned and gouged his features, leaving his gaunt face deep-chiseled and expressionless. That was while he was learning that it took an Apache to catch an Apache. So, for all practical purposes, he became one. Barney Fry taught him everything he knew about the Apache; then he began teaching Fry. He relied on no one entirely, not even Fry. He followed his own judgment, a judgment that his fellow officers looked upon as pure animal instinct. And perhaps they were right. But Travisin understood the steps necessary to survival in an enemy element. They weren't included in Cook's "Cavalry Tactics": you learned them the hard way, and your being alive testified that you had learned well. They said Travisin was more of an Apache than the Apaches themselves. They said he was cold-blooded, sometimes cruel. And they were uneasy in his presence; he had discarded his cotillion demeanor the first year at Fort Thomas, and in its place was the quiet, pulsing fury of an Apache war dance.

This was easy enough for the inquisitive to understand. But there was another side to Eric Travisin.

For three years he had been acting as agent at the Camp Gila subagency, charged with the health and welfare of over two hundred White Mountain Apaches. And in three years he had transformed nomadic hostiles into peaceful agriculturalists. He was a dismounted cavalry officer who sometimes laid it on with the flat of his saber, but he was completely honest. He understood them and took their side, and they respected him for it. It was better than San Carlos.

That's why the conversation at the officers' mess at Fort Thomas, thirty miles southwest, so often dwelled on him: he was a good Samaritan with a Spencer in his hand. They just didn't understand him. They didn't realize that actually he was following the line of least resistance. He was accepting the situation as it was and doing the best job with the means at hand. To Travisin it was that simple; and fortunately he enjoyed it, both the fighting and the pacifying. The fact that it made him a better cavalryman never entered his mind. He had forgotten about promotions. By this time he was too much a part of the savage everyday existence of Apache country. He looked at the harsh, rugged surroundings and liked what he saw.

He shuffled his feet up and down the porch pole and sank deeper into his camp chair. Suddenly in his breast he felt the tenseness. His ears seemed to tingle and strain against an unnatural stillness, and immediately every muscle tightened. But as quickly as the strange feeling came over him, he relaxed. He moved his head no more than two inches, and from the corner of his eye saw the Apache crouched on hands and knees at the corner of the ramada. The Indian crept like an animal across the porch, slowly and with his back arched. A pistol and a knife were at his waist, but he carried no weapon in his hands. Travisin moved his right hand across his stomach and eased open the holster flap. Now his arms were folded across his chest, with his right hand gripping the holstered pistol. He waited until the Apache was less than six feet away before he wheeled from his chair and pushed the long-barreled revolving pistol into the astonished Apache's face.

Travisin grinned at the Apache and holstered the handgun. "Maybe someday you'll do it."

The Indian grunted angrily. With victory almost in his grasp he had failed again. Gatito, sergeant of Travisin's Apache scouts, was an old man, the best tracker in the Army, and it cut his pride deeply that he was never able to win their wager. Between the two men was an unusual bet of almost two years' standing. If at any time, while not officially occupied, the scout was able to steal up to the officer and place his knife at Travisin's back, a bottle of whiskey was his. For such a prize the Indian would gladly crawl through anything. He tried constantly, using every trick he knew, but the officer was always ready. The result was a grumbling, thirsty Indian, but an officer whose senses were razor-sharp. Travisin even practiced staying alive.

Gatito gave the report of the morning patrol and then added, almost as an afterthought, "Chiricahua come. Two miles away."

Travisin wheeled from the office doorway. "Where?"

Gatito spoke impassively. "Chiricahua come. He come with troop from Fort."

Travisin considered the Apache's words in silence, squinting through the afternoon glare toward the wooden bridge across the Gila that was the end of the trail from Thomas. They would come from that direction. "Go get Fry immediately. And turn out your boys."

Chapter Two

SECOND LIEUTENANT William de Both, West Point's newest contribution to the "Dandy 5th," had the distinct feeling that he was entering a hostile camp as he led H troop across the wooden bridge and approached Camp Gila. As he drew nearer to the agency office, the figures in front of it appeared no friendlier. Good God, were they all Indians? After guarding the sixteen hostiles the thirty miles from Fort Thomas, Lieutenant de Both had had enough of Indians for a long time. Even with the H troopers riding four sides, he couldn't help glancing nervously back to the sixteen hostiles and expecting trouble to break out at any moment. After thirty miles of this, he was hardly prepared to face the gaunt, raw-boned Travisin and his sinister-looking band of Apache scouts.

His fellow officers back at Fort Thomas had eagerly informed de Both of the character of the formidable Captain Travisin. In fact, they painted a picture of him with bold, harsh strokes, watching the young lieutenant's face intently to enjoy the mixed emotions that showed so obviously. But even with the exaggerated tales of the officers' mess, de Both could not help learning that this unusual Indian agent was still the best army officer on the frontier. Three months out of the Point, he was only too eager to serve under the best.

Leading his troop across the square, he scanned the ragged line of men in front of the office and on the ramada. All were armed, and all stared at the approaching column as if it were bringing cholera instead of sixteen unarmed Indians. He halted the column and dismounted in front of the tall, thin man in the center. The lieutenant inspected the man's faded blue chambray shirt and gray trousers, and unconsciously adjusted his own blue jacket.

"My man, would you kindly inform the captain that Lieutenant de Both is reporting? I shall present my orders to him." The lieutenant was brushing trail dust from his sleeve as he spoke.

Travisin stood with hands on hips looking at de Both. He shook his head faintly, without speaking, and began to twist one end of his dragoon mustache. Then he nodded to the foremost of the Chiricahuas and turned to Barney Fry.

"Barney, that's Pillo, isn't it?"

"Ain't nobody else," the scout said matter-of-factly. "And the skinny buck on the paint is Asesino, his son-in-law."

Travisin turned his attention to the bewildered lieutenant. "Well, mister, ordinarily I'd play games with you for a while, but under the circumstances, when you bring along company like that, we'd better get down to the business at hand without the monkeyshines. Fry, take care of our guests. Lieutenant, you come with me." He turned abruptly and entered the office.

Inside, de Both pulled out a folded sheet of paper and handed it to Travisin. The captain sat back, propped his boots on the desk and read the orders slowly. When he was through, he shook his head and silently cursed the stupidity of men trying to control a powder-keg situation two thousand miles from the likely explosion. He read the orders again to be certain that the content was as illogical as it seemed.

HEADQUARTERS, DEPARTMENT OF ARIZONA
IN THE FIELD, FORT THOMAS, ARIZONA
August 30, 1880
E. M. Travisin. Capt. 5th Cav. Reg.
Camp Gila Subagency
Camp Gila, Arizona

You are hereby directed, by order of the Department of the Interior, Bureau of Indian Affairs, to place Pillo and the remnants of his band (numbering fifteen) on the Camp Gila White Mountain reservation. The Bureau compliments you on the remarkable job you are doing and has confidence that the sixteen hostile Chiricahuas, placed in your charge, will profit by the example of their White Mountain brothers and become peaceful farmers.

The bearer, Second Lieutenant William de Both, is, as of this writing, assigned to Camp Gila as second in command. Take him under your wing, Eric; he's young, but I think he will make a good officer.

EMON COLLIER
BRIGADIER GENERAL COMMANDING

He looked up at the lieutenant, who was gazing about the bare room, taking in the table, the rolltop desk along the back wall, the rifle rack and three straight chairs. De Both looked no more than twenty-one or -two, pink-cheeked, neat, every inch a West Point gentleman. But already, after only three months on the frontier, his face was beginning to lose that expression of anticipated adventure, the young officer's dream of winning fame and promotion in the field. The thirty miles from Fort Thomas alone presented the field as something he had not bargained for. To Travisin, it wasn't a new story. He'd had younger officers serve under him before, and it always started the same way, ". . . take him under your wing . . . teach him about the Apache." It was always the old campaigner teaching the recruit what it was all about.

To Eric Travisin, at twenty-eight, only seven years out of the Point, it was bound to be amusing. The cavalry mustache made him look older, but that wasn't it. Travisin had been a veteran his first year. It was something that he'd had even before he came West. It was that something that made him stand out in any group of men. It was the strange instinct that made him wheel and draw his handgun when Gatito stole up behind him. It was a combination of many things, but not one of them did Travisin himself understand, even though they made him the youngest captain in Arizona because of it.

And now another one to watch him and not understand. He wondered how long de Both would last.

He said, "Lieutenant, do you know why you've been sent here?"

"No, sir." De Both brought himself to attention. "I do not question my orders."

Travisin was faintly amused. "I'm sure you don't, Lieutenant. I was referring to any rumors you might have heard. . . . And relax."

De Both remained at attention. "I don't make it a practice to repeat idle rumors that have no basis in fact."

Travisin felt his temper rise, but suppressed it from long practice. It wasn't the way to get things done. He circled the desk and drew a chair up behind de Both. "Here, rest your legs." He placed a firm hand on the lieutenant's shoulder and half forced him into the chair. "Mister, you and I are going to spend a lot of time together. We'll be either in this room or out on the desert with nothing to think about except what's in front of us. Conversation gets pretty thin after a while, and you might even make up things just to hear yourself talk. You're the only other Regular Army man here, so you can see it isn't going to be a parade-grounds routine. I've been here for three years now, counting White Mountain Indians and making patrols. Sometimes things get a bit hot; otherwise you just sit around and watch the desert. I probably don't look like much of an officer to you. That doesn't matter. You can keep up the spit and polish if you want, but I'd advise you to relax and play the game without keeping the rule book open all the time. . . . Now, would you mind telling me what in hell the rumors are at Thomas?"

DE BOTH WAS surprised, and disturbed. He fidgeted in his chair, trying to feel official. "Well, sir, under the circumstances . . . Of course, as I said, there is no basis for its authenticity, but the word is that Crook is being transferred back to the Department to lead an expedition to the border. They say that he will probably ask for you. So I am being assigned here to replace you when the time comes. This is, of course, only gossip that is circulating about."

"Do you believe it?"

"Sir, I don't even think about it."

Travisin said, "You mean you don't want to think about it. Sitting by yourself at a Godforsaken Indian agency with almost two hundred and fifty White Mountains living across the street. Not to mention the scouts." He paused and smiled at de Both. "I don't know, Lieutenant, you might even like it after a while."

"I accept my orders, Captain. My desires have nothing to do with my orders."

But Travisin was not listening. Long strides took him to the doorway and he leaned out with a hand against the door frame on each side.

"Fryyyyyyyyyyyy! Hey, Fryyyy!"

★   ★   ★

THE MEN OF H troop looked over to the office as they prepared to mount. Barney Fry left the sergeant and strode toward the agency office. "Come in here, Barney."

The clatter of trotting horses beat across the quadrangle as Fry stepped up on the porch and entered the office. His short strides were slightly pigeon-toed and he held his head tilted down as if he were self-conscious of his appearance. He looked to be in his early twenties, but, like Travisin, his face was a hard, bronzed mask, matured beyond his age. When he took off his gray wide-brimmed hat, thick, black hair clung close to his scalp, smeared with oily perspiration.

"What do you think, Barney?"

Fry leaned against the edge of the desk. "I think probably the same thing you do. Those 'Paches aren't goin' to stay long at Gila even if we'd give them all the beef critters in Arizona. You notice there wasn't any women in the band?"

"Yes, I noticed," Travisin answered. "They'll never learn, will they?" He looked at de Both. "You see, Lieutenant, the Bureau thinks that if they separate them from their families for a while, the hostiles will become good little Indians and make plows out of their Spencers and grow corn to eat instead of drink. What would you do if some benevolent race snatched your women and children from you and sent you to a barren rock pile over a hundred miles away? And do you know why? For something you'd been doing for the past three hundred years. For that simple but enigmatic something that makes you an Apache and not a Navajo. For that quirk of fate that makes you a tiger instead of a Persian cat. Mister, I've got over two hundred White Mountains here raising crops and eating government beef. I can assure you that they're not doing it by nature! And now they sent sixteen Chiricahuas! Sixteen men with the smell of gunpowder still strong in their nostrils and blood lust in their eyes." Travisin shook his head wearily. "And they send them here without their women."

De Both cleared his throat before speaking. "Well, frankly, Captain, I don't see what the problem is. Obviously, these hostiles have done wrong. The natural consequence would be a punishment of some sort. Why pamper them? They're not little children."

"No, they're not little children. They're Apaches," Travisin reflected. "You know, I used to know an Indian up near Fort Apache by the name of Skimitozin. He was an Arivaipa. One day he was sitting in the hut of a white friend of his, a miner, and they were eating supper together. Then, for no reason at all, Skimitozin drew his handgun and shot his friend through the head. Before they hung him he said he did it to show his Arivaipa people that they should never get too friendly with the *blancos*. The Apache has never gotten a real break from the whites. So Skimitozin wanted to make sure that his people never got to the point of expecting one, and relaxing. Mister, I'm here to kill Indians and keep Indians alive. It's a paradox—no question about that—but I gave up rationalizing a long time ago. Most Apaches have always lived a life of violence. I'm not here primarily to convert them; but by the same token I have to be fair—when they are fair to me."

De Both raised an objection. "I see nothing wrong with our treatment of the Indians. As a matter of fact, I think we've gone out of our way to treat them decently." He recited the words as if he were reading from an official text.

Fry broke in. "Go up to San Carlos and spend a week or two," he said. "Especially when the government beef contractors come around with their adjusted scales and each cow with a couple of barrels of Gila water in her. Watch how the 'Pache women try to cut each other up for a bloated cow belly." Fry spoke slowly, without excitement.

Travisin said to the lieutenant, "Fry's not talking about one or two incidents. He's talking about history. You were with Pillo all the way up from Thomas. Did you see his eyes? If you did, you saw the whole story."

★

Chapter Three

THE EARLY AFTERNOON sun blazed heavily against the adobe houses and vacant quadrangle. The air was still, still and oppressive, and seemed to be thickened by the fierce, withering rays of the Arizona sun. To the east, the purplish blur of the Pinals showed hazily through the glare.

Travisin leaned loosely against a support post under the brush ramada. His gray cotton shirt was black with sweat in places, but he seemed unmindful of the heat. His sun-darkened face was impassive, as if asleep, but his eyes were only half closed in the shadow of his hat brim, squinting against the glare in the direction from which Fry would return.

Earlier that morning, the scout and six of his Coyoteros had traveled upriver to inspect the tracts selected by Pillo and his band. The hostiles had erected their wickiups without a murmur of complaint and seemed to have fallen into the alien routines of reservation life without any trouble; but it was their silence, their impassive acceptance of this new life that bothered Travisin. For the two weeks the hostiles had been at Camp Gila, Travisin's scouts had been on the alert every minute of the day. But nothing had happened. When Fry returned, he would know more.

De Both appeared in the office door behind him. "Not back yet?"

"No. He might have stopped to chin with some of the White Mountain people. He's got a few friends there," Travisin said. "Barney's got a little Apache blood in him, you know."

De Both was openly surprised. "He has? I didn't know that!" He thought of the countless times he had voiced his contempt for the Apaches in front of Fry. He felt uncomfortable and a little embarrassed now, though Fry had never once seemed to take it as a personal affront. Travisin read the discomfort on his face. There was no sense in making it more difficult.

★　★　★

"HIS MOTHER was a half-breed," Travisin explained. "She married a miner and followed him all over the Territory while he dug holes in the ground. Barney was born somewhere up in the Tonto country on one of his dad's claims. When he was about eight or nine his ma and dad were killed by some Tontos and he was carried off and brought up in the tribe. That's where he got his nose for scouting. It's not just in his blood like some people think; he learned it, and he learned it from the best in the business. Then, when he was about fifteen, he came back to the world of the whites. About that time there was a campaign operating out of Fort Apache against the Tontos. One day a patrol came across the rancheria where Barney lived and took him back to Fort Apache. All the warriors were out and only the women and children were around. He remembered enough about the white man's life to want to go back to the Indians, but he knew too much about the Apache's life for the Army to let him go; so he's been a guide since that day. He was at Fort Thomas when I arrived there seven years ago, and he's been with me ever since I've been here at Gila."

De Both was deep in thought. "But can you trust him?" he asked. "After living with the Apaches for so long."

"Can you trust the rest of the scouts? Can you trust those rocks and mesquite clumps out yonder?" Travisin looked hard into the lieutenant's eyes. "Mister, you watch the rocks, the trees, the men around you. You watch until your eyes ache, and then you keep on watching. Because you'll always have that feeling that the minute you let down, you're done for. And if you don't have that feeling, you're in the wrong business."

A little past four, Fry and his scouts rode in. He threw off and ran toward the agency office. Travisin met him in the doorway. "They scoot, Barney?"

FRY PAUSED TO catch his breath and wiped the sweat from his face with a grimy, brown hand.

"It might be worse than that. When we got there this morning only a few of Pillo's band were around. I questioned them, but they kept trying to change the subject and get us out of there. I thought they were actin' strange, talkin' more than usual, and then it dawned on me. Gatito had spotted it right away. They'd been drinkin' tizwin. You know you got to drink a whoppin' lot of that stuff to really get drunk. I figure these boys ain't had much yet, cuz they were still too quiet. But the others were probably off at the source of supply so we rode out and tried to cut their sign. We tried every likely spot in the neighborhood until after noon, and we still couldn't find a trace of them."

Travisin considered the situation silently for a moment. "They've probably been at it since they got here. Taking their time to pick a spot we wouldn't find right away. No wonder they've been so quiet." Travisin had much to think about, for a drunken Apache will do strange things. Bloody things. He asked the scout, "What does Gatito think?"

Fry hesitated, and then said, "I don't like the way he was lickin' his lips while we were on the hunt."

Fry did not have to say more. Travisin knew him well enough to know that the scout felt Gatito could bear some extra attention. To de Both, watching the scene, it was a new experience. The captain and the quarter-breed scout talking like brothers. Saying more with eyes and gestures than with words. He looked from one to the other intently, then for the first time noticed the young Apache standing next to Travisin. A moment ago he had not been there. But there had not been a sound or a footstep!

The young brave spoke swiftly in the Apache tongue for almost a minute and then disappeared around the corner of the office. De Both could still see vividly the red calico cloth around thick, black hair, and his almost feminine features.

Fry and Travisin began to talk again, but de Both interrupted.

"What in the name of heaven was that?"

Travisin grinned at the young officer's astonishment. "I thought you knew Peaches. Forgot he hadn't been around for a while."

"Peaches!"

Travisin said, "Let's go inside."

They gathered around his table, lighted cigarettes, and Travisin went on. "I'd just as soon you didn't speak his name aloud around here. You see, that young, gentle-looking Apache has one of the toughest jobs on the reservation. He's an agency spy. Only Fry and I, and now you, know what he is. Not even any of the scouts know. The Indians suspect that someone on their side is reporting to me, but they have no idea who it is. He's got a dangerous job, but it's necessary. If trouble ever breaks out, we have to be able to nip it in the bud. Peaches is the only way for us to determine where the bud is."

"May I ask what he told you just now?"

Travisin drew hard on his cigarette before replying. "He said that he knew much, but he would be back sometime before sunup tomorrow to tell what he knew. He made one last point very emphatic. He said, 'Watch Gatito!'"

A REAR ROOM of the agency office adobe served as sleeping quarters for both of the officers. Their cots were against opposite walls, lockers at the feet, and two large pine-board wardrobes, holding uniforms and personal gear, were flush with the wall running along the heads of their bunks.

A full moon pointed its light through the window frame over de Both's bed, carpeted the plank flooring with a delicate sheen, and reached as far as the gleaming upper portion of Travisin's body, motionless on the cot. One arm was beneath the gray blanket that reached just above his waist, the other was folded across his bare chest.

A floorboard creaked somewhere near. His eyes opened at once and closed just as suddenly. Beneath the blanket his hand groped near his thigh and quietly covered the grip of his pistol. He opened his eyes slightly and glanced across the room. De Both was dead asleep. The latch on the door leading to the front office rattled faintly, and then hinges creaked as the door began to open. Travisin quietly drew his arm from beneath the blanket and leveled the pistol at the doorway. His thumb closed on the hammer and drew it back, and the click of the cocking action was a sharp, metallic sound. The opening-door motion stopped.

"Nantan, do not shoot." The words were just above a whisper.

Travisin threw the blanket from his legs, swung them to the floor and moved to the doorway without a sound. Peaches backed into the office as he approached.

"Chiricahua leave."

"How long?"

"They go maybe five mile now. Gatito go with them."

Travisin stepped back to the doorway and slammed the butt of his pistol against the wooden door. "Hey, mister, roll out!" De Both sat bolt upright. "Be ready to ride in a few minutes," Travisin said, and ran out of the office toward Barney Fry's adobe across the quadrangle.

In less than twenty minutes, thirteen riders streaked out of the quadrangle westward. Behind them, orange light was just beginning to show above the irregular outline of the Pinals. The morning was cool, but still, and the stillness held the promise of the blistering heat of the day to come.

The sun was only a little higher when Travisin and his scouts rode up to four wickiups along the bank of the Gila. Travisin halted the detail, but did not dismount. He sat motionless in the saddle, his senses alert to the quiet. He said something in Apache and one of the scouts threw off and cautiously entered the first wickiup. He reappeared in an instant, shaking his head from side to side. In the third hut, the scout remained longer than usual. When he reappeared he was dragging an unconscious Indian by the legs.

Travisin said, "That one of them, Barney?"

Fry swung down from his pony and leaned over the prostrate Indian, saying a few words in Apache to the scout still holding the Indian's legs. "He's a Chiricahua, Captain. Dead drunk. Must have been drinking for at least two days." He nodded his head toward the Apache scout. "Ningun says there's a jug inside with a little tizwin in it."

Travisin pointed to two of the scouts and then swept his arm in the direction of the fourth wickiup. They kicked their ponies to a leaping start, dashed to the hut and gave it a quick inspection. In a minute they were back.

The scouts watched Travisin intently as he studied the situation. They knew what the signs meant. They sat their ponies now with restless anticipation, fingering their carbines, checking ammunition belts, holding in the small, wiry horses that also seemed to be charged with the excitement of the moment—for there is no love lost between the Coyotero and the Chiricahua. Eric Travisin knew as well as any of them what the sign meant: sixteen drunken Apaches screaming through the countryside with blood in their eyes and a bad taste in their mouths. It was something that had to be stopped before the Indians regained their senses. Now they were loco Apaches, bloodthirsty, but a bit careless. By the next day, unless stopped, they would again be cold, patient guerrilla fighters led by the master strategist, Pillo.

FROM THE DIRECTION of the agency a scout rode into sight beating his pony to a whirlwind pace. He reined in abruptly and shouted something to Fry through the dust cloud.

"We been sleepin', Captain. He says Gatito made off with a dozen carbines and two hundred rounds of forty-fours. Must have sneaked them out sometime last night."

In Travisin, the excitement of what lay ahead was building up continually. Now it was beginning to break through his calm surface. "We're awake now, Barney. I figure they'll either streak south for the Madres right away, or contact their people up near Apache by dodging through the Basin and then heading east for the reservation. I know if I was going to hide out for a while, I'd sure want my wife along. Let's find out which it is."

★

Chapter Four

BY MIDMORNING Travisin's scouts had followed the tracks of the hostiles to an elevated stretch of pines wedged tightly among bare, rolling hills. They halted a few hundred yards from the wooded area, in the open. Before them the land, dotted with mesquite and catclaw, climbed gradually to the pine plateau; and the sun-glare made shimmering waves, hazy and filmy white, as they looked ahead to the contrasting black of the pines. A shallow arroyo cut its way down from the ridge past where the detail stood, finally ending at the banks of the Gila, twelve miles behind them. On both sides of the crusted edges of the arroyo, the unshod tracks they had been following all morning moved straight ahead.

Ningun, the Apache scout, rode up the arroyo a hundred yards, circled and returned. He mumbled only a few words to Fry, who glanced at the pine ridge again before speaking.

"He says the tracks go all the way up. Ain't no other place they could go."

"Does he think they're still up there?" Travisin asked the question without taking his eyes from the ridge.

"He didn't say, but I know he don't think so." Barney Fry pulled out a tobacco plug and bit off a generous chew, mumbling, "And I don't either." He moved the front of his open vest aside with a thumb and dropped the plug into the pocket of his shirt. "I figure it this way, Captain," he said. "They know who's followin' 'em, and they know we ain't about to get caught in a simple jackpot like that one up yonder without flushin' it out first. So they ain't goin' to waste their time settin' a trap that we won't fall right into."

"Sounds good, Barney, only there's one thing that's been troubling me," Travisin said. "Notice how clean the sign's been all the way? Not once have they tried to throw us off the track—and they've had more than one opportunity to at least make it pretty tough. No Apache, no matter if he's drunker than seven hundred dollars, is going to leave a trail that plain—that is, unless he wants to." He looked at the scout, suggesting a reply with his expression, and added, "Now why do you suppose old Pillo would want us to follow him?"

Fry pushed his hat from his forehead and passed the back of his hand across his mouth. It was plain that the captain's words gave him something to think about, but he had been riding with Travisin too long to show surprise with the officer's uncanny familiarity with what an Apache would do at a given time. He was never absolutely sure himself, but for some unexplainable reason Travisin's judgment was almost always right. And when dealing with an unknown quantity, the Apache, this judgment sometimes seemed to reach a superhuman level.

Fry was quiet, busy putting himself in Pillo's place, but de Both spoke up at once. "I take it you're suggesting that the Indians are not really drunk. But what about that unconscious Indian back at the reservation?" He asked the question as if he were purposely trying to shoot holes in the captain's theory.

"No, Lieutenant. I'm only saying what if," Travisin agreed, with a faint smile. "Could be one way or the other. I just want to impress you that we're not chasing Harvard sophomores across the Boston Common. If you ever come up against a better general than Pillo, you can be sure of one thing—he'll be another Apache."

Though he was sure of Fry's and Ningun's judgment, Travisin sent scouts ahead to flank the pine woods before taking his command through.

In another hour they were over the ridge, in the open, descending noisily over the loose gravel that was strewn down the gradual slope that led to the valley below. On level ground again, they followed the tracks to the north, up the raw, rolling valley, flat and straight from a distance; but as they traveled, the sandrock ground buckled and heaved into shallow crevices and ditches every few hundred feet. The monotony of the bleak scene was interrupted only by the grotesque outlines of giant saguaro and low, thick mesquite clumps.

Even in this comparatively open ground, de Both noticed that Travisin and all of the scouts rode half-tensed in their saddles, their eyes sweeping the area to the front and to both sides, studying every rock or shrub clump large enough to conceal a man. It was a vigilance that he himself was slowly acquiring just from noticing the others. Still he was more than willing to let the scouts do the watching. The damned stifling heat and the dazzling glare were enough for a white man to worry about. He mopped his face continually, and every once in a while pulled the white bandanna around his throat up over his nose and mouth. But that caused the heat to be even more smothering. He could feel the Apache scouts laughing at him. How could they remain so damned cool-looking in this heat! With every step of the horses, the dust rose around him and seemed to cling to his lungs until he would cough and cover his nose again with the kerchief. Ahead, but slightly to the east, he studied the jagged, blue outline of a mountain range. The Sierra Apaches. The purplish blue of the mountains and the soft blue of the cloudless sky were the only pleasant tones to redeem the ragged, wild look of the valley.

He pressed his heels into his horse's flanks and rode up abreast of Travisin. The climate and the unyielding country were grinding de Both's nerves raw; he wanted to scream at somebody, anybody.

"I sincerely hope you know where you're going, Captain."

TRAVISIN IGNORED the sarcasm. "You'll feel better after we camp this evening. First day's always the toughest." He was silent for a few minutes, his head swinging in an arc studying the signs that did not even exist to de Both, and then he added, "Those mountains up ahead are the Sierra Apaches. Lot farther than they look. Before we pass them we're going to camp at a rancher's place. His name's Solomon, a really fine old gentleman. I think you'll like him, Bill." It was the first time Travisin had used de Both's first name. The lieutenant looked at him strangely.

★   ★   ★

IT WAS CLOSE to six o'clock when they reached the road leading to Solomon's place. The road cut an arc through the brush flat and then passed through a grove of cottonwoods. From where they stood, they could see the roof of the ranch house through the clearing in the trees made by the road. The house stood a few hundred yards the other side of the cottonwoods, and just to the right of it a few acres of pines edged toward the house from the foothills of the Sierra Apaches towering to the east. Fry pointed to the wide path of trampled brush a hundred feet to the left of the road they were following.

"There's one I wouldn't care to try to figure out. Why didn't they take the road?"

Travisin was watching Ningun circle the cottonwoods and head back. "They're making it a bit *too* easy now," he replied idly.

Ningun made his report to Fry and pointed above the cottonwoods in the direction of the pines. A faint wisp of dark smoke curled skyward in a thin line. Against the glare it was hardly noticeable.

"Know what that means?" Travisin asked. He looked at no one in particular.

Fry answered, "I got an idea."

They dismounted in the cottonwoods and approached the clearing on foot. The ranch house, barn and corral behind it seemed deserted.

Travisin said, "Go take a look, Barney." Fry beckoned to four of the Apache scouts and they followed him into the clearing. They walked across the open space toward the house slowly, all abreast. They made no attempt to conceal themselves by crouching or hunching their shoulders—a natural instinct, but futile precaution with no cover in sight. They walked perfectly erect with their carbines out in front. Suddenly they all stopped and one of the scouts dropped to his hands and knees and put his ear to the earth. He arose slowly, and the others back at the cottonwoods saw them watching the pines more closely as they approached the house. Fry walked up to the log wall next to the front door and placed his ear to it. He made a motion with his right hand and three of the scouts disappeared around the corner of the house. Without hesitating, Fry approached the front door, kicked it open and darted into the dimness of the interior, the fourth Apache scout behind him. In a few moments, Fry reappeared in the doorway and waved to the rest in the cottonwoods.

He was still in the doorway when Travisin brought the others up. "Just the missus is inside" was all he said.

Travisin, with de Both behind him, walked past the scout into the dimly lit ranch house. The room was a shambles, every piece of furniture and china broken. But what checked their gaze was Mrs. Solomon lying in the middle of the floor. Her clothes had been almost entirely ripped from her body and the flesh showing was gouged and slashed with knife wounds. Her scalp had been torn from her head.

De Both stared at the dead woman with a frozen gaze. Then the revulsion of it overcame him and he half turned to escape into the fresh air outside. He checked himself, thinking then of Travisin, and turned back to the room. The captain and the scout studied the scene stoically; but beneath their impassive eyes, almost any kind of emotion could be present. He tried to show the same calm. A cavalry officer should be used to the sight of death. But this was a form of death de Both had not counted on. He wheeled abruptly and left the room.

The next step was the pines. Travisin ordered the horses put in the corral. In case of a fight, they would be better off afoot; though he was sure that Pillo was hours away by now. They threaded through the nearer, sparsely growing pines that gradually grew taller and heavier as they advanced up the almost unnoticeable grade. Soon the pines entwined with junipers and thick clumps of brush so that they could see no more than fifty feet ahead into the dimness. They were far enough into the thicket so that they could no longer see the wisp of smoke, but now a strange odor took its place. The Coyotero scouts sniffed the air and looked at Travisin.

FRY SAID, "I'LL send some of 'em ahead," and without waiting for a reply called an order to Ningun in the Apache tongue. As five of the scouts went on ahead, he said, "Let 'em do a little work for their pay," and propped his carbine against a pine. He eased his back against the same tree and looked at Travisin.

"You know, that's a funny thing back there at the cabin," Fry said, pointing his thumb over his shoulder. "That's only the second time in my life that I ever knew of a 'Pache scalpin' anybody."

"I was thinking about that myself," Travisin answered. "Then I remembered hearing once that Pillo was one of the few Apaches with Quana Parker at Adobe Walls six years ago. Don't know how Apaches got tied up with Commanches, but some Commanche dog soldier might have taught him the trick."

"Well," Fry reflected, picking up his carbine, "that's about the only trick a 'Pache might be taught."

Ningun appeared briefly through the trees ahead and waved his arm. They walked out to where he stood. Fry and Travisin listened to Ningun speak and then looked past his drooping shoulders to where he pointed. The nauseating odor was almost unbearable here. De Both tried to hold his breath as he followed the others into a small clearing. In front of him, Travisin and the scout moved apart as they reached the open ground and de Both was struck with a scene he was to remember to his dying day. He stared wide-eyed, swallowing repeatedly, until he could no longer control the saliva rising in his throat, and he turned off the path to be sick.

Fry scraped a boot along the crumbly earth and kicked sand onto the smoldering fire. The smoke rose heavy and thick for a few seconds, obscuring the grotesque form that hung motionless over the center of the small fire; and then it died out completely, revealing the half-burned body of Solomon suspended head-down from the arc of three thin juniper poles that had been stuck into the ground a few feet apart and lashed together at the tops. The old man's head hung only three feet above the smothered ashes of the fire. His head and upper portion of his body were burned beyond recognition, the black rawness creeping from this portion of his body upward to where his hands were tied tightly to his thighs; there the blackness changed to livid red blisters. All of his clothing had been burned away, but his boots still clung to his legs, squeezed to his ankles where the rawhide thongs wound about them and reached above to the arch of junipers. He was dead. But death had come slowly.

"The poor old man." The words were simple, but Travisin's voice cracked just faintly to tell more. "The poor, poor old man."

Fry looked around the clearing slowly, thinking, and then he said, "Bet he screamed for a bullet. Bet he screamed until his throat burst, and all the time they'd just be dancin' around jabbin' him with their knives and laughin'." Fry stopped and looked at the captain.

Travisin stared at old Solomon without blinking, his jaw muscles tightening and relaxing, his teeth grinding against one another. Only once in a while did Fry see him as the young man with feelings. It was a strange sight, the man fighting the boy; but always the man would win and he would go on as relentlessly as before, but with an added ruthlessness that had been sharpened by the emotional surge. Travisin never dealt in half measures. He felt sorrow for the old man cut to the bottom of his stomach, and he swore to himself a revenge, silently, though the fury of it pounded in his head.

★
Chapter Five

THEY CAMPED AT Solomon's cabin that night, after burying the man and woman, and were up before dawn, in the saddle again on the trail of Pillo. They rode more anxiously now. Caution was still there, for that was instinct with Travisin and the scouts, but every man in the small company could feel an added eagerness, a gnawing urge to hound Pillo's spoor to the end and bring about a violent revenge.

De Both sensed it in himself and saw it easily in the way the Apache scouts clutched their carbines and fingered the triggers almost nervously. He felt the tightness rise in him and felt as if he must shriek to be relieved of the tension. Then he knew that it was the quickness of action mounting within him, that charge placed in a man's breast when he has to go on to kill or be killed. He watched Travisin for a sign to follow, a way in which to react; but as before he saw only the impassive, sun-scarred mask, the almost indolent look of half-closed eyes searching the surroundings for an unfamiliar sign.

By early afternoon, the thrill of the chase was draining from Second Lieutenant William de Both. His legs ached from the long hours in the saddle, and he gazed ahead, welcoming the green valley stretching as far as the eye could see, twisting among rocky hills, looking thick and cool. Over the next rise, they forded the Salt River, shallow and motionless, just west of Cherry Creek, and continued toward the wild, rugged rock and greenery in the distance. De Both heard Fry mention that it was the southern edges of the Tonto Basin, but the name meant little to him.

Toward sundown they were well into the wildness of the Basin. For de Both, the promise of a shady relief had turned into an even more tortuous ride. Through thick, stabbing chapparal and over steep, craggy mounds of rock they made their way. The trees were there, but they offered no solace; they only urged a stronger caution. The sun was falling fast when Travisin stopped the group on the shoulder of a grassy ridge. Below them the ground fell gradually to the west, green and smooth, extending for a mile to a tangle of trees and brush that began to climb another low hill. Behind it, three or four miles in the distance, the facing sun painted a last, brilliant yellow streak across the jagged top of a mountain.

NINGUN JUMPED DOWN from his pony as the others dismounted, and stared across the grass valley for a full minute or more. Then he spoke in English, pointing to the light-streaked mountain of rock. "There you find Pillo."

Fry conversed with him in Apache for a while, shooting an occasional question at one of the other scouts, and then said to Travisin, "They all agree that's most likely where Pillo is. One of 'em says Pillo used to have a rancheria up there. Pro'bly a favorite spot of his." The scout sat down in the grass and reached for his tobacco chew.

Travisin squatted next to him, Indian fashion, and poked the ground idly with a short stick. "It's still following, Barney," he said. "He must have known that at least one of our boys would have heard of this place and remember it. He purposely picked a place we'd be sure to come to, and on top of that he made it double easy to find."

"Well, you got to admit he'll be fair hard to root out, sittin' on top of that hill. Maybe he just wanted a good advantage."

"He had advantages all along the way. Here's the key, Barney. Did he ever once try to get away?" Travisin sat back and watched the outline of the mountain in the fading light. "Now why the devil did he want to bring us here?" He spoke to himself more than to anyone else.

Fry bit off a chew, packing it into his cheek with his tongue. He mumbled, "You've had more luck figurin' the 'Paches than anyone else. You tell me."

"I can't tell you anything, Barney, but I guess one thing's sure. We're going to play Pillo's game just a little longer." He looked up over Fry's shoulder toward the group of scouts. They sat in a semicircle. All wore breechcloths, long moccasins rolled just below the knees, and red calico bands around jet-black hair. Only their different-colored shirts distinguished them. Ningun wore a blue, cast-off army shirt. A leather belt studded with cartridges crossed it over one shoulder. Travisin beckoned to him. "Hey, Ningun. *Aquí!*"

The Apache squatted next to them silently as Travisin began to draw a map in a bare portion of ground with his stick. "Here's where we are and here's that mountain yonder." He indicated, drawing a circle in the earth. "Now you two get together and tell me what's up there and what's in between." He handed the stick to Fry. "And talk fast; it's getting dark."

Not more than an hour later the sun was well behind the western rim of the Basin. The plan had been laid. Travisin and Ningun gave their revolving pistols a last inspection and strode off casually into the darkness of the valley. It struck de Both that they might have been going for an after-dinner stroll.

They kept to the shadows of the trees and rocks as much as possible, Travisin a few steps behind the Apache, who would never walk more than twenty paces without stopping for what seemed like minutes. And then they would go on after the silence settled and began to sing in their ears. Travisin muttered under his breath at the full moon that splashed its soft light on open areas they had to cross. Ningun would walk slowly to the thinnest reaches of the shadows and then dart across the strips of moonlight. For a few seconds he would be only a dark blur in the moonlight and then would disappear into the next shadow. Travisin was never more than ten paces behind him. Soon they were out of the valley ascending the pine-dotted hill. The sand was soft and loose underfoot, muffling their footsteps, but they went on slowly, making sure of each step. In the silence, a dislodged stone would be like a trumpet blast.

On the crest of the hill, Travisin looked back across the valley. The shadowy bulk of the ridge they had left earlier showed in the moonlight, but there was no sign of life on the shoulder. He had not expected to see any, but there was always the young officer. It took more than one patrol to learn about survival in Apache country.

THEY MADE THEIR way down the side of the slope into a rugged country of twisting rock formations and wild clumps of desert growth. The mountain loomed much closer now, a gigantic patch of soft gray streaking down from its peak where the moonlight pressed against it. At first, they progressed much slower than before, for the irregular ground rose and fell away without warning; grotesque desert trees and scattered boulders limited their vision to never more than fifty feet ahead. Though at a slower pace, Ningun went ahead with an assurance that he knew where he was going.

Soon they reached a level, bare stretch that seemed to extend into the darkness without end. Ningun changed his direction to the right for a good five hundred yards, and then turned back toward the mountain and the bare expanse of desert leading toward it. He beckoned to Travisin and slid down the crumbly bank of an arroyo that led out into the desert. In five months it would be a rushing stream, carrying the rain that washed down from the mountain. Now it was a dark path offering a stingy protection up to the door of Pillo's stronghold.

They followed the erratic, weaving course of the arroyo until it turned sharply, as the ground began to rise, and passed out of sight around the southern base of the mountain. The top of the mountain still lay almost a mile above them—up a gradual slope at first, dotted with small trees, then to rougher ground. The last few hundred yards climbed tortuously over steep jagged rock to the mesa above.

Ningun scurried out of the arroyo and disappeared into a small clump of brush a dozen yards away. In a moment his head appeared, and Travisin followed. They crept more cautiously now from cover to cover. A low, mournful sound cut the stillness. Both stopped dead. Travisin waited for Ningun to move, but he remained stone-still for almost five minutes. No sound followed. Ningun shook his head and whispered, "Night bird."

HE LED ON, not straight up, but almost parallel with the base of the mountain, climbing gradually all the time. They had almost reached the steeper grade when the Apache pointed ahead to a black slash that cut into the mountain. Going closer, Travisin made out a narrow canyon that reached into the mountain on an upgrade. It was gouged sharply into the side of the mountain and extended crookedly down the slight grade to the desert below. Ahead, it made a bend in the darkness and was lost to sight. They climbed along the rim of the canyon for a few minutes while Travisin studied its course and depth, then they doubled back, climbing steadily up the mountain. A hundred yards further on, the Apache gave Travisin a sign and disappeared into the darkness. He waited for almost twenty minutes, toward the end beginning to wonder about the Indian, and then he looked to the side and saw Ningun approaching only a few feet away.

The Apache pressed one finger to his lips, then whispered to the captain. Travisin nodded and followed him, creeping slowly up the rocky incline above. They reached a wide ledge, Ningun leading along it to the left before climbing again over a shoulder-high hump that stretched into a long, flat piece of ground. Two hundred yards to the right, the mountain rose higher to a craggy peak, sharp and jagged. Nothing would be up there. Travisin and Ningun were on the mesa. Not far away they heard a pony sneeze.

On this part of the mesa the grass was tall. They crawled along, a foot at a time, toward the sound of the pony. The grass made a slight, stirring noise as they crawled through it, but at that height it could easily be the wind. Every few feet they would sink to their stomachs and lie flat in the grass for a matter of minutes, and then go on, extending a hand slowly to a firm portion of ground before dragging up the legs just as slowly. In this way they covered a portion of the mesa that extended to a scattered line of small boulders. The occasional snort of a pony seemed to come from less than a stone's throw away.

Travisin raised his head gradually an inch at a time until he could look between two of the rocks. From there the ground dipped slightly into a shallow pocket, descending from four sides to form a natural barricade. As he peered over the rocks, the moon passed behind a cloud and he could make out only the dying embers of a cook fire in the middle of the area. As the cloud moved on, the moon began to reappear gradually, the soft light crawling over slowly from the right, first illuminating the pony herd and then extending toward the center of the pocket. In a few seconds the entire camp area was bathed in the light. Travisin felt a weight drop through his breast as he counted sixty-three Chiricahuas.

The amazement of it held his gaze between the two rocks for a longer time than he realized. He jerked his head back quickly and looked at Ningun who had been spying the camp from a similar concealment. As he looked at Ningun he realized that the Apache understood now, just as he did, why Pillo had left such an obvious trail. But this was not the place to discuss it.

Making their way back to the outer edge of the mesa seemed to take even longer, though actually they snaked through the tall grass at a faster pace than before. They were seasoned enough to retain their calm caution, but now time was even more important, if they were to cope with Pillo. In less than two hours the sun would be present to create new problems. At the edge of the mesa Travisin, still crouched, peered cautiously to the ledge below, and then past it, determining the quickest route that would lead them to their planned rendezvous with Fry and the others.

Without speaking, he nudged Ningun and pointed a direction diagonally down the mountainside. The scout rose to his feet silently and placed himself in position to jump to the ledge below. Travisin turned his head for a last look in the direction of the hostile camp. As he did so, he heard a dull thud and an agonizing grunt escape from the scout. He wheeled, instinctively drawing his pistol, and saw Ningun go backward over the edge, an arrow shaft protruding from his chest.

✱ ✱ ✱

TRAVISIN WAS UP and hurling himself at the ledge in one motion. It happened so fast that the Apache aiming his bow on the ledge below was just a blur, but he heard the arrow whine overhead as he landed on the sprawled form of Ningun and was projected off balance toward the Apache a few feet away. The Apache hurled his bow aside with a piercing shriek and went for a knife at his waist just as Travisin brought his pistol up. In the closeness, the front sight caught in the Apache's waistband on the upward swing, and the barrel was pressing into his stomach when he pulled the trigger. The Indian screamed again and staggered back off the ledge. Travisin hesitated a second, searching the mountainside for the best escape, but it was too late. He heard the yelp at the same time he felt the heavy blow at the back of his skull. He heard the wind rush through his ears and saw the orange flash sear across his eyes, and then nothing.

✱

Chapter Six

PILLO WAITED UNTIL the officer opened his eyes and started to prop himself up on his elbows. Then he kicked Travisin in the temple with the side of his moccasined foot. The Indians howled with laughter as Travisin sprawled on his back, shook his head and attempted to rise again. Pillo caught him on the shoulder this time, but still with enough force to slam the officer back against the ground. The other Apaches closed in, a few of them catching Travisin about the head and shoulders with vicious kicks, before Pillo stepped close to Travisin and held his hands in the air. He chattered for some time in Apache, raising and lowering his voice, and at the end they all stepped back; Pillo was still chief, though wizened and scarred with age. Travisin knew enough of the tongue to know that he was being saved for something else. He thought of old Solomon.

Two of the warriors pulled him to his feet and half-dragged him to the center of the rancheria. Most of the Apaches were stripped to breechcloths, streaks of paint on their chests contrasting with the dinginess of their dirt-smudged bodies. They stood about him, silent now, their dark eyes burning with anticipation of what was to come. Asesino, Pillo's son-in-law, walked up to within a foot of the captain, stared at him momentarily and then spat full in his face. Asesino's lips were curling into laughter when Travisin punched him in the mouth and sent him sprawling at the feet of the warriors.

HE ROSE SLOWLY, reaching for his knife, but Pillo again intervened, speaking harshly to his son-in-law. Pillo was the statesman, the general, not a rowdy guerrilla leader. There would be time for blood, but now he must tell this upstart white soldier what the situation was. That it was the Apache's turn.

He began with the usual formality of explaining the Apache position, but went back farther than Cochise and Mangas Coloradas, both in his own lifetime, to list his complaints against the white man. The Apache has no traditional history to fall back on, but Pillo spoke long enough about the last ten years to compare with any plains Indian's war chant covering generations. As he spoke, the other Apaches would grumble or howl, but did not take their eyes from Travisin. The captain stared back at them insolently, his gaze going from one to the next, never dropping his eyes. But he noted more than scowling faces. He saw that though lookouts were posted on the eastern edge of the mesa, the direction from which he and Ningun had come hours before, the western side, was empty of any Apaches.

Pillo was finishing with background now, and becoming more personal. He spoke in a mixture of Spanish and English, relying on Apache when an emphatic point had to be made. He spoke of promises made and broken by the white man. He spoke of Crook, whom the Apache trusted, but who was gone now.

"Look around, white soldier, you see many *Tinneh* here, but you will not live to see the many more that will come. Soon will come Jicarillas, Tontos and many Mescaleros, and the white men will be driven to the north." As he spoke he pushed his open shirt aside and scratched his stomach.

Travisin saw the two animal teeth hanging from his neck by a leather string. It was then that the idea started to form in his mind. It was rash, something he would have laughed at in a cooler moment; but he glanced at the fire that meant torture. He looked across it and saw Gatito. There was the answer! The animal teeth and Gatito.

"Pillo speaks with large mouth, but only wind comes out," Travisin said suddenly, feeling confidence rise at the boldness of his words. "You speak of many things that will happen, but they are all lies, for before any *Tinneh* come I shall drag you and your people back to the reservation, where you will all be punished."

✶ ✶ ✶

PILLO STARTED to howl with laughter, but was cut short by Travisin. "Hold your tongue, old man! I do not speak with the wind. U-sen Himself sent me. He knows what your medicine is." Travisin paused for emphasis. "And I am that medicine!"

Pillo's lips formed laughter, but the sound was not there. The white soldier spoke of his medicine.

"All your people know that your medicine is the gray wolf who protects you, because U-sen has always made Himself known through the gray wolf to guard you from evil. I tell you, old man, if you or any warrior lays a hand on me as I leave here, you will be struck dead by U-sen's arrow, the lightning stroke. If you do not believe me, touch me!"

Pillo was unnerved. An Apache's medicine is the most important part of his existence. Not something to be tampered with. Travisin addressed Pillo again, turning toward Gatito.

"If Pillo does not believe, let him ask Gatito if I do not have power from U-sen. Ask Gatito, who was the best stalker in the Army, if he was ever able to even touch me, though he tried many times. Ask him if I am not the wolf."

The renegade scout looked at Travisin wide-eyed. He had never thought of this before, but it must be true! He remembered the dozens of times he had tried to win his bet with the captain. Each time he had been but a few feet away, when the captain had laughed and turned on him. The thought swept through his mind and was given support by his primitive superstitions and instincts. Pillo and the others watched him and they saw that he believed. Travisin saw, and exhaled slowly through clenched teeth.

He turned from Pillo and walked toward the western rim of the mesa without another word. It had to be bold or not at all. Apaches in his way fell back quickly as he walked through the circle and out of the rancheria. His strides were long but unhurried as he made his way through the tall grass, looking straight ahead of him and never once behind.

The flesh on the back of his neck tingled and he hunched his shoulders slightly as if expecting at any moment to feel the smash of a bullet or an arrow. For the hundred yards he walked with this uncertainty, the spring in him winding, tightening to catapult him forward into a driving sprint. But he paced off the yards calmly, fighting back the urge to bolt. Nearing the mesa rim his neck muscles uncoiled, and he took a deep breath of the thin air.

There on the western side, the mesa edge slanted, without an abrupt drop, into the irregular fall of the mountainside. A path stretched from the mesa diagonally down the side to be lost among rocks and small rises that twisted the path right and left down the long slope.

Travisin was only a few feet from the path when the Apache loomed in front of him coming up the trail. Though many things raced through his mind, he stopped dead only a split second before throwing himself at the Apache. They closed, chest to chest, and Travisin could smell the rankness of his body as they went over the rim and rolled down the path to land heavily against a tree stump. Travisin lost his hold on the Indian but landed on top clawing for his throat. A saber-sharp pain cut through his back and his nostrils filled with dust and sweat-smell. The Apache's face was a straining blur below him, the neck muscles stretching like steel cords. He pulled one hand from the Apache's throat, clawed up a rock the size of his fist and brought it down in the Indian's face in one sweeping motion, grinding through bone and flesh to drive the Indian's scream back down his throat.

As he rose to run down the path, the carbine shot ricocheted off the mesa rim above him. His medicine was broken.

Chapter Seven

AN HOUR BEFORE dawn Fry had finished spotting his scouts along one side of the narrow canyon that gouged into the shoulder of Pillo's mountain stronghold. One scout was a mile behind with the mounts; the others, concealed among the rocks and brush that climbed the canyon wall, were playing their favorite game. An Apache will squat behind a bush motionless all day to take just one shot at an enemy. Here was the promise of a bountiful harvest. Each man was his own troop, his own company, each knowing how to fight the Apache best, for he is an Apache.

They were to meet Travisin and Ningun there at dawn and wait. Wait and watch, under the assumption that sooner or later Pillo would lead his band down from the mountain. The logical trail was through the canyon. And the logical place for a jackpot was here where the canyon narrowed to a defile before erupting out to the base of the mountain.

De Both crouched near Fry, watching him closely, studying his easy calm, hoping that the contagion of his indifference would sweep over him and throttle the gnawing fear in his belly. But de Both was an honest man, and his fear was an honest fear. He was just young. His knees trembled not so much at the thought of the coming engagement, his first, but at the question: Would he do the right thing? What would his reaction be? He knew it would make or break him.

And then, before he could prepare himself, it had begun. Two, three, four carbine shots screamed through the canyon, up beyond their sight. At the same time, there was a blur of motion on the opposite canyon wall not a hundred yards away and the Apache came into sight. He leaped from boulder to rock down the steep wall of the canyon until he was on level ground. He gazed for a few seconds in the direction from which the shots had come, then crossed the canyon floor at a trot and started to scale the other wall from which he would have a better command of the extending defile. He stopped and crouched behind a rock not twenty feet below de Both's position. Then he turned and began to climb again.

OFTEN WHEN YOU haven't time to think, you're better off, your instinct takes over and your body follows through. De Both pressed against the boulder in front of him feeling the coolness of it on his cheek, pushing his knees tight against the ground. He heard the loose earth crumble under the Apache's moccasins as he neared the rock. He heard the Indian's hand pat against the smooth surface of it as he reached for support. And as his heart hammered in his chest the urge to run made his knees quiver and his boot moved with a spasmodic scrape. It cut the stillness like a knife dragged across an emery stone, and it shot de Both to his feet to look full into the face of the Apache.

Asesino tried to bring his carbine up, but he was too late. De Both's arms shot across the narrow rock between them and his fingers dug into the Apache's neck. Asesino fell back, pushing his carbine lengthwise against the blue jacket with a force that dragged the officer over the rock on top of him, and they writhed on the slope, their heads pointing to the canyon floor. The Indian tried to yell, but fingers, bone-white with pressure, gouged vocal cords and only a gurgling squeak passed agonized lips. His arms thrashed wildly, tore at the back of the blue jacket and a hand crawled downward to unexpectedly clutch the bone handle of the knife. Light flashed on the blade as it rose in the air and plunged into the straining blue cloth.

THERE WAS A GASP, an air-sucking moan. De Both rolled from the Apache with his eyes stretched open to see Fry's boot crush against the Indian's cheekbone. His eyes closed then and he felt the burning between his shoulder blades. He felt Fry's hands tighten at his armpits to pull him back up the slope behind the rock. The same hands tore shirt and tunic to the collar and then gently untied the grimy neckerchief to pad it against the wound.

"You ain't bad hurt, mister. You didn't leave enough strength in him to do a good job." And his heavy tobacco breath brushed against the officer's cheek and made him turn his head.

"I feel all right. But . . . what about the blood?"

"I'll fix you up later, mister. No time now. The captain's put in an appearance." He jerked a thumb over his shoulder.

Far down the canyon a lone figure ran, his arms pumping, his head thrown back, mouth sucking in air. It was a long, easy lope paced to last miles without let-up. It was the pace of a man who ran, but knew what he was doing. Death was behind, but the trail was long. As he came nearer to the scouts' positions, Fry raised slightly and gave a low, shrill whistle, then cut it off abruptly. Travisin glanced up the canyon slope without slacking his pace and passed into the shadows of the defile just as the Apaches trickled from the rocks three hundred yards up the canyon. They saw him pass into the narrowness as they swept onto the canyon floor, over fifty strong, screaming down the passage like a cloud of vampires beating from a cavern. Their yells screeched against the canyon walls and whiplashed back and forth in the narrowness.

Fry sighted down his Remington-Hepburn waiting for the hostiles to come abreast. He turned his head slightly and cut a stream of tobacco into the sand. "Captain was sure right about their sign. They was pavin' us a road clean to hell. Have to find out sometime where they all come from." He squinted down the short barrel, his finger taking in the slack on the trigger. "In about one second you can make all the noise you want." The barrel lifted slightly with the explosion and a racing Apache was knocked from his feet. A split second later, nine more carbines blasted into the canyon bottom.

Fry was on his feet after the first shot, pumping bullets into the milling mass of brown bodies as fast as he could squeeze the trigger. The hostiles had floundered at the first shot, tripping, knocking each other down in an effort to reach safety, but they didn't know where to turn. They were caught in their own kind of trap. They screamed, and danced about frantically. A few tried to rush up the slope into the mouth of the murderous fire from the scouts, but they were cut down at once. Others tried to scale the opposite wall, but the steep slope was slow going and they were picked off easily. They dashed about in a circle firing wildly at the canyon wall, wasting their ammunition on small puffs of smoke that rose above the rocks and brush clumps. And they kept dropping, one at a time. Five shots in succession, two, then one. The last bullet scream died away up-canyon. There was the beginning of silence, but almost immediately the air was pierced with a new sound. Throats shrieked again, but with a vigor, with a lust. It was not the agonized scream of the terrified Chiricahua, but the battle yell of the Coyotero scout as he hurled himself down the slope into the enemy. They had earned their army pay; now it was time for personal vengeance.

Half of the hostiles threw their arms into the air as the scouts swarmed into the open, but they came on with knives and gun stocks raised. Savage closed with savage in a grinding melee of thrashing arms and legs in thick dust, the cornered animal, made more ferocious by his fear, battling the hunter who had tasted blood. They came back with their knives dripping, their carbine stocks shattered.

IT TOOK TWO DAYS longer to return to the little subagency on the banks of the Gila, because it is slower travel with wounded men and sixteen Chiricahua hostiles whose legs are roped under the horses' bellies by day and whose hands are lashed to trees by night. Travisin led and was silent.

De Both held himself tense against the searing pain that shot up between his shoulder blades. But oddly enough, he did not really mind the ride home. He looked at the line of sixteen hostiles and felt nothing. No hate. No pity. Slowly it came upon him that it was indifference, and he moved his stained hat to a cockier angle. Boston could be a million miles away and he could be at the end of the earth, but de Both didn't particularly give a damn. He knew he was a man.

Fry chewed tobacco while his listless eyes swept the ground for sign. That's what he was paid for. It kept running through his mind that it was an awful funny thing to go out after sixteen hostiles, meet sixty and still come back with sixteen. Have to tell that one at Lon Scorey's in Globe.

Pillo rode with his chin on his bony chest. He was much older, and the throbbing hole in his thigh didn't help him, either. He was beginning to smell the greenness of decay.

On the afternoon of the fourth day they rode slowly into the quadrangle at Gila. Travisin looked about. Nothing had changed. For a moment he had expected to find something different, and he yearned for something that wasn't there. But he threw aside his longing and slumped back into his role—the role that forced him to be the best Apache campaigner in the Territory.

A cavalry mount stood in front of the agency office and a trooper appeared on the porch as Travisin, Fry and de Both dismounted and walked to the welcome shade of the ramada.

"Compliments of the commanding officer, sir. I've rode from Fort Thomas with this message."

Travisin read the note and turned with a smile to the other two. "Bill, let me tell you one thing if you don't already know it. Never try to figure out the ways of a woman—or the army. This is from Collier. He says the Bureau has decided to return Pillo and his band to his people at Fort Apache. All sixteen of 'em. Certainly is a good thing we've got sixteen to send back."

Fry said, "Yep, you might have got yourself court-martialed. Way it is, if Pillo loses that leg, you'll probably end up back as a looie."

De Both listened and the quizzical look turned to anger. He opened his mouth to speak, but thought better of it and waited until he had cooled off before muttering simply, "Idiots!"

If Travisin was the winking type, he would have looked at Fry and done so. He glanced at Fry with the hint of a smile, but with eyes that said, "Barney, I think we've got ourselves a lieutenant." Then he walked into the office. There are idiotic Bureau decisions, and there are boots that have been on too long.

And along the Gila, the war drums are silent again. But on frontier station, you don't relax. For though they are less in number, they are still Apaches.

2

Apache Medicine

Original title: Medicine
Dime Western Magazine, May 1952

KLEECAN WAS THREE hours out of Cibicu, almost halfway to the Mescalero camp at Chevelon Creek, when he met the Apache.

Ordinarily he welcomed company, for the life of a cavalry scout is lonely enough without the added routine of riding from camp to camp to count reservation heads, and that day the sky was a dismal gray-green to the north, dark and depressing. It made the semidesert surroundings stand out in vivid contrast—the alkali stretches a garish white between low, bleak hills and ghostly, dust-covered mesquite clumps. It was a composite of gray and bright white and dead green that formed a coldness, a penetrating chill that was premature for so early in September, and more than anything else, it made a man feel utterly alone.

But even with the loneliness on him, Kleecan did not welcome the company he saw on the trail ahead. For he had recognized the Apache. It was Juan Pony. And Juan had been drinking mescal.

There wasn't a man in the vicinity of San Carlos who would have blamed Kleecan for not wanting to meet an Apache under such conditions—and especially this one. Juan Pony had a reputation for meanness, and he did everything in his power to keep the reputation alive. And because he was the son of Pondichay, chief of the Chevelon Creek Mescaleros, other Apaches kept out of his way and white men had to use special handling, for Pondichay had a reputation too.

Less than two years before, he had cut a path of fire and blood from Chihuahua to the Little Colorado, and it had taken seven troops of cavalry to subdue thirty-four braves. Twenty-eight civilians and thirteen troopers had been killed during the campaign. Pondichay had lost two men. He was not to be taken lightly; yet the Bureau had merely snatched his carbine from him and given him a few sterile acres of sand along the Chevelon.

Then the Bureau gave the carbine to Kleecan and turned its back, lest Kleecan had to use it to crush the hostile's skull. Pondichay was hungry for war, and he loved his son more than anything on the Apache earth. The least excuse would send Pondichay back on the warpath. That was why men kept out of the way of Juan Pony. But Kleecan had a job to do. He dropped his left elbow to feel the bulge of the handgun under his coat as he reined in before Juan Pony, who had turned his sorrel sideways, blocking the narrow trail.

THE SCOUT could have easily gone around, for the sandy ground was flat on both sides of the trail, but Kleecan had a certain standing to think of. When a man scouts for the cavalry and keeps track of reservation Apaches, he's boss, and he never lets the Apache forget it. Juan Pony had a poor memory, but he had to be reminded with a smile—for his father was still Pondichay.

The scout nodded his head. "*Salmann,* Juan."

Juan Pony shifted his position on the saddle blanket to show full face, but he ignored the scout's greeting of *friend.* Instead, he swung an old Burnside .54 carbine in the scout's direction, aimlessly but with the hint of a threat, and mumbled some words of Mescalero through tight lips. His sharp-featured face was drawn, and his eyes bloodshot, but through his drunkenness it was plain to see what was in his soul. An Apache does not sip mescal like a gentleman. Nor does it have the same effect.

Kleecan caught one of the mumbled words and it was not complimentary. He said, "Juan, you be a good boy and go home. You go on home and I won't report you for tippin' at the mescal."

The Apache nudged the sorrel with his right heel and the horse moved forward and to the side until the naked knee of the Apache was touching the top of the scout's calf-high boot. They were close, two feet separating their faces, and the scout could smell the foulness of the Apache. Rancid body odor and the sour smell of mescal—the result of a three-day binge.

Kleecan wanted to back away, but he sat motionless, his eyes fixed on the Apache's face, his own dark and impassive in the shadow of the narrow-brimmed hat. Kleecan had been smelling mescal and tizwin on the foul breaths of Apaches for almost fifteen years, and it occurred to him that it never did get any sweeter. He noticed a gleam of saliva at the corner of Juan Pony's mouth and he unconsciously passed a knuckle along the bottom of his heavy dragoon mustache.

He said, "I'll ride along with you, Juan. I'm goin' up to Chevelon to see your daddy." Juan Pony did not answer, but continued to stare at him, his eyes tightening into slits. He leaned closer to the scout until his face and coarse, loose-hanging hair were less than a foot from the scout's. Then Juan Pony cleared his throat and spat, full into the dark face beneath the narrow brim, and with it he sneered the word *"Coche!"* with all the hate in his savage soul.

In the desolate country north of San Carlos, when a man meets a drunken Apache and the Apache spits in his face, he does one of two things: smiles, or shoots him.

KLEECAN SMILED. Because he was looking into the future. But with the smile there was a gnawing in his belly, a gnawing and a revulsion and a bitter urge rising within him that he could not stem by simply gritting his teeth. And though he was looking into the future and seeing Pondichay, fifteen years of dealing with the Apache his own way over-ruled five seconds of logic, and his hand formed a fist and he drove it into the sneering face of Juan Pony.

The Apache went backward off the sorrel, still clutching the carbine, and was out of sight the few seconds it took Kleecan's arm to rise and swing down against the rump of the sorrel. The horse bolted off to the side of the trail with the slap to reveal the Apache pushing himself up with one hand, raising the Burnside with the other. Instinct told Kleecan to draw the handgun, but the ugly, omnipotent face of Pondichay was there again and he flung himself from the saddle in one motion to land heavily on the rising form of Juan Pony. The Apache went backward, landing hard on his back, but his legs were doubled against his body and as he hit, one moccasin shot up between the scout's legs and kicked savagely.

Kleecan's fingers were at the Apache's throat, but the fingers stiffened and spread and he imagined a fire cutting through his body, pushing him away from the Indian. He was on his feet for a moment and then sickness rose from his stomach and almost gagged him so that he fell to his knees and doubled up, holding an arm close to his stomach. Juan Pony twisted his mouth into a smile in his drunkenness and raised the Burnside .54. It would tear a large hole in the white scout. He smiled and began to aim.

His cheek was against the smooth stock when he heard the explosion, and he looked up in surprise, for he was certain he had not yet fired. Then he saw the revolving pistol in the outstretched arm in front of him. Juan Pony had underestimated. It was the last thing he saw in his natural life.

It was said of Kleecan that he never let go. That after he was dead he would still take the time to get the man who had killed him, for Kleecan was not expected to die in bed. He dropped the pistol and rolled to his side with his knees almost touching his chest. The pain cut like a saber and with it was the feeling of sickness. But after a few minutes the saliva eased down from his throat and the sharp pain began to turn to a stiffness. He got to his feet slowly and took the first few steps as if he were walking over broken bottles without boots, but he looked at Juan Pony and the glance snatched him back to reality. And he looked with a grim, troubled face, for he knew what the death of the son of an Apache war chief could mean.

The sky was darker, still gray-green but darker, when Kleecan returned to his mare. He saw the storm approaching and the trouble-look seemed to lift slightly from his dark face. The rain would come and wash away the sign. But it would not wash away the urge for revenge in Pondichay, for the old chief was certain to find the body of his son, buried shallow beneath the rocks and brush off-trail. Pondichay would have no sign to explain to him how it had happened, but that would not hold his hand from its work of vengeance. A revenge on any and all that he chanced to meet. As soon as he discovered the bones of his son.

The scout had one leg up in a stirrup when he saw the small beaded deerskin bag in the road. A leather thong attached to it had been broken, and he realized he had ripped it from the Apache's throat when he had been kicked backward. He picked it up and looked the hundred-odd feet to the mesquite clump where he had buried Juan Pony. He hesitated only for a moment and then stuffed the bag into a side coat pocket. He rode off to the east, leading Juan Pony's sorrel. When he had gone almost three miles, he released the horse with a slap on the rump and set off at a gallop, still toward the east.

He pushed his mount hard, for he wanted to reach the Hatch & Hodges Station at Cottonwood Creek before the rain came. Overhead, the sky was becoming blacker.

AT A QUARTER to four Kleecan stopped at the edge of the mesa. In front of him the ground dropped gradually a thousand yards or more to the adobe stagecoach station at Cottonwood Creek. He watched a Hatch & Hodges Concord start to roll, the greasers jump to the sides, and he could faintly hear the shouts of the driver as he reined with one hand and threw gravel at the lead horses with the other. Within a hundred feet the momentum was up and the Concord streaked past the low adobe wall that ringed the station house on four sides. The yells grew fainter and the dust trail stretched and puffed and soon the coach passed from view, following a bend in the Cottonwood, and all that was left was the cylinder of dust that rolled on to the north into the approaching blackness.

Somewhere in the stillness there was the cold-throated howl of a dog coyote. It complemented the dreary blackness pressing from the north like a soul in hell's despair. Kleecan stiffened in the saddle and started to the south into a yellowness that was sun-glare and hazy reflection from the northern storm, and with it the deathlike stillness. Then his eye caught motion. It was a speck, a blur against the yellow-gray, and he knew it to be the dust raised from fast-moving horses. Probably four miles off. Three, four horses. It was hard to tell in the haze. When he reached the bottom of the grade he could no longer see

the dust, but he was sure the riders had been heading for the Hatch &
Hodges Station.

Art McLeverty, the station agent, came out of the doorway and
stood under the front ramada, scratching a massive stomach. His
stubby fingers clawed at a soiled expanse of blue-striped shirt, collar-
less, the neckband frayed, framing a lobster-red neck and above it an
even deeper red, puffy face. Kleecan called it the map of Ireland because he had heard the expression somewhere and knew McLeverty
thought of it as a compliment.

McLeverty sucked in his stomach and yelled in no particular direction, "Roberto! *¡Aquí muy pronto!*" And almost at once a small Mexican
boy was in front of the mount, taking the reins from Kleecan.

The station agent led the way through the doorway and then to the
right to the small mahogany bar that crossed one side of the narrow
room. On the opposite side of the doorway was the long plank table
and eight cane-bottomed Douglas chairs where the stage passengers
ate, and between bar and table, against the back wall, was the rolltop
desk where McLeverty kept his accounts and schedules. Bare, cold to
the eye, grimy from sand blowing through the open doorway, it was
where Kleecan went for a drink when he had the time.

He leaned on the bar and took off his hat, rubbing the back of his
hand over eyes and forehead. Thin, dark hair was smeared against the
whiteness of a receding hairline, but an inch above the eyes the face
turned tan and weather-beaten and the dragoon mustache, waxed at
the tips, accentuated a face that could look ferocious as well as kindly.
With his hat on, straight over his eyes, the brim cut a shadow of hardness over his face and Kleecan looked stern and cold. Without the hat
he looked kindly because the creases at the corners of his eyes cut a
perpetual smile in his light blue eyes. He dropped the hat back onto his
head, loosely.

"Oh, guess I'll have mescal, Art." He said it slowly, as if after deliber-
ation, though he drank mescal every time he came here.

The station agent reached for the bottle of pale liquid and set it in
front of Kleecan, then picked up a thick tumbler and passed it against
his shirt before placing it next to the bottle. McLeverty looked as if he

was memorizing a speech. He was about to say something, but Kleecan had started to talk.

"If you'd slice up a hen and drop her into the mescal when it's brewin', you'd get a little tone to it. Damn white stuff looks like water." He was pouring as he spoke. He cleared his throat and drank down half a tumblerful.

"I don't make it, I only sell it." McLeverty said it hurriedly. He was almost puffing, so anxious to tell something he knew. "Listen, Kleecan! Didn't you hear the news—no, I know you didn't. . . ." And then he blurted it out: "The paymaster got robbed and killed this morning! Indians!" He had said it. Now he relaxed.

KLEECAN HADN'T looked up. He poured another drink. "I'm not kiddin' with you, Art. You ought to watch the Mexes make it. Throw a few pieces of raw chicken in it and your mescal'll turn kind of a yellow. Makes it look like it's got some body."

"Damn it, Kleecan! I said the paymaster got robbed! The paywagon burned and the paymaster, Major Ulrich, and four of the guards shot and scalped as bald as you please. Passengers going up to Holbrook were all talking about it. They said a cavalry patrol'd stopped them on the road from Apache and told them and then asked them if they'd seen anything. And they were all scared to hell 'cause the cavalry lieutenant told them he was sure it was Juan Pony and some Mescaleros, 'cause no one's seen Juan in almost a week. Damn butchers are probably all up in the hills now."

Kleecan took another drink before looking at the Irishman. "What happened to the other two guards? They always ride at least six."

"They think they were carried away by the 'Paches. What else you think! They weren't around!"

"Art, there're only two things wrong with your story," he said. "Number one: Mescaleros don't scalp. You been out here long enough to know that. And it wouldn't be Yavapais, Maricopas, or Pimas, 'cause they've been farmin' so long their boys don't know what a scalp knife looks like—and an Arapaho hasn't been down this far in ten years.

Number two: Just a little more than three hours ago I shot Juan Pony as dead as you can get. And he was too full of mescal to have taken any paymaster."

Kleecan pushed away from the bar and did a half kneebend. "Damn Indian like to ruined me for life."

McLeverty didn't know what to say. He stood behind the bar with his mouth slightly open and watched his story break up into little pieces.

The scout couldn't help smiling. When news reaches a man in a lonely corner like the Cottonwood station, he will tell it to himself over and over, savoring it, waiting, his jaw aching to tell it to the next man that comes in from an even farther corner. He was a little bit sorry he had spoiled the news-breaking for McLeverty.

Kleecan said, "Tell you what, Art. I'll bet you five to three dollars that there weren't any Indians around and that those two missin' guards are in on the deal."

As he spoke his gaze drifted along the front wall and then stopped at the wide window. There was the flat whiteness, the darkness above it, then in the distance the dust cloud. A few moments later he made out three horsemen. His eyes narrowed from habit, years of squinting into the distance, and he judged that two of the riders could be wearing cavalry blue.

"Get the Army up this way much, Art?"

McLeverty followed the scout's gaze out the window. He squinted for a long time, then his eyes became wider as the riders drew closer, and next they were bulging, for McLeverty seldom enough got a troop of cavalry on patrol up this way—let alone two troopers and a civilian— and it was easy to see he was thinking of what Kleecan had said about the other two guards being a part of the holdup.

And Kleecan was thinking of the same thing. He had been making conversation before. Now he wasn't sure. He told himself it was just the timing that made him think that way.

McLeverty couldn't turn his eyes from the window. He just stared. Finally he said, "God, do you suppose those three—"

"Four," Kleecan said. "I'll add another dollar that there're four of them."

TWO TROOPERS and a civilian, dressed for riding, came into the room slowly and glanced around before walking over to the bar. But even in their slight hesitancy they had smiled. They stood at the bar brushing trail dust from their coats, still smiling, and talked about the coming rain and the dark sky, and they offered to buy the station agent and the scout a drink. Kleecan didn't speak because he was trying to picture the happy world these men were living in. It wasn't cynicism. It was just that men didn't ride into an out-of-the-way stage station covered with the grime of hours on horseback and then suddenly react with a brotherly-love spirit that belonged to Christmas Eve. A saddle doesn't treat a man that way.

McLeverty was pushing the bottle across the bar to the three men when the back door opened and the fourth one entered. Like the other civilian his coat was open and a pistol hung at his side. McLeverty looked at the man and then to Kleecan and in the look there was a mixture of suspicion, respect, and fear.

The fourth man saw the suspicion.

"Wanted to use your backhouse," he explained. "Afore I came in and had to go right out again," and he ended the words with a meaningless laugh.

He joined the others at the bar and stood next to Kleecan, who lounged against the bar with his back half turned to the four men. The fourth one slapped the two troopers on the shoulders and told them to pour a drink. The troopers were younger than the two civilians. Big, rawboned men, they wore their uniforms slovenly and didn't seem to care. The man who had come in the back way did most of the talking and most of the drinking.

They had been at the bar for almost fifteen minutes when the lull finally came. They had been talking continually during that time. Talking about uninteresting things in loud voices. There were a few words, then prolonged laughter, and after that silence. The four men lifted their glasses to their lips. It was a way of filling the lull while they thought of something else.

Kleecan turned his head slightly in their direction. "Hear about the paymaster gettin' held up?"

When he said it four drinks were still mouth high. There was the clatter of a shot glass hitting the bar. And the strangled coughing as a drink caught halfway down a throat, and the continued coughing as the liquor hung there and burned. But after the coughing there was silence. Kleecan wasn't paying any attention to them.

The fourth man had his coat open and his right hand was on the pistol butt at his hip. The two troopers glanced at each other and then at Kleecan, who had turned his head in their direction, but they dropped the glance to somewhere in front of them. Only the other civilian was completely composed. He hadn't moved a muscle. He was about Kleecan's age, older than the other three, and wore long dragoon mustaches similar to the scout's.

He looked at Kleecan. "No, mister. Tell us about it. Happen near here?" The man's voice was even, and carried a note of curiosity.

"Happened south of Fort Apache," Kleecan said. "That right, Art?"

McLeverty said, "That's right. The major was coming up from Fort Thomas when these—uh—Indians jumped the train and took five scalps and the pay."

"You don't say," the civilian said. "We've just come from Fort McDowell. Left yesterday and been riding ever since. That's why we haven't heard anything, I guess." He smiled, but not with nervousness.

Kleecan didn't smile. He nodded to the troopers. "You soldiers from Whipple?"

"Yes, they're both from Whipple Barracks." The civilian answered before either trooper could say anything. "You see, my partner and I are to join the survey party on the upper Chevelon, and these two gentlemen"—he pointed to the two troopers with a sweep of his arm—"are our guides."

"You could use another guide," Kleecan said. "You're fifteen miles east of Chevelon."

The civilian looked dumbfounded. He pushed his hat back from his forehead. "No! Why I thought it was due north of here!" There was surprise in his voice. "Well, it's a good thing we stopped in here," he said. "You say we have to go back fifteen miles?"

Kleecan didn't answer. He was staring at the troopers, looking at the regiment number on their collars. And as he looked he couldn't help the feeling that was coming over him. "I didn't know the Fifth was over at McDowell," he said.

The civilian shrugged his shoulders. "You know how the Army moves regiments around."

"I ought to," Kleecan said slowly. "I guide for them."

The silence was heavy in the narrow room. Heavy and oppressing, and because no one spoke the silence acted to strip naked the thoughts of the two men who stood at the bar staring into each other's eyes. The civilian knew his pretense was at an end and he shrugged his shoulders again, but looked in Kleecan's face.

Kleecan stared back at him, and all of a sudden there was a god-awful hate in him and he wanted to yell something, swear, and go for his gun—because the Fifth was at Fort Thomas, and the paywagon guards would be men of the Fifth, but they wouldn't wear their forage caps like that, not without the slant across an eye that meant Manassas and Antietam and a thousand miles of blood-red plains between the Rosebud and the Gila, and there was no survey party on the upper Chevelon for he had taken it out ten days before, and two men didn't go into Mescalero country to survey with two others who pretended to be troopers—not without equipment.

The civilian said, matter-of-factly, "What are you going to do about it?"

Kleecan stood motionless and knew he couldn't do anything about it. But he felt the hot anger drain from his face and he was glad of that, for then he wouldn't move rashly. Four to one wasn't gambling odds.

"Well, if you don't know, I'll tell you," the civilian said. "You're going to get on your horse and start guiding, and you're going to guide us over the best trail right out of Arizona, and you'll ride with that feeling that the least little move you make out of line will be your last. If we go, you go, and you don't look like a martyr to me."

THE RAIN CONTINUED to drizzle in the early dusk. They rode single file along the narrow trail that followed the bend of the lower Chevelon, and they rode in silence, each man with his own thoughts. Kleecan was soaked to the skin. One of the troopers had taken his poncho and now rode huddled, his chin bent into the folds of the collar, his body dry. When it had started to grow dark, Kleecan thought they would stop and find some kind of shelter for the night. He had even suggested it, but the outlaw leader had only laughed and said, "Travel when it's raining and there isn't any sign. You ought to know that, Indian scout. We'll keep on long as the rain lasts, even if we ride all night." That had been almost two hours before.

And it was then that the idea had been born. *Even if we ride all night.* He had had two hours to think it out clearly.

When they came to the Chevelon ford it was almost dark. Kleecan dismounted and walked to the bank of the running creek that was now almost waist deep from the continuous rain. The outlaw leader dismounted with him, but the others stayed on their horses, back under the bow of a cottonwood. From there the two men at the creek bank were only dim shadows. And that was what Kleecan was counting on. He looked at the creek and then to the outlaw and nodded his head, but as he turned to go back to his horse his foot slipped on the loose, sandy bank, throwing him off balance and hard against the outlaw. The man pushed Kleecan aside violently and drew his gun in a clean motion, but not before Kleecan's hand had found the side pocket of his coat.

"Don't do that again. We don't need you that bad."

"The darkness is makin' you spooky. I slipped on the bank."

Nothing more was said.

They made the crossing without mishap and picked up the trail again on the other side. In the darkness they made their way haltingly, brushing sharp chaparral and ducking suddenly as the blackness of a tree limb loomed in front of their faces. Kleecan rode silently and gave no warning call when an obstruction came in the trail, then smiled when he'd hear the curse from one of the outlaws whose face had been swatted by a soaked tree branch. The rain continued to drizzle and they rode on. They were a good two miles from the creek ford when Kleecan called back, "Trail goes left." Then he kicked the mare hard and swerved her to the left to follow the sharp turn in the trail.

The outlaws were taken by surprise momentarily. Their heads were down, shielding their faces from the stinging drizzle, but they heard

Kleecan's mare break into a gallop, and in a body they spurred their own horses, bunching in confusion at the trail bend, then singling out to kick their mounts into a gallop up a sharp, widening rise. The trail dipped again suddenly and the outlaw chief, in the lead, reined in with a jolting motion, swinging an arm over his head. In the dimness he saw heavy, bulky shapes all around him, round and massive. The outlaws instinctively brought their mounts in close together and looked about, squinting into the darkness. Then one of the outlaws made a noise like a deep sigh. It was a moan and an exclamation. Somebody said, "Oh, God!" and another man cursed, but it sounded like a prayer, for there was a plea in it. On the outer rim they saw the hazy shapes of the wicki-ups and on four sides of them they looked down into the faces of Mescalero Apaches.

Kleecan had led them into the middle of Pondichay's rancheria.

The scout still sat his mare, but he was beyond the circle of Apaches. Next to him stood Pondichay, old and somber, too polite to ask outright the meaning of the sudden intrusion. Kleecan greeted him in Mescalero and continued to speak in that tongue, but he kept his eyes on the outlaw chief as he spoke.

For Kleecan told the old chief many things. He told him what a great warrior he was and recounted many of Pondichay's deeds, but slowly his voice saddened and finally he told him how sad he had been to hear of Juan Pony. The old Apache looked up, but Kleecan continued. And he told him that Juan Pony had been murdered. He told him that he had worked great medicine and was able to bring right to this camp the murderers of Juan Pony. His voice became cold and he told him how the murderers had committed the greatest sacrilege of all by taking Juan's *hoddentin* sack, which held the sacred pollen to ward off evil. And he told Pondichay that if he did not believe him, why not look in the chief murderer's pocket and see if the medicine bag was not still there—for it is said that an Apache warrior parts with his *hoddentin* bag only when he is dead.

Kleecan wheeled his horse around. He had made his offering to the gods of destruction.

3

You Never See Apaches . . .

Original Title: Eight Days from Willcox
Dime Western Magazine, September 1952

BY NATURE, ANGSMAN was a cautious man. From the shapeless specks that floated in the sky miles out over the plain, his gaze dropped slowly to the sand a few feet from his chin, then rose again more slowly, to follow the gradual slope that fell away before him. He rolled his body slightly from its prone position to reach the field glasses at his side, while his eyes continued to crawl out into the white-hot nothingness of the flats. Sun glare met alkali dust and danced before the slits of his eyes. And, far out, something moved. Something darker than the monotonous tone of the flats. A pinpoint of motion.

He put the glasses to his eyes and the glare stopped dancing and the small blur of motion cleared and enlarged as he corrected the focus. Two ponies and two pack animals. The mules were loaded high. He made that out right away, but it was minutes before he realized the riders were women. Two Indian women. Behind them the scavenger birds floated above the scattered animal carcasses, circling lower as the human figures moved away.

Angsman pushed himself up from the sand and made his way back through the pines that closed in on the promontory. A few dozen yards of the darkness of the pines and then abruptly the glare was forcing against sand again where the openness of the trail followed the shoulder of the hill. He stopped at the edge of the trees, took his hat off, and rubbed the red line where the sweatband had stuck. His mustache drooped untrimmed toward dark, tight cheeks, giving his face a look of sadness. A stern, sun-scarred sadness. It was the type of face that needed the soft shadow of a hat brim to make it look complete. Shadows to soften the gaunt angles. It was an intelligent, impassive face, in its late thirties. He looked at the three men by the horses and then moved toward them.

Ygenio Baca sat cross-legged in the dust smoking a cigarette, drawing deep, and he only glanced at Angsman as he approached. He drew long on his cigarette, then held it close to his eyes and examined it as some rare object as the smoke curled from his mouth. Ygenio Baca, the mozo, had few concerns.

Ed Hyde's stocky frame was almost beneath his horse's head, with a hand lifted to the horse's muzzle. The horse's nose moved gently against the big palm, licking the salty perspiration from hand and wrist. In the other arm Hyde cradled a Sharps rifle. His squinting features were obscure beneath the hat tilted close to his eyes. Sun, wind, and a week's beard gave his face a puffy, raw appearance that was wild, but at the same time soft and hazy. There was about him a look of sluggishness that contrasted with the leanness of Angsman.

Billy Guay stood indolently with his thumbs hooked in his gun belts. He took a few steps in Angsman's direction and pushed his hat to the back of his head, though the sun was beating full in his face. He was half Ed Hyde's age, a few years or so out of his teens, but there was a hardness about the eyes that contrasted with his soft features. Features that were all the more youthful, and even feminine, because of the long blond hair that covered the tops of his ears and hung unkempt over his shirt collar. Watching Angsman, his mouth was tight as if daring him to say something that he would not agree with.

Angsman walked past him to Ed Hyde. He was about to say something, but stopped when Billy Guay turned and grabbed his arm.

"The dust cloud was buffalo like I said, wasn't it?" Billy Guay asked, but there was more statement of fact than question in his loud voice.

Angsman's serious face turned to the boy, but looked back to Ed Hyde when he said, "There're two Indian women out there cleaning up after a hunting party. The dust cloud was the warriors going home. I suspect they're the last ones. Stragglers. Everyone else out of sight already."

Billy Guay pushed in close to the two men. "Dammit, the cloud could have still been buffalo," he said. "Who says you know so damn much!"

Ed Hyde looked from one to the other like an unbiased spectator. He dropped the long buffalo rifle stock down in front of him. His worn black serge coat strained tight at the armpits as he lifted his hands to pat his coat pockets. From the right one he drew a half-chewed tobacco plug.

For a moment Angsman just stared at Billy Guay. Finally he said, "Look, boy, for a good many years it's been my business to know so damn much. Now, you'll take my word that the dust cloud was an Indian hunting party and act on it like I see fit, or else we turn around and go back."

Ed Hyde's grizzled head jerked up suddenly. He said, "You're dead right, Angsman. There ain't been buffalo this far south for ten years." He looked at the boy and spoke easier. "Take my word for it, Billy." He smiled. "If anybody knows it, I do. Those Indians most likely ran down a deer herd. But hell, deer, buffalo, what's the difference? We're not out here for game. You just follow along with what Angsman here says and we all go home rich men. Take things slow, Billy, and you breathe easier."

"I just want to know why's he got to give all the orders," Billy Guay said, and his voice was rising. "It's us that own the map, not him. Where'd he be without us!"

Angsman's voice was the same, unhurried, unexcited, when he said, "I'll tell you. I'd still be back at Bowie guiding for cavalry who ride with their eyes open and know how to keep their mouths shut in Apache country." He didn't wait for a reply, but turned and walked toward the dun-colored mare. "Ygenio," he called to the Mexican still sitting cross-legged on the ground, "hold the mules a good fifty yards behind us and keep your eyes on me."

EIGHT DAYS OUT of Willcox and the strain was beginning to tell. It had been bad from the first day. Now they were in the foothills of the Mogollons and it was no better. Angsman had thought that as soon as they climbed from the dust of the plains the tension would ease and the boy would be easier to handle, but Billy Guay continued to grumble with his thumbs in his gun belts and disagree with everything that was said. And Ed Hyde continued to say nothing unless turning back was mentioned.

Since early morning their trail had followed this pine-covered crest that angled irregularly between the massive rock peaks to the south and east and the white-gold plain to the west. Most of the ways the trail had held to the shoulder, turning, twisting, and falling with the contour of the hillcrest. And from the west the openness of the plains continued to cling in glaring monotony. Most of the time Angsman's eyes scanned the openness, and the small black specks continued to crawl along in his vision.

The trail dipped abruptly into a dry creek basin that slanted down from between rocky humps looming close to the right. Angsman reined his mount diagonally down the bank, then at the bottom kicked hard to send the mare into a fast start up the opposite bank. The gravel loosened and fell away as hooves dug through the dry crust to clink against the sandy rock. Momentarily the horse began to fall back, but Angsman spurred again and grunted something close to her ear to make the mare heave and kick up over the bank.

He rode on a few yards before turning to wait for the others.

Billy Guay reached the creek bank and yelled across, without hesitating, "Hey, Angsman, you tryin' to pick the roughest damn trail you can find?"

The scout winced as the voice slammed against the towering rock walls and drifted over the flats, vibrating and repeating far off in the distance. He threw off and ran to the creek bank. Billy Guay began to laugh as the echo came back to him. "Damn, Ed. You hear that!" His voice carried clear and loud across the arroyo. Angsman put a finger to his mouth and shook his head repeatedly when he saw Ed Hyde looking his way. Then Hyde leaned close and said something to the boy. He heard Billy Guay swear, but not so loud, and then there was silence.

Now, ten days from the time the message had brought him to the hotel in Willcox, he wasn't so sure it was worth it.

In the hotel room Hyde had come to the point immediately. Anxiety showed on his face, but he smiled when he asked the point-blank question "How'd you like to be worth half a hundred thousand dollars?" With that he waved the piece of dirty paper in front of Angsman's face. "It's right here. Find us the picture of a Spanish sombrero and we're rich." That simply.

Angsman had all the time in the world. He smoked a cigarette and thought. Then he asked, "Why me? There're a lot of prospectors around here."

Hyde did something with his eye that resembled a wink. "You're well recommended here in Willcox. They say you know the country better than most. And the Apaches better than anybody," Hyde said with a hint of self-pride for knowing so much about the scout. "Billy here and I'll give you an equal share of everything we find if you can guide us to one little X on a piece of paper."

Billy Guay had said little that first meeting. He half-sat on the small window ledge trying to stare Angsman down when the scout looked at him. And Angsman smiled when he noticed the boy's two low-slung pistols, thinking a man must be a pretty poor shot with one pistol that he'd have to carry another. And when Billy Guay tried to stare him down, he stared back with the half smile and it made the boy all the madder; so mad that often, then, he interrupted Hyde to let somebody know that he had something to say about the business at hand.

Ed Hyde told a story of a lost mine and a prospector who had found the mine, but was unable to take any gold out because of Indians, and who was lucky to get out with just his skin. He referred to the prospector always as "my friend," and finally it turned out that "my friend" was buffalo hunting out of Tascosa in the Panhandle, along with Ed Hyde, raising a stake to try the mine again, when he "took sick and died." The two of them were out on a hunt when it happened and he left the map to Hyde, "since I saw him through his sickness." Ed Hyde remained silent for a considerable length of time after telling of the death of his friend.

Then he added, "I met Billy here later on and took to him 'cause he's got the nerve for this kind of business." He looked at Billy Guay as a man looks at a younger man and sees his own youth. "Just one thing more, mister," he added. "If you say yes and look at the map, you don't leave our sight."

In the Southwest, lost-mine stories are common. Angsman had heard many, and knew even more prospectors who chased the legends. He had seen a few become rich. But it wasn't so much the desire for gold that finally prompted him to go along. Cochise had promised peace and Geronimo had scurried south to the Sierra Madres. All was quiet in his territory. Too quiet. He had told himself he would go merely as an escape from boredom. Still, it was hard to keep the wealth aspect from cropping into the thought. Angsman saw the years slipping by with nothing to show for them but a scarred Spanish saddle and an old-model Winchester. All he had to do was lead them to a canyon and a rock formation that looked like a Spanish hat.

Two days to collect the equipment and round up a mozo who wasn't afraid to drive mules into that part of Apacheria where there was no peace. For cigarettes and a full belly Ygenio Baca would drive his mules to the gates of hell.

IT WAS ALMOST a mile past the arroyo crossing that Angsman noticed his black specks had disappeared from the open flats. For the past few hundred yards his vision to the left had been blocked by dense pines. Now the plains yawned wide again, and his glasses inched over the vast- ness in all directions, then stopped where a spur jutted out from the hillside ahead to cut his vision. The Indian women had vanished.

Hyde and Billy Guay sat their mounts next to Angsman, who, afoot, swept his glasses once more over the flat. Finally he lowered them and said, more to himself than to the others, "Those Indian women aren't nowhere in sight. They could have moved out in the other direction, or they might be so close we can't see them."

He nodded ahead to where the trail stopped at thick scrub brush and pine and then dipped abruptly to the right to drop to a bench that slanted toward the deepness of the valley. From where they stood, the men saw the trail disappear far below into a denseness of trees and rock.

"Pretty soon the country'll be hugging us tight; and we won't see anything," Angsman said. "I don't like it. Not with a hunting party in the neighborhood."

Billy Guay laughed out. "I'll be go to hell! Ed, this old woman's afraid of two squaws! Ed, you hear—"

Ed Hyde wasn't listening. He was staring off in the distance, past the treetops in the valley to a towering, sand-colored cliff with flying rock buttresses that walled the valley on the other side. He slid from his mount hurriedly, catching his coat on the saddle horn and ripping it where a button held fast. But now he was too excited to heed the ripped coat.

"Look! Yonder to that cliff." His voice broke with excitement. "See that gash near the top, like where there was a rock slide? And look past to the mountains behind!" Angsman and Billy Guay squinted at the distance, but remained silent.

"Dammit!" Hyde screamed. "Don't you see it!" He grabbed his horse's reins and ran, stumbling, down the trail to where it leveled again at the bench. When the others reached him, the map was in his hand and he was laughing a high laugh that didn't seem to belong to the grizzled face. His extended hand held the dirty piece of paper . . . and he kept jabbing at it with a finger of the other hand. "Right there, dammit! Right there!" His pointing finger swept from the map. "Now look at that gold-lovin' rock slide!" His laughter subsided to a self-confident chuckle.

From where they stood on the bench, the towering cliff was now above them and perhaps a mile away over the tops of the trees. A chunk of sandrock as large as a two-story building was gouged from along the smooth surface of the cliff top, with a gravel slide trailing into the valley below; but massive boulders along the cliff top lodged over the depression, forming a four-sided opening. It was a gigantic frame through which they could see sky and the flat surface of a mesa in the distance. On both sides the mesa top fell away to shoulders cutting sharp right angles from the straight vertical lines, then to be cut off there, in their vision, by the rock border of the cliff frame. And before their eyes the mesa turned into a flat-topped Spanish sombrero.

Billy Guay's jaw dropped open. "Damn! It's one of those hats like the Mex dancers wear! Ed, you see it?"

Ed Hyde was busy studying the map. He pointed to it again. "Right on course, Angsman. The flats, the ridge, the valley, the hat." His black-crusted fingernail followed wavy lines and circles over the stained paper. "Now we just drop to the valley and follow her up to the end." He shoved the map into his coat pocket and reached up to the saddle horn to mount. "Come on, boys, we're good as rich," he called, and swung up into the saddle.

Angsman looked down the slant to the darkness of the trees. "Ed, we got to go slow down there," he tried to caution, but Hyde was urging his mount down the grade and Billy Guay's paint was kicking the loose rock after him. His face tightened as he turned quickly to his horse, and then he saw Ygenio Baca leaning against his lead mule vacantly smoking his cigarette. Angsman's face relaxed.

"Ygenio," he said. "Tell your mules to be very quiet."

Ygenio Baca nodded and unhurriedly flicked the cigarette stub down the grade.

They caught up with Hyde and Billy Guay a little way into the timber. The trail had disappeared into a hazy gloom of tangled brush and tree trunks with the cliff on one side and the piney hill on the other to keep out the light.

Angsman rode past them and they stopped and turned in the saddle. Hyde looked a little sheepish because he didn't know where the trail was, but Billy Guay stared back defiantly and tried to look hard.

"Ed, you saw some bones out there on the flats a while back," Angsman said. "Likely they were men who had gold fever." That was all he said. He turned the head of the mare and continued on.

Angsman moved slowly, more cautiously now than before, and every so often he would rein in gently and sit in the saddle without moving, and listen. And there was something about the deep silence that made even Billy Guay strain his eyes into the dimness and not say anything. It was a loud quietness that rang in their ears and seemed unnatural. Moving at this pace, it was almost dusk when they reached the edge of the timber.

The pine hill was still on their left, but higher and steeper. To the right, two spurs reached out from the cliff wall that had gradually dropped until now it was just a hump, but with a confusion of rocky angles in the near distance beyond. And ahead was a canyon mouth, narrow at first, but then appearing to open into a wider area.

As they rode on, Angsman could see it in Ed Hyde's eyes. The map was in his hand and he kept glancing at it and then looking around. When they passed through the canyon mouth into the open, Hyde called, "Angsman, look! Just like it says!"

But Angsman wasn't looking at Ed Hyde. A hundred feet ahead, where a narrow side canyon cut into the arena, the two Indian women sat their ponies and watched the white men approach.

✯   ✯   ✯

ANGSMAN REINED in and waited, looking at them the way you look at deer that you have come across unexpectedly in a forest, waiting for them to bolt. But the women made no move to run. Hyde and Billy Guay drew up next to Angsman, then continued on as Angsman nudged the mare into a walk. They stopped within a few feet of the women, who had still neither moved nor uttered a sound.

Angsman dismounted. Hyde stirred restlessly in his saddle before putting his hands on the horn to swing down, but stopped when Billy Guay's hand tightened on his arm.

"Damn, Ed, look at that young one!" His voice was loud and excited, but as impersonal as if he were making a comment at a girlie show. "She'd even look good in town," he added, and threw off to stand in front of her pony.

Angsman looked at Billy Guay and back to the girl, who was sliding easily from the bare back of her pony. He greeted her in English, pleasantly, and tipped his hat to the older woman, still mounted, who giggled in a high, thin voice. The girl said nothing, but looked at Angsman.

He said, *¿Cómo se llama?* and spoke a few more words in Spanish.

The girl's face relaxed slightly and she said, "Sonkadeya," pronouncing each syllable distinctly.

"What the hell's that mean?" Billy Guay said, walking up to her.

"That's her name," Angsman told him, then spoke to the girl again in Spanish.

She replied with a few Spanish phrases, but most of her words were in a dialect of the Apache tongue. She was having trouble combining the two languages so that the white men could understand her. Her face would frown and she would wipe her hands nervously over the hips of her greasy deerskin dress as she groped for the right words. She was plump and her hair and dress had long gone unwashed, but her face was softly attractive, contrasting oddly with her primitive dress and speech. Her features might have belonged to a white woman—the coloring, too, for that matter—but the greased hair and smoke smell that clung to her were decidedly Apache.

When she finished speaking, Angsman looked back at Hyde. "She's a Warm Springs Apache. A Mimbreño," he said. "She says they're on their way home."

Hyde said, "Ask her if she knows about any gold hereabouts."

Angsman looked at him and his eyes opened a little wider. "Maybe you didn't hear, Ed. I said she's a Mimbre. She's going home from a hunting trip led by her father. And her father's Delgadito," he added.

"Hell, the 'Paches are at peace, ain't they?" Hyde asked indifferently. "What you worried about?"

"Cochise made peace," Angsman answered. "These are Mimbres, not Chiricahuas, and their chief is Victorio. He's never never made peace. I don't want to scare you, Ed," he said looking back to the girl, "but his war lieutenant's Delgadito."

Billy Guay was standing in front of the girl, his thumbs in his gun belts, looking at her closely. "I know how to stop a war," he said, smiling.

"Who's talkin' about war?" Hyde asked. "We're not startin' anything."

"You don't have to stop it, Ed," Angsman said. "You think about finishing it. And you think about your life."

"Don't worry about me thinkin' about my life. I think about it bein' almost gone and not worth a Dixie single. Hell, yes, we're takin' a chance!" Hyde argued. "If gold was easy to come by, it wouldn't be worth nothin'."

"I still know how to stop a war," Billy Guay said idly.

Hyde looked at him impatiently. "What's that talk supposed to mean?" Then he saw how Billy Guay was looking at the girl, and the frown eased off the grizzled face as it dawned on him what Billy Guay was thinking about, and he rubbed his beard. "You see what I mean, Ed," Billy Guay said, smiling. "We take Miss Indin along and ain't no Delgadito or even U.S. Grant goin' to stop us." He looked up at the old woman on the pony. "Though I don't see any reason for carryin' excess baggage."

Angsman caught him by both arms and spun him around. "You guncrazy kid, you out of your mind? You don't wave threats at Apaches!" He pushed the boy away roughly. "Just stop a minute, Ed. You got better sense than what this boy's proposing."

"It's worth a chance, Angsman. Any chance. We're not stoppin' after comin' this far on account of some Indin or his little girl," Hyde said.

"I'd say Billy's got the right idea. I told you he had nerve. Let him use a little of it."

Billy Guay looked toward Angsman's mount and saw his handgun in a saddle holster, then both pistols came out and he pointed them at the scout.

"Don't talk again, Angsman, 'cause if I hear any more abuse I'll shoot you as quick as this." He raised a pistol and swung it to the side as if without aiming and pulled the trigger. The old Indian woman dropped from the pony without a cry.

There was silence. Hyde looked at him, stunned. "God, Billy! You didn't have to do that!"

Billy Guay laughed, but the laugh trailed off too quickly, as if he just then realized what he had done. He forced the laugh now, and said, "Hell, Ed. She was only an Indin. What you fussin' about?"

Hyde said, "Well, it's done now and can't be undone." But he looked about nervously as if expecting a simple solution to be standing near at hand. A solution or some kind of justification. He saw the mining equipment packed on one of the mules and the look of distress left his eyes. "Let's quit talkin' about it," he said. "We got things to do."

Billy Guay blew down the barrel of the pistol he had fired and watched Sonkadeya as she bent over the woman momentarily, then rose without the trace of an emotion on her face. It puzzled Billy Guay and made him more nervous. He waved a pistol toward Ygenio Baca. "Hey, Mazo! Get a shovel and turn this old woman under. No sense in havin' the birds tellin' on us."

THE SCOUT RODE in silence, knowing what would come, but not knowing when. His gaze crawled over the wildness of the slanting canyon walls, brush trees, and scattered boulders, where nothing moved. The left wall was dark, the shadowy rock outlines obscure and blending into each other; the opposite slope was hazy and cold in the dim light of the late sun. He felt the tenseness all over his body. The feeling of knowing that something is close, though you can't see it or hear it. Only the quietness, the metallic clop of hooves, then Billy Guay's loud, forced laughter that would cut the stillness and hang there in the narrowness until it faded out up-canyon. Angsman knew the feeling. It went with campaigning. But this time there was a difference. It was the first time he had ever led into a canyon with such a strong premonition that Apaches were present. Yet, with the feeling, he recognized an eager expectancy. Perhaps fatalism, he thought.

He watched two chicken hawks dodging, gliding in and out, drop toward a brush tree halfway up the slanting right wall, then, just as they were about to land in the bush, they rose quickly and soared out of sight. Now he was more than sure. They were riding into an ambush. And there was so little time to do anything about it.

He glanced at Hyde riding next to him. Hyde couldn't be kept back now. The final circle on his map was just a little figuring from the end of the canyon.

"Slow her down, Ed," Billy Guay yelled. "I can't propose to Miss Indin and canter at the same time." He laughed and reached over to put his hand on Sonkadeya's hip, then let the hand fall to her knee.

He called out, "Yes, sir, Ed, I think we made us a good move."

Sonkadeya did not resist. Her head nodded faintly with the sway of her pony, looking straight ahead. But her eyes moved from one canyon wall to the other and there was the slightest gleam of a smile.

Angsman wondered if he really cared what was going to happen. He didn't care about Hyde or Billy Guay; and he didn't know Ygenio Baca well enough to have a feeling one way or the other. From the beginning Ygenio had been taking a chance like everyone else. He thought of his own life and the odd fact occurred to him that he didn't even particularly care about himself. He tried to picture death in relation to himself, but he would see himself lying on the ground and himself looking at the body and knew that couldn't be so. He thought of how hard it was to take yourself out of the picture to see yourself dead, and ended up with: If you're not going to be there to worry about yourself being dead, why worry at all? But you don't stay alive not caring, and his eyes went back to the canyon sides.

He watched Hyde engrossed in his map and looked back at Billy Guay riding close to Sonkadeya with his hand on her leg. They could be shot from their saddles and not even see where it came from. Or, they could be taken by surprise. His head swung front again and he saw the canyon up ahead narrow to less than fifty feet across. Or they could be taken by surprise!

He flicked the rein against the mare's mane, gently, to ease her toward the right canyon wall. He made the move slowly, leading the others at a very slight angle, so that Hyde and Billy Guay, in their preoccupation, did not even notice the edging. Either to be shot in the head or not at all, Angsman thought.

Now they were riding much closer to the slanting canyon wall. He turned in the saddle to watch Billy Guay, still laughing and moving his hand over Sonkadeya. And when he turned back he saw the half-dozen Apaches standing in the trail not a dozen yards ahead. It was funny, because he was looking at half-naked, armed Apaches and he could still hear Billy Guay's laughter coming from behind.

Then the laughter stopped. Hyde groaned, "Oh, my God!" and in the instant spurred his mount and yanked rein to wheel off to the left. There was the report of a heavy rifle and horse and rider went down.

Angsman's arms were jerked suddenly behind his back and he saw three Apaches race for the fallen Hyde as he felt himself dragged over the rump of the mare. He landed on his feet and staggered and watched one warrior dragging Hyde back toward them by one leg. Hyde was screaming, holding on to the other leg that was bouncing over the rough ground.

Billy Guay had jerked his arms free and stood a little apart from the dozen Apaches aiming bows and carbines at him. His hands were on the pistol butts, with fear and indecision plain on his face.

Angsman twisted his neck toward him, "Don't even think about it, boy. You don't have a chance." It was all over in something like fifteen seconds.

Hyde was writhing on the ground, groaning and holding on to the hole in his thigh, where the heavy slug had gone through to take the horse in the belly. Angsman stooped to look at the wound and saw that Hyde was holding the map, pressed tight to his leg and now smeared with blood. He looked up and Delgadito was standing on the other side of the wounded man. Next to him stood Sonkadeya.

★ ★ ★

DELGADITO WAS NOT dressed for war. He wore a faded red cotton shirt, buttonless and held down by the cartridge belt around his waist; and his thin face looked almost ridiculous under the shabby wide-brimmed hat that sat straight on the top of his head, at least two sizes too small. But Angsman did not laugh. He knew Delgadito, Victorio's war lieutenant, and probably the most capable hit-and-run guerrilla leader in Apacheria. No, Angsman did not laugh.

Delgadito stared at them, taking his time to look around, then said, "Hello. Angs-mon. You have a cigarillo?"

Angsman fished in his shirt pocket and drew out tobacco and paper and handed it to the Indian. Delgadito rolled a cigarette awkwardly and handed the sack to Angsman, who rolled himself one then flicked a match with his thumbnail and lighted the cigarettes. Both men drew deeply and smoked in silence. Finally, Angsman said, "It is good to smoke with you again, Sheekasay."

Delgadito nodded his head and Angsman went on, "It has been five years since we smoked together at San Carlos."

The Apache shook his head slightly. "Together we have smoked other things since then, Angs-mon," and added a few words in the Mimbre dialect.

Angsman looked at him quickly. "You were at Big Dry Wash?"

Delgadito smiled for the first time and nodded his head. "How is your sickness, Angs-mon?" he asked, and the smile broadened.

Angsman's hand came up quickly to his side, where the bullet had torn through that day two years before at Dry Wash, and now he smiled.

Delgadito watched him with the nearest an Apache comes to giving an admiring look. He said, "You are a big man, Angs-mon. I like to fight you. But now you do something very foolish and I must stop you. I mean you no harm, Angs-mon, for I like to fight you, but now you must go home and stop this being foolish and take this old man before the smell enters his leg. And, Angs-mon, tell this old man what befalls him if he returns. Tell him the medicine he carries in his hand is false. Show him how he cannot read the medicine ever again because of his own blood." For a moment his eyes lifted to the heights of the canyon wall. "Maybeso that is the only way, Angs-mon. With blood."

Angsman offered no thanks for their freedom, gratitude was not an Apache custom, but he said, "On the way home I will impress your words on them."

"Tell my words to the old man," Delgadito replied, then his voice became cold. "I will tell the young one." And he looked toward Billy Guay.

Angsman swallowed hard to remain impassive. "There is nothing I can say."

"The mother of Sonkadeya speaks in my ear, Angs-mon. What could you say?" Delgadito turned deliberately and walked away.

Angsman rode without speaking, listening to Hyde's groans as the saddle rubbed the open rawness of his wound. The groans were beginning to erase the scream that hung in his mind and repeated over and over, Billy Guay's scream as they carried him up-canyon.

Angsman knew what he was going to do. He'd still have his worn saddle and old-model carbine, but he knew what he was going to do. Hyde's leg would heal and he'd be back the next year, or the year after; or if not him, someone else. The Southwest was full of Hydes. And as long as there were Hydes, there were Billy Guays. Big talkers with big guns who ended up lying dead, after a while, in a Mimbre rancheria. Angsman would go back to Fort Bowie. Even if it got slow sometimes, there'd always be plenty to do.

4

Red Hell Hits Canyon Diablo

Original Title: Tizwin
10 Story Western Magazine, October 1952

THEY CALLED IT Canyon Diablo, but for no apparent reason. Like everything else it had advantages and disadvantages, good points and bad ones, depending on the time of the day, the season of the year, or who happened to be occupying the canyon at a given time. At this particular time, two hundred feet up the south wall, a solitary disadvantage stood motionless on the narrow ledge, watching the small group of riders on the open plain approach the dark defile that led into the canyon. A dozen feet above his head the rock sloped back abruptly straightening into the flat tableland. Directly below, the wall extended in a sheer drop to the canyon mouth; but a few yards to his right the canyon wall buckled with loose rock and thorn brush, sloping gradually out into the open plain.

A fifty caliber buffalo rifle rested on a waist-high boulder in front of him, pointed in the general direction of the riders. His gaze followed the same line, his face motionless, though the sand-specked hot wind nudged shoulder-length, jet-black hair and forced his eyelids to lower slightly, so that he watched with eyes that were slits against the glare. Eyes that were small, black, bullet-like . . . staring at the riders with a cold-steel hate. It is easy for a Chiricahua Apache to hate. It is doubly so when his vision is filled with the sight of *blanco* horse soldiers.

Lieutenant Gordon Towner reined in his patrol at the signal from the rider fifty yards ahead. Matt Cline, the civilian scout, wheeled his pony and rode back to the officer and six men.

"Did you see him, Lieutenant?"

"Did I see whom?"

Matt Cline's jaw bulged, a wad of tobacco accentuating his creased, ruddy face, and the short brim of his hat was low on his forehead casting a shadow to the tips of his straggly, black mustache. His lips were parted slightly by the tobacco bulge of his jaw and barely moved when he spoke. He pointed ahead to the mouth of the canyon three hundred yards away, and then his arm swept up to the top of the south wall. Pointing up, his lean, heavily veined arm stretched from the sleeve of red flannel underwear. He wore no shirt. His suspenders crossed the sweat-stained, colorless undershirt and attached to dark serge trousers that tucked into high, dust-caked boots. Across his lap he held a Remington-Hepburn.

"See that ledge runnin' along near the top of the wall? Well, not a minute ago one of our little friends was up there." The scout ended with a stream of tobacco juice spurting into the white dust.

The lieutenant pulled the brim of his floppy, gray field hat closer to his eyes and squinted ahead to the canyon entrance. A hundred things raced through his mind, and every one of them was a question. It was his patrol and he was supposed to have the answers. That's why he had a commission. But the face bore a puzzled expression. It was young, and lobster-red, and told openly that he was new to frontier station, though he had learned all the answers at the Point. You hesitate when it's your command, your responsibility. When a dirty old man in an undershirt is studying you to see what you've got, waiting to pick you apart. And if he finds the wrong thing, the buzzards do the rest of the picking.

"Mr. Cline, the primary objective of this patrol is to locate and bring in Trooper Byerlein. If in the process we come across hostiles, it is also the duty of this patrol to scout them and deal with them using the best means at hand. I would judge that there is a rancheria somewhere in that canyon. I don't think their band could be very large, for I know of no Indians at San Carlos that are unaccounted for. Now that we've found one, or possibly a band, we'll have to act quickly before they get away."

"You got it wrong there, Lieutenant," the scout said. "We didn't find him. That Indian found us."

"Perhaps I'm wrong, but I'd observe him to be a lookout. Now he's obviously fled after being seen."

"Only thing wrong with that, Lieutenant, is that you don't observe an Apache when he's on lookout. I don't know what your experience is, but I hear this is your first patrol out of Fort Thomas. You might as well learn right now that when you spot an Apache like that, it's because he wants you to see him. Right now there could be a dozen of 'em hidin' on that rocky grade goin' up to the ledge. If we was to ride to the mouth we'd see him again just a little way further on. Then you'd go further and you'd see him again. Until he led you to the right spot. There'd be a lot of shots and you'd go back to Thomas draped over your horse facedown. If there's anybody left to lead the horse."

And so they learned. The lieutenant faced the scout, but was silent. It wasn't the best thing to have been said in front of his men. Above all, they had to have confidence in him. He waited until he felt the heat of embarrassment drain from his face.

"What do you suggest, then?"

Matt Cline shifted his chew to the other cheek. "Well, it looks like Byerlein's tracks go into the canyon, which means they pro'bly got him. It's one thing trackin' a deserter, but it's another goin' into an Apache rancheria to get him. If he's there he's either dead or half dead, so there's no worry there anymore." He pointed to a splash of green that crept between low hills to the north of where they were standing.

"I think we'd better wait and move over to those pines until Sinsonte shows up. He'll cut our sign over to there without any trouble. Maybe he'll know just what we're up against."

FROM THE EDGE of the pines they watched the canyon entrance across the empty stretch of desert, and the shadowy defile that slashed into the mountainside had eight different meanings. But it flicked through everyone's mind that it was a place where you could die while never seeing what did it. Six enlisted troopers prayed to six interpretations of God that the young lieutenant wasn't a glory seeker . . . at least not on this patrol. So the men sprawled in sand and grass, their bodies relaxed—though it's a singular type of relaxation only a little more than a mile from the Apache. Eyes are ever watchful. The lieutenant and Cline sat a little apart from the men. Towner pulled at the sparse tufts of grass nervously, looking around in every direction, but mostly toward the canyon.

"How do you know you can trust Sinsonte?" It was more than just making conversation. "He's an Apache just like the rest of them. How do you know he isn't eating with that band of hostiles right now?"

"Well, for one thing, army chow's spoiled him," the scout answered. "He probably wouldn't even touch mescal anymore if somebody baked it for him. I been scoutin' with him goin' on five years now and I don't have any reason not to trust him. The day he turn around and lets go with his Sharps at me, why, then I'll quit trustin' him."

Cline smiled at his joke. " 'Course he ain't always been a scout. He was with Cochise ten years ago, shootin' all the whites he could, long as he needed a pony or a few extra rounds, but that was just somethin' in his past. To an Apache, what you did a long time ago hasn't got much bearin' on what you happen to be doin' at the present. And I don't think he got along too well with Cochise, though he was with him since Apache Pass. 'Course, he won't come right out and tell you. See, Sinsonte is a White Mountain Apache, and for some reason—buried somewhere in his past—he's got a full-fledged hate for Chiricahuas. That, along with army rations, is why he's the best tracker at Fort Thomas."

"Uh-huh," Towner grunted. "So you think the hostiles in the canyon are Chiricahuas." It was half question, half statement of fact. The words of a brand-new lieutenant, willing to learn, but wishing he could have picked his own instructor.

Cline said, "I don't see how they could be anythin' else. If they're all accounted for on the reservation, then they must be ones that come up from across the border. When we was roundin' up the bands to bring them to San Carlos and Fort Apache, a bunch of 'em slipped through the net and streaked south for the Sierra Madres, and nobody could dig 'em out of those hills. Now, every once in a while, bands of 'em come raidin' back into Arizona for horses and shells. They're carryin' on a little war with the Mexicans and have to keep their supplies up. Everybody'd just as soon they never come back. They got some good leaders . . . Chatto, Nachez, old Nana and Loco. And now I hear about an upstart medicine man who's gainin' influence. Name's Geronimo. I'd bet the bucks over in that canyon are part of that band."

An hour after sundown, Lieutenant Towner was still sitting at the edge of the pines, repeatedly shifting from one position to another on the sandy ground. Pine-tree shadows striped his soft face and made his eyes seem to shine. They were open wide. It was a long way from Springfield, Mass. A few yards out in the desert there was a muffled scraping sound, and he jumped to his feet, tugging at his holstered revolving pistol. By the time he had gotten it out, Sinsonte was standing next to him. Matt Cline came up from somewhere behind him.

"Did you find 'em?"

Sinsonte stood in front of his pony holding the hackamore close under the animal's head, while the other hand still covered the nostrils. A man can be shot even when approaching a friendly camp.

"I find, nantan." Sinsonte, a little man even for an Apache, stood with narrow, hunched shoulders. He was perhaps fifty years and his eyes were beginning to be rivered with tiny red lines, but in them still was a fire, a fire that belonged to a younger man. Besides the calico red band holding his hair in place, he wore only high Apache moccasins with turned-up toes and a white cotton breechclout. A uniform jacket was lashed in his bedroll for more peaceful days.

The two scouts crouched together at the edge of the desert for a long time, drawing obscure lines in the sand and conversing in a mixture of Apache and Spanish with only an occasional English word. For a few minutes the lieutenant leaned over their map of sand, trying to recognize a mark or hear even a part of their conversation that was understandable. Finally he turned away in disgust.

"Sergeant Lonnigan!" The old sergeant rose from the circle of enlisted men. "Issue half rations all around. No fire. Therefore no coffee." It felt good to bark an order.

Dammit, he was still in command!

"Yes, sir!" Lonnigan snapped his reply. Thirty years in the army. Seven years longer than the shavetail had even existed. But Lonnigan was used to young second lieutenants. He had served under many. He remembered one who was now a general. He remembered two during the march to the sea, and at Shiloh—they were both colonels. And he remembered dozens of others who were dead. For some reason he liked this new Lieutenant Towner, even if he was too straight out of the

manual and didn't know much about Apaches. He remembered a time
not too long ago when he himself had never heard the name Apache.
You learned. And there are little humps of ground out behind the com-
missary building at Thomas to testify for those who didn't.

IN A LITTLE WHILE Cline went over to the lieutenant.

"Sinsonte found them. Chiricahuas. He was only a few dozen yards
from that lookout who tried to lure us in, and he followed him. When
the lookout saw the lure wouldn't work, he headed straight for the
camp to talk it over with the rest of 'em. About fourteen, fifteen. Sinsonte says from Nachez's band, but they're here with a subchief by the
name of Lacayuelo . . . and mister, he's really a bad one. He's even hard
in the eyes of most of the Apaches, and that's sayin' somethin'. I'd
guess the rest of 'em are bad actors just like he is."

"Did he see Byerlein?"

"Yeah, but he was layin' on the ground in the middle of 'em, so Sinsonte don't know if'n he's alive or dead. I'd say he's half of either one."

The lieutenant looked out through the dingy grayness of the moon-
bathed desert to the black slash that was Canyon Diablo, reflecting on
what he had been told. It made it no easier for him, but he turned to
the scout abruptly.

"Mr. Cline, if Sinsonte can sneak up on a band of hostiles without
being detected, then he can lead this patrol in. Perhaps not to their
camp, but at least to a favorable position from which we can make contact without being at a disadvantage. An ever present obligation to pre-
vent the hostiles from committing further depredations in the Territory
cannot be turned aside or put off. My duty is before me, Mr. Cline, and
will be carried out whether you object or not." He paused to give emphasis to his words. "So we're going to get them."

"I don't object, mister. You're the boss. I knew ever since this afternoon that you'd be wantin' to go in, so Sinsonte and I just did a little
figurin' and I think we got an answer."

"How to get in?"

"Yeah," the scout replied. "Sinsonte's leavin' now to snake acrost that
open stretch. In about four hours the moon'll be down low enough for

the rest of us to get acrost. We leave the horses here. And I say take all the men along, no horse guard left behind, 'cause we'll need all the carbines we got. 'Course that's up to you. The idee is to angle from here so as to land us on the north side of the mountain, three miles up from the entrance we saw this afternoon. On the north it slopes up pretty gradual, and there's a trail that winds about halfway up and then cuts down into rocky country and on into the center of the canyon. The trail in's a fair hard one to find, but Sinsonte's goin' to meet us where it starts. He's out layin' the carpet now."

Chapter Two

The White Flag

THE MOON CLAIMED it was near three o'clock when Cline halted the seven cavalrymen on a broad ledge halfway up the mountain slope. It had been hours since anyone had spoken. Neither the tedious climb nor the circumstance allowed for talk. Only once a teeth-clenched curse followed a misstep, and Towner turned long enough to glare at the trooper and curse him out with his eyes. Now could be heard the heavy breathing as each man stretched his neck to gulp the cool mountain air. Below them the desert rolled dimly for miles, and in the distance was a darker shadow. The clump of pines they had left hours before. From the ledge where they stood, a narrow defile slashed into the mountainside, its rock-wall sides rising over a hundred feet. The trail twisted from view thirty-odd yards ahead.

Cline said, "You never see the end of this one until you're there. She bends around so much."

Towner studied the approach. "You followed it before?"

"A few years back, but I don't look forward to walkin' down that aisle not knowin' who I'm goin' to meet." He looked around restlessly. "It beats me where Sinsonte is. If he don't show in ten minutes, we'll have to go on. This ain't no place to be perched when the sun comes out."

By five, the small band had threaded deep into the defile. Sinsonte had not come. The narrow passage had widened considerably, but it was a slow, exerting grind over the sharp rock and through the biting chaparral clumps that dotted the way. Towner had ordered absolute silence, but the order could not mute the metallic scrape of issue boots on hard rock or the rattle of stones kicked along the pathway. They kept their lips sealed and bit off the urge to curse out the army, the Apache, the sun-bleached country and Lieutenant Towner.

They were experienced men, combining one hundred and sixteen years of active service, and they knew what it was to walk up to an enemy. Walking slowly. How to march without speaking, without thinking, the vigilance being inbred. Many soldiers experienced it, but you had to fight Apaches to really know what it meant. Walking down a narrow trail in the heart of a Chiricahua stronghold, a soldier will even smile at the thought of the arid, glaring, baked-sand parade at Fort Thomas. There is a feeling of security there, though you wouldn't go so far as to call it home.

And Gordon Towner had his thoughts. Did Cook say anything about a similar circumstance? It was true, he was afraid, but more of doing the wrong thing, giving the wrong command, than of the Indians. A twenty-three-year-old boy from Springfield, leading his first command against an enemy, Chiricahua Apaches. A command that consisted of a sergeant, five privates and a grizzly old scout who would have to learn more respect for an officer of the United States Army.

The single file column stopped abruptly at the sign of Matt Cline's arm raised above his head. The trail narrowed again to less than ten feet across, and the path was partially blocked by clumps of thick bushes; but it was evident that they were near the end of the passage. Cline was moving ahead to scout the brush when the low moan of a single Apache voice reached them. The scout stopped dead and the voice went on in a broken-tongue chant, groans mixed with the chopped Apache words. He listened for a minute and recognized the death chant and went on, knowing what to expect.

Towner watched him approach the thick bushes and then stop and look to the right. He took a step toward the wall where a pile of loose boulders jutted out into the path, but stopped long enough to wave the others ahead. Behind the jutting rocks, in a shallow niche in the wall,

Sinsonte sat propped against the wall mumbling the death chant through lips smeared with blood. At first glance, it looked as if his whole face had been lacerated, but in another second Towner saw that all the blood poured from his eyes, or where his eyes had been. He moved his legs stretched out in front of him and the feet wobbled loosely, turning too far to the sides, uncontrolled, the way they will when the tendons have been slashed. Sinsonte would never follow another sign.

Cline lifted his revolving pistol and placed it in the old Indian's hand, but he turned quickly to Towner who was looking the other way, swallowing hard to keep down the bile that was rising in his stomach.

"Come on, we got to get out of here." He was about to say more but his sentence was cut short by the singing ricochet of a bullet over their heads.

"They're behind us!" Lonnigan shouted and turned bringing his carbine up.

"Hold your fire, Sergeant! Everybody up!" Towner had his handgun out and waved the men ahead with it. He waited until they had all followed Cline through the bushes, and then sprinted after them.

They scrambled over the rocks into the boulder-strewn clearing, glancing uncertainly at the four canyon walls that seemed to stretch to the sky, offering no avenue of escape. From somewhere to the left a volley of shots split the stillness scattering the soldiers behind the handiest bits of cover. Low clumps of mesquite dotted the clearing, but offered no permanent protection to the troopers.

Matt Cline took a snap shot at a mound of rock and brush fifty yards away over which a thin wisp of smoke was rising, then shouted to the lieutenant to spread the men out and follow him. It took him only a few seconds to grasp the situation and decide what course to take. There was only one choice. With the men behind him, Cline raced for a small clump of trees that grew out from between the rocks at the base of the right side of the box canyon, directly across from where the shots were coming.

Their backs were to the Indians firing from the well-concealed places along the left wall, but they ran well spread out, dodging and ducking, continually changing course to offer as difficult a target as possible. The firing was intense during the fifteen or twenty seconds it took them to reach the trees, but then died off abruptly as the last man vaulted the natural rock barrier and dropped among the trees. Not a hit. It was always a consoling thought that the Apaches never had bullets enough to waste on practice.

THEY TOOK CROUCHED positions five to ten feet apart behind the natural barricade of rocks and trees, pointing their carbines out between the rocks. And they waited. At their backs, the jagged canyon wall, veined with crevices and ledges, loomed skyward.

The lieutenant searched the cliff with his gaze, but could see the top in only one place through the dense trees. Apaches could get up there, but they wouldn't see anyone to fire on. No, the danger was ahead, among the rocks not three hundred yards away—and you couldn't see it. But he was satisfied with his position. It was small, right under the wall and not more than thirty yards wide. It wasn't a position you could hold forever, not without food and water. Still, the young officer was satisfied. There was no place the scout could lead them.

He nudged Cline. "Do you think they'll try to run over us?" He spoke in a low voice, as if afraid the Indians would overhear.

Cline shifted his chew, looking out over the clearing. He only occasionally glanced at the lieutenant. "Mister, I've known Apaches all my life—I even lived with them when I was a boy—but don't ask me what I think they'll do. Nobody knows what an Apache's goin' to do until it's done. I don't think even the Apache himself knows. But," the scout reflected, "I know they ain't goin' to come whoopin' across that open space if it means some of 'em gettin' killed. He's a heller, but he don't stick his neck out."

"Lieutenant!"

Towner and the scout crouched low and crawled to the trooper who had called.

"I think they're comin'. I seen somethin' move," the trooper said, pointing. "About twenty feet from the other side."

The scout squinted hard through the low branches. "Hell, yeah, they're comin'! Look!"

An Apache showed himself for a split second, disappearing into a shallow gully near the spot where the trooper had pointed. Cline threw up the Remington-Hepburn at the same time and fired, the bullet kicking up sand where the Indian had disappeared. "You got to shoot fast or there's nothin' to shoot at." The last word was on his lips when he threw the piece up again and fired.

"Damn, they move fast!"

Individually, then, the soldiers began firing at the darting, crawling, shadowy figures that never remained in sight more than a few seconds. They fired slowly, taking their time, with a patience that started for some of them at the first Bull Run. They knew what they were doing. They knew how to make each shot mean something.

From the opposite ridge came a heavy fire, continuing for almost a minute, keeping the soldiers crouching low behind their defenses.

"Keep shooting, dammit!" Towner screamed down the line. "They're moving up under fire cover!"

He turned to his own position in time to see the blur of a painted face and a red calico band loom in front of him not twenty feet away. The Apache was screaming, coming straight on, bringing a Sharps to his shoulder when Towner raised his handgun and fired. The face disappeared in a crimson flash, and for a split second a picture of Sinsonte passed through his mind. He stared between the rocks where the painted face had been. He saw it still. Gordon Towner had killed his first man . . . and sometimes it will do something to you.

Cline called over, "Good shootin', mister." But Towner didn't hear. He was squeezing off on another creeping shadow. He had been baptized.

They were firing continuously now, seeing more Apaches than there actually were. Every few minutes someone would yell, "I got one!" but most of their bullets whined harmlessly off the rocks and into the brush and sand. On to the middle of the day the cavalrymen pecked away in this fashion, firing sporadically at every cover that might conceal an Indian.

They were holding their own, successfully keeping the hostiles at bay, whittling down their number, except for one disastrous occurrence. An

Apache who had crawled unbelievably close, was shot through the side as he dove for a cover, but the bullet did not stop him. He leaped to his feet and goaded himself on with a frenzied scream that brought him to the top of the barricade. If he was going to die, he didn't intend to die alone.

It all happened in a few seconds. Private Huber jumped up just as the Indian fired his heavy buffalo gun from the waist, and the ball caught the trooper square in the throat. At least four shots ripped through the Indian's body as he swung the heavy rifle like a club and smashed it against the side of a head. He teetered for a moment and then fell forward, still clutching the Sharps, onto the lifeless bodies of Privates Huber and Martz.

And when a man says one cavalryman is worth ten Apaches, he is a fool. It is certain he was not at Canyon Diablo that July day in '78.

SHORTLY AFTER NOON the firing slackened gradually and finally died out altogether. Not an Apache was in sight. They were certain that at least two or three were still out in the middle somewhere, but if they were, the devil himself was hiding them. A hot breeze sang through the canyon, shifting the sand and stirring the mesquite clumps. The movement of the wind was all the more eerie contrasted with the dead stillness of the canyon. There was not a human sound. The sun struck fiercely into the boxed area, the shimmering heat waves mixing with the sand-specked breeze to form a gritty element that you could almost stick with a bayonet. It was hot, blistering hot, and the lack of water made it all the worse. That, and the overpressing reality that out there, somewhere, were Apaches, Chiricahua Apaches with the smell of blood in their nostrils. It set a stage of silence and tortuous, eye-strained waiting.

Towner and Cline squatted next to the two heaps of stones that covered the dead cavalrymen. Since burying Huber and Martz they had spoken less and less. It was getting late in the afternoon. The silence and back-breaking vigilance clung all the heavier, daring conversation or a moment of relaxation. But Towner was getting tired.

"If we ever get out of here I'll send back for them to be buried at Thomas," he said.

"I don't think they'd care one way the other now," the scout replied. "I know I wouldn't. What difference does it make if . . . Well, I'll be damned! Look at that!"

Matt Cline jumped up and pointed with his carbine toward the other side of the canyon. A white flag waved a few times above the grayness of rock, then an Indian stepped cautiously into the open carrying the flag tied to the end of an antiquated Springfield.

As he advanced, five Apaches jumped down from low ledges along the wall, and as they walked slowly toward Towner's position, three more Apaches appeared as if out of nowhere to join them. They had been hiding in the open area since giving up the sneak attack hours before. As the soldiers watched them advance, they wondered how the devil they could have missed seeing the three hiding right out in the open. Towner wondered if it wasn't just an excuse to gather up the warriors who had been stranded. Matt Cline wondered if the Springfield that bore the white flag was loaded.

The nine Apaches were still a few dozen yards away. Matt Cline leaned toward the lieutenant.

"I figure they're out of bullets or they wouldn't be playin' games. I'd say they want to get close, catch us off guard and finish the job with knives. If they had shells they could sit back there for a week and wait for us to come out in the open or die of starvation. It's gotta be a trick. Whatever you do, for God's sake don't trust 'em!"

Towner held his revolving pistol at his side. "Which one's Lacayuelo?"

"That little one with the cavalry jacket on, next to the one carryin' the flag."

A few feet from the defense line the Apaches stopped and Lacayuelo came on alone. His brown chest and stomach showed through the opening of the filthy, buttonless jacket. An empty cartridge belt crossed his chest and left shoulder. And an inane grin showed protruding teeth, forming a parallel with a smear of yellow paint that extended from ear to ear across the bridge of his nose. Like the others of his band he wore Apache moccasins that reached to his knees; but unlike the others whose only covering were light breechclouts, he wore ragged, gray trousers that tucked into his moccasins. His headband, holding back shoulder-length black hair, had once been a bright red, but now was a grease-stained, colorless rag. Three of the others wore small bush clumps attached to their headbands. At two hundred yards you wouldn't see them.

Lacayuelo began gesturing and speaking rapidly in the choppy, sound-picture Apache tongue. Matt Cline listened without interrupting, until he was finished, and then turned to the lieutenant.

"To make it short, he says there's no reason why we can't all be friends. He says just give him and his warriors some shells so they can hunt and keep from going hungry, and everybody'll be happy. He says he can't understand why we attacked him and his peaceful huntin' party."

Towner stared at the Apache. He took his campaign hat off and shook his head. "Does this animal understand English?"

"Enough to get by, but it would take him till Christmas to tell you anything."

The lieutenant continued to stare at Lacayuelo and his eyes narrowed. "Tell him he can go to hell with his hunting. He and his party are under arrest. Tell him he's going back to San Carlos to stand trial for murder."

Cline passed it on to the Chiricahua subchief who grinned and replied in only a few words.

"He says you can't arrest him, because he's here under the protection of a white flag. He says you have too much honor to disregard his sign of truce. He's a sly old devil, throwin' it back in your lap."

"Ask him what he's done with Byerlein."

The scout turned from the Indian after a minute. "He says he doesn't know what you're talkin' about. He says we're the first *blancos* he's seen in two months."

"He does, does he." Towner had not taken his eyes from the subchief since he stepped forward. Now, still looking full into his face, he raised his revolving pistol and pulled back the hammer. "Tell Lacayuelo that white flag or no white flag, I'll shoot his damn eyes out if he doesn't start talking about Byerlein."

Cline hesitated. "Mister, he's got more men than we have."

"He's got more men without bullets. Tell him!"

Cline passed it on and the words made the Apache lurch forward a half a step, but he looked into the muzzle of Towner's gun and stopped dead. He studied the young lieutenant, looking him up and down, taking his own good time; and finally must have decided that the *blanco* wasn't joking, for all at once a broad grin creased his evil, sun-scarred face and he was as friendly as could be. He jabbered to Cline for almost two minutes and then turned abruptly and walked away. The other Apaches followed.

"Where the devil are they going?"

Cline said, "He says he sees you're a friend of the Apache, so he's invitin' us to his rancheria for some refreshments. We're supposed to follow. He's thinkin' of somethin'. I say stay here."

Towner only glanced at him. "When you're in command, Mr. Cline, you can say that. Lonnigan! Spread out behind me. Mr. Cline, you'll walk at my side."

Five cavalrymen and a civilian scout walked slowly across the canyon floor, following the Indians by fifty yards. The sun had begun to drop behind the western canyon wall so that half of the boxed area was in shadow. Towner and the rest strode from the dark into the light and followed the Indians to the other side, then through a narrow defile into a side canyon. They walked into this new clearing where four wickiups stood and a dozen or so ponies were tethered on the other side of the canyon meadow. And they approached the Apaches with almost a swagger, a show of indifference, for they were cavalrymen of the "5th" . . . though they had only nine bullets between them.

Chapter Three

Tizwin

FOR AN APACHE rancheria, this one was comparatively clean, but it only testified that the Indians had not been there very long. The four wickiups were in a semicircle, and two cook fires, close together, were in the center of the half-moon area. Lacayuelo and his warriors sat in an irregular circle between the wickiups and the dead cook fires. He rose to one knee as they approached and beckoned them to join the circle; but Towner stopped the group on the opposite side of the cook fires and watched the Indians pass from one to the next a bulging water bag made from horse intestines.

Towner turned his head slightly. "What are they drinking?"

"Tizwin, most likely," Cline said. "Or mescal." He watched the Indians drink. "I wouldn't put any pesos on it bein' water."

"What the devil's tizwin?"

"Apache corn beer. Knock you back to the States if you drink enough. Makes a worse Indian out of a bad one. I don't know what it'll do to a hardcase like Lacayuelo. He wants us to join 'em."

"Corn beer, eh," the lieutenant muttered, almost to himself. And he had a most uncommon look in his eyes.

Sometimes it seems as if certain men are set aside to do great things while others have to play the role of the fool or the coward, predestined from all eternity. But if you look close into every case, and that means everybody in the world, you'll see a time, a circumstance where a judgment has to be made that either makes or breaks the man. Sometimes luck helps. But it happens often in the army—especially on frontier station—and it was happening now to young Gordon Towner. Fortunately, he knew it. And wasn't afraid to push his luck.

"Mr. Cline, tell the filthy scoundrel that we'll be only too happy to join his soiree." And then to Lonnigan, "Sergeant, turn your bully boys loose. They can drink all they want—long as it's more than the Indians."

They sat where they had stood, on the other side of the ashes of the cook fires, ten to fifteen feet from the Apaches. Lacayuelo sent the water bag over to them—it turned out to be tizwin—but gestured and argued loudly for almost an hour for the *blancos* to join his circle. He was drinking all the time, like everyone else, and finally gave up his pleading when he saw that it was no use. The fly would not venture into the web. Perhaps he felt that ten feet wasn't far anyway.

The soldiers raised their baked-clay cups drink for drink with the Indians, carbines or handguns across laps, eyes ever watchful over the cup brims. It was a strange setting: the savage and the soldier, mortal enemies, drinking tizwin together, each watching for the false move. But the strangest sight was Gordon Towner. He was at least two cupfuls ahead of everyone else. He repeatedly drank down the warm liquid with one toss and raised his empty cup as a sign for more. He drank without speaking, never taking his eyes off the Apache subchief. Lacayuelo met the *blanco* chief's gaze and felt more than distrust. There was a challenge also. And he would try to drink his tizwin as rapidly.

Cline looked at the lieutenant anxiously. The scout was beginning to feel his drinks, and he'd had tizwin before.

"Mister, you'd better take it easy. This stuff'll do somethin' to you."

Towner sat erect with his legs crossed. "Mr. Cline, I may be young, but a long time ago my father taught me to drink like a gentleman. If I didn't think I could out-drink these creatures, I'd resign my commission."

"That's the trouble, they don't drink like gentlemen."

The lieutenant reached for the water bag again. "Play the game, Mr. Cline. Play the game." And oddly enough the words gave the scout confidence.

It was shortly after this that one of the Apaches screamed and leaped to his feet, drawing a knife from his breechclout. Five white men dropped their cups and raised pieces in one motion to cover the Apache who was about to leap over the mound of ashes. The sixth was doing quite another thing. He was laughing, and loud enough to make the Indian stop his motion in midair, so that one of his moccasins came down in the middle of the cook fire, the soft ashes puffing in a cloud of gray smoke. He jerked his foot up instinctively, but too quickly, so that he was thrown off balance back among the other Chiricahuas. Towner laughed all the louder.

Then he stopped abruptly and eyed the subchief coldly. He spoke slowly, carefully, to make certain the old Indian would understand.

"Lacayuelo, why do you bring boys to do the work of men? I have heard many tales of how brave the Apache warriors are, but now I see that these tales must surely be false. For what I have seen of the Apache makes me believe that he is an old woman or a very little boy. You do not sit like men of dignity and calmly drink your tizwin. You scream and jump and would commit murder if you had the chance. That is because your hearts are black. You do not have the hearts of true braves. I have come the distance of twenty sunsets to see the Apache because I have heard so many tales of wonder and bravery. And now I see that he cannot even drink a few cups of tizwin without turning into the desert dog. Surely this is not something a man can be proud of." He glanced at the scout. "Tell these other beasts what I said. I think Lacayuelo understood. Look at his face."

LACAYUELO LISTENED again as Cline repeated the words, and his face grew darker. As he rose to speak, his eyes were bleary from the tizwin, but he controlled his voice well, speaking slowly so that his thick tongue would not jumble the words.

"The *mejor* speaks as man much wiser than his years would have him be. You are young and I start to grow old and I can see what you are doing. Your words have stabbed our hearts. You tell us we are not men. I tell you, I know what you are doing. Still, we will sit and drink tizwin and by'n by I show you Chiricahua is more man than a *blanco*." He spoke gravely, solemnly. "You have called us many names. Now I will show you they are not true. Now you must show me that you are a man, or I shall call you not only woman and little boy, but dead fool!"

The men understood now, fully. It was a contest. They were pitting their ability to drink against the Apaches'. They understood well what would happen to the loser. And they understood that they relied completely on the young Lieutenant Towner to keep the Indians drinking. Occasionally, a man would laugh to himself, *How the devil did I get into this!* But it was a hollow laugh. For the most part there was silence, a deathlike silence, for that's what was in the air. It stretched from one line of men over to the other and it held them transfixed. This was the most serious drinking any trooper had ever done—and it went on and on, into the dusk.

The Indians were becoming dim outlines in the grayness when Towner ordered the fire. Lonnigan worked cautiously, facing the Indians, though his feet were very unsteady. He cursed with a thick tongue the matches that kept going out in his fumbling fingers, but soon he had a good fire going. Across the flames, Towner watched the shadows dance on the faces of the Apaches. In the orange light they were fierce, grotesque, black smudges hiding eyes filmed and bulging with hate; but he noticed other things too. Eyes that closed, opened, then closed again for a longer time. A head would nod. Soon one of the Apaches, without a sound, fell back and lay motionless.

Within the next two hours, three more Indians slumped into unconsciousness. But not without continued prompting from the lieutenant. He drank his cupfuls down without hesitation, and when an Indian faltered for a minute, or would spill the liquid in his drunkenness, Towner was alert to sneer and goad him on to more.

Lacayuelo watched his strength melt away with the hot liquid, but he was powerless to do anything. At one time he began a chant, a song telling of all his warrior deeds; but the *blanco* chief howled with laughter. And when the Apache staggered to his feet to cross the fire, the lieutenant stopped laughing and stared at him silently. It was a look of contempt. A look that said, *I told you you were not a man.* And Lacayuelo fell back to show this insolent *muchacho* what a man really was. But it was becoming more difficult each hour.

The end was near. Lacayuelo knew it. His eyes moved up and down the line of his warriors. Only two were in sitting positions, but their heads drooped chin to chest. Neither had taken a drink in almost an hour. He looked across the dying fire. The scout lay belly-down on the hard ground, his arms outstretched unnaturally pointing in the direction of the three troopers, motionless on their backs. But the sergeant was still awake; head hanging, but awake. He would move slowly, the Indian thought. And the *blanco* chief still faced across the fire, his hat brim low masking his eyes. He could be asleep. . . .

The Indian swayed as he rose to his feet, leaned too far forward and fell to his hands and knees, tripping over the extended foot of one of the prostrate warriors. His head was clear, he could think, but his body would not react with the same accord. He stumbled as he rose again, this time shattering the pottery cup against a rock.

He looked quickly to the *blanco* chief. The form danced and swayed before his blurred vision, but that part which was the head did not move. The eyes still cloaked by the hat brim.

But now there was another motion. He stumbled forward kicking dirt into the dying fire and then stopped dead, swaying on feet spread slightly apart. He squinted hard to make the *blanco* chief stop swinging back and forth, and as the film fell away and the rotating motion slowed, he saw the revolving pistol pointed at his eyes. And through the piercing ring in his ears he heard the hammer click into cock position. It was all over.

Towner watched the old Indian sink to his knees slowly and then fall forward, rolling onto his side. He had the urge to pull the trigger, even though it was not necessary, even though it was all over. From across the glowing pile of ashes there was neither the sign of motion nor the hint of it.

He nudged Lonnigan who lifted his head momentarily, grunted, and then eased his thick body slowly backward until he was lying down. Like the others, he was past caring. Towner stumbled as he crossed the fire, his feet moving as if iron fetters were attached, but he shuffled on until he stood before Lacayuelo. He looked up and down the line of prostrate forms that revolved slowly on the ground, and then back at the subchief, shaking his head and blinking his eyes. All through the night his willpower had been using brute force to goad his body on, lashing the sinking feeling away with, *Show the savages!* Now it was over, and he could feel himself being drawn into the black nothingness of utter exhaustion. But there was one thing more to be done.

He bent over the still form of Lacayuelo and looked at his clothing closely, at the filthy jacket and ragged pants. Then the issue belt caught his eye. It was polished, gleaming. He unbuckled it and drew it off. The first thing he saw was the name on the inside—Byerlein. That was all. He drew his arm back and brought the barrel of the revolving pistol down upon the Indian's skull. And as he staggered down the line of unconscious figures, he brought the weapon down again and again against the heads of the Apaches. When it was finished, he felt better.

IT WAS FORTY miles back to Thomas. Forty blistering, dry miles through the furnace that was central Arizona. Miles that cramped legs and jolted heads already racked by the aftereffects of Apache corn beer. And there were nine Chiricahua hostiles who had to be watched, watched with a sharp eye; though their feet were lashed beneath pony bellies and their skulls throbbed with a brutal pain.

Just before sunset, the riders, caked with alkali dust and heads bowed, rode across the parade at Fort Thomas. Colonel Darck stepped to the front of the ramada before his quarters to receive the lieutenant who had wheeled off toward him.

"You lost some men, Lieutenant." The colonel volunteered only this observation. It could mean anything. His opinion would come later when Towner made his official report. This meeting was simply a courtesy. "You look all in, Mr. Towner. Not used to the weather yet, eh? What do you say to a whiskey before cleaning up?"

The colonel spoke about it for years after. Of course he was polite about it, but it was the idea. The young lieutenant was the only officer Darck ever knew to refuse a whiskey punch after finishing a blistering four-day patrol.

5

The Colonel's Lady

Original Title: Road to Inspiration
Zane Grey's Western, November 1952

MATA LOBO WAS playing his favorite game. He stretched his legs stiffly behind him until his moccasined feet touched rock, and then he pushed, writhing his body against the soft, sandy ground, enjoying an animal pleasure from the blistering sun on his naked back and the feel of warm, yielding earth beneath him. His extended hand touched the stock of the Sharps rifle a few inches from his chin and sighted down the barrel for the hundredth time. The target area had not changed.

Sixty yards down the slope the military road came into view from between the low hills, cutting a sharp, treacherous arc to follow the bend of Banderas Creek on the near side and then to continue, paralleling the base of the hill, making the slow climb over this section of the Sierra Apaches. Mata Lobo's front sight was dead on the sudden bend in the road.

He flexed his finger on the trigger and sighted again, taking in the slack, then releasing it. Not long now. In a few minutes he should hear the faint, faraway rattle of the stage as it weaved across the plain from Rindo's Station at the Banderas Crossing. Six miles across straight, flat desert. And then louder—with a creaking—a grinding, jingling explosion of leather, wood, and horseflesh as the Hatch & Hodges Overland began the gradual climb over the woody western end of the Sierra Apaches, and then to drop to another white-hot plain that stretched the twelve miles to Inspiration, the end of the line. The vision in the mind of Mata Lobo shortened the route by a dozen miles.

Every foot of the road was known to him. Especially this sudden bend at the beginning of the climb. He had scouted it for weeks, timing the stage runs, watching the drivers from his niche on the hill. And through his Apache patience he learned many things.

At the bend, the driver and the shotgun rider were too busy with the team to be watching the hillside. And the passengers, full and comfortable after a meal at Rindo's, would be suddenly jolted into hanging on with the sway of the bouncing Concord as it swept around the sharp curve, with no thought of looking out the windows.

It was the perfect site for ambush, Apache style. Mata Lobo was sure, for he had done it before.

And then it began. He raised himself on his elbows and cocked his ears to the sound that was still a whisper out on the desert. Two miles away. Then louder, and louder; then the straining pitch to the rattling clamor and the stage was starting up the grade.

The Apache pivoted his rifle on the rocks in front of him, making sure of free motion, and then he lined up again the five brass cartridges arranged on the ground near his right hand.

When he looked back to the road the lead horses were coming into view. He waited until the stage was in full sight, slowed down slightly in the middle of the road, and then he fired, aiming at the closer lead horse.

The horse's momentum carried it along for the space of time it took the Apache to inject another cartridge and squeeze off at the other lead animal. The horses swerved against each other, still going, then four pairs of legs buckled at once, and eight other pairs raced on, trampling the fallen horses, but to be tripped immediately in a wild confusion of thrashing legs and screaming horses and grinding brakes.

Next to the driver the shotgun rider was throwing his boot against the brake lever when the coach jackknifed and twisted over, gouging into the dirt road, sending up a thick cloud of dust to cover the scene.

As the dust began to settle, Mata Lobo saw one figure lying next to the overturned Concord, his face upturned to the two right-side wheels, still turning slowly above him. There was a stir of motion farther ahead as a figure crawled along the ground, got to his feet, stumbled, pulled himself frantically across the road in a wild, reeling motion that finally developed into a crouched run. He was almost to the shelter of the creek bank when the buffalo gun screamed again across the hillsides. The impact threw him over the bank to lie facedown at the edge of the creek.

He aimed the rifle again at the overturned stage in time to see the head appear above the door opening. Mata Lobo's finger almost closed on the trigger, but he hesitated, seeing shoulders appear and then the rest of the body.

The man stopped uncertainly, looking around, cocking his ear to the silence. An odd-looking little man, fat and frightened, but not sure of what to be afraid. He clutched a small black case that singled him out as a drummer of some kind. He clutched it protectingly, shielding his means of existence.

When his gaze swept the hillside, perhaps he saw the glint of the rifle barrel, but if he did, it meant nothing to him. There was no reaction. And a second later it was too late. The .50-caliber bullet tore through his body to spin him off the coach.

Again silence settled. This time, longer. The wheels had stopped moving above the sprawled form of the guard.

Still Mata Lobo waited. His eyes, beneath the red calico headband, were nailed to the overturned Concord. He hadn't moved from his position. He sat stone still and waited. Watched and waited and counted.

He counted three dead: the driver, a passenger, and the guard who was in the road next to the coach—he was undoubtedly dead. But the run usually carried more passengers, at least two more, and that bothered the Apache.

Others might still be inside the coach, dead, wounded, or just waiting. Waiting with a cocked pistol. Either way Mata Lobo had to find out. He hadn't laid this ambush for sport alone. He needed bullets, and a shirt, and any glittering trinkets that might catch his eye. But it was the bullets, more than anything else, that finally made him raise himself and slip quietly down the side of the hill.

His Apache sense led him in a wide circle, so that when he approached the Concord, Banderas Creek was behind him. He walked half crouched, slowly, with short toe-to-heel strides, catlike, a coiled spring ready to snap. Mata Lobo was a Chiricahua Apache, well schooled in the ways of war.

He passed the baggage strewn about the ground without a side glance and dropped to his hands and knees as he came to the vertical wall that was the top of the coach. He touched the baggage rack lightly, then, pressing his ear against the smooth surface of the coach top, he remained fixed in this position for almost five minutes. Long, silent minutes.

He was about to rise, satisfied the coach was unoccupied, when he heard the sharp, scraping sound from within. Like someone moving a foot across a board.

He froze again, pressing close, then slowly placed his rifle on the ground beside him and lifted a skinning knife from a scabbard at his back.

He inched his body upward until he was standing, placed a foot on a rung of the baggage rack, and pushed his body up until his head was above the coach. He was confident of his own animal stealth. A gun could be waiting, but he doubted it. Only a fool would have moved, knowing he was just outside. A fool, or a child, or a woman.

Nor was he wrong. The woman was crouched against the roof of the coach, her back arched against the smooth surface, holding with both hands a long-barreled pistol that pointed toward the rear window. She was totally unaware of the Apache staring at her a few feet away, lying belly down on the side of the coach. When she saw him it was too late.

Revolver went up as knife came down, but the knife was quicker and the heavy knob on the handle smashed against her knuckles to make her drop the revolver. Dark, vein-streaked arms reached in to drag her up through the door window. She struggled in his grasp, but only briefly, for he flung her from the coach and leapt down to the road after her.

She sat in the road dust and eyed him defiantly, her lips moving slightly, her eyes not wavering from his face. She screamed for the first time as she rose from the dust, but it was not a scream of fear.

She was almost to her feet when the Apache's hand tightened in her hair to fling her off balance back to the ground. He stood over her and looked down into the dust-streaked face. Then he turned back to the stagecoach.

She watched as he rummaged about the wreckage, sitting motionless, knowing that if she tried to run he would probably not hesitate to kill her. Her hands moved to her hair and unhurriedly brushed back the blond wisps that had been pulled from the tight chignon at the nape of her neck. Her hands moved slowly, almost unconsciously, and then down and in the same lifeless manner brushed the heavy dust from the green jersey traveling-dress, as if her movements were instinctive, not predetermined.

But her eyes were not lifeless. They followed the Apache's every move and narrowed slightly into two thin lines that contrasted sharply with her soft face, like fire on water. Her body moved from habit while her mind showed through her eyes.

She was afraid, but only loathing was on the surface. The fear was the stabbing weight in her breast, an emotion she had learned to control. She could have been in her late twenties, but her chin and the lines near her eyes told of at least six additional years.

Every now and then the Apache would glance back in her direction, but he found her always in the same position. She watched him bend over the still form of the guard lying on his back, and her eyes blinked hard as the Indian brought the stock of his rifle down on the man's forehead, but she did not turn her head.

There was no doubt now that all were dead. Mata Lobo was a thorough man, for his people had been slaying the *blanco* since the first war club smashed through the cumbersome armor of the conquistadors. His deeds were known throughout Apacheria; they whispered the name of the bronco Chiricahua with the bloodlust ever in his breast. There would be no survivor to tell of the lone Apache killer.

The sport of the affair had satisfied him, but he was angry. None of the men had been using a Sharps, so there was no ammunition to be had. He picked up the guard's Winchester, slinging the cartridge belt over his shoulder, but he liked the feel of the heavy buffalo rifle better. In the Sharps he had the confidence that comes only after trial. But he had only two cartridges left for it.

He turned his attention to the drummer, who was sprawled awkwardly next to the coach. With his foot he pushed the body over onto its back. A crimson smear spread over the shirtfront. The Apache opened the black satchel next to the man and emptied the contents onto the ground—needles, scissors, paring knives, and thread—and moved on to the horses.

His next act made the woman turn her head slightly, for with his skinning knife he sliced a large chunk of meat from the rump of a disabled horse and stuffed it into the sample case. Then he stepped to the front of the horse and cut the animal's jugular vein. Soon after, a Chiricahua Apache with a white woman at his side waded up Banderas Creek along the shallows. The woman dragged her legs through the water stiffly, slowly, as if her reluctance to move quickly was an open act of defiance toward the Indian.

The Chiricahua carried two rifles and a bloodstained satchel and wore a clean shirt, the tail hanging below his narrow hips. With every few steps his glance turned to the cold face of the woman. They disappeared three hundred yards upstream, where the creek cut a bend into the blackness of the pines.

It was the point riders of Phil Langmade's C Troop that found the wrecked stagecoach and the dead men, almost two hours later. Twenty days in the field and a brush with Nachee, and because of it they had missed the stage at Rindo's.

They were returning to the garrison at Inspiration, thighs aching from long, stiff hours in the saddle. Grimy, salt-sweat-white, alkali-caked—both their uniforms and their minds—after days of riding through the savage dust-glare of central Arizona. And of the forty mounts, three had ponchos draped over the saddles, bulging and shapeless. All patrols were not routine.

Langmade sent flankers to climb the ridges on both sides, and then went in. The troopers spread out in a semicircle, watching with hollow, lifeless eyes the flankers on the ridge more than the grisly scene on the road. You get used to the sight of death, but never to expecting it.

Langmade dismounted, but Simon Street, the civilian scout, rode up to the dead driver before throwing off. He walked upstream another hundred yards and then came back, approaching the officer from around the coach. The troopers sat still in their saddles, half-asleep, half-ready to throw up a carbine. Habit.

Langmade said, "I don't know if I want to find her inside the coach or not. If she's there, she's dead."

Street's eyes moved slowly over the scene. "You won't find her," he said. "There's a little heel print over on the bank. They went upstream. That's sure. If they went down they'd wind up in the open near Rindo's."

Langmade boosted himself onto the side of the stage and came down almost in the same motion. He nodded his head to the scout and kept it moving in an arc along the top of the near ridge.

"Bet they laid up there waiting," Langmade said. "A month's pay they were Apaches."

Street followed his gaze to the ridge. He just glanced at the officer, his face creased-bronze and old beyond its years, crow's feet where eye met temple, his hat tilted low on his forehead, his eyes in shadow. "You're throwin' your money away, soldier," he said. "Apache."

Langmade looked at him quickly. "Only one?"

"That's all the sign says." Street pointed to the butchered horse. "A war party don't cut just one steak."

He turned his attention back to the ridge. He was looking at the exact spot from which the Apache had fired. Then his gaze fell slowly to sweep across the road to Banderas Creek. And he squinted against the glare as his eyes followed the course of the creek to the bend into the pines.

Langmade pushed his field hat back from his forehead, releasing the hot-steel grip of the sweatband, and watched the scout curiously. Langmade was young, in his mid-twenties, but he was good for a second lieutenant. He didn't talk much and he watched. He watched and he learned. And he knew he was learning from one of the best. But the tension was building inside his stomach, and it wasn't just the after-effects of a twenty-day patrol.

There were three dead men in the road and a woman missing and it had happened because he had failed to bring the patrol in to Rindo's on time. The report would include an account of the brush with Nachee, and that would absolve him of blame. But it wouldn't make it easier for him to face Colonel Darck.

You didn't just look at a stone near your boot toe and say "sorry" to a man whose wife has been carried off by a blood-drunk Apache—even if you weren't to blame.

There it was. Langmade stood motionless, watching the scout. Langmade was in command, a commissioned officer in the United States Army, but he was tired. His bones ached and his mind dragged, weary of fighting the savage country and the elusive Apache who was a part of that country, and always there was so little time.

Learning to fight doesn't come easy with most men. Learning to fight the Apache doesn't come easy with anyone. You watch the veteran until your face takes on the same mask of impassiveness, then you make decisions.

He waited patiently for Street to say something, to give him a lead. He remembered forty troopers who watched the thin gold bars on his shoulders, and he tried to forget his helplessness.

Langmade said, "The colonel was coming from Thomas to meet Mrs. Darck at Inspiration." The scout was aware of this, he knew, but he had to say something. He had to fill the gap until something happened.

Simon Street looked at the officer and a half smile broke the thin line of his mouth. "We'll find her, soldier. It wasn't your fault. People get killed by Apaches every day."

As the words came out, he realized he had said the wrong thing and added, quickly, "Know who this looks like to me?" and then went on when Langmade looked but didn't speak.

"Looks like that bronco Apache we been chasin' on and off for five years. Nochalbestinay. Though the Mexicans named him Mata Lobo. He was a Turkey Creek Chiricahua who'd never get used to reservation life in seven hundred years. Sendin' him to San Carlos was like throwin' a mountain cat a hunk of raw meat and then pullin' all his teeth out."

Street pulled a thin cigar from his pocket and passed his tongue over the crumbling outer layer of tobacco. "You know, at one time there was almost a thousand troops plus a hundred Apache scouts all in the field at one time huntin' him, and no one even saw him. You couldn't ask the dead ones if they saw him or not. An Apache's bad enough, but this one's half devil."

He moved toward the butchered horse. "Boy's got a real yen for steak, ain't he?"

All the time the tension had been building in Langmade. Just standing there with his arms heavy at his sides and the weight pulling down inside his stomach. He had to hesitate until he was sure his voice would come out sounding natural.

"You've got the sign and I've got the men," he said. "Just point the way, Simon. Just point the way."

Street had turned and was walking toward his horse. He stopped and looked back at the officer. "Get your troop back to Inspiration and get a fresh patrol out, soldier."

Street's words were low, directed only to the officer, but Langmade raised his voice almost to a shout when he answered:

"We've got men here—get on his track!"

"I'm not goin' to guide for dead men," the scout answered easily. "If a thousand men can't catch him, you can't count on forty. Maybe just one's the answer. I don't want to tell you how to run your business, son, but if I was you I'd shake it back to Inspiration and get a fresh patrol out."

Street mounted and then looked down at Langmade, who had followed him over to the horse. "The trail's as fresh as you'd want it," he said, nodding toward the butchered horse. "That mare hasn't been dead three hours. And he's got a woman with him to slow him down."

"I've been out longer than that, Simon," Langmade said. "She'll slow him down just so long."

The scout's mouth turned slightly into a smile as he pressed his heels into the mare's flanks. "That's why I got to hurry, soldier."

He walked the mare toward Banderas Creek and kicked her into a gallop as he turned upstream.

AN HOUR BEFORE sunset Simon Street was walking his horse along the winding trail that threaded its way diagonally down the slope of the forest-covered hill that on the western side joined the rocky heights of the Sierra Apaches. This gradual leveling of the sierra was a tangled mass of junipers, gnarled stumps, and rock, rising and falling abruptly from one hillock to the next.

The trail gouged itself laboriously in a general southwesterly direction, fighting rock falls, pine, and prickly pear, finally to emerge miles to the south at Devil's Flats. From the crest, and occasionally down the path, you could see in the distance the whiteness—the bleak, bone-bleached whiteness—that was the flats.

Street had traveled a dozen-odd miles from the ambush, making his way slowly at first along the creek bank, looking for a particular telltale sign. He knew the Apache had followed the creek, leaving no prints, but somewhere he had to come out.

The Apache would cover his tracks from the creek, but he would be coming out at a particular place for a reason. To pick up his mount. And you can't leave a horse tied in one place for any length of time without also leaving a sign. To recognize the place is something else.

Street saw the low tree branch that had been scarred by the hack-amore, and his eyes fell to the particles of horse droppings that had re-mained after the Apache had swept most of it into the denser scrub brush. He was on the trail. From then on it was just a question of think-ing like an Apache.

For the scout, that night, it was the last of his jerked beef and a quar-ter canteen of cold coffee. No fire. Cold, tasteless rations while he pressed his back against a smooth rock that was still warm from the day's heat and dueled his patience against the black pit that was the night.

His Winchester lay across his lap, and the slight pressure on his thighs was a feeling of reassurance against the loneliness of the night. Dead stillness, then the occasional night sound. He could be the only man in the world. Yet, just a few miles ahead, perhaps less, was a bronco Apache who would kill at the least provocation. And with him was a white woman.

Street rubbed the stock of the Winchester idly.

IN THE DUSK Amelia Darck watched the Apache. He crouched over the slab of red horsemeat, sitting on his heels, and hacked at the meat with his skinning knife. He cut off a chunk and stuffed it into his mouth, but the cold blood-taste of the raw meat tightened his throat muscles and he swallowed hard to get it down. He would wait.

He cut the slab of meat into thin strips and spread them out separately on a flat shelf of rock. When he had more time he would jerk the meat properly and have plenty to eat.

He looked toward the white woman and saw her staring at him. Always she stared, and always with the same fixed, strange look on her face. The eyes of the Apache and the white woman met, and Mata Lobo turned his attention back to the meat. The woman continued to stare at the Apache.

She sat on the ground with her arms extended behind her, full weight on her arms, propping her body in a rigid position, unmoving. Her legs extended straight out before her, the ankles lashed together with a strip of rawhide. And she continued to watch the Apache.

Amelia Darck saw an Apache for the first time when she was six years old. His face was vivid in her memory. She remembered once somebody had said, ". . . like glistening bacon rind." And always a dirty cloth headband.

Yuma, Whipple Barracks, Fort Apache, and Thomas. Officers' row on a sun-baked parade. Chiricahua, White Mountain, Mescalero, and Tonto. Thigh-high moccasins and a rusted Spencer. Tizwin drunk, then war drums. And only the red sun-slash in the sky after the patrol had faded into the glare three miles west of Thomas. Shapeless ponchos that used to be men. The old story. And she continued to watch the Apache.

Mata Lobo glanced at the woman, then stood up abruptly and walked toward her. He stooped at her feet, hesitated, then placed the blade of the knife between her ankles and jerked up with the blade, severing the rawhide string.

His face was expressionless, smooth and impassive, as he eased his body to the ground. A face that in the dimness was shadow on stone. His hands pushed against her shoulders until her arms bent slowly and her back was flat against the short, sparse grass.

The hands moved from her shoulder and touched her face gently, the fingers moving on her cheeks like a blind man's identifying an object, and his body eased toward hers.

Her face was the same. The eyes open, infrequently blinking. She smelled the sour dirt-smell of the Apache's body. Then she opened her arms and pulled him to her.

SIMON STREET was up before dawn. He gave his tightening stomach the last of the cold, stale coffee while he waited for the sun to peel back another layer of the morning darkness. It was cold and damp for that time of the year, and when he again started down the trail, a gray mist hung from the lower branches of the trees and lay softly against the grotesque rock lines.

More often now, the ground fell away to the left, the trail hugging the side of the hill in its diagonal descent; and in the distance was a sheet of milky smoke where the mist clung softly to the flats. The trail was narrow and rocky and lined with dense brush most of the way down.

Less than a mile ahead the grade dropped again steeply to the left of the trail, bare of tree or rock, cutting a smooth swatch twenty yards wide through the pines. The mist had evaporated considerably by then and Street could see almost to the bottom of the slide.

First, it was the faintest blur of motion. And then the sound. A sound that could be human.

Simon Street had been riding half tensed for the past dozen years. There was no abrupt stop. He reined in gently with a soothing murmur into the mare's ear, and slid from the saddle, whispering again to the mare as he tied the reins to a pine branch a foot from the ground.

He made his way along the trail until the slope was again thick with brush and trees, and there he began his descent. A yard at a time, making sure of firm ground before each step, bending branches slowly so there would be no warning swish. And every few yards he would hug the ground and wait, swinging his gaze in every direction, even behind.

He had gone almost a hundred yards when he saw the woman.

He crouched low to the sandy ground and crawled under the full branches of a pine, watching the woman almost thirty yards away. She was sitting on something just off the ground, her back resting against the smoothness of a birch tree.

He was approaching her from the rear and could see only part of her head and shoulder resting against the tree trunk. The brush near her cut off the lower part of her body, but there was something strange about her position—her immobility, the way her shoulder was thrown back so tightly against the roundness of the birch. Street had the feeling she was dead. Time would tell.

He lay motionless under the thick foliage and waited, the Winchester in front of him. And Simon Street had his thoughts. You never get used to the sight of a white woman after an Apache has finished with her. An hour later, a week later, a dozen years later, the picture will flash in your memory, vivid, stark naked of hazy forgetfulness.

And the form of the Apache will be there, too, close like the smothering reek of a hot animal, though you may have never seen him. Then you will be sick if you are the kind. Street wasn't the kind, but he didn't look forward to approaching the woman.

After almost a half hour he again began to work his way toward the woman. In that length of time he had not moved. Nor had the woman. If she was dead, the Apache would probably be gone. But that was guessing, and when you guess, you take a chance.

He crawled all the way, slowly, a foot at a time, until he was directly behind the birch. Then he reached up, his hand sliding along the white bark, and touched her shoulder lightly.

Amelia Darck jumped to her feet and turned in the motion. Her face was powder white, her eyes wide, startled; but when she saw the scout the color seemed to creep through her cheeks and her mouth broke into a fragile smile.

"You're late, Mr. Street. I've waited a good many hours."

The scout was momentarily stunned. He knew his face bore a foolish expression, but there was nothing he could do about it.

The woman's face regained its composure quickly and once again she was the colonel's lady. Though there was a drawn look and a darker shadow about the eyes that could not be wiped away with a polite smile.

Then Street saw the Apache. He was lying belly down in the short grass, close behind Mrs. Darck. Street took a step to her side and saw the handle of the skinning knife sticking straight up from the Apache's back. The cotton shirt was deep crimson in a wide smear around the knife handle.

He looked at her again with the foolish look still on his face.

"Mr. Street, I've been sitting up all night with a dead Indian and I'm almost past patience. Would you kindly take me to my husband."

He looked again at the Apache and then to the woman. Disbelief in his eyes. He started to say something, but Amelia Darck went on.

"I've lived out here most of my life, Mr. Street, as you know. I heard Apache war drums long before I attended my first cotillion, but I have hardly reached the point where I have to take an Apache for a lover."

Simon Street saw a thousand troops and a hundred scouts in the field. Then he looked at the slender woman walking briskly up the grade.

6

Law of the Hunted Ones

Original Title: Outlaw Pass
Western Story Magazine, December 1952

★

Chapter One

PATMAN SAW IT first. The sudden flash of sun on metal; then, on the steepness of the hillside, it was a splinter of a gleam that hung unmoving amidst the confusion of jagged rock and brush. Just a dull gleam now that meant nothing, but the first metallic flash had been enough for Virgil Patman.

He exhaled slowly, dropping his eyes from the gleam up on the slanting wall, and let his gaze drift up ahead through the narrowness, the way it would naturally. But his fists remained tight around the reins. He muttered to himself, "You damn fool." Cover was behind, a hundred feet or more, and a rifle can do a lot of pecking in a hundred feet.

The boy doesn't see it, he thought. Else he would have been shooting by now. And then other words followed in his mind. Why do you think the boy's any dumber than you are?

He shifted his hip in the saddle and turned his head halfway around. Dave Fallis was a few paces behind him and to the side. He was looking at his hands on the flat dinner-plate saddle horn, deep in thought.

Patman drew tobacco and paper from his side coat pocket and held his mount in until the boy came abreast of him.

"Don't look up too quick and don't make a sudden move," Patman said. He passed the paper along the tip of his tongue, then shaped it expertly in his bony, freckly fingers. He wasn't looking at the boy, but he could sense his head come up fast. "What did I just tell you?"

He struck a match and held it to the brown paper cigarette. His eyes were on the match and he half-mumbled with the cigarette in his mouth, "Dave, hold on to your nerve. There's a rifle pointing at us. Maybe two hundred feet ahead and almost to the top of the slope." He handed the makings across. "Build yourself one like it was Sunday afternoon on the front porch."

Their horses moved at a slow walk close to the left side that was smooth rock and almost straight up. Here, and as far as you could see ahead, the right side slanted steeply up, gravel, rock and brush thrown violently together, to finally climb into dense pines overhead. Here and there the pines straggled down the slope. Patman watched the boy put the twisted cigarette between his lips and light it, the hand steady, up close to his face.

"When you get a chance," Patman said, "look about halfway up the slope, just this side of that hollow. You'll see a dab of yellow that's prickly pear, then go above to that rock jam and tell me what you see."

Fallis pulled his hat closer to his eyes and looked up-canyon before dragging his gaze to the slope. His face registered nothing, not even a squint with the hat brim resting on his eyebrows. A hard-boned face, tight through the cheeks and red-brown from the sun, but young and with a good mouth that looked as if it smiled most of the time, though it wasn't smiling now. His gaze lowered to the pass and he drew on the cigarette.

"Something shining up there, but I don't make out what it is," he said.

"It's a rifle, all right. We'll take for granted somebody's behind it."

"Indian?"

"Not if the piece is so clean it shines," Patman answered. "Just keep going, and watch me. We'll gamble that it's a white man—and gamble that he acts like one."

Fallis tried to keep his voice even. "What if he just shoots?" The question was hoarse with excitement. *Maybe the boy's not as scared as I am,* Patman thought. *Young and too eager to be afraid. You get old and take too damn much time doing what kept you alive when you were young. Why keep thinking of him,* he thought, *you got a hide too, you know.*

Patman answered, "If he shoots, we'll know where we stand and you can do the first thing that comes to your mind."

"Then I might let go at you," Fallis smiled, "for leading us into this jackpot."

Patman's narrow face looked stone-hard with its sad smile beneath the full mustache. "If you want to make jokes," he said, "go find someone else."

"What're we going to do, Virg?" Fallis was dead serious. It made his face look tough when he didn't smile, with the heavy cheekbones and the hard jawline beneath.

"We don't have a hell of a lot of choices," Patman said. "If we kick into a run or turn too fast, we're likely to get a bullet. You don't want to take a chance on that gent up there being the nervous type. And if we just start shooting, we haven't got anything to hide behind when he shoots back."

He heard the boy say, "We can get behind our horses."

He answered him, "I'd just as soon get shot as have to walk home. You got any objections to just going on like we don't know he's there?"

Fallis shook his head, swallowing. "Anything you say, Virg. Probably he's just out hunting turkeys. . . ." He dropped behind the older man as they edged along the smooth rock of the canyon wall until there was ten feet between their horses.

☆ ☆ ☆

THEY RODE STIFF-BACKED, from habit, yet with an easy looseness of head and arms that described an absence of tension. Part of it was natural, again habit, and part was each trying to convince the other that he wasn't afraid. Patman and Fallis were good for each other. They had learned it through campaigning.

Now, with the tightness in their bellies, they waited for the sound. The clop of their horses' hooves had a dull ring in the awful silence. They waited for another sound.

Both men were half expecting the heavy report of a rifle. They steeled themselves against the worst that could happen, because anything else would take care of itself. The sound of the loose rock glancing down the slope was startling, like a warning to jerk their heads to the side and up the slanting wall.

The man was standing in the spot where Patman had pointed, his rifle at aim, so that all they could see was the rifle below the hat. No face.

"Don't move a finger, or you're dead!" The voice was full and clear. The man lowered the rifle and called, "Sit still while I come down."

He turned and picked his way over the scattered rock, finally half sliding into the hollow that was behind his position. The hollow fell less steeply to the canyon floor with natural rock footholds and gnarled brush stumps to hold on to.

For a moment the man's head disappeared from view, then was there again just as suddenly. He hesitated, watching the two men below him and fifty feet back up the trail. Then he disappeared again into a deeper section of the descent.

Dave Fallis' hand darted to the holster at his hip.

"Hold onto yourself!" Patman's whisper was a growl in his heavy mustache. His eyes flicked to the hollow. "He's not alone! You think he'd go out of sight if he was by himself!"

The boy's hand slid back to the saddle horn while his eyes traveled over the heights above him. Only the hot breeze moved the brush clumps.

The man moved toward them on the trail ahead with short, bow-legged steps, his face lowered close to the upraised rifle. When he was a dozen steps from Patman's horse, his head came up and he shouted, "All right!" to the heights behind them. Fallis heard Patman mumble, "I'll be damned," looking at the man with the rifle.

"Hey, Rondo!" Patman was grinning his sad smile down at the short, bowlegged man with the rifle. "What you got here, a toll you collect from anybody who goes by?" Patman laughed out, with a ring of relief to the laugh. "I saw you a ways back. Your toll box was shining in the sun." He went on laughing and put his hand in his side coat pocket.

The rifle came up full on his chest. "Keep your hand in sight!" The man's voice cut sharply.

Patman looked at him surprised. "What's the matter with you, Rondo? It's me. Virg Patman." His arm swung to his side. "This here's Dave Fallis. We rode together in the Third for the past five years."

Rondo's heavy-whiskered face stared back, the deep lines unmoving as if they had been cut into stone. The rifle was steady on Patman's chest.

"What the hell's the matter with you!" Patman repeated. "Remember me bringing you your bait for sixty days at Thomas?"

Rondo's beard separated when his mouth opened slightly. "You were on the outside, if I remember correctly."

Patman swore with a gruff howl. "You talk like I passed sentence! You damn fool, what do you think a Corporal of the Guard is—a judge?" His head turned to Fallis. "This bent-legged waddie shoots a reservation Indian, gets sixty days, then blames it on me. You remember him in the lock-up?"

"No. I guess—"

"That's right," Patman cut in. "That was before your time."

Rondo looked past the two men.

"That wasn't before my time." The voice came from behind the two men.

HE WAS SQUATTING on a hump that jutted out from the slope, just above their heads and a dozen or so feet behind them, and he looked as if he'd been sitting there all the time. When he looked at him, Fallis thought of a scavenger bird perched on the bloated roundness of a carcass.

It was his head and the thinness of his frame that gave that impression. His dark hair was cropped close to his skull, brushed forward low on his forehead and coming to a slight point above his eyebrows. The thin hair pointed down, as did the ends of a shadowy mustache that was just starting to grow, lengthening the line of his face, a face that was sallow complexioned and squinting against the brightness of the afternoon.

He jumped easily from the hump, his arms outstretched and a pistol in each hand, though he wore only one holster on his hip.

Fallis watched him open-mouthed. He wore a faded undershirt and pants tucked into knee-high boots. A string of red cotton was knotted tight to his throat above the opening of the undershirt. And with it all, the yellowish death's-head of a face. Fallis watched because he couldn't take his eyes from the man. There was a compelling arrogance about his movements and the way he held his head that made Fallis stare at him. And even with the shabbiness of his dress, it stood out. It was there in the way he held his pistols. Fallis pictured a saber-slashing captain of cavalry. Then he saw a black-bearded buccaneer.

"I remember when Rondo was in the lock-up at Fort Thomas." His voice was crisp, but low and he extra-spaced his words. "That was a good spell before you rode me to Yuma, wasn't it?"

Patman shook his head. The surprise had already left his face. He shook his head wearily as if it was all way above him. He said, "If you got any more men up there that I policed, get 'em down and let me hear it all at once." He shook his head again. "This is a real day of surprises. I can't say I ever expected to see you again, De Sana."

"Then what are you doing here?" The voice was cold-clear, but fell off at the end of the question as if he had already made up his mind why they were there.

Patman saw it right away.

It took Fallis a little longer because he had to fill in, but he understood now, looking at De Sana and then to Patman.

Patman's voice was a note higher. "You think we're looking for you?"

"I said," De Sana repeated, "then what are you doing here?"

"Hell, we're not tracking you! We were mustered out last week. We're pointing toward West Texas for a range job, or else sign for contract buffalo hunters."

De Sana stared, but didn't speak. His hands, with the revolving pistols, hung at his sides.

"What do I care if you broke out of the Territory prison?" Patman shouted it, then seemed to relax, to calm himself. "Listen," he said, "we're both mustered out. Dave here has got one hitch in, and I've got more years behind me than I like to remember. But we're out now and what the army does is its own damn business. And what you do is your business. I can forget you like that." He snapped his fingers. " 'Cause you don't mean a thing to me. And that dust-eatin' train ride from Willcox to Yuma, I can forget that too, 'cause I didn't enjoy it any more than you did even if you thought then you weren't going to make the return trip. You're as bad as Rondo here. You think 'cause I was train guard it was my fault you got sent to Yuma. Listen. I treated you square. There were some troopers would have kicked your face in just on principle."

De Sana moistened his lower lip with his tongue, idly, thinking about the past and the future at the same time. A man has to believe in something, no matter what he is. He looked at the two men on the horses and felt the weight of the pistols in his hands. There was the easy way. He looked at them watching him uneasily, waiting for him to make a move.

"Going after a range job, huh?" he said almost inaudibly.

"That's right. Or else hunt buffalo. They say the railroad's paying top rate, too," Patman added.

"How do I know," De Sana said slowly, "you won't get to the next sheriff's office and start yelling wolf."

Patman was silent as his fingers moved over his jaw. "I guess you'll have to take my word that I've got a bad memory," he said finally.

"What kind of memory has your friend got?" De Sana said, looking hard at Dave Fallis.

"You got the biggest pistols he ever saw," Patman answered.

Rondo mounted behind Patman and pointed the way up the narrow draw that climbed from the main trail about a quarter of a mile up. It branched from the pass, twisting as it climbed, but more decidedly bearing an angle back in the direction from which they had come. Rondo had laughed out at Patman's last words. The tension was off now. Since De Sana had accepted the two men, Rondo would too, and went even a step further, talking about hospitality and coffee and words like this calls for a celebration, even though the words were lost on the other three men. The words had no meaning but they filled in and lessened the tension.

☆

Chapter Two

DE SANA WAS still standing in the pass when they left, but when Fallis looked back he saw the outlaw making his way up the hollow.

When the draw reached the end of its climb they were at the top of the ridge, looking down directly to the place where they had held up. Here, the pines were thick, but farther off they scattered and thinned again as they began to stretch toward higher, rockier ground.

De Sana was standing among the trees waiting for them. He turned before they reached him and led the way through the pines. Fallis looked around curiously, feeling the uneasiness that had come over him since meeting De Sana. Then, as he looked ahead, the hut wasn't fifty feet away.

It was a low structure, flat-roofed and windowless, with rough, uneven logs chinked in with adobe mud. On one side was a lean-to where the cooking was done. A girl was hanging strips of meat from the low ceiling when they came out of the pines, and as they approached she turned with a hand on her hip, smoothing a stray wisp of hair with the other.

She watched them with open curiosity, as a small child stares at the mystery of a strange person. There was a delicateness of face and body that accentuated this, that made her look more childlike in her open sensitivity. De Sana glanced at her and she dropped her eyes and turned back to the jerked meat.

"Put the coffee on," De Sana called to her. She nodded her head without turning around. "Rondo, you take care of the mounts and get back to your nest."

Rondo opened his mouth to say something but thought better of it and tried to make his face look natural when he took the reins from the two men and led the horses across the small clearing to the corral, part of which could be seen through the pines a little way off. A three-sided lean-to squatted at one end of the small, fenced area.

"That's Rondo's," De Sana pointed to the shelter. Walking to the cabin he called to the girl again. This time she did not shake her head. Fallis thought perhaps the shoulders tensed in the faded gray dress. Still, she didn't turn around or even answer him.

The inside of the cabin was the same as the outside, rough log chinked with adobe, and a packed dirt floor. A table and two chairs, striped with cracks and gray with age, stood in the middle of the small room. In a far corner was a straw mattress. On it, a blanket was twisted in a heap. Along the opposite wall was a section of log with a board nailed to it to serve as a bench, and next to this was the cupboard: three boxes stacked one on the other. It contained a tangle of clothing, cartridge boxes and five or six bottles of whiskey.

The two men watched De Sana shove his extra pistol into a holster that hung next to the cupboard. The other was on his hip. He took a half-filled bottle from the shelf and went to the table.

"Looks like I'm just in time." Rondo was standing in the doorway, grinning, with a canteen hanging from his hand. "Give me a little fill, *jefe,* to ease sitting on that eagle's nest."

De Sana's head came up and he moved around the table threateningly, his eyes pinned on the man in the doorway. "Get back to the pass!" His hand dropped to the pistol on his hip in a natural movement. "You watch! You get paid to watch! And if you miss anything going through that pass . . ." His voice trailed off, but for a moment it shook with excitement.

"Hell, Lew. Nobody's going to find us way up here," Rondo argued half-heartedly.

Patman looked at him surprised. "Cima Quaine's blood-dogs could track a man all the way to China."

"Aw, San Carlos's a hundred miles away. Ain't nobody going to track us that far, not even 'Pache Police."

De Sana said, "I'm not telling you again, Rondo." Rondo glanced at the hand on the pistol butt and moved out of the doorway.

But as he walked through the pines toward the canyon edge, he held the canteen up to his face and shook it a few times. He could hear the whiskey inside sloshing around sounding as if it were still a good one-third full. Rondo smiled and his mind erased the scowling yellow face. Lew De Sana could go take a whistlin' dive at the moon for all he cared.

THE GIRL'S FINGERS were crooked through the handles of the three enamel cups, and she kept her eyes lowered to the table as she set the coffeepot down with her other hand, placing the cups next to it.

"Looks good," Patman said.

She said nothing, but her eyes lifted to him briefly, then darted to the opposite side of the table where Fallis stood and then lowered just as quickly. She had turned her head slightly, enough for Fallis to see the bruise on her cheekbone. A deep blue beneath her eye that spread into a yellowish caste in the soft hollow of her cheek. There was a lifelessness in the dark eyes and perhaps fear. Fallis kept staring at the girl, seeing the utter resignation that showed in her face and was there even in the way she moved her small body. Like a person who has given up and doesn't much care what happens next. He noticed the eyes when her glance wandered to him again, dark and tired, yet with a certain hungriness in their deepness. No, it wasn't fear.

De Sana picked up the first cup as she filled it and poured a heavy shot from the bottle into it. He set the bottle down and lifted the coffee cup to his mouth. His lips moved, as if tasting, and he said, "It's cold," looking at the girl in a way that didn't need the support of other words. He turned the cup upside down and poured the dark liquid on the floor.

Fallis thought, *What a damn fool. Who's he trying to impress?* He glanced at Patman but the ex-corporal was looking at De Sana as if pouring coffee on the floor was the most normal thing in the world.

As the girl picked up the big coffeepot, her hand shook with the weight and before her other hand could close on the spout, she dropped it back on the table.

"Here, I'll give you a hand," Fallis offered. "That's a big jug."

But just as he took it from the girl's hands, he heard De Sana say, "Leave that pot alone!"

He looked at De Sana in bewilderment. "What? I just want to help her out with the coffeepot."

"She can do her own chores." De Sana's voice was unhurried. "Just put it down."

Dave Fallis felt heat rise up over his face. When he was angry, he always wondered if it showed. And sometimes, as, for instance, now, he didn't care. His heart started going faster with the rise of the heat that tingled the hair on the back of his head and made the words come to his mouth. And he had to spit the words out hard because it would make him feel better.

"Who the hell are you talking to? Do I look like somebody you can give orders to?" Fallis stopped but kept on looking at the thin, sallow face, wishing he could think of something good to say while the anger was up.

Patman moved closer to the younger man. "Slow down, Dave," he said with a laugh that sounded forced. "A man's got a right to run things like he wants in his own house."

De Sana's eyes moved from one to the other, then back to the girl and said, "What are you waiting for?" He kept his eyes on her until she passed through the doorway. Then he said, "Mister, you better have a talk with your boy."

Fallis heard Patman say, "That's just his Irish, Lew. You know, young and gets hot easy." He stared at the old cavalryman—not really old, but twice his own age—and tried to see through the sad face with the drooping mustache because he knew that wasn't Virg Patman talking, calling him by his first name as if they were old friends. What was the matter with Virg? He felt the anger draining and in its place was bewilderment. It made him feel uneasy and kind of foolish standing there, with his big hands planted on the table, trying to stare down the skeletal-looking gunman who looked at him as if he were a kid and would be just wasting his time talking. It made him madder, but the things he wanted to say sounded too loudmouth in his mind. The words seemed blustering, hot air, compared to the cold, slow-spoken words of De Sana.

Now De Sana said, "I don't care what his nationality is. But I think you better tell him the facts of life."

Fallis felt the heat again, but Patman broke in with his laugh before he could say anything.

"Hell, Lew," Patman said. "Let's get back to what we come for. Nobody meant any harm."

De Sana fingered the dark shadow of his mustache thoughtfully, and finally said, hurriedly, "Yeah. All right." Then he added, "Now that you're here, you might as well stay the night and leave in the morning. If you have any stores with you, break them out. This isn't any street mission. And remember, first light you leave."

Later, during the meal, he spoke little, occasionally answering Patman in monosyllables. He never spoke directly to Fallis and only answered Patman when he had to. Finally he pushed from the table before he had finished. He rolled a cigarette moving toward the door. "I'm going out to relieve Rondo," he said. "Don't wander off."

☆　☆　☆

FALLIS WATCHED HIM walk across the clearing and when the figure disappeared into the pines he turned abruptly to Patman sitting next to him.

"What's the matter with you, Virg?"

Patman put his hand up. "Now just slow it down. You're too damn jumpy."

"Jumpy? Honest to God, Virg, you never sucked up to the first sergeant like you did to that little rooster. Back in the pass you read him out when he started jumping to conclusions. Now you're buttering up like you were scared to death."

"Wait a minute." Patman passed his fingers through his thinning hair, his elbow on the table. He looked very tired and his long face seemed to sag loosely in sadness. "If you're going to play brave, you got to pick the right time, else your bravery don't mean a damn thing. These hills are full of heroes, and nobody even knows where to plant the flowers over them. Then you come across a man fresh out of Yuma—out the hard way, too—" he added, "a man who probably shoots holes in his shadow every night and can't trust anybody because it might mean going back to an adobe cell block. He got sent there in the first place because he shot an Indian agent in a hold-up. He didn't kill him, but don't think he couldn't have—and don't think he hasn't killed before."

Patman exhaled and drew tobacco from his pocket. "You run into a man like that, a man who counts his breaths like you count your blessings, and you pick a fight because you don't like the way he treats his woman."

"A man can't get his toes stepped on and just smile," Fallis said testily.

Patman blew smoke out wearily. "Maybe your hitch in the Army was kind of a sheltered life. Brass bands and not having to think. Trailing a dust cloud that used to be Apaches isn't facing Lew De Sana across a three foot table. I think you were lucky."

Fallis picked up his hat and walked toward the door. "We'll see," he answered.

"Wait a minute, Dave." Fallis turned in the doorway.

"Sometimes you got to pick the lesser of evils," the older man said.

"Like choosing between a sore toe or lead in your belly. Remember, Dave, he's a man with a price on his head. He's spooky. And remember this. A little while ago he could have shot both of your eyes out while he was drinking his coffee."

Patience wasn't something Dave Fallis came by naturally. Standing idle ate at his nerves and made him move restlessly like a penned animal. The Army hitch had grated on him this way. Petty routines and idleness. Idleness in the barracks and idleness even in the dust-smothering parade during the hours of drill. Routine that became so much a part of you it ceased being mentally directed.

The cavalry had a remedy for the restless feeling. Four-day patrols. Four-day patrols that sometimes stretched to twenty and by it brought the ailment back with the remedy. For a saddle is a poor place for boredom, and twelve hours in it will bring the boredom back quicker than anything else, especially when the land is flat and vacant, silent but for a monotonous clop, blazing in its silence and carrying only dust and a sweat smell that clung sourly to you in the daytime and chilled you at night. Dave Fallis complained because nothing happened—because there was never any action. He was told he didn't know how lucky he was. That he didn't know what he was talking about because he was just a kid. And nothing made him madder. Damn a man who's so ignorant he holds age against you!

Now he stood in the doorway and looked out across the clearing. He leaned against the doorjamb, hooking his thumbs in his belt, and let his body go loose. The sun was there in front of him over the trees, casting a soft spread of light on the dark hillsides in the distance. Now it was a sun that you could look at without squinting or pulling down your hat brim. A sun that would be gone in less than an hour.

He saw the girl appear and move toward the lean-to at the side of the hut. She walked slowly, listlessly.

Fallis left the doorway and idled along the front of the hut after she had passed and entered the shelter. And when he ducked his head slightly and entered the low-roofed shed, the girl was busy scooping venison stew from the pot and dishing it onto one of the tin plates.

★ ★ ★

SHE TURNED QUICKLY at the sound of his step and almost brushed him as she turned, stopping, her mouth slightly open, her face lower than his, but not a foot separating them.

He was grinning when she turned, but the smile left his face as she continued to stare up at him, her mouth still parted slightly and warm looking, complementing the delicately soft lines of nose and cheekbones. The bruise was not so noticeable now, in the shadows, but its presence gave her face a look of sadness, yet adding luster to the deep brown eyes that stared without blinking.

His hands came up to grip her shoulders, pulling gently as he lowered his face to hers. She yielded against the slight pressure of his hands, drawing closer, and he saw her eyes close as her face tilted back, but as he closed his eyes he felt her shoulders jerk suddenly from his grip and in front of his face now was the smooth blackness of her hair hanging straight about her shoulders.

"Why did you do that?" Her voice was low, and with her back to him, barely audible.

Fallis said, "I haven't done anything yet," and tried to make his voice sound light. The girl made no answer, but remained still, with her shoulder close to him.

"I'm sorry," he said. "Are you married to him?"

Her head shook from side to side in two short motions, but no sound came from her. He turned her gently, his hands again on her shoulders, and as she turned she lowered her head so he could not see her face. But he crooked a finger beneath her chin and raised it slowly to his. His hand moved from her slender chin to gently touch the bruised cheekbone.

"Why don't you leave him?" He half-whispered the words.

For a moment she remained silent and lowered her eyes from his face. Finally she said, "I would have no place to go." Her voice bore the hint of an accent.

"What's worse than living with him and getting beat like an animal?"

"He is good to me—most of the time. He is tired and nervous and doesn't know what he is doing. I remember him when he was younger and would visit my father. He smiled often then and was good to us."

Her words flowed faster now, as if she was anxious to speak, voluntarily lifting her face to look into his with a pleading in her dark eyes that seemed to say, "Please believe what I say and tell me that I am right."

"My father," she went on, "worked a small farm near Nogales which I remember as far back as I am able. He worked hard but he was not a very good farmer, and I always had the feeling that papa was sorry he had married and settled there. You see, my mother was Mexican," and she lowered her eyes as if in apology.

"One day this man rode up and asked if he may buy coffee. We had none, but he stayed and talked long with papa and they seemed to get along very well. After that he came often, maybe two three times a month and always he brought us presents and sometimes even money, which my papa took and I thought was very bad of him, even though I was only a little girl. Soon after that my mother died of sickness, and my papa took me to Tucson to live. And from that time he began going away for weeks at a time with this man and when he returned he would have money and he would be very drunk. When he would go, I prayed to the Mother of God at night because I knew what he was doing.

"Finally, he went away and did not return." Her voice carried a note of despair. "And my prayers changed to ones for the repose of his soul."

Fallis said, "I'm sorry," awkwardly, but the girl went on as if he had not spoken.

"A few months later the man returned and treated me differently." Her face colored slightly. "He treated me older. He was kind and told me he would come back soon and take me away from Tucson to a beautiful place I would love. . . . But it was almost two years after this that the man called Rondo came to me at night and took me to the man. I had almost forgotten him. He was waiting outside of town with horses and made me go with them. I did not know him, he had changed so—his face, and even his voice. We have been here for almost two weeks, and only a few days ago I learned where he had been for the two years."

Suddenly, she pressed her face into his chest and began to cry silently, convulsively.

Fallis's arms circled the thinness of her shoulders to press her hard against his chest. He mumbled, "Don't cry," into her hair and closed his eyes hard to think of something he could say. Feeling her body shaking against his own, he could see only a smiling, dark-haired little girl looking with awe at the carefree, generous American riding into the yard with a war bag full of presents. And then the little girl standing there was no longer smiling, her cheekbone was black and blue and she carried a half-gallon coffeepot in her hands. And the carefree American became a sallow death's-head that she called only "the man."

With her face buried against his chest, she was speaking. At first he could not make out her words, incoherent with the crying, then he realized that she was repeating, "I do not like him," over and over, "I do not like him." He thought, how can she use such simple words? He lifted her head, her eyes closed, and pressed his mouth against the lips that finally stopped saying, "I do not like him."

She pushed away from him lingeringly, her face flushed, and surprised the grin from his face when she said, "Now I must get wood for in the morning."

The grin returned as he looked down at her childlike face, now so serious. He lifted the hand-ax from the wood box, and they walked across the clearing very close together.

Virgil Patman stood in the doorway and watched them dissolve into the darkness of the pines.

Well, what are you going to do? Maybe a man's not better off minding his own business. The boy looks like he's doing pretty well not minding his. But damn, he thought, he's sure making it tough! He stared out at the cold, still light of early evening and heard the voice in his mind again. You've given him a lot of advice, but you've never really done anything for him. He's a good boy. Deserves a break. It's his own damn business how quick he falls for a girl. Why don't you try and give him a hand?

Patman exhaled wearily and turned back into the hut. He lifted De Sana's handgun from the holster on the wall and pushed it into the waist of his pants. From the cupboard he took the boxes of cartridges, loading one arm, and then picked up a Winchester leaning in the front corner that he had not noticed there before. He passed around the cooking lean-to to the back of the hut and entered the pines that pushed in close there. In a few minutes he was back inside the cabin, brushing sand from his hands. Not much, he thought, but maybe it'll help some. Before he sat down and poured himself a drink, he drew his pistol and placed it on the table near his hand.

★

Chapter Three

TWO CENTS KNEW patience. It was as natural to him as breathing. He could not help smiling as he watched the white man, not a hundred feet away and just above him on the opposite slope, pull his head up high over the rim of the rocks in front of him, concentrating his attention off below where the trail broke into the pass. Rondo watched the pass, like De Sana had told him, and if his eyes wandered over the opposite canyon wall, it was only when he dragged them back to his own niche, and then it was only a fleeting glance at almost vertical smooth rock and brush.

Two Cents waited and watched, studying this white man who exposed himself so in hiding. Perhaps the man is a lure, he thought, to take us off guard. His lips straightened into a tight line, erasing the smile. He watched the man's head turn to the trees above him. Then the head turned back and he lifted the big canteen to his mouth. Two Cents had counted, and it was the sixth time the man had done so in less than a half hour. His thirst must be that of fire.

He felt a hand on his ankle and began to ease his body away from the rim that was here thick with tangled brush. He backed away cautiously so that the loose gravel would not even know he was there, and nodded his head once to Vea Oiga who crept past him to where he had lain.

A dozen or so yards back, where the ground sloped from the rim, he stood erect and looked back at Vea Oiga. Even at this short distance he could barely make out the crouched figure.

He lifted the shell belt over his head and then removed the faded blue jacket carefully, smoothing the bare sleeves before folding it next to

Vea Oiga's on the ground. If he performed bravely, he thought, perhaps Cima Quaine will put a gold mark on the sleeves. He noticed Vea Oiga had folded his jacket so the three gold stripes were on top. Perhaps not three all at once, for it had taken Vea Oiga years to acquire them, but just one. How fine that would look. Surely Cima Quaine must recognize their ability in discovering this man in the pass.

Less than an hour before they had followed the trail up to the point where it twisted into the pass, but there they stopped and back-trailed to a gradual rock fall that led up to the top of the canyon. They had tied up there and climbed on foot to the canyon rim that looked across to the other slope. They had done this naturally, without a second thought, because it was their business, and because if they were laying an ambush they would have picked this place where the pass narrowed and it was a hundred feet back to shelter. A few minutes after creeping to the rim, Rondo had appeared with a clatter of gravel, standing, exposing himself fully.

Vea Oiga had whispered to him what they would do after studying the white man for some time. Then he had dropped back to prepare himself. With Cima Quaine and the rest of the Coyotero Apache scouts less than an hour behind, they would just have time to get ready and go about the ticklish job of disposing of the lookout. Two Cents hoped that the chief scout would hurry up and be there to see him climb up to take the guard. He glanced at his castoff cavalry jacket again and pictured the gold chevron on the sleeve; it was as bright and impressive as Vea Oiga's sergeant stripes.

Now he looked at the curled toes of his moccasins as he unfastened the ties below his knees and rolled the legging part of his pants high above his knees and secured them again. He tightened the string of his breechclout, then spit on his hands a half dozen times rubbing the saliva over his arms and the upper part of his body until his dull brown coloring glistened with the wetness. When he had moistened every part of skin showing, he sank to the ground and rolled in the dust, rubbing his arms and face with the sand that clung to the wet skin.

He raised himself to his knees and knelt motionless like a rock or a stump, his body the color of everything around him, and now, just as still and unreal in his concentration.

Slowly his arms lifted to the dulling sky and his thoughts went to U-sen. He petitioned the God that he might perform bravely in what was to come, and if it were the will of U-sen that he was to die this day, would the God mind if it came about before the sun set? To be killed at night was to wander in eternal darkness, and nothing that he imagined could be worse, especially coming at the hands of a white man whom even the other white men despised.

WHEN TWO CENTS had disappeared down through the rocks, Vea Oiga moved back from the rim until he was sure he could not be seen. Then he ran in a crouch, weaving through the mesquite and boulders, until he found another place along the rim that was dense with brush clumps. From here, Rondo's head and rifle barrel were still visible, but now he could also see, down to the right, the opening where the trail cut into the pass. He lay motionless watching the white man until finally the low, wailing call lifted from down-canyon. At that moment he watched Rondo more intently and saw the man's head lift suddenly to look in the direction from which the sound had come; but after only a few seconds the head dropped again, relaxed. Vea Oiga smiled. Now it was his turn.

The figure across the canyon was still for a longer time than usual, but finally the scout saw the head move slowly, looking behind and above to the pines. Vea Oiga rolled to his side and cupped his hands over his mouth. When he saw the canteen come up even with the man's face, he whistled into his cupped hands, the sound coming out in a moan and floating in the air as if coming from nowhere. He rolled again in time to see Two Cents dart from the trail opening across the pass to the opposite slope. He lay motionless at the base for a few minutes. Then as he watched, the figure slowly began to inch his way up-canyon.

By the time the sergeant of scouts had made his way around to where trail met pass, Two Cents was far up the canyon. Vea Oiga clung tight to the rock wall and inched his face past the angle that would show him the pass. He saw the movement. A hump that was part of the ground seemed to edge along a few feet and then stop. And soon he watched this moving piece of earth glide directly under the white man's position and dissolve into the hollow that ran up the slanting wall just past the yellowness of the patch of prickly pear. And above the yellow bloom the rifle could no longer be seen. A splash of crimson spreading in the sky behind the pines was all that was left of the sun.

Vea Oiga turned quickly and ran back up-trail. He stopped on a rise and looked out over the open country, patched and cut with hills in the distance. His gaze crawled out slowly, sweeping on a small arc, and then stopped. There! Yes, he was sure. Maybe they were three miles away, but no more, which meant Cima Quaine would be there in fifteen to twenty minutes. Vea Oiga did not have time to wait for the scouting party. He ran back to the mouth of the pass and there, at the side of the trail, piled three stones one on the other. With his knife he scratched marks on the top stone and at the base of the bottom one, then hurried to the outcropping of rock from which he had watched the progress of his companion. And just as his gaze inched past the rock, he saw the movement behind and above the white man's position, as if part of the ground was sliding down on him.

Vea Oiga moved like a shadow at that moment across the openness of the pass. The shadow moved quickly up the face of the slope and soon was lost among rock and the darkness of the pines that straggled down the slope.

CROSSING THE CLEAR patch of sand, Lew De Sana didn't like the feeling that had come over him. Not something new, just an intensifying of the nervousness that had spread through his body since the arrival of the two men. As if every part of his body was aware of something imminent, but would not tell his mind about it. As he thought about it, he realized that, no, it was not something that had been born with the arrival of the two men. It had been inside of him every day of the two years at Yuma, gaining strength the night Rondo aided him in his escape. And it had been a clawing part of his stomach the night north of Tucson when they had picked up the girl.

He didn't understand the feeling. That's what worried him. The nervousness would come and then go away, but when it returned, he would find that it had grown, and when it went away there was always a part of him that had vanished with it. A part of him that he used to rely on.

One thing, he was honest with himself in his introspection. And undoubtedly it was this honesty that made him see himself clearly enough to be frightened, but still with a certain haze that would not allow him to understand. He remembered his reputation. Cold nerve and a swivel-type gun holster that he knew how to use. In the days before Yuma, sometimes reputation had been enough. And, more often, he had hoped that it would be enough, for he wasn't fool enough to believe completely in his own reputation. But every once in a while he was called on to back up his reputation, and sometimes this had been hard.

Now he wasn't sure. Men can forget in two years. They can forget a great deal, and De Sana worried if he would have to prove himself all over again. It had come to him lately that if this were true, he would never survive, even though he knew he was still good with a gun and could face any situation if he had to. There was this tiredness inside of him now. It clashed with the nervous tension of a hunted man and left him confused and in a desperate sort of helplessness.

Moving through the pines, thoughts ran through his mind, one on top of the other so that none of them made sense. He closed his eyes tightly for a moment, passing his hand over his face and rubbing his forehead as if the gesture would make the racing in his mind stop. He felt the short hair hanging on his forehead, and as his hand lowered, the gauntness of his cheeks and the stubble of his new mustache. He saw the cell block at Yuma and swore in his breath.

His boots made a muffled, scraping sound moving over the sand and pine needles, and, as if becoming aware of the sound for the first time, he slowed his steps and picked his way more carefully through the trees.

The muscles in his legs tightened as he eased his steps on the loose ground. And then he stopped. He stopped dead and the pistol was out in front of him before he realized he had even pulled it. Instinctively his knees bent slightly as he crouched; straining his neck forward he looked through the dimness of the pines, but if there was movement before, it was not there now.

Still, he waited a few minutes to make sure. He let the breath move through his lips in a long sigh and lowered the pistol to his side. He hated himself for his jumpiness. It was the strange tiredness again. He was tired of hiding and drawing when the wind moved the branches of trees. How much can a man take, he wondered. Maybe staying alive wasn't worth it when you had to live this way.

He was about to go ahead when he saw it again. The pistol came up and this time he was sure. Through the branches of the tree in front of him, he saw the movement, a shadow gliding from one clump to the next, perhaps fifty paces up ahead. Now, as he crouched low to the bole of the pine that shielded him, the lines in his face eased. At that moment he felt good because it wasn't jumpiness anymore, and there was another feeling within him that hadn't been there for a long time. He peered through the thick lower branches of the pine and saw the dim shape on the path now moving directly toward him.

He watched the figure stop every few feet, still shadowy in the gloom, then move ahead a little more before stopping to look right and left and even behind. De Sana felt the tightness again in his stomach, not being able to make out what the man was, and suddenly the panic was back. For a split second he imagined one of the shadows that had been haunting him had suddenly become a living thing; and then he made out the half-naked Apache and it was too late to imagine anymore.

He knew there would be a noise when he made his move, but that couldn't be helped. He waited until the Indian was a step past the tree, then he raised up. Coal-black hair flaired suddenly from a shoulder, then a wide-eyed face even with his own and an open mouth that almost cried out before the pistol barrel smashed against the bridge of his nose and forehead.

De Sana cocked his head, straining against the silence, then slowly eased down next to the body of the Indian when no sound reached him. He thought: A body lying motionless always seemed to make it more quiet. Like the deeper silence that seemed to follow gunfire. Probably the silence was just in your head.

He laid his hand on the thin, grimy chest and jerked it back quickly when he felt no movement. Death wasn't something the outlaw was squeamish about, but it surprised him that the blow to the head had killed the Indian. He looked over the half-naked figure calmly and decided there was something there that bothered him. He bent closer in the gloom. No war paint. Not a line. He fumbled at the Indian's holster hurriedly and pulled out the well-kept Colt .44. No reservation-jumping buck owned a gun like that; and even less likely, a Sierra Madre broncho who'd more probably carry a rusted cap and ball at best. He wondered why it hadn't occurred to him right away. Apache police! And that meant Cima Quaine. . . .

He stood up and listened again momentarily before moving ahead quickly through the pines.

He came to the canyon rim and edged along it cautiously, pressing close to the flinty rock, keeping to the deep shadows as much as he could, until he reached the hollow that sloped to the niche that Rondo had dug for himself.

He jumped quickly into the depression that fell away below him and held himself motionless in the darkness of the hollow for almost a minute before edging his gaze over the side and down to the niche a dozen yards below. He saw Rondo sprawled on his back with one booted leg propped on the rock parapet next to the rifle that pointed out over the pass.

There was no hesitating now. He climbed hurriedly, almost frantically, back to the pine grove and ran against the branches that stung his face and made him stumble in his haste. The silence was still there, but now it was heavier, pushing against him to make him run faster and stumble more often in the loose footing of the sand. He didn't care if he made noise. He heard his own forced breathing close and loud and imagined it echoing over the hillside, but now he didn't care because they knew he was here. He knew he was afraid. Things he couldn't see did that to him. He reached the clearing, finally, and darted across the clearing toward the hut.

Chapter Four

VIRGIL PATMAN PUSHED the glass away from his hand when he heard the noise outside and wrapped his fingers around the bone handle of the pistol. The light slanting through the open doorway was weak, almost the last of the sun. He waited for the squat figure of Rondo to appear in this dim square of light, and started slightly when suddenly a thin shape appeared. And he sat bolt upright when next De Sana was in the room, clutching the door frame and breathing hard.

Patman watched him curiously and managed to keep the surprise out of his voice when he asked, "Where's Rondo? Thought you relieved him."

De Sana gasped out the word, "Quaine!" and wheeled to the front corner where the rifle had been. He took two steps and stopped dead. Patman watched the thin shoulders stiffen and raised the pistol with his hand still on the table until the barrel was leveled at the outlaw.

"So you led them here after all." His voice was low, almost a mumble, but the hate in the words cut against the stillness of the small room. He looked directly into Patman's face, as if not noticing the pistol leveled at him. "I must be getting old," he said in the same quiet tone.

"You're not going to get a hell of a lot older," Patman answered. "But I'll tell you this. We didn't bring Quaine and his Apaches here. You can believe that or not. I don't much care. Just all of a sudden I don't think you're doing anybody much good being alive."

De Sana's mouth eased slightly as he smiled. "Why don't you let your boy do his own fighting?" And with the words he looked calmed again, as if he didn't care that a trap was tightening about him. Patman noticed it, because he had seen the panic on his face when he entered. Now he saw this calm returning and wondered if it was just a last-act bravado. It unnerved him a little to see a man so at ease with a gun turned on him and he lifted the pistol a foot off the table to make sure the outlaw had seen it.

"I'm not blind."

"Just making sure, Lew," Patman drawled.

De Sana seemed to relax even more now, and moved his hand to his back pocket, slowly, so the other man wouldn't get the wrong idea. He said, "Mind if I have a smoke?" while he dug the tobacco and paper from his pocket.

Patman shook his head once from side to side, and his eyes squinted at the outlaw, wondering what the hell he was playing for. He looked closely as the man poured tobacco into the creased paper and didn't see any of it shake loose to the floor. The fool's got iron running through him, he thought.

De Sana looked up as he shaped the cigarette. "You didn't answer my question," he said.

"About the boy? He can take care of himself," Patman answered.

"Why isn't he here, then?" De Sana said it in a low voice, but there was a sting to the words.

Patman said, "He's out courting your girlfriend," and smiled, watching the dumbfounded expression freeze on the gunman's face. "You might say I'm giving him a little fatherly hand here," and the smile broadened.

De Sana's thin body had stiffened. Now he breathed long and shrugged his shoulders. "So you're playing the father," he said. Standing half-sideways toward Patman, he pulled the unlit cigarette from his mouth and waved it at the man seated behind the table. "I got to reach for a match, Dad."

"Long as you can do it with your left hand," Patman said. Then added, "Son."

De Sana smiled thinly and drew a match from his side pocket.

Patman watched the arm swing down against the thigh and saw the sudden flame in the dimness as it came back up. And at that split second he knew he had made his mistake.

He saw the other movement, another something swinging up, but it was off away from the sudden flare of the match and in the fraction of the moment it took him to realize what it was, it was too late. There was the explosion, the stab of flame, and the shock against his arm. At the same time he went up from the table and felt the weight of the handgun slipping from his fingers, as another explosion mixed with the smoke of the first and he felt the sledgehammer blow against his side. He went over with the chair and felt the packed-dirt floor slam against his back.

His hands clutched at his side instinctively, feeling the wetness that was there already, then winced in pain and dropped his right arm next to him on the floor. He closed his eyes hard, and when he opened them again he was looking at a pistol barrel, and above it De Sana's drawn face.

Unsmiling, the outlaw said, "I don't think you'd a made a very good father." He turned quickly and sprinted out of the hut.

Patman closed his eyes again to see the swirling black that sucked at his brain. For a moment he felt a nausea in his stomach, then numbness seemed to creep over his body. A prickling numbness that was as soothing as the dark void that was spinning inside his head. *I'm going to sleep,* he thought. But before he did, he remembered hearing a shot come from outside, then another.

CIMA QUAINE WALKED over to him when he saw the boy look up quickly.

Dave Fallis looked anxiously from Patman's motionless form up to the chief scout who now stood next to him where he knelt.

"I saw his eyes open and close twice!" he whispered excitedly.

The scout hunkered down beside him and wrinkled his buckskin face into a smile. It was an ageless face, cold in its dark, crooked lines and almost cruel, but the smile was plain in the eyes. He was bareheaded, and his dark hair glistened flat on his skull in the lantern light that flickered close behind him on the table.

"You'd have to tie rocks to him and drop him in a well to kill Virgil," he said. "And then you'd never be sure." He glanced at the boy to see the effect of his words and then back to Patman. The eyes were open now, and Patman was grinning at him.

"Don't be too sure," he said weakly. His eyes went to Fallis who looked as if he wanted to say something, but was afraid to let it come out. He smiled back at the boy watching the relief spread over his face and saw him bite at his lower lip. "Did you get him?"

Fallis shook his head, but Quaine said, "Vea Oiga was crawling up to take the horses when De Sana ran into the corral and took one without even waiting to saddle. He shot at him, but didn't get him." He twisted his head and looked up at one of the Apaches standing behind him. "When we get home, you're going to spend your next two months' pay on practice shells."

Vea Oiga dropped his head and looked suddenly ashamed and ridiculous with the vermilion sergeant stripes painted on his naked arms. He shuffled through the doorway without looking up at the girl who stepped inside quickly to let him pass.

She stood near the cupboard not knowing what to do with her hands, watching Dave Fallis. One of the half-dozen Coyotero scouts in the room moved near her idly, and she shrank closer to the wall nervously picking at the frayed collar of her dress. She looked about the room wide-eyed for a moment, then stepped around the Apache hurriedly and out through the doorway. She moved toward the lean-to, but held up when she saw the three Apaches inside laughing and picking at the strips of venison that were hanging from the roof to dry. After a while, Fallis got up stretching the stiffness from his legs and walked to the door. He stood there looking out, but seeing just the darkness.

Cima Quaine bent closer to Patman's drawn face. The ex-trooper's eyes were open, but his face was tight with pain. The hole in his side had started to bleed again. Patman knew it was only a matter of time, but he tried not to show the pain when the contract scout lowered close to him. He heard the scout say, "Your partner's kind of nervous," and for a moment it sounded far away.

Patman answered, "He's young," but knew that didn't explain anything to the other man.

"He's anxious to get on after the man," Quaine went on. "How you feel having an avenging angel?" Then added quickly, "Hell, in another day or two you'll be avenging yourself."

"It's not for me," Patman whispered, and hesitated. "It's for himself, and the girl."

Quaine was surprised, but kept his voice down. "The girl? He hasn't even looked at her since we got here."

"And he won't," Patman said. "Until he gets him." He saw the other man's frown and added, "It's a long story, all about pride and getting your toes stepped on." He grinned to himself at the faint sign of bewilderment on the scout's face. Nobody's going to ask a dying man to talk sense. Besides, it would take too long.

After a silence, Patman whispered, "Let him go, Cima."

"His yen to make war might be good as gold, but my boys ain't worth a damn after dark. We can pick up the man's sign in the morning and have him before sundown."

"You do what you want tomorrow. Just let him go tonight."

"He wouldn't gain anything," the scout whispered impatiently. "He's got the girl here now to live with long as he wants."

"He's got to live with himself, too." Patman's voice sounded weaker. "And he doesn't take free gifts. He's got a funny kind of pride. If he doesn't go after that man, he'll never look at that girl again."

Cima Quaine finished, "And if he does go after him, he may not get the chance. No, Virg. I better keep him here. He can come along tomorrow if he wants." He turned his head as if that was the end of the argument and looked past the Coyoteros to see the girl standing in the doorway.

She came in hesitantly, dazed about the eyes, as if a strain was sapping at her vitality to make her appear utterly spent. She said, "He's gone," in a voice that was not her own.

Cima Quaine's head swung back to Patman when he heard him say, "Looks like you don't have anything to say about it."

AT THE FIRST light of dawn, Dave Fallis looked out over the meadow from the edge of timber and was unsure. There was moisture in the air lending a thickness to the gray dawn, but making the boundless stillness seem more empty. Mist will do that, for it isn't something in itself. It goes with lonesomeness and sometimes has a feeling of death. He reined his horse down the slight grade and crossed the gray wave of meadow, angling toward the dim outline of a draw that trailed up the ridge there. It cut deep into the tumbled rock, climbing slowly. After a while he found himself on a bench and stopped briefly to let his horse rest for a moment. The mist was below him now, clinging thickly to the meadow and following it as it narrowed through the valley ahead. He continued on along the bench that finally ended, forcing him to climb on into switchbacks that shelved the steepness of the ridge. And after two hours of following the ridge crown, he looked down to estimate himself a good eight miles ahead of the main trail that stayed with the meadow. He went down the opposite slope, not so steep here, but still following switchbacks, until he was in level country again and heading for the Escudillas in the distance.

The sun made him hurry. For every hour it climbed in the sky lessened his chance of catching the man before the Coyoteros did. He was going on luck. The Coyoteros would use method. But now he wondered if it was so much luck. Vea Oiga had told him what to do.

He had been leading the horse out of the corral and down through the timber when Vea Oiga grew out of the shadows next to him, also leading a horse. The Indian handed the reins to the boy and held back the mare he had been leading. "It is best you take gelding," he whispered. "The man took stallion. Leave the mare here so there is no chance she will call to her lover."

The Apache stood close to him confidently. "You have one chance, man," he said. "Go to Bebida Wells, straight, without following the trail. The man will go fast for a time, until he learns he is not being followed. But at dawn he will go quick again on the main trail for that way he thinks he will save time. But soon he will tire and will need water. Then he will go to Bebida Wells, for that is the only water within one day of here. When he reaches the well, he will find his horse spent and his legs weary from hanging without stirrups. And there he will rest until he can go on."

He had listened, fascinated, while the Indian read into the future and then heard how he should angle, following the draws and washes to save miles. For a moment he wondered about this Indian who knew him so well in barely more than an hour, how he had anticipated his intent, why he was helping. It had made no sense, but it was a course to follow, something he had not had before. The Apache had told him, "Shoot straight, man. Shoot before he sees you."

And with the boy passing from view into the darkness, Vea Oiga led the mare back to the corral, thinking of the boy and the dying man in the hut. Revenge was something he knew, but it never occurred to him that a woman could be involved. And if the boy failed, then he would get another chance to shoot straight. There was always plenty of time.

* * *

THE SUN WAS almost straight up, crowding the whole sky with its brassy white light, when he began climbing again. The Escudillas seemed no closer, but now the country had turned wild, and from a rise he could see the wildness tangling and growing into gigantic rock formations as it reached and climbed toward the sawtooth heights of the Escudillas.

He had been angling to come around above the wells, and now, in the heights again, he studied the ravines and draws below him and judged he had overshot by only a mile. On extended patrols out of Thomas they had often hit for Bebida before making the swing-back to the south. It was open country approaching the wells, so he had skirted wide to come in under cover of the wildness and slightly from behind.

A quarter of a mile on he found a narrow draw dense with pines strung out along the walls, the pines growing into each other and bending across to form a tangled arch over the draw. He angled down into its shade and picketed the gelding about halfway in. Then, lifting the Winchester, he passed out of the other end and began threading his way across the rocks.

A yard-wide defile opened up on a ledge that skirted close to the smoothness of boulders, making him edge sideways along the shadows of the towering rocks, until finally the ledge broadened and fell into a ravine that was dense with growth, dotted with pale yucca stalks against the dark green. He ran through the low vegetation in a crouch and stopped to rest at the end of the ravine where once more the ground turned to grotesque rock formations. Not a hundred yards off to the left, down through an opening in the rocks, he made out the still, sand-colored water of a well.

More cautiously now, he edged through the rocks, moving his boots carefully on the flinty ground. And after a dozen yards of this he crept into the narrowness of two boulders that hung close together, pointing the barrel of the Winchester through the aperture toward the pool of muddy water below.

He watched the vicinity of the pool with a grimness now added to his determination; he watched without reflecting on why he was there. He had thought of that all morning: seeing Virg die on the dirt floor. . . . But the outlaw's words had always come up to blot that scene. "I think you better teach him the facts of life." Stepping on his toes while he was supposed to smile back. It embarrassed him because he wanted to be here because of Virg. First Virg and then the girl. He told himself he was doing this because Virg was his friend, and because the girl was helpless and couldn't defend herself and deserved a chance. That's what he told himself.

But that was all in the past, hazy pictures in his mind overshadowed by the business at hand. He knew what he was doing there, if he wasn't sure why. So that when the outlaw's thin shape came into view below him, he was not excited.

He did not see where De Sana had come from, but realized now that he must have been hiding somewhere off to the left. De Sana crouched low behind a scramble of rock and poked his carbine below toward the pool, looking around as if trying to determine if this was the best position overlooking the well. His head turned, and he looked directly at the aperture behind him, where the two boulders met, studying it for a long moment before turning back to look down his carbine barrel at the pool. Dave Fallis levered the barrel of the Winchester down a fraction and the front sight was dead center on De Sana's back.

He wondered why De Sana had taken a carbine from the corral lean-to and not a saddle. Then he thought of Vea Oiga who had fired at him as he fled. And this brought Vea Oiga's words to memory. "Shoot before he sees you."

Past the length of the oiled gun barrel, he saw the Y formed by the suspenders and the faded underwear top, darkened with perspiration. The short-haired skull, thin and hatless. And at the other end, booted long legs, and toes that kicked idly at the gravel.

For a moment he felt sorry for De Sana. Not because the barrel in front of him was trained on his back. He watched the man gaze out over a vastness that would never grow smaller. Straining his eyes for a relentless something that would sooner or later hound him to the ground. And he was all alone. He watched him kick his toes for something to do and wipe the sweat from his forehead with the back of his hand. De Sana perspired like everyone else. That's why he felt sorry for him. He saw a man, like a thousand others he had seen, and he wondered how you killed a man.

The Indian had told him, "Shoot before he sees you." Well, that was just like an Indian.

He moved around from behind the rocks and stood there in plain view with the rifle still pointed below. He felt naked all of a sudden, but brought the rifle up a little and called, "Throw your gun down and turn around!"

And the next second he was firing. He threw the lever and fired again—then a third time. He sat down and ran his hand over the wetness on his forehead, looking at the man who was now sprawled on his back with his carbine across his chest.

He buried the gunman well away from the pool and scattered rocks around so that when he was finished you'd wouldn't know that a grave was there. He took the outlaw's horse and his guns. That would be enough proof. On the way back he kept thinking of Virg and the girl. He hoped that Virg would still be alive, but knew that was too much to ask. Virg and he had had their good times and that was that. That's how you had to look at things.

He thought of the girl and wondered if she'd think he was rushing things if he asked her to go with him to the Panhandle, after a legal ceremony. . . .

And all the way back, not once did he think of Lew De Sana.

7

Cavalry Boots

Zane Grey's Western, December 1952

ON THE MORNING of May the tenth, 1870, four troops of cavalry, out of Fort Bowie and at full strength, met a hundred-odd Mimbreño Apaches under Chee about a mile east of what used to be Helena. Cavalry met Apache on open, flat terrain—which happened seldom enough—and they cut the Indians to ribbons. Only Chee and a handful of his warriors escaped.

On the official record the engagement is listed as the Battle of Dos Cabezas. But strictly speaking the title is misleading, for the twin peaks of Dos Cabezas were only a landmark to the south. The engagement broke the back of an Apache uprising, but that is not the important point. The Reservation at San Carlos is mute testimony that all uprisings did fail.

No, the importance of the Dos Cabezas action is in how it happened to come about; and the record is not complete on that score—though there is a statement in the record meant to explain how cavalry was able to meet guerrilla Apache away from his mountain stronghold. And there is mention of the unnatural glow in the night sky that attracted both cavalry and Apache. But still, the record is incomplete.

Stoneman himself, Brigadier General, Department of Arizona, was at Bowie at the time. That is why much of the credit for the engagement's success is given to him. However, the next week at Camp Grant, Stoneman made awards connected with the action. The Third United States Dragoons received a unit citation. A Lieutenant R. A. Gander was cited for bravery; it being consolation for a shattered left leg. One other award was made. And therein lies the strange story of the Dos Cabezas affair.

This is how it happened.

A<small>LWAYS</small>, <small>IT IS</small> preceded by quiet.

The silence creeps over the gray gloom that is the desert at night and even the natural night sounds are not there. Off, far off, against the blackness of a mountainside there appears the orange-red smear of a bonfire. From a distance it is a flickering point of light, cold and alone. And then—

THE APACHES ARE UP!

It is a scream down the length of the barracks adobe.

Through the window, Kujava sees the thin slash of red in the blackness to the east and he pulls his boots on mechanically, grimly.

Then he is First Sergeant Kujava, swinging through the barracks with a booming voice and a leather gauntlet slashing at sleeping feet. Kujava knows men. He asks them if they want to be late to die and he does it with a roar of a laugh so they cannot refuse. With the recruits, it is effective. They leap up and yell and laugh with an eagerness that means they are new to frontier station.

And it shows they do not know the Apache.

Others remain motionless, but with eyes open, seeing the desert and the dust-covered mesquite and the alkali and the screaming whiteness of the sun all combined in a shimmering, oppressing haze that sears the eyeballs of a white man until a knot tightens around his forehead. That, and salt sweat and the gagging nitrogen smell of the animals beneath them. Stillness, and never an Apache in sight. These are the ones who have been in as long as Kujava.

On Bud Nagle, the dawn rousing had a bewildering effect. He sat bolt upright on his cot and saw the first sergeant running down the narrow aisle, but what the sergeant was calling made no sense to him. He frowned and rubbed his eyes at the commotion, then fell back slowly on his cot and remained motionless. But he did not see the desert.

There was a cobblestone street with store fronts and restaurants, and it was east of the Mississippi.

By the end of his first month Bud Nagle had known he was not a cavalryman. He knew he was not a soldier of any kind, but after seven months, it was too late to do anything about it, and even the office door in Milwaukee that bore the legend *L. V. Nagle, Attorney,* could not prevail against it. Enlistments do not dissolve, even if the recruit realizes he is out of place; and especially were they not dissolving that spring of 1870 when Apacheria, from the Dragoons to the San Andres, was vibrating with the beat of hundreds of war drums. The Apaches were up and Cochise would not be stopped.

Now he saw the street again. The shouting, laughing people and the ordinarily shy girls who giggled and threw their arms around the returning soldiers and kissed them right on the street. Right on Wisconsin Avenue. He remembered the deep-blue uniforms and the glistening boots and the one-eyed angle of the kepis, and he could hardly wait.

The uniforms disappeared from the cobblestone street. They had been gone for almost five years, but never from the mind of Bud Nagle. Smiling girls and glistening boots.

By the time he found out how long issue boots kept a shine, it was too late. He was in Apache country.

Now he opened his eyes and looked full into the awe-inspiring face of the first sergeant. Deep-brown hollow cheeks and full cavalry mustache.

"Get off that bunk 'fore I kick your comfort-lovin' butt across the parade!" And he was off down the aisle.

It was always the same. Kujava pulled him from his cot, drilled him until his legs shook with weakness. The corporal swore and gave him extra duty, full pack, four hours on the parade. He was always the handiest when their ire was up and he never learned to keep his mouth shut. The fact that nothing he did was ever done in a military fashion made it doubly easy for the noncoms, and the contagion of their bullying even spread to the ranks.

He was easy to insult and seemed even to invite it. He was not a soldier among soldiers. He tried to act like a man without looking like one. And he complained. That's part of Army life: a big part. But he whined when he should have bitched like a man. Soldiers know soldiers. They didn't know Bud Nagle.

After only three weeks at Camp Grant he found himself alone. From habit, he continued a pathetic campaign to join the ranks, but at night, in the darkness of the barracks, when in the quietness he could think, Bud Nagle understood that he hated the Army and the men in it. He hated both to the depths of his soul.

BY MIDAFTERNOON B Troop was almost thirty miles south of Camp Grant. To the southwest were the Dragoons, and to the east, the Chiricahuas, looming hazy but ominous in the distance. Somewhere up in the towering rocks was the stronghold of Cochise. This wide semidesert corridor was the gateway to Sonora. Through it passed the Apache raiders into Mexico. Stoneman's Department of Arizona was shaking off its winter lethargy by sending patrols to every corner of the frontier.

Lieutenant R. A. Gander, riding at the head of B Troop, waited until the twin peaks of Dos Cabezas faced him from an eleven o'clock angle, less than a mile to the south, then he rested the patrol for an hour before turning east. B Troop was at the south end of its patrol. It would swing eastward for a few miles, then swing again slightly north and bivouac near Fort Bowie at the mouth of Apache Pass. From there, the last leg was the thirty miles back to Grant.

Soon they were in the foothills of the Chiricahuas. The mountains rose high above them to the south, and on all sides now were timbered hills and massive rock formations through which the trail twisted and climbed, seldom in sight ahead for more than a hundred yards.

It was dangerous country to take a patrol through. Gander knew that, but sometimes you had to offer a little bait in the business of fighting Indians. That, and the fact that a young officer tends to become careless after too many months of garrison duty. He becomes eager. Gander had not seen an Apache in six months.

He rode with the self assurance that he was a natural leader. They don't give commissions to everyone. He was following patrol instructions to the letter, a routine laid down by a much higher authority than his own, and Lieutenant Gander had complete faith in his superiors. At the Point that had become as natural to him as walking.

He had sent point riders ahead to safeguard against ambush, with explicit orders to make frequent contact.

No danger of being cut off. It was strict military procedure, always on the alert. It was patrol precaution, outlined and detailed in the Manual. So Gander was confident.

Unfortunately, Chee had not read the Manual. Nor had any of his Mimbreño Apaches.

Chee knew everything he needed to know about Lieutenant Gander and his forty-man patrol. He had known it before the troop was five miles south of Grant. The size of the patrol, their equipment, and their experience. In the endless expanse of Arizona sky there were thin wisps of smoke and sudden flashes of the sun's reflection caught on polished metal. That morning the signals had been many and Chee moved over a hundred warriors from the *rancheria* high up in the Chiricahuas to the foothills.

He scattered them along both sides of the trail where the irregular road suddenly opened up and sloped into a flat, broad area almost a mile long and three hundred yards wide. He hid his warriors behind rock and scrub brush hours before the patrol reached Dos Cabezas and swung eastward into the foothills. And he laid his ambush with contempt for the soldier who was fool enough to establish a pattern of operation in enemy territory.

Chee made no sign when Gander's point riders came into view from the narrow, sloping trail. His face was unlined and impassive, but in the calmness of his dark face there was an eye-squinting sternness that told of other things. It told of his father, Mangas Coloradas, who had been shot in the back as he lay on the ground tied hand and foot. Trussed up and shot from behind after he had accepted a white flag.

SERGEANT KUJAVA, leading point, sent a rider out to the extremities on both sides of the open space. He rode in silence, his head swiveling from one side to the other, taking in every rock and tree clump, his eyes climbing the steel walls of brush and rock that revolted against the sandy flatness to rise abruptly on both sides and finally stretch into rolling foothills. He paid no attention to Bud Nagle riding at his side. He had stopped lecturing him at Dos Cabezas.

He walked his mount slowly, and every so often he stood up in the stirrups and gazed straight ahead. And in the alert mind of First Sergeant Kujava there was an uneasiness. He didn't like the stillness.

Bud Nagle wiped the palm of his hand across his mouth and then pulled his hat brim closer to his eyes while his tongue felt along the dryness that crusted his lips. He swore feebly against the country and made his mind to go far away where there was greenness and a cool breeze and streetcar tracks.

His dull eyes fell to his uniform shirt that was fading from the saturation of body salt. His head rolled to the side and he looked at boots that could be any color under the crust of white dust.

At the north end of the pocket, where rock and brush squeezed in again to resume its rugged stinginess, the narrowness brought the two outriders in to join the sergeant and Nagle. Ahead, the trail sloped gradually through a rock pass and then broadened into a timber-flanked aisle that stretched into the distance and finally ended in a yellowness that was the plain.

Kujava held the riders up and turned in his saddle to see the patrol just entering the open area.

"Stretch your legs," he told them. "They're too far behind. That's how you get cut off."

The two outriders dismounted and led their mounts to the side of the trail where a clump of pines cast a triangle of shade. They sat on the ground and stretched stiff legs out in front of them.

Kujava turned his horse around. He slouched in the saddle, one leg hooked over the saddle horn, and watched the hazy line of blue approaching in the distance. He watched the patrol reach the midpoint of the pocket, and the unnatural silence gnawed at his brain and made the ring seem sharper in his ears. He swung his boot back to the stirrup, uneasy, wanting to be ready, and as he did so he heard the *click*.

Not wood, like a twig snapping. It was metal grinding against metal, and it was sharp and clear enough to send the flash of honest fear through his body and jerk him to the reaction of a man who knows combat. He yanked rein to drag his mount about sharply and tugged his carbine from its boot in the motion, for a Spencer will make that very click when the breech is opened, and the click is loud if the piece is rusted—rusted and uncared for, like the carbine an Apache would have!

He shouted and swung up the carbine, but the shout was drowned in a crash of gunfire and the motion was lost in the phantasm of a hundred impressions as the basin exploded its ambush and caught B Troop by the throat.

Kujava shouted and fired and shouted, and he saw his outriders sprawled in their triangle of shade. And he saw Bud Nagle still sitting his horse with both hands frozen to the saddle horn, his back a ramrod and his eyes popped open in white circles of fear and disbelief.

"Nagle, ride! Ride!" Kujava's arm swung as he screamed at the stiff-bodied trooper and struck him across the shoulder.

"Get out of here—ride like hell to Bowie—before they're on to us!"

Nagle moved and seemed to be suddenly drenched with the excitement so that it washed through him and took with it his nerve and his reason.

And the simplicity of Bud Nagle said, "I don't know where it is."

Strange things happen in combat. Kujava's jaw dropped and he wanted to laugh, even with the firing—because of the firing, but it was only for an instant.

He swung his carbine against the rump of Nagle's mount, sending it into a jolting start down the narrow trail.

"Ride, dammit! Ride!"

His hands were frozen to the saddle horn, his eyes still wide open, seeing nothing, as his mount broke through the rocky narrowness in a gallop, sliding almost sideways in the loose gravel, careening from one rock wall to the other until hoofs struck firm ground at the bottom and raced on, momentum up, along the timber-lined aisle.

He strained his eyes against the distance as if this would draw the safety of it closer to him; as if he would be shielded from the pressing blackness of the heavy timber by holding his neck rigid to look only straight ahead. In a way it was a comfort, but because of it he didn't see the four ponies come out of the timber behind him. Four ponies painted for war and carrying Mimbreño Apaches.

He reached the end of the aisle and swung out onto the open plain, riding into the vastness, unsure of the direction, kicking his mount frantically toward the low horizon. Hoofs pounded packed sand and the sound vibrated against his mind to keep the knot tight inside of him, taking the place of the excitement of combat that was now a faint rattle far behind.

In his fear he was unmindful of time, his eyes straining against the distance. Then, in the haze, the horizon changed.

A dark line interrupted the monotonous tone of the plains, stretching and taking shape. It came closer yard by yard and finally there it was. A town. A real town!

He was a mile or more away when the shot rapped from behind. He turned to see the Apaches less than two hundred yards behind, then kicked hard and angled for the frame structures in the distance.

The Mimbres closed the gap by another two dozen yards before Bud Nagle reached the edge of the town, and as he wheeled to head into the street, a second shot slapped against the wide openness like a barrel stave against concrete, and horse and rider went down.

Bud Nagle was stunned. He sat in the dust shaking his head while the dust and his mind cleared. He wanted to rest, but the rumble of the ponies behind him jerked him stumbling to his feet. He tried to run before he was all the way up and he fell to his hands and knees, crawled, then rose to his feet again and ran a few yards yelling at the top of his voice before he stumbled again, sprawling full length in the thick dust of the road.

The dust filled his open mouth and choked his screams for help, muffling the words to make them incoherent and all the more pitiful. He screamed and choked and drove his legs so savagely that he fell again as he reached the three steps to a porch, hitting his knees against the steps repeatedly until he climbed to the porch and lunged through the swing-type doors of the building.

He stopped in the gloom of the interior, throwing out his arms to rest against a support post in the middle of the room. His body sagged with relief as he put his head against the post, trying to catch his breath.

A hoarseness came out of his throat forming the words, "Apaches—Apaches! Right outside town!"

The silence answered him. And it was so loud and mocking that the breath caught in his throat.

He lifted his head slowly because he knew what he would see and he didn't want to see it. Finally he straightened his head and looked at the dust that couldn't be less than a dozen years old. It covered every surface of the bare room.

He made his head swing along an arc, taking in the rectangular strip of lighter-colored flooring where the bar had stood, and on toward the front of the room. His body moved and a boot scraped the gritty floor.

His shoulders jerked upward and his whole body tensed in an unnatural rigid position. His gaze sank into a dingy front corner and he kept his eyes on the shadowed line where wall met wall, as if by seeing nothing, nothing would see him. Slowly, neck muscles relaxed and the line of his jaw eased. He turned his eyes to the doorway.

A patch of dirty gray light showed through the opening above the louvered doors. Below, a square of the front porch stood out vividly, framed by the blackness of the doors and the dismal gloom of the inside of the room. The doors hung silently against the evening light, rickety and fragile because of the louvers, forming a thin, flimsy barrier against the outside.

He knew he was alone in a one-block town—alone with four Apaches.

And the desolate, stone-silent town squeezed in through the darkening gloom with a ring to its silence that was overbearing, and it pushed the thin figure back into the shadows.

The uniform hung loose and empty-looking as he backed away, lifting his feet gently, holding his arms close to his sides. His right arm brushed the holster on his hip and he glanced down and up quickly as if afraid to take his eyes from the doorway. But his drawn face relaxed slightly as he fumbled at the holster and drew the long-barreled revolving pistol.

Suddenly he stopped. A sharpness jolted against his spine, and he wheeled, discharging the heavy pistol wildly. He fired four times, running, stumbling toward the stairway along the back wall. The explosions slammed against the empty room, bouncing from wall to wall in an ear-splitting din, and with it was the sharp clattering of broken glass. He raced up the stairs, leaving the barroom alone, bare but for the center post against which he had bumped.

And again the silence.

In the upstairs room he pressed stiff-backed to the wall just inside the door while his chest heaved and his head jerked in spasms from the door to the front windows that were dim gray squares outlining the evening. Slowly he edged along the wall until he reached a corner window and pressed his cheek to the frame.

From the angle he could see almost the entire length of the block-long town. Adobe and clapboard squatted side by side, gaunt and ugly and with a flimsy coldness that proclaimed their unoccupancy. Ramadas extended from most of the building fronts, rickety and drooping, pushing out into the street to squeeze the dirt road into a rutted narrowness. The ramadas hid most of the lower windows and doorways that lined the street, casting a deeper shadow in the fast-falling gloom.

Then, from somewhere below, there was creak of a board bending on a rusted nail. He froze to the wall and the sound stopped.

It tightened every nerve and muscle in his body; but he moved his legs, his hand shaking with the weight of the revolving pistol. He made his way across the room to the door and looked out to the dim landing, leaning over the railing and listened, but only the ragged cut of his breath interrupted the stillness. He backed from the stairway along the short hall that ended a few feet behind him.

A glass-paned door opened to an outside landing with a decaying stairway falling steeply to the ground. The last of the evening light seeped into the narrowness between the two buildings and lost most of its strength filtering through the grimy panes of the door glass. He glanced over his shoulder through one of the panes seeing only the landing and the rotting board wall of the next building, which was a livery stable.

He approached the blackness of the stairwell again, and as he leaned forward the muffled sound came from below. It was faint, far-away, like leather on wood, but it rasped against his spine like an off-chord and he felt his neck hairs bristle.

He stood rigid, working his mouth to scream, but the scream came out a moan, and the moan a sob, and he kept saying, "Please God— please God—please God—" until he finally turned, slamming into the door, smashing his pistol through the glass panes when the door would not open at once, kicking boots and knees against the door panel.

Then he was out and down the stairs, stopping a moment in the narrow alley to swing his head both ways. An instant later he disappeared through the side door of the next building.

In the upper hall a vague shadow emerged from the blackness of the stairwell to the landing where Bud Nagle had stood. The figure was obscure, but the last of the evening's faint light showed dimly on the head of the Mimbreño war lance.

A MIMBREÑO APACHE is not a fanatic. He will not throw his life away. If mortally wounded, the chances are he will put aside precaution to make his last act that of killing a white man. Many white men will do the same. It is not fanaticism; it is complete resignation. Fatalism with fate staring you in the face.

A Mimbre is a little man, less than five-seven, but he is an oiled-leather cord with rock-tight knots all the way down. He wears a calico band to hold back shoulder-length hair, and his moccasins reach the midpoint of his thighs. He wears a cotton breechclout and his upper body is painted vermilion. Paint on dirt.

His God is U-sen, and he is the best natural guerrilla fighter in the world. He is a strategist. He lives to kill—and he plans it every hour he's awake while he drinks tizwin to make sure the kill-urge will not go away. And don't you forget it: *He does not throw his life away.*

That is why the three shadows converged on the stable, but without a war cry, without assault. There was not even the hint of noise. The shadows were unreal, blending with the gloom. They moved to the side of the building to join the fourth shadow standing in the narrow alley. The phantom shapes fused together to become a part of the deeper shadow close to the side of the stable.

In a few minutes the obscure figures reappeared, moving quickly, taking definite shape upon reaching the street, then fading again, passing under the ramadas on the other side. And in the narrow alley there was a flicker of light. A wavering, dancing speck of light. Then, vivid orange against black as the fire gradually climbed the decaying wall of the stable.

It was a matter of only a few minutes. The fire scaled the side wall slowly at first; small orange tongues, scattered along the dry surface, finally ate into each other and erupted into a brilliant mass of flame.

For the figure crouched inside the stable there was no choice. He edged out of a stall and moved toward the front of the stable, watching the fire, fascinated, until the flames reached the loft above him and the heat pressed close and smothering.

For a few minutes he forgot about the Apaches, his mind coping with just one thing at a time, and not relating the fire to the Indians. He was completely fascinated, moving toward the front slowly, reluctant to take his eyes from the dancing flames, until the heat licked close and he turned to find himself at the front entrance.

Hiding was out of the question. Swept out by the fire and the panic that strapped his mind and made his heart hammer against his chest.

Panic and no choice.

It made him throw his shoulder against the heavy swing door and force his body through the narrow opening. He hesitated a long second, then ran to the left, hitting the duckboard sidewalk in four strides, then up the steps of the barroom porch. He hesitated again in the deep shadows of the ramada, glanced back toward the stable grinding his teeth together to keep from crying out, then ran across the porch.

At the end of the porch he glanced back again, and that was his mistake.

He turned to break into a run, but the stairs were there and he pitched forward, throwing his arms out in front of him. There was the half-scream and the explosion and that was all. He lay faceup. A thin hole in his chest showed where he had shot himself. And the toes of his issue boots pointed to the red glow that was spreading in the sky.

IT WAS THE same glow that brought Apache and cavalry to meet the next morning on the flat plain east of the town of Helena.

Cause and effect is natural. Cavalry followed the glow in the night sky for an obvious reason. That was why there was a garrison at Fort Bowie. Chee brought his Mimbres through a mistake in judgment. Fire in the sky to the northeast, the direction of Fort Bowie. And Cochise, with over two hundred Chiricahuas, was on the warpath in that general direction. It was easy for Chee to abandon one ambushed troop for a chance to assist in the sack of a whole garrison.

An error in judgment and overeagerness. And when Chee discovered his error it was too late. He was in the open. One of Stoneman's scouts learned this from a Mimbre who survived the battle. The story influenced Stoneman's reasoning. There is no question of that.

That afternoon they found Bud Nagle. His gun empty and his body mutilated. The right hand and foot hacked off. There was only one conclusion to be reached.

At Camp Grant the next week, Stoneman awarded him posthumously the medal that bears Minerva's head. The Medal of Honor.

Regimental pride is a strange thing. A soldier will cling to it because it is important, and he will even let it bias his mind. West of the San Andres there was little else but regimental pride.

Stoneman gave Nagle the Medal of Honor because he had sacrificed his life for his troop. He had fired the town to signal the Bowie garrison, thereby giving his own life. Stoneman even hinted that Nagle signaled with the intention of luring Chee. He did not state it flatly, but moved around it with tactical terms.

That's what regimental pride will do. A hero. His name listed forever on the Roll of Honor of B Troop, Third United States Dragoons. And many believed it—even knowing Bud Nagle— Yes, that's what regimental pride will do.

8

Under the Friar's Ledge

Dime Western Magazine, January 1953

STRUGGLES' ATTITUDE toward the Sangre del Santo story was one of complete indifference. At the time he first heard the story, he was contract surgeon at Fort Huachuca with no time for chasing lost mine legends. It was common knowledge that Struggles had more than a superficial interest in precious metals—it was evident in the way he wangled assignments to extended patrols and would have his pan out at every water stop, and the leaves on which he went into the Dragoons alone with a pack mule and a shovel—but prospecting, to Struggles, was a world apart from chasing legends. Lost mines were for fools, or anyone too lazy to swing a pick and build a sluice box. Listening to the tale, Struggles' rough-grained campaigner's face would wrinkle like soft leather and a half smile would frame the cigar that was clamped between his teeth.

But that was while he was still at Huachuca. That was before he met Juan Solo.

In Soyopa, which is in the state of Sonora, there was another story related along with the one of Sangre del Santo. It concerned Juan Solo who made his home in Soyopa, and very simply, it told that Juan Solo, the Indian-Mexican, knew the exact location of the lost mine. And once a year, they said, he would bring to the tienda a half bar of solid silver weighing one thousand ounces, a weight not used since the departure of the Spanish. And the storekeeper, who was becoming very rich, would allow Juan to purchase whatever he pleased for the rest of the year.

When questioned about the mine, Juan Solo would smile, just as Doctor Struggles was doing at that very time up at Fort Huachuca, and he would shake his head and walk away.

They said that Juan Solo was one of Gokliya's Apaches until Gokliya turned wild and the Mexicans began calling him *Hieronymo*. They said Juan was lazy by nature and became tired of running, so he left the band and became Mexican. But changing his nationality did not erase from his memory the mine he had discovered hiding out in the Sierra Madre with Gokliya. And finally, after the Apache war chief was packed off to Florida, Juan Solo was free to visit his secret mine.

They said he could have been the richest man in Mexico, but his only concern was for mescal and a full bean pot to answer the growl in his belly. Spending any more would have been wasteful. On one occasion, two men resentful of Juan's niggardly attitude followed him into the range when he left for his annual collection. One came back a month later—with his mind still in the hills. The other never returned. It was a long time before anyone tried it again . . . but that was when Struggles entered the story. . . .

In 1638, the Sangre del Santo was mining more silver than any diggings in New Spain with free, Indian labor. But perhaps the Spanish overseers and their protecting garrison were somewhat more demanding than was ordinarily common. The story has it that a Franciscan friar, Tomas Maria, could stand the inhuman treatment of the Tarahumare laborers no longer and so caused them to revolt.

It is said the Spanish killed Tomas Maria for putting thoughts into the heads of the Tarahumares; and after the uprising, in which the Spanish were taken by surprise and annihilated, the Indians found the padre's body and laid it away inside the entrance to the mine. Then they sealed it and defaced the mountainside so there would be no trace of the entrance. The adobe quarters of the Spanish were caved in and spread about until they again became part of the land. The country was restored, and the legend of Tomas Maria's spirit protecting the mine was handed down from father to son.

In Soyopa, the villagers crossed themselves when the name Tomas

Maria was mentioned. Then someone would smile and say that the padre and Juan Solo must indeed be good friends, and then everyone would smile. . . .

On a morning in early summer, Juan Solo left Soyopa prodding his burro unhurriedly in the direction that pointed toward the wild, climbing Sierra Madre.

A month before, Struggles had entered Sonora and started down the Bavispe. It had taken a long time to shake soldiering out of his life.

He had been contract surgeon all through most of the campaigns, from before Apache Pass to Crook's border expedition, and in those days he was too busy doctoring to give in completely to the urge that had been growing since his first year in the Southwest. Sometimes the troopers kidded him about it and accused him of knowing every rock within a five mile radius of Thomas, Bowie and Fort Huachuca. Struggles took it with a smile because there was little enough to laugh about at that time.

He wasn't a fanatic about gold. Some men eat and breathe it and know nothing else. Struggles simply thought prospecting was a good idea. Sun and fresh air, hard work, enough excitement to keep your blood circulating regularly and the chance of becoming rich for life. Finally, after almost twenty years of campaigning, he reasoned that his obligation to the Army was at an end. He had served long enough that no one could say he had signed up just for the free transportation.

He worked the Dragoons for almost a year with only a few pyrite showings and then a trace that would die out before it had hardly started. It was enough discouragement to make him look for a new field. He decided to point south and follow the Bavispe down through Sonora, keeping the Sierra Madre on his left, working the foothills until he had the feel of the country, then go deeper into the range.

Five days after Juan Solo left his pueblo, Struggles found him in a barranca. They did not speak, because Juan was unable to. He was spread on his back in the middle of the depression, stripped, his hands and feet fastened with rawhide and pegged deep into the sand. Near him were the ashes of a fire over which his feet had been held before he was staked to the ground.

They spoke of it for a long time after in Soyopa. How Juan Solo rode out one morning on his burro and returned a week later tied to the animal with the American leading it, along with his own, and how the American stayed on with Juan at his adobe and tended him until his sickness passed.

STRUGGLES DID NOT consider saving Juan's life a special act of charity. He would have done the same for anyone. Nor did the man's reluctance to explain completely what had occurred bother Struggles. At first, all Juan offered in explanation was that an American, a man whom he had trusted as a friend, caught him unaware and performed this torture on him. Struggles accepted this without pressing conversation and gradually, as his wounds healed, Juan Solo became more at ease. A natural friendship was developing, in spite of their extremely opposite backgrounds.

Finally, one day when Juan's burns were almost healed, he said to Struggles: "That was a good thing you did before." It was his way of thanking Struggles for saving his life.

The surgeon brushed it off. "No more than any man would have done," he said.

Juan Solo frowned. "It is not of such a simple nature. There was a good thing you did before."

Struggles waited while Juan Solo unhurriedly formed the words in his mind.

"Once," Juan began, "I had a friend who desired to be rich. He begged me to show him silver, so I took him into the hills. But even being a friend, I blindfolded his eyes lest avarice lead him back for more, though I meant to give him plenty enough. For two days I walked behind his burro picking up the kernels of maize that he was dropping to mark the trail. And at the end of that time, I unbound his eyes and returned to him all the maize he had dropped, saying such a wasteful man would indeed not know how to use silver. And there I left him, discovering that he was no friend.

"The next time I went out from the pueblo, he was waiting for me and he took me and demanded that I show him the place of the silver. He had Mexican men with him, and at his word they built a fire to abuse the truth from me, as if the words would come from my feet; but I would not speak, so they left me to die."

Juan Solo's eyes did not leave Struggles' hard-lined face. He went on, "Now I have learned that friendship is not simply of words. Man, I will show you silver; as much as your burro can carry will be yours. And there will be no blindfold."

Struggles cleared his throat and felt a flush of embarrassment. "Juan, I didn't treat you for a fee." And then was sorry he had said it when the Indian's sleepy eyes opened suddenly.

But his voice remained even when he said, "To a friend, you offer a gift. You do not repay him." He hesitated. "And I say *offer*, for you need not accept it. Approaching El Sangre del Santo is not the same as entering the great city of Chihuahua. Often there is danger."

Struggles' cigar almost slipped from his mouth. "You know where it is?" he asked, amazed.

The Indian nodded his head.

Sketchily then, the story of the mine formed in the surgeon's head. He relaxed in his chair, putting the pieces together. He had almost forgotten the legend of Tomas Maria.

"What about the padre who acts as watchman?" he asked cautiously. "Is he the danger you spoke of?"

Juan Solo smiled faintly. "Here they say that he and I are good friends. No, the danger is from those who would take all the wealth from the poor padre."

Struggles smiled at the Indian and said, "I imagine he gets pretty lonely up there," but Juan Solo only shrugged his shoulders. Struggles added, "I mean your ex-friend, the American."

The Indian nodded. "After leaving me the thought would come to him that if I died his chance of discovering the mine would be remote. So he would return and find that someone had taken me. First he would curse, then inquire discreetly through one of his men if I had been brought to Soyopa; and finding this to be so, his choice would then be to wait for me to go out again and then to follow."

"Well, you're just guessing now," Struggles said.

Juan Solo shrugged again. "Perhaps."

On the fourth day after leaving the pueblo, Juan's conjecture came back to Struggles suddenly. From that afternoon on, there was little room in his mind for doubting the Indian's word.

They were in high, timbered country moving their horses and pack mules single file along a trail that cut into the pines, climbing to distant rimrock. Where the slope leveled, they came out onto a bench that opened up for a dozen yards revealing, down over the tops of the lower pines and dwarf oaks, the country they had left hours before. In the timber it was cool; but below, the sandy flats and the scattered rock eruptions were all the same glaring yellow, hazy through a dust that hung motionless. At first, Struggles thought he was seeing sun spots from the glare.

He blinked before squinting again and now he was certain there were no sun spots. Far off against the yellow glare, a confused number of moving specks were pointing toward the deep shadows of a barranca. Juan Solo was watching with the palm of his hand shading his eyes.

He looked at the surgeon when the specks passed out of sight. "Now there is no doubt," he said.

Struggles' rough face turned to him quickly. "Why, that could be anybody."

"Señor Doctor," Juan said quietly. "This is my country."

AT SUNDOWN they stopped long enough to eat a cold supper, then moved on into a fast-falling gloom. The country was level now, but thick with brush; mesquite clumps which in the evening dimness clung ghostlike to the ground and were dead silent with no breeze to stir them. Struggles, riding behind the Indian, felt his eyes stretched open unnaturally and told himself to quit being a damn fool and relax.

He chewed on the end of the dead cigar and let his stomach muscles go loose, but still a tension gripped him which his own steadying words could not detach. They were being followed. He knew that now, and didn't have to close his eyes to picture what would happen if they were overtaken. But there was more to the feeling than that. It was also the country—the climbing, stretching, never-ending wildness of the country. The Sierra Madre was like the sea, he thought. Both of them deathless, monotonously eternal, and so indifferent in their magnitude that either could accept the dust of all the world's dead and not have the decency to show it in posture. He thought: *Now I know what people mean about wanting to die in bed.* But again he told himself to shut up, because it was foolish to talk.

There was only a soft squeak of saddle leather and the muffled clop of hoofs on sand, and ahead, the dim figure of Juan Solo moving silently, rhythmically to the sounds.

The dusk thickened into night, and later Struggles could feel the ground beneath him changing though he could make out nothing in the darkness. There was a closeness above him along with the more broken ground, so that he sensed rather than observed that they were passing into rockier country.

And when first morning light reflected in the sky, Struggles saw that they were deep into a canyon. Ahead, it twisted out of sight, but beyond the rim a wall of mountain rose a thousand feet into the sky, tapering into a slender pinnacle at one end of its unbalanced crest. It seemed close enough to hit with a stone, but it was at least two miles beyond the canyon.

Juan Solo reined in gently and raised his arm toward the peak, pointing a finger. "Señor Doctor," he said. "Be the first American to observe El Sangre del Santo . . . and know it."

Struggles was unprepared. "That's it?" he said incredulously; then wondered why he had expected it to appear differently. Lost mines needn't look like lost mines. Looking at the peak he thought of the legend, trying to picture what had taken place here; but then he thought of the other that he had been thinking all night, and he glanced uneasily behind him.

Juan Solo watched him. "They are many hours behind," he said, "since they could not follow in the night. So, if it is not abusive to you, I say we should go quickly to the mine and leave before they arrive, continuing on in the widest circle that ends again where we started. Thus they will not know that they have been to El Sangre and left it. And later, when they see us surrounded by seven hundred bottles of mescal—" the Indian could not keep from grinning—"they will scratch their heads and turn and gaze out at the mountains that say nothing, and they will scratch their thick heads again."

Just past the canyon bend, Juan angled toward the shadowy vein of a crevice, the base overgrown with brush, which entered into a defile twisting through a squeezed-in narrowness to finally emerge in open country again at the base of the mountain.

From the ledge, Struggles' gaze lifted to the thin spire of rock, then dropped slowly, inching down with the speck that was Juan Solo descending the steep, narrow path of a rock slide that made a sweeping angle from the peak to the ledge where Struggles stood, then lost itself completely in a scatter of boulders on a bench fifty feet below. Struggles moved to the edge and glanced at the animals on the bench then on down the grade to the canyon they had left a few hours before, squinting hard, before looking back at Juan Solo.

And as the Indian reached the ledge, Struggles shook his head, then pressed his sleeve against his forehead and exhaled slowly. "I'm worn out just watching you," he said.

The Indian swung from his shoulder a blanket gathered into the shape of a sack. "Climbing for such that is up there is never wearing," he said. He untied the blanket ends and let them drop, watching Struggles, as the surgeon looked with astonishment at the dull-gleaming heap of candlesticks, chalices and crosses; all ornately tooled and some decorated with precious stones.

"These and more were placed in the sepulchre of Tomas Maria," Juan Solo said. "Along with the silver that had already been fashioned into bars when the restoration took place."

Struggles picked up a slender cruciform and ran his fingers over the baroque carvings. "It's unbelievable," he said, looking at Juan Solo. "These articles should be in a museum."

Juan Solo shook his head and there was the hint of a smile softening the straight lips of his mouth. "Then what would Tomas Maria have? These were only for if your mind doubted," he said, gathering the blanket and swinging it over his shoulder. "Now I will get your silver." And started up the slope.

Struggles felt a tingle of nervousness now; a restless urge to move about or at least face the solidness of the rock wall, as if by not seeing, the sprawling openness of the grade would not make him feel so naked. It stretched below him in a vast unmoving silence that seemed to hold time in a vacuum.

For a few minutes he watched Juan Solo almost a hundred feet above him. And when he again looked out over the slope, he saw it immediately, the thin dust thread in the distance on what only a few minutes before was a landscape as still as a painting. He watched it grow as it approached, squinting hard until he was sure, then he cupped his hands to his mouth and shouted, "Juan!" sharply. And when he saw the figure look down, he pointed out to the dust trail until he was certain Juan saw it, then went over the ledge, sliding down to the bench in a shower of loose gravel that made the animals shy at their halters and back away from the slope.

He moved them in quickly as best he could under a jutting of rock and pulled his carbine from its boot before moving back to the ledge.

☆　☆　☆

THE BENCH WAS a good thousand yards up the slope from the basin floor, and from there the riders were only dots against the ragged country, indistinguishable, disappearing behind brush now and again; but finally Struggles could make out six of them following the switchbacks single-file up the grade. He pushed his carbine out over the rocks watching the front door close as they approached. There was no back door. He had no doubt as to who they were, and still they kept coming, making no attempt to stay behind cover. From a hundred yards they all looked Mexican. One of them started to wave his sombrero and suddenly there was a pistol shot from above.

Struggles looked up, going flat behind the rocks, and saw Juan Solo down on the ledge again swinging his pistol in an arc before firing twice more; and when Struggles lifted his head above the rocks, he saw only a lone figure running after the horses that were scattering far down the grade. Nothing moved along the slope where the riders had been. Beyond the scattered rock and brush, the solitary figure was slowly rounding up the horses one at a time and leading them behind the shelter of a rise.

Struggles swung his carbine across a straight line waiting for something to move. They couldn't stay down forever. But for the next few minutes nothing happened.

Then, he saw the sombrero lift hesitantly above a rock for a full second before disappearing. After a few moments, the crown was edging up again when the pistol shot sounded from above and echoed back from down the slope. The hat disappeared again and someone yelled, "Hold your fire!" and next a white cloth was waving back and forth over the rock.

A man stepped out from behind the covering holding the cloth and motioned to the side until another man moved out hesitantly to join him as he started up the grade waving the cloth. He carried only a holstered pistol, but the second man held a Winchester across the crook of his arm. They came on slowly until they were in short-pistol range.

Struggles put his sights square in the center of the first man's chest and thought how easy it would be, but then he called, "That's good enough!"

The one with the rifle hesitated, but the other didn't break his stride.

"I said that's far enough!"

He stopped then, less than fifty feet away. A willow-root straw was down close to his eyes shading his features, but you could see that he was an American. There was an easiness about him, standing in the open in a relaxed slouch; and Struggles thought, *He looks like a red-dirt farmer leaning against the corner on Saturday night. Only there's no matchstick in his mouth and a gun's only six inches from his hand.*

The one with the Winchester, a Mexican, moved up next to him and stood sideways so that the cradled barrel was pointing up to the ledge. The American followed the direction of the barrel, then looked where he thought Struggles to be.

"Tell that crazy Indian to do something with his nerves," he called.

Struggles lifted his head slightly from the rear sight. "You're the one making him nervous, not me."

"There doesn't have to be trouble—that's what I mean." He pushed the straw up from his eyes. "Why don't you come out in the open?"

Struggles' cheek pressed against the stock again. "You better get to the point pretty soon." And with the words saw the American's face break into a smile.

"Well, the point is, you're sitting on a pile of silver and I want it." His smile broadened and he added, "And the edge of the point is that we're six and you're two."

"Only when you come to get us, it's going to cost you something," Struggles said.

"Not if we sit back in the shade and wait for your tongues to swell up."

"You look a little too skinny to be good at waiting."

The American nodded to the ledge. "Ask Juan how good I am at waiting. I used up a lot of my patience while my vaqueros scratched for your sign, but I still got some left."

Struggles admitted, "It didn't take you too long at that."

"Your boy isn't the only one who knows the country." He was waving the white cloth idly. "Look," he said. "Here's how it is. You either sit and die of thirst, or else get on your mounts and ride the hell out. Of course, for my own protection I'd have to ask both of you to leave your guns behind."

Struggles said, "You don't have a high regard for our reasoning, do you?"

The man shrugged. "I'm not talking you into anything." He waited a few moments, then turned and walked down the slope. The Mexican backed down, keeping the Winchester high.

Struggles fingered the trigger lightly and wondered what that principle was based on—about not shooting a man in the back. And when the straw hat was out of range he still had not thought of it.

Through the heat of the afternoon Struggles' mind talked to him, making conversation; but always an argument resulted, and his mind was poor company because it kept telling him that he was afraid. When the heat began to lift, a breeze stirred lazily over the bench and made a faint whispering sound as it played through the crevices above. And finally, the bench lost its shape in darkness.

It was cool relief after the glaring white light of the afternoon; but with the darkness, the slope that was still a painting now came alive and was something menacing.

Struggles crawled back to the slope and stood up, cupping his hands to his mouth, and whispered, "Juan," then gritted his teeth as the word cut the silence.

He waited, but nothing happened. He brought up his hands again, but jumped back quickly as a stream of loose shale clattered down from above. And as if on signal, two rifles opened up from below. Struggles went flat and inched back to the rim as the firing kept up, spattering against the flinty slope.

WHEN IT STOPPED, he raised his head above the rocks, but there was only the darkness. *They're not a hundred feet away,* he thought. *Waiting for us to move.* He settled down again, pressing close to the rock barrier. Well, they were going to have a long wait. But now he wondered if he was alone. Since the firing there had been no sound from above. Had something happened to Juan?

Time lost its meaning after a while and became only something that dragged hope with it as it went nowhere.

Sometime after midnight, Struggles started to doze off. His head nodded and his chin was almost on his chest, but even then a consciousness warned him and he jerked his head up abruptly. He moved it from side to side now, shaking himself awake; and as his face swung to the left he saw the pinpoint of a gleam up on the mountainside.

He came to his feet, fully awake now, but blinked his eyes to make sure. The light was moving down with crawling slowness from the peak, flickering dully, but growing in intensity as it inched down the rock slide path that Juan Solo had climbed earlier.

After a few minutes Struggles saw a torch, with the flame dancing against the blackness of the slope, and as it descended to the ledge the shape of a man was illuminated weirdly in the flickering orange light it cast.

The figure moved to the edge, holding up a baroque cross whose end was the burning torch—the figure of a man wearing the coarse brown robes of a Franciscan friar.

He held the cross high overhead and spoke one sentence of Castilian, the words cold and shrill in the darkness.

"Leave this Blood of the Saint or thus your souls shall plunge to the hell of the damned!"

His arm swung back and the torch soared out into the night and down until it hit far below on the slope in a shower of bursting sparks. The figure was gone in the darkness.

Quiet settled again, but a few minutes later gunfire came from down the slope. And shortly after that, the sound of horses running hard, and dying away in the distance.

The rest of the night Struggles asked himself questions. He sat unmoving with the dead cigar stub still in his mouth and tried to think it out, applying logic. Finally he came to a conclusion. There was only one way to find out the answers to last night's mystery.

At the first sign of morning light he rose and started to climb up the slope toward the ledge.

This would answer both questions—it was the only way.

He was almost past caring whether or not the American and his men were still below. Almost. He climbed slowly, feeling the tenseness between his shoulder blades because he wasn't sure of anything. When he was nearing the rim, a hand reached down to his arm and pulled him up the rest of the way.

"Juan."

The Indian steadied him as he got to his feet. "You came with such labor, I thought you sick."

And at that moment Struggles did feel sick. Weak with relief, he was, suddenly, for only then did he realize that somehow it was all over.

He exhaled slowly and his grizzled face relaxed into a smile. He looked past Juan Solo and the smile broadened as his eyes fell on the torn blanket with the pieces of rope coiled on top of it.

"Padre, you ought to take better care of your cassock," Struggles said, nodding toward the blanket.

Juan Solo frowned. "Your words pass me," he said, looking out over the slope; and added quickly, "Let us find what occurred with the American."

Struggles was dead certain that Juan knew without even having to go down from the ledge.

Not far down the grade they found him, lying on his face with stiffened fingers clawed into the loose sand. Near his body were the ashes of the cruciform, still vaguely resembling—even as the wind began to blow it into nothingness—the shape of a cross.

Struggles said, "I take it he didn't believe in the friar, and wouldn't listen to his men who did."

Juan Solo nodded as if to say, *So you see what naturally happened,* then said, "Now there is plenty of time for your silver, Señor Doctor," and started back up the grade.

Struggles followed after him, trying to picture Tomas Maria, and thinking what a good friend the friar had in Juan Solo.

9

The Rustlers

Original Title: Along the Pecos
Zane Grey's Western, February 1953

MOST OF THE time there was dead silence. When someone did say something it was never more than a word or two at a time: *More coffee?* Words that were not words because there was no thought behind them and they didn't mean anything. Words like *getting late*, when no one cared. Hardly even noises, because no one heard.

Stillness. Six men sitting together in a pine grove, and yet there was no sound. A boot scraped gravel and a tin cup clanked against rock, but they were like the words, little noises that started and stopped at the same time and were forgotten before they could be remembered.

More coffee? And an answering grunt that meant even less.

Five men scattered around a campfire that was dead, and the sixth man squatting at the edge of the pines looking out into the distance through the dismal reflection of a dying sun that made the grayish flat land look petrified in death and unchanged for a hundred million years.

Emmett Ryan stared across the flats toward the lighter gray outline in the distance that was Anton Chico, but he wasn't seeing the adobe brick of the village. He wasn't watching the black speck that was gradually getting bigger as it approached.

All of us knew that. We sat and watched Emmett Ryan's coat pulled tight across his shoulder blades, not moving body or head. Just a broad smoothness of faded denim. We'd been looking at the same back all the way from Tascosa and in two hundred miles you can learn a lot about a back.

The black speck grew into a horse and rider, and as they moved up the slope toward the pines the horse and rider became Gosh Hall on his roan. Emmett walked over to meet him, but didn't say anything. The question was on his broad, red face and he didn't have to ask it.

Gosh Hall swung down from the saddle and put his hands on the small of his back, arching against the stiffness. "They just rode in," he said, and walked past the big man to the dead fire. "Who's got all the coffee?"

Emmett followed him with his eyes and the question was still there. It was something to see that big, plain face with the eyes open wide and staring when before they'd always been half-closed from squinting against the glare of twenty-odd years in open country. Now his face looked too big and loose for the small nose and slit of an Irish mouth. You could see the indecision and maybe a little fear in the wide-open eyes, something that had never been there before.

We'd catch ourselves looking at that face and have to look at something else, quick, or Em would see somebody's jaw hanging open and wonder what the hell was wrong with him. We felt sorry for Em—I know I did—and it was a funny feeling to all of a sudden see the big TX ramrod that way.

Gosh looked like he had an apron on, standing over the dead fire with his hip cocked and the worn hide chaps covering his short legs. He held the cup halfway to his face, watching Em, waiting for him to ask the question. I thought Gosh was making it a little extra tough on Em; he could have come right out with it. Both of them just stared at each other.

Finally Emmett said, "Jack with them?"

Gosh took a sip of coffee first. "Him and Joe Anthony rode in together, and another man. Anthony and the other man went into the Senate House and Jack took the horses to the livery and then followed them over to the hotel."

"They see you?"

"Naw, I was down the street under a ramada. All they'd see'd be shadow."

"You sure it was them, Gosh?" I asked him.

"Charlie," Gosh said, "I got a picture in my head, and it's stuck there 'cause I never expected to see one like it. It's a picture of Jack and Joe

Anthony riding into Magenta the same way a month ago. When you see something that's different or hadn't ought to be, it sticks in your head. And they was on the same mounts, Charlie."

Emmett went over to his dun mare and tightened the cinch like he wanted to keep busy and show us everything was going the same. But he was just fumbling with the strap, you could see that. His head swung around a few inches. "Jack look all right?"

Gosh turned his cup upside down and a few drops of coffee trickled down to the ashes at his feet. "I don't know, Em. How is a man who's just stole a hundred head of beef supposed to look?"

Emmett jerked his body around and the face was closed again for the first time in a week, tight and redder than usual. Then his jaw eased and his big hands hanging at his sides opened and closed and then went loose. Emmett didn't have anything to grab. Some of the others were looking at Gosh Hall and probably wondering why the little rider was making it so hard for Em.

Emmett asked him, "Did you see Butzy?"

"He didn't ride in. I 'magine he's out with the herd." Gosh looked around. "Neal still out, huh?"

Neal Whaley had gone in earlier with Gosh, then split off over to where they were holding the herd, just north of Anton Chico. Neal was to watch and tell us if they moved them. Emmett figured they were holding the herd until a buyer came along. There were a lot of buyers in New Mexico who didn't particularly care what the brand read, but Emmett said they were waiting for a top bid or they would have sold all the stock before this.

Ned Bristol and Lloyd Cohane got up and stretched and then just stood there awkwardly looking at the dead fire, their boots, and each other. Lloyd pulled a blue bandanna from his coat pocket and wiped his face with it, then folded it and straightened it out thin between his fingers before tilting his chin up to tie it around his neck. Ned pushed his gun belt down lower on his hips and watched Emmett.

Dobie Shaw, the kid in our outfit, went over to his mount and pulled his Winchester from the boot and felt in the bag behind the saddle for a box of cartridges. Dobie had to do something too.

Ben Templin was older; he'd been riding better than thirty years.

He eased back to the ground with his hands behind his head tilting his hat over his face and waited. Ben had all the time in the world.

Everybody was going through the motions of being natural, but fidgeting and acting restless and watching Emmett at the same time because we all knew it was time now, and Emmett didn't have any choice. That was what forced Emmett's hand, though we knew he would have done it anyway, sooner or later. But maybe we looked a little too anxious to him, when it was only restlessness. It was a long ride from Tascosa. A case of let's get it over with or else go on home—one way or the other, regardless of whose brother stole the cows.

Gosh Hall scratched the toe of his boot through the sand, kicking it over the ashes of the dead fire. "About that time, ain't it, Em?"

Emmett exhaled like he was very tired. "Yeah, it's about that time." He looked at every face, slowly, before turning to his mare.

IT'S ROUGHLY a hundred and thirty miles from Tascosa, following the Canadian, to Trementina on the Conchas, then another thirty-five miles south, swinging around Mesa Montosa to Anton Chico, on the Pecos. Counting detours to find water holes and trailing the wrong sign occasionally, that's about two hundred miles of sun, wind, and New Mexico desert—and all to bring back a hundred head of beef owned by a Chicago company that tallied close to a quarter million all over the Panhandle and north-central Texas.

The western section of the TX Company was headquartered at Sudan that year, with most of the herds north of Tascosa and strung out west along the Canadian. Emmett Ryan was ramrod of the home crew at Sudan, but he spent a week or more at a time out on the grass with the herds. That was why he happened to be with us when R. D. Perris, the company man, rode in. We were readying to go into Magenta for a few when Perris came beating his mount into camp. Even in the cool of the evening the horse was flaked white and about to drop and Perris was so excited he could hardly get the words out. And finally when he told his story there was dead silence and all you could hear was R. D. Perris breathing like his chest was about to rip open.

Jack Ryan and Frank Butzinger—Frank, who nobody ever gave

credit for having any sand—and over a hundred head of beef hadn't been seen on the west range for three days. R. D. Perris had said, "The tracks follow the river west, but we figured Jack was taking them to new grass. But then the tracks just kept on going. . . ."

Emmett was silent from that time on. He asked a few questions, but he was pretty sure of the answers before he asked them. There was that talk for weeks about Jack having been seen in Tascosa and Magenta with Joe Anthony. And there weren't many people friendly with Joe Anthony. In his time, he'd had his picture on wanted dodgers more than once. Two shootings for sure, and a few holdups, but the holdups were just talk. Nobody ever pinned anything on him, and with his gunhand reputation, nobody made any accusations.

Gosh Hall had seen them together in Magenta and he told Emmett to his face that he didn't like it; but Emmett had defended him and said Jack was just sowing oats because he was still young and hadn't got his sense of values yet. But Lloyd Cohane was there that time at the line camp when Emmett dropped in and chewed hell out of Jack for palling with Joe Anthony. Then came the time Emmett walked into the saloon in Tascosa with his gun out and pushed it into Joe Anthony's belly before Joe even saw him and told him to ride and keep riding.

Jack was there, drunk like he usually was in town, but he sobered quick and followed Anthony out of the saloon when Emmett prodded him out, and laughed right in Emmett's face when Em told him to stay where he was. And he was laughing and weaving in the saddle when he rode out of town with Anthony.

Until that night Perris came riding in with his story, Em hadn't seen his brother. So you know what he was thinking; what all of us were thinking.

Riding the two hundred miles to find the herd was part of the job, but knowing you were trailing a friend made the job kind of sour and none of us was sure if we wanted to find the cattle. Jack Ryan was young and wild and drank too much and laughed all the time, but he had more friends than any rider in the Panhandle.

Like Ben Templin said: "Jack's a good boy, but he's got an idea life's just a big can-can dancer with four fingers of scootawaboo in each hand." And that was about it.

★　★　★

THE SPLOTCH of white that was Anton Chico from a distance gradually got bigger and cleared until finally right in front of us it was gray adobe brick, blocks of it, dull and lifeless in the cold late sunlight. Emmett slowed us to a walk the last few hundred feet approaching the town's main street and motioned Ben Templin up next to him.

"Ben," he said, "you take Dobie with you and cut for that back street yonder and come up behind the livery. Don't let anybody see you and hush the stableman if he gets loud about what you're doing. Maybe Butzy'll come along, Ben—if he isn't there already."

I looked at Emmett watching Ben Templin and Dobie Shaw cut off, and there it was. His old face again. All closed and hard with the crow's feet streaking from the corners of his eyes. And his mouth tight like it used to be when he thought and ordered men at the same time, because he always knew what he was doing. You could see Emmett knew what he was doing now, that he'd set his mind. And when Emmett Ryan set his mind his pride saw to it that it stayed set.

Emmett walked his mount down the left side of the narrow main street with the rest of us strung out behind. When he veered over to a hitchrack about halfway down the second block, we veered with him and tied up, straggled along before two store fronts.

Em stepped up on the boardwalk and moved leisurely toward the Senate House hotel almost at the end of the block. He stopped as he crossed the alley next to the hotel and nodded to Lloyd Cohane, then bent his head toward the alley and moved it in a half-circle over his big shoulders. Lloyd moved off down the alley toward the back of the hotel.

"Go on with him, Ned," Em whispered. "Stick near the kitchen door and if anybody but the cook comes out shoot his pants off."

Ned moved off after Lloyd, both carrying carbines. Em looked at Gosh and me, but didn't say anything. He just looked and that meant we were with him and supposed to back up anything he did. Then he turned toward the hotel and slipped his revolver out in the motion. Gosh moved right after him and pointed the barrel of his Winchester out in front of him.

Two idlers sitting in front of the hotel stared at us trying to make out they weren't staring, and as soon as we passed them I heard their chairs scrape and their footsteps hurrying down the boards. A man across the street pushed through the saloon doors without even putting his hands out. A rider slowed up in front of the hotel as if about to turn in and then he kicked his mount into a trot down the street.

In the hotel lobby you could still hear the horse clopping down the street and it made the lobby seem even more quiet and comfortable, feeling the coolness inside and picturing the horse on the dusty street. But there was the clerk with his mouth open watching Emmett walk toward the café entrance, his spurs chinging with each step.

It seemed like, for a show like this, everything was moving too fast. The next thing, we were in the café part and Jack Ryan and Joe Anthony and the other man were looking at us like they couldn't believe their eyes.

None of them moved. Jack's jaw was open with a mouthful of beef, his eyes almost as wide open as his mouth. The other man had a taco in his fingers raised halfway to his mouth and he just held it there. Didn't move it up or down. Joe Anthony's right hand was around a glass of something yellow like mescal. His left hand was below the level of the table. The three of them had their hats on, pushed back, and they looked dirty and tired.

Jack chewed and swallowed hard and then he smiled. "Damn, Em, you must have flown!"

The other man looked at us one at a time slowly, then shrugged his shoulders and said, "What the hell," and shoved the taco in his mouth.

Joe Anthony wiped the back of his hand over his mouth and moved the hand back, smoothing the long mustaches with the knuckle of his index finger. The other hand was still under the table.

Emmett held his revolver pointed square at Joe Anthony and seemed to be unmindful of the other two men. Lloyd and Ned came through the kitchen door and moved around behind Emmett.

"Get up," Em ordered. "And take off your belts."

Somebody's chair scraped, but Joe Anthony said, "Hold it!" and it was quiet.

Anthony was staring back at Emmett. "Do I look like a green kid to you, Ryan?" he said, and half smiled. "You're not telling anybody what to do, cowboy."

"I said get up," Em repeated.

Joe Anthony kept on smiling like he thought Emmett was a fool. He shook his head slowly. "Ryan, the longer you stand there, the shorter your chances are of leaving here on your two feet."

"You're all mouth," Emmett said. "Just mouth."

The outlaw's expression didn't change. His face was good-looking in a swarthy kind of way, but gaunt and hungry-looking with pale, shallow eyes like a man who forgot where his conscience was, or that he ever had one.

His smile sagged a little and he said, "Ryan, let's quit playing. You ride the hell out of here before I shoot you."

"I'm not playing," Emmett said, leveling the revolver. "Get up, quick."

"Ryan," Joe Anthony whispered impatiently, "I've had a Colt leveled on your belly since the second you come through that doorway."

I thought I knew Emmett Ryan, but I didn't know him as well as I supposed. His face didn't change its expression, but his finger moved on the trigger and the room filled with the explosion. His thumb yanked on the hammer and he fired again right on top of the first one.

Joe Anthony went back with his chair, fell hard and lay still. His pistol was still in the holster on his right hip.

Emmett looked down at him. "You're all mouth, Anthony. All mouth."

Nobody said anything after that. We were looking at Em and Em was looking at Joe Anthony stretched out on the floor. I heard steps behind me and there was Dobie Shaw tiptoeing in and looking like he'd dive out the window if anybody said anything.

Emmett waved his gun at the other man and glanced at his brother. "Who's this?"

Jack spoke easily. "Earl Roach. We picked him up for a trail driver. He didn't know it was rustled stock."

Roach was unfastening his gun belt. He shot a look toward Jack. "Boy," he said, "you take care of your troubles and I'll take care of mine."

Dobie Shaw moved up behind Emmett hesitantly and waited for the big foreman to look his way. "Mr. Ryan—Ben's holding Butzy over to the livery." He went on hurriedly trying to get the whole story out be-

fore Em asked any questions. "Butzy walked right in and didn't move after Ben throwed down on him, but there was another one back a ways
and he turned and rode like hell when he saw me and Ben with our
guns out. Me and Ben didn't even get a shot at him 'fore he was round
the corner and gone."

"All right, Dobie. You go on back with Ben." Emmett hesitated and
glanced at Jack like he was making up his mind all over again, but the
doubt passed off quickly. He said, "We'll be over directly. You go on and
tell Ben to keep Butzy right there."

FRANK BUTZINGER was flat against the boards of a stall, though Ben
Templin was standing across the open part of the stable smoking a cigarette with his carbine propped against the wall. Ben wasn't paying any
attention to him, but even in the dim light you could see Butzy was
about ready to die of fright.

Gosh Hall pushed Jack and Earl Roach toward the stall that Butzy
was in and mumbled something, probably swearing. Jack looked
around at him with a half smile and shook his head like a father playing
Indians with his youngster. Humoring him.

Emmett stood out in the open part with the rest of us spread around
now. He said, "You sell the stock yet?"

"A few," Jack answered. "We got almost a hundred head."

"You got the money?"

"What do you think?"

The foreman motioned to Gosh Hall. "Get some line and tie their
hands behind them."

The little cowboy's face brightened and he moved into the stall lifting
a coil of rope from the side wall. When he pulled his knife and started to
cut it into pieces, the stableman came running over. He'd been standing
in the front doorway, but I hadn't noticed him there before.

He ran over yelling, "Hey, that's my rope!"

Gosh reached out, laughing, and grabbed one of his braces and
snapped it against his faded red-flannel undershirt. "Get back, old
man, you're interfering with justice." Then he pushed the man hard
against the stall partition.

Emmett took hold of his elbow and pulled him out toward the front of the livery. "You stay out here," he said. "This isn't any of your business." He turned from the man and nodded his head to the stalls where three horses were.

The stable was large, high-ceilinged, with stalls lining both sides. The open area was wide, but longer than it was wide, with heavy timbers overhead reaching from lofts on both sides that ran the length of the stable above the stalls. The stable was empty but for the three horses toward the back.

"Bring those horses up here." Em said it to no one in particular.

When Dobie and Ned and I led the mounts up, I heard Lloyd ask Em if he should go get our horses. Em shook his head, but didn't say anything.

Lloyd said, "Shouldn't we be getting out to the stock, Em?"

"We got time. Neal's watching the cows," Em reminded him. "The man that was with Butzy spread his holler if there were any others out there. They'd be halfway to Santa Fe by now."

He turned on Gosh impatiently. "Come on, get 'em mounted."

I picked up one of their saddles from the rack and walked up behind Gosh, who was pushing the three men toward the horses.

"Look out, Gosh. Let me get the saddles on before you get in the way. You can't throw 'em on with your arms behind your back."

Gosh twisted his mouth into a smile and looked past me at Emmett. There was a wad of tobacco in his cheek that made his thin face lopsided, like a jagged rock with hair on it. He shifted the wad, still smiling, and then spit over to the side.

"You tell him, Em," he said.

Emmett looked at me with his closed-up, leathery face. He stared hard as if afraid his eyes would waver. "They don't need the saddles."

Gosh swatted me playfully with the end of rope in his hand. "Want me to paint you a picture, Charlie?" He laughed and walked out through the wide entrance.

Gosh didn't have to paint a picture. Ben Templin dropped his cigarette. Lloyd and Ned and Dobie just stared at Emmett, but none of them said anything. Em stood there like a rock and stared back like he was defying anybody to object.

The boys looked away and moved about uncomfortably. They weren't about to go against Emmett Ryan. They were used to doing what they were told because Em was always right, and weren't sure that he wasn't right even now. A hanging isn't an uncommon thing where there is little law. Along the Pecos there was less than little. Still, it didn't rub right—even if Em was following his conscience, it didn't rub right.

I hesitated until the words were in my mouth and I'd have had bit my tongue off to hold them back. "You setting yourself up as the law?" It was supposed to have a bite to it, but the words sounded weak and my voice wasn't even.

Emmett said, "You know what the law is." He beckoned to the coil of rope Gosh had hung back on the boards. "That's it right there, Charlie. You know better than that." Emmett was talking to himself as well as me, but you didn't remind that hardheaded Irishman of things like that.

"Look, Em. Let's get the law and handle this right."

"It's black and white, it's two and two, if you steal cows and get caught you hang."

"Maybe. But it's not up to you to decide. Let's get the law."

"I've already decided," was all he said.

The stable hand crept up close to us and waited until there was a pause. "The deputy ain't here," the old man said. "He rode down to Lincoln yesterday morning to join the posse." He waited for someone to show interest, but no one said a word. "They're getting a posse up on account of there's word Bill Bonney's at Fort Sumner."

He stepped back looking proud as could be over his news. I could have kicked his seat flat for what he said.

Gosh came back with two coiled lariats on his arm and a third one in his hands. He was shaping a knot at one end of it.

Earl Roach looked at Gosh, then up to the heavy rafter that crossed above the three horses, then Jack's head went up too.

Gosh spit and grinned at them, forming a loop in the second rope. "What'd you expect'd happen?"

Jack kept his eyes on the rafter. "I didn't expect to get caught."

"Jack's always smiling into the sunshine, ain't he?" Gosh pushed Earl Roach toward his horse. "Mount up, mister."

Roach jerked his shoulder away from him. "I look like a bird to you? You want me up on that horse, you'll have to put me up."

"Earl, I'll put you up and help take you down."

When he got to Butzy and offered him a leg up, Butzy made a funny sound like a whine and started to back away, but Gosh grabbed him by his shirt before he took two steps. Butzy looked over Gosh's bony shoulder, his eyes popping out of his pasty face.

"Em, what you fixin' to do?" His voice went up a notch, and louder. "What you fixin' to do? You just scarin' us, Em?"

If it was a joke, Butzy didn't want to play the fool, but you could tell by his voice what he was thinking. Em didn't answer him.

Gosh finished knotting the third rope and handed it to Dobie, who looked at it like he'd never seen a lariat before.

Gosh said, "Make yourself useful and throw that rope over the rafter."

He went out and brought his horse in and mounted so he could slip the nooses over their heads, but he stood in the stirrups and still couldn't reach the tops of their heads. Emmett told him to get down and ordered Ben Templin to climb up and fix the ropes. Ben did it, but Em had to tell him three times.

Before he jumped down, Ben lighted cigarettes and gave them to Jack and Earl. Butzy was weaving his head around so Ben couldn't get one in his mouth. Just rolling his head around with his eyes closed, moaning.

Gosh looked up at him and laughed out loud. "You praying, Butzy?" he called out. "Better pray hard, you ain't got much time," and kept on laughing.

Ben Templin made a move toward Gosh, but Emmett caught his arm.

"Hold still, Ben." He looked past him at Gosh. "You can do what you're doing with your mouth shut."

Gosh moved behind the horses with the short end of rope in his hand. He edged over behind Earl Roach's horse. "Age before beauty, I always say."

Butzy's eyes opened up wide. "God, Em! Please Em—please—honest to God—I didn't know they was stealing the herd! Swear to God,

Em, I thought Perris told Jack to sell the herd. Please, Em—I—let me go and I'll never show my face again. Please—"

"You'll never show it anyway where you're going," Gosh cracked.

Earl Roach was looking at Butzy with a blank expression. His head turned to Jack, holding his chin up to ease his neck away from the chafe of the rope. "Who's your friend?"

Jack Ryan's lips, with the cigarette hanging, formed a small smile at Roach. "Never saw him before in my life." His young face was paler than usual, you could see it through beard and sunburn, but his voice was slow and even with that little edge of sarcasm it usually carried.

Roach shook his head to drop the ash from his cigarette. "Beats me where he come from," he said.

Ben Templin swore in a slow whisper. He mumbled, "It's a damn waste of good guts."

Lloyd and Ned and Dobie were looking at the two of them like they couldn't believe their eyes and then seemed to all drop their heads about the same time. Embarrassed. Like they didn't rate to be in the same room with Jack and Earl. I felt it too, but felt a mad coming on along with it.

"Dammit, Em! You're going to wait for the deputy!" I knew I was talking, but it didn't sound like me. "You're going to wait for the deputy whether you like it or not!"

Emmett just stared back and I felt like running for the door. Emmett stood there alone like a rock you couldn't budge and then Ben Templin was beside him with his hand on Em's arm, but not just resting it there, holding the forearm hard. His other hand was on his pistol butt.

"Charlie's right, Em," Ben said. "I'm not sure how you got us this far, or why, but ain't you or God Almighty going to hang those boys by yourself."

They stood there, those two big men, their faces not a foot apart, not telling a thing by their faces, but you got the feeling if one of them moved the livery would collapse like a twister hit it.

Finally Emmett blinked his eyes, and moved his arm to make Ben let go.

"All right, Ben." It was just above a whisper and sounded tired. "We've all worked together a long time and have always agreed—if it was a case of letting you in on the agreeing. We won't change it now."

Gosh came out from behind the horses. Disappointed and mad. He moved right up close to Emmett. "You going to let this woman—"

That was all he got a chance to say. Emmett swung his fist against that bony tobacco bulge and Gosh flattened against the board wall before sliding down into a heap.

Emmett started to walk out the front and then he turned around. "We're waiting on the deputy until tomorrow morning. If he don't show by then, this party takes up where it left off."

He angled out the door toward the Senate House, still the boss. The hardheaded Irishman's pride had to get the last word in whether he meant it or not.

THE DEPUTY got back late that night. You could see by his face that he hadn't gotten what he'd gone for. Emmett stayed in his room at the Senate House, but Ben Templin and I were waiting at the jail when the deputy returned—though I don't know what we would have done if he hadn't—with two bottles of the yellowest mescal you ever saw to ease his saddle sores and dusty throat.

We told him how we'd put three of our boys in his jail—just a scare, you understand—when they'd got drunk and thought it'd be fun to run off with a few head of stock. Just a joke on the owner, you understand. And Emmett Ryan, the ramrod, being one of them's brother, he had to act tougher than usual, else the boys'd think he was playing favorites. Like him always giving poor Jack the wildest broncs and making him ride drag on the trail drives.

Em was always a little too serious, anyway. Of course, he was a good man, but he was a big, red-faced Irishman who thought his pride was a stone god to burn incense in front of. And hell, he had enough troubles bossing the TX crew without getting all worked up over his brother getting drunk and playing a little joke on the owners—you been drunk like that, haven't you, Sheriff? Hell, everybody has. A sheriff with guts enough to work in Bill Bonney's country had more to do than chase after drunk cowpokes who wouldn't harm a fly. And even if they were serious, what's a few cows to an outfit that owns a quarter million?

And along about halfway down the second bottle— So why don't we turn the joke around on old Em and let the boys out tonight? We done you a turn by getting rid of Joe Anthony. Old Em'll wake up in the morning and be madder than hell when he finds out, and that will be some sight to see.

The deputy could hardly wait.

In the morning it was Ben who had to tell Em what happened. I was there in body only, with my head pounding like a pulverizer. The deputy didn't show up at all.

We waited for Emmett to fly into somebody, but he just looked at us, from one to the next. Finally he turned toward the livery.

"Let's go take the cows home," was all he said.

Not an hour later we were looking down at the flats along the Pecos where the herd was. Neal Whaley was riding toward us.

Emmett had been riding next to me all the way out from Anton Chico. When he saw Neal, he broke into a gallop to meet him, and that was when I thought he said, "Thanks, Charlie."

I know his head turned, but there was the beat of his horse when he started the gallop, and that mescal pounding at my brains. Maybe he said it and maybe he didn't.

Knowing that Irishman, I'm not going to ask him.

10

Three-Ten to Yuma

Dime Western Magazine, March 1953

HE HAD PICKED up his prisoner at Fort Huachuca shortly after midnight and now, in a silent early morning mist, they approached Contention. The two riders moved slowly, one behind the other.

Entering Stockman Street, Paul Scallen glanced back at the open country with the wet haze blanketing its flatness, thinking of the long night ride from Huachuca, relieved that this much was over. When his body turned again, his hand moved over the sawed-off shotgun that was across his lap and he kept his eyes on the man ahead of him until they were near the end of the second block, opposite the side entrance of the Republic Hotel.

He said just above a whisper, though it was clear in the silence, "End of the line."

The man turned in his saddle, looking at Scallen curiously. "The jail's around on Commercial."

"I want you to be comfortable."

Scallen stepped out of the saddle, lifting a Winchester from the boot, and walked toward the hotel's side door. A figure stood in the gloom of the doorway, behind the screen, and as Scallen reached the steps the screen door opened.

"Are you the marshal?"

"Yes, sir." Scallen's voice was soft and without emotion. "Deputy, from Bisbee."

"We're ready for you. Two-oh-seven. A corner . . . fronts on Commercial." He sounded proud of the accommodation.

"You're Mr. Timpey?"

The man in the doorway looked surprised. "Yeah, Wells Fargo. Who'd you expect?"

"You might have got a back room, Mr. Timpey. One with no windows." He swung the shotgun on the man still mounted. "Step down easy, Jim."

The man, who was in his early twenties, a few years younger than Scallen, sat with one hand over the other on the saddle horn. Now he gripped the horn and swung down. When he was on the ground his hands were still close together, iron manacles holding them three chain lengths apart. Scallen motioned him toward the door with the stubby barrel of the shotgun.

"Anyone in the lobby?"

"The desk clerk," Timpey answered him, "and a man in a chair by the front door."

"Who is he?"

"I don't know. He's asleep . . . got his brim down over his eyes."

"Did you see anyone out on Commercial?"

"No . . . I haven't been out there." At first he had seemed nervous, but now he was irritated, and a frown made his face pout childishly.

Scallen said calmly, "Mr. Timpey, it was your line this man robbed. You want to see him go all the way to Yuma, don't you?"

"Certainly I do." His eyes went to the outlaw, Jim Kidd, then back to Scallen hurriedly. "But why all the melodrama? The man's under arrest—already been sentenced."

"But he's not in jail till he walks through the gates at Yuma," Scallen said. "I'm only one man, Mr. Timpey, and I've got to get him there."

"Well, dammit . . . I'm not the law! Why didn't you bring men with you? All I know is I got a wire from our Bisbee office to get a hotel room and meet you here the morning of November third. There weren't any instructions that I had to get myself deputized a marshal. That's your job."

"I know it is, Mr. Timpey," Scallen said, and smiled, though it was an effort. "But I want to make sure no one knows Jim Kidd's in Contention until after train time this afternoon."

Jim Kidd had been looking from one to the other with a faintly amused grin. Now he said to Timpey, "He means he's afraid somebody's going to jump him." He smiled at Scallen. "That marshal must've really sold you a bill of goods."

"What's he talking about?" Timpey said.

Kidd went on before Scallen could answer. "They hid me in the Huachuca lockup 'cause they knew nobody could get at me there . . . and finally the Bisbee marshal gets a plan. He and some others hopped the train in Benson last night, heading for Yuma with an army prisoner passed off as me." Kidd laughed, as if the idea were ridiculous.

"Is that right?" Timpey said.

Scallen nodded. "Pretty much right."

"How does he know all about it?"

"He's got ears and ten fingers to add with."

"I don't like it. Why just one man?"

"Every deputy from here down to Bisbee is out trying to scare up the rest of them. Jim here's the only one we caught," Scallen explained— then added, "alive."

Timpey shot a glance at the outlaw. "Is he the one who killed Dick Moons?"

"One of the passengers swears he saw who did it . . . and he didn't identify Kidd at the trial."

Timpey shook his head. "Dick drove for us a long time. You know his brother lives here in Contention. When he heard about it he almost went crazy." He hesitated, and then said again, "I don't like it."

Scallen felt his patience wearing away, but he kept his voice even when he said, "Maybe I don't either . . . but what you like and what I like aren't going to matter a whole lot, with the marshal past Tucson by now. You can grumble about it all you want, Mr. Timpey, as long as you keep it under your breath. Jim's got friends . . . and since I have to haul him clear across the territory, I'd just as soon they didn't know about it."

Timpey fidgeted nervously. "I don't see why I have to get dragged into this. My job's got nothing to do with law enforcement. . . ."

"You have the room key?"

"In the door. All I'm responsible for is the stage run between here and Tucson—"

Scallen shoved the Winchester at him. "If you'll take care of this and the horses till I get back, I'll be obliged to you . . . and I know I don't have to ask you not to mention we're at the hotel."

He waved the shotgun and nodded and Jim Kidd went ahead of him through the side door into the hotel lobby. Scallen was a stride behind him, holding the stubby shotgun close to his leg. "Up the stairs on the right, Jim."

Kidd started up, but Scallen paused to glance at the figure in the armchair near the front. He was sitting on his spine with limp hands folded on his stomach and, as Timpey had described, his hat low over the upper part of his face. You've seen people sleeping in hotel lobbies before, Scallen told himself, and followed Kidd up the stairs. He couldn't stand and wonder about it.

Room 207 was narrow and high-ceilinged, with a single window looking down on Commercial Street. An iron bed was placed the long way against one wall and extended to the right side of the window, and along the opposite wall was a dresser with washbasin and pitcher and next to it a rough-board wardrobe. An unpainted table and two straight chairs took up most of the remaining space.

"Lay down on the bed if you want to," Scallen said.

"Why don't you sleep?" Kidd asked. "I'll hold the shotgun."

The deputy moved one of the straight chairs near to the door and the other to the side of the table opposite the bed. Then he sat down, resting the shotgun on the table so that it pointed directly at Jim Kidd sitting on the edge of the bed near the window.

He gazed vacantly outside. A patch of dismal sky showed above the frame buildings across the way, but he was not sitting close enough to look directly down onto the street. He said, indifferently, "I think it's going to rain."

There was a silence, and then Scallen said, "Jim, I don't have anything against you personally . . . this is what I get paid for, but I just want it understood that if you start across the seven feet between us, I'm going to pull both triggers at once—without first asking you to stop. That clear?"

Kidd looked at the deputy marshal, then his eyes drifted out the window again. "It's kinda cold too." He rubbed his hands together and the three chain links rattled against each other. "The window's open a crack. Can I close it?"

Scallen's grip tightened on the shotgun and he brought the barrel up, though he wasn't aware of it. "If you can reach it from where you're sitting."

Kidd looked at the windowsill and said without reaching toward it, "Too far."

"All right," Scallen said, rising. "Lay back on the bed." He worked his gun belt around so that now the Colt was on his left hip.

Kidd went back slowly, smiling. "You don't take any chances, do you? Where's your sporting blood?"

"Down in Bisbee with my wife and three youngsters," Scallen told him without smiling, and moved around the table.

There were no grips on the window frame. Standing with his side to the window, facing the man on the bed, he put the heel of his hand on the bottom ledge of the frame and shoved down hard. The window banged shut and with the slam he saw Jim Kidd kicking up off of his back, his body straining to rise without his hands to help. Momentarily, Scallen hesitated and his finger tensed on the trigger. Kidd's feet were on the floor, his body swinging up and his head down to lunge from the bed. Scallen took one step and brought his knee up hard against Kidd's face.

The outlaw went back across the bed, his head striking the wall. He lay there with his eyes open looking at Scallen.

"Feel better now, Jim?"

Kidd brought his hands up to his mouth, working the jaw around. "Well, I had to try you out," he said. "I didn't think you'd shoot."

"But you know I will the next time."

For a few minutes Kidd remained motionless. Then he began to pull himself straight. "I just want to sit up."

Behind the table Scallen said, "Help yourself." He watched Kidd stare out the window.

Then, "How much do you make, Marshal?" Kidd asked the question abruptly.

"I don't think it's any of your business."

"What difference does it make?"

Scallen hesitated. "A hundred and fifty a month," he said, finally, "some expenses, and a dollar bounty for every arrest against a Bisbee ordinance in the town limits."

Kidd shook his head sympathetically. "And you got a wife and three kids."

"Well, it's more than a cowhand makes."

"But you're not a cowhand."

"I've worked my share of beef."

"Forty a month and keep, huh?" Kidd laughed.

"That's right, forty a month," Scallen said. He felt awkward. "How much do you make?"

Kidd grinned. When he smiled he looked very young, hardly out of his teens. "Name a month," he said. "It varies."

"But you've made a lot of money."

"Enough. I can buy what I want."

"What are you going to be wanting the next five years?"

"You're pretty sure we're going to Yuma."

"And you're pretty sure we're not," Scallen said. "Well, I've got two train passes and a shotgun that says we are. What've you got?"

Kidd smiled. "You'll see." Then he said right after it, his tone changing, "What made you join the law?"

"The money," Scallen answered, and felt foolish as he said it. But he went on, "I was working for a spread over by the Pantano Wash when Old Nana broke loose and raised hell up the Santa Rosa Valley. The army was going around in circles, so the Pima County marshal got up a bunch to help out and we tracked Apaches almost all spring. The marshal and I got along fine, so he offered me a deputy job if I wanted it." He wanted to say that he started for seventy-five and worked up to the one hundred and fifty, but he didn't.

"And then someday you'll get to be marshal and make two hundred."

"Maybe."

"And then one night a drunk cowhand you've never seen will be tearing up somebody's saloon and you'll go in to arrest him and he'll drill you with a lucky shot before you get your gun out."

"So you're telling me I'm crazy."

"If you don't already know it."

Scallen took his hand off the shotgun and pulled tobacco and paper from his shirt pocket and began rolling a cigarette. "Have you figured out yet what my price is?"

Kidd looked startled, momentarily, but the grin returned. "No, I haven't. Maybe you come higher than I thought."

Scallen scratched a match across the table, lighted the cigarette, then threw it to the floor, between Kidd's boots. "You don't have enough money, Jim."

Kidd shrugged, then reached down for the cigarette. "You've treated me pretty good. I just wanted to make it easy on you."

The sun came into the room after a while. Weakly at first, cold and hazy. Then it warmed and brightened and cast an oblong patch of light between the bed and the table. The morning wore on slowly because there was nothing to do and each man sat restlessly thinking about somewhere else, though it was a restlessness within and it showed on neither of them.

The deputy rolled cigarettes for the outlaw and himself and most of the time they smoked in silence. Once Kidd asked him what time the train left. He told him shortly after three, but Kidd made no comment.

Scallen went to the window and looked out at the narrow rutted road that was Commercial Street. He pulled a watch from his vest pocket and looked at it. It was almost noon, yet there were few people about. He wondered about this and asked himself if it was unnaturally quiet for a Saturday noon in Contention . . . or if it were just his nerves. . . .

He studied the man standing under the wooden awning across the street, leaning idly against a support post with his thumbs hooked in his belt and his flat-crowned hat on the back of his head. There was something familiar about him. And each time Scallen had gone to the window—a few times during the past hour—the man had been there.

He glanced at Jim Kidd lying across the bed, then looked out the window in time to see another man moving up next to the one at the post. They stood together for the space of a minute before the second man turned a horse from the tie rail, swung up, and rode off down the street.

The man at the post watched him go and tilted his hat against the sun glare. And then it registered. With the hat low on his forehead Scallen saw him again as he had that morning. The man lying in the armchair . . . as if asleep.

He saw his wife, then, and the three youngsters and he could almost feel the little girl sitting on his lap where she had climbed up to kiss him good-bye, and he had promised to bring her something from Tucson. He didn't know why they had come to him all of a sudden. And after he had put them out of his mind, since there was no room now, there was an upset feeling inside as if he had swallowed something that would not go down all the way. It made his heart beat a little faster.

Jim Kidd was smiling up at him. "Anybody I know?"

"I didn't think it showed."

"Like the sun going down."

Scallen glanced at the man across the street and then to Jim Kidd. "Come here." He nodded to the window. "Tell me who your friend is over there."

Kidd half rose and leaned over looking out the window, then sat down again. "Charlie Prince."

"Somebody else just went for help."

"Charlie doesn't need help."

"How did you know you were going to be in Contention?"

"You told that Wells Fargo man I had friends . . . and about the posses chasing around in the hills. Figure it out for yourself. You could be looking out a window in Benson and seeing the same thing."

"They're not going to do you any good."

"I don't know any man who'd get himself killed for a hundred and fifty dollars." Kidd paused. "Especially a man with a wife and young ones. . . ."

Men rode into town in something less than an hour later. Scallen heard the horses coming up Commercial, and went to the window to see the six riders pull to a stop and range themselves in a line in the middle of the street facing the hotel. Charlie Prince stood behind them, leaning against the post.

Then he moved away from it, leisurely, and stepped down into the street. He walked between the horses and stopped in front of them just below the window. He cupped his hands to his mouth and shouted, *"Jim!"*

In the quiet street it was like a pistol shot.

Scallen looked at Kidd, seeing the smile that softened his face and was even in his eyes. Confidence. It was all over him. And even with the manacles on, you would believe that it was Jim Kidd who was holding the shotgun.

"What do you want me to tell him?" Kidd said.

"Tell him you'll write every day."

Kidd laughed and went to the window, pushing it up by the top of the frame. It raised a few inches. Then he moved his hands under the window and it slid up all the way.

"Charlie, you go buy the boys a drink. We'll be down shortly."

"Are you all right?"

"Sure I'm all right."

Charlie Prince hesitated. "What if you don't come down? He could kill you and say you tried to break. . . . Jim, you tell him what'll happen if we hear a gun go off."

"He knows," Kidd said, and closed the window. He looked at Scallen standing motionless with the shotgun under his arm. "Your turn, Marshal."

"What do you expect me to say?"

"Something that makes sense. You said before I didn't mean a thing to you personally—what you're doing is just a job. Well, you figure out if it's worth getting killed for. All you have to do is throw your guns on the bed and let me walk out the door and you can go back to Bisbee and arrest all the drunks you want. Nobody's going to blame you with the odds stacked seven to one. You know your wife's not going to complain. . . ."

"You should have been a lawyer, Jim."

The smile began to fade from Kidd's face. "Come on—what's it going to be?"

The door rattled with three knocks in quick succession. Abruptly the room was silent. The two men looked at each other and now the smile disappeared from Kidd's face completely.

Scallen moved to the side of the door, tiptoeing in his high-heeled boots, then pointed his shotgun toward the bed. Kidd sat down.

"Who is it?"

For a moment there was no answer. Then he heard, "Timpey."

He glanced at Kidd, who was watching him. "What do you want?"

"I've got a pot of coffee for you."

Scallen hesitated. "You alone?"

"Of course I am. Hurry up, it's hot!"

He drew the key from his coat pocket, then held the shotgun in the crook of his arm as he inserted the key with one hand and turned the knob with the other. The door opened and slammed against him, knocking him back against the dresser. He went off balance, sliding into the wardrobe, going down on his hands and knees, and the shotgun clattered across the floor to the window. He saw Jim Kidd drop to the floor for the gun. . . .

"Hold it!"

A heavyset man stood in the doorway with a Colt pointing out past the thick bulge of his stomach. "Leave that shotgun where it is." Timpey stood next to him with the coffeepot in his hand. There was coffee down the front of his suit, on the door, and on the flooring. He brushed at the front of his coat feebly, looking from Scallen to the man with the pistol.

"I couldn't help it, Marshal—he made me do it. He threatened to do something to me if I didn't."

"Who is he?"

"Bob Moons . . . you know, Dick's brother. . . ."

The heavyset man glanced at Timpey angrily. "Shut your damn whining." His eyes went to Jim Kidd and held there. "You know who I am, don't you?"

Kidd looked uninterested. "You don't resemble anybody I know."

"You didn't have to know Dick to shoot him!"

"I didn't shoot that messenger."

Scallen got to his feet, looking at Timpey. "What the hell's wrong with you?"

"I couldn't help it. He forced me."

"How did he know we were here?"

"He came in this morning talking about Dick and I felt he needed some cheering up; so I told him Jim Kidd had been tried and was being taken to Yuma and was here in town . . . on his way. Bob didn't say anything and went out, and a little later he came back with the gun."

"You damn fool." Scallen shook his head wearily.

"Never mind all the talk." Moons kept the pistol on Kidd. "I would've found him sooner or later. This way everybody gets saved a long train ride."

"You pull that trigger," Scallen said, "and you'll hang for murder."

"Like he did for killing Dick. . . ."

"A jury said he didn't do it." Scallen took a step toward the big man. "And I'm damned if I'm going to let you pass another sentence."

"You stay put or I'll pass sentence on you!"

Scallen moved a slow step nearer. "Hand me the gun, Bob."

"I'm warning you—get the hell out of the way and let me do what I came for."

"Bob, hand me the gun or I swear I'll beat you through that wall."

Scallen tensed to take another step, another slow one. He saw Moons's eyes dart from him to Kidd and in that instant he knew it would be his only chance. He lunged, swinging his coat aside with his hand, and when the hand came up it was holding a Colt. All in one motion. The pistol went up and chopped an arc across Moons's head before the big man could bring his own gun around. His hat flew off as the barrel swiped his skull and he went back against the wall heavily, then sank to the floor.

Scallen wheeled to face the window, thumbing the hammer back. But Kidd was still sitting on the edge of the bed with the shotgun at his feet.

The deputy relaxed, letting the hammer ease down. "You might have made it, that time."

Kidd shook his head. "I wouldn't have got off the bed." There was a note of surprise in his voice. "You know, you're pretty good. . . ."

At two-fifteen Scallen looked at his watch, then stood up, pushing the chair back. The shotgun was under his arm. In less than an hour they would leave the hotel, walk over Commercial to Stockman, and then up Stockman to the station. Three blocks. He wanted to go all the way. He wanted to get Jim Kidd on that train . . . but he was afraid.

He was afraid of what he might do once they were on the street. Even now his breath was short and occasionally he would inhale and let the air out slowly to calm himself. And he kept asking himself if it was worth it.

People would be in the windows and the doors, though you

wouldn't see them. They'd have their own feelings and most of their hearts would be pounding . . . and they'd edge back of the door frames a little more. The man out on the street was something without a human nature or a personality of its own. He was on a stage. The street was another world.

Timpey sat on the chair in front of the door and next to him, squatting on the floor with his back against the wall, was Moons. Scallen had unloaded Moons's pistol and placed it in the pitcher behind him. Kidd was on the bed.

Most of the time he stared at Scallen. His face bore a puzzled expression, making his eyes frown, and sometimes he would cock his head as if studying the deputy from a different angle.

Scallen stepped to the window now. Charlie Prince and another man were under the awning. The others were not in sight.

"You haven't changed your mind?" Kidd asked him seriously.

Scallen shook his head.

"I don't understand you. You risk your neck to save my life, now you'll risk it again to send me to prison."

Scallen looked at Kidd and suddenly felt closer to him than any man he knew. "Don't ask me, Jim," he said, and sat down again.

After that he looked at his watch every few minutes.

At five minutes to three he walked to the door, motioning Timpey aside, and turned the key in the lock. "Let's go, Jim." When Kidd was next to him he prodded Moons with the gun barrel. "Over on the bed. Mister, if I see or hear about you on the street before train time, you'll face an attempted murder charge." He motioned Kidd past him, then stepped into the hall and locked the door.

They went down the stairs and crossed the lobby to the front door, Scallen a stride behind with the shotgun barrel almost touching Kidd's back. Passing through the doorway he said as calmly as he could, "Turn left on Stockman and keep walking. No matter what you hear, keep walking."

As they stepped out into Commercial, Scallen glanced at the ramada where Charlie Prince had been standing, but now the saloon porch was an empty shadow. Near the corner two horses stood under a sign that said EAT, in red letters; and on the other side of Stockman the signs continued, lining the rutted main street to make it seem narrower. And beneath the signs, in the shadows, nothing moved. There was a whisper of wind along the ramadas. It whipped sand specks from the street and rattled them against clapboard, and the sound was hollow and lifeless. Somewhere a screen door banged, far away.

They passed the café, turning onto Stockman. Ahead, the deserted street narrowed with distance to a dead end at the rail station—a single-story building standing by itself, low and sprawling, with most of the platform in shadow. The westbound was there, along the platform, but the engine and most of the cars were hidden by the station house. White steam lifted above the roof, to be lost in the sun's glare.

They were almost to the platform when Kidd said over his shoulder, "Run like hell while you're still able."

"Where are they?"

Kidd grinned, because he knew Scallen was afraid. "How should I know?"

"Tell them to come out in the open!"

"Tell them yourself."

"Dammit, *tell* them!" Scallen clenched his jaw and jabbed the short barrel into Kidd's back. "I'm not fooling. If they don't come out, I'll kill you!"

Kidd felt the gun barrel hard against his spine and suddenly he shouted, "Charlie!"

It echoed in the street, but after there was only the silence. Kidd's eyes darted over the shadowed porches. "Dammit, Charlie—hold on!"

Scallen prodded him up the warped plank steps to the shade of the platform and suddenly he could feel them near. "Tell him again!"

"Don't shoot, Charlie!" Kidd screamed the words.

From the other side of the station they heard the trainman's call trailing off, ". . . Gila Bend. Sentinel, Yuma!"

The whistle sounded loud, wailing, as they passed into the shade of the platform, then out again to the naked glare of the open side. Scallen squinted, glancing toward the station office, but the train dispatcher was not in sight. Nor was anyone. "It's the mail car," he said to Kidd. "The second to last one." Steam hissed from the iron cylinder of the engine, clouding that end of the platform. "Hurry it up!" he snapped, pushing Kidd along.

Then, from behind, hurried footsteps sounded on the planking, and, as the hiss of steam died away—"Stand where you are!"

The locomotive's main rods strained back, rising like the legs of a grotesque grasshopper, and the wheels moved. The connecting rods stopped on an upward swing and couplings clanged down the line of cars.

"Throw the gun away, brother!"

Charlie Prince stood at the corner of the station house with a pistol in each hand. Then he moved around carefully between the two men and the train. "Throw it far away, and unhitch your belt," he said.

"Do what he says," Kidd said. "They've got you."

The others, six of them, were strung out in the dimness of the platform shed. Grim faced, stubbles of beard, hat brims low. The man nearest Prince spat tobacco lazily.

Scallen knew fear at that moment as fear had never gripped him before; but he kept the shotgun hard against Kidd's spine. He said, just above a whisper, "Jim—I'll cut you in half!"

Kidd's body was stiff, his shoulders drawn up tightly. "Wait a minute . . ." he said. He held his palms out to Charlie Prince, though he could have been speaking to Scallen.

Suddenly Prince shouted, "Go down!"

There was a fraction of a moment of dead silence that seemed longer. Kidd hesitated. Scallen was looking at the gunman over Kidd's shoulder, seeing the two pistols. Then Kidd was gone, rolling on the planking, and the pistols were coming up, one ahead of the other. Without moving Scallen squeezed both triggers of the scattergun.

Charlie Prince was going down, holding his hands tight to his chest, as Scallen dropped the shotgun and swung around drawing his Colt. He fired hurriedly. *Wait for a target!* Words in his mind. He saw the men under the platform shed, three of them breaking for the station office, two going full length to the planks . . . one crouched, his pistol up. *That one! Get him quick!* Scallen aimed and squeezed the heavy revolver and the man went down. *Now get the hell out!*

Charlie Prince was facedown. Kidd was crawling, crawling frantically and coming to his feet when Scallen reached him. He grabbed Kidd by the collar savagely, pushing him on, and dug the pistol into his back. "Run, damn you!"

Gunfire erupted from the shed and thudded into the wooden caboose as they ran past it. The train was moving slowly. Just in front of them a bullet smashed a window of the mail car. Someone screamed, "You'll hit Jim!" There was another shot, then it was too late. Scallen and Kidd leapt up on the car platform and were in the mail car as it rumbled past the end of the station platform.

Kidd was on the floor, stretched out along a row of mail sacks. He rubbed his shoulder awkwardly with his manacled hands and watched Scallen, who stood against the wall next to the open door.

Kidd studied the deputy for some minutes. Finally he said, "You know, you really earn your hundred and a half."

Scallen heard him, though the iron rhythm of the train wheels and his breathing were loud in his temples. He felt as if all his strength had been sapped, but he couldn't help smiling at Jim Kidd. He was thinking pretty much the same thing.

11

The Big Hunt

Original Title: Matt Gordon's Boy
Western Story Magazine, April 1953

IT WAS A SHARPS .50, heavy and cumbrous, but he was lying at full length downwind of the herd behind the rise with the long barrel resting on the hump of the crest so that the gun would be less tiring to fire.

He counted close to fifty buffalo scattered over the grass patches, and his front sight roamed over the herd as he waited. A bull, its fresh winter hide glossy in the morning sun, strayed leisurely from the others, following thick patches of gamma grass. The Sharps swung slowly after the animal. And when the bull moved directly toward the rise, the heavy rifle dipped over the crest so that the sight was just off the right shoulder. The young man, who was still not much more than a boy, studied the animal with mounting excitement.

"Come on, granddaddy . . . a little closer," Will Gordon whispered. The rifle stock felt comfortable against his cheek, and even the strong smell of oiled metal was good. "Walk up and take it like a man, you ugly monster, you dumb, shaggy, ugly hulk of a monster. Look at that fresh gamma right in front of you. . . ."

The massive head came up sleepily, as if it had heard the hunter, and the bull moved toward the rise. It was less than eighty yards away, nosing the grass tufts, when the Sharps thudded heavily in the crisp morning air.

The herd lifted from grazing, shaggy heads turning lazily toward the bull sagging to its knees, but as it slumped to the ground the heads lowered unconcernedly. Only a few of the buffalo paused to sniff the breeze. A calf bawled, sounding *nooooo* in the open-plain stillness.

Will Gordon had reloaded the Sharps, and he pushed it out in front of him as another buffalo lumbered over to the fallen bull, sniffing at the blood, nuzzling the bloodstained hide: and, when the head came up, nose quivering with scent, the boy squeezed the trigger. The animal stumbled a few yards before easing its great weight to the ground.

Don't let them smell blood, he said to himself. They smell blood and they're gone.

He fired six rounds then, reloading the Sharps each time, though a loaded Remington rolling-block lay next to him. He fired with little hesitation, going to his side, ejecting, taking a cartridge from the loose pile at his elbow, inserting it in the open breech. He fired without squinting, calmly, killing a buffalo with each shot. Two of the animals lumbered on a short distance after being hit, glassy eyed, stunned by the shock of the heavy bullet. The others dropped to the earth where they stood.

Sitting up now, he pulled a square of cloth from his coat pocket, opened his canteen, and poured water into the cloth, squeezing it so that it would become saturated. He worked the wet cloth through the eye of his cleaning rod, then inserted it slowly into the barrel of the Sharps, hearing a sizzle as it passed through the hot metal tube. He was new to the buffalo fields, but he had learned how an overheated gun barrel could put a man out of business. He had made sure of many things before leaving Leverette with just a two-man outfit.

Pulling the rod from the barrel, he watched an old cow sniffing at one of the fallen bulls. Get that one quick . . . or you'll lose a herd!

He dropped the Sharps, took the Remington, and fired at the buffalo from a sitting position. Then he reloaded both rifles, but fired the Remington a half-dozen more rounds while the Sharps cooled. Twice he had to hit with another shot to kill, and he told himself to take more time. Perspiration beaded his face, even in the crisp fall air, and burned powder was heavy in his nostrils, but he kept firing at the same methodical pace, because it could not last much longer, and there was not time to cool the barrels properly. He had killed close to twenty when the blood smell became too strong.

The buffalo made rumbling noises in the thickness of their throats, and now three and four at a time would crowd toward those on the ground, sniffing, pawing nervously.

A bull bellowed, and the boy fired again. The herd bunched, bumping each other, bellowing, shaking their clumsy heads at the blood smell. Then the leader broke suddenly, and what was left of the herd was off, from stand to dead run, in one moment of panic, driven mad by the scent of death.

The boy fired into the dust cloud that rose behind them, but they were out of range before he could reload again.

It's better to wave them off carefully with a blanket after killing all you can skin, the boy thought to himself. But this had worked out all right. Sometimes it didn't, though. Sometimes they stampeded right at the hunter.

He rose stiffly, rubbing his shoulder, and moved back down the rise to his picketed horse. His shoulder ached from the buck of the heavy rifles, but he felt good. Lying back there on the plain was close to seventy or eighty dollars he'd split with Leo Cleary . . . soon as they'd been skinned and handed over to the hide buyers. Hell, this was easy. He lifted his hat, and the wind was cold on his sweat-dampened forehead. He breathed in the air, feeling an exhilaration, and the ache in his shoulder didn't matter one bit.

Wait until he rode into Leverette with a wagon full of hides, he thought. He'd watch close, pretending he didn't care, and he'd see if anybody laughed at him then.

✱   ✱   ✱

HE WAS MOUNTING when he heard the wagon creaking in the distance, and he smiled when Leo Cleary's voice drifted up the gradual rise, swearing at the team. He waited in the saddle, and swung down as the four horses and the canvas-topped wagon came up to him.

"Leo, I didn't even have to come wake you up." Will Gordon smiled up at the old man on the box, and the smile eased the tight lines of his face. It was a face that seemed used to frowning, watching life turn out all wrong, a sensitive boyish face, but the set of his jaw was a man's . . . or that of a boy who thought like a man. There were few people he showed his smile to other than Leo Cleary.

"That cheap store whiskey you brought run out," Leo Cleary said. His face was beard stubbled, and the skin hung loosely seamed beneath tired eyes.

"I thought you quit," the boy said. His smile faded.

"I have now."

"Leo, we got us a lot of money lying over that rise."

"And a lot of work. . . ." He looked back into the wagon, yawning. "We got near a full load we could take in . . . and rest up. You shooters think all the work's in knocking 'em down."

"Don't I help with the skinning?"

Cleary's weathered face wrinkled into a slow smile. "That's just the old man in me coming out," he said. "You set the pace, Will. All I hope is roaming hide buyers don't come along . . . you'll be wanting to stay out till April." He shook his head. "That's a mountain of back-breaking hours just to prove a point."

"You think it's worth it or not?" the boy said angrily.

Cleary just smiled. "Your dad would have liked to seen this," he said. "Come on, let's get those hides."

Skinning buffalo was filthy, back-straining work. Most hunters wouldn't stoop to it. It was for men hired as skinners and cooks, men who stayed by the wagons until the shooting was done.

During their four weeks on the range the boy did his share of the work, and now he and Leo Cleary went about it with little conversation. Will Gordon was not above helping with the butchering, with hides going for four dollars each in Leverette, three dollars if a buyer picked them up on the range.

The more hides skinned, the bigger the profit. That was elementary. Let the professional hunters keep their pride and their hands clean while they sat around in the afternoon filling up on scootawaboo. Let them pay heavy for extra help just because skinning was beneath them. That was their business.

In Leverette, when the professional hunters laughed at them, it didn't bother Leo Cleary. Maybe they'd get hides, maybe they wouldn't. Either way it didn't matter much. When he thought about it, Leo Cleary believed the boy just wanted to prove a point—that a two-man outfit could make money—attributing it to his Scotch stubbornness. The idea had been Will's dad's—when he was sober. The old man had almost proved it himself.

But whenever anyone laughed, the boy would feel that the laughter was not meant for him but for his father.

Leo Cleary went to work with a frown on his grizzled face, wetting his dry lips disgustedly. He squatted up close to the nearest buffalo and with his skinning knife slit the belly from neck to tail. He slashed the skin down the inside of each leg, then carved a strip from around the massive neck, his long knife biting at the tough hide close to the head. Then he rose, rubbing the back of his knife hand across his forehead.

"Yo! Will . . ." he called out.

The boy came over then, leading his horse and holding a coiled riata in his free hand. One end was secured to the saddle horn. He bunched the buffalo's heavy neck skin, wrapping the free end of line around it, knotting it.

He led the horse out the whole length of the rope, then mounted, his heels squeezing flanks as soon as he was in the saddle.

"Yiiiiiii!" He screamed in the horse's ear and swatted the rump with his hat. The mount bolted.

The hide held, stretching, then jerked from the carcass, coming with a quick sucking, sliding gasp.

They kept at it through most of the afternoon, sweating over the carcasses, both of them skinning, and butchering some meat for their own use. It was still too early in the year, too warm, to butcher hindquarters for the meat buyers. Later, when the snows came and the meat would keep, they would do this.

They took the fresh hides back to their base camp and staked them out, stretching the skins tightly, flesh side up. The flat ground around the wagon and cook fire was covered with staked-out hides, taken the previous day. In the morning they would gather the hides and bind them in packs and store the packs in the wagon. The boy thought there would be maybe two more days of hunting here before they would have to move the camp.

For the second time that day he stood stretching, rubbing a stiffness in his body, but feeling satisfied. He smiled, and even Leo Cleary wasn't watching him to see it.

At dusk they saw the string of wagons out on the plain, a black line creeping toward them against the sunlight dying on the horizon.

"Hide buyers, most likely," Leo Cleary said. He sounded disappointed, for it could mean they would not return to Leverette for another month.

The boy said, "Maybe a big hunting outfit."

"Not at this time of day," the old man said. "They'd still have their hides drying." He motioned to the creek back of their camp. "Whoever it is, they want water."

Two riders leading the five Conestogas spurred suddenly as they neared the camp and rode in ahead of the six-team wagons. The boy watched them intently. When they were almost to the camp circle, he recognized them and swore under his breath, though he suddenly felt self-conscious.

The Foss brothers, Clyde and Wylie, swung down stiff legged, not waiting for an invitation, and arched the stiffness from their backs. Without a greeting Clyde Foss's eyes roamed leisurely over the staked-out hides, estimating the number as he scratched at his beard stubble. He grinned slowly, looking at his brother.

"They must a used rocks . . . ain't more than forty hides here."

Leo Cleary said, "Hello, Clyde . . . Wylie," and watched the surprise come over them with recognition.

Clyde said, "Damn, Leo, I didn't see you were here. Who's that with you?"

"Matt Gordon's boy," Leo Cleary answered. "We're hunting together this season."

"Just the two of you?" Wylie asked with surprise. He was a few years older than Clyde, calmer, but looked to be his twin. They were both of them lanky, thin through face and body, but heavy boned.

Leo Cleary said, "I thought it was common talk in Leverette about us being out."

"We made up over to Caldwell this year," Clyde said. He looked about the camp again, amused. "Who does the shooting?"

"I do." The boy took a step toward Clyde Foss. His voice was cold, distant. He was thinking of another time four years before when his dad had introduced him to the Foss brothers, the day Matt Gordon contracted with them to pick up his hides.

"And I do skinning," the boy added. It was like *What are you going to do about it!* the way he said it.

Clyde laughed again. Wylie just grinned.

"So you're Matt Gordon's boy," Wylie Foss said.

"We met once before."

"We did?"

"In Leverette, four years ago." The boy made himself say it naturally. "A month before you met my dad in the field and paid him for his hides with whiskey instead of cash . . . the day before he was trampled into the ground. . . ."

☆   ☆   ☆

THE FOSS BROTHERS met his stare, and suddenly the amusement was gone from their eyes. Clyde no longer laughed, and Wylie's mouth tightened. Clyde stared at the boy and said, "If you meant anything by that, you better watch your mouth."

Wylie said, "We can't stop buffalo from stampedin'." Clyde grinned now.

"Maybe he's drunk . . . maybe he favors his pa."

"Take it any way you want," the boy said. He stood firmly with his fists clenched. "You knew better than to give him whiskey. You took advantage of him."

Wylie looked up at the rumbling sound of the wagon string coming in, the ponderous creaking of wooden frames, iron-rimmed tires grating, and the never-changing off-key leathery rattle of the traces, then the sound of reins flicking horse hide and the indistinguishable growls of the teamsters.

Wylie moved toward the wagons in the dimness and shouted to the first one, "Ed . . . water down!" pointing toward the creek.

"You bedding here?" Leo Cleary asked after him.

"Just water."

"Moving all night?"

"We're meeting a party on the Salt Fork . . . they ain't going to stay there forever." Wylie Foss walked after the wagons leading away their horses.

Clyde paid little attention to the wagons, only glancing in that direction as they swung toward the stream. Stoop shouldered, his hand curling the brim of his sweat-stained hat, his eyes roamed lazily over the drying hides. He rolled a cigarette, taking his time, failing to offer tobacco to the boy.

"I guess we got room for your hides," he said finally.

"I'm not selling."

"We'll load soon as we water . . . even take the fresh ones."

"I said I'm not selling."

"Maybe I'm not asking."

"There's nothing making me sell if I don't want to!"

The slow smile formed on Clyde's mouth. "You're a mean little fella, aren't you?"

Clyde Foss dropped the cigarette stub and turned a boot on it. "There's a bottle in my saddle pouch." He nodded to Leo Cleary, who was standing off from them. "Help yourself, Leo."

The old man hesitated.

"I said help yourself."

Leo Cleary moved off toward the stream.

"Now, Mr. Gordon . . . how many hides you say were still dryin'?"

"None for you."

"Forty . . . forty-five?"

"You heard what I said." He was standing close to Clyde Foss, watching his face. He saw the jaw muscles tighten and sensed Clyde's shift of weight. He tried to turn, bringing up his shoulder, but it came with pain-stabbing suddenness. Clyde's fist smashed against his cheek, and he stumbled off balance.

"Forty?"

Clyde's left hand followed around with weight behind it, scraping his temple, staggering him.

"Forty-five?"

He waded after the boy then, clubbing at his face and body, knocking his guard aside to land his fists, until the boy was backed against his wagon. Then Clyde stopped as the boy fell into the wheel spokes, gasping, and slumped to the ground.

Clyde stood over the boy and nudged him with his boot. "Did I hear forty or forty-five?" he said dryly. And when the boy made no answer— "Well, it don't matter."

He heard the wagons coming up from the creek. Wylie was leading the horses. "Boy went to sleep on us, Wylie." He grinned. "He said don't disturb him, just take the skins and leave the payment with Leo." He laughed then. And later, when the wagons pulled out, he was laughing again.

Once he heard voices, a man swearing, a never-ending soft thudding against the ground, noises above him in the wagon. But these passed, and there was nothing.

He woke again, briefly, a piercing ringing in his ears, and his face throbbed violently though the pain seemed to be out from him and not within, as if his face were bloated and would soon burst. He tried to open his mouth, but a weight held his jaws tight. Then wagons moving . . . the sound of traces . . . laughter.

It was still dark when he opened his eyes. The noises had stopped. Something cool was on his face. He felt it with his hand— a damp cloth. He sat up, taking it from his face, working his jaw slowly.

The man was a blur at first . . . something reflecting in his hand. Then it was Leo Cleary, and the something in his hand was a half-empty whiskey bottle.

"There wasn't anything I could do, Will."

"How long they been gone?"

"Near an hour. They took all of them, even the ones staked out." He said, "Will, there wasn't anything I could do. . . ."

"I know," the boy said.

"They paid for the hides with whiskey." The boy looked at him, surprised. He had not expected them to pay anything. But now he saw how this would appeal to Clyde's sense of humor, using the same way the hide buyer had paid his dad four years before.

"That part of it, Leo?" The boy nodded to the whiskey bottle in the old man's hand.

"No, they put three five-gallon barrels in the wagon. Remember . . . Clyde give me this."

The boy was silent. Finally he said, "Don't touch those barrels, Leo."

He sat up the remainder of the night, listening to his thoughts. He had been afraid when Clyde Foss was bullying him, and he was still afraid. But now the fear was mixed with anger, because his body ached and he could feel the loose teeth on one side of his mouth when he tightened his jaw, and taste the blood dry on his lips and most of all because Clyde Foss had taken a month's work, four hundred and eighty hides, and left three barrels of whiskey.

Sometimes the fear was stronger than the anger. The plain was silent and in its darkness there was nothing to hold to. He did not bother Leo Cleary. He talked to himself and listened to the throb in his temples and left Leo alone with the little whiskey he still had. He wanted to cry, but he could not because he had given up the privilege by becoming a man, even though he was still a boy. He was acutely aware of this, and when the urge to cry welled in him he would tighten his nerves and call himself names until the urge passed.

Sometimes the anger was stronger than the fear, and he would think of killing Clyde Foss. Toward morning both the fear and the anger lessened, and many of the things he had thought of during the night he did not now remember. He was sure of only one thing: He was going to get his hides back. A way to do it would come to him. He still had his Sharps.

He shook Leo Cleary awake and told him to hitch the wagon.

"Where we going?" The old man was still dazed, from sleep and whiskey.

"Hunting, Leo. Down on the Salt Fork."

HUNTING WAS GOOD in the Nations. The herds would come down from Canada and the Dakotas and winter along the Cimarron and the Salt and even down to the Canadian. Here the herds were big, two and three hundred grazing together, and sometimes you could look over the flat plains and see thousands. A big outfit with a good hunter could average over eighty hides a day. But, because there were so many hunters, the herds kept on the move.

In the evening they saw the first of the buffalo camps. Distant lights in the dimness, then lanterns and cook fires as they drew closer in a dusk turning to night, and the sounds of men drifted out to them on the silent plain.

The hunters and skinners were crouched around a poker game on a blanket, a lantern above them on a crate. They paid little heed to the old man and the boy, letting them prepare their supper on the low-burning cook fire and after, when the boy stood over them and asked questions, they answered him shortly. The game was for high stakes, and there was a pot building. No, they hadn't seen the Foss brothers, and if they had, they wouldn't trade with them anyway. They were taking their skins to Caldwell for top dollar.

They moved on, keeping well off from the flickering line of lights. Will Gordon would go in alone as they neared the camps, and, if there were five wagons in the camp, he'd approach cautiously until he could make out the men at the fire.

From camp to camp it was the same story. Most of the hunters had not seen the Fosses; a few had, earlier in the day, but they could be anywhere now. Until finally, very late, they talked to a man who had sold to the Foss brothers that morning.

"They even took some fresh hides," he told them.

"Still heading west?" The boy kept his voice even, though he felt the excitement inside of him.

"Part of them," the hunter said. "Wylie went back to Caldwell with three wagons, but Clyde shoved on to meet another party up the Salt. See, Wylie'll come back with empty wagons, and by that time the hunters'll have caught up with Clyde. You ought to find him up a ways. We'll all be up there soon . . . that's where the big herds are heading."

They moved on all night, spelling each other on the wagon box. Leo grumbled and said they were crazy. The boy said little because he was thinking of the big herds. And he was thinking of Clyde Foss with all those hides he had to dry . . . and the plan was forming in his mind.

Leo Cleary watched from the pines, seeing nothing, thinking of the boy who was out somewhere in the darkness, though most of the time he thought of whiskey, barrels of it that they had been hauling for two days and now into the second night.

The boy was a fool. The camp they had seen at sundown was probably just another hunter. They all staked hides at one time or another. Seeing him sneaking up in the dark they could take him for a Kiowa and cut him in two with a buffalo gun. And even if it did turn out to be Clyde Foss, then what?

Later, the boy walked in out of the darkness and pushed the pine branches aside and was standing next to the old man.

"It's Clyde, Leo."

The old man said nothing.

"He's got two men with him."

"So . . . what are you going to do now?" the old man said.

"Hunt," the boy said. He went to his saddlebag and drew a cap-and-ball revolver and loaded it before bedding for the night.

In the morning he took his rifles and led his horse along the base of the ridge, through the pines that were dense here, but scattered higher up the slope. He would look out over the flat plain to the south and see the small squares of canvas, very white in the brilliant sunlight. Ahead, to the west, the ridge dropped off into a narrow valley with timbered hills on the other side.

The boy's eyes searched the plain, roaming to the white squares, Clyde's wagons, but he went on without hesitating until he reached the sloping finish of the ridge. Then he moved up the valley until the plain widened again, and then he stopped to wait. He was prepared to wait for days if necessary, until the right time.

From high up on the slope above, Leo Cleary watched him. Through the morning the old man's eyes would drift from the boy and then off to the left, far out on the plain to the two wagons and the ribbon of river behind them. He tried to relate the boy and the wagons in some way, but he could not.

After a while he saw buffalo. A few straggling off toward the wagons, but even more on the other side of the valley where the plain widened again and the grass was higher, green-brown in the sun.

Toward noon the buffalo increased, and he remembered the hunters saying how the herds were moving west. By that time there were hundreds, perhaps a thousand, scattered over the grass, out a mile or so from the boy who seemed to be concentrating on them.

Maybe he really is going hunting, Leo Cleary thought. Maybe he's starting all over again. But I wish I had me a drink. The boy's downwind now, he thought, lifting his head to feel the breeze on his face. He could edge up and take a hundred of them if he did it right. What's he waiting for! Hell, if he wants to start all over, it's all right with me. I'll stay out with him. At that moment he was thinking of the three barrels of whiskey.

"Go out and get 'em, Will," he urged the boy aloud, though he would not be heard. "The wind won't keep forever!"

Surprised, then, he saw the boy move out from the brush clumps leading his horse, mount, and lope off in a direction out and away from the herd.

"You can't hunt buffalo from a saddle . . . they'll run as soon as they smell horse! What the hell's the matter with him!"

HE WATCHED the boy, growing smaller with distance, move out past the herd. Then suddenly the horse wheeled, and it was going at a dead run toward the herd. A yell drifted up to the ridge and then a heavy rifle shot followed by two reports that were weaker. Horse and rider cut into the herd, and the buffalo broke in confusion.

They ran crazily, bellowing, bunching in panic to escape the horse and man smell and the screaming that suddenly hit them with the wind. A herd of buffalo will run for hours if the panic stabs them sharp enough, and they will stay together, bunching their thunder, tons of bulk, massive bellowing heads, horns, and thrashing hooves. Nothing will stop them. Some go down, and the herd passes over, beating them into the ground.

They ran directly away from the smell and the noises that were now far behind, downwind they came and in less than a minute were thundering through the short valley. Dust rose after them, billowing up to the old man, who covered his mouth, coughing, watching the rumbling dark mass erupt from the valley out onto the plain. They moved in an unwavering line toward the Salt Fork, rolling over everything, before swerving at the river—even the two canvas squares that had been brilliant white in the morning sun. And soon they were only a deep hum in the distance.

Will Gordon was out on the flats, approaching the place where the wagons had stood, riding slowly now in the settling dust.

But the dust was still in the air, heavy enough to make Leo Cleary sneeze as he brought the wagon out from the pines toward the river.

He saw the hide buyers' wagons smashed to scrap wood and shredded canvas dragged among the strewn buffalo hides. Many of the bales were still intact, spilling from the wagon wrecks; some were buried under the debris.

Three men stood waist deep in the shallows of the river, and beyond them, upstream, were the horses they had saved. Some had not been cut from the pickets in time, and they lay shapeless in blood at one end of the camp.

Will Gordon stood on the bank with the revolving pistol cocked, pointed at Clyde Foss. He glanced aside as the old man brought up the team.

"He wants to sell back, Leo. How much, you think?"

The old man only looked at him, because he could not speak.

"I think two barrels of whiskey," Will Gordon said. He stepped suddenly into the water and brought the long pistol barrel sweeping against Clyde's head, cutting the temple.

"Two barrels?"

Clyde Foss staggered and came to his feet slowly.

"Come here, Clyde." The boy leveled the pistol at him and waited as Clyde Foss came hesitantly out of the water, hunching his shoulders. The boy swung the pistol back, and, as Clyde ducked, he brought his left fist up, smashing hard against the man's jaw.

"Or three barrels?"

The hide buyer floundered in the shallow water, then crawled to the bank, and lay on his stomach, gasping for breath.

"We'll give him three, Leo. Since he's been nice about it."

Later, after Clyde and his two men had loaded their wagon with four hundred and eighty hides, the old man and the boy rode off through the valley to the great plain.

Once the old man said, "Where we going now, Will?"

And when the boy said, "We're still going hunting, Leo," the old man shrugged wearily and just nodded his head.

12

Long Night

Zane Grey's Western, May 1953

NEAR THE CREST of the hill, where the road climbed into the timber, he raised from the saddle wearily and turned to look back toward the small, flickering pinpoints of light.

The lights were people, and his mind gathered faces. A few he had seen less than a half hour before; but now, to Dave Boland, all of the faces were expressionless and as cold as the lights. They seemed wide-eyed and innocently, stupidly vacant.

He rode on through the timber with what was left of a hot anger, and now it was just a weariness. He had argued all afternoon and into the evening. Argued, reasoned, threatened and finally, pleaded. But it had ended with "I'm sorry, I've got my supper waiting for me," and a door slammed as soon as his back was turned.

He felt alone and inadequate, and for a moment a panic swept him, leaving his forehead cold with perspiration. The worst was still ahead, telling Virginia.

Wheelock had been in the hotel dining room and he had approached the big rancher hesitantly and told him he was sorry to bother him. . . .

"Mr. Wheelock, I paid you prompt for that breeding. The calf was too big, that's why it died. I did everything I could. If you'll breed her again—"

"I heard the calf strangled. Son, when you help a delivery, loop your rope around the head then bring it good and tight along the jaws, and a few turns on the forelegs if they're out." He drew circles in the air with his fork. "Then you don't strangle them to death." And he laughed with a mouthful of food when he said, finally, "The breeding fee generally doesn't include advice on how to deliver."

E. V. Timmons leaned back from the rolltop and palmed his hands thoughtfully as if he were offering a prayer. He looked at the ceiling for a long time with a tragic cast to his eyes. When he spoke it was hesitantly, as if it pained him, but with conviction. . . .

"Buying trends are erratic these days, Dave. Tomorrow, demand might drop on a big item and I'd have a heavy inventory on my hands and no place to unload. It means you have to maintain a working capital."

Tom Wylie was sympathetic when he told him about most of his stock dying from rattleweed poisoning.

"That's mean stuff in March, Dave. Got to keep your stock out of it. You know, the best way to get rid of it is to cut the crowns a few inches below the soil surface. It generally won't send up new tops." He asked Boland if he had seen Timmons. And after that he kept his sympathy.

John Avery was in the hotel business. He was used to walls and space limitations. "If my cows got into rattleweed I'd put fences up to keep them the hell out. You got to organize, boy!" Avery's supper was waiting for him. . . .

Virginia would understand.

Hell, what else could she do? He saw her pale, small-boned face that now, somehow, seemed sharper and more drawn with their child only a few days or a week away. She would smile a weak smile, twisting the hem of her apron—and it would mean nothing. Virginia smiled from habit. She smiled every time he brought her bad news. But always with the same sad expression in the eyes. Sometime, in the future, perhaps there would be a real reason to smile. He wondered if she would be able to. Now, with the baby coming . . .

Virginia had waited tables in a restaurant in Sudan because she had to support herself after her folks died suddenly. She was a great kidder and all the riders liked her. Broadminded, they said. He used to pass through Sudan a few times a year when most of the Company herds were grazed near the Canadian. After a while, he went out of his way and even made excuses to go there. She never kidded with him . . .

When he told the others about it, they said, "She's a nice girl—but who wants a nice girl? You get bone-tired pushing steers from the Nueces to Dodge; but, son, you can throw off along the way anytime you want—"

It had been raining hard for the past few minutes when finally he led his mare into the long, rickety shed, unsaddled and pitch-forked some hay.

The rain, he thought, shaking his head. The one thing I don't need is rain. He tried to see humor in it, though it was an irritation. Like an annoying, tickling fly lighting on a broken leg.

He walked up the slight grade toward the dim shape of the adobe house, passing the empty chicken coops, then skirted Virginia's vegetable garden, moving around toward the front of the house. He saw a light through a curtained side window. At the front of the house he called, "It's me," so as not to startle her, then lifted the latch on the door and pushed in.

Virginia Boland stood next to the oilcloth-covered table. She twisted the hem of her apron—she did it deliberately, her fingers tensed white straining at the material—and her eyes were wide. No smile softened the pale, oval face. Her dark dress was ill-fitting about her narrow shoulders and bosom as if it were sizes too large, then rounded, bulging with her pregnancy to lose any shape it might have had before.

Boland said, taking his hat off, "I guess I don't have to tell you what happened."

"Dave—" Her voice was small, and now almost a whisper. Her eyes still wide.

He came out of his coat and brushed it half-heartedly before throwing it to a chair.

"I saw all of them, Ginny."

"Dave—"

He looked at her curiously now across the few feet that separated them. . . . There was something in her voice. And suddenly he knew she wasn't saying his name in answer to his words. He moved to her quickly and held her by the shoulders.

"Is it time? Are you ready now?"

She shook her head, looking at him imploringly as if she were saying something with her eyes, but she didn't speak.

She didn't have to.

"Hello, Davie boy." The voice came from behind Virginia.

He stood in the doorway of the partitioned bedroom with the curtain draped over his shoulder. The white cloth dropped to the floor showing only part of him; damp and grimy, trail dust streaked and smeared over clothes that had not been changed for days. A yellow slicker was draped over his lower arm and his hand would have gone unnoticed if the long pistol barrel were not sticking out from the raincoat.

"Been a long time, hasn't it!" he said, and came into the room carefully, lifting the slicker from his arm to drape it over a straight chair. "I almost didn't recognize little Ginny with her new shape." He grinned, winking at Boland. "You didn't waste any time, did you?"

Boland stared at the man self-consciously, feeling a nervousness that was edged with fear, but he made himself smile.

"Jeffy, I almost didn't recognize you," he said.

"Wait'll you see Red." His head turned to the side and he called to the bedroom, "Red, come on out!"

Boland looked toward the curtained doorway and then to the dirt-caked figure next to him. "I wouldn't have known you by sight, but your voice—"

"You didn't forget that Cimarron crossing two years ago, did you?"

"Of course I remember," Boland said. "You saved my life." He tried to show friendship and appreciation at the same time and smiled when he said, "What are you doing here, Jeffy?"

"You're a regular babe in the woods, aren't you?" His head turned again. "Red! Dammit!"

He hesitated in the doorway, leaning against the partition, and then came into the room, straining to move his legs and holding his arms tight to his stomach as if his insides would fall out with a heavy step. He was as filthy as the other man, but his grime-streaked, bearded face was sickly white and his jaw muscles clenched as he eased himself down onto the cot which stood against the side wall nearer the two men.

He leaned back until his head and shoulders were against the adobe, then blew his breath out in a low groan. He held his right elbow to his side protectingly, and from under his arm a dark, wet stain reached in a smear almost to the buttons on his shirt.

Boland looked at Jeffy who was leaning against their small table with his arms folded and the pistol pointing up past his shoulder and heard him say, "Red's sick."

He glanced at his wife who was holding her hands close to her waist and then he moved closer to the cot. "How are you, Red?"

The man shook his head wearily, but didn't speak.

Leaning over him, Boland said in subdued surprise, "That's a gun-shot wound!"

Jeffy came off the table now and pushed Boland away from the cot. "You want to know everything," he said, and glanced down at Red. "Keep your eyes open. You're not that bad hurt."

"What's the matter with you!" Boland flared. "He's been shot clean through."

Jeffy shrugged. "Tell him something he doesn't know."

Boland turned on him angrily. "What happened! If you're going to dirty up my house, you're going to tell me what happened!"

"You're forgetting about that Cimmaron crossing." Jeffy smiled. He was near forty with a thin, wizened face made lopsided by a tobacco wad; and now he took off his shapeless hat to show a receding hairline and a high, white forehead that looked obscenely naked because of its whiteness. He looked at Boland's wife, wiping his mouth with the back of his hand.

"Honey, he ever tell you how I pulled him out from under the cows? Deep water after a flash flood and they was millin' in the stream—" He grinned at her as if there was a secret between them. "You'd still be shaking your tail in that Sudan hash-house if it wasn't for me."

"Saving my life doesn't bless anything you've got to say to my wife." Boland had felt the temper hot in his face, but he calmed himself. Now his voice was lower, but there was an edge to it still.

"And it doesn't give you leave to walk in my house with your gun out and start pushing everybody around. I know you're in some trouble. With your dirty mind and Red's drinking it could be almost anything. Now I'm telling you, Jeffy, start acting right or move on."

Jeffy shook his head sadly. "That's some way to talk after all the time Red and me and you bunked together."

"What did you do, Jeffy?"

There was a pause and his face became serious. "Held up a man and Red shot him when he went for his gun."

"Where'd it happen?"

As suddenly as he had become serious, his face grinned again and he said, "You always did have a long nose." He looked over to the cot and said, "Red!" surprising the man's eyes open.

"I'm not going to tell you again. Keep your eyes open." He lifted his slicker from the chair and shrugged an arm into it. "Pull your gun and hold it on them, while I take a look around. I might even go all the way toward town, so don't get jumpy if I'm gone a couple hours."

He started for the door, buttoning the slicker with one hand, then looked at Virginia. "Honey, you have some coffee on for when I get back. Like you used to." He grinned at her showing tobacco-yellowed teeth and shook his head reminiscently. "You sure used to throw it around in that café."

She looked away from him to her husband. Neither of them spoke.

"Your joining society's changed you, honey. There was a time when we couldn't shut you up." They heard the rain when he opened the door, then the sound was closed off again and he was gone.

In the room's abrupt silence Red drew his pistol, but his hand fell to the cot and the fingers closed on the handle loosely. He did not cock it.

Looking at him, Boland tried to picture him killing a man. Neither he nor Jeffy were ever good citizens, he thought. But they never robbed or killed before. He had worked with them for a couple of years when he first started riding for the T. & N. M. Cattle Company and he had not particularly liked them then; but his dislikes were based on small, personal things—Jeffy always making dirty remarks, and Red getting sloppy drunk any chance he had. Both had been lazy and never did any more than they had to.

And now—they had to flop themselves right on top of his other troubles.

Virginia moved over to the stove and lighted the fire under the coffeepot. She said to him, "Are you hungry, Dave?"

He shook his head. "Not very." *And I've got to worry about Ginny on top of all of it.* And then he thought: *or, are you feeling sorry for yourself?*

"Are you?" Her head nodded to the man on the cot.

"I don't think I'd hold it."

Boland asked him now, "When were you shot, Red?"

"Yesterday, in Clovis. Somebody musta recognized me and told the marshal. He hit me by surprise."

"Right after you killed this man?"

"Hell, that was months ago in Dodge. We been hiding since. Went into Clovis yesterday for grub and somebody seen us." He was breathing easier and went on, "We lost them last night. Damn marshal hit me by surprise—"

Boland said, "I suppose you were drunk in Dodge."

Red grinned sheepishly. "Fact is, I don't even remember shootin' the man."

"But Jeffy told you you did."

"Yeah, Jeffy said I was actin' mean and—"

"And lost your nerve and shot him when you didn't have to."

Red looked surprised. "Yeah. That's just what he said."

Boland waited, watching the man think it over. Then, "You starting to get any notions in your head?" It occurred to him then for the first time. He had been thinking Red was a damn fool hiding all that time because of Jeffy—unless his face was plastered all over the country. Otherwise, how would anyone in Clovis have known him? Then it hit him: a reward!

Virginia moved past him holding the coffeepot and a porcelain cup. She handed the cup to Red. "Try some coffee. Maybe you'll feel better."

"I don't think I'd hold it."

"Well, try, anyway."

He held the cup over his lap in his left hand and she leaned closer to pour the coffee. Suddenly she moved the pot to the side and emptied the scalding coffee on Red's gun hand.

His hand went up as he screamed and the gun flew over the foot of the cot, and in the instant she pushed the palm of her hand over his mouth forcing his head against the wall and muffling his scream.

Boland came up with the gun. He did it without thinking; and now, as he leveled it in Red's face he looked at Virginia with disbelief in his wide-open eyes. They followed her as she moved across the room, replaced the coffeepot on the stove and returned to stand awkwardly near the cot. She bit her lower lip nervously, watching the man.

The violent motion had ripped open his wound and now it was bleeding again. He hugged his arm to his side, groaning, with his scalded hand held limply in front of him.

Virginia's head lowered closer to his and she said, "I'm sorry," embarrassedly.

For another moment Boland continued to stare at her, but now with curiosity in place of surprise, as if he wasn't quite sure he knew this woman he had married.

He handed her the pistol. "Want me to cock it?"

"I can do that."

"If he budges, shoot him quick."

He moved toward the door and hesitated momentarily before turning back to Virginia. He kissed her mouth softly and looking into her face as he drew away, her features seemed not so sharp and pointed. And there was more color to her skin. He moved to the door anxiously, but glanced at her again before going out.

The rain had worn itself to a cold drizzle and there was no moon to make shadows in the blackness. He moved around the house slowly, cautiously, and hugged the adobe as he passed the garden. His pistol was in the saddlebag hanging in the barn-shed and now he thought: why in hell didn't I bring it in! No, then Jeffy would have it now. But he wouldn't know it was in the saddlebag. I've to get the gun—and then Jeffy. But where is he?

He reached the back of the house and crouched down in the dead silence, looking in the direction of the barn-shed. He waited, listening for a sound, and after a few minutes he could make out an oblong, hazy outline. He thought of Virginia now and he didn't feel so alone. Even the business of the afternoon, when it crept into his mind, didn't cause a sinking feeling, and he went over everything calmly. It puzzled him, because he was used to feeling alone. He thought of the reward again. . . .

He arose abruptly and sprinted across the back section toward the barn. He ran half-crouched, even though it was dark. At the side of the doorway, he pressed his back to the wall and listened. He waited again, then slowly inched his head past the opening. It was darker within. He stepped inside quickly and as he did, felt the gun barrel jab into his spine.

"You must be dumber than I thought you were," Jeffy said.

☆   ☆   ☆

VIRGINIA BACKED toward the table slowly, her free hand feeling for the edge, and when her fingers touched the smooth oilcloth she moved around it so that now the table was between her and the man on the cot. She did not take her eyes from the sprawled figure as she reached behind for the chair. There was a flutter of movement within her and she held the pistol with both hands, sitting down quickly. She trained the front sight on the man and saw it tremble slightly against the background of his body.

He closed his eyes suddenly, grinding his teeth together, and when he opened them they were dark hollows in his bloodless face. His mouth opened as if he would say something, but he blew his breath out wearily and moved a boot until it slid off the cot to the floor. His teeth clenched as it hit the flooring.

He brought his left hand over to the wound, his face tightening as his fingers touched the blood-smear of shirt that was stuck fast to the wound. It was still bleeding and now a dark stain was forming on the light wool blanket that covered the mattress.

She watched the stain spreading on the blanket where it touched his side and again she felt the squirm of life within her. She felt suddenly faint.

She remembered the afternoon her mother had given her the blanket and how she'd folded it into the chest with her linens and materials. She had seated herself on the chest then and clasped her hands contentedly, listing her possessions in her mind and thinking, smiling: now all I need is a husband. She had giggled then, she remembered.

For the bed, they used Dave's heavy army blankets. The cot served as a sofa and deserved something bright and dressy enough for the front room.

Red lifted his boot to the cot, and stretched it out tensely, and as the heel slid over the blanket a streak of sand-colored clay followed the heel in a thin crumbling line.

And then she no longer recognized the blanket. It became something else with this man sprawled on top of it. It became part of him with his blood staining it. And she saw the man and the blanketed cot as one. The wound was in the center. It was the focal point.

His face grimaced again with the pain and he groaned.

She said softly, "Haven't you done anything for it?"

He was breathing through his mouth as if his lungs were worn out and there was a pause before he said, "I stuffed my bandanna inside till it got soaked through, then I threw it away."

She stared at the bloodstain without speaking. Then, suddenly, she laid the pistol on the table and went over to the stove.

Red watched her pour water from a kettle into a shallow, porcelain pan before reaching for a towel that hung from a wall rack. His eyes drifted to the gun on the table and his body strained as if he would rise, but as Virginia turned and moved toward him, he relaxed.

She caught the slight movement and stopped halfway to the cot, her eyes going from the man to the table. She hesitated for a moment, then went on to the cot where she kneeled down, placing the pan on the floor.

She poured water on the wound and pulled at the shirt gently, working it loose. When it was free she tore the shirt up to the armpit, exposing the raw wound. It looked swollen and tender, fire-red around the puncture then darkening into a surrounding purplish-blue.

She looked into his face briefly. "Didn't your *friend* offer to help you?"

"He had to worry about getting us out."

"After he got you in."

Red said, irritably, "I've got a mind of my own."

She held the wet cloth to the wound then took it away, wringing the strained water from it. "Then why don't you use it?" she said calmly.

Red looked at her hard, then flared, "Maybe Jeffy was right. Maybe since you quit swingin' your tail in a hash-house, all of a sudden you're somebody else."

Virginia's head remained lowered over the pan as she rinsed out the cloth, squeezing it into the water. "You don't have any cause to talk like that."

She went to the wall rack and brought back a dry cloth and neither of them spoke as she folded it and pressed it gently against the wound.

And as she did this, Red's eyes lowered to the streak of clay on the blanket and he brushed it off carefully. He looked at the bloodstain and said in a low voice, "I'm sorry about your cover." He was silent for a moment then said, almost dazedly, "I'm going to die—"

She made no answer and now his eyes lifted to her faded blond hair and then over her head to roam about the room. He was thinking about the soiled blanket and now he saw the raveling poplin curtains that looked flimsy and ridiculous next to the drab adobe. On the board partition there was a print of a girl in a ballet costume, soft-shadowed color against the rough boards. And over by the far wall was the grotesquely fat stove, its flue reaching up through the low ceiling.

He said, "You got it pretty hard, haven't you?"

She hesitated before saying, "We get by."

"Well," he said, glancing around again, "I wouldn't say you had the world by the tail."

Virginia looked up quickly. There was a rattling of knocks on the door and from outside she heard, "Honey, give that gun back to Red like a good girl."

☆ ☆ ☆

JEFFY CAME THROUGH the doorway prodding Boland before him. He glared at Red who was holding his gun on his lap carelessly. "You're some watchdog."

Red said nothing, but then he gagged as if he would be sick. He breathed hard with his mouth open to catch his breath and then seemed to sag within himself. His eyes were open, but lifeless.

"It's a good thing I tested you out, Red."

Red was silent for a moment. Then he said, "Jeffy, did I shoot that man in Dodge?"

"I told you you did." He looked at Red curiously.

"But I don't remember doing it."

"How many things you ever done do you remember?"

"I thought I'd remember killing a man."

Jeffy rolled the tobacco on his tongue, looking around the room. Then he shrugged and sent a stream of it to the floor. "I'm not going to argue with you, Red. I don't have time." He glanced at Virginia. "Honey, how'd you like to go for a ride?"

There was a silence then, and Jeffy laughed to fill it. "You don't think I'm riding out of here without some protection!" He looked at Boland. "Davie, would you take a pot at me with your woman hangin' onto my cantle?"

Boland's face was white. For a moment there had been a fury inside of him, but his brain had fought it and now he felt only panic. There was a plea in his voice when he said, "My wife's going to have a baby."

Jeffy grinned at him. "All the more reason."

"Jeffy."

He glanced at Red who seemed suddenly wide awake.

"Jeffy, you're just scaring, aren't you?"

"What do you think?"

He looked at him, squinting, as if he were trying to read his mind. "You'd take that girl on horseback the way she is?"

"Red, if I had a violin I'd accompany you." He started toward Virginia.

And with his movement the gun turned in Red's lap, and the room filled with the roar as it went off. He cocked to fire again, but there was no need. He looked at Jeffy lying facedown on the floor and said incredulously, "He would have done it!"

He let the pistol fall to the floor. "There," he said to Virginia. "Keep your coffeepot away from here."

Boland looked at Jeffy and then picked up the pistol. Virginia smiled at him wearily and sat down at the table, propping her elbows on it. He said to her, "Maybe you better get some sleep."

"Dave."

He turned to Red.

"I'm going to die, Dave."

Boland remained silent.

"Do me a favor and don't holler law until the morning. Then it won't matter."

"All right, Red." Then he said, "I don't want to sound like a gravepicker, but how much have you and Jeffy got on your heads?"

Red looked at him, surprised. "Reward?"

Boland nodded.

"Why, nothin'. What made you think so?"

"You said somebody identified you in Clovis."

"Well, it was probably somebody used to know us."

Now that he had asked him, Boland was embarrassed. But, strangely, there was no disappointment and at that moment it surprised him. He grinned at Virginia. "I guess you don't get anything for nothing."

She smiled back at him and didn't look so tired. "You should know that by now."

For a few minutes there was silence. They could hear Red's breathing, but it was soft and even. Suddenly, Boland said, "Ginny, you know I haven't been home more'n an hour!"

Virginia nodded. "And it seemed like the whole, long night." Her eyes smiled at him and she said, softly, "When you're telling our grandchildren about it, maybe you can stretch it a little bit."

13

The Boy Who Smiled

Gunsmoke, June 1953

WHEN MICKEY SEGUNDO was fourteen, he tracked a man almost two hundred miles—from the Jicarilla Subagency down into the malpais.

He caught up with him at a water hole in late afternoon and stayed behind a rock outcropping watching the man drink. Mickey Segundo had not tasted water in three days, but he sat patiently behind the cover while the man quenched his thirst, watching him relax and make himself comfortable as the hot lava country cooled with the approach of evening.

Finally Mickey Segundo stirred. He broke open the .50-caliber Gallagher and inserted the paper cartridge and the cap. Then he eased the carbine between a niche in the rocks, sighting on the back of the man's head. He called in a low voice, "Tony Choddi . . ." and as the face with the wide-open eyes came around, he fired casually.

He lay on his stomach and slowly drank the water he needed, filling his canteen and the one that had belonged to Tony Choddi. Then he took his hunting knife and sawed both of the man's ears off, close to the head. These he put into his saddle pouch, leaving the rest for the buzzards.

A week later Mickey Segundo carried the pouch into the agency office and dropped the ears on my desk. He said very simply, "Tony Choddi is sorry he has caused trouble."

I remember telling him, "You're not thinking of going after McKay now, are you?"

"This man, Tony Choddi, stole stuff, a horse and clothes and a gun," he said with his pleasant smile. "So I thought I would do a good thing and fix it so Tony Choddi didn't steal no more."

With the smile there was a look of surprise, as if to say, "Why would I want to get Mr. McKay?"

A few days later I saw McKay and told him about it and mentioned that he might keep his eyes open. But he said that he didn't give a damn about any breed Jicarilla kid. If the kid felt like avenging his old man, he could try, but he'd probably cash in before his time. And as for getting Tony Choddi, he didn't give a damn about that either. He'd got the horse back and that's all he cared about.

After he had said his piece, I was sorry I had warned him. And I felt a little foolish telling one of the biggest men in the Territory to look out for a half-breed Apache kid. I told myself, Maybe you're just rubbing up to him because he's important and could use his influence to help out the agency . . . and maybe he knows it.

Actually I had more respect for Mickey Segundo, as a human being, than I did for T. O. McKay. Maybe I felt I owed the warning to McKay because he was a white man. Like saying, "Mickey Segundo's a good boy, but, hell, he's half Indian." Just one of those things you catch yourself doing. Like habit. You do something wrong the first time and you know it, but if you keep it up, it becomes a habit and it's no longer wrong because it's something you've always been doing.

McKay and a lot of people said Apaches were no damn good. The only good one was a dead one. They never stopped to reason it out. They'd been saying it so long, they knew it was true. Certainly any such statement was unreasonable, but damned if I wouldn't sometimes nod my head in agreement, because at those times I'd be with white men and that's the way white men talked.

I might have thought I was foolish, but actually it was McKay who was the fool. He underestimated Mickey Segundo.

That was five years ago. It had begun with a hanging.

EARLY IN THE morning, Tudishishn, sergeant of Apache police at the Ji-carilla Agency, rode in to tell me that Tony Choddi had jumped the boundaries again and might be in my locale. Tudishishn stayed for half a dozen cups of coffee, though his information didn't last that long. When he'd had enough, he left as leisurely as he had arrived. Hunting renegades, reservation jumpers, was Tudishishn's job; still, it wasn't something to get excited about. Tomorrows were for work; todays were for thinking about it.

Up at the agency they were used to Tony Choddi skipping off. Usually they'd find him later in some shaded barranca, full of tulapai.

It was quiet until late afternoon, but not unusually so. It wasn't often that anything out of the ordinary happened at the subagency. There were twenty-six families, one hundred eight Jicarillas all told, under my charge. We were located almost twenty miles below the reservation proper, and most of the people had been there long before the reservation had been marked off. They had been fairly peaceful then, and remained so now. It was one of the few instances where the Bureau allowed the sleeping dog to lie; and because of that we had less trouble than they did up at the reservation.

There was a sign on the door of the adobe office which described it formally. It read: D. J. MERRITT—AGENT, JICARILLA APACHE SUBAGENCY—PUERCO, NEW MEXICO TERRITORY. It was a startling announcement to post on the door of a squat adobe sitting all alone in the shadow of the Nacimentos. My Apaches preferred higher ground and the closest jacales were two miles up into the foothills. The office had to remain on the mail run, even though the mail consisted chiefly of impossible-to-apply Bureau memoranda.

Just before supper Tudishishn returned. He came in at a run this time and swung off before his pony had come to a full stop. He was excited and spoke in a confusion of Apache, Spanish, and a word here and there of English.

Returning to the reservation, he had decided to stop off and see his friends of the Puerco Agency. There had been friends he had not seen for some time, and the morning had lengthened into afternoon with tulapai, good talking, and even coffee. People had come from the more remote jacales, deeper in the hills, when they learned Tudishishn was there, to hear news of friends at the reservation. Soon there were many people and what looked like the beginning of a good time. Then Señor McKay had come.

McKay had men with him, many men, and they were looking for Mickey Solner—the squaw man, as the Americans called him.

Most of the details I learned later on, but briefly this is what had happened: McKay and some of his men were out on a hunting trip. When they got up that morning, McKay's horse was gone, along with a shotgun and some personal articles. They got on the tracks, which were fresh and easy to follow, and by that afternoon they were at Mickey Solner's jacale. His woman and boy were there, and the horse was tethered in front of the mud hut. Mickey Segundo, the boy, was honored to lead such important people to his father, who was visiting with Tudishishn.

McKay brought the horse along, and when they found Mickey Solner, they took hold of him without asking questions and looped a rope around his neck. Then they boosted him up onto the horse they claimed he had stolen. McKay said it would be fitting that way. Tudishishn had left fast when he saw what was about to happen. He knew they wouldn't waste time arguing with an Apache, so he had come to me.

When I got there, Mickey Solner was still sitting McKay's chestnut mare with the rope reaching from his neck to the cottonwood bough overhead. His head drooped as if all the fight was out of him, and when I came up in front of the chestnut, he looked at me with tired eyes, watery and red from tulapai.

I had known Solner for years, but had never become close to him. He wasn't a man with whom you became fast friends. Just his living in an Apache rancheria testified to his being of a different breed. He was friendly enough, but few of the whites liked him—they said he drank all the time and never worked. Maybe most were just envious. Solner was a white man gone Indian, whole hog. That was the cause of the resentment.

His son, Mickey the Second, stood near his dad's stirrup looking at him with a bewildered, pathetic look on his slim face. He held on to the stirrup as if he'd never let it go. And it was the first time, the only time, I ever saw Mickey Segundo without a faint smile on his face.

"Mr. McKay," I said to the cattleman, who was standing relaxed with his hands in his pockets, "I'm afraid I'll have to ask you to take that man down. He's under bureau jurisdiction and will have to be tried by a court."

McKay said nothing, but Bowie Allison, who was his herd boss, laughed and then said, "You ought to be afraid."

Dolph Bettzinger was there, along with his brothers Kirk and Sim. They were hired for their guns and usually kept pretty close to McKay. They did not laugh when Allison did.

And all around the clearing by the cottonwood were eight or ten others. Most of them I recognized as McKay riders. They stood solemnly, some with rifles and shotguns. There wasn't any doubt in their minds what stealing a horse meant.

"Tudishishn says that Mickey didn't steal your horse. These people told him that he was at home all night and most of the morning until Tudishishn dropped in, and then he came down here." A line of Apaches stood a few yards off and as I pointed to them, some nodded their heads.

"Mister," McKay said, "I found the horse at this man's hut. Now, you argue that down, and I'll kiss the behind of every Apache you got living around here."

"Well, your horse could have been left there by someone else."

"Either way, he had a hand in it," he said curtly.

"What does he say?" I looked up at Mickey Solner and asked him quickly, "How did you get the horse, Mickey?"

"I just traded with a fella." His voice shook, and he held on to the saddle horn as if afraid he'd fall off. "This fella come along and traded with me, that's all."

"Who was it?"

Mickey Solner didn't answer. I asked him again, but still he refused to speak. McKay was about to say something, but Tudishishn came over quickly from the group of Apaches.

"They say it was Tony Choddi. He was seen to come into camp in early morning."

I asked Mickey if it was Tony Choddi, and finally he admitted that it was. I felt better then. McKay couldn't hang a man for trading a horse.

"Are you satisfied, Mr. McKay? He didn't know it was yours. Just a matter of trading a horse."

McKay looked at me, narrowing his eyes. He looked as if he were trying to figure out what kind of a man I was. Finally he said, "You think I'm going to believe them?"

It dawned on me suddenly that McKay had been using what patience he had for the past few minutes. Now he was ready to continue what they had come for. He had made up his mind long before.

"Wait a minute, Mr. McKay, you're talking about the life of an innocent man. You can't just toy with it like it was a head of cattle."

He looked at me and his puffy face seemed to harden. He was a heavy man, beginning to sag about the stomach. "You think you're going to tell me what I can do and what I can't? I don't need a government representative to tell me why my horse was stolen!"

"I'm not telling you anything. You know Mickey didn't steal the horse. You can see for yourself you're making a mistake."

McKay shrugged and looked at his herd boss. "Well, if it is, it isn't a very big one—leastwise we'll be sure he won't be trading in stolen horses again." He nodded to Bowie Allison.

Bowie grinned, and brought his quirt up and then down across the rump of the chestnut.

"Yiiiiiiiiii . . ."

The chestnut broke fast. Allison stood yelling after it, then jumped aside quickly as Mickey Solner swung back toward him on the end of the rope.

☆　☆　☆

IT WAS TWO weeks later, to the day, that Mickey Segundo came in with Tony Choddi's ears. You can see why I asked him if he had a notion of going after McKay. And it was a strange thing. I was talking to a different boy than the one I had last seen under the cottonwood.

When the horse shot out from under his dad, he ran to him like something wild, screaming, and wrapped his arms around the kicking legs trying to hold the weight off the rope.

Bowie Allison cuffed him away, and they held him back with pistols while he watched his dad die. From then on he didn't say a word, and when it was over, walked away with his head down. Then, when he came in with Tony Choddi's ears, he was himself again. All smiles.

I might mention that I wrote to the Bureau of Indian Affairs about the incident, since Mickey Solner, legally, was one of my charges; but nothing came of it. In fact, I didn't even get a reply.

Over the next few years Mickey Segundo changed a lot. He became
Apache. That is, his appearance changed and almost everything else
about him—except the smile. The smile was always there, as if he knew
a monumental secret which was going to make everyone happy.

He let his hair grow to his shoulders and usually he wore only a
frayed cotton shirt and breechclout; his moccasins were Apache—
curled toes and leggings which reached to his thighs. He went under
his Apache name, which was Peza-a, but I called him Mickey when I saw
him, and he was never reluctant to talk to me in English. His English
was good, discounting grammar.

Most of the time he lived in the same jacale his dad had built, providing for his mother and fitting closer into the life of the rancheria
than he did before. But when he was about eighteen, he went up to the
agency and joined Tudishishn's police. His mother went with him to
live at the reservation, but within a year the two of them were back.
Tracking friends who happened to wander off the reservation didn't set
right with him. It didn't go with his smile.

Tudishishn told me he was sorry to lose him because he was an expert tracker and a dead shot. I know the sergeant had a dozen good
sign followers, but very few who were above average with a gun.

He must have been nineteen when he came back to Puerco. In all
those years he never once mentioned McKay's name. And I can tell you
I never brought it up either.

I saw McKay even less after the hanging incident. If he ignored me
before, he avoided me now. As I said, I felt like a fool after warning him
about Mickey Segundo, and I'm certain McKay felt only contempt for
me for doing it, after sticking up for the boy's dad.

McKay would come through every once in a while, usually going on
a hunt up into the Nacimentos. He was a great hunter and would go
out for a few days every month or so. Usually with his herd boss, Bowie
Allison. He hunted everything that walked, squirmed, or flew and I'm
told his ranch trophy room was really something to see.

You couldn't take it away from the man; everything he did, he did
well. He was in his fifties, but he could shoot straighter and stay in the
saddle longer than any of his riders. And he knew how to make money.
But it was his arrogance that irked me. Even though he was polite, he

made you feel far beneath him. He talked to you as if you were one of the hired help.

One afternoon, fairly late, Tudishishn rode in and said that he was supposed to meet McKay at the adobe office early the next morning. McKay wanted to try the shooting down southwest toward the malpais, on the other side of it, actually, and Tudishishn was going to guide for him.

The Indian policeman drank coffee until almost sundown and then rode off into the shadows of the Nacimentos. He was staying at one of the rancherias, visiting with his friends until the morning.

McKay appeared first. It was a cool morning, bright and crisp. I looked out of the window and saw the five riders coming up the road from the south, and when they were close enough I made out McKay and Bowie Allison and the three Bettzinger brothers. When they reached the office, McKay and Bowie dismounted, but the Bettzingers reined around and started back down the road.

McKay nodded and was civil enough, though he didn't direct more than a few words to me. Bowie was ready when I asked them if they wanted coffee, but McKay shook his head and said they were leaving shortly. Just about then the rider appeared coming down out of the hills.

McKay was squinting, studying the figure on the pony.

I didn't really look at him until I noticed McKay's close attention. And when I looked at the rider again, he was almost on us. I didn't have to squint then to see that it was Mickey Segundo.

McKay said, "Who's that?" with a ring of suspicion to his voice.

I felt a sudden heat on my face, like the feeling you get when you're talking about someone, then suddenly find the person standing next to you.

Without thinking about it I told McKay, "That's Peza-a, one of my people." What made me call him by his Apache name I don't know. Perhaps because he looked so Indian. But I had never called him Peza-a before.

He approached us somewhat shyly, wearing his faded shirt and breechclout but now with a streak of ochre painted across his nose from ear to ear. He didn't look as if he could have a drop of white blood in him.

"What's he doing here?" McKay's voice still held a note of suspicion, and he looked at him as if he were trying to place him.

Bowie Allison studied him the same way, saying nothing.

"Where's Tudishishn? These gentlemen are waiting for him."

"Tudishishn is ill with a demon in his stomach," Peza-a answered. "He has asked me to substitute myself for him." He spoke in Spanish, hesitantly, the way an Apache does.

McKay studied him for some time. Finally, he said, "Well . . . can he track?"

"He was with Tudishishn for a year. Tudishishn speaks highly of him." Again I don't know what made me say it. A hundred things were going through my head. What I said was true, but I saw it getting me into something. Mickey never looked directly at me. He kept watching McKay, with the faint smile on his mouth.

McKay seemed to hesitate, but then he said, "Well, come on. I don't need a reference . . . long as he can track."

They mounted and rode out.

McKay wanted prongbuck. Tudishishn had described where they would find the elusive herds and promised to show him all he could shoot. But they were many days away. McKay had said if he didn't have time, he'd make time. He wanted good shooting.

Off and on during the first day he questioned Mickey Segundo closely to see what he knew about the herds.

"I have seen them many times. Their hide the color of sand, and black horns that reach into the air like bayonets of the soldiers. But they are far."

McKay wasn't concerned with distance. After a while he was satisfied that this Indian guide knew as much about tracking antelope as Tudishishn, and that's what counted. Still, there was something about the young Apache. . . .

"TOMORROW, WE begin the crossing of the malpais," Mickey Segundo said. It was evening of the third day, as they made camp at Yucca Springs.

Bowie Allison looked at him quickly. "Tudishishn planned we'd follow the high country down and come out on the plain from the east."

"What's the matter with keeping a straight line," McKay said. "Keeping to the hills is longer, isn't it?"

"Yeah, but that malpais is a blood-dryin' furnace in the middle of August," Bowie grumbled. "You got to be able to pinpoint the wells. And even if you find them, they might be dry."

McKay looked at Peza-a for an answer.

"If Señor McKay wishes to ride for two additional days, that is for him to say. But we can carry our water with ease." He went to his saddle pouch and drew out two collapsed, rubbery bags. "These, from the stomach of the horse, will hold much water. Tomorrow we fill canteens and these, and the water can be made to last five, six days. Even if the wells are dry, we have water."

Bowie Allison grumbled under his breath, looking with distaste at the horse-intestine water sacks.

McKay rubbed his chin thoughtfully. He was thinking of prongbuck. Finally he said, "We'll cut across the lava."

Bowie Allison was right in his description of the malpais. It was a furnace, a crusted expanse of desert that stretched into another world. Saguaro and ocotillo stood nakedly sharp against the whiteness, and off in the distance were ghostly looming buttes, gigantic tombstones for the lava waste. Horses shuffled choking white dust, and the sun glare was a white blistering shock that screamed its brightness. Then the sun would drop suddenly, leaving a nothingness that could be felt. A life that had died a hundred million years ago.

McKay felt it and that night he spoke little.

The second day was a copy of the first, for the lava country remained monotonously the same. McKay grew more irritable as the day wore on, and time and again he would snap at Bowie Allison for his grumbling. The country worked at the nerves of the two white men, while Mickey Segundo watched them.

On the third day they passed two water holes. They could see the shallow crusted bottoms and the fissures that the tight sand had made cracking in the hot air. That night McKay said nothing.

In the morning there was a blue haze on the edge of the glare; they could feel the land beneath them begin to rise. Chaparral and patches of toboso grass became thicker and dotted the flatness, and by early afternoon the towering rock formations loomed near at hand. They had then one water sack two thirds full; but the other, with their canteens, was empty.

Bowie Allison studied the gradual rise of the rock wall, passing his tongue over cracked lips. "There could be water up there. Sometimes the rain catches in hollows and stays there a long time if it's shady."

McKay squinted into the air. The irregular crests were high and dead still against the sky. "Could be."

Mickey Segundo looked up and then nodded.

"How far to the next hole?" McKay asked.

"Maybe one day."

"If it's got water. . . . Then how far?"

"Maybe two day. We come out on the plain then near the Datil Mountains and there is water, streams to be found."

McKay said, "That means we're halfway. We can make last what we got, but there's no use killing ourselves." His eyes lifted to the peaks again, then dropped to the mouth of a barranca which cut into the rock. He nodded to the dark canyon which was partly hidden by a dense growth of mesquite. "We'll leave our stuff there and go on to see what we can find."

They unsaddled the horses and ground-tied them and hung their last water bag in the shade of a mesquite bush.

Then they walked up-canyon until they found a place which would be the easiest to climb.

They went up and they came down, but when they were again on the canyon floor, their canteens still rattled lightly with their steps. Mickey Segundo carried McKay's rifle in one hand and the limp, empty water bag in the other.

He walked a step behind the two men and watched their faces as they turned to look back overhead. There was no water.

The rocks held nothing, not even a dampness. They were naked now and loomed brutally indifferent, and bone dry with no promise of moisture.

The canyon sloped gradually into the opening. And now, ahead, they could see the horses and the small fat bulge of the water bag hanging from the mesquite bough.

Mickey Segundo's eyes were fixed on the water sack. He looked steadily at it.

Then a horse screamed. They saw the horses suddenly pawing the ground and pulling at the hackamores that held them fast. The three horses and the pack mule joined together now, neighing shrilly as they strained dancing at the ropes.

And then a shape the color of sand darted through the mesquite thicket, so quickly that it seemed a shadow.

Mickey Segundo threw the rifle to his shoulder. He hesitated. Then he fired.

The shape kept going, past the mesquite background and out into the open.

He fired again and the coyote went up into the air and came down to lie motionless.

It only jerked in death. McKay looked at him angrily. "Why the hell didn't you let me have it! You could have hit one of the horses!"

"There was not time."

"That's two hundred yards! You could have hit a horse, that's what I'm talking about!"

"But I shot it," Mickey Segundo said.

When they reached the mesquite clump, they did not go over to inspect the dead coyote. Something else took their attention. It stopped the white men in their tracks.

They stared unbelieving at the wetness seeping into the sand, and above the spot, the water bag hanging like a punctured bladder. The water had quickly run out.

Mickey Segundo told the story at the inquiry. They had attempted to find water, but it was no use; so they were compelled to try to return.

They had almost reached Yucca Springs when the two men died. Mickey Segundo told it simply. He was sorry he had shot the water bag, but what could he say? God directs the actions of men in mysterious ways.

The county authorities were disconcerted, but they had to be satisfied with the apparent facts.

McKay and Allison were found ten miles from Yucca Springs and brought in. There were no marks of violence on either of them, and they found three hundred dollars in McKay's wallet. It was officially recorded that they died from thirst and exposure.

A terrible way to die just because some damn Apache couldn't shoot straight. Peza-a survived because he was lucky, along with the fact that he was Apache, which made him tougher. Just one of those things.

Mickey continued living with his mother at the subagency. His old Gallagher carbine kept them in meat, and they seemed happy enough just existing.

Tudishishn visited them occasionally, and when he did they would have a tulapai party. Everything was normal.

Mickey's smile was still there but maybe a little different.

But I've often wondered what Mickey Segundo would have done if that coyote had not run across the mesquite thicket. . . .

14

The Hard Way

Zane Grey's Western, August 1953

TIO ROBLES STRETCHED stiffly on the straw mattress, holding the empty mescal bottle upright on his chest. His sleepy eyes studied Jimmy Robles going through his ritual. Tio was half smiling, watching with amusement.

Jimmy Robles buttoned his shirt carefully, even the top button, and pushed the shirttail tightly into his pants, smooth and tight with no blousing about the waist. It made him move stiffly the few minutes he was conscious of keeping the clean shirt smooth and unwrinkled. He lifted the gun belt from a wall peg and buckled it around his waist, inhaling slowly, watching the faded cotton stretch tight across his stomach. And when he wiped his high black boots it was with the same deliberate care.

Tio's sleepy smile broadened. "Jaime," he spoke softly, "you look very pretty. Are you to be married today?" He waited. "Perhaps this is a feast day that has slipped my mind." He waited longer. "No? Or perhaps the mayor has invited you to dine with him."

Jimmy Robles picked up the sweat-dampened shirt he had taken off and unpinned the silver badge from the pocket. Before looking at his uncle he breathed on the metal and rubbed its smooth surface over the tight cloth of his chest. He pinned it to the clean shirt, studying the inscription cut into the metal that John Benedict had told him read *Deputy Sheriff.*

Sternly, he said, "You drink too much," but could not help smiling at this picture of indolence sprawled on the narrow bed with a foot hooked on the window ledge above, not caring particularly if the world ended at that moment.

"Why don't you stop for a few days, just to see what it's like?"

Tio closed his eyes. "The shock would kill me."

"You're killing yourself anyway."

Tio mumbled, "But what a fine way to die."

Jimmy left the adobe hut and crossed a backyard before passing through the narrow dimness of two adobes that squeezed close together, and when he reached the street he tilted his hat closer to his eyes against the afternoon glare and walked up the street toward Arivaca's business section. This was a part of Saturday afternoon. This leaving the Mexican section that was still quiet, almost deserted, and walking up the almost indiscernible slope that led to the more prosperous business section.

Squat gray adobe grew with the slope from Spanishtown into painted, two-story false fronts with signs hanging from the ramadas. Soon, cowmen from the nearer ranges and townspeople who had quit early because it was Saturday would be standing around under the ramadas, slapping each other on the shoulder thinking about Saturday night. Those who hadn't started already. And Jimmy Robles would smile at everybody and be friendly because he liked this day better than any other. People were easier to get along with. Even the Americans.

Being deputy sheriff of Arivaca wasn't a hard job, but Jimmy Robles was new. And his newness made him unsure. Not confident of his ability to uphold the law and see that the goods and rights of these people were protected while they got drunk on Saturday night.

The sheriff, John Benedict, had appointed him a month before because he thought it would be good for the Mexican population. One of their own boys. John Benedict said you performed your duty "in the name of the law." That was the thing to remember. And it made him feel uneasy because the law was such a big thing. And justice. He wished he could picture something other than that woman with the blindfold over her eyes. John Benedict spoke long of these things. He was a great man.

Not only had he made him deputy, but John Benedict had given him a pair of American boots and a pistol, free, which had belonged to a man who had been hanged the month before. Tio Robles had told him to destroy the hanged man's goods, for it was a bad sign; but that's all Tio knew about it. He was too much *Mexicano.* He would go on sweating at the wagonyard, grumbling, and drinking more mescal than he could hold. It was good he lived with Tio and was able to keep him out of trouble. Not all, some.

His head was down against the glare and he watched his booted feet move over the street dust, lost in thought. But the gunfire from up-street brought him to instantly. He broke into a slow trot, seeing a lone man in the street a block ahead. As he approached him, he angled toward the boardwalk lining the buildings.

SID ROMAN STOOD square in the middle of the street with his feet planted wide. There was a stubble of beard over the angular lines of his lower face and his eyes blinked sleepily. He jabbed another cartridge at the open cylinder of the Colt, and fumbled trying to insert it into one of the small openings. The nose of the bullet missed the groove and slipped from his fingers. Sid Roman was drunk, which wasn't unusual, though it wasn't evident from his face. The glazed expression was natural.

Behind him, two men with their hats tilted loosely over their eyes sat on the steps of the Samas Café, their boots stretched out into the street. A half-full bottle was between them on the ramada step. A third man lounged on his elbows against the hitch rack, leaning heavily like a dead weight. Jimmy Robles moved off the boardwalk and stood next to the man on the hitch rack.

Sid Roman loaded the pistol and waved it carelessly over his head. He tried to look around at the men behind him without moving his feet and stumbled off balance, almost going down.

"Come on . . . who's got the money!" His eyes, heavy lidded, went to the two men on the steps. "Hey, Walt, dammit! Put up your dollar!"

The one called Walt said, "I got it. Go ahead and shoot," and hauled the bottle up to his mouth.

Sid Roman yelled to the man on the hitch rack, "You in, Red?" The man looked up, startled, and stared around as if he didn't know where he was.

Roman waved his pistol toward the high front of the saloon across the street. SUPREME, in foot-high red letters, ran across the board hanging from the top of the ramada. "A dollar I put five straight in the top loop of the *P*." He slurred his words impatiently.

Jimmy Robles heard the man next to him mumble, "Sure, Sid." He looked at the sign, squinting hard, but could not make out any bullet scars near the *P*. Maybe there was one just off to the left of the *S*. He waited until the cowman turned and started to raise the Colt.

"Hey, Sid." Jimmy Robles smiled at him like a friend. "I got some good targets out back of the jail."

Aiming, Sid Roman turned irritably, hot in the face. Then the expression was blank and glassy again.

"How'd you know my name?"

Jimmy Robles smiled, embarrassed. "I just heard this man call you that."

Roman looked at him a long time. "Well you heard wrong," he finally said. "It's Mr. Roman."

A knot tightened the deputy's mouth, but he kept the smile on his lips even though its meaning was gone. "All right, mester. It's all the same to me." John Benedict said you had to be courteous.

The man was staring at him hard, weaving slightly. He had heard of Sid Roman, old man Remillard's top hand, but this was the first time he had seen him close. He stared back at the beard-grubby face and felt uneasy because the face was so expressionless—looking him over like he was a dead tree stump. Why couldn't he get laughing drunk like the Mexican boys, then he could be laughing, too, when he took his gun away from him.

"Why don't you just keep your mouth shut," Roman said, as if that was the end of it. But then he added, "Go on and sweep out your jail-house," grinning and looking over at the men on the steps.

The one called Walt laughed out and jabbed at the other man with his elbow.

Jimmy Robles held on to the smile, gripping it with only his will now. He said, "I'm just thinking of the people. If a stray shot went inside, somebody might get hurt."

"You saying I can't shoot, or're you just chicken scared!"

"I'm just saying there are many people on the street and inside there."

"You're talking awful damn big for a dumb Mex kid. You must be awful dumb." He looked toward the steps, handling the pistol idly. "He must be awful dumb, huh, Walt?"

Jimmy Robles heard the one called Walt mumble, "He sure must," but he kept his eyes on Roman, who walked up to him slowly, still looking at him like he was a stump or something that couldn't talk back or hear. Now, only a few feet away, he saw a glimmer in the sleepy eyes as if a new thought was punching its way through his head.

"Maybe we ought to learn him something, Walt. Seeing he's so dumb." Grinning now, he looked straight into the Mexican boy's eyes. "Maybe I ought to shoot his ears off and give 'em to him for a present. What you think of that, Walt?"

Jimmy Robles's smile had almost disappeared. "I think I had better ask you for your gun, mester." His voice coldly polite.

Roman's stubble jaw hung open. It clamped shut and his face colored, through the weathered tan it colored as if it would burst open from ripeness. He mumbled through his teeth, "You two-bit kid!" and tried to bring the Colt up.

Robles swung his left hand wide as hard as he could and felt the numbing pain up to his elbow the same time Sid Roman's head snapped back. He tried to think of courtesy, his pistol, the law, the other three men, but it wasn't any of these that drew his hand back again and threw the fist hard against the face that was falling slowly toward him. The head snapped back and the body followed it this time, heels dragging in the dust off balance until Roman was spread-eagled in the street, not moving. He swung on the three men, pulling his pistol.

They just looked at him. The one called Walt shrugged his shoulders and lifted the bottle that was almost empty.

WHEN JOHN BENEDICT closed the office door behind him, his deputy was coming up the hall that connected the cells in the rear of the jail.

He sat down at the rolltop desk, hearing the footsteps in the bare hall-way, and swiveled his chair, swinging his back to the desk.

"I was over to the barbershop. I saw you bring somebody in," he said to Jimmy Robles entering the office. "I was all lathered up and couldn't get out. Saw you pass across the street, but couldn't make out who you had."

Jimmy Robles smiled. "Mester Roman. Didn't you hear the shooting?"

"Sid Roman?" Benedict kept most of the surprise out of his voice. "What's the charge?"

"He was drinking out in the street and betting on shooting at the sign over the Supreme. There were a lot of people around—" He wanted to add, "John," because they were good friends, but Benedict was old enough to be his father and that made a difference.

"So then he called you something and you got mad and hauled him in."

"I tried to smile, but he was pointing his gun all around. It was hard."

John Benedict smiled at the boy's serious face. "Sid call you chicken scared?"

Jimmy Robles stared at this amazing man he worked for.

"He calls everybody that when he's drunk." Benedict smiled. "He's a lot of mouth, with nothing coming out. Most times he's harmless, but someday he'll probably shoot somebody." His eyes wandered out the window. Old man Remillard was crossing the street toward the jail. "And then we'll get the blame for not keeping him here when he's full of whiskey."

Jimmy Robles went over the words, his smooth features frowning in question. "What do you mean we'll get blamed?"

Benedict started to answer him, but changed his mind when the door opened. Instead, he said, "Afternoon," nodding his head to the thick, big-boned man in the doorway. Benedict followed the rancher's gaze to Jimmy Robles. "Mr. Remillard, Deputy Sheriff Robles."

Remillard's face was serious. "Quit kidding," he said. He moved to-ward the sheriff. "I'm just fixing up a mistake you made. Your memory must be backing up on you, John." He was unexcited, but his voice was heavy with authority. Remillard hadn't been told no in twenty years, not by anyone, and his air of command was as natural to him as breathing. He handed Benedict a folded sheet he had pulled from his inside coat pocket, nodding his head toward Jimmy Robles.

"You better tell your boy what end's up."

He waited until Benedict looked up from the sheet of paper, then said, "I was having my dinner with Judge Essery at the Samas when my foreman was arrested. Essery's waived trial and suspended sentence. It's right there, black and white. And kind of lucky for you, John, the judge's in a good mood today." Remillard walked to the door, then turned back. "It isn't in the note, but you better have my boy out in ten minutes." That was all.

John Benedict read the note over again. He remembered the first time one like it was handed to him, five years before. He had read it over five times and had almost torn it up, before his sense returned. He wondered if he was using the right word, *sense.*

"Let him out and give him his gun back."

Jimmy Robles smiled, because he thought the sheriff was kidding. He said, "Sure," and the "John" almost slipped out with it. He propped his hip against the edge of his table-desk.

"What are you waiting for?"

Jimmy Robles came off the table now, and his face hung in surprise. "Are you serious?"

Benedict held out the note. "Read this five times and then let him go."

"But I don't understand," with disbelief all over his face. "This man was endangering lives. You said we were to protect and . . . " His voice trailed off, trying to think of all the things John Benedict had told him.

Sitting in his swivel chair, John Benedict thought, Explain that one if you can. He remembered the words better than the boy did. Now he wondered how he had kept a straight face when he had told him about rights, and the law, and seeing how the one safeguarded the other. That was John Benedict the realist. The cynic. He told himself to shut up. He did believe in ideals. What he had been telling himself for years, though having to close his eyes occasionally because he liked his job.

Now he said to the boy, "Do you like your job?" And Jimmy Robles looked at him as if he did not understand.

He started to tell him how a man elected to a job naturally had a few obligations. And in a town like Arivaca, whose business depended on spreads like Remillard's and a few others, maybe the obligations were a little heavier. It was a cowtown, so the cowman ought to be able to have what he wanted. But it was too long a story to go through. If Jimmy Robles couldn't see the handwriting, let him find out the hard way. He was old enough to figure it out for himself. Suddenly, the boy's open, wondering face made him mad.

"Well, what the hell are you waiting for!"

JIMMY ROBLES pushed Tio's empty mescal bottle to the foot of the bed and sat down heavily. He eased back until he was resting on his spine with his head and shoulders against the adobe wall and sat like this for a long time while the thoughts went through his head. He wished Tio were here. Tio would offer no assistance, no explanation other than his biased own, but he would laugh and that would be better than nothing. Tio would say, "What did you expect would happen, you fool?" And add, "Let us have a drink to forget the mysterious ways of the American." Then he would laugh. Jimmy Robles sat and smoked cigarettes and he thought.

Later on, he opened his eyes and felt the ache in his neck and back. It seemed like only a few moments before he had been awake, clouded with his worrying, but the room was filled with a dull gloom. He rose, rubbing the back of his neck, and, through the open doorway that faced west, saw the red streak in the gloom over the line of trees in the distance.

He felt hungry, and the incident of the afternoon was something that might have happened a hundred years ago. He had worn himself out thinking and that was enough of it. He passed between the buildings to the street and crossed it to the adobe with the sign EMILIANO'S. He felt like enchiladas and tacos and perhaps some beer if it was cold.

He ate alone at the counter, away from the crowded tables that squeezed close to each other in the hot, low-ceilinged café, taking his time and listening to the noise of the people eating and drinking. Emiliano served him, and after his meal set another beer—that was very cold—before him on the counter. And when he was again outside, the air seemed cooler and the dusk more restful.

He lighted a cigarette, inhaling deeply, and saw someone emerge from the alley that led to his adobe. The figure looked up and down the street, then ran directly toward him, shouting his name.

Now he recognized Agostino Reyes, who worked at the wagonyard with his uncle.

The old man was breathless. "I have hunted you everywhere," he wheezed, his eyes wide with excitement. "Your uncle has taken the shotgun that they keep at the company office and has gone to shoot a man!"

Robles held him hard by the shoulders. "Speak clearly! Where did he go!"

Agostino gasped out, "Earlier, a man by the Supreme insulted him and caused him to be degraded in front of others. Now Tio has gone to kill him."

Jimmy ran with his heart pounding against his chest, praying to God and His Mother to let him get there before anything happened. A block away from the Supreme he saw the people milling about the street, with all attention toward the front of the saloon. He heard the deep discharge of a shotgun and the people scattered as if the shot were a signal. In the space of a few seconds the street was deserted.

He slowed the motion of his legs and approached the rest of the way at a walk. Nothing moved in front of the Supreme, but across the street he saw figures in the shadowy doorways of the Samas Café and the hotel next door. A man stepped out to the street and he saw it was John Benedict.

"Your uncle just shot Sid Roman. Raked his legs with a Greener. He's up there in the doorway laying half dead."

He made out the shape of a man lying beneath the swing doors of the Supreme. In the dusk the street was quiet, more quiet than he had ever known it, as if he and John Benedict were alone. And then the scream pierced the stillness. "God Almighty somebody help me!" It hung there, a cold wail in the gloom, then died.

"That's Sid," Benedict whispered. "Tio's inside with his pistol. If anybody gets near that door, he'll let go and most likely finish off Sid. He's got Remillard and Judge Essery and I don't know who else inside. They didn't get out in time. God knows what he'll do to them if he gets jumpy."

"Why did Tio shoot him?"

"They say about an hour ago Sid come staggering out drunk and bumped into your uncle and started telling him where to go. But your uncle was just as drunk and he wouldn't take any of it. They started swinging and Sid got Tio down and rubbed his face in the dust, then had one of his boys get a bottle, and he sat there drinking like he was on the front porch. Sitting on Tio. Then the old man come back about an hour later and let go at him with the Greener." John Benedict added, "I can't say I blame him."

Jimmy Robles said, "What were you doing while Sid was on the front porch?" and started toward the Supreme, not waiting for an answer.

John Benedict followed him. "Wait a minute," he called, but stopped when he got to the middle of the street.

On the saloon steps he could see Sid Roman plainly in the square of light under the doors, lying on his back with his eyes closed. A moan came from his lips, but it was almost inaudible. No sound came from within the saloon.

He mounted the first step and stood there. "Tio!"

No answer came. He went all the way up on the porch and looked down at Roman. "Tio! I'm taking this man away!"

Without hesitating he grabbed the wounded man beneath the arms and pulled him out of the doorway to the darkened end of the ramada past the windows. Roman screamed as his legs dragged across the boards. Jimmy Robles moved back to the door and the quietness settled again.

He pushed the door in, hard, and let it swing back, catching it as it reached him. Tio was leaning against the bar with bottles and glasses strung out its smooth length behind him. From the porch he could see no one else. Tio looked like a frightened animal cowering in a dead-end ravine, more pathetic in his ragged and dirty cotton clothes. His rope-soled shoes edged a step toward the doorway, with his body moving in a crouch. The pistol was in front of him, his left hand under the other wrist supporting the weight of the heavy Colt and, the deputy noticed now, trying to keep it steady.

Tio waved the barrel at him. "Come in and join your friends, Jaime." His voice quivered to make the bravado meaningless.

Robles moved inside the door of the long barroom and saw Remillard and Judge Essery standing by the table nearest the bar. Two other men stood at the next table. One of them was the bartender, wiping his hands back and forth over his apron.

Robles spoke calmly. "You've done enough, Tio. Hand me the gun."

"Enough?" Tio swung the pistol back to the first table. "I have just started."

"Don't talk crazy. Hand me the gun."

"Do you think I am crazy?"

"Just hand me the gun."

Tio smiled, and by it seemed to calm. "My foolish nephew. Use your head for one minute. What do you suppose would happen to me if I handed you this gun?"

"The law would take its course," Jimmy Robles said. The words sounded meaningless even to him.

"It would take its course to the nearest cottonwood," Tio said. "There are enough fools in the family with you, Jaime." He smiled still, though his voice continued to shake.

"Perhaps this is my mission, Jaime. The reason I was born."

"You make it hard to decide just which one is the fool."

"No. Hear me. God made Tio Robles to his image and likeness that he might someday blow out the brains of Señores Rema-yard and Essery." Tio's laugh echoed in the long room.

Jimmy Robles looked at the two men. Judge Essery was holding on to the table and his thin face was white with fear, glistening with fear. And for all old man Remillard's authority, he couldn't do a thing. An old Mexican, like a thousand he could buy or sell, could stand there and do whatever he desired because he had slipped past the cowman's zone of influence, past fearing for the future.

Tio raised the pistol to the level of his eyes. It was already cocked. "Watch my mission, Jaime. Watch me send two devils to hell!"

He watched fascinated. Two men were going to die. Two men he hardly knew, but he could feel only hate for them. Not like he might hate a man, but with the anger he felt for a principle that went against his reason. Something big, like injustice. It went through his mind that if these two men died, all injustice would vanish. He heard the word in his mind. His own voice saying it. Injustice. Repeating it, until then he heard only a part of the word.

His gun came out and he pulled the trigger in the motion. Nothing was repeating in his mind, now. He looked down at Tio Robles on the floor and knew he was dead before he knelt over him.

He picked up Tio in his arms like a small child and walked out of the Supreme into the evening dusk. John Benedict approached him and he saw people crowding out into the street. He walked past the sheriff and behind him heard Remillard's booming voice. "That was a close one!" and a scattering of laughter. Fainter then, he heard Remillard again. "Your boy learns fast."

He walked toward Spanishtown, not seeing the faces that lined the street, hardly feeling the limp weight in his arms.

The people, the storefronts, the street—all was hazy—as if his thoughts covered his eyes like a blindfold. And as he went on in the darkness he thought he understood now what John Benedict meant by justice.

15

The Last Shot

Original Title: A Matter of Duty
Fifteen Western Tales, September 1953

FROM THE SHADE of the pines, looking across the draw, he watched the single file of cavalrymen come out of the timber onto the open bench. The first rider raised his arm and they moved at a slower pace down the slope, through the green-tinged brush. The sun made small flashes on the visors of their kepis and a clinking sound drifted faintly across the draw.

He had come down the same way a few minutes before and now he was certain that they would stay on his trail. Watching them, he sat his sorrel mare unmoving, his young face sun-darkened and clean-lined and glistening with perspiration, though the air was cool. A Sharps lay across his lap and he gripped it hard, then looked about quickly as if searching for a place to hide it. Instead he swung the stock against the sorrel's rump and guided her away from the rim, breaking into a run as they crossed a meadow of bear grass toward the darkness of a pine stand. And as he drew near, a rider, watching him closely, came out of the pines.

Lou Walker, the young man, swung his mount close to the other rider and pushed the rifle toward him.

"Give me your carbine, Risdon!"

"What happened?" the man said. Ed Risdon was close to fifty. He sat heavily in his saddle and his round, leathery face studied Walker calmly.

"I missed him."

"How could you miss? All you had to do was aim at his beard."

"His horse spooked as I fired. It reared up and I hit it in the withers."

"They see you?"

"I was up in the rocks and when I missed they took out after me. Give me the carbine. If I get caught they'll see it hasn't been fired."

"What if I get caught?" Risdon said.

"You won't if you scat."

Risdon drew the short rifle from its saddle scabbard and handed it to Lou Walker, exchanging it for Walker's Sharps. "Maybe," he said, "I'd better stay with you."

"Get home and tell Beckwith what happened—and get that gun out of here."

Risdon hesitated. "What'll I tell Barbara?"

Walker stared at him. "I don't like it any more than you do."

"I think maybe it's getting senseless," Risdon answered.

"Think what you want—just get the hell out of here."

Walker nudged the mare with his knee and rode away from Risdon, back toward the rim. As he neared it he looked around, across the meadow, to make certain Risdon was gone. He could hear the cavalrymen below him now, the clinking sound of their approach sharp in the crisp air, and waited until they could see him up through the trees before he started off, following the rim. There was a shout, then another, and when the carbine shot rang behind him he knew they had reached the crest. He swung from the high ground then, zigzagging down through the scattered piñons, guiding the reins loosely.

A quarter of the way from the bottom the dwarf pines gave up to brush and hard rock. Walker spurred toward the open slope, glancing over his shoulder, seeing the flashes of blue uniforms up through the trees. He heard the carbine report and the whine as the bullet glanced off rock. Then another. A third kicked up sand a few yards in front of the mare and she swerved suddenly on the slope. He tried to hold her in, but the mare was already side-slipping on the loose shale. Suddenly she was falling and Walker went out of the saddle. He tried to twist his body in the air—then he struck the slope and rolled. . . .

THERE WAS A stable smell of leather and damp horsehide. Again his body slammed against the ground and the shock of it brought open his eyes. They had carried him draped across a saddle and when they reached the others, a trooper threw his legs over the horse and he landed on his back.

He heard a voice say, "Sergeant!" close over him. He looked up and the trooper spat to the side. "He's awake."

Now there were other faces that looked down at him and they were all the same—shapeless kepis, tired, curious eyes, dirt in crease lines, and two- or three-day beards. Though there were some faces without the stubble, they were boys with the expressions of men. The blue uniforms were covered with fine dust and the jackets seemed ill-fitting, with buttons missing, and from the shoulders hung the oblong, leather-covered, wooden cases that hold seven cartridge tubes for a Spencer carbine.

And then another uniform was standing over him. Alkali dust made the Union blue seem faded, but the jacket held firmly to chest and shoulders and a full, red beard reached to the second button. The red beard moved.

"Mister, we owe you an apology, though I don't imagine it makes your head feel any better."

Walker relaxed slowly, sitting up, then came to his feet and stood in front of the red beard which was even with his own chin. But his leg buckled under him and he sat down again, feeling the stabbing in his right knee. He winced, but kept his eyes on the officer. He had imagined McGrail to be a much taller man and now he was surprised. *Stories make a man taller than he is. . . .* Then he felt better because Major McGrail was not unusually tall. Still, he was uneasy. Perhaps because he had tried to kill him not a half hour before.

"Your knee?" McGrail said.

Walker nodded, then said, "Where's my horse?"

"It was past saving."

"You didn't have a right to fire on me."

McGrail smiled faintly. "I'm told you had a damn uncommon guilty way of running when ordered to halt."

"I didn't hear anything."

"Perhaps you weren't listening."

"I don't wear a uniform."

"Did you ever?"

"Are you holding a trial?"

"Someone shooting at me arouses a fair amount of curiosity."

"So your men chased out and spotted me and thought I was the one."

McGrail said nothing. He extended his left hand to the side and the sergeant stepped quickly, placing in it the carbine he'd been holding.

McGrail handed the carbine to Walker. "We took the liberty of examining it," he said. "You see, the bullet struck my mount. From something with a large bore—a Sharps perhaps."

And mine's a carbine that hasn't been fired."

"A Perry that hasn't been fired," McGrail corrected. "A Confederate make, isn't it?"

"As far as I know, this gun doesn't know north from south."

"I suppose not." McGrail smiled. "Which way are you going?" he said then.

"Valverde."

"Well, I can repay some inconvenience by offering you a remount home."

"I didn't say it was my home."

"In fact—" McGrail smiled "—you haven't said anything."

THE UNION CAVALRY Station, Valverde, New Mexico, was a mile north of the pueblo. McGrail swung his troop in that direction as they approached Valverde and Lou Walker sat his mount for some time watching the dust rise behind the line of cavalry. Then he went on—though the image of McGrail, red beard and tired eyes, remained in his mind.

Before reaching the plaza, he turned into a side street and tied the borrowed mount in front of a one-story adobe and went through the doorway that said EAT above it in large faded letters.

The man behind the bar looked up and nodded as he entered and the waiter, who was Mexican and wore a stained apron, also nodded. There were no patrons in the room, but Walker passed through it to a back room which was smaller and had only three tables. And as he sat down, the Mexican appeared in the doorway.

"You're limping."

"My horse threw me."

"That's a bad thing." The waiter considered this and then said, "What pleases you?"

"Brandy and coffee."

His knee was becoming stiff and was sensitive when he touched it. He rubbed it idly, becoming used to it, until the waiter returned and placed his tray on the table. The waiter poured coffee from a small porcelain pot, then raised the brandy bottle.

"In the coffee?"

He shook his head and watched as the waiter poured brandy into a glass. He looked up as a man came through the doorway.

Walker nodded and said, "Beckwith."

The man, in his mid-forties, was thin and he wore a heavy mustache that made his drawn face seem even narrower.

He said, "What's that?"

"Brandy."

"You better watch it." Sitting down, Beckwith's hand flicked against the waiter's arm. "We'll see you," he said and waited until the scuffing sound of the waiter's sandals had faded out of the room while he watched Walker closely.

"I saw McGrail ten minutes ago."

"I missed him."

"That's like telling me I've got eyes. All you had to do was aim at his beard."

"That's what Risdon said."

"Where is he?"

"He went back to del Norte."

"He was supposed to stay with you," Beckwith said.

"He went back to tell you what happened. I didn't know you were here."

"You don't seem too concerned about this."

"I'm tired," Walker said.

Beckwith stared at him without expression, coldly. "Listen," he said after a moment. "Every day that man stays alive, the Yankees get more to fight with. Not just beef and remounts, but recruits he sweet-talks into joining Sam Grant—" Beckwith paused.

"You've heard of a place called Five Forks—in Virginia?"

"Go on."

"A week ago Pickett got his pants beat off there. Fitz Lee's Cavalry was cut to pieces."

"Then it's nearly over," Walker said quietly.

"Hell no it ain't! Kirby Smith's still holding out in Mississippi. We got more land than just Virginia."

"And how many more lives?" Walker said.

"Quitting?"

"All of a sudden I'm tired." Beneath the table his hand rubbed the knee.

"Or is it scared?" Beckwith said.

"Leave me alone for a while."

"1 asked you a question."

Walker's face hardened. "Where've you been for four years, Beckwith—del Norte? Or did you get over to Tascosa once. Tell me what you do to keep from getting scared?"

After a moment he said, "My knee's turning stiff."

"That's too bad," Beckwith said.

"Everything's too bad."

"You haven't answered me," Beckwith said. "What are you going to do?"

Walker drank off the brandy and dropped his arm heavily. "Kill him," he said finally.

HE TOOK A ROOM at the hotel and stretched out on the bed without removing his clothes, just his coat and boots. He hung his shoulder holster on the foot of the bed, but took out the handgun and placed it next to his leg; and he was asleep before he could think of the war or of Beckwith, the Confederate agent who'd never seen a skirmish, or McGrail, who had to be killed because he was a valuable Yankee officer. He did think of Barbara, Risdon's daughter, but it was only for a few minutes.

It was early morning when he awoke and before he opened his eyes he felt the stiffness in his knee. Without moving his leg he knew it was swollen: then, when he raised it, it began to throb.

It was the same leg a year ago. No, he thought now. Yellow Tavern was eleven months ago. He had been with a Texas Volunteer company assigned to Stuart's Cavalry. The defense of Richmond.

They could have stayed in the redoubts and waited, but that wasn't Stuart. He came out and threw his sabers in Sheridan's face at Yellow Tavern—straight on into the Whitworths the Yankees had captured and turned on them—and it wasn't enough. Sheridan wasn't McClellan. Walker remembered Stuart going down, shot through the lungs, and then his own mount was down and he was conscious only of the scalding pain in his right leg.

It was during his stay in the Richmond hospital that the civilian had come and asked him strange questions about how he thought about things, and finally began talking about soldiers without uniforms. "Spying?" he'd asked. Call it what you want, the civilian said. There's more than one way to fight a war.

They had picked him because he was a Texan, could speak some Spanish, and his war record was good. Three months later he was in Paso del Norte, with Beckwith's organization, buying guns for the Cause. Ed Risdon guided for them. Risdon had traded goods down through Chihuahua and Sonora for over fifteen years. He knew the country and he brought them through each time. About one trip a month.

His daughter, Barbara, waited in del Norte, watching for Lou Walker. Between trips they were together most of the time.

Then one day, that was two weeks ago, Beckwith told him what had to be done about McGrail. For only two troops of blue-bellies his command was doing a mountain of harm, getting men and supplies headed east safely. That would have to be stopped.

Beckwith is a strange man, he thought. He can become fanatical about the Cause, though he's never been east of the Panhandle. That's it, he thought now. That makes the difference. He didn't see the Wilderness, or Cold Harbor, or Yellow Tavern.

The morning wore on and he began to feel hungry, but his body ached and he remained on the bed, smoking cigarettes when it would occur to him, not moving his leg. He wasn't worried about the knee.

He was dozing again when the light knocks sounded on the door and he sat upright with the suddenness of it and winced, feeling the muscles pull in his knee.

"Who is it?" His palm covered the bone handle of the pistol next to him.

A girl's voice answered him.

HE WAS OFF the bed, went to the door, opened it, and the girl was in his arms. Close to her cheek he said, "Barbara—" but her mouth brushed against his and that was all he said. For a moment they clung together, then he drew her inside and closed the door.

"How'd you find me?"

"Beckwith told us."

"Your father's with you?"

She nodded. Her dark hair was pulled back tightly into a chignon and it made her face seem delicately small. "I told him I wanted to be with you."

"That must have touched him," Walker said. He led her to the bed and sat down next to her. There was no chair in the room and he felt suddenly embarrassed at being alone with her, and at the same time he was conscious of his uncombed hair and the two-day beard, even though he knew it would not matter to her.

"Lou, you hurt your leg!"

Her gaze remained on his knee, but she said, "You're going to try again, aren't you?"

"You're not supposed to know about that."

Her eyes lifted to his, frowning. "What good will it do?"

"If I knew all the whys, I'd be wearing yellow epaulettes with fringe."

"One more dead man isn't going to help anything."

"You didn't talk to Beckwith very long."

For a moment the girl was silent. "We're leaving," she said then.

"For where?"

"I don't know—toward California."

"Your dad's idea?"

"Partly. But maybe I'm more worn out than he is." She looked at him longingly. "Lou—come with us."

"You know better than that."

"Why?"

"I'd be a deserter."

Her eyes begged him again, but she said nothing and finally her head lowered and she stared at her hands in her lap. Walker made a cigarette and smoked it in the silence, trying to rationalize going with them: but he could not.

The girl was rising when they heard the footsteps outside the door. Then the three knocks.

"Walker?" Beckwith's voice came from the hall.

Walker looked at the girl, then went to the door and opened it. Risdon stood in the doorway. Behind him, Beckwith said, "Go on," and Risdon moved into the room. Beckwith followed a step behind, with the barrel of his pistol pressed into the man's back.

Beckwith looked at the girl and then to Walker. "Lou," he said. "You're about the most resourceful man I know, even when you're sick."

The girl had gone to her father and now she looked at him with frightened surprise. "You told him!"

"I had to. I don't want him saying we're running away."

"What do you call it?" Beckwith said.

"I'm getting too old to play soldierboy," Risdon said.

"You think you can just walk away?"

"He's not in the army," Walker said now. "He can leave any time he feels like it!"

"With all he knows about us?" Beckwith asked.

"God, if you can't trust him, who can you!"

"Lou, I wonder about that more and more every day."

"Cut out the foolishness!"

"Were you going, too?"

"No."

"Just take your word for it?" Beckwith's thin face was expressionless. "Lou," he said, "I'm not play-actin'. You know what they do to deserters."

"What's he deserting from?"

"Me," Beckwith said quietly. He added, then, "Lou, I'll have to take your word about you not going—but get over on the bed out of the way." Walker hesitated and Beckwith turned the pistol on him threateningly. "I can include you as easily as not."

Walker backed against the bed and eased down, keeping his right leg stiffly in front of him. As he sank to the bed, something hard dug against his thigh. His hand moved to the side of his leg, then stopped. It was his pistol.

Risdon was watching his daughter and now he was about to speak: it was on his face.

"Keep it to yourself," Beckwith said to him. "I don't want to hear any more."

"What are you going to do?" Walker asked him quietly. His hand was on the pistol butt now, close under his leg.

"What I have to," Beckwith said. "We can't take chances on either of them."

"Here?"

"Out somewhere."

Walker's fingers closed around the pistol grip. He hesitated, because he wanted to do this the right way, and he wasn't sure what that was. He heard Risdon say, "Beckwith—" and saw the agent's head turn toward Risdon. At that moment, Walker raised the pistol and cocked it.

Beckwith heard the click and his head swung back. He looked at Walker as if what he saw could not be possible.

Walker held the pistol dead on the agent's chest. "I'm not going to try to convince you of anything," he said. "Just let go of the gun."

The surprise passed and Beckwith's drawn face scowled. "You're making the biggest mistake of your life."

"If you don't think I'd shoot, hold on to that gun for three more seconds."

Beckwith's pistol was pointed midway between Risdon and Walker. His eyes held on Walker's face, trying to read something there. Then, slowly, his arm lowered and when his hand reached his side, the fingers opened and the pistol dropped to the floor.

Risdon stooped, picked it up and glanced at Beckwith as he rose.

"You just lost yourself a job."

"You've got to take him with you," Walker said now. "Drop him at maybe Cuchillo—by the time he finds help you'll have all the distance you'd need."

Risdon frowned. "You're coming now, aren't you?"

Walker shook his head.

The girl looked at him in disbelief. "Lou, why would you stay now?"

"The same reason as before."

"But it's different now!"

"Why is it? I'm still a soldier. I haven't been serving under a private flag of Beckwith's."

The girl continued to look at him with the plea in her eyes, but now there was nothing she could say.

Risdon shrugged. "Well, you can't fight that."

Walker pulled on his boots, then lifted the shoulder holster from the bedpost and slipped his arm through it and inserted the handgun. He picked up his coat and moved to the girl.

"If you don't understand," he said quietly, "then I don't know what I can say."

She looked up into his face, but without smiling, and then she kissed him.

Risdon said, "She's tryin'." His eyes followed Walker moving to the door. "Lou," he said. "We thought we'd follow the Rio Grande to Cuchillo then bear west toward Santa Rita."

Unexpectedly, Walker smiled, but he said nothing going out the door.

AT YELLOW TAVERN he had killed a Union soldier. Perhaps he had killed others, but the one at Yellow Tavern was the only one he was sure of. It had been at close range, firing down into the soldier's face as the Yankee's bayonet thrust caught in his horse's mane. He fired and the blue uniform disappeared. That simple. What he was about to do no longer seemed a part of war, because the man had a name and was not just a blue uniform.

He rode out from Valverde to the cavalry station at a walk, moving the borrowed mount unhurriedly, his right leg hanging out of the stirrup. Nearing the adobes a trooper rode by and shouted, but the sound of his running mount covered the words.

The sunlight on the gray adobe was cold, because there was no one about and there were no sounds. Over the row of bare houses, far to the north, reaching into the clouds, was the whiteness of Sangre de Cristo. This, too, caused the cavalry station to seem drab. Walker knew a patrol was out. Perhaps McGrail had taken it. For a moment he felt relief, but knew that would solve nothing.

He went through a doorway above which a wooden shingle read: HEADQUARTERS—VALVERDE STATION—COS, D & E—9TH US CAVALRY.

At the desk a sergeant looked up and momentarily there was recognition on his face. But he said nothing, he only listened to the name that was given him, then stepped into the next room and closed the door behind him.

He reappeared almost immediately. "The major will see you," and stepped aside to let Walker pass.

McGrail's back was turned. He stood at the window behind his desk, looking out at the sand and glare.

He did not turn, but when the door closed, he said, "I've been expecting you."

Walker hesitated. "Why?"

McGrail turned then. He was holding a revolving pistol in his right hand, and with the other he was wiping a cloth along the barrel.

"To return the horse you borrowed," he said. "Why else?"

Walker was silent. The surprise was on his face for a brief moment. It passed, and still he did not say anything.

"How's the leg?"

"Stiff."

"I suppose it would be."

McGrail moved the cloth slowly, steadily along the pistol barrel. Abruptly he said, "You wouldn't know the whereabouts of a man named Beckwith, would you?"

Walker was startled. "Should I?"

"You're not one for answering questions, are you?"

Walker unbuttoned his coat and drew tobacco from his shirt. He made a cigarette and replaced the tobacco, leaving his coat open.

"I could never wear a shoulder holster," McGrail said. "Would always feel bound."

Walker exhaled cigarette smoke. "You get used to anything."

"I thought you might have heard of this Beckwith," McGrail said. "I'm rather anxious to meet him, myself—you see, he's a Confederate agent."

"Why are you telling me that?"

McGrail shrugged. "Just conversation. Thought you might be interested. You see, this Beckwith thinks he's been putting something over on us, but there are as many people in Valverde giving information to me as there are to him." McGrail was relaxed. His eyes were not tired now, and his full red beard had been combed and trimmed.

"People like waiters and bartenders?" Walker said.

"All kinds of people, doing their bit." McGrail smiled.

Walker dropped his cigarette to the plank flooring and stepped on it and saw the major frown. "If you have something to say, say it."

McGrail hesitated, watching Walker closely. He had been leaning against the front of his desk. Now he moved around it and, next to the window, unrolled a wall map by pulling a short cord. He beckoned to Walker with the handgun.

He moved forward hesitantly and watched McGrail point with his left hand to a dot on the map, but he could not read the name because of McGrail's hand. But east and north of the dot there were other names that could be read. Five Forks, Malvern Hill, Seven Pines. And suddenly he felt the skin prickle on the nape of his neck and between his shoulders.

"We heard less than an hour ago," McGrail said quietly. "On the morning of April ninth, here at Appomattox, Lee surrendered to General Grant. Mr. Walker, the war is over."

The room was silent. Walker's eyes remained on the map, unmoving. *The war's over,* he said in his mind, and repeated the words. *The war's over.* He felt relief. He waited for something else, but that was all.

He felt only relief. *How are you supposed to feel when you lose a war?* he thought. He looked at McGrail now and watched the cavalryman step to his desk and lay his pistol there. He felt his own pistol, heavy beneath his left arm, and now his hand dropped slowly from his coat front.

"I just now sent a man to Valverde," McGrail said. "You must have passed him. News travels slowly out here, doesn't it?" he said now. "You know April the ninth was two days ago—the day before we found you in that draw."

The cavalryman began arranging papers that were scattered over the polished surface of his desk. He looked up at Walker who was staring at him strangely.

"Mr. Walker, if you'll excuse me, I've a mountain of reports to wade through that have to be done today. That was all you wanted, wasn't it? To return the horse?"

Walker hesitated. "As a matter of fact, there was something else."

McGrail looked up again. "Yes?"

"I wondered if you might have a rig I could buy," Walker said. A grin was forming through the beard stubble. "It's hard going astride, with one leg dragging. You see, I've got a long way to go—down the Rio Grande to Cuchillo, then west toward Santa Rita—"

16

Blood Money

Original Title: Rich Miller's Hand
Western Story Magazine, October 1953

THE YUMA SAVINGS and Loan, Asunción Branch, was held up on a Monday morning, early. By eight o'clock the doctor had dug the bullet out of Elton Goss's middle and said if he lived, then you didn't need doctors anymore—the age of miracles was back. By nine Freehouser, the Asunción marshal, had all the facts—even the identity of the five holdup men—thanks to the Centralia Hotel night clerk's having been awake to see four of them come down from their rooms just after sunup. Then, he had tried to make the faces register in his mind, but even squinting and wrinkling his forehead did no good. The fifth man had been in the hotel lobby most of the night and the clerk knew for sure who he was, but didn't at the time associate him with the others. Later, when Freehouser showed him the WANTED dodgers, then he was dead sure about all of them.

Four were desperadoes. Well known, though with beard bristles and range clothes they looked like anybody else. First, the Harlan brothers, Ford and Eugene. Ford was boss: Eugene was too lazy to work. Then Deke, an old hand whose real name was something Deacon, though no one knew what for sure. And the fourth, Sonny Navarez, wanted in Sonora by the *rurales;* in Arizona, by the marshal's office. He, like the others, had served time in the territorial prison at Yuma.

As far as Freehouser was concerned, they weren't going back to Yuma if he caught them. Not with Elton Goss dying and his dad yelling for blood.

The fifth outlaw was identified as Rich Miller, a rider from down by Four Tanks. Those who knew of him said he was weathered good for his age, though not as tough as he thought he was. A boy going on eighteen and getting funny ideas in his brain because of the changing chemistry in his body. The bartender at the Centralia said Rich had been in and out all day, looking like he was mad at somebody. So they judged Rich had gotten drunk and was talked into something that was way over his head.

A hand from F-T Connected, which was out of Four Tanks, said Rich Miller'd been let go the day before, when the old man caught him drunk up at a line shack and not tending his fences. So what the Centralia bartender said was probably true. Freehouser said it was just too damn bad for him, that's all.

Monday afternoon the marshal's posse was in Four Tanks, then heading east toward the jagged andesite peaks of the Kofas. McKelway, the law at Four Tanks, had joined the posse, bringing five men with him, and offering a neighborly hand. But he became hard-to-hold eager when he found out who they were after. The Fords, Deke, and Navarez had dead-or-alive money on them. McKelway knew Rich Miller and said he just ought to have his nose wiped and run off home. But Freehouser looked at it differently.

This was armed robbery. Goss, the bank manager, and his son Elton, who clerked for him, were hauled out of bed by two men—they turned out to be Eugene Harlan and Deke. Ford Harlan and Sonny Navarez were waiting at the rear door of the bank. The robbery would have come off without incident if Elton hadn't gone for a gun in a desk drawer. The elder Goss wasn't sure which one shot him. Then they were gone, with twelve thousand dollars.

They rode around front and Rich Miller came out of the Centralia to join them. He'd been sitting at the window, asleep, the clerk thought, wearing off a drunk. He was used to having riders do that. When the rooms were filled up he didn't care. But Rich Miller suddenly came alive and swung onto a mount the Mexican was leading. So all that time he must have been watching the front to see no one sneaked up on them.

McKelway said a boy ought to be allowed one big mistake before he was called hard on something he'd done. Besides, Rich Miller's name didn't bring any reward money.

Tuesday morning, the twenty-man posse was deep in the Kofas. Gray rock towering on all sides, wild country, and now, no trail. Freehouser decided they would split up, climb to higher ground, and wait. Just look around. He sent a man back to Four Tanks to wire Yuma and Aztec in case the outlaws got through the Kofas. But Freehouser was sure they were still in the mountains, somewhere.

Wednesday morning his hunch paid off. One of McKelway's men spotted a rider, and the posse closed in by means of a mirror-flash system they'd planned beforehand. The rider turned out to be Ford Harlan.

Wednesday afternoon Ford Harlan was dead.

He had led them a chase most of the morning, slipping through the man net, but near noon he turned into a dead-end canyon, a deserted mine site that once had been Sweet Mary No. 1. Ford Harlan had been urging his mount up a slope above the mine works, toward an adobe hut perched on a ledge about three hundred yards up, when Freehouser cupped his hands and called for him to halt. He kept on. A moment later Jim Mission, McKelway's deputy, knocked him out of the saddle with a single shot from his Remington.

Then McKelway and Mission volunteered to bring Ford Harlan down. McKelway tied a white neckerchief to the end of his Sharps for a truce flag and they went up. Freehouser had said if you want to get Ford, you might as well go a few more steps and ask the rest if they want to give up. They were almost to the body when the pistol fire broke from above. They scrambled down fast and when they reached the posse, Freehouser was smiling.

They were all up there, Eugene and Deke and the Mexican and Rich Miller. One of them had lost his nerve and opened up. You could see it on Freehouser's face. The self-satisfaction. They were trapped in an old assay shack with a sheer sandstone wall towering behind it—thin shadow lines of crevices reaching to slender pinnacles—and only one way to come down. The original mine opening was on the same shelf; probably they'd hid their horses there.

Freehouser was a contented man; he had all the time in the world to figure how to pry them out of the 'dobe. He even listened to McKelway and admitted that maybe the kid, Rich Miller, shouldn't be hung with the others—if he didn't get shot first.

Some of the posse went back home, because they had jobs to hold down, but the next day, others came out from Asunción and Four Tanks to see the fun.

☆　☆　☆

IT SEEMED NATURAL that Deke should take over as boss. There was no discussing it; no one gave it a thought. Ford was dead. Eugene was indifferent. Sonny Navarez was Mexican, and Rich Miller was a kid.

The boy had wondered why Deke wasn't the boss even before. Maybe Deke didn't have Ford's nerve, but he had it over him in age and learning. Still, a man gets old and he thinks of too many what-ifs. And sometimes Deke was scary the way he talked about fate and God pulling little strings to steer men around where they didn't want to go.

He was at the window on the right side of the doorway, which was open because there was no door. Eugene and Deke were at the left front window. He could hear Sonny Navarez behind him moving gear around, but the boy did not take his eyes from the slope.

Deke lounged against the wall, his face close to the window frame, his carbine balanced on the sill. Eugene was a step behind him. He was a heavy-boned man, shoulders stretching his shirt tight, and tall, though Deke was taller when he wasn't lounging. Eugene pulled at his shirt, sticking to his body with perspiration. The sun was straight overhead and the heat pushed into the canyon without first being deflected by the rimrock.

The Mexican drew his carbine from his bedroll and moved up next to Rich Miller, and now the four of them were looking down the slope, all thinking pretty much the same thing, though in different ways.

Eugene Harlan broke the silence. "I shouldn't of fired at them."

It could have gone unsaid. Deke shrugged. "That's under the bridge."

"I wasn't thinking."

Deke did not bother to look at him. "Well, you better start."

"It wasn't my fault. Ford led 'em here!"

"Nobody's blaming you for anything. They'd a got us anyway, sooner or later. It was on the wall."

Eugene was silent, and then he said, "What happens if we give ourselves up?"

Deke glanced at him now. "What do you think?"

Sonny Navarez grinned. "I think they would invite us to the rope dance."

"Ford's the one shot that boy in the bank," Eugene protested. "They already got him."

"How would they know he's the one?" Deke said.

"We'll tell them."

Deke shook his head. "Get a drink and you'll be doing your nerves a favor."

Sonny Navarez and Rich Miller looked at Deke and both of them grinned, but they said nothing and after a moment they looked away again, down the slope, which fell smooth and steep. Slightly to the left, beyond an ore tailing, rose the weathered gray scaffolding over the main shaft; below it, the rickety structure of the crushing mill and, past that, six rusted tanks cradled in a framework of decaying timber. These were roughly three hundred yards down the slope. There was another hundred to the clapboard company buildings straggled along the base of the far slope.

A sign hanging from the veranda of the largest building said SWEET MARY NO. 1—EL TESORERO MINING CO.—FOUR TANKS, ARIZONA TERR. Most of the possemen now sat in the shade of this building.

Deke raised his hat again and passed a hand over his bald head, then down over his face, weathered and beard stubbled, contrasting with the delicate whiteness of his skull. Rich Miller's eyes came back up the slope, hesitating on Ford Harlan's facedown body. Then he removed his hat, passed a sleeve across his forehead, and replaced the curled brim low over his eyes.

He heard Eugene say, "You can't tell what they'll do."

"They won't send us back to Yuma," Deke said. "That's one thing you can count on. And it costs money to rig a gallows. They'd just as lief do it here, with a gun—appeals to the sporting blood."

Sonny Navarez said, "I once shot a mountain sheep in this same canyon that weighed as much as a man."

"Right from the start there were signs," Deke said. "I was a fool not to heed them. Now it's too late. Something's brought us to die here all together, and we can't escape it. You can't escape your doom."

Sonny Navarez said, "I think it was twelve thousand dollars that brought us."

"Sure it was the money, in a way," Deke said. "But we're so busy listening to Ford tell how easy money's restin' in the bank, waitin' to be sent to Yuma, we're not seein' the signs. Things that've never happened before. Like Ford insisting we got to have five—so he picks up this kid—"

Rich Miller said, "Wait a minute!" because it didn't sound right.

Deke held up his hand. "I'm talking about the signs—and Ford all of a sudden gettin' the urge to go on scout when he never done anything like that before. It was all working toward this—and now there's nothing we can do about it."

"I ain't going to get shot up just because you got a crazy notion," Eugene said.

Deke shook his head, wearily. "It's sealed up now. After fate shows how it's going, then it's too late."

"I didn't shoot that man in the bank!"

"You think they'll bother to ask you?"

"Damn it, I'll tell 'em—and they'll have to prove I did it!"

"If you can get close enough to 'em without gettin' shot," Deke said quietly. He brought out field glasses from his saddlebags, which were below the window, and put the glasses to his face, edging them along the men far below in front of the company buildings.

Rich Miller said to him, "What do you see down there?"

"Same thing you do, only bigger."

"I think," Sonny Navarez said to Deke, "that you are right in what you have said, that they will try hard to kill us—but this boy is not one of us. I think if he would surrender, they would not kill him. Prison, perhaps, but prison is better than dying."

"You worry about yourself," Rich Miller said.

"The time to be brave," the Mexican said, "is when they are handing out medals."

"You heard him," Deke said. "Worry about your own hide. The more people we got, the longer we last. There's nothing that says if you're going to get killed, you got to hurry it up."

Rich Miller watched Eugene move back to the table along the rear wall and pick up the whiskey bottle that was there. The boy passed his tongue over dry lips, watching Eugene drink. It would be good to have a drink, he thought. No, it wouldn't. It would be bad. You drank too much and that's why you're here. That's why you're going to get shot or hung.

But he could not sincerely believe what Deke had said. That one way of the other, this was the end. Down the slope the posse was very far away—dots of men that seemed too small to be a threat. He did not feel sorry about joining the holdup, because he did not let himself think about it. He did feel something resembling sorry for the man in the bank. But he shouldn't have reached for the gun. I wonder if I would have, he thought.

It wasn't so bad up here in the 'dobe. Plenty of water and grub. Maybe we'll have some fun. Look at that crazy Mexican, talking about hunting mountain sheep.

If you were in jail you could say, all right, you made a mistake; but how do you know if you've made a mistake when you're still alive and got two thousand dollars in your pants? My God, a man can do just about anything with two thousand dollars!

FREEHOUSER SAT in the shade, not saying anything. McKelway came to him, biting on his pipe idly, and after a while pointed to the mine-shaft scaffolding and said how a man with a good rifle might be able to draw a bead and throw something in that open doorway if he was sitting way up there on top.

Freehouser studied the ore tailings, furrowed and steep, that extended out from the slope on both sides of the hut. If a man was going up to that 'dobe, he'd have to go straight up, right into their guns. Maybe McKelway had something. Soften them up a bit.

STANDING BY the windows, watching the possemen not moving, became tiresome. So one by one they would go back to the table and take a drink. Rich Miller took his turn and it tasted good. But he did not drink much.

Still, the time dragged on—until Eugene thought of something. He went to his gear and drew a deck of cards.

Sonny Navarez said, "I have not played often."

"Stand by the window awhile," Deke told him. "Then somebody'll spell you. You got enough cash to learn with."

Eugene shook his head, thinking of his brother, who had taken twice as much as the others because the holdup had been his idea. "Damn Ford had four thousand in his bags. . . ."

They started playing, using matches for chips, each one worth a dollar. Rich Miller said the stakes were big . . . he'd never played higher than nickel-dime before; but he began winning right off and he changed his tune. Most of the time they played five-card stud. Deke said it separated the men from the boys and he looked at Rich Miller when he said it. Deke played with a dumb face, but would smile after the last card was dealt—as if the last card always twinned the one he had in the hole. And he lost every hand. Eugene and Rich Miller took turns winning the pots, and after a while Deke stopped smiling.

"We're raising the stakes," he said finally. "Each stick's worth ten dollars." Deke's cut was down to a few hundred dollars.

Eugene took a drink and wiped his mouth and grinned. "Ain't you losing it fast enough?"

Rich Miller grinned with him.

Deke said, "Just deal the cards."

McKELWAY REACHED the platform on top of the shaft scaffolding and dropped the line to haul up the rifles—his own Sharps and Jim Mission's roll-block Remington. He was glad Jim Mission was coming up with him. Jim was company and could shoot probably better than he could.

When Jim reached the platform the two men nodded and smiled, then loaded their rifles and practice-sighted on the doorway. McKelway said, Try not to hit the boy, though knocking off any of the others would be doing mankind a good turn, and Jim Mission said it was all right with him.

EUGENE GOT UP from the table unsteadily, tipping back his chair; he was grinning and stuffing currency into his pants pockets. In two hours he had won every cent of Deke's and Rich Miller's money. They remained seated, watching him sullenly, thinking it was a damn fool thing to try and win back all your losings in a couple of hands. Eugene took another pull at the bottle and wiped his mouth and looked at them, but he only grinned.

"Sonny!" He called to the Mexican lounging beside the window. "Your turn to get skinned."

The Mexican shook his head. "I could not oppose such luck."

"Come on!"

Sonny Navarez shook his head again and smiled.

Harlan looked at him steadily, frowning. "Are you going to play?"

"Why should I give you my money?"

"You don't come over here, I'll come get you."

The Mexican did not smile now and the room was silent. Rich Miller started to rise, but Deke was up first. "Gene, you want to fight somebody—there's plenty outside."

Eugene ignored him and kept on toward Sonny. The Mexican's hand edged toward his holstered pistol.

"Gene, you sit down now," Deke said tensely.

Eugene stepped into the rectangle of sunlight carpeting in from the doorway. He was stepping out of it when the rifle cracked and sang in the open stillness. Eugene's hands clawed at his face and he dropped without uttering a sound.

★ ★ ★

MCKELWAY RELOADED quickly. He had got one of them, he was sure of that. And it hadn't looked like the boy, else he wouldn't have fired. Jim Mission told him it was good shooting. After that McKelway did some figuring.

From the crest of the ore tailing in front of them, they'd be only about fifty yards from the hut. The only trouble was, they'd be out in the open. He told Jim Mission about it and he said why not go up after dark; then if they didn't see anything they'd still be close enough to shoot at sounds. McKelway said he was just waiting for Jim to say it.

THERE WAS NO poker the rest of the afternoon. Deke had dragged Eugene by his boots out of the doorway and placed him against a side wall with his hands on his chest, not crossed, but pushed inside his coat. He took the money out of Eugene's pockets—six thousand dollars—and laid it on the table. Then he sat down and looked at it.

Rich Miller pressed close to the wall by the window, studying the slope, wondering where the man with the rifle was. His eyes hung on the weathered shaft scaffolding, and now he wasn't so sure if there'd be any fun.

Once Deke said, "Now it's starting to show itself," but they didn't bother to ask him what.

Sonny Navarez stayed by a window. He would look at Eugene's body, but most of the time he was watching the dying sun. Rich Miller noticed this, but he figured the Mexican was thinking about God—or heaven or hell—because there was a dead man in the room. Sonny had crossed himself when Eugene was cut down, even though he would have killed him himself a minute before.

The sun was below the canyon rim, though the sky still reflected it red and orange, when Sonny Navarez pulled his pistol.

Deke was raising the bottle. He glanced at the Mexican, but only momentarily. He took a long swallow then and extended the bottle to Rich Miller. But the boy was staring at Sonny Navarez. Deke's head turned abruptly. Sonny's long-barreled .44 was pointing toward them.

Deke took his time putting down the bottle. He looked up again. "What's the idea?"

The Mexican said, "When it is dark I'm leaving."

Deke nodded to the pistol. "You think we're going to try and stop you?"

"You might. I am taking the money."

"You're wasting your time."

Sonny Navarez shrugged. "*Qué va*—it's worth a try. From no matter where you die, it's the same distance to hell."

"You wouldn't have a chance," Rich Miller said. "There's somebody out there close with a rifle dead on this place."

"For this money a man will brave many things," the Mexican said. "And—I am not leaving until dark." Then he told them to face the wall, and when they did, he picked up the bundles of oversize bills and stuffed them inside his jacket.

Rich Miller said, "Do you think you'll get through?"

"Probably no."

Deke said, "You're a damn fool."

"If I get out," Sonny Navarez said, "I will visit a priest and give his church part of the money, and not rob again."

"It's too late for that," Deke said. "It's too late for anything."

No," the Mexican insisted. "I will be very sorry for this crime. With the money that is left after the church I will buy my mother a house in Hermosillo and after that I will recite the rosary every day."

Deke shook his head. "Things are going the way they are for a reason we don't know. But nothing you can do will change it."

The Mexican shrugged and said, "*Qué va*—"

It was almost full dark when Sonny Navarez moved to the doorway. He stood next to the opening and holstered his pistol and lifted his carbine, which was there against the wall. He levered a shell into the breech and stepped into the opening, crouching slightly. He hesitated, as if listening, then turned to the two men at the table and nodded. As he was turning back, the rifle shot rang in the dim stillness and echoed up-canyon. Sonny Navarez doubled, sinking to his knees, and hung there momentarily, as if in prayer, before falling half through the doorway.

LATER, MCKELWAY and Mission climbed down from the ore tailing and reported to Freehouser. The marshal said three out of five men wasn't bad for one day's work. They were sitting on the porch, cigarettes glowing in the darkness, when the rider came in from Asunción. He told them that Elton Goss was going to pull through.

Freehouser laughed and said, well, he guessed the age of miracles was back. A good one on the doctor, eh?

The news made everybody feel pretty good, because Elton was a nice boy. McKelway mentioned that it would also make it a whole lot easier on Rich Miller.

LOOKING OUT into the night, the boy could just barely make out the shapes of the mine structures and the cyanide vats, which Deke had told him held 250 tons of ore and had to be hauled all the way across the desert from Yuma. How did he say it? The ore'd pour into the crusher—jaws and rollers that'd beat it almost to powder—then pass into the vats and get leached in cyanide for nine days. Five pounds of cyanide to the ton of water, that was it. He thought, *What's the sense in re-membering that?*

It's a strange thing, Rich Miller thought now, *how in two days a man can change from a thirty-a-month rider to an outlaw and not even feel it. Almost like the man has nothing to do with it. Just a rope pulling you into things.*

He remembered earlier in the day, being eager, looking forward to doing some long-range shooting, but seeing the situation apart from himself. He wondered how he could have thought this. Now there were two dead men in the room—that was the difference.

Later on, he got to thinking about Eugene breaking the poker game and about the Mexican. It occurred to him that both of them, for a short space of time, had all of the money, and now they were dead. Ford had taken the biggest cut, and he was dead. Toward morning he dozed and when he awoke, Deke was sitting, leaning against the wall below the other window.

Deke was silent and Rich Miller said, for something to say, "When they going to try for us?"

"When they get good and damn ready."

Rich Miller was silent and after a while he said, "We could take a chance and give up—you know, not like surrenderin'—with the idea of gettin' away later on when they ain't a hundred of 'em around."

"You know what I told you."

"But you ain't dead sure about that."

"I'd say I'm a little older than you are."

Rich Miller did not answer. Damn, he hated for someone to tell him that. As if old men naturally knew more than young ones. Taking credit for being older when they didn't have anything to do with it.

"What're you thinking about?" Deke said.

"Giving up."

Deke exhaled slowly. "You saw what happens if you go through that door."

"There's other ways."

"Like what?"

"Wavin' a flag."

"You wave anything out that door," Deke said quietly, "I'll kill you."

HE'S CRAZY, RICH thought. *He's honest-to-God crazy and doesn't know it.* Deke had butted the table against the wall under the window and now they sat opposite each other, Deke on one side of the window, the boy on the other. Deke had divided the eight thousand dollars between them and said they were going to play poker to keep their minds from blowing away. He placed his pistol on the edge of the table.

They stayed fairly close at first, each winning about the same number of pots, but after a while the boy began to win more often. In the quietness he thought of many things—like not being able to give himself up—and then he remembered something which had occurred to him earlier.

"Deke," the boy said, "you know why Sonny and Eugene got killed?"

"I've been telling you why. 'Cause they were destined to."

"But why?"

"No one knows that."

"I do." The boy watched the older man closely. "Because they had the money." He paused. "Ford had most of it, and he was the first. Eugene had all but Sonny's when he got hit. Then Sonny took all of it and he lasted less than an hour."

Deke said nothing, but his sunken expression seemed more drawn.

They played on in silence and slowly Rich Miller was taking more and more of the money. Deke seemed uncomfortable and he said quietly that he guessed it just wasn't his day. In less than an hour he was down to two hundred and fifty dollars.

"You might clean me out," Deke said.

Rich Miller said nothing and dealt the cards. The first ones down, then a queen to Deke and a jack to himself. He looked at his hole card. A ten of diamonds. Deke bet fifty dollars on the queen.

"You must have twin girls," the boy said.

"You know how to find out."

Rich Miller's next card was a king. Deke's an ace. He bet fifty dollars again. Their fourth cards were low and no help, but Deke pushed in all the money he had.

"That's on a hunch," he said.

Rich Miller dealt the last cards—a queen to Deke, making it an ace, a five, and two queens. He gave himself a second king.

"What you show beats me," Deke said, grinning. He pushed away from the table and stood up. "You got it all, boy. You know what that means."

"It means I'm giving up."

"It's too late. You explained it yourself a while ago—the man who gets the money gets killed!" Deke was grinning deeply. "Now I don't have anything."

"You're dead sure you'll be last."

"As sure as a man can be. It's the handwriting."

"What good'll it do you?"

"Who knows?"

"You're so dead sure, go stand in that doorway."

Deke was silent.

"What about your handwritin'? The pattern says you'll be the last, and even then, who knows? That all the bunk?"

Deke hesitated momentarily, then walked slowly toward the doorway. He stopped next to it, stiffly. Then he moved out.

Rich Miller's eyes stayed on Deke as his hand moved across the table. He lifted Deke's pistol from the table edge and swung it out the window and fired in the direction of the scaffolding.

A high-pitched, whining report answered the shot and hung longer in the air. Deke staggered, turning back into the room, and had time to look at the boy in wide-eyed amazement. Then he was dead.

The boy returned to the window after getting his carbine and, with his bandanna tied to the end of the barrel, waved it in a slow arc back and forth. Once they started up the slope he sat back in the chair and idly turned over his hole card, the ten.

The possemen were drawing closer, up to Ford Harlan's body now. He flipped Deke's hole card. It landed on top of the two queens. Three ladies.

He rose and moved to the doorway as he saw the men nearing the shelf, then glanced down at Deke and shook his head. I sure am crazy, he thought. I never heard before of a man cheating to lose.

He walked through the doorway with his hands above his head.

17

Trouble at Rindo's Station

Original Title: Rindo's Station
Argosy, October 1953

★

Chapter One

THERE WAS A TIME when Bonito might have fired at the rider far below on the road, and for no other reason than to test his carbine, since the rider was a white man. He had done this many times before—sometimes for a shirt, or a fresh horse, usually for ammunition, though a reason was not necessary. But now there was something on the Mescalero's mind. He held his fire and urged his pony down the piñon slope.

From high up he had recognized Ross Corsen—the lank figure slouched in the McClellan saddle, head down against the glare, hat low over his eyes. And now, as the Mescalero closed in, Corsen looked up, though he had seen him long before, when Bonito was still high up the slope.

"*Sik-isn,*" Bonito said. The word was a hiss between his lips. Strands of hair hung from the shadow of a high-crowned hat, thick, glistening hair accentuating the yellowish cast of his skin and the pock scars that roughened heavy-boned features. A frayed, sweat-stained shirt covered his chest, but his legs were naked, for he wore only a breechclout, and the curled toes of his moccasins hung beneath the pony's belly, ridiculously close to the ground. A carbine was across his lap.

Ross Corsen smiled at the Apache's greeting and studied the broad, ugly face. "Now you call me *brother,*" he said in Spanish. "You must want something." He had not seen the Mescalero in almost a year, not since the four-day chase down to the border, and a glimpse of Bonito far off, not running any longer because he was safely in Mexico. Bonito had killed two Coyotero policemen during a tulapai drunk. That had started it. On the run for the border, he killed two more men, plus four horses that didn't belong to him. Now he was back and Corsen studied him, wondering why.

The Apache spoke a slow, guttural Spanish and said, as if in the middle of his thoughts, "We have suffered unfairly from your hand; all of us have"—he used the Apache word *tinneh,* which meant all of the people and in its meaning described the blood tie which bound them together—"and from the other man, the one who directs you. You think only of yourselves."

"And when did you begin thinking of others?" Corsen said.

"Those are my people at Pinaleño," Bonito answered him.

Corsen shrugged. "I won't argue with you. What you do now is no concern of mine. I can't do a thing to you or for you, but maybe suggest you go home and get drunk, which is what you'll probably do anyway."

"And where is our home, Cor-sen?"

"You know as well as I do."

"At San Carlos, where there is little to eat?"

Corsen nodded to the Maynard carbine across the Apache's lap. "Maybe in Mexico. You can't have one of those at San Carlos."

"Yes, in Sonora and Chihuahua where it is a business of profit to take the hair of the Apache, the government paying for our scalps."

Corsen shook his head. "Look, I no longer am in charge of the Pinaleño Reservation. The government man has discharged me." He thought for words that would explain it clearly to the Apache. "He is the one, Mr. Sellers, who has taken your guns and decided that you live on government beef."

"Some of the government beef," Bonito corrected. "He sells most of it to others for his own profit."

"That is not true of all reservations. You know I treated your people fairly."

"But you are no longer there and soon it will be true of all reservations."

The words were familiar to Corsen. No, not so much the words as the idea: he had argued this very thing with Sellers three days before, straining his patience to explain to the Bureau of Indian Affairs supervisor exactly what an Apache is. What kind of thinking animal he is. How much abuse he will take before all the peace talks in the world will not stop him. And he had lost the argument because, even if reason was not on Sellers's side, authority was. He threw it in Sellers's face, accusing him of selling government rations for his own profit, and Sellers laughed, daring him to prove it—then fired him. He would have quit. You can't go on working for a man like that. He decided that he didn't care anyway.

For that matter it was strange that he should. Ross Corsen knew Apaches because he had fought them. He had been in charge of the Coyotero trackers at Fort Thomas for four years. And after that, for three years—until the day before yesterday—he had been in charge of the Mescalero Subagency at Pinaleño, thirty miles south of Thomas.

He didn't care. The hell with it. That's what he told himself. Still he kept wondering what had brought Bonito back. He thought: Leave him alone. If he came back to help his people, let him work it out his own Apache way. You tried. But instead he asked carefully, "Why would a warrior of Bonito's stature return now to a reservation? They haven't forgotten what you did. If you're caught, they'll hang you."

"Then I would die—which the people are doing now on the reservation, under Bil-Clin who calls himself their chief." Bonito's eyes half closed and he went on. "Let me tell you a story, Cor-sen, which happened long ago. There was a young man of the Mescalero, who was a great hunter and slayer of his enemies. From raids to Mexico he would return to his rancheria with countless ponies and often with women who would then do his bidding. And many of these he gave to his chief out of honor.

"One day he returned from war gravely wounded and his hands empty, but he noticed that still this chief, who was the son of a chief and he the son of one before him, received more spoils than anyone, yet without endangering himself by being present on the raid. Now this grieved the warrior. He would not offend his chief, but he was beginning to think this unjust.

"On a day after his wound had healed, he was walking in a deep canyon with this in his thoughts and as it grew unbearable he cried out to U-sen why should this be, and immediately a spirit appeared before him. Now, this spirit questioned the warrior, asking him how a man became chief, and the warrior answered that it was blood handed from father to son. And the spirit asked him where in the natural order was this found? Did one lobo wolf lead the pack because of his blood? The warrior thought deeply of this and gradually he realized that chieftainship of blood was not just. It was the place of the bravest warrior to lead—not for his own sake, but for the good of all.

"You know what he did, Cor-sen?" Bonito paused then. "He returned to the rancheria and challenged his chief and fought him to the death with his knife. Two others opposed him, and he killed these also. With this the people realized that it was as it should be and the warrior was acclaimed chief of Mescaleros.

"That was the first time, Cor-sen, but it has happened many times since. When one is no longer deserving to be chief, then another opposes him. Sometimes the opposed chief steps aside; often it is settled with a knife."

Corsen was silent. Then he said, "At Pinaleño Bil-Clin is still a strong chief. And he is wise enough not to lead his people in a war he cannot win."

Bonito's heavy face creased into a grim smile. "Is he strong . . . and wise?" Then he said, his tone changing, "Do you go away from here?"

"Perhaps." Corsen looked at the Apache curiously.

"It would be wise," Bonito said, "if you went far from here." He turned his pony then and loped off.

ROSS CORSEN followed the road to Rindo's and the Mescalero's parting words hung in his mind like a threat, and for a while the words made him angry. The running of their tribe was no concern of his. Not now. But it implied more than just Bonito opposing Bil-Clin. There was something else. Bonito was a renegade. He was vicious even in the eyes of his own people. Not the type to be followed as a leader unless the people were desperate. Unless he came just at the right time. And it occurred to Corsen: like now, with a man they don't know taking over the agency . . . and with unrest on every reservation in Arizona, I'd like to stay, just to handle Bonito. . . . But again, the hell with it. Working under Sellers wasn't worth it.

He planned to go up to Whipple Barracks and talk to someone about a guide contract. He would leave his horse at Rindo's and catch the stage there, and while he was waiting he'd have a while to be with Katie.

★

Chapter Two

THE HATCH & HODGES' Central Mail section had headquarters at Fort McDowell. From there, one route angled northwest to Prescott. The Central Mail swung in an arc southeast. From McDowell the route skirted the Superstitions to Apache Junction, then continued on, changing teams at Florence, White Tanks, Gila Ford, and Rindo's. Thomas was the last stop, the southern terminal.

Rindo's Station had been constructed with the Apaches in mind. An oblong, thick-walled adobe building had an open stable shed at one end. The corral, holding the spare stage teams, connected behind the stable. And circling the station, out fifty-odd yards, was an adobe wall. It was thick, chest high. At the east end of the yard a stand of aspen had been hacked down and only the trunks remained. Beyond the wall the country was flat on three sides—alkali dust and heat waves shimmering over stubbles of desert growth—but to the east the ground rose gradually, barren, pale yellow climbing into deep green where piñon sprouted from the hillside.

Corsen had skirted the base of the hill and now he was in sight of Rindo's. He nudged his mount to a trot.

Someone was in the doorway. Another figure came from the dark line of the shed and moved to the gate which was in the north side of the wall. He could make out the man in the doorway now—Billy Teachout, the station agent. And as the gate swung open there was the Mexican, Delgado, in white peon clothes.

"Hiiiii, man!"

"Señor Delgado, keeper of the horses!"

Corsen reached down and slapped the old Mexican's thin shoulder, then dismounted.

"God of my life, it has been months!"

"Three or four weeks."

"It seems months."

Corsen grinned at the old man, at the tired eyes that were now stretched open showing thin lines of veins, smiling at the sight of a friend.

Billy Teachout moved a few steps into the yard, thumbs hooked behind his suspender straps. "Ross, get in here out of the sun!"

"Let the keeper of the horses take yours," Delgado said, still smiling. "We will talk together after."

Corsen followed the station agent's broad back into the house and opened his eyes wide to the interior dimness. It was dark after the sun glare. He pushed his hat brim from his eyes and stood looking at the familiar whitewashed walls, the oblong pine table, and Douglas chairs at one end of the room, the squat stove in the middle, and the red-painted pine bar at the other end. Billy Teachout edged his large frame sideways, with an effort, through the narrow bar opening.

"You wouldn't have beer," Corsen said.

"It's about six months to Christmas," Billy answered, and leaned his forearms onto the bar. He was in no hurry. Time meant little, and it showed in his loose, heavy build, in his round, clean-shaven face that he most always kept out of the sun's reach unless it was stage time. He had worked in the Prescott office until Al Rindo's death two years before, then had been transferred here. Al Rindo had died of a heart attack, but Billy Teachout said it was sunstroke and he'd be damned if he'd let it happen to him. He had Katie to think of, his sister's girl who had come to live with him after her folks passed on.

It wasn't a bad life. Five stages a week for him and Katie; Delgado and his wife to take care of. Change horses; keep them curried; feed the passengers. Nothing to it—as long as the Apaches minded.

"You can have yellow mescal or bar whiskey," Billy said.

"One's as bad as the other." Corsen put his elbows on the bar. "Whiskey."

"Kill any bugs you got."

Corsen took a drink and then rolled a cigarette. "Where's Katie?"

"Prettyin'. She saw you two miles away. After Delgado all week, you don't look so bad."

☆   ☆   ☆

CORSEN GRINNED, relaxing the hard line of his jaw. A young face, leathery and immobile until a smile would soften the eyes that were used to sun glare, and ease the set face that talked eye to eye with the Apache and showed nothing. Corsen knew his business. He knew the Apache—his language, often even his thoughts—and the Apache respected him for it. Corsen, the Indian agent. He could make natural-born raiders at least half satisfied with a barren government land tract. The Corsens were few and far between, even in Arizona.

"Billy, I just saw Bonito."

"God—he's returned to the reservation?"

"I don't know—or much care. I'm leaving."

"What?"

"Sellers fired me day before yesterday. He's got somebody else for the job."

"Got somebody else! Those are Mescaleros!"

"I'm through arguing with him. Sellers is reservation supervisor. He can run things how he likes and hire who he likes. I should have quit long ago."

"Who's taking your place?"

"A man named Verbiest."

"Somebody looking for some extra change."

"He might be all right."

Billy Teachout shook his head wearily. To him it was another example of cheap politics, knowing the right people. Agency posts were being handed out to men who cared nothing for the Indians. There was profit to be made by short-rationing their charges and selling the government beef and grain to homesteaders, or back to the Army. Even that had been done.

"Sellers has been trying to get rid of you for a long time. Finally he made it," Billy Teachout said. He shook his head again. "Your Mescaleros aren't going to take kindly to this."

"Verbiest might know what he's doing," Corsen said. Then, "But if he doesn't, you better keep your windows shut till he hangs a few of them and they calm down again."

"Where you going? I might just close up and go with you."

"What about the stage line?"

"The hell with it. I'm getting too old for this kind of thing."

Corsen smiled. "I'm going up to Whipple to see about a guide contract."

"So if you can't nurse them, you fight them."

"Either one's a living."

"Ross—"

He turned to see Katie standing in the doorway that led to the kitchen. His gaze rested on her face—tanned, freckled, clear-eyed, a face that smiled often, but now held on his earnestly.

"Ross, I heard what you were telling Billy."

"I can't work for that man anymore."

"Can't you find something else around here?"

"There isn't anything."

"Fort Thomas. Why can't you guide out of there?"

Corsen shrugged. "There's a chance, but I'd still have to go through the department commander's office at Whipple."

"Ross . . ." Her voice was a whisper.

It showed on her face that was not eager now and seemed even pale beneath the sun coloring. The face of a girl, sensitive nose and mouth, but in her clear, blue, serious eyes the awareness of a woman.

Katie was nineteen. She had known Ross Corsen for almost three years, meeting him the day after she had arrived to live with her uncle. And she expected to marry him, even though he never mentioned it. She knew how he felt. Ross didn't have to say a word. It was in the way he looked at her, in the way he had kissed her for the first time only a few weeks ago—a small, soft, lingering, inexperienced kiss. She loved Corsen; very simply she loved him, because he was a man, respected as a man, and because he was a boy at the same time. Perhaps just as she was girl and woman in one.

"Are you coming back?"

"Of course I am."

"What if you're stationed somewhere far away?"

"I'll come and get you," he answered.

Billy Teachout looked at them, from one to the other. "Maybe I've been inside too much." To the girl he said, "Has he behaved himself?"

"Billy," Corsen said, "I was going to ask you. This is all of a sudden—" Then, to Katie, "I'm taking the stage." He smiled faintly. "If I leave my horse here, I've got to come back."

✯ ✯ ✯

"THE STAGE!" Delgado was in the doorway momentarily. The screen door banged and he was gone.

It came in from the east, a thin sand trail, a shadow leading the dust that rose furiously into a billowing tail.

Delgado was swinging out with the grayed wooden gate. Then the stage, rumbling in an arc toward the opening, and the hoarse-throated voice of Ernie Ball, the driver.

"Delgadooo!"

The little Mexican was in front of the lead horses now, reaching for reins close to the bit rings.

"Delgado, you half-a-man! Hold 'em, *chico!*"

Ernie Ball was off the box, grinning, wiping the back of a gnarled hand over his mouth, smoothing the waxed tips of his full mustache. His palm slapped the thin wood of the coach door, then swung it open to bang on its hinges.

"Rindo's Station!"

Billy Teachout came out carrying a paintbrush and a bucket half full of axle grease. Ross and Katie were already outside.

"You're late," Billy told the driver.

Ernie Ball pulled a dull gold watch from his vest pocket. "Seven minutes! That's the earliest I've been late." He replaced the watch and dipped a thumb and forefinger daintily into the grease bucket, then twirled the tips of his mustache between the fingers.

"Ross, how are you? Katie, honey." He touched his hat brim to the girl.

Ross Corsen was looking past the stage driver to the man coming out of the coach—the familiar black broadcloth suit and flat-crowned hat. The man reached the ground and there it was, the bland expression, the carefully trimmed mustache. He carried a leather business case tightly and carefully under his arm.

W. F. Sellers. Field supervisor. Southwest Area. Bureau of Indian Affairs.

"Fifteen minutes," Ernie Ball was saying, "for those going on. Time enough for a drink if the innkeeper's feelin' right. Hey, Billy!" His voice changed as he turned to Sellers. "End of the line for you and your friend."

Another man was out of the coach. He stepped down uncertainly and moved next to Sellers. Two others came down, squinting at the glare— thin-lipped, sun-darkened men in range clothes. They stretched and looked about idly, then moved beyond the back of the stage, walking the stiffness from their legs.

Sellers had not taken his eyes from Corsen.

"I thought you might have had the politeness of staying to meet your successor."

Corsen looked at the other man now. "Mr. Verbiest," he said, "I hope you know what you're doing."

"I've instructed Mr. Verbiest on how the agency should be run," Sellers said.

"Then you both ought to make a nice profit," Billy Teachout said mildly.

Sellers stared at him narrowly. "All we want from you is a couple of horses."

"What for?"

"None of your damn business."

Verbiest said, smiling, "We're riding north to the San Carlos Agency. I'd like to take a look at how a smooth-running reservation operates."

"Sellers'll learn you without riding way up there," Ernie Ball said. "All you need is some spare weights to heavy your scale for when you're passing out the 'Paches their beef." Ernie laughed and looked at Teachout. "Hey, Billy?"

"You're insinuating something that could get you into a great deal of trouble in court," Sellers told the stage driver.

"Insinuatin'!"

Sellers turned on Billy Teachout. "I said two horses. Good ones!"

"I'm not the stable hand. Wait for Delgado or get them yourself."

Sellers's face showed no reaction. But he said quietly, "Mr. Teach-out, you're through here—as of the next time I get to Prescott."

The station agent shrugged. "While I'm waiting, I'll go inside and pour drinks for those that wants."

Corsen relaxed, exhaling slowly, and watched them all go inside. It was a relief not to have to put up with Sellers anymore. Just seeing him had made his stomach tighten. He glanced at Katie.

"This is a poor way to say good-bye."

"For how long, Ross?"

"Maybe a few months."

The screen door slammed. Corsen remembered the two men in range clothes then. They must have just gone in. Then he was looking at Katie, at the expression changing on her face, eyes alive, looking at something behind him. He turned sharply.

Standing a few feet away was one of the men in range clothes. He stood with his legs spread, as if bracing himself, a short man in faded Levi's, holding a pistol dead on Corsen's stomach.

★

Chapter Three

"RAISE YOUR HANDS up." He motioned with the pistol. "You too, honey." He came forward slowly.

"I'm not armed," Corsen said.

"Take your coat off and drop it."

Corsen took off the worn buckskin and let it fall. He backed up as the man motioned with the pistol, then watched him trample on the coat to make certain there was no gun in it.

"Inside now," the man said.

His partner stood one legged, his left boot on a chair, leaning slightly, elbow on knee, hand holding the pistol idly.

Billy Teachout was behind the bar. Ernie Ball, Sellers, and Verbiest stood in front of it, all with their arms raised. Three pistols were on the floor, along with the business case Sellers had been carrying. Ygenia, Delgado's wife, stood in the kitchen doorway, unable to move.

The one on the chair waved Ross and Katie toward the others. They moved across the room and stood by the front window. "Buz," he said then, "round up that Mexican. He's outside somewhere."

Ernie Ball was squinting at the gunman. "Your face is starting to ring a bell, but your name don't register."

"How would you know my name?"

"You entered Ed Fisher in the book when you paid your fare at Thomas."

The gunman shrugged. "That'll do. . . . What're you carrying this trip?"

"Mail."

"That all?"

"Swear to God. It's on the rack if you want to look."

The one called Buz came in through the kitchen, pushing past the Mexican woman.

"He ain't in sight. Not anywhere."

Corsen glanced out at the yard. Just the stage was there. The horses had been taken away, but the change team had not yet been harnessed.

"That's all right," Fisher said. "Hand me your gun and go through their pockets. We got to move."

He watched Buz search them, stuffing bills and coins into his pockets as he went along. "About how much?" he asked when he had finished.

"Not more than a hundred and fifty."

"What about that satchel there?" He pointed to the business case on the floor.

INSTANTLY SELLERS said, "Those are government papers!" More calmly he said, "Bureau statistics."

Ed Fisher said, "Buz, open it up."

The gunman lifted the case and looked at Fisher with surprise. "If there's writin' in here, it's cut on stone." He carried it to the table and unfastened the straps and opened it. He brought out something folded in newspaper and unwrapped it carefully. A leather pouch. He pulled the thongs quickly, eagerly, and dumped the pouch upside-down on the table. The coins came out in a shower.

"Ed! Mint silver!"

Fisher was grinning at Sellers. "How much, Buz?"

"Four, five, six pouches . . . about two thousand!"

Corsen was looking out of the window. There was something, a movement high up on the slope. Then, hearing Buz, he glanced quickly at Sellers. That was it, plain enough. Sellers didn't make that kind of money with a Bureau job. It could only come from selling Indian rations. But now, as the others watched Buz at the table, Corsen's eyes narrowed, looking out into the glare again, and now he could make out the movement. Far out, coming down from the slope, reaching the flat stretch now, were tiny specks, dots against the sand glare that he knew were riders. They were coming from where he had seen Bonito that morning, and suddenly, abruptly, Corsen realized who the riders were.

Ed Fisher was saying, "Get two horses and run off the others. One's saddled already." He looked at the men in front of him. "Whose mount is that in the shed, the chestnut?"

Corsen looked from the window as the screen door slammed behind Buz going out. "The chestnut's mine," he said.

"Thanks for the use."

"You're not going anywhere."

Fisher looked at him quickly, then smiled, his eyes going to Katie. "If you want to play Mister Brave for your girl, wait for when I got more time."

"It's not me that's stopping you," Corsen said, "but I'll tell you again—you're not going anywhere."

"You can talk plainer than that."

"All right. Call to your partner."

"What'll that prove?"

"Just see if he's still there."

Fisher, yelled, "Hey—Buz!"

There was a silence, then boot scuffing and Buz was at the door. "What?"

Fisher looked at Corsen, then back to Buz. "Nothing. Hurry up."

Buz looked at him queerly and moved off again.

"Now what?" Fisher said.

"It'll come," Corsen said. "He hasn't seen them yet."

"Seen who?"

And there it was, as if answering his question—the sound of running, boots on packed sand. Buz's voice yelling, hoarse with panic. Then he was at the door, stumbling against it. "'Paches!"

☆ ☆ ☆

"STAY WHERE YOU ARE!" Fisher held his pistol on the men at the bar and backed toward the door. He glanced out. "How many?"

"Six of them! Let me in!"

"Keep watching!"

Through the window Corsen could now see the cluster of riders plainly, walking their ponies. They were in no hurry—not six, but five, coming across the flat stretch.

"They're peaceful." It was Sellers who said this. "There hasn't been a war party around here in over a year."

Corsen looked at him. "They're twenty miles off the reservation."

"They've been known to wander, but when they do, they have to be taught a lesson. That was your trouble, Corsen—too easy on them. Verbiest, you come along with me and see how it's done."

Corsen said quietly, "Bonito doesn't learn very fast."

"Bonito?" Sellers showed surprise. "He's down in the Madres."

"He wasn't this morning when I talked to him."

"And you're just now telling me?"

"I was fired."

Fisher glanced out the door again, then back, his eyes stopping on Sellers. "Have you got something to do with them?"

Sellers did not answer, but Teachout said, "He's with the Bureau of Indian Affairs."

"Then this is your party, mister," Fisher said, looking at Sellers.

"I'm not obligated to confront known hostiles. That's common sense."

Fisher moved out of the doorway. "You don't have a choice. Get out there and find out what they want." He waved the long-barreled pistol. "Come on, all of you except the women. They stay here."

In the yard Corsen glanced back once at the two outlaws in the doorway. Then they had reached the adobe wall and his gaze swung back to the five Mescaleros who had reined in a hundred paces beyond the wall.

Bonito was a pony's length ahead of the others. He did not resemble the man Corsen had talked to earlier. The flop-brimmed hat was gone and now his coarse face was paint-streaked—a line of ochre from ear to ear crossing the bridge of his nose, another over his chin. His headband was yellow, bright against long hair glistening with oil. Only one thing about him was the same—the Maynard across his lap.

Behind him were Bil-Clin, chief at the Pinaleño Agency, Bil-Clin's son, Sunshine, and two other Indians. All four were armed with old-model carbines.

Corsen's eyes remained on the Mescaleros, but he said to Sellers, "Let's see you go out and teach them a lesson."

Sellers did not reply at first. He kept his eyes on the five Apaches, waiting, expecting them to make a move. Then he said, "All right. Ask him what he wants."

Corsen hesitated. He wanted to make it hard for Sellers, not offer any assistance, but there was Katie and the others to think of. He boosted himself over the wall, then motioned to the Apaches to come on.

They moved forward, Bonito still in the lead, and when they were less than ten feet from the wall Bonito raised his arm and they stopped there. "Cor-sen, we speak to each other again."

"But this time not by accident."

"You told me before that you were not with this one now." Bonito's eyes shifted to Sellers.

"These are not ordinary circumstances," Corsen answered. "Tell me why you are here and I'll relate it to him."

Bonito waited, then nodded toward Sellers. "There is the reason."

"What would you have me tell him?"

"Tell him that he will come with us, until *pesh-e-gar*—many of them—are brought here tomorrow."

"Rifles!"

"Enough for as many of us that could stand in line from here to the house there. And many bullets for the *pesh-e-gar*. This one"—he nodded again to Sellers—"will remain with us until they are brought and the ones who bring them depart again. Then he will be released and my people will go with me from Pinaleño across the Bravos and there we will fight the *Nakai-yes*."

Corsen turned to the others. "He says he needs guns to make war on the Mexicans." Then to Bonito. "You would, of course, not use the guns on this side of the Bravos."

Bonito nodded solemnly.

"The guns would have to be acquired at Fort Thomas. How do you know the Army would let you have them? Perhaps this man isn't worth a hundred rifles."

Bonito's face barely moved as he spoke. "Killing this one would be a reward in itself."

Corsen paused. "What if he refuses to go with you?"

"At Pinaleño you would find only the women and the children." He turned his head, indicating the dense pines of the higher slope. "The warriors are here, Cor-sen. You are six. Then two men in the house and two women. If he does not come with us, then we will come into your house there—"

Corsen concealed his surprise. "You observe our number well."

Bonito said, "I have been here longer than a full day, waiting for this time. And you see I did not count the Mexican man. He has agreed to remain with us until this one comes to take his place."

Corsen glanced at Billy Teachout. "He says they've got Delgado."

"Oh-my-God—"

Sellers moved closer to Corsen.

"What else does he want?"

"He wants you."

"Me!"

"We get you back in exchange for about a hundred rifles," Corsen added. "I don't know what makes him think you're worth that many."

"Tell him," Sellers said evenly, "that if he doesn't get back to Pinaleño by sundown he'll be shot. Along with Bil-Clin and his boy."

"Pinaleño has moved here," Corsen answered. "The braves are up in the pines. If you don't go with them they'll swarm down all over us."

"They wouldn't get across the wall," Sellers sneered. "There aren't a dozen rifles among the pack of them."

"You forgot, we don't have any."

Sellers was silent. Then, "All right. When the stage doesn't arrive at Gila Ford this evening they'll know something's wrong and send help."

Corsen said, "There are three men at the Gila Ford Station."

"Then they'll get more help!" Sellers said angrily.

"In what—three or four days?"

"What's the matter?" Sellers taunted. "You scared?"

Corsen ignored the remark. "What about Delgado?"

Sellers shrugged. "One thing at a time. Tell him we'll go back and think it over, and let him know."

Corsen told him, and as they were turning to go he looked at Bil-Clin. "Now the chief of the Mescaleros follows the words of a bandit."

Bil-Clin shifted his eyes and did not reply.

Chapter Four

KATIE CAME OUT from the kitchen, edging by Buz, who was in the doorway, and went to Corsen. She had served them food and had now finished washing the dishes. Corsen was at the front window, looking off to the east, watching for a movement to change the monotony of the plain.

She stood close to him and he asked in a low voice, "How's Ygenia?"

"She's praying."

He wanted to say something consoling that she could take to Ygenia, but there was nothing. The Apaches had Delgado. They would keep him until Sellers turned himself over to them. And that was not likely to happen.

KATIE'S FACE was close to his. Serious, searching eyes repeating the question he could not answer. She had been in the kitchen most of the time and she did not know all that had happened since the men had returned. Fisher was in the doorway, a silhouette against the faint outside dusk. Buz was by the kitchen door, holding his gun on the others at the bar end of the room, keeping an eye on Billy Teachout, who was in the kitchen watching the corral and yard.

"Ross, why doesn't he force Sellers to go to the Indians?"

"Fisher would have to shoot him first," Ross said quietly. "This business about the rifles is the long chance. Bonito would like to have them, but I think he'd just as soon have Sellers—for one long day. Sellers knows it. You can't force him to go. No matter what he's stolen, he's a white man. Handing him to Bonito wouldn't be right."

"How long will he wait, Ross?"

"Bonito? He'll send us a message tonight, most likely. And if we don't act on it he'll come at sunup."

"The outlaw would have to give you guns then," Katie said.

Corsen nodded. "He's holding off as long as he can, waiting for a miracle. I feel kind of sorry for him. He can't fight off Bonito with just one man, but if he gives us guns he's through. He loses either way."

They were silent then, standing close to each other.

Corsen's gaze would come in from the dim plain and go about the room.

Fisher, in the doorway, glanced now and then at Sellers. You have to give him credit, Corsen thought. Sitting on the edge of his nerves until the last possible minute.

Buz looks hard, but he leans on Fisher. He could never do this alone. They thought they had something good, and it turns out to be the worst jackpot they could fall into. Let them stew in it.

Billy and Ernie are men who know patience because they do more than just live here: they're part of the country. They'll sit through something like this and not show it.

Verbiest is afraid to open his mouth. His voice would give him away. He's so scared, he can taste it.

And Sellers. He'll never believe he's through—and maybe he isn't. He's got his life at stake, plus a government post and two thousand dollars in government silver. The money must have come from selling agency stores. He'll scheme, confident that he'll think of something to pull him out of this.

Bonito has nothing to lose. With a hundred warriors, and nothing to lose, he will probably win.

Strips of gray light crossed the room from the doorway and the windows. Outside, the moonlight showed the station yard in dim, unmoving stillness, bounded by the adobe wall, a pale line against the darkness beyond. Corsen looked out of the window again, then moved toward Fisher. He saw the dull gleam of a pistol barrel bear on him and he said, "Ed. A word with you."

"Come ahead," Fisher said quietly.

"It'll be dark in a few minutes," Corsen said. "You'd better give us our guns."

"I'll take my chances for a while."

"You won't be able to watch us in the dark—and you're not going to use a lamp with Bonito outside."

Fisher was silent. Then, "I'm trying to think it out," he said wearily.

"You don't have a choice," Corsen told him. "Those are Mescaleros. You're old enough to know how they behave when they're up."

"No, I don't. Not the way I know what would happen if you people had guns. Buz and I would turn our backs once—"

"All right," Corsen said. "Then give back all the money you took."

"Tell them I was just kiddin', eh?"

"I'm thinking about two women being here," Corsen said, "and a hundred Mescaleros out there. Make up your mind one way or the other—but do it before it's too late."

☆ ☆ ☆

THE SOUND CAME to them gradually. It came faintly, growing out of the darkness, at first a muffled sound, now the unmistakable clop of a horse moving at a slow walk. A chair scraped in the room. Fisher's voice rasped, "Quiet!"

In the stillness Fisher cocked his head, listening, then whispered close to Corsen's cheek, "It's stopped."

Corsen waited. "At the gate," he said.

"It's a trick." Fisher was talking to himself. "A damn Apache trick."

"Maybe it is." Corsen paused. "And maybe it isn't, Ed," he said quietly. "If I was to go out there, would you hold your gun that way?"

"You're crazy."

"Let's find out." Corsen pushed through the screen door without a sound and was moving across the yard. He walked unhurriedly, because if Bonito was behind the wall, running would not make a difference; the yard was open, and gray with moonlight. He reached the gate and stood with his hand on the heavy latch.

Fisher watched him tensely. He felt someone close to him and glanced to see the girl. Billy Teachout was behind her. They looked at Fisher, then out toward the gate, and they did not speak.

In the darkness someone said, "What is it?" excitedly.

At a window Ernie Ball's voice hissed. "Shhhhh!"

They watched Corsen lift the iron latch. Then the shadowy figure pushed against the gate and the squeak of the hinges was a mournful screech with no other sounds in the night. Corsen went through the opening, and for the moment he was out of sight Katie held her breath. Then the gate swung wide and he was there again, leading the larger, darker shadow of a horse. A rider was atop the horse, head down, swaying gently with the movement of the horse's shoulders and flanks. Corsen closed the gate and came on, holding the horse close under the muzzle by a hackamore.

"Who is it?" from inside the doorway.

Fisher was in the yard now. He looked at Corsen, then toward the rider, questioningly.

Corsen went to the rider, raised his arms, and said gently, "Come, *viejo.*" The small figure toppled hesitantly, stiffly, into Corsen's arms.

He heard someone behind him say, "Delgado—"

They carried him inside to a bedroom and eased him down onto the bed. And when the lamp was lighted next to the bed, no one recognized Delgado.

"Mary, Virgin and Mother," Ygenia said, close to Delgado's cheek, kneeling on the floor and stroking her hand gently over his head. When Katie came in with a basin of water, she mopped his face, washing the blood away. She moved the cloth over his eyes very gently and when she took it away she gasped and uttered the name of the Mother of God again.

Delgado's face was knife scarred, small marks crisscrossing his cheeks. His nose was broken, that was evident, and his right eye was no longer in the socket.

His head came off the blanket, then fell back as the thin lines of his face tightened. He said, almost inaudibly, "Ross."

"I'm here," Corsen said close to his cheek. "Don't talk now. Say it in the morning."

Delgado breathed. "Bonito did this to me. There were others who beat at me and stuck me with their knives, but it was Bonito who did this." His hand waved close to his face.

"As I gathered the fresh team, one of them broke away and I went after it afoot because this one was a friend and would come if I approached with gentleness. But this time he went a greater distance. When he was near the piñon he stopped and let me approach, and at that moment the barbarians came from out of the pines. Almost as if this friend had lured me to them—"

Corsen said gently, "Tell this in the morning."

Delgado turned his head, opening his left eye. "If you are here to listen." He waved his hand again. "Bonito did this to me. He impressed upon me that when he comes he will take the remainder of my sight. I would not like that to happen. He said that you had failed him. Now he will enter this house with the coming of the sun. . . ."

Silence then. Corsen rose as Ygenia began to stroke Delgado's head. Fisher appeared in the doorway.

"Your guns are on the table," he said quietly.

Chapter Five

Corsen pushed his gun belt lower on his hips and picked up the Winchester leaning against the support post. He heard the screen door close softly and peered into the darkness around the coach which they had pushed into the stable shed. A figure was moving along the front of the house toward him.

It was Fisher. "There better be two of us out here. The east side of the house is a blind spot. And when the shootin' starts," he added, "I don't hanker to be in the same room with that thievin' government man. He could swing his barrel two feet and let go, easy as not." He looked at Corsen's carbine and holstered pistol. "You had them out here?"

"With the saddle," Corsen said.

"Where's your horse? It was here."

"I took it around to the corral. I'd rather have it run off than hit."

They rolled straw bales from the back wall of the shed to the front and piled them three high for some protection. There were no doors on the stable shed. It was built out from the station house four wagons wide. Ernie's coach was in the first stall nearest the house. Corsen went to the small window at the far end of the shed and Fisher stopped near him, looking out into the night.

"Might they come before dawn?"

"I've never heard of it," Corsen answered. "But don't put that down in your book as a rule. Bonito might have told Delgado dawn to put us off guard."

"That was something, what he did to him."

Corsen said quietly, "Delgado was lucky. Bonito's showing off. He wants us to think he's got full control of the situation. Even to letting a prisoner go, knowing he'll get him back again."

"He could convince me."

"I'm not so sure he has." Corsen paused. "If I could talk to Bil-Clin—I don't see how he could help but resent this renegade's coming up and taking over. If we could get Bil-Clin alone. . . ."

Fisher said nothing.

Sometimes when you wait, the time goes slow, Corsen thought, but now it is going fast, so fast it isn't time anymore, but something else. That was a month ago that I told Katie I would come and get her. And Billy was surprised because he hadn't known what was going on. It seems like a month, but it was yesterday afternoon. Now he pictured himself with Katie at night, her face in soft shadows. She was in the room with Ygenia and Delgado, and a pistol. The door was bolted. If they broke through the door, then she would fire the pistol until it was empty. Then, in a timeless time she would pray. Pray that it would not take long for Ygenia and for herself. She would not use the gun on herself to make it quick.

Even if he had asked her to, she would not. She doesn't even show this. There may be a little of it in her eyes, but it isn't in her voice. You're lucky, Ross. But how can you be lucky and unlucky at the same time?

But now more time had passed and there was an orange streak in the east and the sky was no longer full dark, and suddenly shadows were coming over the wall. Shadows that were the shapes of men, but without sound and without the gleam of weapons. They dropped and clung close to the wall. Now some were coming forward!

"Oh, my God!" Fisher had seen them.

From the house, "They're coming!" and the hurried report of a rifle. A pause, now a staccato of rifle fire and suddenly the station yard erupted into wild sound—whining gun reports and the full-throated scream of the Mescalero war cry and the whinnying of horses.

Down the carbine barrel Corsen squinted at three warriors coming zigzagging toward the shed. Then the outside two were out of vision and he fired. The Mescalero fell in his tracks. As he levered, the other two tuned abruptly and were back to the wall as he aimed again. One of them was on the wall, and he brought the barrel up an inch and squeezed the trigger, and the warrior dropped to the other side. The third one was over, out of sight. And as suddenly as the firing had started, it stopped.

Corsen glanced both ways, surprised. Two, three, four of them were down and the rest had retreated. They're feeling us out, he thought. Seeing how many guns we have.

Fisher exhaled a long sigh. "We drove them off."

"The first time," Corsen said. "Now Bonito knows what we have and he'll scratch his head till something comes out of it."

Fisher looked up suddenly. "There!"

It was the Apache Corsen had hit first, now crawling toward the wall, dragging his left leg. Fisher raised his pistol.

"Hold it!" Corsen squinted hard at the Apache. "That's Bil-Clin's boy!"

Corsen waited until Sunshine reached the wall. Then, as the Apache raised himself slowly, painfully, with his weight on his right leg, Corsen raised the carbine and fired.

The bullet sang, ricocheting off the wall, and white dust spattered above the boy's head as he sank down.

Corsen levered a shell into the breech, his eyes on Sunshine. Watch him. Watch him like a hawk. He's got a broken leg, but he can be over that wall in one jump.

The next moment Sunshine was pushing up with his arms and his one good leg. But it was a feint, for he lunged suddenly to the side. Corsen was ready. He swung the barrel and placed the next shot a foot in front of Sunshine. Pieces of adobe splattered on the Apache's hair, and now he sat down and stared toward the shed.

Corsen said, "Watch along the wall, Ed. I'm going out. You edge toward the house."

Fisher said, "What?"

"If this works," Corsen said hurriedly, "I'll give you a signal. When I do, bring the men out. Just the men!"

Sunshine had not moved, and now Corsen said, "Here we go." He handed the Winchester to Fisher and pushed over the straw bales. Going over them, he drew his pistol and walked out into the open yard with the handgun pointed toward Sunshine. When he was in the middle of the yard he stopped.

"Bil-Clin!"

There was no answer, though he knew they were on the other side of the wall.

He shouted again, "Bil-Clin!" Then he said in Spanish, "My gun is on your son!" His eyes shifted above Sunshine. Stillness. A bare line of adobe—and then Bil-Clin was standing a dozen paces to the left, head and shoulders above the wall. Corsen's eyes went to him.

"Come over the wall."

Bil-Clin's arms came up and he raised himself to the top of the wall and dropped to the inside. He did not look at his son, but approached Corsen.

"Bil-Clin," Corsen said, "call Bonito and the others."

The Apache said a word in Mescalero and suddenly his warriors were at the wall. They had stood up and were now a line of bare chests and war paint and thick blue-black hair with cloth bands over the foreheads. Bonito stood among them, but he was alone. He lifted his Maynard and rested it on the wall.

"Come in, Bonito," Corsen said. And when the renegade did not move he glanced at Bil-Clin, then cocked his pistol. "Order him to come in—if you're still the chief."

Bil-Clin looked at his son now, for the first time. The boy's eyes, between stripes of yellow paint, were on Corsen. Bil-Clin spoke again in Mescalero and it was evident that his words were for Bonito. But Bonito did not answer.

Corsen tightened. He could feel it in his stomach, but he made his voice sound calm. "Bonito, you are now chief?"

Still the Apache said nothing.

"Yesterday you told me that chieftainship of the Mescalero is not a thing of heredity, but a position earned by the one most capable in war. In fighting. So, Bonito, are you chief?"

Bonito did not move. Corsen was looking at him now, but he glanced away momentarily toward Ed Fisher, and nodded to him.

"Let me tell you something, Bonito. There are others who live here now—some with authority that seems to contradict yours. How can you be a chief if you have opposed only this old man, Bil-Clin?"

★   ★   ★

HE GLANCED TOWARD the house and saw them coming out now.

"What about the government man, Bonito? He tells me you are a woman—a filthy pig of a woman with the diseases of animals. Unfit to live. And he has much authority. Perhaps he is the true chief here?"

Bonito's eyes had gone to Sellers as he appeared in the doorway. The eyes held on the man, narrowing, and then Bonito was over the wall.

"How would you have it, Cor-sen?"

"Whatever is customary."

"With the knife, then."

"I'll tell him." Corsen turned to the men in front of the station house. "Sellers, Bonito says you're afraid to fight him alone."

Sellers was startled. "You're crazy!"

"Ask him."

"Fight him with what?"

"Knives."

"Now I know you're crazy."

"You want to convince him you're boss, don't you? Beat him in a fair fight, the way they have to pick their chiefs sometimes."

Fisher moved a step toward Sellers and, as he did so, brought the Winchester up and down in a short motion and Sellers's pistol was out of his hand. He looked at Fisher with complete surprise, watching the outlaw pick up the pistol.

"I'll hold it for you while you're teaching that red son a lesson."

"Corsen! Tell him I won't fight him, that we don't do this in our government."

"Bonito," Corsen translated, "he says he does not have a knife."

BONITO REACHED behind him and drew a dull-gleaming blade from his waistband. His arm swung low. The knife scraped, bouncing over the sand to stop near Sellers.

"Corsen, tell that savage—"

"Listen," Corsen said, "this started because of you and Bonito. So you and he are going to finish it."

"He's fought this way all of his life. I wouldn't have a chance!"

Corsen shrugged. "You can't tell."

Bonito was handed a knife and without hesitating he stepped toward Sellers.

Fisher stooped, picked up the knife at Sellers's feet, and put it in his hand. "If you make it, I'll buy you a drink."

"Wait a minute, Ross!" Sellers backed up. "Ross, tell him I won't do it—"

But Bonito was in front of him now.

The Mescalero lowered his head, hunching his shoulders, and brought the knife up in front of him, looking up at Sellers's face through half-closed eyes.

"Ross!"

The blade flashed, a short swipe of naked arm that was out and in before anyone could see what had happened.

Sellers screamed. His left cheek was slashed from ear to mouth.

"Ross!"

Bonito feinted toward Sellers's head. Going back, Sellers brought

up his arm, but the blade dropped. It flashed low under his guard and
flicked a short arc across the sucked-in stomach. Sellers's vest opened
from pocket to pocket and he screamed again and this time turned and
started to run. But he came up short, pushed, jolted back to face Bonito
by Teachout, who stood behind him.

"You're going the wrong way," Teachout said.

"Let me go!"

Bonito stood waiting.

Corsen's gaze went from him to Sellers. "Are you through?"

Sellers, blood smeared over his face, was breathing hard, holding
his stomach. "Ross." He gasped. "Shoot him! Now, while he's still!"

"Are you quitting?" Corsen said.

"God! Shoot him!"

Corsen said calmly, "Fight him, or else get out."

Sellers looked at him strangely, taken by surprise. "Get out?"

"That's right. Ride out of here and take Verbiest with you. Forget
you ever worked for the Bureau. There are seven people here to testify
you're not fit for the job. Now, either fight him or write yourself off."

Sellers hesitated, fingering the cut across his stomach, his eyes on
Corsen. Then his gaze went slowly to Bonito, who stood unmoving,
watching him. Gradually Sellers's grip loosened around the knife, and
as it dropped from his hand he turned abruptly and walked to the station house. The screen door banged.

"Now," Bonito said coldly, "there is no more doubt."

"It is still in my mind," Corsen said mildly. He lowered the pistol
he'd been holding on Sunshine and turned to Bonito. He added,
pointedly, "I have seen women fight before. Usually it proves nothing."

Bonito's eyes narrowed. "Say your words straight, Cor-sen."

Corsen stopped a stride from the Apache. He raised his hand and
swung the open palm hard against Bonito's face. The Apache was taken
off guard and staggered back, but he did not go down.

"Is that straight enough?"

Corsen looked back at Ed Fisher and swung the pistol underhand
toward him, and as he turned back to Bonito he shifted his feet suddenly and came around with his right fist smashing against the
Apache's face. And this time Bonito went down.

"Maybe that's a little straighter." Then, looking toward Bil-Clin, Corsen said, "Is this your chief?"

Bonito came to one knee. His mouth was half open with numbness, but he smiled and said, "All right. Corsen."

Behind him he heard Fisher say, "Here's the knife." Corsen half turned as if to look at Fisher, but it was a short movement. He pivoted, swinging his left hand, and again caught Bonito on the face as he was rising.

The Apache went down, rolling away from Corsen's reach, but as he came up Corsen was there. He swung a right and then a left to the Apache's head to beat him down again.

Bonito looked up at him, propping himself with his elbows; his face was cut at both eyes and his mouth swollen. And now he considered what to do next—how to fight this man whose not using a weapon was an insult. He brought his knees up under him, then one foot, watching Corsen closely.

Corsen moved a step closer, clenching his fists. Bonito will pull something this time, he thought. Bonito was rising, then suddenly throwing himself at Corsen's legs. Corsen dodged and kicked out, but his boot caught Bonito's shoulder and now the Apache was rolling. Corsen started after him, then stopped dead as Bonito jumped to his feet.

Fisher yelled, "You want it now, Ross?"

Corsen shook his head. This was the way to beat him, if it could be done. He started toward Bonito, thinking: Carry it to him. Once he starts calling the play, you're through. Watch his eyes. They'll tell you a snap second before he moves. He moved close to Bonito, tensed, watching the yellow-filmed eyes, smelling the animal smell of the man, seeing the eyes now and not the face.

Corsen drew his arm back slowly, knotting the fist. He shifted his weight suddenly, swinging the fist—*the eyes*—then just as suddenly threw himself to the side. Bonito's knife jabbed viciously, but Corsen was not there. And as the Apache came around to find him, in that split second Corsen was ready. He went back on his left foot, his body balanced, and then his weight shifted and his boot kicked savagely into Bonito's loins. The Apache gasped and stopped dead in his tracks, bending, holding his stomach.

And that was it. Corsen hit him with one fist, then the other, and as Bonito started to sag he caught the Apache's arm and drove his right fist straight into the paint-streaked face. The Apache went down, dropping the knife, and landed heavily on his back.

"There, Bil-Clin, is your chief," Corsen said. He went over to Sunshine and knelt beside him, examining the shinbone that his bullet had broken.

Bil-Clin was standing next to him now. It was hard for him to speak, even if it was not an outright apology, for he was Mescalero, but he said, "What would you have us do?"

Corsen rose and looked at Bil-Clin. "If you wish, we will get an American doctor for your son. But now go back to Pinaleño and take your dead."

"And you will come, Cor-sen?"

CORSEN'S GAZE went over the line of Apaches at the wall. Immobile faces, streaks of vermilion and bright yellow, and looking at them he was angry. But he thought: These are Mescaleros. You know what they are. You know what they can do. You were lucky today, but don't push your luck, and perhaps because of it make some cavalry patrol officer, who isn't even out here yet, push his. And he nodded slowly, wearily, to Bil-Clin and said, "Yes. I will come."

The others were standing almost in a line. Teachout and Ernie Ball, Ed Fisher and his partner and Verbiest.

Maybe this will straighten Fisher out, Corsen thought. He's a man you'd buy a drink for, even after he's robbed you. Verbiest made a mistake, but he knows it and he won't make it again. . . .

And then he did not think of them anymore. Katie was in the doorway and he walked toward the house.

18

Saint with a Six-Gun

Original Title: The Hanging of Bobby Valdez
Argosy, October 1954

INSIDE THE HOTEL café, Lyall Quinlan sat at the counter having his breakfast. Every once in a while he would look over at Elodie Wells. Elodie had served him, but now her back was to him; she was looking out the big window over the lower part that was green painted and said REGENT CAFÉ in white—looking across the street to the Tularosa jail. Horses and wagons were hitched there and down the street both ways, and behind the jailhouse in the big yard where everybody was now, that's where they were hanging Bobby Valdez.

Out on the street there wasn't a sound. Inside now, just the noise of Lyall Quinlan's palm popping the bottom of the ketchup bottle until it flowed out over his eggs. Elodie scowled at him as if she was trying to hear something and Lyall was interrupting the best part. Lyall just smiled at her, a young-kid smile, and began eating his eggs. Elodie, like about everybody in Tularosa, had been excited all week long waiting for this day to come—a whole week while Bobby Valdez sat in his cell with Lyall Quinlan guarding him. Elodie was mad because she had to work this morning. Lyall felt pretty good, so he just went on eating his eggs. . . .

☆ ☆ ☆

BOHANNON, THE Tularosa marshal, brought in Bobby Valdez Thursday afternoon and right away sent a man to Las Cruces to fetch Judge Metairie. Bohannon didn't have a doubt Valdez would not be bound over for trial, and he was right. Friday morning a coroner's jury decided that one Roberto Eladio Viscarra y Valdez did willfully commit murder—judging from the size hole in the forehead of one Harley Tanner (deceased) and the .41-caliber Colt gun found on the accused when he was apprehended the next day. A witness testified that he saw Bobby Valdez pull this same Colt and let go at Tanner in a fashion that in no way resembled self-defense.

Everybody agreed it was about time a smart-aleck gunman like Bobby Valdez was brought to justice and made to pay the penalty. The only ones who'd cry would be some of the girls who couldn't see his handgun for his brown eyes. It was a shame he had to hang, being only twenty-two, but that's what would happen. He didn't have to be bad.

Saturday morning, Criminal Sessions Court, the Honorable Benson Metairie presiding, was called to order in the lobby of the Regent Hotel. The courthouse at Las Cruces would have been better, but that meant transporting Bobby Valdez almost a hundred miles. A year ago he'd gotten away when they were taking him there from Mesilla, and Mesilla was like just across the field.

VALDEZ WAIVED counsel, though there wasn't an attorney in Tularosa to defend him if he'd wanted one. Judge Metairie said it was just as well. Since the case was cut and dried, why waste time with a lot of litigating?

The court called up a witness who swore he'd seen Bobby Valdez plain as day come out of the Regent Café that Wednesday evening, which established the accused's presence in town the night of the shooting.

The star witness took the stand and said he was crossing the street to have a word with his friend Harley Tanner, who was standing right in front of this hotel, when Bobby Valdez came out of the shadows of the adobe building, called Tanner a dirty name, and, when Tanner came around, pulled his gun and shot him. Then Valdez lit out.

Bohannon suggested stepping outside to reenact the crime, but Judge Metairie said everybody knew what the front of the Regent Hotel looked like and the fierce sun this time of day wasn't going to make it any plainer. "Just close your eyes, Ed, and make a picture," the judge told Bohannon.

It was stated that the next morning Bohannon's posse followed Valdez's sign till they caught up with him about noon near the Mescalero reservation line. Valdez's horse had lamed and left Bobby out in the open, as Bohannon said, "with his pants down, so to speak."

Judge Metairie called a man who was referred to as a character witness and this man described seeing Bobby Valdez shoot two men during the White Sands bank holdup last Christmastime. Another character witness was on the Butterfield stage that was held up last June between Lordsburg and Continental. Surer'n hell it was Bobby Valdez who'd opened the door with that .41 Colt gun in his hand, and no polka-dot bandanna over his nose was going to argue it wasn't. Two more men sat down on the Douglas-chair witness stand with like stories.

Judge Metairie looked at his watch and asked what time was the stage back to Las Cruces, and when somebody told him not till three o'clock, he said that they might as well adjourn for dinner then and let the jury reach their verdict over a nice meal—though he didn't see where they'd have much thinking to do.

Court reconvened at one-thirty. The jury foreman stood up, waited for the talking to die, then said how they allowed Bobby Valdez sure couldn't be anything else but guilty.

Judge Metairie nodded, gaveled the register desk to restore order, waited until the quiet could be felt, then in the voice of doom sentenced Roberto Eladio Viscarra y Valdez, on the morning one week from this day, to be hanged by the neck until dead.

Criminal Sessions Court was closed and most people felt Judge Metairie had turned in a better-than-usual performance.

Saturday evening Lyall Quinlan went on duty at the Tularosa Jail.

It came about because Bohannon was scheduled to play poker and Quinlan arrived just at the right time. He came looking for the job; still, he was taken by surprise when Bohannon offered it to him, "temporarily, you understand," because he'd been turned down so many times before. Lyall Quinlan wanted to be a lawman, but Bohannon always put him off with the excuse that he already had an assistant, Barney Groom, and Barney served the purpose even if he was an old man.

But Bohannon was thinking maybe an extra night man ought to be on with Valdez upstairs, a man to sit up there and watch him. He was supposed to play cards tonight, which disallowed him. Then, lo and behold, there was young Lyall Quinlan coming in the door!

"Lyall, you musta heard me wishin' for you." Then, seeing the astonishment come over the boy's face—a thin face with big, self-conscious eyes—he thought: Hell, Lyall's all right. Even if he doesn't pack much weight, he's honest. And he rode in the posse that brought in Valdez. An eager boy like him'd make a good deputy! For what he considered would be a temporary period, Bohannon convinced himself that Quinlan would do just fine. Tomorrow he could always kick him the hell out. . . .

"Barney, give Lyall here a scattergun and tell him what to do," and Bohannon was gone.

Lyall Quinlan sat up all night watching Bobby Valdez. That is, most of the time he sat in the cane-bottom chair—it was in the hallway facing the one cell they had upstairs—he was keeping his eyes on Valdez, who hardly paid him any attention. Whenever Lyall would start to get sleepy, he'd get up, crook the sawed-off scattergun under his arm, and pace up and down in the short hallway.

The first time he did it, Bobby Valdez, who was lying on his back with his eyes closed, opened them, turned his head enough to see Lyall, and told him to shut up. It was his boots making the noise. But Lyall went right on walking up and down. Valdez called on one of the men saints then and asked him why did all keepers of jails wear squeaky boots? The lamp hanging out in the hall didn't seem to bother him, only Lyall's boots.

When Lyall kept on walking, the Mexican said something else, half smiling—a low-voiced string of soft-spoken Spanish.

Lyall edged closer to the cell and said through the heavy iron bars, "Hush up!"

Valdez went to sleep right after that and Lyall sat in the chair again, feeling pretty good, not so tense anymore.

Let him try something, Lyall thought, watching the sleeping Mexican, feeling the shotgun across his lap. I'd blast him before he got through the door. He practice-swung the gun around. Cut him right in half. Boy, it was heavy. Only about fifteen inches of barrel left and really heavy. Imagine what that'd do to a man!

He kept watching the sleeping man, his eyes going from the high black boots to the lavender shirt and the dark face, the composed, soft-featured dark face.

How can he sleep? Next Saturday he's going to swing from the end of a rope and he's laying there sleeping. Well, some people are built different. If he wasn't different he wouldn't be in that cell. But he ain't more'n a year older than I am. How could he have already done so much in his life? And killed the men he has? Two at White Sands, one in Mesilla. Tanner. Lyall's thumb went over the tips of his fingers. That's four. Then two more way over to Pima County. At least six, though some claim nine and ten. And Elodie thrilled to death because she served him his dinner the night he shot Tanner. They say he was something with the girls—which about proves that they don't use their heads for much more than a place to grow hair.

Well, he just better not try to come out of that cell. About a minute later Lyall went over and jiggled the door to make sure it was still locked.

Barney Groom came up when it was daylight, and seeing Lyall just sitting there he blinked like he couldn't believe what his eyes told him. "You awake?"

Lyall rose. "Of course."

"Son, you mean you've been awake all night?"

"I thought I was hired to watch this prisoner."

Old Barney Groom shook his head.

"What's the matter?"

"Nothin'," Barney said. Then, "Bohannon's downstairs."

Lyall said, "He want to see me?"

"When you go out he won't be able to help it," said Barney.

"Well, and when should I come back?"

"I ain't the timekeeper. Ask Bohannon about that."

They heard footsteps on the stairs and then Bohannon was in the hallway, yawning, scratching his shirtfront.

Barney Groom said, "Ed, this boy stayed awake all night!"

Bohannon stopped scratching, though he didn't drop his hand. He looked at Lyall Quinlan, who nodded and said, "Mr. Bohannon."

The marshal squinted in the dim light. It was plain he'd been drinking, the way his eyes looked filmy, though he stood there with his feet planted and didn't sway a bit. Finally he said, "You don't say!"

"All night," Barney Groom said.

Bohannon looked at him. "How would you know?"

"He was awake when I come up."

Bohannon said nothing.

"Mr. Bohannon," Lyall said, "I didn't go to sleep."

"Maybe you did and maybe you did not."

Bobby Valdez had been watching them. Now he swung his legs off the bunk. He stood up and moved toward the bars. "He's telling the truth," the Mexican said.

Bohannon put his cold eyes on Valdez for a moment, then looked back at Lyall Quinlan.

Valdez shrugged. "It don't make any difference to me," he said. "But make him grease his boots if he's going to walk all night."

Barney Groom moved a step toward the cell as if threatening Valdez. "You got any more requests?"

"Yes," the Mexican said right away. "I want to go to church."

"What?" Barney Groom said, then was embarrassed for having looked like he'd taken the Mexican seriously, and added, "Sure. I'll send the carriage around."

Valdez looked at him without expression. "This is Sunday."

Bohannon was squinting and half smiling. "Any special denomination, Brother Valdez?"

"Listen, man," Valdez said, "this is Sunday, and I have to go to mass."

Bohannon asked, "You go to mass every Sunday?"

"I've missed some."

Bohannon, with the half smile, went on studying him. Then he said, "Tell you what. We'll douse you with a bucket of holy water instead."

Bohannon and Groom left right after that. Lyall was to stay until one or the other came back from breakfast.

When he was alone again, Lyall looked at Valdez sitting on the bunk. Even after the words were ready he waited a good ten minutes before saying them. "The nearest church is down to White Sands," he told Valdez. "You can't blame the marshal for not wanting to ride you all the way down there."

Valdez looked up.

"It's so far," Lyall Quinlan said. He looked toward the window at the end of the hallway, then back to Valdez. "I appreciate you telling the marshal I was awake all night. I think something like that sets pretty good with him."

Bobby Valdez looked at Lyall curiously. Then his expression softened to a smile, as if he'd suddenly become aware of a new interest, and he said, "Anytime, friend."

When Bohannon came back he sent Lyall across the street to the Regent to get Valdez's breakfast. After he'd given the tray to Valdez, Bohannon deputized him, but mentioned how it was a temporary appointment until the Citizens Committee passed on it. "Now, if you was to keep an extra-special eye on Brother Valdez, I'd have to recommend you as fit, wouldn't I?" He patted Lyall's shoulder and said now was as good a time as any to start the new appointment. "We'll see how you handle yourself alone."

Lyall thought it was a funny way to do things, but he'd have plenty of time for sleep later on. When opportunity knocks on the door you got to open it, he told himself. So he stayed on at the jail, sitting downstairs this time, until midafternoon when Bohannon came back.

"Now get yourself some shut-eye, boy," the marshal told him "so you'll be in fit shape for tonight."

Lyall's mother told him they were making a fool out of him, but Lyall didn't have time to argue. He just said this was what he always wanted to do—a hell of a lot better than working behind a store counter, though he didn't use quite those words. Lyall's mother used mother arguments, but finally there was nothing she could do but shake her head and let him go to bed.

HE WENT BACK on duty at nine, sitting in the cane-bottom chair, not hearing a sound from Barney Groom downstairs. Bobby Valdez was more talkative. He talked about horses and girls and the terrible fact that he hadn't gotten to church that day; then made a big to-do admiring Lyall for the way he could go so long without sleep. That was fine.

But pretty soon Bobby Valdez went to sleep and that night Lyall walked up and down the little hallway even more than he had the first night. Two or three times he almost went to sleep, but he kept moving and blinking his eyes. He found a way of propping the shotgun between his leg and the chair arm, so that the trigger guard dug into his thigh and that kept him awake whenever he sat down to rest.

In the morning Bohannon came up the stairs quietly, but Lyall heard him and said, "Hi, Mr. Bohannon," when the marshal tiptoed in.

Lyall slept all day Monday and after that he was all right, not having any trouble keeping awake that night. Bobby Valdez talked to him until late and that helped.

Tuesday he ate his supper at the Regent Café before going to work. He mentioned weather to Elodie and how the food was getting better, but didn't once refer to the silver deputy star on his shirtfront. Elodie tried to be unconcerned, too, but finally she just had to ask him, and Lyall answered, "Why, sure, Elodie, I've been a deputy marshal since last Saturday. Didn't you know that?"

Elodie had to describe how Bobby Valdez came in for dinner the night he shot Tanner. "He sat right on that very stool you're on and ate tacos like he didn't have a worry in the world. Real calm."

Lyall said, "Uh-huh, but he's kind of a little squirt, ain't he?" and walked out casually, knowing Elodie was watching after him with her mouth open.

TUESDAY NIGHT Valdez told Lyall how his being in the cell had all come about—how he'd started out an honest vaquero down in Sonora, but got mixed up with some unprincipled men who were chousing other people's cows. Bobby Valdez said, by the name of a saint, he didn't know anything about it, but the next thing the *rurales* were chasing him across the border. About a year later, in Contention, Arizona, he killed a man. It was in self-defense and he was acquitted; but the man had a friend, so he ended up killing the friend too. And after that it was just one thing leading to another. Everybody seemed to take him wrong . . .

couldn't get an honest job . . . so what was a young man supposed to do?

The way he described it made Lyall Quinlan shake his head and say it was a shame.

Wednesday night Bobby Valdez only nodded to Lyall when he came on duty. The Mexican was sitting on the edge of the bunk, elbows on his knees, staring at his hands as he washed them together absently.

He's finally realizing he's going to die, Lyall thought. You have to leave a man alone when he's doing that. So for over an hour no one spoke.

When Lyall did speak it was because he wanted to make it little easier for Valdez. He said, "All people have to die. That's the best way to look at it."

Valdez looked up, then nodded thoughtfully.

"You got to look at it," Lyall went on, "like, well, just something that happens to everybody."

"I've done that," the Mexican said. "What torments me now is that I have not confessed."

"You didn't have to," Lyall said. "Judge Metairie found out the facts without you confessing."

"No, I mean to a priest."

"Oh."

"It is a terrible thing to die without absolution."

"Oh."

It was quiet then, Lyall frowning, the Mexican looking at his hands. But suddenly Bobby Valdez looked up, his face brightening, and he said, as if it had just occurred to him, "My friend, would *you* bring a priest to me?"

"Well—I'll tell Mr. Bohannon in the morning. I'm sure he'll—"

"No!" Valdez stood up quickly. "I cannot take the chance of letting him know!" His voice calmed as he said, "You know how he makes fun of things spiritual—that about the holy water, and calling me 'Brother.' What if he should refuse this request? Then I would die in the state of mortal sin just because he does not understand. My friend," he said just above a whisper, "surely you can see that he must not know."

"Well—" Lyall said.

"In White Sands," Valdez said quickly, "there is a man called Sixto Henriquez who knows the priest well. At the mescal shop they'll tell you where he lives. Now, all you would have to do is tell Sixto to send the priest late Friday night after it is very quiet, and then it will be accomplished."

Lyall hesitated.

"Then," Valdez said solemnly, "I would not die in sin."

Lyall thought about it some more and finally he nodded.

He woke up at noon for the ride to White Sands. He'd have to hurry to be back in time to go on duty; but he would have hurried anyway because he didn't feel right about what he was doing, as if it was something sneaky. At the mescal shop the proprietor directed him, in as few words as were necessary, to the adobe of Sixto Henriquez. Lyall was half afraid and half hoping Sixto wouldn't be home. But there he was, a thin little man in a striped shirt who didn't open the door all the way until Lyall mentioned Valdez.

After Lyall had told why he was there, Henriquez took his time rolling a cigarette. He lit it and blew out smoke and then said, "All right."

Lyall rode back to Tularosa feeling a lot better. That hadn't been hard at all.

When he went on duty that night he said to Bobby Valdez, "You're all set," and would just as soon have let it go at that, but Valdez insisted that he tell him everything. He told him. There wasn't much to it—how the man just said, "All right." But Valdez seemed to be satisfied.

Friday morning Lyall stopped at the Regent Café for his breakfast. Elodie was serving the counter. She was frowning and muttering about being switched to mornings just the day before Bobby Valdez's hanging.

Lyall told her, "A nice girl like you don't want to see a hanging."

"It's the principle of it," she pouted. The principle being everybody in Tularosa was excited about Bobby Valdez hanging whether they had a stomach for it or not.

"Lyall, don't you get scared up there alone with him?" she said with a little shiver that might have been partly real.

"What's there to be scared of? He's locked in a cell."

"What if one of his friends should come to help him?" Elodie said.

"How could a man like that have friends?"

"Well—I worry about you, Lyall."

Lyall stopped being calm, his whole face grinning. "Do you, Elodie?"

And that's what Lyall was thinking about when he went on duty Friday night. About Elodie.

Barney Groom was sitting at Bohannon's rolltop with his feet propped up, looking like he was ready to go to sleep. He said to Lyall, "'Night's the last night. After the hanging we can relax a little."

Lyall went upstairs and sat down in the cane-bottom chair still thinking about Elodie: how she looked like a little girl when she pouted. A deputy marshal can probably support a wife, he thought. Still, he wasn't so sure, since Bohannon hadn't mentioned salary to him yet.

Bobby Valdez said, "This is the night the priest comes."

Lyall looked up. "I almost forgot. Bet you feel better already."

"As if I have risen from the dead," Bobby Valdez said.

Later on—Lyall didn't have a timepiece on him but he estimated it was shortly after midnight—he heard the noise downstairs. Not a strange noise; it was just that it came unexpectedly in the quiet. He looked over at Bobby Valdez. Still asleep. For the next few minutes it was quiet again.

Then he heard footsteps on the stairs. It must be the priest, Lyall thought, getting up. He'd told the man to tell the priest to just walk by Barney, who'd probably be asleep, and if he wasn't, just explain the whole thing. So Barney was either asleep or had agreed.

Lyall wasn't prepared for the robed figure that stepped into the hallway. He'd expected a priest in a regular black suit; but then he remembered the priest at White Sands was the kind who wore a long robe and sandals.

Lyall said, "Father?"

That end of the hallway was darker and Lyall couldn't see him very well, and now as he came forward, Lyall still couldn't see his face because the cowl, the hood part of the robe, was up over his head. His arms were folded, with his hands up in the big sleeves.

"Father?"

"My son."

Lyall turned to the cell. "He's right here, Father." Valdez was standing at the bars and it struck Lyall suddenly that he hadn't heard Valdez get up. He turned his head to look at the priest and felt the gun barrel jab against his back.

"Place your weapon on the floor," the voice behind him said.

Bobby Valdez added, "My son," smiling now.

✮ ✮ ✮

THE MAN BEHIND Lyall reached past him to hand the ring of jail keys to Valdez. As he did, the cowl fell back and Lyall saw the man he'd talked to in White Sands. Sixto Henriquez.

Valdez said, "Whether you could get a robe was the thing that bothered me."

"A gift," Sixto said. "Hanging from his clothesline."

Lyall heard them, but he wouldn't let himself believe it. He wanted to say, "Wait a minute! Come on, now, this wasn't supposed to happen!"

Thinking of Bohannon and Elodie and the nights walking in the hallway, suddenly knowing he'd done the wrong thing, and too late to do anything about it. "Wait a minute . . . I was trying to help you!" But not saying it because it had been his own damn, stupid fault, and he was so aware of it now, he had to bite his lip to keep from yelling like a kid.

Valdez came out of the cell and picked up the shotgun Lyall had dropped. He said to Lyall, "Now my soul feels better."

He motioned Sixto toward the stairs. "Go first and see how it is with the old one."

"He sleep," Sixto said, and patted the barrel of his pistol.

"Let's be sure," Bobby Valdez said. He watched Sixto go through the doorway and listened to him start down the stairs. He looked at Lyall again, smiling. "You can mark this to experience."

If Valdez had backed out, holding the gun on Lyall, it wouldn't have happened. Even if he had just warned Lyall not to yell out or follow them—but he just turned and started walking out, *knowing* Lyall wouldn't dare try to stop him. And that's where Bobby Valdez made his mistake.

Lyall saw the man's back like a slap in the face. Even though he was scared, all of a sudden the knots inside him got too tight to stand. No

thinking now about how it happened or what might happen—just an
overpowering urge to get him!

He lunged at the back that was moving away. Three long strides and
his arms were around Valdez's neck, jerking, swinging him off his feet.
He heard the shotgun clatter against the wall and hit the floor.

Tight against him, Bobby Valdez was turning his body. Lyall let go
with one arm, brought it down quick, and drove it as hard as he could
into the stomach almost against him. Valdez gasped and started to sag.
Then footsteps on the stairs. Lyall scrambled for the shotgun, came up
with it, and was at the doorway in time to see Sixto partway up the stairs,
but as he raised the shotgun there was a swirl of robes and Sixto was at
the bottom again. There was the sound of him running through the office, then nothing. Lyall came around fast. Valdez was almost on him,
coming in low, diving for Lyall's legs—and he dove right into the shotgun barrel swung hard against his skull.

Lyall just stood there breathing for a minute before he dragged
Bobby Valdez back to the cell and hefted him onto the bunk.

"Mr. Valdez," Lyall said out loud, "that's one *you* can mark to experience."

He went downstairs after that. Barney Groom was slouched in his
chair, out cold. Lyall went to the doorway; he stepped outside to have a
look around, and there was the friar's robe. It was in the road over by
the hitch rack. Lyall gathered it up quick. He brought it back in the office and hung it beneath his rain slicker that was hooked on a peg.
Then he breathed easier.

ELODIE TURNED AWAY from the window. "It's over, Lyall," she said
gravely. "They're starting to come out on the street."

Lyall glanced at her. "Is that right, Elodie?" he said, then put a little
more ketchup on his eggs. Scrambled eggs were good that way; this
morning they tasted even better. He ate them, half smiling, remembering Bohannon coming that morning. Bohannon frowning at Barney
Groom, Barney trying to figure how he got his head bumped when he
was sound asleep.

Then when they went upstairs—that was really something. Bohannon saying, "Maybe he's sick," seeing Valdez's white face and the side of his head swollen like a lopsided melon. And Barney Groom saying, "Maybe the same bug bit me, bit him."

Then what Bohannon said to him when they went downstairs again—that was the best.

"Now, Lyall, you done a fair job, though just sitting up there trying to keep awake wasn't much of a test. Tell you what"—Bohannon pulled a folded sheet of paper from his vest pocket—"last night I got a note from the White Sands marshal telling about the padre there getting his outfit stolen off the clothesline and would I assign a man to it since he's busy collecting taxes." Bohannon chuckled. "Have to keep the padres happy. Now, Lyall, if you could prove to me you're smart enough to get that padre's robe back for him, I'll see you're made a permanent deputy. And that's my solemn word."

Lyall pretended he didn't see Bohannon wink at Barney Groom. He said, "Yes, sir, I'll sure try." Just as serious as he could.

19

The Captives

Film Title: *The Tall T*
Argosy, February 1955

★

Chapter One

HE COULD HEAR the stagecoach, the faraway creaking and the muffled rumble of it, and he was thinking: It's almost an hour early. Why should it be if it left Contention on schedule?

His name was Pat Brennan. He was lean and almost tall, with a deeply tanned, pleasant face beneath the straight hat brim low over his eyes, and he stood next to his saddle, which was on the ground, with the easy, hip-shot slouch of a rider. A Henry rifle was in his right hand and he was squinting into the sun glare, looking up the grade to the rutted road that came curving down through the spidery Joshua trees.

He lowered the Henry rifle, stock down, and let it fall across the saddle, and kept his hand away from the Colt holstered on his right leg. A man could get shot standing next to a stage road out in the middle of nowhere with a rifle in his hand.

Then, seeing the coach suddenly against the sky, billowing dust hanging over it, he felt relief and smiled to himself and raised his arm to wave as the coach passed through the Joshuas.

As the pounding wood, iron, and three-team racket of it came swaying toward him, he raised both arms and felt a sudden helplessness as he saw that the driver was making no effort to stop the teams. Brennan stepped back quickly, and the coach rushed past him, the driver, alone on the boot, bending forward and down to look at him.

Brennan cupped his hands and called, *"Rintoooon!"*

The driver leaned back with the reins high and through his fingers, his boot pushing against the brake lever, and his body half turned to look back over the top of the Concord. Brennan swung the saddle up over his shoulder and started after the coach as it ground to a stop.

He saw the company name, HATCH & HODGES, and just below it, *Number 42* stenciled on the varnished door; then from a side window, he saw a man staring at him irritably as he approached. Behind the man he caught a glimpse of a woman with soft features and a small, plumed hat and eyes that looked away quickly as Brennan's gaze passed them going up to Ed Rintoon, the driver.

"Ed, for a minute I didn't think you were going to stop."

Rintoon, a leathery, beard-stubbled man in his mid-forties, stood with one knee on the seat and looked down at Brennan with only faint surprise.

"I took you for being up to no good, standing there waving your arms."

"I'm only looking for a lift a ways."

"What happened to you?"

Brennan grinned and his thumb pointed back vaguely over his shoulder. "I was visiting Tenvoorde to see about buying some yearling stock and I lost my horse to him on a bet."

"Driver!"

Brennan turned. The man who had been at the window was now leaning halfway out of the door and looking up at Rintoon.

"I'm not paying you to pass the time of day with"—he glanced at Brennan—"with everybody we meet."

Rintoon leaned over to look down at him. "Willard, you ain't even part right, since you ain't the man that pays me."

"I chartered this coach, and you along with it!" He was a young man, hatless, his long hair mussed from the wind. Strands of it hung over his ears, and his face was flushed as he glared at Rintoon. "When I pay for a coach I expect the service that goes with it."

Rintoon said, "Willard, you calm down now."

"Mr. Mims!"

Rintoon smiled faintly, glancing at Brennan. "Pat, I'd like you to meet Mr. Mims." He paused, adding, "He's a bookkeeper."

Brennan touched the brim of his hat toward the coach, seeing the woman again. She looked to be in her late twenties and her eyes now were wide and frightened and not looking at him.

His glance went to Willard Mims. Mims came out of the doorway and stood pointing a finger up at Rintoon.

"Brother, you're through! I swear to God this is your last run on any line in the Territory!"

Rintoon eased himself down until he was half sitting on the seat. "You wouldn't kid me."

"You'll see if I'm kidding!"

Rintoon shook his head. "After ten years of faithful service the boss will be sorry to see me go."

Willard Mims stared at him in silence. Then he said, his voice calmer, "You won't be so sure of yourself after we get to Bisbee."

Ignoring him, Rintoon turned to Brennan. "Swing that saddle up here."

"You hear what I said?" Willard Mims flared.

Reaching down for the saddle horn as Brennan lifted it, Rintoon answered, "You said I'd be sorry when we got to Bisbee."

"You remember that!"

"I sure will. Now you get back inside, Willard." He glanced at Brennan. "You get in there, too, Pat."

Willard Mims stiffened. "I'll remind you again—this is *not* the passenger coach."

Brennan was momentarily angry, but he saw the way Rintoon was taking this and he said calmly, "You want me to walk? It's only fifteen miles to Sasabe."

"I didn't say that," Mims answered, moving to the coach door. "If you want to come, get up on the boot." He turned to look at Brennan as he pulled himself up on the foot rung. "If we'd wanted company we'd have taken the scheduled run. That clear enough for you?"

Glancing at Rintoon, Brennan swung the Henry rifle up to him and said, "Yes, sir," not looking at Mims; and he winked at Rintoon as he climbed the wheel to the driver's seat.

A moment later they were moving, slowly at first, bumping and swaying; then the road seemed to become smoother as the teams pulled faster.

Brennan leaned toward Rintoon and said, in the noise, close to the driver's grizzled face, "I wondered why the regular stage would be almost an hour early, Ed, I'm obliged to you."

Rintoon glanced at him. "Thank Mr. Mims."

"Who is he, anyway?"

"Old man Gateway's son-in-law. Married the boss's daughter. Married into the biggest copper claim in the country."

"The girl with him his wife?"

"Doretta," Rintoon answered. "That's Gateway's daughter. She was scheduled to be an old maid till Willard come along and saved her from spinsterhood. She's plain as a 'dobe wall."

Brennan said, "But not too plain for Willard, eh?"

Rintoon gave him a side glance. "Patrick, there ain't nothing plain about old man Gateway's holdings. That's the thing. Four years ago he bought a half interest in the Montezuma Copper Mine for two hundred and fifty thousand dollars, and he's got it back triple since then. Can you imagine anyone having that much money?"

Brennan shook his head. "Where'd he get it, to start?"

"They say he come from money and made more by using the brains God gave him, investing it."

Brennan shook his head again. "That's too much money, Ed. Too much to have to worry about."

"Not for Willard, it ain't," Rintoon said. "He started out as a bookkeeper with the company. Now he's general manager—since the wedding. The old man picked Willard because he was the only one around he thought had any polish, and he knew if he waited much longer he'd have an old maid on his hands. And, Pat"—Rintoon leaned closer—"Willard don't talk to the old man like he does to other people."

"She didn't look so bad to me," Brennan said.

"You been down on Sasabe Creek too long," Rintoon glanced at him again. "What were you saying about losing your horse to Tenvoorde?"

"Oh, I went to see him about buying some yearlings—"

"On credit," Rintoon said.

Brennan nodded. "Though I was going to pay him some of it cash. I told him to name a fair interest rate and he'd have it in two years. But he said no. Cash on the line. No cash, no yearlings. I needed three hundred to make the deal, but I only had fifty. Then when I was going he said, 'Patrick'—you know how he talks—'I'll give you a chance to get your yearlings free,' and all the time he's eyeing this claybank mare I had along. He said, 'You bet your mare and your fifty dollars cash, I'll put up what yearlings you need, and we'll race your mare against one of my string for the winner.'"

Ed Rintoon said, "And you lost."

"By a country mile."

"Pat, that don't sound like you. Why didn't you take what your fifty would buy and get on home?"

"Because I needed these yearlings plus a good seed bull. I could've bought the bull, but I wouldn't have had the yearlings to build on. That's what I told Mr. Tenvoorde. I said, 'This deal's as good as the stock you're selling me. If you're taking that kind of money for a seed bull and yearlings, then you know they can produce. You're sure of getting your money.'"

"You got stock down on your Sasabe place," Rintoon said.

"Not like you think. They wintered poorly and I got a lot of building to do."

"Who's tending your herd now?"

"I still got those two Mexican boys."

"You should've known better than to go to Tenvoorde."

"I didn't have a chance. He's the only man close enough with the stock I want."

"But a bet like that—how could you fall into it? You know he'd have a pony to outstrip yours."

"Well, that was the chance I had to take."

They rode along in silence for a few minutes before Brennan asked, "Where they coming from?"

Rintoon grinned at him. "Their honeymoon. Willard made the agent put on a special run just for the two of them. Made a big fuss while Doretta tried to hide her head."

"Then"—Brennan grinned—"I'm obliged to Mr. Mims, else I'd still be waiting back there with my saddle and my Henry."

Later on, topping a rise that was thick with jack pine, they were suddenly in view of the Sasabe station and the creek beyond it, as they came out of the trees and started down the mesquite-dotted sweep of the hillside.

Rintoon checked his timepiece. The regular run was due here at five o'clock. He was surprised to see that it was only ten minutes after four. He remembered then, his mind picturing Willard Mims as he chartered the special coach.

Brennan said, "I'm getting off here at Sasabe."

"How'll you get over to your place?"

"Hank'll lend me a horse."

As they drew nearer, Rintoon was squinting, studying the three adobe houses and the corral in back. "I don't see anybody," he said. "Hank's usually out in the yard. Him or his boy."

Brennan said, "They don't expect you for an hour. That's it."

"Man, we make enough noise for somebody to come out."

Rintoon swung the teams toward the adobes, slowing them as Brennan pushed his boot against the brake lever, and they came to a stop exactly even with the front of the main adobe.

"Hank!"

Rintoon looked from the door of the adobe out over the yard. He called the name again, but there was no answer. He frowned. "The damn place sounds deserted," he said.

Brennan saw the driver's eyes drop to the sawed-off shotgun and Brennan's Henry on the floor of the boot, and then he was looking over the yard again.

"Where in hell would Hank've gone to?"

A sound came from the adobe. A boot scraping—that or something like it—and the next moment a man was standing in the open doorway.

He was bearded, a dark beard faintly streaked with gray and in need of a trim. He was watching them calmly, almost indifferently, and leveling a Colt at them at the same time.

He moved out into the yard and now another man, armed with a shotgun, came out of the adobe. The bearded one held his gun on the door of the coach. The shotgun was leveled at Brennan and Rintoon.

"You-all drop your guns and come on down." He wore range clothes, soiled and sun bleached, and he held the shotgun calmly as if doing this was not something new. He was younger than the bearded one by at least ten years.

Brennan raised his revolver from its holster and the one with the shotgun said, "Gently, now," and grinned as Brennan dropped it over the wheel.

Rintoon, not wearing a handgun, had not moved.

"If you got something down in that boot," the one with the shotgun said to him, "haul it out."

Rintoon muttered something under his breath. He reached down and took hold of Brennan's Henry rifle lying next to the sawed-off shotgun, his finger slipping through the trigger guard. He came up with it hesitantly, and Brennan whispered, barely moving his lips, "Don't be crazy."

Standing up, turning, Rintoon hesitated again, then let the rifle fall. "That all you got?"

Rintoon nodded. "That's all."

"Then come on down."

Rintoon turned his back. He bent over to climb down, his foot reaching for the wheel below, and his hand closed on the sawed-off shotgun. Brennan whispered, "Don't do it!"

Rintoon mumbled something that came out as a growl. Brennan leaned toward him as if to give him a hand down. "You got two shots. What if there're more than two of them?"

Rintoon grunted, "Look out, Pat!" His hand gripped the shotgun firmly.

Then he was turning, jumping from the wheel, the stubby scatter-gun flashing head-high—and at the same moment a single revolver shot blasted the stillness. Brennan saw Rintoon crumple to the ground, the shotgun falling next to him, and he was suddenly aware of powder smoke and a man framed in the window of the adobe.

The one with the shotgun said, "Well, that just saves some time," and he glanced around as the third man came out of the adobe. "Chink, I swear you hit him in midair."

"I was waiting for that old man to pull something," said the one called Chink. He wore two low-slung, crossed cartridge belts and his second Colt was still in its holster.

Brennan jumped down and rolled Rintoon over gently, holding his head off the ground. He looked at the motionless form and then at Chink. "He's dead."

Chink stood with his legs apart and looked down at Brennan indifferently. "Sure he is."

"You didn't have to kill him."

Chink shrugged. "I would've, sooner or later."

"Why?"

"That's the way it is."

The man with the beard had not moved. He said now, quietly, "Chink, you shut your mouth." Then he glanced at the man with the shotgun and said, in the same tone, "Billy-Jack, get them out of there," and nodded toward the coach.

☆

Chapter Two

KNEELING NEXT to Rintoon, Brennan studied them. He watched Billy-Jack open the coach door, saw his mouth soften to a grin as Doretta Mims came out first. Her eyes went to Rintoon, but shifted away quickly. Willard Mims hesitated, then stepped down, stumbling in his haste as Billy-Jack pointed the shotgun at him. He stood next to his wife and stared unblinkingly at Rintoon's body.

That one, Brennan was thinking, looking at the man with the beard—that's the one to watch. He's calling it, and he doesn't look as though he gets excited. . . . And the one called Chink. . . .

Brennan's eyes went to him. He was standing hip-cocked, his hat on the back of his head and the drawstring from it pulled tight beneath his lower lip, his free hand fingering the string idly, the other hand holding the long-barreled .44 Colt, pointed down but cocked.

He wants somebody to try something, Brennan thought. He's itching for it. He wears two guns and he thinks he's good. Well, maybe he is. But he's young, the youngest of the three, and he's anxious. His gaze stayed on Chink and it went through his mind: Don't even reach for a cigarette when he's around.

The one with the beard said, "Billy-Jack, get up on top of the coach."

Brennan's eyes raised, watching the man step from the wheel hub to the boot and then kneel on the driver's seat. He's number-three man, Brennan thought. He keeps looking at the woman. But don't bet him short. He carries a big-gauge gun.

"Frank, there ain't nothing up here but an old saddle."

The one with the beard—Frank Usher—raised his eyes. "Look under it."

"Ain't nothing there either."

Usher's eyes went to Willard Mims, then swung slowly to Brennan. "Where's the mail?"

"I wouldn't know," Brennan said.

Frank Usher looked at Willard Mims again. "You tell me."

"This isn't the stage," Willard Mims said hesitantly. His face relaxed then, almost to the point of smiling. "You made a mistake. The regular stage isn't due for almost an hour." He went on, excitement rising in his voice, "That's what you want, the stage that's due here at five. This is one I chartered." He smiled now. "See, me and my wife are just coming back from a honeymoon and, you know—"

Frank Usher looked at Brennan. "Is that right?"

"Of course it is!" Mims's voice rose. "Go in and check the schedule."

"I'm asking this man."

Brennan shrugged. "I wouldn't know."

"He don't know anything," Chink said.

Billy-Jack came down off the coach and Usher said to him, "Go in and look for a schedule." He nodded toward Doretta Mims. "Take that woman with you. Have her put some coffee on, and something to eat."

Brennan said, "What did you do with Hank?"

Frank Usher's dull eyes moved to Brennan. "Who's he?"

"The station man here."

Chink grinned and waved his revolver, pointing it off beyond the main adobe. "He's over yonder in the well."

Usher said, "Does that answer it?"

"What about his boy?"

"He's with him," Usher said. "Anything else?"

Brennan shook his head slowly. "That's enough." He knew they were both dead and suddenly he was very much afraid of this dull-eyed, soft-voiced man with the beard; it took an effort to keep himself calm. He watched Billy-Jack take Doretta by the arm. She looked imploringly at her husband, holding back, but he made no move to help her. Billy-Jack jerked her arm roughly and she went with him.

Willard Mims said, "He'll find the schedule. Like I said, it's due at five o'clock. I can see how you made the mistake"—Willard was smiling—"thinking we were the regular stage. Hell, we were just going home . . . down to Bisbee. You'll see, five o'clock sharp that regular passenger-mail run'll pull in."

"He's a talker," Chink said.

Billy-Jack appeared in the doorway of the adobe. "Frank, five o'clock, sure as hell!" He waved a sheet of yellow paper.

"See!" Willard Mims was grinning excitedly. "Listen, you let us go and we'll be on our way"—his voice rose—"and I swear to God we'll never breathe we saw a thing."

Chink shook his head. "He's somethin'."

"Listen, I swear to God we won't tell *anything*!"

"I know you won't," Frank Usher said. He looked at Brennan and nodded toward Mims. "Where'd you find him?"

"We just met."

"Do you go along with what he's saying?"

"If I said yes," Brennan answered, "you wouldn't believe me. And you'd be right."

A smile almost touched Frank Usher's mouth. "Dumb even talking about it, isn't it?"

"I guess it is," Brennan said.

"You know what's going to happen to you?" Usher asked him tonelessly.

Brennan nodded, without answering.

Frank Usher studied him in silence. Then, "Are you scared?"

Brennan nodded again. "Sure I am."

"You're honest about it. I'll say that for you."

"I don't know of a better time to be honest," Brennan said.

Chink said, "That damn well's going to be chock full."

Willard Mims had listened with disbelief, his eyes wide. Now he said hurriedly, "Wait a minute! What're you listening to him for? I told you, I swear to God I won't say one word about this. If you don't trust him, then keep him here! I don't know this man. I'm not speaking for him, anyway."

"I'd be inclined to trust him before I would you," Frank Usher said.

"He's got nothing to do with it! We picked him up out on the desert!"

Chink raised his .44 waist high, looking at Willard Mims, and said, "Start running for that well and see if you can make it."

"Man, be reasonable!"

Frank Usher shook his head. "You aren't leaving, and you're not going to be standing here when that stage pulls in. You can scream and carry on, but that's the way it is."

"What about my wife?"

"I can't help her being a woman."

Willard Mims was about to say something, but stopped. His eyes went to the adobe, then back to Usher. He lowered his voice and all the excitement was gone from it. "You know who she is?" He moved closer to Usher. "She's the daughter of old man Gateway, who happens to own part of the third richest copper mine in Arizona. You know what that amounts to? To date, three quarters of a million dollars." He said this slowly, looking straight at Frank Usher.

"Make a point out of it," Usher said.

"Man, it's practically staring you right in the face! You got the daughter of a man who's practically a millionaire. His only daughter! What do you think he'll pay to get her back?"

Frank Usher said, "I don't know. What?"

"Whatever you ask! You sit here waiting for a two-bit holdup and you got a gold mine right in your hands!"

"How do I know she's his daughter?"

Willard Mims looked at Brennan. "You were talking to that driver. Didn't he tell you?"

Brennan hesitated. If the man wanted to bargain with his wife, that was his business. It would give them time; that was the main thing. Brennan nodded. "That's right. His wife is Doretta Gateway."

"Where do you come in?" Usher asked Willard Mims.

"I'm Mr. Gateway's general manager on the Montezuma operation."

Frank Usher was silent now, staring at Mims. Finally he said, "I suppose you'd be willing to ride in with a note."

"Certainly," Mims quickly replied.

"And we'd never see you again."

"Would I save my own skin and leave my wife here?"

Usher nodded. "I believe you would."

"Then there's no use talking about it." Mims shrugged and, watching him, Brennan knew he was acting, taking a long chance.

"We can talk about it," Frank Usher said, "because if we do it, we do it my way." He glanced at the house. "Billy-Jack!" Then to Brennan, "You and him go sit over against the wall."

Billy-Jack came out, and from the wall of the adobe Brennan and Willard watched the three outlaws. They stood in close, and Frank Usher was doing the talking. After a few minutes Billy-Jack went into the adobe again and came out with the yellow stage schedule and an envelope. Usher took them and, against the door of the Concord, wrote something on the back of the schedule.

He came toward them folding the paper into the envelope. He sealed the envelope and handed it with the pencil to Willard Mims. "You put Gateway's name on it and where to find him. Mark it personal and urgent."

Willard Mims said, "I can see him myself and tell him."

"You will," Frank Usher said, "but not how you think. You're going to stop on the main road one mile before you get to Bisbee and give that envelope to somebody passing in. The note tells Gateway you have something to tell him about his daughter and to come alone. When he goes out, you'll tell him the story. If he says no, then he never sees his daughter again. If he says yes, he's to bring fifty thousand in U.S. scrip divided in three saddlebags, to a place up back of the Sasabe. And he brings it alone."

Mims said, "What if there isn't that much cash on hand?"

"That's his problem."

"Well, why can't I go right to his house and tell him?"

"Because Billy-Jack's going to be along to bring you back after you tell him. And I don't want him someplace he can get cornered."

"Oh. . . ."

"That's whether he says yes or no," Frank Usher added.

Mims was silent for a moment. "But how'll Mr. Gateway know where to come?"

"If he agrees, Billy-Jack'll give him directions."

Mims said, "Then when he comes out you'll let us go? Is that it?"

"That's it."

"When do we leave?"

"Right this minute."

"Can I say good-bye to my wife?"

"We'll do it for you."

Brennan watched Billy-Jack come around from the corral, leading two horses. Willard Mims moved toward one of them and they both mounted. Billy-Jack reined his horse suddenly, crowding Mims to turn with him, then slapped Mims's horse on the rump and spurred after it as the horse broke to a run.

Watching them, his eyes half closed, Frank Usher said, "That boy puts his wife up on the stake and then he wants to kiss her good-bye." He glanced at Brennan. "You figure that one for me."

Brennan shook his head. "What I'd like to know is why you only asked for fifty thousand."

Frank Usher shrugged. "I'm not greedy."

Chapter Three

CHINK TURNED AS the two horses splashed over the creek and grew gradually smaller down the road. He looked at Brennan and then his eyes went to Frank Usher. "We don't have a need for this one, Frank."

Usher's dull eyes flicked toward him. "You bring around the horses and I'll worry about him."

"We might as well do it now as later," Chink said.

"We're taking him with us."

"What for?"

"Because I say so. That reason enough?"

"Frank, we could run him for the well and both take a crack at him."

"Get the horses," Frank Usher said flatly, and stared at Chink until the gunman turned and walked away.

Brennan said, "I'd like to bury this man before we go."

Usher shook his head. "Put him in the well."

"That's no fit place!"

Usher stared at Brennan for a long moment. "Don't push your luck. He goes in the well, whether you do it or Chink does."

Brennan pulled Rintoon's limp body up over his shoulder and carried him across the yard. When he returned, Chink was coming around the adobe with three horses already saddled. Frank Usher stood near the house and now Doretta Mims appeared in the doorway.

Usher looked at her. "You'll have to fork one of these like the rest of us. There ain't no lady's saddle about."

She came out, neither answering nor looking at him.

Usher called to Brennan, "Cut one out of that team and shoot the rest," nodding to the stagecoach.

Minutes later the Sasabe station was deserted.

They followed the creek west for almost an hour before swinging south toward high country. Leaving the creek, Brennan had thought: Five more miles and I'm home. And his eyes hung on the long shallow cup of the Sasabe valley until they entered a trough that climbed winding ahead of them through the hills, and the valley was no longer in view.

Frank Usher led them single file—Doretta Mims, followed by Brennan, and Chink bringing up the rear. Chink rode slouched, swaying with the movement of his dun mare, chewing idly on the drawstring of his hat, and watching Brennan.

Brennan kept his eyes on the woman much of the time. For almost a mile, as they rode along the creek, he had watched her body shaking silently and he knew that she was crying. She had very nearly cried mounting the horse—pulling her skirts down almost desperately, then sitting, holding on to the saddle horn with both hands, biting her lower lip and not looking at them. Chink had sidestepped his dun close to her and said something, and she had turned her head quickly as the color rose from her throat over her face.

They dipped down into a barranca thick with willow and cottonwood and followed another stream that finally disappeared into the rocks at the far end. And after that they began to climb again. For some time they rode through the soft gloom of timber, following switchbacks as the slope became steeper, then came out into the open and crossed a bare gravelly slope, the sandstone peaks above them cold pink in the fading sunlight.

They were nearing the other side of the open grade when Frank Usher said, "Here we are."

Brennan looked beyond him and now he could make out, through the pines they were approaching, a weather-scarred stone-and-log hut built snugly against the steep wall of sandstone. Against one side of the hut was a hide-covered lean-to. He heard Frank Usher say, "Chink, you get the man making a fire and I'll get the woman fixing supper."

There had not been time to eat what the woman had prepared at the stage station and now Frank Usher and Chink ate hungrily, hunkered down a dozen yards out from the lean-to where Brennan and the woman stood.

Brennan took a plate of the jerky and day-old pan bread, but Doretta Mims did not touch the food. She stood next to him, half turned from him, and continued to stare through the trees across the bare slope in the direction they had come. Once Brennan said to her, "You better eat something," but she did not answer him.

When they were finished, Frank Usher ordered them into the hut.

"You stay there the night . . . and if either of you comes near the door, we'll let go, no questions asked. That plain?"

The woman went in hurriedly. When Brennan entered he saw her huddled against the back wall near a corner.

The sod-covered hut was windowless, and he could barely make her out in the dimness. He wanted to go and sit next to her, but it went through his mind that most likely she was as afraid of him as she was of Frank Usher and Chink. So he made room for himself against the wall where they had placed the saddles, folding a saddle blanket to rest his elbow on as he eased himself to the dirt floor. Let her try and get hold of herself, he thought; then maybe she will want somebody to talk to.

He made a cigarette and lit it, seeing the mask of her face briefly as the match flared, then he eased himself lower until his head was resting against a saddle, and smoked in the dim silence.

Soon the hut was full dark. Now he could not see the woman, though he imagined that he could feel her presence. Outside, Usher and Chink had added wood to the cook fire in front of the lean-to and the warm glow of it illuminated the doorless opening of the hut.

They'll sit by the fire, Brennan thought, and one of them will always be awake. You'd get about one step through that door and *bam*. Maybe Frank would aim low, but Chink would shoot to kill. He became angry thinking of Chink, but there was nothing he could do about it and he drew on the cigarette slowly to make himself relax, thinking: Take it easy: you've got the woman to consider. He thought of her as his responsibility and not even a doubt entered his mind that she was not. She was a woman, alone. The reason was as simple as that.

He heard her move as he was snubbing out the cigarette. He lay still and he knew that she was coming toward him. She knelt as she reached his side.

"Do you know what they've done with my husband?"

He could picture her drawn face, eyes staring wide open in the darkness. He raised himself slowly and felt her stiffen as he touched her arm. "Sit down here and you'll be more comfortable." He moved over to let her sit on the saddle blanket. "Your husband's all right," he said.

"Where is he?"

"They didn't tell you?"

"No."

Brennan paused. "One of them took him to Bisbee to see your father."

"My father?"

"To ask him to pay to get you back."

"Then my husband's all right." She was relieved, and it was in the sound of her voice.

Brennan said, after a moment, "Why don't you go to sleep now? You can rest back on one of these saddles."

"I'm not tired."

"Well, you will be if you don't get some sleep."

She said then, "They must have known all the time that we were coming."

Brennan said nothing.

"Didn't they?"

"I don't know, ma'am."

"How else would they know about . . . who my father is?"

"Maybe so."

"One of them must have been in Contention and heard my husband charter the coach. Perhaps he had visited Bisbee and knew that my father . . ." Her voice trailed off because she was speaking more to herself than to Brennan.

After a pause Brennan said, "You sound like you feel a little better."

He heard her exhale slowly and he could imagine she was trying to smile.

"Yes, I believe I do now," she replied.

"Your husband will be back sometime tomorrow morning," Brennan said to her.

She touched his arm lightly. "I *do* feel better, Mr. Brennan."

He was surprised that she remembered his name. Rintoon had mentioned it only once, hours before. "I'm glad you do. Now, why don't you try to sleep?"

She eased back gently until she was lying down and for a few minutes there was silence.

"Mr. Brennan?"

"Yes, ma'am."

"I'm terribly sorry about your friend."

"Who?"

"The driver."

"Oh. Thank you."

"I'll remember him in my prayers," she said, and after this she did not speak again.

Brennan smoked another cigarette, then sat unmoving for what he judged to be at least a half hour, until he was sure Doretta Mims was asleep.

Now he crawled across the dirt floor to the opposite wall. He went down on his stomach and edged toward the door, keeping close to the wall. Pressing his face close to the opening, he could see, off to the right side, the fire, dying down now. The shape of a man wrapped in a blanket was lying full length on the other side of it.

Brennan rose slowly, hugging the wall. He inched his head out to see the side of the fire closest to the lean-to, and as he did he heard the unmistakable click of a revolver being cocked. Abruptly he brought his head in and went back to the saddle next to Doretta Mims.

★

Chapter Four

IN THE MORNING they brought Doretta Mims out to cook; then sent her back to the hut while they ate. When they had finished they let Brennan and Doretta come out to the lean-to.

Frank Usher said, "That wasn't a head I seen pokin' out the door last night, was it?"

"If it was," Brennan answered, "why didn't you shoot at it?"

"I about did. Lucky thing it disappeared," Usher said. "Whatever it was." And he walked away, through the trees to where the horses were picketed.

Chink sat down on a stump and began making a cigarette.

A few steps from Doretta Mims, Brennan leaned against the hut and began eating. He could see her profile as she turned her head to look out through the trees and across the open slope.

Maybe she *is* a little plain, he thought. Her nose doesn't have the kind of a clean-cut shape that stays in your mind. And her hair—if she didn't have it pulled back so tight she'd look a little younger, and happier. She could do something with her hair. She could do something with her clothes, too, to let you know she's a woman.

He felt sorry for her, seeing her biting her lower lip, still staring off through the trees. And for a reason he did not understand, though he knew it had nothing to do with sympathy, he felt very close to her, as if he had known her for a long time, as if he could look into her eyes— not just now, but anytime—and know what she was thinking. He realized that it was sympathy, in a sense, but not the feeling-sorry kind. He could picture her as a little girl, and self-consciously growing up, and he could imagine vaguely what her father was like. And now—a sensitive girl, afraid of saying the wrong thing; afraid of speaking out of turn even if it meant wondering about instead of knowing what had happened to her husband. Afraid of sounding silly, while men like her husband talked and talked and said nothing. But even having to listen to him, she would not speak against him, because he was her husband.

That's the kind of woman to have, Brennan thought. One that'll stick by you, no matter what. And, he thought, still looking at her, one that's got some insides to her. Not just all on the surface. Probably you would have to lose a woman like that to really appreciate her.

"Mrs. Mims."

She looked at him, her eyes still bearing the anxiety of watching through the trees.

"He'll come, Mrs. Mims. Pretty soon now."

Frank Usher returned and motioned them into the hut again. He talked to Chink for a few minutes and now the gunman walked off through the trees.

Looking out from the doorway of the hut, Brennan said over his shoulder, "One of them's going out now to watch for your husband." He glanced around at Doretta Mims and she answered him with a hesitant smile.

Frank Usher was standing by the lean-to when Chink came back through the trees some time later. He walked out to meet him.

"They coming?"

Chink nodded. "Starting across the slope."

Minutes later two horses came into view crossing the grade. As they came through the trees, Frank Usher called, "Tie up in the shade there!" He and Chink watched the two men dismount, then come across the clearing toward them.

"It's all set!" Willard Mims called.

Frank Usher waited until they reached him. "What'd he say?"

"He said he'd bring the money."

"That right, Billy-Jack?"

Billy-Jack nodded. "That's what he said." He was carrying Rintoon's sawed-off shotgun.

"You didn't suspect any funny business?"

Billy-Jack shook his head.

Usher fingered his beard gently, holding Mims with his gaze. "He can scare up that much money?"

"He said he could, though it will take most of today to do it."

"That means he'll come out tomorrow," Usher said.

Willard Mims nodded. "That's right."

Usher's eyes went to Billy-Jack. "You gave him directions?"

"Like you said, right to the mouth of that barranca, chock full of willow. Then one of us brings him in from there."

"You're sure he can find it?"

"I made him say it twice," Billy-Jack said. "Every turn."

Usher looked at Willard Mims again. "How'd he take it?"

"How do you think he took it?"

Usher was silent, staring at Mims. Then he began to stroke his beard again. "I'm asking you," he said.

Mims shrugged. "Of course, he was mad, but there wasn't anything he could do about it. He's a reasonable man."

Billy-Jack was grinning. "Frank, this time tomorrow we're sitting on top of the world."

Willard Mims nodded. "I think you made yourself a pretty good deal."

Frank Usher's eyes had not left Mims. "You want to stay here or go on back?"

"What?"

"You heard what I said."

"You mean you'd let me go . . . now?"

"We don't need you anymore."

Willard Mims's eyes flicked to the hut, then back to Frank Usher. He said, almost too eagerly, "I could go back now and lead old man Gateway out here in the morning."

"Sure you could," Usher said.

"Listen, I'd rather stay with my wife, but if it means getting the old man out here faster, then I think I better go back."

Usher nodded. "I know what you mean."

"You played square with me. By God, I'll play square with you."

Mims started to turn away.

Usher said, "Don't you want to see your wife first?"

Mims hesitated. "Well, the quicker I start traveling, the better. She'll understand."

"We'll see you tomorrow then, huh?"

Mims smiled. "About the same time." He hesitated. "All right to get going now?"

"Sure."

Mims backed away a few steps, still smiling, then turned and started to walk toward the trees. He looked back once and waved.

Frank Usher watched him, his eyes half closed in the sunlight. When Mims was almost to the trees, Usher said, quietly, "Chink, bust him."

Chink fired, the .44 held halfway between waist and shoulders, the long barrel raising slightly as he fired again and again until Mims went down, lying still as the heavy reports faded into dead silence.

★

Chapter Five

FRANK USHER WAITED as Billy-Jack stooped next to Mims. He saw Billy-Jack look up, nodding his head.

"Get rid of him," Usher said, watching now as Billy-Jack dragged Mims's body through the trees to the slope and there let go of it. The lifeless body slid down the grade, raising dust, until it disappeared into the brush far below.

Frank Usher turned and walked back to the hut.

Brennan stepped aside as he reached the low doorway. Usher saw the woman on the floor, her face buried in the crook of her arm resting on one of the saddles, her shoulders moving convulsively as she sobbed.

"What's the matter with her?" he asked.

Brennan said nothing.

"I thought we were doing her a favor," Usher said. He walked over to her, his hand covering the butt of his revolver, and touched her arm with his booted toe. "Woman, don't you realize what you just got out of?"

"She didn't know he did it," Brennan said quietly.

Usher looked at him, momentarily surprised. "No, I don't guess she would, come to think of it." He looked down at Doretta Mims and nudged her again with his boot. "Didn't you know that boy was selling you? This whole idea was his, to save his own skin." Usher paused. "He was ready to leave you again just now . . . when I got awful sick of him way down deep inside."

Doretta Mims was not sobbing now, but still she did not raise her head.

Usher stared down at her. "That was some boy you were married to, would do a thing like that."

Looking from the woman to Frank Usher, Brennan said, almost angrily, "What he did was wrong, but going along with it and then shooting him was all right?"

Usher glanced sharply at Brennan. "If you can't see a difference, I'm not going to explain it to you." He turned and walked out.

Brennan stood looking down at the woman for a few moments, then went over to the door and sat down on the floor just inside it. After a while he could hear Doretta Mims crying again. And for a long time he sat listening to her muffled sobs as he looked out at the sunlit clearing, now and again seeing one of the three outlaws.

He judged it to be about noon when Frank Usher and Billy-Jack rode out, walking their horses across the clearing, then into the trees, with Chink standing looking after them.

They're getting restless, Brennan thought. If they're going to stay here until tomorrow, they've got to be sure nobody's followed their sign. But it would take the best San Carlos tracker to pick up what little sign we made from Sasabe.

He saw Chink walking leisurely back to the lean-to. Chink looked toward the hut and stopped. He stood hip-cocked, with his thumbs in his crossed gun belts.

"How many did that make?" Brennan asked.

"What?" Chink straightened slightly.

Brennan nodded to where Mims had been shot. "This morning."

"That was the seventh," Chink said.

"Were they all like that?" he asked.

"How do you mean?"

"In the back."

"I'll tell you this: Yours will be from the front."

"When?"

"Tomorrow before we leave. You can count on it."

"If your boss gives you the word."

"Don't worry about that," Chink said. Then, "You could make a run for it right now. It wouldn't be like just standing up gettin' it."

"I'll wait till tomorrow," Brennan said.

Chink shrugged and walked away.

After a few minutes Brennan realized that the hut was quiet. He turned to look at Doretta Mims. She was sitting up, staring at the opposite wall with a dazed expression.

Brennan moved to her side and sat down again. "Mrs. Mims, I'm sorry—"

"Why didn't you tell me it was his plan?"

"It wouldn't have helped anything."

She looked at Brennan now pleadingly. "He could have been doing it for all of us."

Brennan nodded. "Sure he could."

"But you don't believe that, do you?"

Brennan looked at her closely, at her eyes puffed from crying. "Mrs. Mims, you know your husband better than I did."

Her eyes lowered and she said quietly, "I feel very foolish sitting here. Terrible things have happened in these two days, yet all I can think of is myself. All I can do is look at myself and feel very foolish." Her eyes raised to his. "Do you know why, Mr. Brennan? Because I know now that my husband never cared for me; because I know that he married me for his own interest." She paused. "I saw an innocent man killed yesterday and I can't even find the decency within me to pray for him."

"Mrs. Mims, try and rest now."

She shook her head wearily. "I don't care what happens to me."

There was a silence before Brennan said, "When you get done feeling sorry for yourself I'll tell you something."

Her eyes came open and she looked at him, more surprised than hurt.

"Look," Brennan said. "You know it and I know it—your husband married you for your money; but you're alive and he's dead and that makes the difference. You can moon about being a fool till they shoot you tomorrow, or you can start thinking about saving your skin right now. But I'll tell you this—it will take both of us working together to stay alive."

"But he said he'd let us—"

"You think they're going to let us go after your dad brings the money? They've killed four people in less than twenty-four hours!"

"I don't care what happens to me!"

He took her shoulders and turned her toward him. "Well, I care about me, and I'm not going to get shot in the belly tomorrow because you feel sorry for yourself."

"But I can't help!" Doretta pleaded.

"You don't know if you can or not. We've got to keep our eyes open and we've got to think, and when the chance comes we've got to take it quick or else forget about it." His face was close to hers and he was still gripping her shoulders. "These men will kill. They've done it before and they have nothing to lose. They're going to kill us. That means we've got nothing to lose. Now, you think about that a while."

He left her and went back to the door.

Brennan was called out of the hut later in the afternoon, as Usher and Billy-Jack rode in. They had shot a mule deer and Billy-Jack carried a hindquarter dangling from his saddle horn. Brennan was told to dress it down, enough for supper, and the rest to be stripped and hung up to dry.

"But you take care of the supper first," Frank Usher said, adding that the woman wasn't in fit condition for cooking. "I don't want burned meat just 'cause she's in a state over her husband."

After they had eaten, Brennan took meat and coffee in to Doretta Mims.

She looked up as he offered it to her. "I don't care for anything."

He was momentarily angry, but it passed off and he said, "Suit yourself." He placed the cup and plate on the floor and went outside to finish preparing the jerky.

By the time he finished, dusk had settled over the clearing and the inside of the hut was dark as he stepped inside.

He moved to her side and his foot kicked over the tin cup. He stooped quickly, picking up the cup and plate, and even in the dimness he could see that she had eaten most of the food.

"Mr. Brennan, I'm sorry for the way I've acted." She hesitated. "I thought you would understand, else I'd never have told you about— about how I felt."

"It's not a question of my understanding," Brennan said.

"I'm sorry I told you," Doretta Mims said.

He moved closer to her and knelt down, sitting back on his heels. "Look. Maybe I know how you feel, better than you think. But that's not important. Right now you don't need sympathy as much as you need a way to stay alive."

"I can't help the way I feel," she said obstinately.

Brennan was momentarily silent. He said then, "Did you love him?"

"I was married to him!"

"That's not what I asked you. While everybody's being honest, just tell me if you loved him."

She hesitated, looking down at her hands. "I'm not sure."

"But you wanted to be in love with him, more than anything."

Her head nodded slowly. "Yes."

"Did you ever think for a minute that he loved you?"

"That's not a fair question!"

"Answer it anyway!"

She hesitated again. "No, I didn't."

He said, almost brutally, "Then what have you lost outside of a little pride?"

"You don't understand," she said.

"You're afraid you can't get another man—is that what it is? Even if he married you for money, at least he married you. He was the first and last chance as far as you were concerned, so you grabbed him."

"What are you trying to do, strip me of what little self-respect I have left?"

"I'm trying to strip you of this foolishness! You think you're too plain to get a man?"

She bit her lower lip and looked away from him.

"You think nobody'll have you because you bite your lip and can't say more than two words at a time?"

"Mr. Brennan—"

"Listen, you're as much woman as any of them. A hell of a lot more than some, but you've got to realize it! You've got to do something about it!"

"I can't help it if—"

"Shut up with that I-can't-help-it talk! If you can't help it, nobody can. All your life you've been sitting around waiting for something to happen to you. Sometimes you have to walk up and take what you want."

Suddenly he brought her to him, his arms circling her shoulders, and he kissed her, holding his lips to hers until he felt her body relax slowly and at the same time he knew that she was kissing him.

His lips brushed her cheek and he said, close to her, "We're going to stay alive. You're going to do exactly what I say when the time comes, and we're going to get out of here." Her hair brushed his cheek softly and he knew that she was nodding yes.

★
Chapter Six

DURING THE NIGHT he opened his eyes and crawled to the lighter silhouette of the doorway. Keeping close to the front wall, he looked out and across to the low-burning fire. One of them, a shadowy form that he could not recognize, sat facing the hut. He did not move, but by the way he was sitting Brennan knew he was awake. You're running out of time, Brennan thought. But there was nothing he could do.

The sun was not yet above the trees when Frank Usher appeared in the doorway. He saw that Brennan was awake and he said, "Bring the woman out," turning away as he said it.

Her eyes were closed, but they opened as Brennan touched her shoulder, and he knew that she had not been asleep. She looked up at him calmly, her features softly shadowed.

"Stay close to me," he said. "Whatever we do, stay close to me."

They went out to the lean-to and Brennan built the fire as Doretta got the coffee and venison ready to put on.

Brennan moved slowly, as if he were tired, as if he had given up hope; but his eyes were alive and most of the time his gaze stayed with the three men—watching them eat, watching them make cigarettes as they squatted in a half circle, talking, but too far away for their voices to be heard. Finally, Chink rose and went off into the trees. He came back with his horse, mounted, and rode off into the trees again but in the other direction, toward the open grade.

It went through Brennan's mind: He's going off like he did yesterday morning, but this time to wait for Gateway. Yesterday on foot, but today on his horse, which means he's going farther down to wait for him. And Frank went somewhere yesterday morning. Frank went over to where the horses are. He suddenly felt an excitement inside of him, deep within his stomach, and he kept his eyes on Frank Usher.

A moment later Usher stood up and started off toward the trees, calling back something to Billy-Jack about the horses—and Brennan could hardly believe his eyes.

Now. It's now. You know that, don't you? It's now or never. God help me. God help me think of something! And suddenly it was in his mind. It was less than half a chance, but it was something, and it came to him because it was the only thing about Billy-Jack that stood out in his mind, besides the shotgun. *He was always looking at Doretta!*

She was in front of the lean-to, and he moved toward her, turning his back to Billy-Jack sitting with Rintoon's shotgun across his lap.

"Go in the hut and start unbuttoning your dress." He half whispered it and saw her eyes widen as he said it. "Go on! Billy-Jack will come in.

Act surprised. Embarrassed. Then smile at him." She hesitated, starting to bite her lip. "Damn it, go on!"

He poured himself a cup of coffee, not looking at her as she walked away. Putting the coffee down, he saw Billy-Jack's eyes following her.

"Want a cup?" Brennan called to him. "There's about one left."

Billy-Jack shook his head and turned the sawed-off shotgun on Brennan as he saw him approaching.

Brennan took a sip of the coffee. "Aren't you going to look in on that?" He nodded toward the hut.

"What do you mean?"

"The woman," Brennan said matter-of-factly. He took another sip of the coffee.

"What about her?" Billy-Jack asked.

Brennan shrugged. "I thought you were taking turns."

"What?"

"Now, look, you can't be so young, I got to draw you a map—" Brennan smiled. "Oh, I see. . . . Frank didn't say anything to you. Or Chink. . . . Keeping her for themselves. . . ."

Billy-Jack's eyes flicked to the hut, then back to Brennan. "They were with her?"

"Well, all I know is Frank went in there yesterday morning and Chink yesterday afternoon while you were gone." He took another sip of the coffee and threw out what was left in the cup. Turning, he said, "No skin off my nose," and walked slowly back to the lean-to.

He began scraping the tin plates, his head down, but watching Billy-Jack. Let it sink through that thick skull of yours. But do it quick! Come on, move, you animal!

There! He watched Billy-Jack walk slowly toward the hut. God, make him move faster! Billy-Jack was out of view then beyond the corner of the hut.

All right. Brennan put down the tin plate he was holding and moved quickly, noiselessly, to the side of the hut and edged along the rough logs until he reached the corner. He listened first before he looked around. Billy-Jack had gone inside.

He wanted to make sure, some way, that Billy-Jack would be looking at Doretta, but there was not time. And then he was moving again—along the front, and suddenly he was inside the hut, seeing the back of Billy-Jack's head, seeing him turning, and a glimpse of Doretta's face, and the sawed-off shotgun coming around. One of his hands shot out to grip the stubby barrel, pushing it, turning it up and back violently, and the other hand closed over the trigger guard before it jerked down on Billy-Jack's wrist.

Deafeningly, a shot exploded, with the twin barrels jammed under the outlaw's jaw. Smoke and a crimson smear, and Brennan was on top of him wrenching the shotgun from squeezed fingers, clutching Billy-Jack's revolver as he came to his feet.

He heard Doretta gasp, still with the ringing in his ears, and he said, "Don't look at him!" already turning to the doorway as he jammed the Colt into his empty holster.

Frank Usher was running across the clearing, his gun in his hand.

Brennan stepped into the doorway leveling the shotgun. "Frank, hold it there!"

Usher stopped dead, but in the next second he was aiming, his revolver coming up even with his face, and Brennan's hand squeezed the second trigger of the shotgun.

Usher screamed and went down, grabbing his knees, and he rolled to his side as he hit the ground. His right hand came up, still holding the Colt.

"Don't do it, Frank!" Brennan had dropped the scattergun and now Billy-Jack's revolver was in his hand. He saw Usher's gun coming in line, and he fired, aiming dead center at the half-reclined figure, hearing the sharp, heavy report, and seeing Usher's gun hand raise straight up into the air as he slumped over on his back.

Brennan hesitated. Get him out of there, quick. Chink's not deaf.

He ran out to Frank Usher and dragged him back to the hut, laying him next to Billy-Jack. He jammed Usher's pistol into his belt. Then, "Come on!" he told Doretta, and took her hand and ran out of the hut and across the clearing toward the side where the horses were.

They moved into the denser pines, where he stopped and pulled her down next to him in the warm sand. Then he rolled over on his stomach and parted the branches to look back out across the clearing.

The hut was to the right. Straight across were more pines, but they were scattered thinly, and through them he could see the sand-colored expanse of the open grade. Chink would come that way, Brennan knew. There was no other way he could.

★

Chapter Seven

CLOSE TO HIM, Doretta said, "We could leave before he comes." She was afraid, and it was in the sound of her voice.

"No," Brennan said. "We'll finish this. When Chink comes we'll finish it once and for all."

"But you don't know! How can you be sure you'll—"

"Listen, I'm not sure of anything, but I know what I have to do." She was silent and he said quietly, "Move back and stay close to the ground."

And as he looked across the clearing his eyes caught the dark speck of movement beyond the trees, out on the open slope. There he was. It had to be him. Brennan could feel the sharp knot in his stomach again as he watched, as the figure grew larger.

Now he was sure. Chink was on foot leading his horse, not coming straight across, but angling higher up on the slope. He'll come in where the trees are thicker, Brennan thought. He'll come out beyond the lean-to and you won't see him until he turns the corner of the hut. That's it. He can't climb the slope back of the hut, so he'll have to come around the front way.

He estimated the distance from where he was lying to the front of the hut—seventy or eighty feet—and his thumb eased back the hammer of the revolver in front of him.

There was a dead silence for perhaps ten minutes before he heard, coming from beyond the hut, "Frank?" Silence again. Then, "Where the hell are you?"

Brennan waited, feeling the smooth, heavy, hickory grip of the Colt in his hand, his finger lightly caressing the trigger. It was in his mind to fire as soon as Chink turned the corner. He was ready. But it came and it went.

It went as he saw Chink suddenly, unexpectedly, slip around the corner of the hut and flatten himself against the wall, his gun pointed toward the door. Brennan's front sight was dead on Chink's belt, but he couldn't pull the trigger. Not like this. He watched Chink edge slowly toward the door.

"Throw it down, boy!"

Chink moved and Brennan squeezed the trigger a split second late. He fired again, hearing the bullet thump solidly into the door frame, but it was too late. Chink was inside.

Brennan let his breath out slowly, relaxing somewhat. Well, that's what you get. You wait, and all you do is make it harder for yourself. He could picture Chink now looking at Usher and Billy-Jack. That'll give him something to think about. Look at them good. Then look at the door you've got to come out of sooner or later.

I'm glad he's seeing them like that. And he thought then: How long could you stand something like that? He can cover up Billy-Jack and stand it a little longer. But when dark comes. . . . If he holds out till dark he's got a chance. And now he was sorry he had not pulled the trigger before. You got to make him come out, that's all.

"Chink!"

There was no answer.

"Chink, come on out!"

Suddenly gunfire came from the doorway and Brennan, hugging the ground, could hear the swishing of the bullets through the foliage above him.

Don't throw it away, he thought, looking up again. He backed up and moved over a few yards to take up a new position. He'd be on the left side of the doorway as you look at it, Brennan thought, to shoot on an angle like that.

He sighted on the inside edge of the door frame and called, "Chink, come out and get it!" He saw the powder flash, and he fired on top of it, cocked and fired again. Then silence.

Now you don't know, Brennan thought. He reloaded and called

out, "Chink!" but there was no answer, and he thought: You just keep digging your hole deeper.

Maybe you did hit him. No, that's what he wants you to think. Walk in the door and you'll find out. He'll wait now. He'll take it slow and start adding up his chances. Wait till night? That's his best bet—but he can't count on his horse being there then. I could have worked around and run it off. And he knows he wouldn't be worth a damn on foot, even if he did get away. So the longer he waits, the less he can count on his horse.

All right, what would you do? Immediately he thought: I'd count shots. So you hear five shots go off in a row and you make a break out the door, and while you're doing it the one shooting picks up another gun. But even picking up another gun takes time.

He studied the distance from the doorway to the corner of the hut. Three long strides. Out of sight in less than three seconds. That's if he's thinking of it. And if he tried it, you'd have only that long to aim and fire. Unless . . .

Unless Doretta pulls off the five shots. He thought about this for some time before he was sure it could be done without endangering her. But first you have to give him the idea.

He rolled to his side to pull Usher's gun from his belt. Then, holding it in his left hand, he emptied it at the doorway. Silence followed.

I'm reloading now, Chink. Get it through your cat-eyed head. I'm reloading and you've got time to do something.

He explained it to Doretta unhurriedly—how she would wait about ten minutes before firing the first time; she would count to five and fire again, and so on until the gun was empty. She was behind the thick bole of a pine and only the gun would be exposed as she fired.

She said, "And if he doesn't come out?"

"Then we'll think of something else."

Their faces were close. She leaned toward him, closing her eyes, and kissed him softly. "I'll be waiting," she said.

Brennan moved off through the trees, circling wide, well back from the edge of the clearing. He came to the thin section directly across from Doretta's position and went quickly from tree to tree, keeping to the shadows until he was into thicker pines again. He saw Chink's horse off to the left of him. Only a few minutes remained as he came out of the trees to the off side of the lean-to, and there he went down to his knees, keeping his eyes on the corner of the hut.

The first shot rang out and he heard it whump into the front of the hut. One . . . then the second . . . two . . . he was counting them, not moving his eyes from the front edge of the hut . . . three . . . four . . . be ready. . . . Five! Now, Chink!

He heard him—hurried steps on the packed sand—and almost immediately he saw him cutting sharply around the edge of the hut, stopping, leaning against the wall, breathing heavily but thinking he was safe. Then Brennan stood up.

"Here's one facing you, Chink."

He saw the look of surprise, the momentary expression of shock, a full second before Chink's revolver flashed up from his side and Brennan's finger tightened on the trigger. With the report Chink lurched back against the wall, a look of bewilderment still on his face, although he was dead even as he slumped to the ground.

Brennan holstered the revolver and did not look at Chink as he walked past him around to the front of the hut. He suddenly felt tired, but it was the kind of tired feeling you enjoyed, like the bone weariness and sense of accomplishment you felt seeing your last cow punched through the market chute.

He thought of old man Tenvoorde, and only two days ago trying to buy the yearlings from him. He still didn't have any yearlings.

What the hell do you feel so good about?

Still, he couldn't help smiling. Not having money to buy stock seemed like such a little trouble. He saw Doretta come out of the trees and he walked on across the clearing.

20

No Man's Guns

Western Story Roundup, August 1955

AS HE DREW near the mass of tree shadows that edged out to the road he heard the voice, the clear but hesitant sound of it coming unexpectedly in the almost-dark stillness.

"Cliff—"

His right knee touched the booted Springfield and he thought of it calmly, instinctively, drawing it left-handed in his mind, as he slowed the sorrel to a walk. Now at the edge of the shadows he saw a man with a rifle.

The man called uncertainly, "Cliff?"

"You got the wrong party," he answered, and neck-reined the sorrel toward the trees.

Less than twenty feet away the rifle came up suddenly. "Who are you?"

"My name's Mitchell."

The rifle barrel hung hesitantly. "You better light down."

Astride the McClellan saddle, Dave Mitchell didn't move. He sat with his shoulders pulled back, yet he was relaxed. Narrow hips, sun-darkened, thin-lined features beneath the slightly turned-up forward brim of a faded Stetson and everything about him said *Cavalry.* Everything but the rough-wool gray suit he wore. His coat was unbuttoned and his dark shirt was unmistakably Army issue.

"You're camped back in there?" Mitchell asked, and he was thinking, watching the man studying him: I'm the wrong man and now he doesn't know what to do. The man with the rifle didn't reply and

Mitchell said, "I'm ready to camp the night. If you already got a place, maybe I could join you."

For a moment the man didn't answer. Then the rifle, a long-barreled Remington, waved in a short arc. "Light down."

Mitchell let his right rein fall as he came off the sorrel. The rifle waved again. The man stood aside and Mitchell walked past him leading the sorrel. They moved through the trees, thinly scattered aspen, then cottonwood as the ground began to slope gradually, and Mitchell knew there'd be a creek close by. Unexpectedly, then, he saw the broad clearing and a wagon illuminated by firelight.

The ribbed canvas covering of it formed a pale background for the two figures who stood watching him approach. A man, his legs slightly apart and his hand covering the butt of a holstered revolver. A woman was next to him and she watched Mitchell with open curiosity as he entered the clearing.

"Rady's brought us a guest," the woman said.

The man with the rifle was next to Mitchell now. "Hyatt, he says he wants to camp." The woman walked to the fire, but Hyatt, his hand still on the revolver, didn't move. Nor did he answer, and his eyes remained on Mitchell. "He said he was ready to camp the night," Rady added, "so I thought—"

"Open your coat," Hyatt said. "Hold it open."

Slowly Mitchell spread the coat open. "I'm not armed."

"He's got a carbine on the horse," Rady said.

Hyatt glanced at him. "Go back where you were."

MITCHELL DROPPED the rein and walked toward the low-burning fire as the woman extended a porcelain cup toward him and said, "Coffee?" Behind him he heard Rady's footsteps in the dry leaves, then fading to nothing, and he felt Hyatt watching him as he took the cup of coffee, his hand momentarily touching the woman's.

"You drink your coffee, then move off," Hyatt said. He was in his early thirties, but a week-old beard stubble darkened his face, adding ten years to his appearance. His face was drawn into tight, sunken cheeks and he looked as if he'd never smiled in his life. To the woman he said, "I'll tell you when we start giving coffee to everybody who goes by."

Mitchell hesitated, letting the sudden tension inside him subside, and he thought, Don't let him rile you. Don't even tell him to go to hell. He said to Hyatt, "I'll leave in a minute."

"You'll leave sooner if I say so."

Maybe you ought to tell him, at that, Mitchell thought. Just to see what he'd do. But he heard the woman say, "Hy, don't talk like that," and he turned to the fire again.

"You shut your mouth!" Hyatt told her.

Mitchell sipped his coffee, his eyes on the woman. Her face was lit by the firelight and it shone warmly and cleanly. He watched her glance at Hyatt but not answer him and he said to her, mildly, "I don't want to start a family argument."

"We'll ignore him, then," the woman said. She smiled and the smile was faintly in her eyes. She'd impressed Mitchell as a woman who smiled little, and the soft radiance that came briefly into her eyes surprised him. Still, she fell into a type in Mitchell's mind: small, frail looking, a woman who picked at her food yet was strong and you wondered what kept her going. Light hair, thin, delicately formed features, and dark shadows beneath the eyes. A serious kind, a woman who loved strongly and simply. A woman who spoke little. This, Mitchell believed, was the most interesting type of all. The most feminine, even while sometimes reminding you of a little boy. At least the most appealing. Perhaps the kind to marry.

She said, "Could I ask where you're going?"

"Home," Mitchell answered. No, she didn't exactly fit the type. She talked too freely.

"Where is that?"

"Banderas. I just left Whipple Barracks yesterday. Discharged."

"I thought so," the woman said. "Just the way you stand."

"I suppose some of it's bound to rub off, after twelve years."

"You don't look that old."

"Older'n you. I'm almost thirty-one."

"Were you an officer?"

"No, ma'am. Sergeant."

"You're going home to your folks?"

"Yes, ma'am. My dad has a place near Banderas."

"They'll be glad to see you."

Mitchell half turned as Hyatt said, "How do we know you're from Whipple?"

"I just told you I was."

"What proof you got?"

"I don't have to show you anything."

Hyatt's hand hung close to his holster. "You don't think so, huh?"

"Look," Mitchell said. "Why don't you quit standing on your nerves."

"Let's see your proof," Hyatt said.

Mitchell glanced at the woman. "You ought to keep him locked up."

The woman half smiled. "Do you have discharge papers?"

Mitchell's hand slipped into his open coat and patted his shirt pocket. "Right here."

"Why don't you show him?" the woman said. "So we'll have a little peace."

✫　✫　✫

MITCHELL SHOOK his head. "It's a matter of principle now." A matter of principle. And a matter of twelve years someone telling you what to do. You can take it when you're being paid to take it. But this one isn't paying, Mitchell thought. Take that handgun off him and bend it over his head? No, just get out. You don't have any business here.

The woman said, "Men are always talking about principle, or honor."

"Well, I'm through talking about it tonight," Mitchell said. He handed the empty cup to her. "Much obliged. I'm moving on now." She looked at him, but said nothing.

He saw her eyes shift suddenly.

Behind you!

It snapped in his mind and he heard the movement and he wheeled, bringing up his arms, throwing himself low at Hyatt who was almost on top of him. His shoulder slammed into Hyatt's knees and he drove forward as the pistol barrel came down against his spine. His arms clamped Hyatt's legs and he came up suddenly, His boots digging into the sand, throwing Hyatt's legs over his shoulder. Hyatt landed on his back, rolling over almost as he struck the ground, frantically reaching for the revolver knocked from his hand, almost touching it as Mitchell dropped on top of him.

They rolled in the sand, Hyatt's fingers tearing through Mitchell's shirt, clawing at his throat. Mitchell's hand found the revolver. He threw it spinning across the sand and his fist came back to slam against Hyatt's face. He pushed himself free, rolling, rising to his feet, and as Hyatt came up he swung hard against his jaw. Hyatt staggered. He started to go down and Mitchell hit him again, holding him momentarily with his left hand as his right clubbed into the upturned face. Hyatt's head snapped back and he went down.

Mitchell turned to the woman. He was breathing heavily and his left hand was pressed to the small of his back. "Are you married to him?" he asked.

She shook her head. "Not really."

Mitchell hesitated. If he turned away he'd never see this woman again. Something made him ask, "Do you love him?"

She looked at him, her face softly impassive in the firelight. "You'd better move along," she said quietly.

For a moment Mitchell's eyes remained on her, as if he were reluctant to leave. He turned to the sorrel, then hesitated again and walked over to Hyatt.

"Mister, you brought this on yourself. Your man out there thought I was somebody named Cliff and he brought me in because he was too scared to do anything else. I don't care who you are. . . . I don't care who Cliff is—" Mitchell broke off. "If you want to know the truth, I think you're crazy." He glanced momentarily at the woman before telling Hyatt, "Maybe you got some good points, but if you do you keep them a secret."

Hyatt's head came up slowly. He watched Mitchell go to his sorrel and mount. He watched him silently, his hand covering a folded piece of paper on the ground beneath him. A square of paper folded four times just to fit into a shirt pocket.

Mitchell urged the sorrel into the trees, letting it have its head, but holding it enough to reach the road farther down from where Rady would be. The woman stayed in his mind: standing in the firelight, her eyes meeting his and not lowering even when he continued to stare at her.

Some woman.

✻ ✻ ✻

HIS BODY CAME alive as the shot sounded behind him and his hand instinctively went to the booted carbine. He turned in the saddle drawing the Springfield, the sorrel sidestepping nervously, kicking the dry leaves, throwing its head. There were other sounds in the leaves and suddenly a man's voice: "Throw up your hands!" And almost with the words Mitchell was dragged from the saddle. Men were all around him in the darkness, two holding his arms, and as he tried to rise a fist came from nowhere, stinging hard against his face.

A rifle barrel jabbed into his back and he was taken through the trees, a man holding each arm. There were more men at the clearing and the nearest ones stepped aside as Mitchell was brought in. One man was building the fire. Another was climbing the wagon wheel, now looking inside. The rest stood in a semicircle around Hyatt and the woman.

The man holding Mitchell's left arm shouted, "Dyke, we got the other one!"

Mitchell saw one of the men turn and nod his head, then beckon them to come closer. He stood relaxed, a tall man wearing a stiff-brimmed hat low and straight over his eyes, and a tawny tip-twisted mustache that in the firelight blended with the weathered cut of his features. His coat was open, a dark coat . . . and then Mitchell saw it. The deputy star against the dark cloth and everything was suddenly perfectly clear.

Hyatt was saying, "What're you doing! We're camped here and you barge in, shooting—"

A man said, "You scrambled for that gun quick enough."

"How'd I know who you were?"

"You know now." The man laughed. Mitchell looked from this man to the others. There were perhaps a dozen in the group, but only Dyke and two or three more wore deputy stars.

"Listen"—Hyatt's voice calmed—"I think you could've announced yourselves, that's all. You're looking for somebody and you want to ask some questions, that it?"

Dyke shook his head. "I don't have any questions."

Hyatt's eyes shifted along the line of men. "We're on our way down to Tucson. I'm going in business with a man down there."

Dyke said nothing. His eyes were on Hyatt, studying him.

"In the freight business," Hyatt said. "This man's already got contracts."

"Are you through?" Dyke said then.

Hyatt frowned. "What do you mean?"

"I'll tell a story now," Dyke said. "It starts the day before yesterday when the Hatch & Hodges was held up an hour out of Mojave. One of the passengers, Mr. J. A. Hicks, was shot and killed when he raised an objection. Now, this Mr. Hicks was owner of the Mogollon Cattle Company—Slash M—of which I'm foreman. Mr. Hicks, besides being boss, was my best friend . . . which doesn't mean much to the story aside from it's the reason I was deputized to take out a posse."

Hyatt said, "I'm sorry to hear that, but—"

"I'm not finished," Dyke stated. "You see, these holdup men separated after the robbery. We spent a whole day scratching for sign and finally we got on one we were pretty sure of. Last night we caught up with a man named Cliff something. Now, at first he said he didn't know anything about it."

☆   ☆   ☆

DYKE'S EYES HADN'T left Hyatt's. "I hit this man twice. The second one broke his jaw and after that he wrote down what we wanted to know. How he was to meet his friends tonight, and where. A woman and two men posing as travelers. A man named James Rady; another by the name of Hyatt Earl."

"Well?" Hyatt said. His voice was controlled, and it told nothing of what he might be thinking.

Dyke brought a match out of his vest pocket and wedged it into the corner of his mouth, shaking his head as he did. "That's all there is to the story."

Hyatt hesitated. "Now what?"

"Now, Mr. Earl," Dyke said mildly, his eyes lifting then, "we're going to hang you right on that cottonwood over there."

"What're you talking about, hanging! You don't even know—" Hyatt broke off. He looked at Dyke and at his men and for a long moment he was silent, gaining control of himself. He said then, calmly, almost defiantly, "You got to take us to trial. That's what the law says."

The matchstick moved under Dyke's full mustache. "Mr. Earl, are you telling me what I have to do?"

That was it. The futility of arguing showed briefly on Hyatt's face. He asked, "What about the woman?"

Dyke shook his head. "This Cliff said she didn't want any part of it, but you forced her into it. We're not bothered about her. Just you and Rady there." He nodded directly at Mitchell.

Mitchell frowned. Hurriedly then his eyes swept the clearing. Rady wasn't here! He called to Dyke, "I'm not Rady! He's the one with the Remington . . . was out by the road."

Dyke studied him before answering. "There wasn't anybody out there."

"Then he got away, but I sure as hell ain't Rady!"

"Who're you supposed to be?"

"Dave Mitchell. I just rode in a little while ago looking to camp." He saw Hyatt watching him, a grin softening the dark bearded face.

"Rady," Hyatt said, "are you drunk or something?"

Mitchell stared at him with disbelief. "What's the matter with you? Tell them who I am!"

Hyatt shook his head. "There's no use in that, Rady. Let's own up . . . take our medicine like men."

Mitchell's eyes went to Dyke. "Listen. This man's crazy. I suspected it before. Now I'm sure."

"If I was in your shoes," said Dyke, "I might pull the same stunt."

Mitchell paused. "All right"—his glance went to the woman—"ask her."

She looked at Mitchell, then shook her head. "He's not Rady. His name is Mitchell."

Dyke said, "Uh-huh, and you're Mrs. Mitchell."

"I never saw him before this evening."

"Claire," Hyatt said sympathetically, "there's no use. Rady's got to take his medicine just the same way I do."

The woman's face was cold and showed no emotion. "He had a fight with this man Mitchell and lost. That's why he wants to see him hang."

"Claire! . . . Rady and I were just kidding! You thought we really meant it?"

Mitchell looked at Dyke again. "You said that holdup was day before yesterday. I can prove I was at Whipple then. I was just discharged yesterday."

"What's your proof?" Dyke asked.

"Ask anybody at Whipple!"

"Rady," Hyatt said, "delaying it a few days ain't going to help any, they'll still hang you. Let's get it over with."

Mitchell's expression changed suddenly and his hand went to his chest. "My discharge order! It's dated yesterday!"

"Keep your hand out of that coat!" Dyke snapped. He nodded to one of the men near Mitchell. "Take a look."

The man stepped in front of Mitchell. His hand went over the shirt, then to the inside coat pocket. "Nothing," he said over his shoulder.

Mitchell's hand came up. He felt the empty pocket, and the part of his shirt that was torn—

"Listen, while we were fighting my shirt was ripped. The paper fell out, that's what happened. Look around there, right where you're standing!"

Dyke continued to study Mitchell, but some of his men moved about, looking at the ground and scuffing the sand with their boots. A man said, "I don't see nothin'," and another said, "Not around here." Watching them, the tension building and becoming unbearable. Mitchell suddenly tore himself from the men holding him. They started after him and Dyke called, "Let him go!"

Mitchell came on, his eyes searching the ground, then dropped to his hands and knees, his fingers brushing the sand, smoothing it, and carefully he covered the area where the fight had taken place. He came up slowly and sat back on his heels. "It's not here," he said wearily. Then: "Wait! When I was pulled off my horse—" He came to his feet quickly.

Dyke asked, "You ever on the stage?"

"I'm telling you the truth!" Mitchell screamed. "Can't you see that!"

"I see a man fighting awful hard," Dyke replied, "for a life he don't deserve."

"What do you expect me to do!" Mitchell paused then. He breathed in and out and said, more calmly, "I swear to Almighty God I had nothing to do with that holdup."

"That's what this Cliff said," Dyke answered. "Before I broke his jaw."

"Rady," Hyatt spoke up, "you don't want that to happen to you, do you?"

Mitchell ignored him. Still looking at Dyke he said, "Isn't there a doubt in your mind?" Dyke didn't answer and in the silence their eyes held.

Then, behind Mitchell, a man said, "Let's have some coffee first." Dyke's eyes lifted. He nodded and walked toward the fire, finished with Mitchell.

☆ ☆ ☆

HYATT AND THE woman were moved over by the wagon. Then Mitchell was brought over. They tied Hyatt's and Mitchell's hands behind their backs and made them sit down, the woman between them.

There was nothing to be said. In silence they watched Dyke's men build another fire close to the cottonwood tree they would use. Two men entered the clearing carrying riatas, uncoiling them as they crossed to the tree. Mitchell saw his sorrel and a bay brought in and the saddles were taken off both horses.

Now what do you do? he thought.

Tell him!

I did tell him! He's hard-shelled and mean because Hyatt killed his friend and that's all he can think about. But he's calm about it, isn't he? Judge and jury wrapped into one hard-bitten weathered face. His mind is the law and he can be as calm as he pleases, knowing his way is the only way.

Twelve years of campaigning and you're going to die under another man's name. Nobody knowing . . . no, two people knowing who you are. The woman—Claire—and Hyatt.

Two feet away and you can't even touch him. Get up quick and butt his face in with your head! No . . . come on, think straight now. Now isn't a time to think about revenge. Forget about him. You're going to die and that's all there is to it.

He said it in his mind, feeling each word: I'm going to die. More slowly then: I am going to die.

All right, now you know it. You always knew it, but now you know it. Come on, think straight. I *am* thinking straight. Go to hell with that thinking straight business! There's no *straight* way to think when you're going to die. What did you think about the other time? The first and only and supposedly last other time.

Nervous and not liking it, not believing that it was happening to him, but holding himself together nevertheless and thinking over and over again that it was a shame to die alone. Alone, because the Coyotero tracker didn't count. You couldn't talk about last things in sign language. Dos Fuegos had taken out a buckskin pouch in which he carried his *hoddentin,* the sacred pollen made from tule that would ward off evil, and with that he had readied himself.

CORPORAL MITCHELL then, Corporal Mitchell and a Coyotero tracker called Dos Fuegos—the two of them riding point and cut off from the others and their mounts shot from under them. Then holding flat to the ground, lying behind the mound and looking across to the rock-scrambled sand-glaring dead-silent slope where the Mimbres were. Lying unmoving—wondering if the patrol would find them.

The Mimbres came—a few at a time, running, dodging, firing carbines; and they drove them back to cover. The second rush came before they had time to reload—but so did D Company, brought by the firing, and that was that.

Sergeant Mitchell, the next month, and less talkative.

But, Mitchell thought, you really didn't learn anything that time. Not that you could apply to this one. Only that dying is important to you and if you can't do it in bed, sometime far in the future, then have it happen during a heroic act with a great number of people watching. Don't talk foolish. You're going to die, that's all . . . so do it as well as you can.

He thought of his father and mother and for a few minutes he prayed.

The woman touched his arm and he looked up. "I'm sorry . . . I wish there was something I could do."

"I wish there was too," Mitchell answered. "I wonder if you'd do me a favor."

"What is it?"

"Sometime look up my father in Banderas, R. F. Mitchell, and let him know what happened."

She nodded slowly. "All right."

Hyatt leaned forward. "Rady, your folks don't live in Banderas."

"You've got a real sense of humor," Mitchell said, mildly.

Momentarily Hyatt frowned. "You've calmed down some."

Mitchell didn't reply. He saw Dyke, standing by the big cottonwood tree, motion to the men guarding them, and now they were pulled to their feet. Hyatt turned to the woman. "Claire, we say good-bye now."

"Hy, tell them who he is."

Hyatt grinned. "Honey, I did."

"I think I'm glad they're hanging you," she said.

Hyatt shrugged. One of the possemen took Mitchell's arm. He looked at the woman and their eyes held lingeringly. Come on, he thought. You couldn't say it in minutes, so don't say it at all. He turned and followed Hyatt across the clearing and he knew that the woman was watching him.

"Get 'em up," Dyke ordered.

THEY WERE LIFTED onto the horses and a mounted man rode between them and adjusted the riata loops over their heads. Dyke looked up at them. "Mr. Rady seems to've lost his fight."

Hyatt grinned. "He's turned honest."

Mitchell looked at him. "You proved your point. Now you're wearing it out."

Hyatt's eyes narrowed. For a moment he was silent and he watched Mitchell curiously. "You ever see a hanging?" he asked then.

Mitchell shook his head. "No."

"If your neck don't bust, you strangle awhile." His eyes stayed on Mitchell. "You scared?"

Mitchell shrugged. "Probably, the same as you are."

A bewildered look crossed Hyatt's face. Apparently he had expected

Mitchell to panic now, to lose control of himself pleading for his life, but he was at ease and he sat the sorrel without moving. He leaned closer so that only Mitchell could hear him say, "Rady's ten miles away by now; but in another minute he'll be legally, officially dead."

"I'd say I was doing him some favor," Mitchell answered.

Hyatt hesitated, and the cloud of uncertainty clouded his face again. He wanted to whisper, but his voice rasped. "You're going to *hang*! You understand that? Hang!"

Mitchell nodded. "The same as you are."

Hyatt's teeth clenched. He was about to say more, but he stopped.

Mitchell looked down at Dyke. "He's going to foam at the mouth in a minute."

Dyke shook his head. "He don't have that long."

But now Hyatt was looking at Mitchell calmly, without bewilderment, and without the brooding anger that had been a knife edge inside of him since the fight. That had started to die as they sat by the wagon. He had tried to bring it back by taunting Mitchell, but it was no use. His anger was dead and even the memory of it seemed senseless and unimportant. Mitchell was a man. Give him credit for it.

That's how it happened. That's what caused Hyatt to say, unexpectedly, "Reach in the side of my boot; the right one."

Dyke looked at him. "What for?"

"Just do it!"

Hyatt's eyes returned to Mitchell. "You either got more guts than any man I ever saw . . . or else you're the dumbest."

Dyke's two fingers came out of the boot lifting the folded sheet of paper. He unfolded it and his eyes went over it slowly.

The two granite-faced men, at the very gates of a hot and waiting hell, stared stonily down at the executioner.

Dyke read it completely: the formal phrasing of the discharge order, the written-in-ink portion that described the soldier, and the scrawled, illegible signature at the bottom. He looked at the date again. Then, and only then, did he look at Mitchell.

Their eyes met briefly before Dyke turned away. He said to the men near him, "Take him down and untie him," and started toward the edge of the trees, walking with his head down. He stopped then and turned. "Hyatt Earl too. We're taking him to Mojave."

When his hands were cut loose, Mitchell walked over to Dyke. "Can I have my order now?"

Dyke handed it to him. "Listen, if I tried to tell you I'm sorry—"

Mitchell turned away. Don't listen to that, he thought. You might hit him. Don't even think of Hyatt. He looked over at the woman and saw her watching him. Then stopped. He'd have plenty of time to talk to her. And he thought, feeling the relief, but still holding himself calm: You've carried it this far. Hang on one more minute.

He turned back to Dyke and said, "Don't take it so hard, we all make mistakes."

21

The Rancher's Lady

Original Title: The Woman from Tascosa
Western Magazine, September 1955

THEY CAME TO Anton Chico on the morning stage, Willis Calender and his son, Jim; the man getting out of the coach first, stretching the stiffness from his back and squaring the curled-brim hat lower over his eyes, and then the boy, hesitating, squinting, rubbing his eyes before jumping down to stand close to his dad. It had been a long, all-night trip from the Puerto de Luna station and a six-hour ride in the wagon before that up from the Calender place in the Yeso Creek country.

Willis Calender had come to Anton Chico to marry a woman he'd never met except in letters. Three letters from him—the first two to get acquainted, the third to ask her to be his wife. She'd answered all of them, saying, yes, she was interested in the marriage state and finally she thought living down on the Yeso would be just fine. Which was exactly what the marriage broker said she would say. Her name was Clare Conway and she was to come over from Tascosa and meet Willis.

He brought Jim along because Jim was eleven, old enough to make the trip without squirming and wanting to stop every second mile, and because he was anxious for Jim to meet this woman before she became his mother. Then, the trip back to Yeso Creek would give the boy time to get used to her. Just bringing her home suddenly and saying, well, Jim, here's your new ma walking in the door, would be expecting too much of the boy; like asking him to pretend everything was still the same. Jim had been good friends with his mother—though he didn't cry at the funeral with all the people around—and he had a picture of her in his mind as fresh as yesterday. Willis Calender knew it, and this was the only thing about remarrying that bothered him.

Little Molly was different. Molly was three when her mother died, and Willis wasn't sure if the little girl even remembered her still. The first few days with the new mother might be difficult, but it would only be a matter of time. It didn't require the kind of getting used to her that it did with Jim; so Molly had been left home with their three-mile-away neighbors, the Granbys. Molly was four now, though, and she needed a mother. She was the main reason Willis Calender had written to the Santa Fe marriage broker, who was said to have the confidence of every eligible woman from the Panhandle to the Sangre de Cristos.

The boy looked about the early-morning street and then to his dad, who was raising his arms to take the mail sack the driver was lowering. He saw the dark suit coat strain across the shoulders and half expected to hear it rip but hoped it wouldn't, because it was his father's only coat that made up a suit. Usually it was hanging with mothballs in the pockets because cattle aren't fussy about how a man looks. It was funny to see his dad wearing it. When was the last time? Then he remembered the bright, silent afternoon of the funeral.

Maybe she won't be here, the boy thought, watching the driver come down off the wheel and take the mail sack and go up the steps of the express office. A man in range clothes was standing there against a post, and as the boy looked that way, their eyes met. The man said, "Hello, Jimmy," his mouth forming a funny half-smile in the beard stubble that covered his mouth and jaw.

As Calender looked up, surprise seemed to sadden his weathered face. He put his big hand behind the boy's shoulder and moved him forward toward the steps and said, "Hello, Dick." Only that.

Dick Maddox was still against the post, his thumbs crooked in his belt. Another man in range clothes was on the other side of the post from him. Maddox nodded and said, "Will." Then added, "I'm surprised you brought your boy along."

"Why would that be?" Calender said.

"Well, it ain't many boys see their dad get married."

"How'd you know about that?"

"Things get around," Maddox said easily. "You know, I was surprised Clare didn't ask one of us fellas to give her away."

☆ ☆ ☆

CALENDER LOOKED at the man steadily, trying to hide his surprise, and hesitated so it wouldn't show in his voice. "You know Miss Conway?"

Maddox glanced at the man next to him. "He says do I know *Miss* Conway." Both of them grinned. "Well, I'd say anybody who's followed the Canadian to Tascosa knows *Miss* Conway, and that's just about everybody."

The words came like a slap in the face, but Calender thought: Hold on to yourself. And he kept his voice natural when he said, "What do you mean by that?"

Maddox straightened slightly against the post. "You're marrying her, you must've known she worked at the Casa Grande."

Calender was suddenly conscious of his boy looking up at him. He said, "Come on, Jim." And, glancing at Dick Maddox: "We've got to move along."

They started up the street toward the two-story hotel, and Maddox called, "What time's the wedding?" The man with him laughed. Calender heard them but he didn't look around.

When they were farther up the street, the boy said, "Who was that man?"

"Maddox is his name," Calender said. "He used to be old man Granby's herd boss. Now I guess he works around here."

They were silent, and then the boy said, "Why'd you get mad when he started talking about *her*?"

"Who got mad?"

"Well, it looked like it."

"Most of the time that man doesn't know what he's talking about," Will Calender said. "Maybe I looked mad because I had to stand there and be civil while he wasted air."

"All he said was other people knew her," the boy said.

"All right, let's not talk about it any more."

"I didn't see anything wrong in that."

Calender didn't answer.

"Maybe he was good friends with her."

Calender turned on the boy suddenly, but his judgment held him, and after a moment he spoke quietly: "I said let's not talk about it any more."

But it stayed in his mind, and now there was an urgency inside him, an impatience to meet this woman face to face and try to read there what her past had been. It was strange. From the letters he had never doubted she was anything but a good woman, but now— And with this uncertainty the fear began to grow, the fear that he'd see something on her face, some mark of an easy woman.

Damn Maddox! Why'd he have to say it in front of the boy! But he could be just talking, insinuating what isn't so, Calender thought. A man like that ought to have his tongue cut out. All he's good for is drink and talk. Ask old man Granby, he got his bellyful of Maddox and fired him.

They went into the hotel, into the quiet, dim lobby with its high-beamed ceiling. Their eyes lifted to the second-floor balcony which extended all the way around, except for the front side, so that all of the hotel's eleven rooms looked down on the lobby, where, around the balcony support posts, were cane-bottom Douglas chairs and cuspidors and here and there parts of newspapers. The room was empty, except for the man behind the desk who watched them indifferently. His hair glistened flat on an angle over his forehead, and a matchstick barely showed in the corner of his mouth.

"Miss Conway," Will Calender said. The name was loud in the high-ceilinged room, and he felt embarrassed hearing himself say it.

"You're Mr. Calender?"

"That's right." Calender thought: How does he know my name? He stared at the room clerk closely. If he starts to grin, I'll hit him.

"Miss Conway is in number five." The clerk nodded vaguely up the balcony.

Calender hesitated. "Would she be—up yet?"

The clerk started to grin, and Calender thought: Watch yourself, boy. But the clerk just said, "Why don't you go up and knock on the door?"

The boy frowned, watching his father climb the stairs and move along the balcony. He was walking funny, like his feet hurt. Maybe she won't be there, the boy thought hopefully. Maybe she changed her mind. No, she'll be there. He pictured her coming down the stairs, then smiling and patting his cheek and saying, "So this is *Jimmy.*" A smile that would be gone and suddenly come back again. "My, but Jimmy is a fine-looking young man. How old are you, Jimmy?" She'll be fat and smelly like Mrs. Granby and those other ladies down on Yeso Creek. How come all women get so fat? All except Ma. She wasn't fat and she smelled nice and she never called me Jimmy. He felt a funny feeling re-membering his mother, the sound of her voice and the easy way she did things without complaining or getting excited. What did Molly have to have a mother for? She's gotten along for a year without one.

He saw the door open, but caught only a glimpse of the woman. His father went inside then, but the door remained open.

The room clerk grinned and winked at the boy. "Now, if that was me, I think I'd close the door."

A moment later they came out of the room. The boy watched his fa-ther close the door and follow the woman along the balcony to the stairs and then down. The woman was younger than he'd imagined her, much younger, with a funny hat and blond hair fixed in a bun. And she wasn't fat; if anything, skinny. Her face was slender, the skin pale-clear and her eyes seemed sad. The boy looked at her until she got close.

"This here is my son," Will Calender said. "We left Molly at the Granbys'. She's only four years old"—he smiled self-consciously—"like I told you in the letters."

The woman smiled back at him. She seemed ill at ease but she said, "How do you do?" to the boy, and her voice was calm and without the false enthusiasm of Will Calender's.

The boy said, "Ma'am," not looking at her face now but noticing her slender white hands holding the ends of the crocheted shawl in front of her.

A silence followed, and Will Calender suggested that they could get something to eat. He had intended mentioning Maddox's name up in the room then watch her reaction, but there hadn't been time. She didn't look like the kind Maddox hinted she was, did she? Maybe Mad-dox was just talking. She was better-looking than he'd expected. Those eyes and that low, calm voice. Dick Maddox better watch his mouth.

They went to the café next door for breakfast. Calender and the boy ordered eggs and meat, but Clare Conway just took coffee, because she wasn't very hungry. Most of the time they ate in silence. Every now and then Will Calender could hear himself chewing and he'd move his fork on the plate or stir at his coffee with the spoon scraping the bottom of the cup. Clare said the coffee was very good. And, maybe a minute later: It's going to be a nice day. It's so dry out here you can stand the extra heat.

Then it was Will's turn. Where you from originally? . . . New Orleans. . . . I never been there but I hear it's a nice town. . . . It's all right. . . . Silence. . . . How long'd you live in Tascosa? . . . Five years. My husband was with one of the cattle companies. . . . Oh. . . . He died three years ago. . . . Silence. . . . That's right, you told me in your letter. . . . That's right, I did. . . . Silence. . . . What've you been doing since then? . . . I took a position. . . . Calender's jaw was set. . . . At the Casa Grande? . . . Clare Conway blushed suddenly. She nodded and took a sip of coffee in the silence.

There were two men at a table near them and Will Calender had the feeling one nudged the other, and they both grinned, looking over, then looked away quickly when Calender shot a glance toward them.

Calender passed the back of his hand across his mouth and cleared his throat. "Miss Conway, I planned on ordering some stores this morning, long as I was here. They're hauled down to Puerto de Luna, and I pick 'em up there. Some seed and flour"—he cleared his throat again—"and I have to speak to the justice yet." He looked quickly toward the front window, though it wasn't necessary because Clare's eyes were on her coffee cup.

"Jim, here, will stay with you." The boy looked at him with a plea in his eyes, and Will scowled. Then he rose and walked out without looking at the woman.

Standing in front of the hotel, Dick Maddox looked over toward the café as Calender came out, putting on his hat. Maddox glanced at the three men with him, and they grinned as he looked back toward Calender, who was coming toward them now.

"You married yet, Will?"

Calender glanced at Maddox's closed face, at the beard bristles and the cigarette and the eyes in the shadow of the hat brim. "Not yet," he said, and looked straight ahead again, not slowing his stride.

Maddox waited until he was looking at Calender's back. He drew on the cigarette and exhaled and said slowly, "Some men will marry just about anything."

Calender's boots sounded on the planking one, two, three, then stopped. He came around. "Do you mean me, Dick?"

★ ★ ★

A SMILE TOUCHED the corner of Dick Maddox's mouth. "Old man Granby used to have a saying: If the shoe fits, wear it."

"You can talk plainer than that."

"How plain, Will?"

"Talk like a man for a change."

"Well, as a man, I'm wondering if you're going to go ahead and marry this—*Miss* Conway." One of the men behind him laughed but cut it off.

"What if I am?"

Maddox shrugged. "Every man to his own taste."

Calender stepped closer to him. "Dick, if I was married to that woman and you said what you have—you'd be dead right now."

"That's opinion, Will." Maddox smiled because he was sure he could take Will Calender and he wanted to make sure the three men with him knew it.

Calender said, "The point is, I'm not married to her yet. Not yet. If you don't come out with what's on your mind now, you better not come out with it about two hours from now."

Maddox shook his head. "You're a warnin' man, Will."

"What did she do in Tascosa?" Calender said bluntly.

Maddox hesitated, grinning. "Worked at the Casa Grande."

"And that's what?"

"You never been to Tascosa?"

"I just never saw the place."

"Well, the Casa Grande's where a sweaty trail hand goes for his drink, gamblin', and girls." Maddox paused. "I could draw you a picture, Will."

"Dick, if you're pullin' a joke—"

"Ask anybody in town."

Calender looked at the hat-brim shadow and the eyes, the eyes that held without wavering. Then he turned and went up the street.

From his office window, Hillpiper, the Anton Chico Justice of the Peace, watched Will Calender cross the street. The office was above the jail and offered a view of sun, dust, and adobe; there was nothing else to see in Anton Chico, unless you were looking down the streets east, then you'd see the Pecos.

Hillpiper sat down at his desk, hearing the boots on the stairs, and when the knock came he said, "Come in, Will."

"How'd you know it was me?"

"Sit down." Hillpiper smiled. "You had an appointment for this morning, and I've got a window." Hillpiper wore silver-rim spectacles for close work, but he looked over them to Calender sitting across the desk from him.

Calender said, "You know what everybody in town's saying?"

Hillpiper shook his head. "Not everybody."

"They're talking about this woman I'm to marry."

"I'll say it again. Not everybody."

Calender's raw-boned face was tightening, and his voice was louder. "How can they know so much about her—and me, the man that's to marry her, not know anything?"

"It's happened before," Hillpiper said.

"You heard what they're saying?"

"I heard Maddox in the saloon last night. Is he the everybody you're talking about?"

"He's enough. But it's what she is!" Calender said savagely. "What she didn't tell in her letters!"

"Three letters," Hillpiper said mildly. Calender had told him about it when he made the arrangements and set the date: the marriage broker in Santa Fe writing to him, then writing to the woman. Hillpiper had told him it was all right as far as he was concerned, since he didn't see why two people had to love each other to get along. Love's something that might come, but if it didn't—look at all the marriages getting on without it. And Calender had said, That's right. I never thought of that. See, my little girl's the main reason.

"In three letters," Hillpiper went on, "a woman hardly has time to open up her heart."

"She could have told me what she did!"

"Just what does she do, Will?"

"You heard Maddox."

"I want to hear it from you."

"She worked at the Casa Grande!" Calender flared. "How do you want me to say it?"

Hillpiper put his palms on the desk and leaned forward. "All right, Will, she worked in a saloon. She danced with trail hands, maybe sang a little and smiled more than was natural to get the boys to buy the extra drink they'd a bought anyway. And that's all she's done, regardless of how Maddox makes a dozen words sound like a whole story. Why she did that kind of work, I don't know. Maybe she had to because there was nothing else for a girl to do and she still had to eat like anybody else. Maybe it killed her to do it. Or"—Hillpiper's voice was quieter and he shrugged—"maybe she liked doing it. Maybe she forgot where she carried her morals—assuming what she was doing is morally wrong. By most men's standards it is wrong for a female to work in a saloon, your standards too or you wouldn't be here with your face tied in a knot. But those same men have a hell of a good time with the females when they're at the Casa Grande."

Hillpiper smiled faintly. "You were always a little stricter than most men anyway, Will. Seems like most of your life you've been a hard-working, Bible-reading family man, with no time for places like the Casa Grande. You've sweated your ranch into something pretty nice, something most other men wouldn't have the patience or the guts to do. And I can see you not wanting to chance ruining all you've built— ranch or family. That's why I was a little surprised when you of all people came in with this mail-order romance idea. I suspect, now that I think about it, you had the idea if a girl wants to get married she's the simon-pure family type and nothing else. You had a good woman before, Will; so you expected one just as good this time."

Hillpiper leaned a little closer, his eyes on Calender's weathered face. "Will," Hillpiper said. "You might be shocked a little bit, but when you get to heaven you're going to see a lot of faces you never expected to see. Folks who got up there on God's standards and not man's. For all you know, you're liable to even see Dick Maddox—though I suppose that would be stretching divine mercy a little thin."

Anton Chico's Justice of the Peace leaned back in his swivel chair, his coat opening to show a gold watch chain across his vest. His hand came out of a side pocket with a cigar, and with a match from a vest pocket he lit it, puffing a cloud of smoke. When he looked up, Calender was standing.

"What've you decided, Will?"

"I've got my kids to think about."

"It's your problem." Hillpiper said this in a kindly way, stating a fact. "If you've decided not to go through with it, that's your business."

Will Calender nodded. "I suppose I should pay her stage fare back to Tascosa."

"That would be nice, Will," Hillpiper said mildly.

Calender thanked him and went out, down the stairs and into the street. Crossing to the other side, he felt awkward and self-conscious. The suit coat held tight across the shoulders and he could feel his big hands hanging too far out of the sleeves, and with nothing to hold on to.

It's gotten hot, he thought, pulling his hat lower. Maybe the dryness makes it easier on some people, but it's still hot. And then he thought: I'd better tell her before I buy the stage ticket.

DICK MADDOX was still in front of the hotel, but now more men were there. It had gotten around that Maddox was having some fun with Will Calender, so they drifted over casually from here and there, the ones who knew Maddox standing closest to him, laughing at what he said. The rest were all along the hotel's shady ramada. One of the men saw Calender coming and he nudged Maddox, who looked up, then pretended he wasn't concerned, until Calender was close to the hotel entrance.

"You change your mind, Will?"

Calender stopped and breathed out wearily, "If you showed as much concern for your own business, you'd be a well-to-do man."

"You can't take kiddin', can you?"

"Why should I have to?"

"You got a lot to learn, Will."

Calender shrugged, because he was tired of this, and went inside.

The boy was sitting alone, with his heels hooked in the wooden rungs of the chair. When he saw his father he jumped up quickly.

Calender looked about to be certain the woman was not in the lobby.

"Where is she?" he asked the boy.

"She went upstairs. All of a sudden she just started crying and went upstairs."

"What?"

"It was when they started talking. We were sitting here, and then her chin started to shake—you know—and then she run upstairs."

"Who was talking? The men outside?" The boy nodded hurriedly, and Calender could see that he was frightened and trying to hide it and at the same time was not sure what it was all about.

"What did they say?"

"Just one of them, the rest were laughing most of the time. He was telling them"—the boy said it slowly as if he'd memorized it—"he said some women didn't know their place. They think they can live in the gutter then go out when they want and brush against people like nothing's coming off. He was talking loud so we could hear every word and he said a man would be a fool to marry a woman like that and have her brushing against his kids with her gutter ways. It was like that, what he said. Then he spoke your name and he said he'd bet anybody five dollars American you'd changed your mind now about getting married. That's when she run upstairs."

The boy frowned, looking at his father, watching his eyes go up to the room. "Why'd he have to say things like that? We were sitting here talking—getting acquainted."

Calender looked at the boy and saw that he was grinning.

"You know she never once asked me how old I was or if I knew my reader or things like that. She talked to me about affairs and interesting things like I was grown up, like Ma used to do. And, Pa, she called me *Jim*! Can you imagine that? She called me *Jim*! If her hair was darker and her nose a little different, I'd swear she was Ma!"

"Don't say things like that!" Calender was conscious of his voice, and he said quietly, "There's the difference of night and day."

"Well, her voice is different too, and maybe she's a speck taller, though that could be the hat. I never seen Ma in a regular hat. But outside of that, they sure are alike."

"You know what you're saying, comparing this woman with your mother?"

The boy looked at him questioningly, but the trace of a smile was still on his face. "I'm just saying they're alike, that's all. Maybe they don't look so much alike, but they sure are alike." The boy smiled; he was sure his explanation was clear because he understood it so well himself.

Calender was looking at the boy closely now. "What if she's done something bad?"

"Pa, little Molly's doing bad things all the time. That's just the way girls are. Most times they're not doing serious things, so they have more time to get theirselves into trouble."

Calender's eyes remained on the boy. Calender asked: "You think Molly will like her?"

"Couple of bad women like them will get along just fine." The boy grinned.

Calender left him abruptly, going up the stairs. In a few minutes he came back down, and in front of him was Clare Conway.

They walked across the lobby. Nearing the door, the woman hesitated and looked up at Will Calender. She was unsure and afraid. It was in her wide-open eyes, in the way her fingers held the ends of the crocheted shawl. Then she moved on again as if not under her own power—when Will touched her elbow and said to the boy, "Come on, Jim."

And when they were out on the ramada the woman's eyes were looking down at her hands; she could feel Will Calender holding her elbow, she could feel the guiding pressure of his hand, and moved to the right along the ramada, along the line of silent men, hearing only her footsteps and the footsteps of the man at her side. The hand on her elbow tightened. She was being turned gently, and there was no longer the sound of footsteps and when she looked up a man was close in front of her, a man with heavy beard bristles.

"Miss Conway," Calender said. "This is Mr. Maddox. He's had such a keen interest in our business, I thought you might like to meet him."

"Now, Will—" Maddox said, looking at Calender strangely.

"And, Dick," Calender went on, "this is Miss Conway. Isn't there something you wanted to say to her?"

"Will—"

"Maybe you'd just like to tip your hat like a gentleman."

Maddox was staring at Calender almost dumbfounded, but slowly his face relaxed as he realized what Calender was doing in front of all these men and he said mildly, grinning, "Now, Will, I don't know if I want to do that or not."

Calender's fist came around suddenly, unexpectedly, driving against Maddox's jaw, changing the smile to lopsided surprise and sending him back off the ramada into the street. Calender followed, and hit him again and this time Maddox went down, his hat falling off in front of him. Maddox started to rise, but Calender came for him again. Maddox hesitated, then eased down and sat in the street, looking up at Calender.

"One other thing, Dick," Will said. "I hear you're taking bets there isn't going to be a wedding today." He glanced back at the crowd of men in the shade. "Who's holding the stakes?"

There was a silence, then someone called, "Nobody'd bet him."

Calender beckoned to the man. "Come here." He brought a five-dollar gold piece out of his pants pocket and gave it to the man. "Dick Maddox'll give you one just like this. Now you add the two up and have that much ready for me when I get back."

He walked to the ramada. The tension was gone. Some of the men were whispering and talking, some just looking out at Maddox still sitting in the street.

The boy's face was beaming as he watched his father. Clare came toward him.

"You ripped the seam of your coat up the back," she said.

He felt her hand on his back pulling the cloth together. "Gives me a little more room," he said, conscious of the men watching him.

"It's your good coat, though," the woman said. "I'll mend it soon as we get home."

22

Jugged

Original Title: The Boy from Dos Cabezas
Western Magazine, December 1955

STAN CASS, HIS elbows leaning on the edge of the rolltop desk, glanced over his shoulder as he said, "Take a look how I made this one out."

Marshal John Boynton had just come in. He was standing in the front door of the jail office, one finger absently stroking his full mustache. He looked at his regular deputy, Hanley Miller, who stood next to a chair where a young man sat leaning forward looking at his hands.

"What's the matter with him?" Boynton said, ignoring Stan Cass.

Hanley Miller put his hand on the back of the chair. "A combination of things, John. He's had too many, been beat up, and now he's tired."

"He looks tired," Boynton said, again glancing at the silent young man.

Stan Cass turned his head. "He looks like a smart-aleck kid."

Boynton walked over to Cass and picked up the record book from the desk. The last entry read:

NAME: Pete Given
DESCRIPTION: Ninteen. Medium height and build. Brown hair and eyes. Small scar under chin.
RESIDENCE: Dos Cabezas
OCCUPATION: Mustanger
CHARGE: Drunk and disorderly
COMMENTS: Has to pay a quarter share of the damages in the Continental Saloon whatever they are decided to be.

Boynton handed the record book to Cass. "You spelled *nineteen* wrong."

"Is that all?"

"How do you know he has to pay a quarter of the damages?"

"Being four of them," Cass said mock seriously. "I figured to myself: Now, if they have to chip in for what's busted, how much would—"

"That's for the judge to say. What were they doing here?"

"They delivered a string to the stage line," Cass answered. He was a man in his early twenties, clean shaven, though his sideburns extended down to the curve of his jaw. He was smoking a cigarette and he spoke to Boynton as if he were bored.

"And they tried to spend all the profit in one night," Boynton said.

Cass shrugged indifferently. "I guess so."

Boynton's finger stroked his mustache and he was thinking: Somebody's going to bust his nose for him. He asked, civilly, "Where're the other three?"

Cass nodded to the door that led back to the first-floor cell. "Where else?"

Hanley Miller, the regular night deputy, a man in his late forties, said, "John, you know there's only room for three in there. I was wondering what to do with this boy." He tipped his head toward the quiet young man sitting in the chair.

"He'll have to go upstairs," Boynton said.

"With Obie Ward?"

"I guess he'll have to." Boynton nodded to the boy. "Pull him up."

Hanley Miller got the sleepy boy on his feet.

Cass shook his head watching them. "Obie Ward's got everybody buffaloed. I'll be a son of a gun if he ain't got everybody buffaloed."

Boynton's eyes dropped to Cass, but he did not say anything.

"I'm just saying that Obie Ward don't look so tough," Cass said.

"Act like you've got some sense once in a while," Boynton said now. He had hired Cass the week before as an extra night guard—the day they brought in Obie Ward—but he was certain now he would not keep Cass. Tomorrow he would look around for somebody else. Somebody who didn't talk so much and didn't have such a proud opinion of himself.

"All I'm saying is he don't look so tough to me," Cass repeated.

Boynton ignored him. He looked at the young man, Pete Given, standing next to Hanley now with his eyes closed, and he heard his deputy say, "The boy's asleep on his feet."

"He looks familiar," Boynton said.

"We had him here about three months ago."

"Same thing?"

Hanley nodded. "Delivered his horses, then stopped off at the Continental. Remember, his wife come here looking for him. He was here five days because the judge was away and she got here court day. Pretty little thing with light-colored hair? Not more'n seventeen. Come all the way from Dos Cabezas by herself."

"Least he had sense enough to get a good woman," Boynton said. He seemed to hesitate. Then: "You and I'll take him up." He slipped his revolver from its holster and placed it on the desk. He took young Pete Given's arm then and raised it up over his shoulder, glancing at his deputy again. "Hanley, you come behind with your shotgun."

Cass watched them go through the door and down the hall to the back of the jail to the outside stairway, and he was thinking: Won't even wear his gun up there, he's so scared. That's some man to work for, won't even wear his gun when he goes in Ward's cell. He shook his head and said the name again, contemptuously. Obie Ward. He'd pull his tough act on me just once.

PETE GIVEN OPENED his eyes. Lying on his right side his face was close to the wall and for a moment, seeing the chipped and peeling adobe and smelling the stale mildewed smell of the mattress which did not have a cover on it, he did not know where he was. Then he remembered, and he closed his eyes again.

The sour taste of whiskey coated his mouth and he lay very still, waiting for the throbbing to start in his head. But it did not come. He raised his head and moved closer to the wall and felt the edge of the mattress cool and firm against his cheek. Still the throbbing did not come. There was a dull tight feeling at the base of his skull, but not the shooting sharp pain he had expected. That was good. He moved his toes and could feel his boots still on and there was no blanket covering him.

They just dumped you here, he thought. He made saliva in his mouth and kept swallowing until his mouth did not feel sticky and some of the sour taste went away. Well, what did you expect?

It's about all you deserve, buddy. No, it's more'n you deserve.

You'll learn, huh?

He thought of his wife, Mary Ellen, and his eyes closed tighter and for a moment he tried not to think of anything.

How do I do this? How do I get something good, then kick it away like it's not worth anything?

What'll you tell her this time?

"Mary Ellen, honest to gosh, we just went in to get one drink. We sold the horses and got something to eat and figured one drink before starting back. Then Art said one more. All right, just one, I told him. But, you know, we were relaxed—and laughing. That's hard work running a thirty-horse string for five days. Harry got in a blackjack game. The rest of us were just sitting relaxed. When you're sitting like that the time seems to go faster. We had a few drinks. Maybe four—five at the most. Like I said, we were laughing and Art was telling some stories. You know Art, he keeps talking—then there's a commotion over at the blackjack table and we see Harry haulin' off at this man. And—"

And Mary Ellen will say, "Just like the last time," not raising her voice or seeming mad, but she'll keep looking you right in the eye.

"Honey, those things just happen. I can't help it. And it wasn't just like last time."

"The result's the same," she'll say. "You work hard for three months to earn decent money then pay it all out in fines and damages."

"Not all of it."

"It might as well be all. We can't live on what's left."

"But I can't help it. Can't you see that? Harry got in a fight and we had to help him. It's just one of those things that happens. You can't help it."

"But it seems a little silly, doesn't it?"

"Mary Ellen, you don't understand."

"Doesn't throwing away three months' profit in one night seem silly to you?"

"You don't understand."

You can be married to a girl for almost a year and think you know her and you don't know her at all. That's it. You know how she talks, but you don't know what she's thinking. That's a big difference. But there's some things you can't explain to a woman anyway.

He felt a little better. Facing her would not be pleasant—but it still wasn't his fault.

He rolled over, momentarily studying the ceiling, then he let his head roll on the mattress and he saw the man on the other bunk watching him. He was sitting hunched over, making a cigarette.

Pete Given closed his eyes and he could still see the man. He didn't seem big, but he had a stringy hard-boned look. Sharp cheekbones and dull-black hair that was cut short and brushed forward to his forehead. No mustache, but he needed a shave and it gave the appearance of an almost full-grown mustache.

He opened his eyes again. The man was drawing on the cigarette, still watching him.

"What time you think it is?" Given asked.

"About nine." The man's voice was clear though he barely moved his mouth.

Given said, "If you were one of them over to the Continental I'd just as soon shake hands this morning."

The man did not reply.

"You weren't there, then?"

"No," he said now.

"What've they got you for?"

"They say I shot a man."

"Oh."

"Fact is, they say I shot two men, during the Grant stage holdup."

"Oh."

"When the judge comes tomorrow, he'll set a court date. Give the witnesses time to get here." He stood up, saying this. He was tall, above average, but not heavy.

"Are you"—Given hesitated—"Obie Ward?"

The man nodded, drawing on the cigarette.

"Somebody last night said you were here. I'd forgot about it." Given spoke louder, trying to make his voice sound natural, and now he raised himself on an elbow.

Obie Ward asked, "Were you drinking last night?"

"Some."

"And got in a fight."

Given sat up, swinging his legs off the bunk and resting his elbows on his knees. "One of my partners got in trouble and we had to help him."

"You don't look so good," Ward said.

"I feel okay."

"No," Ward said. "You don't look so good."

"Well, maybe I just look worse'n I am."

"How's your stomach?"

"It's all right."

"You look sick to me."

"I could eat. Outside of that I got no complaint." Given stood up. He put his hands on the small of his back and stretched, feeling the stiffness in his body. Then he raised his arms straight up, stretching again, and yawned. That felt good. He saw Obie Ward coming toward him, and he lowered his arms.

Ward reached out, extending one finger, and poked it at Pete Given's stomach. "How's it feel right there?"

"Honest to gosh, it feels okay." He smiled looking at Ward, to show that he was willing to go along with a joke, but he felt suddenly uneasy. Ward was standing too close to him and Given was thinking: What's the matter with him?—and the same moment he saw the beard-stubbled face tighten.

Ward went back a half step and came forward, driving his left fist into Given's stomach. The boy started to fold, a gasp coming from his open mouth, and Ward followed with his right hand, bringing it up solidly against the boy's jaw, sending him back, arms flung wide, over the bunk and hard against the wall. Given slumped on the mattress and did not move. For a moment Ward looked at him, then picked up his cigarette from the floor and went back to his bunk.

He was sitting on the edge of it when Given opened his eyes—smoking another cigarette, drawing on it and blowing the smoke out slowly.

"Are you sick now?"

Given moved his head, trying to lift it, and it was an effort to do this. "I think I am."

Ward started to rise. "Let's make sure."

"I'm sure."

✯ ✯ ✯

WARD RELAXED AGAIN. "I told you so, but you didn't believe me. I been watching you all morning and the more I watched, the more I thought to myself: Now there's a sick boy. Maybe you ought to even have a doctor."

Given said nothing. He stiffened as Ward rose and came toward him.

"What's the matter? I'm just going to see you're more comfortable." Ward leaned over, lifting the boy's legs one at a time, and pulled his boots off, then pushed him, gently, flat on the bunk and covered him with a blanket that was folded at the foot of it. Given looked up, holding his body rigid, and saw Ward shake his head. "You're a mighty sick boy. We got to do something about that."

Ward crossed the cell to his bunk, and standing at one end, he lifted it a foot off the floor and let it drop. He did this three times, then went down to his hands and knees and, close to the floor, called, "Hey, Marshal!" He waited. "Marshal, we got a sick boy up here!" He rose, winking at Given, and sat down on his bunk.

Minutes later a door at the back end of the hallway opened and Boynton came toward the cell. A deputy with a shotgun, his day man, followed him.

"What's the matter?"

Ward nodded. "The boy's sick."

"He ought to be," Boynton said.

Ward shrugged. "Don't matter to me, but I got to listen to him moaning."

Boynton looked toward Given's bunk. "A man that don't know how to drink has got to expect that." He turned abruptly. Their steps moved down the hall and the door slammed closed.

"No sympathy," Ward said. He made another cigarette, and when he had lit it he walked over to Given's bunk. "He'll come back in about two hours with our dinner. You'll still be in bed, and this time you'll be moaning like you got belly cramps. You got that?"

Staring up at him, Given nodded his head stiffly.

At a quarter to twelve Boynton came up again. This time he ordered Ward to lie down flat on his bunk. He unlocked the door then and remained in the hall as the day man came in with the dinner tray and placed it in the middle of the floor.

"He still sick?" Boynton stood in the doorway holding a sawed-off shotgun.

Ward turned his head on the mattress. "Can't you hear him?"

"He'll get over it."

"I think it's something else," Ward said. "I never saw whiskey hold on like that."

"You a doctor?"

"As much a one as you are."

Boynton looked toward the boy again. Given's eyes were closed and he was moaning faintly. "Tell him to eat something," Boynton said. "Maybe then he'll feel better."

"I'll do that," Ward said. He was smiling as Boynton and his deputy moved off down the hall.

Lying on his back, his head turned on the mattress, Given watched Ward take a plate from the tray. It looked like stew.

"Can I have some?" Given said.

Chewing, Ward shook his head.

"Why not?"

Ward swallowed. "You're too sick."

"Can I ask you a question?"

"Go ahead."

"How come I'm sick?"

"You haven't figured it?"

"No."

"I'll give you a hint. We'll get our supper about six. Watch the two that bring it up."

"I don't see what they'd have to do with me."

"You don't have to see."

Given was silent for some time. He said then, "It's got to do with you busting out."

Obie Ward grinned. "You got a head on your shoulders."

Boynton came up a half hour later. He stood in the hall and when his deputy brought out the tray, his eyes went from it to Pete Given's bunk. "The boy didn't eat a bite," Boynton observed.

Ward raised up on his elbow. "Said he couldn't stand the smell of it." He watched Boynton look toward the boy, then sank down on the bunk again as Boynton walked away. When the door down the hall closed, Ward said, "Now he believes it."

It was quiet in the cell after that. Ward rolled over to face the wall and Pete Given, lying on his back, remained motionless, though his eyes were open and he was studying the ceiling.

He tried to understand Obie Ward's plan. He tried to see how his being sick could have anything to do with Ward's breaking out. And he thought: He means what he says, doesn't he? You can be sure of that much. He's going to bust out and you got a part in it and there ain't a damn thing you can do about it. It's that simple, isn't it?

OBIE WARD WAS RIGHT. At what seemed close to six o'clock they heard the door open at the end of the hall and a moment later Stan Cass and Hanley Miller were standing in front of the cell. Hanley opened the door and stood holding a sawed-off shotgun as Cass came in with the tray.

Cass half turned to face Ward sitting on his bunk, then went down to one knee, lowering the tray to the floor, and he did not take his eyes from Ward. He rose then and turned as he heard groans from the other bunk.

"What's his trouble?"

Ward looked up. "Didn't your boss tell you?"

"He told me," Cass said, "but I believe what I see."

"Help yourself, then."

Cass turned sharply. "You shut your mouth till I want to hear from you!"

"Yes, sir," Ward said. His dark face was expressionless.

Cass stared at him, his thumbs hooked in his gun belt. "You think you're somethin', don't you?"

Ward's head moved from side to side. "Not me."

"I'd like to see you pull somethin'," Cass said. His right hand opened and closed, moving closer to his hip. "I'd just like to see you get off that bunk and pull somethin'."

Ward shook his head. "Somebody's been telling you stories."

"I think they have," Cass said. He hesitated, then walked out, slamming the door shut.

Ward called to him through the bars, "What about the boy?"

"You take care of him," Cass said, moving off. Hanley Miller followed, looking back over his shoulder.

Ward waited until the back door closed, then picked up a plate and began to eat and not until he was almost finished did he notice Given watching him.

"Did you see anything?"

Given came up on his elbow slowly. He looked at the tray on the floor, then at Ward. "Like what?"

"Like the way that deputy acted."

"He wanted you to try something."

"What else?"

Given pictured Cass again in his mind. "He was wearing a gun." Suddenly he seemed to understand and he said, "The marshal wasn't wearing any, but this one was!"

Ward grinned. "And he knows you're sick. First his boss told him, then he saw it with his own eyes." Ward put down the plate and he made a cigarette as he walked over to Given's bunk. "I'll tell you something else," he said, standing close to the bunk. "I've been here seven days. For seven days I watch. I see the marshal. He knows what he's doing and he don't wear a gun when he comes in here. A man out in the hall with a scattergun's enough. Then this other one they call Cass. He walks like he can feel his gun on his hip. He's not used to it, but it feels good and he'd like an excuse to use it. He even wears it in here, though likely he's been told not to. What does that tell you? He's sure of himself, but he's not smart. He wants to see me try something—and he's sure he can get his gun out if I do. For seven days I see this and there's nothing I can do about it—until this morning."

Given nodded thoughtfully, but said nothing.

"This morning I saw you," Ward went on, "and you looked sick. There it was."

Given nodded again. "I guess I see."

"We let the marshal know about it. He tells Cass when he comes on duty. Cass comes up and sure enough, you're sick."

"Yeah?"

"Then Cass comes up the next time—understand it'll be dark outside by then: he brings supper up at six, but he must go out to eat after that because he doesn't come back for the tray till almost eight—and he's not surprised to see you even sicker."

"How does he see that?"

"You scream like your stomach's been pulled out and you roll off the bunk."

"Then what?"

"Then you don't have to do anything else."

Given's eyes held on Ward's face. He swallowed and said, as evenly as he could, "Why should I help you escape?" He saw it coming and he tried to roll away, but it was too late and Ward's fist came down against his face like a mallet.

He was dazed and there was a stinging throbbing over the entire side of his face, but he was conscious of Ward leaning close to him and he heard the words clearly. "I'll kill you. That reason enough?"

After that he was not conscious of time. His eyes were closed and for a while he dozed off. Then, when he opened his eyes, momentarily he could remember nothing and he was not even sure where he was, because he was thinking of nothing, only looking at the chipped and peeling adobe wall and feeling a strange numbness over the side of his face.

His hand was close to his face and his fingers moved to touch his cheekbone. The skin felt swollen hard and tight over the bone, and just touching it was painful. He thought then: Are you afraid for your own neck? Of course I am!

But it was more than fear that was making his heart beat faster. There was an anger inside of him. Anger adding excitement to the fear and he realized this, though not coolly, for he was thinking of Ward and Mary Ellen and himself as they came into his mind, not as he called them there.

Ward had said, Roll off the cot.

All right.

He heard the back door open and instantly Ward muttered, "You awake?" He turned his head to see Ward sitting on the edge of the bunk, his hands at his sides gripping the mattress. He heard the footsteps coming up the hall.

"I'm awake."

"Soon as he opens the door," Ward said, and his shoulders seemed to relax.

As soon as he opens the door.

He heard Cass saying something and a key rattled in the lock. The squeak of the door hinges—

He groaned, bringing his knees up. His heart was pounding and a heat was over his face and he kept his eyes squeezed closed. He groaned again, louder this time, and doing it he rolled to his side, hesitated at the edge of the mattress, then let himself fall heavily to the floor.

"What's the matter with him!"

Four steps on the plank floor vibrated in his ear. A hand took his shoulder and rolled him over. Opening his eyes, he saw Cass leaning over him.

Suddenly then, Cass started to rise, his eyes stretched open wide, and he twisted his body to turn. An arm came from behind hooking his throat, dragging him back, and a hand was jerking the revolver from its holster.

HANLEY MILLER tried to push away from the bars to bring up the shotgun. It clattered against the bars and on top of the sound came the deafening report of the revolver. Hanley doubled up and went to the floor, clutching his thigh.

Cass's mouth was open and he was trying to scream as the revolver flashed over his head and came down. The next moment Ward was throwing Cass's limp weight aside. Ward stumbled, clattering over the tray in the middle of the floor, almost tripping.

Given saw Ward go through the wide-open door. He glanced then at Hanley Miller lying on the floor. Then, looking at Ward's back, the thought stabbed suddenly, unexpectedly, in his mind—

Get him!

He hesitated, though the hesitation was in his mind and it was part of a moment. Then he was on his feet, moving quickly, silently, in his stocking feet, stooping to pick up the sawed-off shotgun, turning and seeing Ward near the door. Now Given was running down the hallway, now swinging open the door that had just closed behind Ward.

Ward was on the back-porch landing, starting down the stairs, and he wheeled, bringing up the revolver as the door opened, as he saw Pete Given on the landing, as he saw the stubby shotgun barrels swinging savagely in the dimness.

Ward fired hurriedly, wildly, the same moment the double barrels slashed against the side of his head. He screamed as he lost his balance and went down the stairway. At the bottom he tried to rise, groping momentarily, feverishly, for his gun. As he came to his feet, Pete Given was there—and again the shotgun cut viciously against his head. Ward went down, falling forward, and this time he did not move.

Given sat down on the bottom step, letting the shotgun slip from his fingers. A lantern was coming down the alley.

Boynton appeared in the circle of lantern light. He looked from Obie Ward to the boy, not speaking, but his eyes remained on Given until he stepped past him and went up the stairs.

A man stooped next to him, extending an already rolled cigarette. "You look like you want a smoke."

Given shook his head. "I'd swallow it."

The man nodded toward Obie Ward. "You took him by yourself?"

"Yes, sir."

"That must've been something to see."

"I don't know—it happened so fast." In the crowd he heard Obie Ward's name over and over—someone asking if he was dead, a man bending over him saying no . . . someone asking, "Who's that boy?" and someone answering, "I don't know, but he's got enough guts for everybody."

Boynton appeared on the landing and called for someone to get the doctor. He came down and Given stood up to let him pass. The man who was holding the cigarette said, "John, this boy got Obie all by himself."

Boynton was looking at Ward. "I see that."

"More'n I would've done," the man said, shaking his head.

"More'n most anybody would've done," Boynton answered. He looked at Given then, studying him openly. He said then, "I'll recommend to the judge we drop the charges against you."

Given nodded. "That'd be fine."

"Anxious to get home to your wife?"

"Yes, sir."

For a moment Boynton was silent. His expression was mild, but his eyes were fastened on Pete Given's face as if he were trying to read something there, some mark of character that would tell him about this boy.

"On second thought," Boynton said abruptly, "I'll tear your name right out of the record book, if you'll take a deputy job. You won't even have to put a foot in court."

Given looked up. "You mean that?"

"I got two jobs open," Boynton said. He hesitated before adding, "Look, it's up to you. Probably I'll tear your name out even if you don't take the job. Seeing the condition of Obie Ward, I wouldn't judge you're a man who's going to be pressured into anything."

Given's face showed surprise, but it was momentary, his mouth relaxing into a slow grin—almost as if the smile widened as Boynton's words sank into his mind—and he said, "I'll have to go to Dos Cabezas and get my wife."

Boynton nodded. "Will she be happy about this?"

Pete Given was still smiling. "Marshal, you and I probably couldn't realize how happy she'll be."

23

Moment of Vengeance

Original Title: The Waiting Man
Saturday Evening Post, April 21, 1956

AT MIDMORNING six riders came down out of the cavernous pine shadows, down the slope swept yellow with arrowroot blossoms, down through the scattered aspen at the north end of the meadow, then across the meadow and into the yard of the one-story adobe house.

Four of the riders dismounted, three of these separating as they moved toward the house; the fourth took his rope and walked off toward the mesquite-pole corral. The horses in the enclosure stood and watched as he opened the gate.

Ivan Kergosen, still mounted, motioned to the open stable shed that was built out from the adobe. The sixth man rode up to it, looked inside, then continued around the corner and was out of sight.

Now Kergosen, tight-jawed and solemn, saw the door of the adobe open. He watched Ellis, his daughter, come out to the edge of the ramada shade, ignoring the three men, who stepped aside to let her pass.

"We've been expecting you," she said. Her voice was calm and her smile, for a moment, seemed genuine, but it faded too quickly. She touched her dark hair, smoothing it as a breeze rose and swept across the yard.

"Where is he?" Kergosen said.

Her gaze lifted, going out across the open sunlight of the meadow to the far west corner, to the windmill that stood out faintly against a dark background of pines.

"He's at the stock tank," Ellis said. "But he'll come in now."

Mr. Kergosen's hands were gripped one over the other on the saddle horn. He stared at his daughter in silence, his mustache hiding his mouth, but not the iron-willed anger in his eyes and in the tight line of his jaw.

"Whether he does or not," Kergosen said, "you're going back with me."

"I'm married now, Pa."

"Don't talk foolish."

"Married in Willson. By a priest."

"We'll talk about that at home."

"I am home!"

"Girl, this isn't going to be a public debate."

"Then why did you bring an audience?" She was sorry as soon as she said it. "Pa, I don't mean disrespect. Phil and I were married in Willson five days ago. He bought stock, drove it here, and we intend to raise it." Her father stared at her, saying nothing, and to fill the silence she added, "This is my home now, where I've come to live with my husband."

Leo Pyke, one of the three men standing near her, the curled brim of his hat straight and low over his eyes, said, "Looks more like a wickiup. Someplace a 'Pache would bring his squaw." He grinned, leaning against a support post, staring at Ellis.

Mr. Kergosen did not look up, but said, "Shut up, Leo."

"It's no fit place," Pyke said, straightening. "That's all I'm saying."

"Phil has work to do on it," Ellis said defensively. "He's already put on a new roof." She looked quickly at her father. "That's what I mean. We didn't just run off and get married. We've planned for it. Phil paid down on the house and property more than a month ago at the Dos Mesas bank. Since then we've be making it livable."

"Behind my back," Kergosen said.

Ellis hesitated. "Phil wanted to ask your permission. I told him it wouldn't do any good."

"How did you suppose that?" her father asked.

"I've lived with you for eighteen years, Pa. I know you."

"Can you say you know Phil Treat as well?"

"I know him," Ellis said simply.

"As far as I'm concerned," Kergosen said, "he qualifies as a man. But certainly not as the man who marries my daughter."

Ellis asked, "And I have nothing to say about it?"

"We're not discussing it here," Kergosen said.

He had hired Treat almost a year ago, during the time he was having trouble with the San Carlos Reservation people. He lost two men that spring and roughly two dozen head of beef to raiding parties. The Apache police did nothing about it, though they knew his stock was being taken to San Carlos. So Ivan Kergosen went to Fort Thomas and hired a professional tracker whose government contract had expired, and went after them himself. They turned out to be Chiricahuas and the scout ran down every last one of them.

The scout's name was Phil Treat. He had been a soldier, buffalo hunter, and cavalry guide, and had earned a reputation as a gunfighter by killing three men: two of them at Tascosa when they tried to steal his hides; the third one at Anton Chico, New Mexico—an Army deserter who drew his gun, refusing to go back to Apache land. Only three, but the shootings were done well, with witnesses, and it took no more than that to establish a reputation.

And after the trouble was past, Phil Treat stayed on with Mr. Kergosen. He was passing fair with cattle, a good horsebreaker, and an A-1 hunter; so Kergosen paid him top wages and was pleased to have such a man around. But as a hired hand; not as a son-in-law.

All his life Ivan Kergosen had worked hard and prayed hard, asking God for guidance. He built his holdings according to a single-minded interpretation of God's will, respecting Him more as a God of Justice than a God of Mercy. And his good fortune, he believed, was God in His justice rewarding him, granting him success in life for adhering to Divine Will. It had taken Ivan Kergosen thirty years of working and fighting—fighting the land, the Apache, and anyone who tried to take from his land—to build the finest spread in the Pinaleño Valley. He built this success for his own self-respect, for his wife who was now deceased, and for his daughter, Ellis—not for a sign-reading gunfighter who'd spent half of his life killing buffalo, the other tracking Apache, and who now, somehow, contrary to all his plans, had married his daughter.

He heard Leo Pyke's voice and he was brought back to the here and now. "Fixing the house while he was working for you, Mr. Kergosen," Pyke was saying. "No telling the amount of sneaky acts he's committed."

The man who had gone to the corral came out, leading a saddled and bridled dun horse. He looked back over his shoulder, then at Mr. Kergosen, and called, "He's coming now!"

Ellis was aware then of the steady cantering sound. She saw Leo Pyke and the two men with him—Sandal, who was a Mexican, and Grady, a bearded, solemn-faced man—look out past the corral, and she said, "In a moment you can say it to his face, Leo. About being sneaky."

She looked up in time to see her husband swing past the corral, coming toward her. She watched him dismount stiffly. He let the reins drop, passed his hand over his mouth, then up to his hat brim, and loosened it from his forehead. He turned his back to the three men in the ramada shade as if intentionally ignoring them; then looked from Ellis to her father and said, "Well?"

And now Ivan Kergosen was faced with the calm, deliberate gaze of this man. He saw that Phil Treat was not wearing a gun; he saw that he was trail dirty and had moved slowly, to stand now, tall but stooped, with his hands hanging empty.

He could handle this man. Kergosen was sure of that now, but he respected him and he had planned this meeting carefully. Leo Pyke, who openly disliked Treat, and Sandal and Grady, who had been with him longer than any of his other riders, would deal with Treat if he objected. No, there would be no trouble. But he formed his words carefully before he spoke.

Then he said, "You made a mistake. So did my daughter. But both mistakes are corrected as of this moment. Ellis is going home and you have ten minutes to pack your gear and get out. Clear?"

"And my stock?" Treat said.

"You're selling your stock to me," Kergosen said, "so there' be nothing to delay you." His hand went into his coat and came out with a folded square of green paper. "My draft on the Willson Bank to cover the sale of your yearling stock. Thirty head. When you draw the money, the canceled draft is my receipt." He extended his hand. "Take it." Treat did not move and Kergosen's wrist flicked out and the folded paper floated—fell to the ground. "Pick it up," Kergosen said. "Your time's running out." He looked at Ellis then. "Mount up."

★ ★ ★

ELLIS ALMOST SPOKE, frightened, angry, and unsure of herself now, but she looked at her husband and waited.

Treat stood motionless, still gazing up at Kergosen. "You have five men and I have myself," he said. "That makes a difference, doesn't it?"

"If this is unjust," Kergosen said, "then it's unjust. I'll say it only once more. Your time's running out."

Treat's eyes moved to Ellis. "Do what he says." He saw the bewildered look come over her face, and he said, "Go home with him, Ellis, and do what he tells you." Treat paused. "But don't speak one solitary word to him as long as you're under his roof. Not till I come for you." He said this quietly in the brittle silence that hung over the yard, and now he saw Ellis nod her head slowly.

He looked up at Kergosen, who was staring at him intently. "Mr. Kergosen, we can't argue with you and we can't fight you, but take Ellis home and you'll know she isn't just your daughter anymore."

"You don't threaten me," Kergosen said.

"No," Treat said, "you've got iron fists, a hundred and thirty square miles of land, and you sit there like it's the high seat of judgment. But you live with Ellis now, if you can."

Kergosen said, "Pick up that draft."

Treat shook his head.

"As God is my judge, I mean you no harm," Kergosen said. "But you don't leave me a choice."

He nodded to Leo Pyke as he reined his bay in a tight circle and rode out. Ellis had mounted and now she followed him, looking back past the two riders who fell in behind her as she passed the corral and started across the meadow.

They were not yet out of sight, but nearing the aspen stands when Pyke said to Sandal and Grady, "So he won't pick it up."

Treat looked at him, then stooped, without loss of dignity, unhurriedly, and picked up the draft. "If it bothers you," he said.

Pyke grinned. "He's not so big now, is he?"

The Mexican rider, Sandal, said, "Like a field hand. I thought he was something with a gun."

"A story he made up," the third man, Grady, said.

Pyke said to Sandal, "Move his horse out of the way."

Sandal winked at Grady. "And the Henry, uh?" He led Treat's clay-bank to the corral and lifted the Henry rifle from the saddle boot as he shooed him in. He walked back to them, studying the rifle, holding it at belt level. Without looking at them, as if not aiming, he flipped the lever down and up and fired past them, and the right front window of the adobe shattered.

Sandal looked up, smiling. "This is no bad gun."

Across the meadow two of Kergosen's riders were moving the herd away from the stock tank. Treat watched them, turning his back to Sandal. There was time. These men would do as they pleased, whether he objected or not. Wait and say nothing, he thought. Wait and watch and keep track of the score.

He remembered a patrol out of Fort Thomas coming to a spring, and a Coyotero Apache guide whose name was Pesh-klitso. The guide had said to him in Spanish, "We followed the barbarian for ten days; two men died, three horses died; we have no food and we killed no barbarian. Yet we could have waited for them here. Our stomachs would be full, the two men and the horses would still be alive, and we would take them when they came." He'd asked the Coyotero how he knew they would come, and the guide answered, "The land is not that broad. They would come sooner or later." Which meant, if not today, then to-morrow; if not this year, then the next.

He had known many Pesh-klitsos at San Carlos, and at Tascosa, when they carried Sharps rifles and hunted buffalo—hunted them by waiting, then killed them. And the more patience you had the more you killed.

Treat waited and watched. He watched Grady go into the adobe and saw the left front window erupt with a spray of broken glass as a chair came through. He saw Sandal break off two of the chair legs with the heel of his boot, then walk into the adobe, and a moment later the Henry was firing again. With the reports, the ear-ringing din and the clicking cocking sound of the lever, he heard glass and china shat-tering, falling from the shelves. Then the sound of a Colt and a dull, clanging noise; sooty smoke billowed from the open doorway and he knew they had shot down the stove chimney.

Grady came out, fanning the smoke in front of him. He mounted his horse, sidestepped it to the ramada, fastened the loop of his rope to a support post, and spurred away. The post ripped out, bouncing, scraping a dust rise, and the mesquite-pole awning sagged partway to the ground. Sandal came out of the adobe, running, ducking his head. He watched Grady circle to come back, went to his own horse, fastened his rope to the other support post, and dragged it away. The ramada collapsed, swinging, smashing, against the adobe front, and the mesquite poles broke apart.

Watching Treat, Leo Pyke said, "You letting them get away with that? All this big talk about you, and you don't even open your mouth."

Grady and Sandal walked their horses in. Treat glanced at them, then back to Pyke. "I don't have anything to say."

"Listen," Pyke said. "I've put up with that closemouth cold-water way of yours a long time. I've watched men stand clear of you, afraid they'd step too close and you'd come to life. I watched Mr. Kergosen, then Ellis, won over to your sly ways. But all that time I was seeing through you—looking clean through, and there was nothing there to see. No backbone, no guts, no nothing."

Sandal was grinning, leaning over his saddle horse. "Eat him up, Layo!"

Pyke's eyes did not leave Treat. "If you were worth it, I'd take my gun off and beat hell out of you."

Treat's eyebrows raised slightly. "Would you, Leo?"

"You damn bet I would."

Sandal said, "Go ahead, man. Do it."

"Shut your mouth!" Pyke threw the words over his shoulder.

"The vision of being segundo returns with the return of the daughter," Sandal said, grinning again. To Grady, next to him, he said, "How would you like to work for this one every day?"

Grady shook his head. "She can't marry him now. And that's the only way he'd get to be Number Two."

"I think she married him," Sandal said, nodding at Treat, "to escape this one."

"I said shut up!" Pyke screamed, turning half around, but at once he looked back at Treat. "You ride out, right now. And if I ever see you this close again, I'll talk to you with a gun. You hear me!"

★ ★ ★

NINE DAYS AFTER that, R. C. Hassett, the county deputy assigned to Dos Mesas, was told of the disappearance of two of Ivan Kergosen's riders. On Saturday, two days before, they'd spent the evening in town. They started back home at eleven o'clock and had not been seen since.

Hassett thought it over the length of time it took him to strap on his holster and take a Winchester down from the wall rack. Then he rode out to Phil Treat's place. Entering the yard, he heard a hammering sound coming from the adobe. He saw that a new ramada had been constructed. As he reined toward the adobe, Phil Treat stepped out of the doorway, a Henry rifle under his arm.

"So you're rebuilding," Hassett said. "I heard about what happened."

His eyes held on Treat as he stepped out of the saddle, letting his reins trail. He brushed open his coat and took a tobacco plug from his vest pocket, bit off a corner of it, and returned the plug to the pocket. His coat remained open, the skirt held back by the butt of his revolver. He had been a law officer for more than two dozen years and he was in no particular hurry.

"I wasn't sure you'd be here," said Hassett. "But something told me to find out."

"You're not looking for me," Treat said.

"No; two of Mr. Kergosen's boys."

Treat called toward the adobe, "Come out a minute!"

Hassett watched as Grady and Sandal appeared in the doorway, then came outside. Grady's bearded face was bruised, one eye swollen and half closed, and he limped as he took the few steps out to the end of the ramada shade. There was no mark on Sandal.

"These the men?" asked Treat. Hassett nodded.

"Ivan reported them lost."

"Not lost," Treat said. "They quit him to work for me."

"Without drawing their pay?"

"That's none of my business," Treat answered.

Hassett's gaze moved to the adobe. "Grady, I didn't know you were a carpenter."

The bearded man hesitated before saying, "I'm swearing out a complaint on one Phil Treat."

Hassett nodded, moving the tobacco from one cheek to the other. "It's your privilege, Grady; though I'd say you got off easy."

"This man forced us—" Grady began.

Hassett held up his hand. "In my office." He looked at Treat then. "You come in, too, and state your complaint. I make out a writ and serve it on Ivan. The writ orders him to court on such and such a date. You're there to claim your wife with proof of legal marriage."

"And if Mr. Kergosen doesn't appear?" asked Treat.

"He's no bigger than I am," Hassett said. "I see that he does next time."

"But that doesn't calm his mind, does it?"

"That's your problem," Hassett said.

Treat almost smiled. "You said it as simply as it can be said."

"All right," Hassett said. "You've been told." He moved around his horse, stepped up into the saddle, then looked down at Treat again. "Let me ask you something. How come Grady looks the way he does and there isn't a mark on Sandal?"

"I talked to Grady first," Treat said.

"I see," Hassett said. "I'll ask you something else. How come Ivan didn't come here looking for these two?"

"I guess he doesn't know I'm still here."

Hassett looked down at Treat. "But he'll know it now, won't he?" He turned and rode out of the yard.

That afternoon, after they had finished the inside repairs, Sandal and Grady were released. They rode out, riding double, and watching them, Treat pictured them approaching the great U-shaped adobe that was Mr. Kergosen's home, then dismounting and standing in the sunlight as Ivan came down the steps from the veranda.

Sandal would tell it: how they were ambushed riding back from Dos Mesas, how Treat had appeared in front of them, coming out of the trees with the Henry; how Grady's horse had been hit when they tried to run, and had fallen on Grady and injured his ankle; how they had been taken back to his adobe and forced to rebuild the ramada and patch the furniture and the stove. And Sandal would describe him as some kind of demon, a *nagual* who never slept and seldom spoke as he held them with a Henry rifle for two days and two nights.

Ivan Kergosen would turn from them, his eyes going to Ellis sitting on the shaded veranda, reading or sewing or staring out over the yard. She would not look at him, but he would detect the beginning of a smile. Only this, on the tenth day of her silence.

You have a woman, Treat thought, picturing her. *You have one and you don't have one.* He thought of the time he had first spoken to her, the times they rode together and the time he first kissed her.

And now they'll come again. But not Grady, because his ankle will put him to bed. Outwait an old man, he thought. *Wait while an old man realizes he is not God, or God's avenging angel, God's right hand. Which could take no longer than your lifetime,* he thought.

He took dried meat, a canteen, a blanket, the Henry, and a holstered Colt revolver and went out into the corral to wait for them.

☆ ☆ ☆

THERE WERE FIVE that came. They reached Treat's adobe at dusk, spreading out as they approached it, coming at it from both sides of the corral, two of the riders circling the stable shed and the adobe before entering the yard. Sandal dismounted and went into the adobe. He came out with a kerosene lantern and held it as Pyke struck a match and lit it.

"Who's going to do it?" asked Sandal.

"You're holding the fire," Pyke said.

"Not me." Sandal shook his head.

"Just throw it in. Hit the wall over the bed."

"Not me. I've done enough to that man."

"What about what he did to you?"

"He had reason."

Pyke stepped out of the saddle. He jerked the lantern away from Sandal and walked to the door. His hand went to the latch, then stopped.

"Layo!" Sandal's voice.

Pyke looked over his shoulder, saw Sandal not looking at him, but staring out toward the corral, and he turned full around, holding the lantern by the ring handle.

He saw Treat crossing the yard toward him. In the dusk he could not see the man's features, but he knew it was Treat. He saw Treat's hands hanging empty and he saw the revolver on his right leg. Now Sandal was moving the horses, holding the reins and whack-slapping at the rump of one to force both of them to the side. The horses of the three riders still mounted moved nervously, and the riders watched Treat, seeing him looking at Leo Pyke. Then, thirty feet from the ramada, Treat stopped.

"Leo, you tore my house down once. Once is enough."

Pyke was at ease. "You're going to stop us?"

"The last time you stated that you'd talk with a gun if I ever came close again." Treat glanced at Sandal when Pyke said nothing. "Is that right?"

"Big as life," the Mexican said.

Treat's gaze returned to Pyke. "Well?"

"You got me at an unfair advantage," Pyke said carefully. "A lantern in my hand. All the light full on me."

"You came here to burn down my house," Treat said, standing motionless. "You're holding the fire, as you told Sandal. You've four men backing you and you call it a disadvantage."

"Three men backing him," Sandal said.

Beyond him one of the mounted riders said, "This part of it isn't our fight."

And Sandal added, "Just Layo's."

"Wait a minute." Pyke was taken by surprise. "You all work for Mr. Kergosen. He says run him out, we do it!"

"But not carry him out," the one who had spoken before said. "You threatened him, Leo; then it's your fight, not ours. And if you think he's got an unfair advantage, put the lantern down."

"So it's like that," Pyke said.

"You got two feet," Sandal said. "Stand on them. Show us how the segundo would do it."

"Listen, you chili picker! You're through!"

"Sure, Layo. Now talk to that boy out there."

"Mr. Kergosen's going to run every damn one of you!" Pyke half

turned to face them, shifting the lantern to his left hand, the light swaying across Sandal and the chestnut color of his horse.

"We'll talk to him," Sandal said.

Pyke stared at him. "You know what you done, you and the rest? You
jawed yourself out of jobs. You see how easy a new one is to find.
Mr. Kergosen's going to be burned, but sure as hell I'm going to"—his
feet started to shift—"tell him!"

As he said it, Pyke was spinning on his toes, swinging the lantern
hard at Treat, seeing it in the air, then going to his right, but seeing
Treat moving, with the revolver suddenly in his hand, and at that moment Treat fired.

Pyke was half around when the bullet struck him. He stumbled back
against the front of the adobe, came forward drawing, bringing up his
Colt, then half turned, falling against the adobe as Treat fired again
and the second bullet hit him.

The revolver fell from Pyke's hand and he stood against the wall
staring at Treat, holding his arms bent slightly, but stiffly against his
sides, as if afraid to move them. He had been shot through both arms,
both just above the elbow.

Treat walked toward him. "Leo," he said, "you've got two things to
remember. One, you're not coming back here again. And two, I could've
aimed dead center." He turned from Pyke to Sandal. "If you want to do
him a good turn, tie up his arms and take him to a doctor. The rest of
you," he said to the mounted men, "can tell Mr. Kergosen I'm still here."

HE WAS TOLD, and he came the next morning, riding into the yard with
a shotgun across his lap. He rode up to Treat, who was standing in front
of the adobe, and the shotgun was pointing down at him when Kergosen drew in the reins. They looked at each other in the clear morning sunlight, in the yellow, bright stillness of the yard.

"I could pull the trigger," Kergosen said, "and it would be over."

"Over for me," Treat said. "Not for you or Ellis."

Kergosen sat heavily in the saddle. He had not shaved this morning
and his eyes told that he'd had little sleep. "You won't draw a gun
against me?"

"No, sir."

"Why?"

"If I did, I'd have to live with Ellis the rest of my life the way you're doing now."

"So you're in a hole."

"But no deeper than the one you're in."

Kergosen studied him. "I underestimated you. I thought you'd run."

"Because you told me to?"

"That was reason enough."

"You're too used to giving orders," Treat said. "You've been Number One a long time and you've forgotten what it's like to have somebody contrary to you."

"I didn't get where I am having people contrary to me," Kergosen stated. "I worked and fought and earned the right to give orders, but I prayed to God to lead me right, and don't you forget that!"

"Mr. Kergosen," Treat said quietly, "are you afraid I can't provide for your daughter?"

"Provide!" Kergosen's face tightened. "An Apache buck provides. He builds a hut for his woman and brings her meat. Any man with one hand and a gun can provide. We're talking about my daughter, not a flat-nosed Indian woman—and you have to put up a damn sight more than meat and a hut!"

Treat said, "You think I won't make something of myself?"

"Mister, all you've proved to me is that you can read sign and shoot." Kergosen paused before asking, "Why didn't you sign a complaint to get Ellis back? Don't you know your rights? That what I'm talking about. You can track a renegade Apache, you can stand off five men with a Colt, but you don't know how to live with a white man!"

"Mr. Kergosen," Treat said patiently, "I could've got a writ. I could've prosecuted you for tearing down my house. I could've killed Leo Pyke with almost a clear conscience. I could've done a lot of things."

"But you didn't," Kergosen said.

"No, I waited."

"If you're waiting for me to die of old age—"

"Mr. Kergosen, I'm interested in your daughter, not your property. We can get along just fine with what we're building on."

"Which is nothing," Kergosen said.

"When you started," Treat asked, "what did you have?"

"When I married I had over one hundred square miles of land. Miles, mister, not acres. I was going on forty years old, sure of myself and not a kid anymore."

"I'm almost thirty, Mr. Kergosen."

"I'll say it again: And you've got nothing."

"Nothing but time."

"Listen," Kergosen said earnestly. "You don't count on the future like it's nothing but years to fill up. You fill them up, good or bad, according to your ability and willingness to sweat, but you're sure of that future before you ask a woman to face it with you."

Treat said, "You had somebody picked for Ellis?"

"Not by name, but a man who can offer her something."

"So you planned her future, and it turned out different."

"Damn it, I try to do what's right!"

"According to your rules."

"With God's help!"

"Mr. Kergosen," Treat said, "I don't mean disrespect, but I think you've rigged it so God has to take the blame for your mistakes. Ellis and I made a mistake. We admit it. We should've come to you first. We would've got married whether you said yes or no, but we still should've come to you first. The way it is now, it's still up to you, but now you're in an embarrassing position with the Almighty. Ellis and I are married in the eyes of the same God that you say's been guiding you all this time, thirty years or more. All right, you and Him have been getting along fine up to now. But now what?"

Kergosen said nothing.

"We could probably argue all day," Treat said, "but it comes down to this: You either go home and send out some more men, or you use that scattergun, or you come inside and have some coffee, and we'll talk it over like two grown-up men."

Kergosen stared at him. "I admire your control, Mr. Treat."

"I've learned how to wait, Mr. Kergosen. If it comes down to that, I'll outwait you. I think you know that."

Kergosen was silent for a long moment. He looked down at his hands on the shotgun and exhaled, letting his breath out slowly, wearily, and he seemed to sit lower on the saddle.

"I think I'm getting old," he said quietly. "I'm tired of arguing and tired of fighting."

"Maybe tired of fighting yourself," Treat said.

Kergosen nodded faintly. "Maybe so."

Treat waited, then said, "Mr. Kergosen, I'm anxious to see my wife."

Kergosen's face came up, out of shadow, deep-lined and solemn, but the hard tightness was gone from his jaw. He shifted his weight and came down off the saddle, and on the ground he handed the shotgun to Treat.

"Phil," he said, "this damn thing's getting too heavy to hold."

From his pocket Treat brought out the bank draft Kergosen had given him. He handed it over, saying, "So is this, Mr. Kergosen."

They stood for a moment. Kergosen's hand went into his pocket with the bank draft and when they moved toward the adobe, the bitterness between them was past. It had worn itself to nothing.

24

Man with the Iron Arm

Original Title: The One Arm Man
Complete Western Book, September 1956

★

Chapter One

CHRIS AND KITE and Vicente were already half down the slope when we came out of the trees—three riders spread out and running hard, waving their sombreros like they could smell the mescal we'd been talking about all morning. This new man, Tobin Royal, was next to me holding in his big sorrel I think just to show he could hold himself, too, if he wanted. He was smoking a cigarette and squinting through the smoke curling up from it.

At the bottom of the grade, looking bleached white in the big open sunlight, were the adobes of Brady's Store: one main structure and a few scattered out-buildings and a corral. Brady's served as a Hatch & Hodges stage-line stop, besides being a combination store and saloon for the half dozen one-loop ranchers in the vicinity. The one we worked for—the El Centro Cattle Company—was bigger than all of them put together twice and just the eastern tip of it came close to touching Brady's Store. Chris and Kite and Vicente and this Tobin Royal and I were gathering stock from the east range, readying for a trail drive and we felt we deserved some of Brady's mescal long as it was handy.

By the time Tobin and I rode into the yard, the others had gone into the saloon side of the adobe and I saw a bare-headed, dark-haired man leading their three horses over to the open stable shed that attached to the adobe. He looked around, hearing us ride in, and I saw then that he had only one arm. For a moment he stood looking at us; then he turned, leading the horses away, moving slow like he either had all the time in the world or else his mind was on something else.

As we swung off, this Tobin Royal called over to him, "Hey, boy, two more here!" But the one-armed man kept going like he hadn't heard. Tobin stood looking at the rumps of the three horses moving into the stable. He let his reins drop and he moved a half dozen slow strides toward the stable. A quirt was thonged to his left wrist and it hung limp at his side opposite the long-barreled Navy Colt on his right hip.

He was a slim, good-looking boy, but he never smiled unless he said something he thought was funny, and he liked to pose, as he was doing now with the quirt and his hat tilted forward and the low-slung Navy Colt. In the few weeks he'd been with us I'd learned this about him.

I started to bring the horses and he turned his head. "You keep them horses over there."

"What's the difference? I'll take them over."

"Just stay where you are." His gaze went back to the stable as the one-armed fellow came out of the shadow into the sunlight again, and for a moment Tobin just stared at the man.

"Are you deaf or something?"

✯ ✯ ✯

THE MAN TURNED to Tobin and his eyes looked tired. They were watery, and with the bits of straw sticking to his shirt and pants he looked as if he'd just slept off a drunk in the stable. He was about thirty, a year one way or the other. He didn't answer Tobin, but came on toward me.

"I asked you a question!"

He stopped then and looked at Tobin.

"I asked you," Tobin said, "if you were deaf."

"No, I'm not deaf."

"You work here?"

The man nodded.

"You're supposed to answer when somebody calls."

"I'll try to remember that," the man said.

The temper rose in Tobin's face again. "Listen, don't talk like that to me! I'll kick your hind end across the yard!"

The tired eyes looked at me momentarily. He came on then and took the reins and started back toward the stable with the horses. Tobin called to him, "Water and rub 'em down now . . . you hear me?" He stood looking after the horses for a time, then finally he turned and started for the adobe as I did.

"You didn't have to talk to him like that."

Tobin shook his head disgustedly. "Judas, I hate a slow-moving, worthless man."

"He had only one arm," I said.

"What difference does that make?"

"Maybe it makes him feel bad."

"It don't make him walk slower."

"Well maybe some men it does."

Tobin opened the door and walked in ahead of me over to the bar that was along the left-hand wall where Chris and Kite and Vicente stood leaning and drinking mescal, and he said, "Whiskey," to Brady standing behind the bar.

Brady was looking toward me, waiting for Tobin to get out of the way. "How you been, Uncle?" Brady said to me.

"Fair," I told him. "How've you been?"

"Good." He smiled now, that big, loose-faced, double-chinned smile of his. "It's nice to see you again."

"I want whiskey," Tobin said.

Brady looked at him. "I heard you, Sonny. You can't wait till I tell a friend hello?"

I got to the bar before Tobin could say anything. "Joe, this is Tobin Royal, a new man with us."

Tobin nodded and Joe Brady said glad-to-meet-you, because he was a businessman. He sat the whiskey bottle on the bar and poured a drink out of it. Tobin emptied the hooker, and touched the bottle with the glass for another. But this one, after Brady poured it, he took to one of the three tables that were along the other wall, where the stage passengers ate. He sat down with the drink in front of him and started making a cigarette.

Joe Brady nudged the mescal bottle toward me. "What's he trying to prove?"

"That he's older than he is," I answered. I could hear Vicente telling a vaquero story and Chris and Kite were listening, knowing what the ending was, but waiting for it anyway. They didn't have much to say to Tobin, because the first day he joined us he had a fight with Kite. Kite had been a Tascosa buffalo skinner, a big rawboned boy, but Tobin licked him good. Tobin always stayed a few steps out from them, like he didn't want to be mistaken for just an ordinary rider.

"I see you got a new man too," I said to Brady.

"That's John Lefton," Brady said. "He came here on the stage a few weeks ago . . . got off like he expected to see something. As it turned out, he'd paid the fare as far as his money would take him . . . which was to here."

"What's he running away from?"

"Did you see him close?"

"You mean the one arm?"

Brady nodded. "That's what I *think* he's running from."

"Well, it's too bad. How'd he lose it?"

"In the War."

"Well," I said again, "it's better to lose it that way than, say, in a corn-crusher. What side was he on?"

"Union."

"Don't hold it against him, Joe."

"Hell, the War's been over for eight years."

"You felt sorry for him and gave him a job?"

Brady shrugged. "What else could I do?"

"He looks like he drinks."

"He about draws his wages in mescal. But he does his work . . . better'n the Mex boy and even took over the bookkeeping."

"It's a terrible thing to see a man down like that."

I heard the screen door open behind me and Brady mumbled, "Here he is."

★
Chapter Two

I HALF TURNED as he went by, walking to the back part of the adobe where Brady's rolltop desk was next to the door that led to the store part. He was carrying a push-broom.

Brady called over the bar, "John, you don't have to do that now."

"It's all right," he answered. His voice sounded natural, but like there wasn't a speck of enthusiasm in him if he ever wanted to bring it out.

"No," Brady said. "Wait till later. These people will just mess up the place anyhow."

He nodded, then leaned the push-broom against the wall and stood at the desk with his back to us.

"I never know how to talk to him," Brady half whispered.

"Mr. Brady—"

Brady looked up and saw John Lefton at the end of the bar now. As he walked down to him, Chris and Kite and Vicente stopped talking. They stood at the bar pretending like they weren't trying to hear what was said, as Brady and the one-armed man talked for a minute. Then Brady came back for the mescal bottle and poured him a good shot of it.

"I wonder what he's trying to forget," I said, when Brady was opposite me again.

"His wife," Brady said, and didn't add anything to that for a minute. Then he said, "He's been here three weeks and he's gotten three letters from her, forwarded from the last town he stayed in, but he hasn't answered one."

"How do you know it's his wife . . . he told you?"

Brady hesitated. "I read one of the letters."

"Joe!"

He gritted his teeth, meaning for me to keep my voice down. "After he got the last one he started drinking and kept it up till it put him asleep. He was sitting at that table there and the letter was right in front of him. Listen . . . I just stood there trying to figure him out, wanting to help him, but I couldn't help him till I knew what his trouble was. Finally I decided, hell, there's only one way to do it, read the letter."

"Go on."

"She asked him why he never answered any of her letters and when he was going to send for her, and telling how much she loved him," Brady paused. "You see it now?"

I COULD SEE IT all right. Him coming back from the War lacking an arm and somehow figuring he'd be a burden and being sensitive about how he looked. Then running away to prove himself . . . then doing more running than proving. Promising to send for her at first, but each day knowing it would be harder as the time passed. Her at home waiting while he wanders around losing his self-respect. That would be eight years of waiting now.

"Maybe," I said, "he don't want her anymore."

Brady shook his head. "You never saw him read the letters."

About a minute later, this Tobin Royal came up next to me and slapped his left-handed quirt down on the bar. "Give me another one," he said.

Brady said civilly, "You haven't paid for the first two yet."

"We'll settle when I'm through," Tobin told him. He drank off part of the whiskey that Brady poured and stood fiddling with what was left, turning the glass between two fingers. His eyes lifted as Brady moved down the bar to where John Lefton was standing and poured him another mescal.

Tobin leaned away from the bar to look at Lefton. He came back then and said, loud enough for everybody to hear, "I guess even a man without all his parts can drink mescal."

I couldn't believe he'd said it, but there it was and at that moment the room was quiet as night. I half whispered to Tobin, "What'd you say that for?" But he didn't answer me. He moved from the bar the next moment and went down to stand next to Lefton who glanced at him, but looked down at his drink again.

"Before you go sloppin' up the mescal juice," Tobin said, "I want to understand my horse is cared for. You rubbed him good?"

Lefton was raising the mescal glass, ignoring Tobin, and suddenly Tobin's quirt came up and lashed down on Lefton's arm and the mescal glass went slamming skidding over the bar.

"I asked you a question," Tobin said.

For a shaded second Lefton's face came alive, but as fast as it came the anger faded from his eyes and he looked down at his wrist, holding it tightly to his stomach. "No," he answered then. "I didn't rub down your horse."

"Do it now," Tobin said.

Brady moved toward them. "Wait a minute! You don't order my help around!"

"He wants to do it," Tobin answered. "Don't you?"

Lefton's eyes raised. "It's all right, Mr. Brady."

"I'll tip him something," Tobin grinned. He looked at Lefton again. "One hand's as good as two for rubbing down a horse, ain't it?"

Lefton hesitated. Before he could answer Tobin's quirt came down cracking against the bar edge and Lefton went back half a step.

"You're not much for answering questions, are you?"

Lefton's eyes raised momentarily. "I'll tend to your horse."

Tobin grinned. "I want to ask you something else." He waited to make Lefton speak.

"All right," Lefton said.

"Where did you leave your arm?"

Again Lefton hesitated and you had the urge to poke him to make him hurry up and answer. "On Rock Creek," he said then. "East of Cemetery Ridge."

"What was your outfit?"

"Seventh Michigan."

Tobin's face brightened. "Damn, I thought you looked like a blue-belly! One of Wade Hampton's boys cut you good, didn't he?" He looked around at the rest of us and said, "A brother of mine was with Wade, all the way to Yellow Tavern."

Lefton didn't say a word and Tobin studied him. "What rank did you hold?"

"Lieutenant."

"From lieutenant of cavalry to rubbin' down horses," Tobin said. He stuck out his quirt as Lefton started to walk past him. "I didn't say you could go!" The quirt moved across Lefton's chest and the tip of it poked at the empty right sleeve.

"Above the elbow," Tobin said. "Were you right-handed or left?"

"Right."

"Now that'd be a hardship," Tobin said. "Teaching the left what the right used to know." The quirt end kept slapping gently at the empty sleeve as he spoke. "But the left's good enough for sloppin' mescal juice, huh?"

Lefton did not answer.

"You hear me?"

"Yes . . . it's good enough."

"I thought stable boys were supposed to say yes *sir.*"

"That's enough!" Brady said. His big face was red and had a tight look about the mouth. "You leave him alone now!"

Tobin looked at Brady. "You ought to learn your stable boy proper respect."

"This man isn't a stable boy!"

"Then how come he wants to rub down my horse?"

This was carrying it too far. I knew Tobin could lick me eight ways from breakfast with one hand, but now I could feel the anger up in my throat and I had to say something.

"Tobin . . . you stop that kind of talk and act like a human being for once in your life!"

He took the time to look my way. "Uncle, are you telling me what to do?"

"I can't talk any plainer!"

He grinned . . . didn't get mad . . . just grinned and said, "Uncle, you know better than that. You don't tell me what to do. Not you or any man here." He turned to Lefton again. "I'm the only one doing any telling, ain't that right?"

He poked Lefton with the quirt and Lefton nodded, though he was looking at the floor.

"Let me hear you say it."

Lefton nodded again. "Yes . . . that's right."

Tobin waited. "Yes . . . what?"

Then it was like seeing this Lefton give up the last shred of pride he owned, and you had to turn your head because you knew he was going to say it, and you didn't want to be looking at him because you weren't sure if you'd feel sorry for him anymore.

We heard it all right, the hollow sounding, *"Yes sir—"*

And after it, Tobin saying, "Now you find your left-handed curry-comb and go on out and rub my horse."

Chapter Three

ALL THE WAY back to our headquarters, later on, with the two-hundred-odd head we'd gathered, not one of us said a word to Tobin, though he made some remarks when we stopped that night as to how fine his big sorrel looked even if it had been curried by a left-handed stable boy.

As I said, we'd come over to the east range to gather and by the time we'd got back to the home ranch the trail drive was about to get under way and, thank the Lord, we saw little of Tobin for the next forty-some-odd days. Chris and Kite and Vicente and I were swing riders when we were on the move; but Tobin, because he was a new man, had to ride drag and eat dust all the way.

We left Sudan, where the El Centro main herd was headquartered, about the first of May, and it wasn't till the middle of June that I had my bath in the Grand Central Hotel in Ellsworth.

I'll tell you the truth: I thought of that one-armed man about every day of the drive, though I never talked about him to the others.

Still, I knew they were thinking about him the way I was. Picturing him standing there with his one arm held tight against his belly after Tobin had quirted him—holding it like that because he didn't have another hand to rub the sting with. Maybe we should all have jumped Tobin and beat his hide off, but that wouldn't have proved anything. I think we were all waiting to see this one-armed man stand his ground and fight back, and though he wouldn't have had a chance, at least he would have felt better after.

Why did Tobin lay it on him? I don't know. I've seen men like Tobin before and since, but not many, thank the Lord. That kind always has to be proving something that other people don't even bother about. Maybe Tobin did it to show us he had no use for a man who couldn't stand on his own two feet. Maybe he did it just so he could see how low a man could slip. Then he could say to himself, "Tobin, boy, you'll never be like that, even if both your arms were gone."

And probably Tobin would be judging himself right. No one could say that he wasn't like a piece of rawhide. He was hard on himself even, would take the meanest horse in the remuda and be the last one in at night just so he could say he worked harder than anybody else. But that's all you could say for him.

And why did John Lefton, a man who had been a cavalry officer and gone through the war, stand there and take it? That I don't know either. Maybe he had *too much* pride.

After running for eight years, it was a long way to look back to what he was. And the mescal would blur it to make it farther. I remember sitting in the tub in the Grand Central Hotel and saying, "The hell with him," like that was final. But it wasn't that easy. There was something about him that told you that at least one time he had been much man.

We did see John Lefton again.

No . . . I don't want to jump to it. I'll tell it the way it happened.

We came back from Ellsworth and most of that fall Chris and me worked a company herd up on the Canadian near Tascosa. Then toward the middle of November we were ordered back to Sudan. One day, right after we were back, the company man, C. H. Felt, said he was sending us over to the east range with a wagon full of alfalfa to scatter for the winter graze. I asked him who was going and he said Chris and Kite and Vicente . . . that's right, and Tobin Royal.

THAT'S HOW THE same five of us come to ride down that gray windy grade into Brady's yard that November afternoon.

No one was in sight, not even the dog we could hear barking off somewhere behind the adobes. Kite swung down and took my reins as I dismounted. Vicente took Chris's. That left Tobin Royal to care for his own. He was still riding that big sorrel.

Chris and I went inside the adobe and right away Chris said, "Something's different here."

"You just never seen the place empty, is all."

He kept looking all around to see if he could place what it was. Then I started looking around and it was an unnaturally long moment before it dawned on me what it was.

The place was *clean*. Not just swept clean and dusted, but there was wax on the bar and three tables and fresh paint on the places it belonged.

"Chris, the place is *clean*. That's what it is!"

He didn't answer me. Chris was looking down to the back end where the rolltop and the door was. A woman, a black-haired, slim-built, prettier-than-ordinary woman, closed the door and came toward us.

She came right up and gave us a little welcome smile, and said, "May I serve you gentlemen something to eat?" Her voice was pleasant, but she seemed to be holding back a little.

Chris said, "Eat?"

And I said, "We ate at camp, ma'am," touching my hat. "We were thinking of a drink."

She smiled again and you could tell that one was put on. "The bar is Mr. Brady's department," she said and started to turn. "He can't be far. I'll see if I can find him." She started to walk to the back, and that's when Kite and Vicente and Tobin Royal came in.

She looked around, but must have reasoned they were with Chris and me, because she went on then until Tobin called out, "Hey . . . where you going?"

She stopped, turning full around as Tobin brushed past us saying, "Now that old man's using his head," meaning Brady, I guess.

The smile didn't show this time, but she said, "May I serve you something to eat?"

Tobin grinned. "Not to eat."

"I don't serve the bar," the woman said. "Mr. Brady does that."

"Uh-huh," Tobin said. Then he laughed out loud. "Like you never been behind a bar before! What're you doing here then?"

"I'm here," she said quietly, "with my husband."

"You're married to *Brady*?"

"I'm Mrs. Lefton."

"Lefton!" Tobin's mouth hung open. "You're married to that one-armed stable boy!"

The color came up over her face like she'd been slapped, but she didn't say a word. Tobin was grinning and shaking his head like it was the funniest thing he'd ever heard of. "Listen," he said to her. "You get me a whiskey drink and I'll tell you something about your husband you probably don't know."

Right then Brady came in behind us. His coat was on and he was breathing in and out like he'd hurried. From the look on his face you could tell he'd seen our horses and the El Centro brand and the chances were good he knew who he'd find.

The woman said quickly, "Is my husband coming?" and now sounded frightened and as if she were trying hard to keep from crying.

Tobin added, "Or is he busy cleaning the stable?"

"He's breaking a horse," Brady stated.

I said, "Breaking a *horse?*"

Brady turned on me. "That's what I said, breaking a horse!"

Tobin must have been as surprised as any of us; but he wouldn't show it. He just shrugged. "Well, I guess one wing's as good as two for that anyway." Without her expecting it he grabbed Mrs. Lefton's arm. "Honey, your husband waits on me. Why shouldn't you?" He gave her a little push toward the bar and that snaky quirt of his slapped back-handed across where her bustle was.

Brady said something, but I don't know what . . . because I heard a step behind me. I just glanced, then came full around realizing who it was. John Lefton.

★

Chapter Four

BUT NOT THE John Lefton we had seen the last time. He didn't have on a hat and his wool shirt was dirty from sweat and dust. His hair was cut shorter than before and hung down a little over his forehead; his jaw was clean-shaved, but he was wearing a full-grown cavalry kind of mustache.

That's where the big difference was: the mustache, and the eyes that were dark and clear and looking straight ahead to Tobin.

He walked past us and as he did I saw the quirt hanging from his wrist. I remembered Brady saying that he'd been breaking a horse, but somehow you got the idea he was wearing it for another reason.

He walked right up to Tobin and said, without wasting breath, "Mr. Royal, I've been waiting some months to see you again."

Tobin was half smiling, but you could tell it was put on, while he tried to figure out the change in this man. Tobin moved a little bit. He cocked his hip and leaned his hand on the bar to show he was relaxed.

"First," John Lefton said, "I want to thank you for what you did."

Tobin frowned then. "What'd I do?"

"If you don't know," Lefton said, "I'm not going to explain it. But you must know what I'm going to give you."

Tobin still looked puzzled. He didn't say anything and suddenly Lefton's quirt slashed across Tobin's hand on the edge of the bar.

"You know now?"

Tobin knew. Maybe he couldn't believe it, but he knew and in the instant he was pushing himself from the bar, dipping that stung hand to get at the Navy Colt. The barrel was just clear of the holster when Lefton's quirt cracked Tobin's wrist like a pistol shot, and slapped the Colt right out of his hand. For a moment Tobin was wide open, not sure what to do. Then he saw it coming and tried to cover, but not soon enough and Lefton's quirt lashed across his face cutting him from cheekbone to nose. The quirt came back, catching him across the forehead and his hat went spinning.

Tobin threw up his arms to cover his face, but now Lefton let go of the quirt. He came up with a fist under Tobin's jaw, and when Tobin's guard came apart, the same fist chopped back-handed, like a counterpunch, and smacked hard. This man knew how to fight. The fist swung low again, into Tobin's belly, and when he doubled up, Lefton's knee came up against his jaw. That straightened Tobin good. When he was just about upright the fist came around like a sledgehammer and the next second Tobin was spread-eagle on the floor.

He must have been conscious, though I don't know how; for then

Lefton looked down at him and said, "You know what you're going to do now, don't you? As soon as you find a left-handed currycomb."

We just stood there until he got Tobin to his feet and out the door; then Brady said, "Mrs. Lefton, you've got yourself a man." And the way he said *man*, it meant everything it could mean plus how Joe Brady felt about the matter.

Mrs. Lefton smiled. "I've known that for some time," she said mildly—to tell us that there had never been any doubt about it as far as she was concerned. She excused herself right after that.

As soon as the door closed behind her, Brady, like a little kid with a story to tell, filled in the part we didn't know about.

He said on that day last May, after we'd gone, Lefton came back in and poured himself a mescal drink. But he didn't drink it. He just stared at it for the longest time. Maybe fifteen or twenty minutes. Suddenly, then, he swept the drink off and brought his fist down on the bar hard enough to break a bone. He held on to the bar then with his head down and Brady said he thought the man was going to cry. But he never did, and after a minute he went outside.

THE CHANGE IN him began right after that, Brady told. It was as if Tobin's quirt had jolted him back to reality. He found himself at deep bottom and now there was only one direction to go, if he had the guts.

Not until a few days later, Brady said, did he realize that Lefton had stopped drinking. He started drawing his wages, did his work all right, and about the middle of July he disappeared for three days. When he came back he had four mustangs on a string. The next day he built a mesquite corral off back of the adobes and that night he wrote a letter to his wife.

By the time his wife arrived, the end of August, Lefton had broken and sold better than a dozen horses. Understand now, when he started this he didn't know the first thing about breaking horses. What happened was, the time he disappeared, he went to Sudan to find something to invest in with the money he'd saved. He happened to talk to a mustanger who told him there was money in horse trading if he could stand getting his insides jolted up.

Lefton hired a couple of Tonkawa boys to scare up green horses and from that day on he was in business. The mustanger in Sudan taught him a few things, but most of it Lefton learned himself. The hard way. He took a beating from those horses, but he never quit and Brady said it was like watching a man do penance. Maybe Lefton felt the same way about it, I don't know.

Brady said that two weeks ago, when Lefton's count had reached forty sold he'd wondered why Lefton stayed around instead of expanding and locating where business would be better. Brady said today, though, he understood why Lefton had *wanted* to stay.

We all agreed that what we saw that afternoon was one of the finest experiences of our lives. Still, neither Chris, Kite, Vicente or me ever talked about it to anyone. You couldn't tell the second part without telling the first, and we still didn't want to do that.

Tobin Royal stayed with us. I'll give him credit for that. Working with us after what we'd seen. After that day he didn't talk so much. But those times he did start, after a few drinks or something, I'd look at him and touch my cheek. His fingers would go up and feel where the quirt had lashed him and he would shut up. There was no scar there, but maybe there was to Tobin. One that would always stay with him.

25

The Longest Day of His Life

Western Novel and Short Stories, October 1956

Chapter One

New Job

THROUGH THE down-pointed field glasses, his gaze inched from left to right along the road that twisted narrowly through the ravine. Where he sat, hunched forward with his legs crossed and with his elbows resting on raised knees to steady the field glasses, the ground dropped away before him in a long grassy sweep; though across from him the slope climbed steeply into dwarf oak and above the trees a pale-orange wall of sandstone rose seamed and shadowed into sun glare. Below and to the right, the road passed into tree shadow and seemed to end there.

"How far to Glennan's place?"

"About four miles," the man who was next to him kneeling on one knee said. He was twice the age of the man with the field glasses, nearing fifty, and studying the end of the ravine his eyes half closed, tightening his face in a teeth-clenched grimace. His name was Joe Mauren, in charge of road construction for the Hatch & Hodges Stage Line Company.

"Past the trees," Mauren said, "the road drops down through a draw for maybe two miles. You come to grass then and you think you're out of it, but follow the wagon tracks and you go down through another pass. Then you're out and you'll see the house back off a ways. It's built close to deep pinyon and sometimes you can't see it for shadows, but you will this time of day."

"Then twelve miles beyond it to the Rock of Ages mine," Steve Brady, the man with the field glasses, said.

"About that," Mauren said.

The field glasses moved left again. "Will you have to do any work along here?"

"No, those scrub oaks catch anything that falls."

"Just back where you're working now."

"That's the only dangerous place."

"The mine's been hauling through for three months," Brady said. "Rock slides don't worry them."

"The driver of an eight-team ore wagon isn't a stage full of passengers," Mauren said. "If we expect people to ride over this stretch, we have to make it near presentable."

"So two miles back to your construction site and eight back of that to Contention," Steve Brady said. He lowered the field glasses. "Twenty-six miles from Contention to Rock of Ages."

"You'll go far," Mauren said dryly.

"I see why we need a stop at Glennan's place," Brady said.

Mauren nodded. "To calm their nerves and slack their thirst."

"Will Glennan serve whiskey?"

"He blame well better," Mauren said, rising. "Else you don't give him the franchise. That's an unwritten rule, boy." He watched Brady get to his feet, brushing his right leg and the seat of his pants.

"New job, new suit," Mauren said. "And by the time you get to Glennan's the suit's going to be powder-colored instead of dark gray."

Brady turned, his free hand brushing the lapels now. "Does it look all right?"

"About a size too small. You look all hands, Steve. Like you're ready to grab something." Mauren almost smiled. "Like that little Kitty Glennan."

"She must be something, the way you talk."

"It'll make the tears run out of your eyes, Steve. She's that pretty."

"The suit's all right then, huh?"

"Take the shooter off and you'll be able to button it." Mauren was looking at the Colt that Brady wore on his right hip.

"It feels good open," Brady said.

Mauren studied him up and down. "Suits are fine, but you get used to wearing them and before you know it you're up in Prescott behind a desk. Like your pa."

"That might'n be so bad."

"You try it, boy. A week and you'd go back to driving or shotgun riding just to get away." They mounted their horses and Mauren said, "You've wasted enough time. Now do something for your pay."

"I'll try and come back this way," Brady said.

"Do that now," Mauren answered. He reined tightly and moved off through the pinyon pine.

FOR A MOMENT Brady watched him, then slipped the glasses into a saddlebag, tight-turned his own mount and slanted down the slope to the road below. He reached the end of the ravine and followed the double wagon ruts into the trees, feeling the relief of the shade now and he pushed his hat up from his forehead, thinking then: Maybe I should've got a new one. The tan Stetson was dusty and dark-stained around the band, but it felt good.

The fact was, everything felt good. It was good to be here and good to see the things there were to see and good to be going where he was going.

He thought of Mr. Glennan whom he had never seen before—Mr. J. F. Glennan—and tried to picture him.

"Mr. Glennan, my name's Brady, with Hatch and Hodges, come with the franchise agreement for you to sign." No—

"Hello Mr. Glennan, my name's Brady, with Hatch and Hodges—you sure got a nice place. Fine for a stage stop, trees for shade and not much building on to do. Here's the agreement, Mr. Glennan. I think you'll like working for"—no—"being with the company. Take me. I been with Hatch and Hodges for eight years; since I was a sixteen-year-old boy."

Then what?

"Yes, sir. I like it very much. See, my father is general manager up to Prescott. He said, 'Steve, if you're going to work for me you're going to start at the bottom and pull your ownself up.' Which is what I did—starting as a stable boy in the Prescott yard."

He thought: He's not interested in that.

But thought then: You got to talk, don't you? You have to be friendly.

"Then I went out, Mr. Glennan. Went to work for Mr. Rindo who's agent up on the Gila Ford to San Carlos run. Then my Uncle Joe Mauren, who isn't my uncle but that's what I call him, made me his shotgun messenger. Uncle Joe drove then. Now he's in charge of all construction. But when I was with him he taught me everything there is to know—how to drive, how to read sign, how to shoot. . . . But you met him! Mr. Mauren? The one first talked to you a couple weeks ago?"

See, he thought. You talk enough and it comes right back to where you started.

"So then I drove a stage for four years and then, just last week, was named a supervisor for the Bisbee to Contention section and for this new line that goes up to Rock of Ages. And that's why I'm the one calling on you with the franchise agreement."

See? Right back again.

You talk all your life and you don't worry about it, he thought. But when it's your job to talk then you worry like it's some new thing to learn. Like it's harder than hitting something with a Colt gun or driving a three-team stage.

★

Chapter Two

Two with Guns

A QUARTER OF a mile ahead of Brady, two riders came down through the rocks and scrub brush to the mouth of the draw. They dismounted, leaving their horses in the trees, came out to the edge of the wagon ruts at the point where they entered the open meadow, and looked back up the draw.

The younger of the two, his hat low and straight over his eyes, and carrying a Henry rifle, said, "He'll be along directly." They moved back to the shadowed cover of the pine trees and stood there to wait.

"You don't know who he is," the second man said. "Why take a chance?"

"Where's the chance?" the younger man said. "If he moves funny I'll bust him."

"Ed wouldn't waste his time on one man."

"The hell with Ed."

"Ed looks for the big one."

"You don't know how big a thing is till you try it," the younger man said. He paused, raising the Henry carefully, pointing the barrel out through the pine branches. "There he is, Russ, look at him."

They watched Brady come out of the trees at the end of the draw and start across the meadow. For a moment the younger man studied him, his face relaxed but set in a tight-lipped grin. He said then, "He don't look like much. Maybe I'll skin him and take his hide."

"While you're talking to yourself, he's moving away," the other man said.

"All right, Russ, you're in such a big hurry." He raised the Henry to his shoulder and called out, "Hold it there!"

Brady reined in, half turning his mount.

"Don't look around!"

The younger man came out almost to the road, to the left of and slightly behind Brady. "Take your coat off, then the gun belt." Moving closer, keeping the Henry sighted on Brady's back, he watched Brady pull off the coat. "Now let it drop," he said.

"It'll get all dirty."

"Drop it!"

Brady obeyed, then unbuckled his gun belt and let it fall next to the coat.

"Now the Winchester."

Brady drew it from the saddle boot and lowered it stock down.

"You got business around here?"

"If I do it's mine," Brady answered. "Nobody else's."

He tried to turn, hearing the quick steps behind him, but caught only a glimpse of the man before he was pulled off the saddle, and as he hit the ground and tried to roll away, the barrel of the Henry chopped against the side of his head to stop him.

The rifle barrel prodded him then. "Get up. That didn't hurt."

Brady pushed himself up slowly with a ringing in his ears and already a dull, hard pain in his temple. He felt the rifle barrel turn him to face the horse.

"Now stand like that while you take your shirt off and drop your pants."

"I can't go around without any clothes—" He felt the hand suddenly on his collar, pulling, choking him, then jerking and the shirt ripped open down the back. Behind him the man laughed.

"You don't know what you can do till you try," the man with the Henry said.

Brady pulled off the shirt without unbuttoning it, used his heels to work off his boots, let his pants drop then stepped into the boots again. He stood now in his long white underwear, wearing boots and hat, and staring at the smooth leather of his saddle close in front of him.

The second man came out of the trees. "Let him go now," he said.

"When I'm ready."

"You're ready now. Let him go."

"Russ, you're the nervous type." The Henry swung back on Brady— "Go on!"—then raised slightly as Brady stepped into the saddle, and the younger man said, "Don't he cut a fine figure, Russ?" He stood grinning, looking up at Brady, then moved toward him and yelled, "Kick him! Go on, *run!*"

As Brady started off, the man called Russ went back into the trees for the horses. When he came out, Brady was halfway across the meadow and the younger man was going through Brady's pockets.

"How much?" Russ asked.

"Ten dollars plus and some papers."

"What kind of papers?"

"How'd I know?"

"Bring them along, for Ed to look over."

"You can have them," the younger man said. He began unbuckling his gun belt and Russ frowned. "Where're you going?"

"Steppin' out, with my new suit on."

"Listen, you know what Ed said—"

"Russ, I don't care what old Ed thinks or says." He winked, grinning, kicking off his boots. "That's a fine-looking girl down there."

☆ ☆ ☆

As JOE MAUREN had described it, the Glennan place was almost hidden in deep tree shadow: a stand of aspen bordering the front yard, pinyon close behind the house and beyond, on higher ground, there were tall ponderosa pines. The house was a one-story log structure with a shingle roof but an addition to it, built out from the side and back to form an L, was of adobe brick. A stable shed, also adobe and joined to the addition by twenty feet of fence, stood empty, its doors open.

Brady passed through the aspen, noticing the empty shed, then moved his gaze to the house, expecting the door to open, but thinking: Unless everybody's gone.

You're doing fine your first day.

Straight out from the door of the log house he reined in, waited a moment then started to dismount.

"Stay up!"

Over his shoulder Brady caught a glimpse of the girl standing at the corner of the house. She was holding a shotgun.

"You don't have to turn around, either!"

Brady shook his head faintly. He didn't move. Twice in one day.

The girl said, "You're a friend of Albie's, aren't you?"

"I never heard of him." Brady started to turn.

The shotgun barrel came up. "Keep your eyes straight!"

Brady shrugged. "I know what you look like anyway."

"Fine, then you don't have to be gawking around."

"Your head'd come up to about my nose," Brady said. "You look more boy than girl, but you got a pretty face with nice blond hair and dark eyes and eyebrows that don't match your hair."

"Albie told you that," the girl said. "You talk just like him."

"Miss Glennan, I'll take an oath I don't know any Albie." He cleared his throat before saying, "My name's Stephen J. Brady of the Hatch and Hodges Company come here to see your dad with the agreement—"

"You don't have any clothes on!"

Brady turned in the saddle to look at her and this time she said nothing to stop him. Her lips were parted and her eyes held him with open astonishment. He had time to take in details—the dark eyes that looked almost black, and her face and arms warm brown against the whiteness of her blouse and her hair that was pale yellow and combed back and tied with a black ribbon—seeing all this before the shotgun tightened on him again.

Brady said, "You've seen men's underwear before. What're you looking so shocked for?"

"Not with you in them," the girl said.

"I thought maybe I could borrow a pair of your brother's pants—"

"How'd you know I had a brother?"

"You got two. The little one, Mike, is in school down in Bisbee. The big one, Paul, whose pants I want to borrow till I get up to Rock of Ages and buy my own, is in the Army. Farrier Sergeant Paul J. Glennan, with the Tenth down to Fort Huachuca."

The girl's eyes narrowed as she studied him. "You know a lot about my family."

"More'n Albie could've told me?"

The girl said nothing.

"I told you I was with Hatch and Hodges," Brady said. "A while back a man took my clothes, guns, and papers, and that's why I'm sitting here like this. But I can still prove I'm from Hatch and Hodges, and here to see your father."

"How?"

"All right," Brady said. "Your father's name is John Michael Glennan, born in Jackson, Michigan, in . . . 1837. Same town your mother's from. Your dad served with the late George Custer and was wounded in the Rock Creek fight at Gettysburg. Your brother Paul was born in '62. You came along in '65; then six years later your dad brought the family out here. You first settled up north near Cabezas, but there weren't enough trees there to suit him, so you came down here and been here ever since.

"Your dad's raised stock, but it never paid him much. Twice he wintered poorly and another year the market was down; so now he'd like to just raise horses and on the side, for steady money, run a stage line stop. Paul'll be out of the Army in six months; Mike out of school in a year.

Your name's Catherine Mary Glennan and every word my Uncle Joe Mauren said about you is true."

"If it's a trick, it's a good one," the girl said. "You knowing all that."

"Sister, I'm trying to do my job, but I can't do it without my pants or my papers. Add to that your dad's not here anyway."

"How do you know that?"

"The stable door's open and your team and wagon's gone."

"They'll be back soon," the girl said quickly.

"Then I'll wait to talk to him."

"But I don't know when."

"You just said *soon*." Brady watched her. "Look, if you're worried about being alone with me I'll move along; but all I got to say is your dad must not want this franchise very much, else he'd be here."

"He *does* want it!" The girl moved toward him. "He had to drive my mother over near Laurel. There's a lady there about to deliver and Ma'd promised to help. But my dad said if you came, to explain it to you so there'd be no misunderstanding, because he does want to have that . . . whatever you call it."

"So you don't know when he'll be home."

"Probably tomorrow."

"Why didn't you tell me that before?" Brady said. " 'Stead of this business about he'll be back soon."

"Because I didn't know who you were," the girl said angrily. "In fact, I still don't. All I'm sure of is you're a man sitting there in your underwear and not much of a man at that to let somebody take your clothes right off you."

"He had a gun," Brady said.

"So did you!"

"But he had his first." Brady's hand went to the side of his face. "And he laid it across me early in the proceedings."

"Oh—"

"That's all right. Just leave me have the pants."

"And something to eat?" She was calm again and her eyes opened inquiringly. "You can ride around back, water your horse and yourself, and come in the back door."

"So the neighbors won't see me?" Brady said.

Chapter Three

Fine-Looking Girl

SHE SMILED at him and after that—while she looked for her brother's pants; while Brady came out of the bedroom pulling up the faded green suspenders and asking her how he looked and she saying like a man who'd already been married twenty years; while they ate pancakes and drank coffee; while they just sat talking about everything in general and asking harmless-sounding questions about one another—they were at ease with each other and both seemed to enjoy it.

He explained how he had been robbed and told to ride on. How he had crossed the meadow then stopped, thinking about going back. But, one, it was good country to hide in; how would he find them? Two, even if he did, he had no gun. And three, which was part of two, they could even be laying for him, waiting to shoot him out of the saddle if he came back.

It was just poor luck, Brady said. But you had to expect so much of that in life; and if it happens the first day of a new job, maybe it's just the Almighty warning you not to be too cocky or full of yourself, else He'll whittle you down to size in one minute's time.

Catherine Mary said she'd never thought of that before, though she knew God moved in mysterious ways. Maybe He even sent Albie here as a warning, she said. A way of telling her to be cautious of the men she met until the right one came along. Albie was easy to see through. He smiled a lot and said nice things, but it was all on the surface.

And where had he come from? Two weeks ago, the first time he came by with another man. Her father was home and they'd stayed only long enough to water their horses, saying they were on their way to a job. Then a few days later, when just her mother and she were at the house, the younger one came back.

That was when he told his name and said he liked this part of the country very much and maybe he'd just stay around. But the way he looked at you and the sweet way he talked, you knew he was thinking something else. The third time he came, there wasn't any doubt about that.

She was alone in the stable when he walked in and right away started talking about how quiet and nice it was and wasn't she lonely never seeing a young man for weeks at a time? Then he tried to kiss her, so sure of himself that she almost had to laugh; but it wasn't funny when he put his arms around her and gave her one of those awful wet kisses. Then he let go and stepped back as if to say there, now you've been kissed you won't fight it anymore.

She didn't fight. She ran and got the shotgun and Albie rode out fast yelling back something about letting her cool off a while.

But what was he doing around here? That was the question. Where had he been living for the past two weeks?

Brady and the girl heard the horse at the same time and both looked at each other across the table, both taken by surprise and thinking no, it couldn't be. For a moment there was no sound. Then, "Kitty!"

She stood up quickly, looking at Brady. "It's him."

Brady said, "Boy, that's something, isn't it?" He was a few steps behind her going to the door, but close to her as she reached it raising the latch. He pulled the door open, stepping outside after her, and the first thing he saw was his new suit.

ALBIE WAS WEARING it. Albie glancing at the doorway as he swung his right leg over the horse, as the girl stepped out into the sunlight saying, "We were just talking about you." And as Albie's foot touched the ground and he started to turn, Brady reached him.

"But no need for talk now," Brady said. He saw the puzzled frown on Albie's face, his mouth slightly open and his eyes asking a question in the shadow of the curled, forward-tilted hat brim. His expression changed suddenly to recognition and at that moment Brady hit him, his right fist jerking up, slamming into the changing, tightening expression.

Albie stumbled against his horse, half turning to catch himself with both palms slapping against the saddle, but his horse side-stepped nervously and in the moment that Albie hung off balance Brady's left fist drove into his ribs, cocked again as his right hand pulled Albie around, then hooked solidly into his jaw. Albie stumbled back off balance and this time he went down. He rolled to his side as he struck the ground, his right hand going to his hip, pulling back the coat, then hesitated.

Brady stood over him. "Try it, I'll stomp you right into the ground."

Albie looked up, squinting and rubbing the side of his jaw. "You her brother?"

"I got one thing to say to you," Brady answered. "Take my suit off."

"If you're not a kin of hers," Albie said, "you better be careful how you talk."

"Just take it off," Brady said.

He looked up, glancing again at the girl as she called, "There's somebody coming."

He was aware of the faint hoofbeat sound then, far off, but clear in the open stillness; and already halfway across the meadow, coming toward them from the pinyon slope that was perhaps four hundred yards away but seemed closer, he saw two riders. Directly behind them in the distance, the wagon trail was a thin sand-colored line coming down out of the dark mass of pinyon. They had descended that road, Brady judged, the same way he had come not an hour before.

Albie was on his elbow, turned now and watched them approach. Brady saw the grin forming on his mouth as they drew closer and again he glanced at the girl. "Who are they?"

She stood motionless, one hand shading her eyes from the sun glare. A breeze moved the fullness of her skirt and her hand dropped to hold the bleached cotton material against her leg.

"I'm not sure," she answered.

"He knows them," Brady said.

She studied them intently before her expression changed. "Yes . . . the one on the left, he was with Albie the first time."

"Russ," Albie said, pushing himself up to a sitting position. "Russ is my ma and the other one's my pa." He laughed then and called out, "Hey, Ma, this boy's pickin' on me!" He came to one knee as the riders came out of the aspen stand, reining their horses to a walk.

The one called Russ, slouched easily in the saddle but with a Winchester across his lap said, "Albie, you're never going to learn."

Albie came to his feet, brushing the seat of his pants. He was grinning and said, "Learn what, Ma?"

"That boy's about to take his suit back."

"Like hell he is," Albie said.

Brady stepped toward him as he spoke and as Albie glanced around, Brady's left hand slammed into his face. Brady was on him as he went down, pressing his knee into his stomach, and when he rose he was holding the Colt Albie had been wearing. He saw that it was his own.

"I told you," Russ said.

Brady looked up at the two riders. "Either of you object?"

Russ shook his head. "Not us. It's your suit, I guess you can take it if you want."

"My Winchester, too," Brady said.

★

Chapter Four

Private Business

RUSS HESITATED. His right hand was through the lever and the barrel pointed just off from Brady. The second rider, who was bearded and wore a low-crowned, stiff-brimmed hat, held his hands one over the other on the saddle horn.

He said, "Russell, give Mr. Brady his piece." He spoke without straining to be heard and now his eyes moved from Brady—who was studying him curiously as he moved toward Russ to take the extended Winchester—to the girl and one hand lifted easily to touch his hat brim.

"You must be Kitty I've heard so much about." And as she nodded he said, "Has Albie been a botheration to you, Miss Glennan?"

"I have to tell you that he has," the girl said seriously. "And being his father, you should know about the things he's been doing—"

The bearded man's palm raised to interrupt her. "No, ma'am, I'll admit I took Albie in and treated him as blood kin, but there's no relationship between us." His eyes went to Brady then returned. "Ask Mr. Brady there, he'll tell you who I am. Though he knows me by a part of my life I've been struggling to forget."

Studying the bearded man, Brady frowned. "We've met before?"

"Bless your heart," the bearded man said. "It's a good feeling to know you can outlive the remembrance of past sins." He touched his hand to his hat brim again, looking at the girl. "My name is Edward Moak, ma'am, once a desperate outlaw, thieving and living off monies that were never rightfully mine, but never killing anybody you understand, until the day five years and five months ago I ran into this same Mr. Steve Brady and he ended my evil ways with one barrel-load of his scattergun." He looked at Brady. "Am I in the recollection of your past now, Mr. Brady?"

"On the Sweet-Mary to Globe run," Brady said, studying Edward Moak, picturing him as he had been: heavier, and with only a mustache. "You've changed some."

"Yuma will do that to a man," Edward Moak said. "Cutting cell blocks out of solid rock will change a man physically, and it can cleanse him spiritually if he'll let it." His eyes went to the girl. "Which I did, Miss Glennan. I let it. The evil oozed out of my skin in honest labor and I felt newly baptized and born again in the bath of my own perspiration."

"Amen," Albie said. He was standing now. He had taken off Brady's coat and cartridge belt and now he stepped out of the pants and let them fall in the dust.

"You see," Moak said. "Albie's smart-alecky because he was raised in bad company and hasn't learned a sense of proper values. That's why I've taken up guiding him, so he'll profit by my experiences and not have to learn the Yuma way." Moak's eyes dropped to his hands on the saddle horn. "It's an easy road for some people, Miss Glennan; but others have to fight the devil every step of the way." He looked up then. "Say, are your folks here, Miss Glennan? Albie's told me about them and I'd be proud to make their acquaintance."

The girl shook her head. "They won't be back until tomorrow."

"That's a shame," Moak said. "Well, maybe some other time." He looked at Brady then. "I almost forgot, I still have something of yours." He stepped out of the saddle and walked around the two horses toward Brady, his legs moving swiftly in high boots. He wore a Colt on his right hip and as his hand moved to his inside coat pocket there was a glimpse of leather, a shoulder holster under his left arm. Brady saw it; but now his eyes were on Edward Moak's face, trying to read something there, but seeing only an easy grin in the short-trimmed beard.

"You've changed some yourself," Moak said. "Grown taller and filled out. You know I didn't get much of a look at you at the holdup." His grin broadened. "All I saw was that scattergun swingin' on me and then my whole left arm hurting like fire and next thing I was on the ground."

HE HELD THE ARM up stiffly. "Can only bend her about six inches, but I say that's little enough to pay for learning the way of righteousness.

"But I got a good look at you at the trial," Moak went on. "Remember, we were on facing sides of those two tables, only you on the right side and me on the wrong. Yes, sir, I got a good look at you that day. Heard you testify, heard you swear your name to be Stephen J. Brady—"Then, not an hour ago, Russell hands me a billfold taken out of the wildness of Albie's youth, and the first thing I see when I open it is the name Stephen J. Brady." Moak shook his head. "I swear for all the country it's a small damn world."

"So it was in your mind to return the billfold," Brady prompted.

"To right a wrong," Moak agreed solemnly. "Though I didn't suspect I'd find you this easy. I figured to pick up young Albie here then go on toward Rock of Ages on the hunch you'd gone that way."

"Just a hunch?" asked Brady.

"Well," said Moak, "I couldn't help reading in your billfold you're a line superintendent—which is a fine thing going from shotgun messenger to line super in just five years and five months—so I felt you'd go there, Rock of Ages being your closest station." Moak paused. "You were, weren't you?"

"In time," Brady said.

"You're staying here a while?"

"I think so."

"You could ride with us," Moak said, "seeing we're both going the same way."

Their eyes held as they spoke. Brady was thinking, feeling the Colt in his right hand and the Winchester in his left pointed to the ground but with his finger through the trigger guards: *Watch him. Keep watching him.* And he said, "No, you go on. I haven't made plans yet."

"We'll be glad to wait on you, Mr. Brady," Moak said softly.

"You must have plenty of spare time," Brady said.

The grin showed in Moak's beard. "We're waiting on a business deal to go through."

"Damned if we aren't," said Albie. He was smiling, standing in his long underwear with hands on thin hips, and he winked at Moak as the bearded man glanced stern-faced at him.

Brady caught it. He said then, "I have private business here with Miss Glennan, so you all go on."

Moak's eyebrows raised. "Now why didn't you say that before? Sure we will." He turned to his horse, motioning Albie to his, then took his time stepping into the saddle. As he neck-reined to turn he said, "Mr. Brady, I'm looking forward to seeing you again."

He rode away, past the front of the house, along the edge of the dense pines with Russell catching up to him then, Albie following and looking back as they neared the far point of trees. Brady and the girl watched them all the way as they followed the curve of the valley north.

As they rounded the edge of trees and passed from sight the girl said, "He was lying, wasn't he?"

Brady looked at her. "How do you know?"

"Just the way he talked. And the little things," the girl said. "His friends, his two guns."

"You didn't miss anything."

"The way he kept staring at you."

"Like in the courtroom," Brady said.

"I'll bet he was mean that day."

"Swore to hunt me and kill me," Brady said. "Which you didn't hear him mention today. He carried on so, screaming and trying to get at me, it took four deputies to take him out."

"That was before he was born again," the girl said.

"Yeah," Brady said, "before he sweated out the badness."

They smiled at the same time and the girl said, "It's not funny, but it's kind of, isn't it?"

"That part is," Brady said. "But I'll bet what he's doing around here isn't funny." He watched the girl go over to his suit and pick it up, shaking out the dust. He watched her fold it over her arm as her eyes met his again.

"We could have some coffee," she said, "and talk about it."

Chapter Five

So They'll Be Back

THEY MOVED the table to the front window and sat next to each other facing it with the Winchester propped against the table edge.

Brady told her about the attempted stage holdup five years ago: how he had shot Ed Moak and how his Uncle Joe Mauren had gotten another man who lived only a few hours with a .45 bullet inside him. He told her what he knew about Ed Moak, things that were brought out at the trial and things he learned about him afterward: That he'd been an outlaw and a gunslinger as far back as anyone knew anything about him; had killed six men for sure, though some put it as high as ten. That he had a reputation for talking mildly and smiling when he talked, and everybody agreed that if a man wore two guns and no badge and did that, you'd better look out for him.

The girl said, So we take for granted he hasn't been reborn. And Brady said, Without even having to mention it.

There was only one reason Ed Moak would be here, would have stayed around for over two weeks, Brady concluded. Because money shipments took this road up to the Rock of Ages mine to meet the once-a-month payroll. There couldn't be any other reason and Moak almost admitted it himself when he said, "We're waiting on a business deal to go through," and Albie laughed and said something. By that time Moak must have been sure of himself and he wasn't so worried about us wondering what he was doing here.

You see, Brady explained, before that he didn't know who was around and he was slick, careful as could be. But then he made you tell that your father was gone till tomorrow and right after that he started to change, not too much, but as if it really didn't matter what we believed anymore. He was sure then that at least somebody he couldn't see wasn't aiming a gun at him.

And he might have made a play then, but by that time I was on guard, holding a Colt and a Winchester and he knew I'd use them—with a stiff left arm to testify to the fact.

So they made the show of riding away. It didn't have to be done then and there, face to face, not when they know they got all night.

The girl asked, "But why wouldn't they just leave for good?"

"With the odds in their favor?"

"But they wouldn't dare plan a holdup now. They're *known*."

"Only by us," Brady said.

"We're still enough to testify against them," the girl said earnestly. "They know that much."

She remembered being frightened in front of Edward Moak, then amused, considering it an unusual experience, one that would make good telling, especially if you described it almost casually. And for a moment she had even pictured herself doing this. But now, realizing it and not wanting to realize it, looking at Brady's face and waiting for him to say something that would relieve the nervous feeling tightening in her stomach, she knew that it was not over.

"Moak must have a good plan," Brady said, "to stay around here studying the land for two weeks. He's not going to waste it because of one man. Especially if the man's the same one almost shot his arm off one time. Then there's Albie. His pride's hurt and the only way to heal it is to bust me. So they'll be back."

The girl's eyes were open wide watching him. "And we just wait for them?"

"I've thought it out," Brady said. "First, I can't leave you here alone. As you said, you know their names. But two of us running for it would be hard put, not knowing where they are."

"You're saying you could make it alone," the girl said. "But I'd slow you down."

Brady nodded. "I'll say it's likely, but we'll never know because I'm not about to leave you alone."

"Mr. Brady, I'm scared. I don't know what I'd do if you left."

"I said I wouldn't. Listen, we're staying right here and that narrows down the possibilities. If they want us they'll have to come in here and they'll have to do it before tomorrow morning . . . before your dad's due back or anybody else who might happen along. Like my Uncle Joe Mauren."

The girl was silent for a moment. "But if they don't see you ride out they'll think you're . . . spending the night."

Brady smiled. "All right, you worry about our good names and I'll worry about our necks. If Ed Moak believes that, that's fine. He'd think we don't suspect he's still around and he might tend to be careless."

Her eyes, still on his face, were open wide and she bit at her lower lip nervously thinking over his words.

"You're awful calm about it," she said finally.

"Maybe on the outside," Brady answered.

HE LEFT THE HOUSE twice that afternoon. The first time out the front door and around to the back, taking his time while his eyes studied the trees that began to close in less than a hundred feet away, just beyond the barn and the smaller outbuildings. He took his horse to the barn before returning to the house.

Less than forty feet away, directly he went to the barn, counting eighteen steps diagonally to the right from the house to the barn door. He milked the single cow in the barn, fed the horses—three, counting his own—checked the rear door which had no lock on it, then took the grain bucket he had used and propped it against the front door with a short-handled shovel. He picked up the milk pail and went out, squeezing past the door that was open little more than a foot.

His eyes went to the back of the stable that was directly across from the barn then along the fence to the house. He walked to the right, passed a corn crib that showed no corn in it through the slats, then turned to the house and went inside, bolting the back door.

They waited and now there was little to talk about. He told her one of them might try sneaking up through the barn to get their horses; but there wasn't much they could do about that. He told her about propping the grain bucket against the door and what he would do and what she would do if they heard it fall. Maybe they wouldn't hear it though. There were a lot of maybe's and he told her the best thing to do was not even think about it and just wait.

"Maybe they've gone and won't come," the girl said.

"That's right, maybe they've gone and won't even come."

Though neither of them believed that.

They watched the darkness creep in long shadows down out of the trees and across the meadow. It came dingy and dark gray over the yard bringing with it a deep silence and only occasional night sounds. When the room was dim the girl rose and brought a lamp to the table, but Brady shook his head and she sat down again without lighting it.

Now neither of them spoke and after a time Brady's hand moved to hers on the table. His fingers touched her fingers lightly. His hand covered hers and held it. They sat this way for a long time, at first self-consciously aware of their hands together, then gradually relaxing, still not speaking, but feeling the nearness of one another and experiencing in the touch of their hands a strange warm intimate feeling, as if they had known each other for years and not just hours.

They sat this way as Brady's fingers moved and rubbed the back of her hand lightly, feeling the small bones and the smoothness of her skin, and when her hand turned their palms came together and held firmly. They sat this way until the faraway sound of a falling bucket clanged abruptly out of the darkness.

Brady came to his feet. He heard the girl gasp and he said, "Hold on to yourself. Remember now, you stay in here. You don't open the door unless you hear my voice."

He went out the front door, closing it quietly, now moving along the front of the house. At the corner he drew his Colt, eased back the hammer, hesitated only a brief moment before crouching and running along the fence to the front of the stable. He stopped to listen, then moved again, around the stable and along its adobe side to the back corner and now he went down to one knee.

Less than forty feet away directly across from him, the door of the barn came slowly open. Someone hesitated in the black square of the opening before coming out cautiously, keeping close to the front of the barn until he reached the corner. Brady waited, his eyes going from the dark figure to the open doorway, but no one followed.

You know who it is, Brady thought, raising, aiming the Colt. You know blame well who it is. He's alone because he ran out of patience. Too young and full of fire to sit and wait. All right. That's fine. Albie, you're digging your own hole and that's just fine.

He watched the figure leave the barn: side-stepping cautiously out of the deep shadow, facing the house with his drawn gun, but edging one step at a time toward the dim outline of the corn crib.

Don't give him a chance, Brady thought. But as his hand tightened on the trigger he called out, "Albie—"

Albie fired. There was no hesitation, no indecision. With the sound of his name, his gun hand swung across his body and fired and with the movement he was running, going down as he reached the corn crib.

Silence.

So you learn, Brady thought. But you don't make the same mistake twice. He stepped out past the corner of the stable bringing up the Colt and lining the barrel on the empty corn crib.

Three times in quick succession he aimed and fired, moving the Colt from right to left across the shape of the crib. The sounds clashed in the darkness: the heavy ring of the Colt, the ripping, whining of the bullets splintering the slats and with the third shot a howl of pain.

Brady moved quickly across the yard to the corner of the barn. He loaded the Colt, listening, watching the crib, then edged around the corner, dropped to his hands and knees and crept toward the crib. Albie was on his knees doubled over holding his arms tight to his stomach when Brady pressed the Colt into his back.

"Get up, Albie."

"I can't move." The words came out in short grunts.

"You're going to move one more time," Brady said.

He took Albie's gun then went quickly across to the house and called the girl's name. The door opened and he saw the relief in her eyes and saw her about to speak, but he said, "Albie's not going to last."

"Oh—" He saw her bite her lower lip.

"Listen—but maybe we can still use him." Brady spoke hurriedly, but quietly, telling her what to do: to hold Albie's gun on him and not move it even though he was doubled over with a bullet through his middle. And after that Brady ran to the barn. He went through it seeing only the cow, then out the rear door and across the wagon ruts into the trees. A dozen yards back in the pines he found their horses picketed with Albie's. He led them back to the barn and came out the front leading only Albie's.

The girl's eyes were open wide. "He's hurt terribly bad."

Brady said nothing. Albie screamed as Brady stooped and pulled him to his feet and made him mount the horse. Brady said then, "Listen to me. We're giving you a chance. Go get some help. You hear me, go get Ed to take care of you." He slapped the horse's rump, jumped after it and slapped again and the horse broke into a gallop—with Albie doubled over, his hands gripping the saddle horn—and rounded the corner of the stable.

Taking the girl's hand, Brady led her through the house, opened the front door then stood in the doorway, his hand holding her arm.

"I don't understand," she said.

"Listen a minute." They could still hear Albie's horse, though faintly now in the distance. "Going straight across," Brady said. "Telling us where Mr. Moak's waiting."

Chapter Six

Two to One Odds

NOW THINK about it some more, Brady thought. He was by the window again staring out at the masked, unmoving shapes in the darkness and hearing the small sounds of the girl who was in the kitchen, beyond the blanket that draped the doorway. Kitty. No—Catherine Mary. Brady said

Catherine Mary again to himself, listening to the sound of it in his mind.

All right, and what're the odds on calling her that tomorrow?

Two to one now. Getting better. But now what will they do? You know what you'll do, but what about them? Was Albie on his own? Maybe. Or part of a plan. Maybe. One of them is back in the trees and the other one's in front, across the meadow. Maybe. Could you run for it now, both of you? Maybe. Or will Ed Moak run for it? Hell no. One, two, three, four maybe's and a hell no—so the changing of the odds doesn't change your situation any. You still sit and wait. But now he knows you're not asleep.

He moved around the table to the side of the window and looked diagonally out across the yard. The aspen stand showed ghostly gray lines and a mass of branches and beyond it, in the smoked light of part of a moon, the meadow was mist gray and had no end as it stretched to nothing.

"Will he die?" the girl asked. She had made no sound coming to stand close to him.

"I think he will," Brady said. The girl did not speak and he said then, "I didn't want to kill him. I wanted to shoot him. I mean I was trying to shoot him because I had to, but killing him or seeing him dead wasn't in my mind."

His eyes moved to her face. She was staring out at the night and Brady said, "You feel sorry for him now."

"I can't help it." Her voice was low and with little tone.

"Listen, I felt sorry for him when I put him on the horse. He was just a poor kid going to die and I didn't like it one bit—but all the time I kept thinking, we're still in it. There's no time out for burying the dead and saying Our Fathers because Ed Moak is still here and knowing it is the only thing in the whole world that's important."

"Unless he's gone," the girl said.

"I just finished adding up the maybe's," Brady said. "You want to know how many there are?"

"I'm sorry."

"No, I shouldn't have said that."

She turned to him. "You remind me a lot of my older brother."

"I hope that's good."

She smiled. "I believe everybody likes Paul. He's never put on or anything."

"Yeah?" There was a silence before Brady said, "You know, I was thinking, you haven't once cried or carried on or—you know, like you'd think a girl would."

"All girls don't act like that."

"I guess not." Brady said then, "You can learn a lot in a few hours, can't you?"

"Things that might've taken months," the girl said.

"Or years."

"It's funny, isn't it?"

"It's strange—"

"That's what I mean."

Brady said, "I've been thinking about you more than about Ed Moak."

☆　☆　☆

HER FACE WAS CLOSE to his, but now she looked out the window not knowing what to say.

"I didn't have any trouble telling you that," Brady said. "Which is something, for me."

She looked at him again, her face upturned calmly now and again close to his. "What is it you're telling me, Mr. Brady?"

"You know."

"I want to hear it."

"It would sound funny."

"That's all right."

He leaned closer and kissed her, holding her face gently between his hands. He kissed her again, hearing the soft sound of it and feeling the clinging response of her lips. His hands dropped to her waist as her arms went up and around his neck and they remained this way even after they had kissed, after his lips had brushed her cheek and whispered close to her ear.

"See?"

"It didn't sound funny."

"What's your ma and dad going to say?"

"They'll say it's awful sudden."

"Will they object?"

"Mr. Brady, are you proposing?"

He smiled, leaning back to look at her. "That's what you call the natural thing, when you're proposing and don't even know you're doing it."

"Then you are."

"1 guess so."

"Can you be sure," she said seriously, "knowing a person just a few hours?"

"We could wait if you want. Say about a week."

"Now you're fooling."

"Not very much."

Catherine Mary smiled now. "I think this has been the fastest moving day of my life."

"But the longest," Brady said. "And it's not even over yet." He saw her smile fade and again he remembered Ed Moak and the other man; he pictured them in the darkness, waiting and not speaking.

He thought angrily: Why does he have to be here? Why should a man who you've seen once before in your life have a chance to ruin your life? He felt restless and suddenly anxious for Moak to come. He wanted this over with; but he made himself think about it calmly because there was nothing he could do but wait.

ALL NIGHT HE remained at the window, occasionally rising, stretching, moving about when the restlessness would return, though most of the time he sat at the table staring out at the darkness, now and again turning to look at the girl who was asleep, covered with a blanket and curled in a canvas-bottomed chair she had moved close to the table. (He had told her to go to bed, but she argued that she wouldn't be able to sleep and she sat in the canvas chair as a compromise. After some time she fell asleep.) Brady waited and the hours dragged.

But to the girl, the night was over suddenly. Something awakened her. She opened her eyes, saw Brady bending over her, felt his hand on her shoulder and beyond him saw the tabletop and the window glistening coldly in the early morning sunlight.

His expression was calm, though grave and quietly determined and when he spoke his words brought her up in the chair and instantly awake.

"They're coming now," Brady said.

"Where?"

"From across. Riding over like it's a social call." He watched her as she leaned close to the table, looking out and seeing them already approaching the aspen stand. "Catherine Mary, I want you to stay inside with the shotgun."

"What're you going to do?"

"Listen to me now—hold the shotgun on Russell. Then I won't have to worry about him." He hesitated uncertainly. "Are you afraid to use it?"

"No—"

"All right, and the Winchester's here on the table."

Facing the window he felt her hand on his arm, but now he moved to the door, not looking at her, and stepped outside before she could say anything more. He watched them coming through the aspen stand, walking their horses into the yard where, perhaps thirty feet from Brady, they stopped.

"Well, you sure must've had plenty of business," Ed Moak said easily. He swung down and still holding the reins moved a few steps ahead of his horse. "We didn't figure to see you still here."

Moak's words came unexpectedly, catching Brady off guard. He had pictured the bearded man calling bluntly for a fight; but this was something else. "It got late," Brady said. "I thought I might as well stay here."

"I can't say's I blame you," Moak said.

"What do you mean by that?"

Moak shrugged, almost smiling. "Not important. What we came for was to ask if you've seen young Albie hereabouts."

Talk to him, Brady thought hesitantly, in this one moment trying to see through Moak's intention; and said, "Haven't seen him."

"He rode out last night not saying for where and never come back."

"I can't help you," Brady said.

"Maybe Miss Glennan saw him."

"She would've said something about it."

"I suppose." Moak shifted his weight from one foot to the other. Standing in front of his horse the reins were over his left shoulder and pulled down in front of him with both hands hanging on the leather straps idly just above his belt line. His coat was open.

When you least expect it, Brady was thinking. That's when it'll come. His hands felt awkwardly heavy and he wanted to do something with them, but he let them hang, picturing now in his mind his right hand coming up with the Colt, cocking it, firing it. Then swinging it on Russell. Aim, he thought. You have to take your time. You have to hurry and take your time.

Moak shifted his feet again. "Russell, we might as well go on." The mounted man said nothing, but he nodded, glancing from Brady to Moak. "What about it?" Moak said to Brady again. "Does it suit your complexion to ride with us?"

"I've business with Mr. Glennan," Brady said. "He's coming along directly."

Moak grinned, glancing at Russell again. "Brady still don't want our company. . . . Well, we'll have to just go on without him."

Now, Brady thought.

He watched Moak turn, looping the right rein over the horse's head. He moved to the saddle, his left hand holding the reins and now reaching for the saddle horn. He stood close to the horse, about to step into the stirrup. And then was turning, pushing away the saddle as his right hand came out of his coat—

And as he had practiced it in his mind Brady drew the Colt, thumbed the hammer, brought it to arm's length, saw the shocked surprise of Moak's face over the front sight, saw the flash of metal in his hand, saw him falling away as the metal came up, shifted the front sight inches, all this in one deliberate nerve-straining motion—and pulled the trigger.

Russell saw the Colt pointed at him then. He shook his head. "Not me, sonny, this was just Ed's do." He dismounted and the Colt followed him to where Moak lay sprawled on his back.

"You can still see the surprise," Russell said. "He's dead, but he still don't believe it." He looked at Brady then. "I warned him. I said you'd be ready and wouldn't get caught on one foot. But all night long he sat rubbing his bad arm and saying what he was going to do to you. Said you'd break up in little pieces with the wait and he'd get you when the right time came.

"Then Albie stole off and come back dead in his saddle. Ed didn't talk for a while. Then he said how he'd ride in at daylight like we didn't know anything about Albie and take you by surprise. I told him again you'd be wide awake, but he wouldn't listen and now he's lying there."

Brady said, "You were planning to hold up a mine payroll, weren't you?"

"You can't prove anything like that," Russell answered.

"Well, it doesn't matter now anyway."

"Listen, I wasn't with him on this. You can't prove that either."

"No, now you're on our side, now it's over."

"I'm not on anybody's side."

"All right, just get out of here."

"We'll bury him first," Russell said. "Back in the trees there."

"I'm telling you to get out! Take him and get out of here right now—you hear me!"

Russell stared at him, then shrugged and said, "All right," quietly. He lifted Moak's body, straining, pushing him belly-down up over the saddle; then looked at Brady again and said, "Why don't you go buy yourself a drink."

"I'm all right."

"Sure you are. But it wouldn't do no harm." Russell mounted and rode out of the yard leading Moak's horse.

Brady watched them until they were out of sight. He closed his eyes and he could still see Moak's legs hanging stiffly and his arms swinging and bouncing with the slow jogging motion of the horse—and he thought: God have mercy on him. And on Albie.

He holstered the Colt then raised his arm and rubbed his sleeve over his forehead, feeling tired and sweaty and feeling a fullness in his stomach that made him swallow and swallow again. And God help *me*, he thought.

He heard the girl behind him before he turned and saw her—not smiling, but looking at him seriously, with her lips parted, almost frowning, her gaze worried and not moving from his face.

"Are you all right?"

"I guess so."

Looking at the girl he knew that if he wasn't all right now, at least he would be. In time.

26

The Nagual

Original Title: The Accident at John Stam's
2-Gun Western, November 1956

OFELIO OSO—WHO had been a vaquero most of his seventy years, but who now mended fences and drove a wagon for John Stam—looked down the slope through the jack pines seeing the man with his arms about the woman. They were in front of the shack which stood near the edge of the deep ravine bordering the west end of the meadow; and now Ofelio watched them separate lingeringly, the woman moving off, looking back as she passed the corral, going diagonally across the pasture to the trees on the far side, where she disappeared.

Now Mrs. Stam goes home, Ofelio thought, to wait for her husband.

The old man had seen them like this before, sometimes in the evening, sometimes at dawn as it was now with the first distant sun streak off beyond the Organ Mountains, and always when John Stam was away. This had been going on for months now, at least since Ofelio first began going up into the hills at night.

It was a strange feeling that caused the old man to do this; more an urgency, for he had come to a realization that there was little time left for him. In the hills at night a man can think clearly, and when a man believes his end is approaching there are things to think about.

In his sixty-ninth year Ofelio Oso broke his leg. In the shock of a pain-stabbing moment it was smashed between horse and corral post as John Stam's cattle rushed the gate opening. He could no longer ride, after having done nothing else for more than fifty years; and with this came the certainty that his end was approaching. Since he was of no use to anyone, then only death remained. In his idleness he could feel its nearness and he thought of many things to prepare himself for the day it would come.

Now he waited until the horsebreaker, Joe Slidell, went into the shack. Ofelio limped down the slope through the pines and was crossing a corner of the pasture when Joe Slidell reappeared, leaning in the doorway with something in his hand, looking absently out at the few mustangs off at the far end of the pasture. His gaze moved to the bay stallion in the corral, then swung slowly until he was looking at Ofelio Oso.

The old man saw this and changed his direction, going toward the shack. He carried a blanket over his shoulder and wore a willow-root Chihuahua hat, and his hand touched the brim of it as he approached the loose figure in the doorway.

"At it again," Joe Slidell said. He lifted the bottle which he held close to his stomach and took a good drink. Then he lowered it, and his face contorted. He grunted, "Yaaaaa!" but after that he seemed relieved. He nodded to the hill and said, "How long you been up there?"

"Through the night," Ofelio answered. *Which you well know,* he thought. *You, standing there drinking the whiskey that the woman brings.*

Slidell wiped his mouth with the back of his hand, watching the old man through heavy-lidded eyes. "What do you see up there?"

"Many things."

"Like what?"

Ofelio shrugged. "I have seen devils."

Slidell grinned. "Big ones or little ones?"

"They take many forms."

Joe Slidell took another drink of the whiskey, not offering it to the old man, then said, "Well, I got work to do." He nodded to the corral where the bay stood looking over the rail, lifting and shaking his maned head at the man smell. "That horse," Joe Slidell said, "is going to finish gettin' himself broke today, one way or the other."

Ofelio looked at the stallion admiringly. A fine animal for long rides, for the killing pace, but for cutting stock, no. It would never be trained to swerve inward and break into a dead run at the feel of boot touching stirrup. He said to the horsebreaker, "That bay is much horse."

"Close to seventeen hands," Joe Slidell said, "if you was to get close enough to measure."

"This is the one for Señor Stam's use?"

Slidell nodded. "Maybe. If I don't ride him down to the house before supper, you bring up a mule to haul his carcass to the ravine." He jerked his thumb past his head, indicating the deep draw behind the shack. Ofelio had been made to do this before. The mule dragged the still faintly breathing mustang to the ravine edge. Then Slidell would tell him to push, while he levered with a pole, until finally the mustang went over the side down the steep-slanted seventy feet to the bottom.

OFELIO CROSSED the pasture, then down into the woods that fell gradually for almost a mile before opening again at the house and outbuildings of John Stam's spread. That *jinete*—that breaker of horses—is very sure of himself, the old man thought, moving through the trees. Both with horses and another man's wife. He must know I have seen them together, but it doesn't bother him. No, the old man thought now, it is something other than being sure of himself. I think it is stupidity. An intelligent man tames a wild horse with a great deal of respect, for he knows the horse is able to kill him. As for Mrs. Stam, considering her husband, one would think he would treat her with even greater respect.

Marion Stam was on the back porch while Ofelio hitched the mules to the flatbed wagon. Her arms were folded across her chest and she watched the old man because his hitching the team was the only activity in the yard. Marion Stam's eyes were listless, darkly shadowed, making her thin face seem transparently frail, and this made her look older than her twenty-five years. But appearance made little difference to Marion. John Stam was nearly twice her age; and Joe Slidell—Joe spent all his time up at the horse camp, anything in a dress looked good to him.

But the boredom. This was the only thing to which Marion Stam could not resign herself. A house miles away from nowhere. Day following day, each one utterly void of anything resembling her estimation of living. John Stam at the table, eyes on his plate, opening his mouth only to put food into it. The picture of John Stam at night, just before blowing out the lamp, standing in his yellowish, musty-smelling long underwear. "Good night," a grunt, then the sound of even, open-mouthed breathing. Joe Slidell relieved some of the boredom. Some. He was young, not bad looking in a coarse way, but, Lord, he smelled like one of his horses!

"Why're you going now?" she called to Ofelio. "The stage's always late."

The old man looked up. "Someday it will be early. Perhaps this morning."

The woman shrugged, leaning in the door frame now, her arms still folded over her thin chest as Ofelio moved the team and wagon creaking out of the yard.

But the stage was not early; nor was it on time. Ofelio urged the mules into the empty station yard and pulled to a slow stop in front of the wagon shed that joined the station adobe. Two horses were in the shed with their muzzles munching at the hay rack. Spainhower, the Butterfield agent, appeared in the doorway for a moment. Seeing Ofelio he said, "Seems you'd learn to leave about thirty minutes later." He turned away.

Ofelio smiled, climbing off the wagon box. He went through the door, following Spainhower into the sudden dimness, feeling the adobe still cool from the night and hearing a voice saying: "If Ofelio drove for Butterfield, nobody'd have to wait for stages." He recognized the voice and the soft laugh that followed and then he saw the man, Billy-Jack Trew, sitting on one end of the pine table with his boots resting on a Douglas chair.

Billy-Jack Trew was a deputy. Val Dodson, his boss, the Doña Ana sheriff, sat a seat away from him with his elbows on the pine boards. They had come down from Tularosa, stopping for a drink before going on to Mesilla.

Billy-Jack Trew said in Spanish, "Ofelio, how does it go?"

The old man nodded. "It passes well," he said, and smiled, because Billy-Jack was a man you smiled at even though you knew him slightly and saw him less than once in a month.

"Up there at that horse pasture," the deputy said, "I hear Joe Slidell's got some mounts of his own."

Ofelio nodded. "I think so. Señor Stam does not own all of them."

"I'm going to take me a ride up there pretty soon," Billy-Jack said, "and see what kind of money Joe's askin'. Way the sheriff keeps me going I need two horses, and that's a fact."

Ofelio could feel Spainhower looking at him, Val Dodson glancing now and then. One or the other would soon ask about his nights in the hills. He could feel this also. Everyone seemed to know about his going into the hills and everyone continued to question him about it, as if it were a foolish thing to do. Only Billy-Jack Trew would talk about it seriously.

* * *

AT FIRST, OFELIO had tried to explain the things he thought about: life and death and a man's place, the temptations of the devil and man's obligation to God—all those things men begin to think about when there is little time left. And from the beginning Ofelio saw that they were laughing at him. Serious faces straining to hold back smiles. Pseudosincere questions that were only to lead him on. So after the first few times he stopped telling them what occurred to him in the loneliness of the night and would tell them whatever entered his mind, though much of it was still fact.

Billy-Jack Trew listened, and in a way he understood the old man. He knew that legends were part of a Mexican peon's life. He knew that Ofelio had been a vaquero for something like fifty years, with lots of lonesome time for imagining things. Anything the old man said was good listening, and a lot of it made sense after you thought about it awhile—so Billy-Jack Trew didn't laugh.

With a cigar stub clamped in the corner of his mouth, Spainhower's puffy face was dead serious looking at the old man. "Ofelio," he said, "this morning there was a mist ring over the gate. Now, I heard what that meant, so I kept my eyes open and sure'n hell here come a gang of elves through the gate dancin' and carryin' on. They marched right in here and hauled themselves up on that table."

Val Dodson said dryly, "Now, that's funny, just this morning coming down from Tularosa me and Billy-Jack looked up to see this be-ootiful she-devil running like hell for a cholla clump." He paused, glancing at Ofelio. "Billy-Jack took one look and was half out his saddle when I grabbed him."

Billy-Jack Trew shook his head. "Ofelio, don't mind that talk."

The old man smiled, saying nothing.

"You seen any more devils?" Spainhower asked him.

Ofelio hesitated, then nodded, saying, "Yes, I saw two devils this morning. Just at dawn."

Spainhower said, "What'd they look like?"

"I know," Val Dodson said quickly.

"Aw, Val," Billy-Jack said. "Leave him alone." He glanced at Ofelio, who was looking at Dodson intently, as if afraid of what he would say next.

"I'll bet," Dodson went on, "they had horns and hairy forked tails like that one me and Billy-Jack saw out on the sands." Spainhower laughed, then Dodson winked at him and laughed too.

BILLY-JACK TREW WAS watching Ofelio and he saw the tense expression on the old man's face relax. He saw the half-frightened look change to a smile of relief, and Billy-Jack was thinking that maybe a man ought to listen even a little closer to what Ofelio said. Like maybe there were double meanings to the things he said.

"Listen," Ofelio said, "I will tell you something else I have seen. A sight few men have ever witnessed." Ofelio was thinking: All right, give them something for their minds to work on.

"What I saw is a very hideous thing to behold, more frightening than elves, more terrible than devils." He paused, then said quietly, "What I saw was a *nagual*."

He waited, certain they had never heard of this, for it was an old Mexican legend. Spainhower was smiling, but half-squinting curiosity was in his eyes. Dodson was watching, waiting for him to go on. Still Ofelio hesitated and finally Spainhower said, "And what's a *nagual* supposed to be?"

"A *nagual*," Ofelio explained carefully, "is a man with strange powers. A man who is able to transform himself into a certain animal."

Spainhower said, too quickly, "What kind of an animal?"

"That," Ofelio answered, "depends upon the man. The animal is usually of his choice."

Spainhower's brow was deep furrowed. "What's so terrible about that?"

Ofelio's face was serious. "One can see you have never beheld a *nagual.* Tell me, what is more hideous, what is more terrible, than a man—who is made in God's image—becoming an animal?"

There was silence. Then Val Dodson said, "Aw—"

Spainhower didn't know what to say; he felt disappointed, cheated.

And into this silence came the faint rumbling sound. Billy-Jack Trew said, "Here she comes." They stood up, moving for the door, and soon the rumble was higher pitched—creaking, screeching, rattling, pounding—and the Butterfield stage was swinging into the yard. Spainhower and Dodson and Billy-Jack Trew went outside, Ofelio and his *nagual* forgotten.

No one had ever seen John Stam smile. Some, smiling themselves, said Marion must have at least once or twice, but most doubted even this. John Stam worked hard, twelve to sixteen hours a day, plus keeping a close eye on some business interests he had in Mesilla, and had been doing it since he'd first visually staked off his range six years before. No one asked where he came from and John Stam didn't volunteer any answers.

Billy-Jack Trew said Stam looked to him like a red-dirt farmer with no business in cattle, but that was once Billy-Jack was wrong and he admitted it himself later. John Stam appeared one day with a crow-bait horse and twelve mavericks including a bull. Now, six years later, he had himself way over a thousand head and a *jinete* to break him all the horses he could ride.

Off the range, though, he let Ofelio Oso drive him wherever he went. Some said he felt sorry for Ofelio because the old Mexican had been a good hand in his day. Others said Marion put him up to it so she wouldn't have Ofelio hanging around the place all the time. There was always some talk about Marion, especially now with the cut-down crew up at the summer range, John Stam gone to tend his business about once a week, and only Ofelio and Joe Slidell there. Joe Slidell wasn't a bad-looking man.

The first five years John Stam allowed himself only two pleasures: he drank whiskey, though no one had ever seen him drinking it, only buying it; and every Sunday afternoon he'd ride to Mesilla for dinner at the hotel. He would always order the same thing, chicken, and always sit at the same table. He had been doing this for some time when Marion started waiting tables there. Two years later, John Stam asked her to marry him as she was setting down his dessert and Marion said yes then and there. Some claimed the only thing he'd said to her before that was bring me the ketchup.

Spainhower said it looked to him like Stam was from a line of hard-headed Dutchmen. Probably his dad had made him work like a mule and never told him about women, Spainhower said, so John Stam never knew what it was like *not* to work and the first woman he looked up long enough to notice, he married. About everybody agreed Spainhower had something.

They were almost to the ranch before John Stam spoke. He had nodded to the men in the station yard, but gotten right up on the wagon seat. Spainhower asked him if he cared for a drink, but he shook his head. When they were in view of the ranch house—John Stam's leathery mask of a face looking straight ahead down the slope—he said, "Mrs. Stam is in the house?"

"I think so," Ofelio said, looking at him quickly, then back to the rumps of the mules.

"All morning?"

"I was not here all morning." Ofelio waited, but John Stam said no more. This was the first time Ofelio had been questioned about Mrs. Stam. Perhaps he overheard talk in Mesilla, he thought.

IN THE YARD John Stam climbed off the wagon and went into the house. Ofelio headed the team for the barn and stopped before the wide door to unhitch. The yard was quiet; he glanced at the house, which seemed deserted, though he knew John Stam was inside. Suddenly Mrs. Stam's voice was coming from the house, high pitched, excited, the words not clear. The sound stopped abruptly and it was quiet again. A few minutes later the screen door slammed and John Stam was coming across the yard, his great gnarled hands hanging empty, threateningly, at his sides.

He stopped before Ofelio and said bluntly, "I'm asking you if you've ever taken any of my whiskey."

"I have never tasted whiskey," Ofelio said and felt a strange guilt come over him in this man's gaze. He tried to smile. "But in the past I've tasted enough mescal to make up for it."

John Stam's gaze held. "That wasn't what I asked you."

"All right," Ofelio said. "I have never taken any."

"I'll ask you once more," John Stam said.

Ofelio was bewildered. "What would you have me say?"

For a long moment John Stam stared. His eyes were hard though there was a weariness in them. He said, "I don't need you around here, you know."

"I have told the truth," Ofelio said simply.

The rancher continued to stare, a muscle in his cheek tightening and untightening. He turned abruptly and went back to the house.

The old man thought of the times he had seen Joe Slidell and the woman together and the times he had seen Joe Slidell drinking the whiskey she brought to him. Ofelio thought: He wasn't asking about whiskey, he was asking about his wife. But he could not come out with it. He knows something is going on behind his back, or else he suspicions it strongly, and he sees a relation between it and the whiskey that's being taken. I think I feel sorry for him; he hasn't learned to keep his woman and he doesn't know what to do.

Before supper Joe Slidell came down out of the woods trail on the bay stallion. He dismounted at the back porch and he and John Stam talked for a few minutes looking over the horse. When Joe Slidell left, John Stam, holding the bridle, watched him disappear into the woods and for a long time after, he stood there staring at the trail that went up through the woods.

Just before dark John Stam rode out of the yard on the bay stallion. Later—it was full dark then—Ofelio heard the screen door again. He rose from his bunk in the end barn stall and opened the big door an inch, in time to see Marion Stam's dim form pass into the trees.

He has left, Ofelio thought, so she goes to the *jinete*. He shook his head thinking: This is none of your business. But it remained in his mind and later, with his blanket over his shoulder, he went into the hills where he could think of these things more clearly.

He moved through the woods hearing the night sounds which seemed far away and his own footsteps in the leaves that were close, but did not seem to belong to him; then he was on the pine slope and high up he felt the breeze. For a time he listened to the soft sound of it in the jack pines. Tomorrow there will be rain, he thought. Sometime in the afternoon.

He stretched out on the ground, rolling the blanket behind his head, and looked up at the dim stars thinking: More and more every day, *viejo*, you must realize you are no longer of any value. The horse-breaker is not afraid of you, the men at the station laugh and take nothing you say seriously, and finally Señor Stam, he made it very clear when he said, "I don't need you around here."

Then why does he keep me—months now since I have been dismounted—except out of charity? He is a strange man. I suppose I owe him something, something more than feeling sorry for him which does him no good. I think we have something in common. I can feel sorry for both of us. He laughed at this and tried to discover other things they might have in common. It relaxed him, his imagination wandering, and soon he dozed off with the cool breeze on his face, not remembering to think about his end approaching.

To the east, above the chimneys of the Organ range, morning light began to gray-streak the day. Ofelio opened his eyes, hearing the horse moving through the trees below him: hooves clicking the small stones and the swish of pine branches. He thought of Joe Slidell's mustangs. One of them has wandered up the slope. But then, the unmistakable squeak of saddle leather and he sat up, tensed. It could be anyone, he thought. Almost anyone.

He rose, folding the blanket over his shoulder, and made his way down the slope silently, following the sound of the horse, and when he reached the pasture he saw the dim shape of it moving toward the shack, a tall shadow gliding away from him in the half light.

The door opened. Joe Slidell came out, closing it quickly behind him. "You're up early," he said, yawning, pulling a suspender over his shoulder. "How's that horse carry you? He learned his manners yesterday . . . won't give you no trouble. If he does, you let me have him back for about an hour." Slidell looked above the horse to the rider. "Mr. Stam, why're you lookin' at me like that?" He squinted up in the dimness. "Mr. Stam, what's the matter? You feelin' all right?"

"Tell her to come out," John Stam said.

"What?"

"I said tell her to come out."

"Now, Mr. Stam—" Slidell's voice trailed off, but slowly a grin formed on his mouth. He said, almost embarrassedly, "Well, Mr. Stam, I didn't think you'd mind." One man talking to another now. "Hell, it's only a little Mex gal from Mesilla. It gets lonely here and—"

John Stam spurred the stallion violently; the great stallion lunged, rearing, coming down with thrashing hooves on the screaming man. Slidell went down covering his head, falling against the shack boards. He clung there gasping as the stallion backed off; the next moment he was crawling frantically, rising, stumbling, running; he looked back seeing John Stam spurring and he screamed again as the stallion ran him down. John Stam reined in a tight circle and came back over the motionless form. He dismounted before the shack and went inside.

Go away, quickly, Ofelio told himself, and started for the other side of the pasture, running tensed, not wanting to hear what he knew would come. But he could not outrun it, the scream came turning him around when he was almost to the woods.

Marion Stam was in the doorway, then running across the yard, swerving as she saw the corral suddenly in front of her. John Stam was in the saddle spurring the stallion after her, gaining as she followed the rail circle of the corral. Now she was looking back, seeing the stallion almost on top of her. The stallion swerved suddenly as the woman screamed going over the edge of the ravine.

Ofelio ran to the trees before looking back. John Stam had dismounted. He removed bridle and saddle from the bay and put these in the shack. Then he picked up a stone and threw it at the stallion, sending it galloping for the open pasture.

The old man was breathing in short gasps from the running, but he hurried now through the woods and did not stop until he reached the barn. He sat on the bunk listening to his heart, feeling it in his chest. Minutes later John Stam opened the big door. He stood looking down at Ofelio while the old man's mind repeated: Mary, Virgin and Mother, until he heard the rancher say, "You didn't see or hear anything all night. I didn't leave the house, did I?"

Ofelio hesitated, then nodded slowly as if committing this to memory. "You did not leave the house."

John Stam's eyes held threateningly before he turned and went out. Minutes later Ofelio saw him leave the house with a shotgun under his arm. He crossed the yard and entered the woods. Already he is unsure, Ofelio thought, especially of the woman, though the fall was at least seventy feet.

WHEN HE HEARD the horse come down out of the woods it was barely more than an hour later. Ofelio looked out, expecting to see John Stam on the bay, but it was Billy-Jack Trew walking his horse into the yard. Quickly the old man climbed the ladder to the loft. The deputy went to the house first and called out. When there was no answer he approached the barn and called Ofelio's name.

He's found them! But what brought him? Ah, the old man thought, remembering, he wants to buy a horse. He spoke of that yesterday. But he found them instead. Where is Señor Stam? Why didn't he see him? He heard the deputy call again, but still Ofelio did not come out. He remained crouched in the darkness of the barn loft until he heard the deputy leave.

The door opened and John Stam stood below in the strip of outside light.

Resignedly, Ofelio said, "I am here," looking down, thinking: He was close all the time. He followed the deputy back and if I had called he would have killed both of us. And he is very capable of killing.

John Stam looked up, studying the old man. Finally he said, "You were there last night; I'm sure of it now . . . else you wouldn't be hiding, afraid of admitting something. You were smart not to talk to him. Maybe you're remembering you owe me something for keeping you on, even though you're not good for anything." He added abruptly, "You believe in God?"

Ofelio nodded.

"Then," John Stam said, "swear to God you'll never mention my name in connection with what happened."

Ofelio nodded again, resignedly, thinking of his obligation to this man. "I swear it," he said.

The rain came in the late afternoon, keeping Ofelio inside the barn. He crouched in the doorway, listening to the soft hissing of the rain in the trees, watching the puddles forming in the wagon tracks. His eyes would go to the house, picturing John Stam inside alone with his thoughts and waiting. They will come. Perhaps the rain will delay them, Ofelio thought, but they will come.

The sheriff will say, Mr. Stam this is a terrible thing we have to tell you. What? Well, you know the stallion Joe Slidell was breaking? Well, it must have got loose. It looks like Joe tried to catch him and . . . Joe got under his hooves. And, Mrs. Stam was there . . . we figured she was up to look at your new horse—saying this with embarrassment. She must have become frightened when it happened and she ran. In the dark she went over the side of the ravine. Billy-Jack found them this morning. . . .

He did not hear them because of the rain. He was staring at a puddle and when he looked up there was Val Dodson and Billy-Jack Trew. It was too late to climb to the loft.

Billy-Jack smiled. "I was around earlier, but I didn't see you." His hat was low, shielding his face from the light rain, as was Dodson's.

Ofelio could feel himself trembling. He is watching now from a window. Mother of God, help me.

Dodson said, "Where's Stam?"

Ofelio hesitated, then nodded toward the house.

"Come on," Dodson said. "Let's get it over with."

Billy-Jack Trew leaned closer, resting his forearm on the saddle horn. He said gently, "Have you seen anything more since yesterday?"

Ofelio looked up, seeing the wet smiling face and another image that was in his mind—a great stallion in the dawn light—and the words came out suddenly, as if forced from his mouth. He said, "I saw a *nagual!*"

Dodson groaned. "Not again," and nudged his horse with his knees.

"Wait a minute," Billy-Jack said quickly. Then to Ofelio, "This *nagual,* you actually saw it?"

The old man bit his lips. "Yes."

"It was an animal you saw, then."

"It was a *nagual.*"

Dodson said, "You stand in the rain and talk crazy. I'm getting this over with."

Billy-Jack swung down next to the old man. "Listen a minute, Val." To Ofelio, gently again, "But it was in the form of an animal?"

Ofelio's head nodded slowly.

"What did the animal look like?"

"It was," the old man said slowly, not looking at the deputy, "a great stallion." He said quickly, "I can tell you no more than that."

Dodson dismounted.

Billy-Jack said, "And where did the *nagual* go?"

Ofelio was looking beyond the deputy toward the house. He saw the back door open and John Stam came out on the porch, the shotgun cradled in his arm. Ofelio continued to stare. He could not speak as it went through his mind: He thinks I have told them!

Seeing the old man's face, Billy-Jack turned, then Dodson.

Stam called, "Ofelio, come here!"

Billy-Jack said, "Stay where you are," and now his voice was not gentle. But the hint of a smile returned as he unfastened the two lower buttons of his slicker and suddenly he called, "Mr. Stam! You know what a *nagual* is?" He opened the slicker all the way and drew a tobacco plug from his pants pocket.

Dodson whispered hoarsely, "What's the matter with you!"

Billy-Jack was smiling. "I'm only askin' a simple question."

John Stam did not answer. He was staring at Ofelio.

"Mr. Stam," Billy-Jack Trew called, "before I tell you what a *nagual* is I want to warn you I can get out a Colt a helluva lot quicker than you can swing a shotgun."

OFELIO OSO DIED at the age of ninety-three on a ranch outside Tularosa. They said about him he sure told some tall ones—about devils, and about seeing a *nagual* hanged for murder in Mesilla . . . whatever that meant . . . but he was much man. Even at his age the old son relied on no one, wouldn't let a soul do anything for him, and died owing the world not one plugged peso. And wasn't the least bit afraid to die, even though he was so old. He used to say, "Listen, if there is no way to tell when death will come, then why should one be afraid of it?"

27

The Kid

Original Title: The Gift of Regalo
Western Short Stories, December 1956

I REMEMBER looking out the window, hearing the wagon, and saying to Terry McNeil and Delia, "Here comes Repper." And when the wagon came even with the porch, I saw the boy. He was sitting with his legs hanging over the end-gate, but he came forward when Max Repper motioned to him.

That was the first time any of us laid eyes on the boy, and I'll tell you frankly we weren't positive at first it was a boy, even though Max Repper referred to a "him," saying, "Don't let his long hair fool you," and even though up close we could see the features didn't belong to a girl. Still, with the extent of my travel bounded by the Mogollon Rim country, central Sonora, the Pecos River, and the Kofa Mountains—north, south, east, and west respectively—I wasn't going to confine my judgment to this being either just a boy or a girl. There are many things in the world I haven't seen, and the way Terry McNeil was keeping his mouth closed I suspect he was reserving judgment on the same grounds.

Terry was in to buy stores for his prospecting site in the Dragoons. He came in usually about every two weeks, but by the little bit he'd buy it was plain he came for Delia more than for flour and salt-meat.

It was just the three of us in the store when Max Repper came— Terry, taking his time like he was planning to outfit an expedition; Deelie, my girl-child, helping him and hoping he'd take all day; and me. Me being the first line of the sign outside that says PATTERSON GENERAL SUPPLIES. BANDERAS, ARIZONA, TERR.

Now, this Max Repper was a man who saddle-tamed horses on a little place he had a few miles up the creek. He sold them to anybody who needed a horse; sometimes a few to the Cavalry Station at Dos Fuegos, though most often their remounts were all matched and came down from Whipple Barracks. So Max Repper sold mainly to the one hundred and eighty-odd souls who lived in and around Banderas.

He also operated a livery here in the settlement, but even Max admitted it wasn't a paying proposition and ordinarily he wasn't one to come right out and say he was holding a bad guess. Max was a hard-nosed individual, like a man had to be to mustang for a living; but he also had a mile-high opinion of himself, and if any living creature sympathized with him it'd have to have been one of his horse string. Though the way Max broke a horse, the possibility of that was even doubtful.

Repper came in with the boy behind him and he said to me, "Pat, look what the hell I found."

I asked him, "What is it?"

And he said, "Don't let the long hair fool you. It's a boy . . . a *white* boy."

We had to take Max's word for it at first, for that boy cut the strangest figure I ever saw. Maybe twelve years old, he was, with long dark hair hanging to his shoulders Apache style, matted and tangled, but he didn't have on a rag headband and that's why you didn't think of Apache when you looked at him, even though his skin was weathered mahogany and the rest of his getup might have been Indian. His shirt was worn-out cotton and open all the way down, no buttons left; his pants were buckskin, homemade by Indian or Mexican, you couldn't tell which, and he wasn't wearing shoes.

The bare feet made you feel sorry for him even after you looked close and saw something half wild about him. You wondered if the mind was translating what the eyes saw into man-talk or into some kind of gray-shadowed animal understanding.

TERRY McNEIL WAS toward the back, leaning on the counter close to Delia. They were just looking. I got up from the desk (it was by the front window and served as "office" for the Hatch & Hodges Line's Banderas

station), but I just stood there, not wanting to go up and gawk at the
boy like he was P. T. Barnum's ten-cent attraction.

"The good are rewarded," Max Repper said. He grinned showing
his crooked yellow teeth, which always took the humor out of anything
funny he ever said. "I was thinking about hiring a boy when I found this
one." He looked at the boy standing motionless. "He's going to work
for me free."

I asked now, "Where'd you find him?"

"Snoopin' around my stores."

"Where's he from?"

"Damn' if I know. He don't even talk."

Max pulled the boy forward by the shoulder right up in front of me
and said, "What do you judge his breed to be?" Like the boy was a paint
mustang with spots Max hadn't ever seen before.

I asked him again where he'd found the boy and he told how a few
nights ago he'd heard something in the lean-to back of his shack, and
had eased out there in his sock feet and jabbed a Henry in the boy's
back as he was taking down Max's fresh jerky strings.

He kept the boy tied up the rest of the night and fed him in the
morning, watched him stuff jerked venison into his mouth, asked him
where he came from, and got only grunts for answers.

He put the boy to work watering his corral mounts, and the way the
boy roughed the horses told Max maybe there was Apache in his background. But Max didn't know any Apache words and the boy wasn't
volunteering any. Max thought of Spanish. The only trouble was he
didn't know Spanish either.

The second night the boy tried to run away and Max (grinning as he
told it) beat him blue. The third morning Max decided (reluctantly)
he'd have to bring the boy in for shoeing. Shoes cost money, but bare-
footed a boy don't work so good—not on a south Arizona horse ranch.

I realized then Max was honest-to-goodness planning on keeping
the boy, but I mentioned, just to make sure, "I suppose you'll take him
to Dos Fuegos and turn him over to the Army."

"What for? He don't belong to them."

"He don't belong to you either."

"He sure as hell does. Long as I feed him."

I told Max, "Maybe the Army can trace where this boy came from."

But Repper said he'd tried for two days to get something out of the boy, and if he couldn't, then no lousy Army man could expect to.

"The kid's had his chance to talk," Max said. "If he don't want to, all right, then. I'll draw him pictures of what to do and push him to'ard it."

Max sat the boy down on a stool and I handed the shoes to him and he jammed them on the boy's feet until he thought he'd found the right size. When Max started to button one of them up the boy yanked his foot away and grunted like it hurt him. Max reached up and swatted the boy across the face and he kept still then.

I remember thinking: He handles the boy like he would a wild mustang, not like a human being. And Terry McNeil must have been thinking the same thing. He came up to us, then knelt down next to the boy, ignoring Max Repper, who was ready to put on the other shoe.

The boy looked at Terry and seemed to back off, maybe just a couple of inches on the outside, but the way he tensed you knew an iron door slammed shut inside of him.

Max said, "What in the name of George H. Hell you think you're doing?" Max had no use for Terry—but I'll tell you about that later.

Terry looked up at Repper and said, "I thought I'd just talk to him."

Max most probably wanted to kick Terry in the teeth, especially now, worn out from trying on shoes, and on general principle besides. Terry was the kind of boy who never let anything bother him, never raised his voice, and I know for a fact that burned Max, especially when they had differences of opinion, which was about every other time they ran into each other.

Max was near the end of his short-sized temper, but he held on and forced out a laugh to show Terry what he thought of him and said to me, "Pat, I'm going to buy myself a drink."

I kept just a couple of bottles for customers who didn't have time to get down to the State House. Serving Max, I watched Terry and the boy.

Terry was sitting cross-legged in front of him now slipping off the shoe Max had buttoned up. He took another from the pile of shoes and tried it on, the boy letting him, watching curiously, and I could hear Terry saying something in that slow, quiet way he talked. First, I thought it was Spanish, and maybe it was, but the little bit I could hear after that was a low mumble . . . then bit-off crisp words like *sik-isn* and *nakai-*yes and *pesh-klitso,* though not used together. The kind of talk you hear up at the San Carlos Reservation.

Then Terry leaned close to the boy and for a while I couldn't see the boy's face. Terry leaned back and said something else; then he touched the boy's arm, holding it for a moment, and when he stood up the boy's eyes followed him and they no longer had that locked iron door behind them.

Terry came over to us and said, "The boy was taken from the Mexican village of Sahuaripa something like three years ago. He was out watching the men herd cattle when a Chiricahua raiding party hit them. They killed the others and carried off the boy."

Max didn't speak, so I said, "I thought he was white."

Terry nodded his head. "His Mexican father told him that his real parents had died when he was a small boy. The Mexican had hired out to them as a guide, but they both died of a fever on the way to wherever they were going. So the Mexican went home to Sahuaripa and took the boy with him. He explained to the boy that he and his wife had never had a child, but they had prayed, and he believed the boy to be God's answer. They named the boy Regalo."

Max said, "You expect me to believe that?"

Terry shrugged. "Why shouldn't you?"

Max just looked at Terry, then grinned and shook his head slowly like saying: You think I was born last week? Terry might have told him what he thought, but Repper stomped out, dragging the boy and his new shoes with him.

I said to Terry, "The boy really tell you that?"

"Sure he did."

"What about the past three years?"

"He's been with Chiricahuas. Made blood son of Juh, who's chief of the whole red she-bang." Terry said the boy had wandered off on a lone hunt; his horse lamed and he was cutting back home when he came across Max's place.

"Terry," I said, "I imagine a boy could learn a lot of mean things from Chiricahuas."

And Terry said, "That's why I'm almost tempted to feel sorry for old Max."

Terry went back to outfitting for his expedition, but now he actually put his list down and asked Deelie to fill it. He didn't stay more than ten minutes after that, talking to Deelie, telling her what the boy said. And when he was gone I asked Deelie what his big hurry was.

"I never saw a man so eager to get back to a mine camp," I said.

"Terry's anxious to make this one pay," Deelie said. There was a soft smile on her face and she dropped her eyes quick, which was Deelie's way of telling you she had a secret—though I suspected it was something more akin to wishful thinking. Terry McNeil was never too anxious about anything.

He took everything in long, easy strides, even pretty little seventeen-year-old things like Deelie. I know he was taken with her, ever since the first day he set foot here, which was two years ago. He came through on his way to Dos Fuegos, riding dispatch for General Stoneman, and stopped off to buy a pound of Arbuckle's (he said that ration coffee put him to sleep); Deelie waited on him and I remember he looked at her like she was the only woman between Whipple Barracks and the border. Deelie ate it up and stood by the window after he was gone. Three weeks later he showed up again with a shovel, a pick, and boards for a sluice box; and said he'd once seen a likely placer up in the Dragoons and he'd always wanted to test it and now he was going to.

He must have saved his dispatch-riding money, because the first year and a half he paid his store bill cash and carry though he never struck anything likelier than quartz. Lately, he hadn't been buying so much.

I NEVER HAVE disrespected him for not wanting to work steady. That's his business. Max Repper called him a saddle tramp—not to his face—but whenever he referred to Terry. You see, the big war between those two started over Deelie. Max thought he had priority, even though Deelie practically told him right out she didn't care for him. Then Terry came along and Deelie about strained her back putting on extra charm. Max saw this and blamed Terry for stealing her affections. Max himself, being close to pushing forty and with those yellow snag teeth, couldn't have stole her affections with seven hundred Henry rifles.

Maybe Deelie and Terry were closer now than when they first met, but I didn't judge so close as to make Terry *run* back to his diggings to work on the marriage stake. Right after he left, it dawned on me that he would have to pass Repper's place on the way. So that was probably why he left on the run: to look in there. Repper was burning when he left, and a man of his sour nature was likely to take out his anger even on a boy.

Terry came back about three weeks later. He tied his horse, stood on the porch, and took time to stretch the saddle kinks out of his back while Deelie waited behind the counter dying. And when he came in she gave him a smile brighter than the sun flash of a U.S. Army heliograph. Deelie's smile would come right up from her toes.

"Terry!"

He gave her a nice smile.

I told him, "You look happy enough, but not like you're ready to celebrate pay dirt."

"Getting warmer, Mr. Patterson," he said. Which is what he always said.

"Have you seen the boy?" I asked. And was a little surprised when he nodded right away.

"Saw him this morning."

"How so?"

"Well," Terry said, "I was over to Dos Fuegos last week, and you know that big black-haired lieutenant, the married one with the little boy?" I nodded. "He sold me one of his son's shirts. A red one from St. Louis."

"And you gave it to the boy."

Terry nodded. "Regalo."

"You rode all the way over to Dos Fuegos to buy a shirt for the boy."

"A red one—"

"From St. Louis. How'd he like it?"

"He liked it fine."

"How'd Repper like it?"

"He was in the shack."

Terry asked me if I'd seen the boy and I told him no. Repper had kept to his horse camp since the first time he brought the boy in. Terry said the boy looked all right in body, but not in his eyes.

✶ ✶ ✶

LATER ON, AFTER I'd closed up, the three of us were sitting in back having something to eat—Deelie showing off what a good cook she was—when I heard someone at the front door.

Everyone in Banderas knows what time I close; still, it could have been something special, so I walked up front through the dark store and opened the door.

Maybe you've guessed it. I sure didn't. It was the boy, Regalo. He just stood there and I had to take him by the arm and bring him inside. Then, when we reached the light, I saw what was the matter.

He had on the red shirt but the back of it was almost in shreds, and crisscrossing his bare skin were raw welts, ugly red-looking burns like a length of manila had been sanded across his back a couple of dozen times.

Terry was up out of the chair and we eased the boy into it and made him lean forward over the table. Terry knelt down close to him and started to talk in Spanish. Ordinarily I know some, but not the way Terry was running the words together. Then the boy spoke. While he did, Deelie went out and came back with some cocoa butter and she spread it over his back gently without batting an eye. I think right then she advanced seven hundred feet in Terry McNeil's estimation.

The boy said, Terry told us, that Repper had come out of the house and when he saw the new shirt he tried to rip it off the boy, but Regalo ran. That made Repper mad and when he caught him at the barn he reached a hackamore line off a nail and laid it across the boy's back until his arm got tired.

Leaning over the table, the boy didn't cry or whimper, but you knew his back stung like fire.

Terry was saying, let's fix him some eggs, when we heard the door again . . . then heavy footsteps and there was Max Repper in the doorway with his Henry rifle square on us.

"The boy's coming with me." That's all he said. He took Regalo by the arm, yanked him out of the chair, marched him through the front part, and out the door. It happened so fast, I hardly realized Max had been there.

Terry was in the doorway looking up toward the front door. He didn't say a word. Probably he was thinking he should have done something, even if it had happened fast and Max was holding a Henry. Whatever he was thinking, he made up his mind fast. Terry took one last glance at Deelie and was gone.

Of course we knew where he was going. First to the boardinghouse for his gun, then to the livery, then to Repper's place. We didn't want him to do it . . . but at the same time, we did. The only thing was, someone else should be there. I figured whatever was going to happen ought to have a witness. So I saddled up and rode out about fifteen minutes behind Terry.

I thought I might catch him on the road, but didn't see a soul and finally I cut off to Repper's. There was Terry's claybank and just over the rump a cigarette glow where Terry was leaning next to the front door.

"He's not here?"

Terry shook his head.

"But we would have passed him on the road," I said.

"Well," Terry said, "he's got to come sooner or later."

As it turned out, it was just after daybreak when we heard the wagon.

Crossing the yard Max looked at us, but he kept on heading the team for the barn. We walked toward him, approaching broadside, then Max turned the team straight on toward the barn door and we could see the wagon bed. Regalo wasn't in it.

Max stepped off the wagon and waited for us with his hands on his hips.

"He ain't here."

Terry asked him, "What happened?"

"He jumped off the wagon and I lost him in the dark."

"And you've been looking for him."

Max grinned that ugly grin of his. "Sure," he said. "A man don't like to lose his top hand."

Then, glancing at Terry, seeing a look on the boy's face I'd never witnessed before, I knew Max Repper was about to lose his top teeth.

Sure enough. Terry took two steps and a little shuffle dance and hit Max square in the mouth. Max went back, but didn't go down and now he came at Terry. Terry had his right cocked, waiting, and he started to throw it. Max put up his guard and Terry held the right, but his left came around wide and clobbered Max on the ear. Then the right followed through, straightening him up, and the left swung wide again and smacked solid against his cheekbone. Max didn't throw a punch. He wanted to at first, then he was kept too busy trying to cover up. I thought Terry's arms would drop off before Max caved in. Then, there it was, for a split second—Max's chin up like he was posing for a profile—and Terry found it with the best-timed, widest-swung roundhouse I've ever seen.

Max went down and he didn't move. Terry stepped inside the barn and came out with a hackamore. He looked down at Max and started to roll him over with his boot. But then he must have thought, What good will it do— He turned away, dropping the hackamore on top of Repper.

All Terry said was "Long as the boy got away . . . that's the main thing."

AFTER THAT EVERYTHING was quiet for a while. Of course what had happened made good conversation, and wherever you'd go somebody would be talking about the half-wild white boy who'd lived with Apaches. And they talked about Max Repper and Terry. Everybody agreed that was a fine thing Terry did, loosening Max's teeth . . . but Terry better watch himself, the way Max holds on to a grudge with both hands and both feet.

Terry went back to his diggings and Deelie wore her tragic look like he was off to the wars. Max would come in about once a week still, but now he didn't talk so much. Ordered what he wanted and got out.

Then one day a man named Jim Hughes came in and told how he'd seen the boy.

Jim had a one-loop outfit a few miles beyond Repper's place. I told him it was probably just a stray reservation buck, but he said no, he came through the willows to the creek off back of his place and there was the boy lying belly down at the side of the creek. The boy jumped up surprised not ten feet away from him, scrambled for his horse, and was gone. And Jim said the boy was wearing a red shirt, the back of it all ripped.

Max heard about it too. The next day he was in asking whether I'd seen the boy. He talked about it like he was just making conversation, but Max wasn't cut out to be an actor. He wanted to find that boy so bad, he could taste it, and it showed through soon as he started talking.

Within the next few days the boy was seen two more times. First by a neighbor of Jim Hughes's who lived this side of him, then a day later by a cavalry patrol out of Dos Fuegos. They gave chase, but the boy ran for high timber and got away. Both times the boy's red shirt was described.

Now there was something to talk about again; everybody speculating what the boy was up to. The cavalry station received orders from the commandant at Fort Huachuca to bring the boy in and be pretty damn quick about it. It didn't look good to have a boy running around who'd been stolen by the Indians. This was something for the authorities. Down at the State House Saloon they were betting five to one the cavalry would never find him, and they had some takers.

Most people figured the boy was out to get Max Repper and was sneaking around waiting for the right time.

I had the hunch the boy was looking for Terry McNeil. And when Terry finally came in again (it had been almost a month), I told him so.

He was surprised to hear the boy had been seen around here and said he couldn't figure it out. Thought the boy would be glad to get away.

"Why would he want to go back to Apaches?" I asked him.

"He lived with them," Terry said.

"That doesn't mean he liked them," I said. "I could see him going back to those Mexican people, but Sahuaripa's an awful long way off and probably he couldn't find his way back."

Terry shook his head. "But why would he be hanging around here?"

"I still say he's looking for you."

"What for?"

"Maybe he likes you."

Terry said, "That doesn't make sense."

"Maybe he likes red shirts."

"Well," Terry said, "I could look for him."

"It would be easier to let him find you," I said.

"If that's what he wants to do."

"Why don't you just sit here for a while," I suggested. "The boy knows you come here. If he wants you, then sooner or later he'll show up."

Terry thought about it, making a cigarette, then agreed finally that he wouldn't lose anything by staying.

Right in front of me Deelie threw her arms around his neck and kissed him about twelve times. I thought: If that's what having him around just a little while will do, what would happen if he agreed to stay on for life?

☆ ☆ ☆

DURING THE NEXT four days nothing happened. There weren't even claims of seeing the boy. Terry said, well, the boy's probably a hundred miles away now. And I said, Either that or else he's closing in now and playing it more careful. Repper came in once and when he saw Terry he got suspicious and hung around a long time, though acting like Terry wasn't even there.

The night of the sixth day we were sitting out on the porch talking and smoking, like we'd been doing every evening, and I remember saying something about working up energy to go to bed, when Terry's hand touched my arm. He said, "Somebody's standing between those two buildings across the street."

I looked hard, but all I saw was the narrow deep shadow between the two adobes. And I was about to tell Terry he was mistaken when this figure appeared out of the shadows. He stood there for a minute close to one of the adobes, then started across the street, walking slowly.

He came to the steps and hesitated; but when Terry stood up and said, "Regalo," softly, the boy came up on the porch.

Deelie turned the lamp up as we went inside and I heard Terry asking the boy if he was hungry. The boy shook his head. Then we all just stood there not knowing what to say, trying not to stare at the boy. He was wearing the torn red shirt and looking at Terry like he had something to tell him but didn't know the right words.

Then he reached into his shirt, suddenly starting to talk in Spanish. He pulled something out wrapped in buckskin, still talking, and handed it to Terry. Then he stopped and just watched as Terry, looking embarrassed, unwrapped the little square of buckskin.

Terry looked at the boy and then at me, his eyes about to pop out of his head, and I saw what he was holding . . . a raw gold nugget.

It must have been the size of two shot glasses; way, way bigger than any I'd ever had the pleasure of seeing. Terry put it on the counter, stepped back, and looked at it like he was beholding the palace of the king of China.

He just stared, and the boy started talking again in that rapid-fire Spanish like he was trying to say everything at once. Terry looked at the boy and he stared some more until the boy stopped talking.

"What'd he say?" I asked him.

Terry took a minute to look over at me. "He says this is mine and that he'll show me a lot more. A place nobody knows about . . ."

I could believe that. You don't find nuggets that size out in the road. And it made sense the boy might know of a mine. It was common talk that any Apache could be a rich man, the way he knew the country—the whereabouts of mines worked by the Spanish two and three hundred years ago. Sure Indians knew about them, but they weren't going to tell whites and be crowded off their land quicker than it was already happening. In three years with Chiricahuas, Regalo could have learned plenty.

I said, "Terrence, you and that red shirt have made a valuable friendship."

☆   ☆   ☆

TERRY WAS STILL about three feet off the ground. He said then, "But he claims he wants to live with me!"

"Well, taking him in is the least you can do, considering—"

"But I can't—"

He stopped there. I turned around to see what Terry was looking at and there was Max Repper in the doorway, with his Henry. Max was grinning, which he hadn't done in a month, and he came forward keeping the barrel trained at Terry.

"I knew he'd show," Repper said, "soon as I saw you hanging around. I came for two things. Him"—he swung the barrel to indicate the boy—"and my nugget."

"Yours?" I said.

"The boy stole it from me."

"You never saw it before you peeked in that window."

"That's your say," Repper answered.

Terry said, "What do you want with the boy?"

"I got work for him till the reservation people take him away."

"He doesn't belong on a reservation," Terry said.

"That's not my worry." Repper shrugged. "That's what they're saying at Dos Fuegos will happen to him."

Terry shook his head slowly, saying, "That wouldn't be right."

Repper lifted the Henry a little higher. "Just hand me the nugget."

Terry hesitated. Then he said, "You come and take it."

"I can do that too," Repper said. He was concentrating on Terry and started to move toward him. His eyes went to the nugget momentarily, two seconds at best, and as they did the boy went for him. He was at Repper's throat in one lunge, dragging him down. Terry moved then, pushing the rifle barrel up and against Repper's face. Repper went down, the boy on top of him, and then a knife was in Regalo's hand.

Deelie screamed and Terry lifted the boy off of Repper, saying, "Wait a minute!" Then, in Spanish, he was talking more quietly, calming the boy.

Repper sat up with his hand to his face. He had a welt across his forehead where the rifle barrel hit, but he was more mad than hurt. He said, "You think I'm going to let you get away with this?"

Terry was himself again. He said, "I don't think you got a choice."

"I haven't?" Max said. "I'll make damn sure he gets put the hell on that reservation."

"If you can prove he's Indian," Terry answered.

Max gave us his sly look. "Either way," he said. "If he ain't Indian then he's white, with white kin, and no authority's going to let him get adopted by a saddle tramp who ain't worked in two years."

It was a good thing Max was sitting down when he said that. Max was through, and he probably knew it, but if Terry wanted the boy, then he'd sure make it plain hell for Terry to keep him.

I told Repper, "That's up to the authorities. The thing is, this boy's got no recollection of white kin and the only other person who knew his parents is dead. And he's said himself he wants to live with Terry."

Max grinned. "And I imagine Terry wants the boy, and his nugget, to live with him. But like I said, the authorities won't see it that way."

And then Deelie had something to say. She was looking at Max Repper, but I think talking to Terry, and she said, "No, they wouldn't let the boy live with a saddle tramp who hasn't worked in two years . . . but I'm sure they would agree that a successful mining man of Mr. McNeil's character would be more than they could hope for . . . especially since he'll be married within the week."

That was exactly how Deelie did it. I've often wondered if she ever thought Terry married her just so he could raise the boy. I didn't think he did, knowing Terry, and I doubt if Deelie really cared . . . long as she had him.

28

Only Good Ones

Western Roundup, New York, Macmillan, 1961
(*Western Writers of America Anthology*)

PICTURE THE GROUND rising on the east side of the pasture with scrub trees thick on the slope and pines higher up. This is where everybody was. Not all in one place but scattered in small groups: about a dozen men in the scrub, the front-line men, the shooters who couldn't just stand around. They'd fire at the shack when they felt like it or, when Mr. Tanner passed the word, they would all fire at once. Other people were up in the pines and on the road which ran along the crest of the hill, some three hundred yards from the shack across the pasture. Those watching made bets whether the man in the shack would give himself up or get shot first.

It was Saturday and that's why everybody had the time. They would arrive in town that morning, hear about what had happened, and, shortly after, head out to the cattle-company pasture. Almost all of the men went out alone, leaving their families in town: though there were a few women who came. The other women waited. And the people who had business in town and couldn't leave waited. Now and then somebody came back to have a drink or their dinner and would tell what was going on. No, they hadn't got him yet. Still inside the line shack and not showing his face.

But they'd get him. A few more would go out when they heard this. Also a wagon from De Spain's went out with whiskey. That's how the saloon was set up in the pines overlooking the pasture and why nobody went back to town after that.

Barely a mile from town those going out would hear the gunfire, like a skirmish way over on the other side of a woods, thin specks of sound, and this would hurry them. They were careful, though, topping the slope, looking across the pasture, getting their bearings, then peering to see who was present. They would see a friend and ask about this Mr. Tanner and the friend would point him out.

The man there in the dark suit: thin and bony, not big but looking like he was made of gristle and hard to kill, with a mustache and a thin nose and a dark dusty hat worn square over his eyes. That was him. Nobody had ever seen him before that morning. They would look at Mr. Tanner, then across the pasture again to the line shack three hundred yards away. It was a little bake-oven of a hut, wood framed and made of sod and built against a rise where there were pines so the hut would be in shade part of the day. There were no windows in the hut, no gear lying around to show anybody lived there. The hut stood in the sun now with its door closed, the door chipped and splintered by all the bullets that had poured into it and through it.

Off to the right where the pine shapes against the sky rounded and became willows, there in the trees by the creek bed, was the man's wagon and team. In the wagon were the supplies he had bought that morning in town before Mr. Tanner spotted him.

Out in front of the hut, about ten or fifteen feet, was something on the ground. From the slope three hundred yards away nobody could tell what it was until a man came who had field glasses. He looked up and said, frowning, it was a doll: one made of cloth scraps, a stuffed doll with buttons for eyes.

The woman must have dropped it, somebody said.

The woman? the man with the field glasses said.

A Lipan Apache woman who was his wife or his woman or just with him. Mr. Tanner hadn't been clear about that. All they knew was she was in the hut with him and if the man wanted her to stay and get shot, that was his business.

Bob Valdez, twenty years old and town constable for three weeks, carrying a shotgun and glad he had something to hold on to, was present at the Maricopa pasture. He arrived about noon. He told Mr. Tanner who he was, speaking quietly and waiting for Mr. Tanner to answer.

Mr. Tanner nodded but did not shake hands and turned away to say something to an R. L. Davis, who rode for Maricopa when he was working. Bob Valdez stood there and didn't know what to do.

He watched the two men. Two of a kind, uh? Both cut from the same stringy hide and looking like father and son: Tanner talking, never smiling, hardly moving his mouth; R. L. Davis standing hip-cocked, posing with his revolver and rifle and a cartridge belt over his shoulder and the funneled, pointed brim of his sweaty hat nodding up and down as he listened to Mr. Tanner, smiling at what Mr. Tanner said, laughing out loud while still Mr. Tanner did not even show the twitch of a lip. Bob Valdez did not like R. L. Davis or any of the R. L. Davises he had met. He was civil, he listened to them, but, God, there were a lot of them to listen to.

A Mr. Beaudry, who leased land to the cattle company, was there. Also Mr. Malsom, manager of Maricopa, and a horsebreaker by the name of Diego Luz, who was big for a Mexican but never offensive and he drank pretty well.

Mr. Beaudry, nodding and also squinting so he could picture the man inside the line shack, said, "There was something peculiar about him. I mean having a name like Orlando Rincon."

"He worked for me," Mr. Malsom said. He was looking at Mr. Tanner. "I mistrusted him and I believe that was part of it, his name being Orlando Rincon."

"Johnson," Mr. Tanner said.

"I hired him two, three times," Mr. Malsom said. "For heavy work. When I had work you couldn't kick a man to doing."

"His name is Johnson," Mr. Tanner said. "There is no fuzz-head by the name of Orlando Rincon. I'm telling you, this one is a fuzz-head from the Fort Huachuca Tenth fuzz-head cavalry and his name was Johnson when he killed James C. Baxter a year ago and nothing else."

He spoke as you might speak to young children to press something into their minds. This man had no warmth and he was probably not very smart. But there was no reason to doubt him.

Bob Valdez kept near Mr. Tanner because he was the center of what was going on here. They would discuss the situation and decide what to do. As the law-enforcement man he, Bob Valdez, should be in on the discussion and the decision. If someone was to arrest Orlando Rincon or Johnson or whatever his name was, then he should do it; he was town constable. They were out of town maybe, but where did the town end? The town had moved out here now; it was the same thing.

Wait for Rincon to give up. Then arrest him.

If he wasn't dead already.

"Mr. Malsom." Bob Valdez stepped toward the cattle-company manager, who glanced over but looked out across the pasture again, indifferent.

"I wondered if maybe he's already dead," Valdez said.

Mr. Malsom, standing heavier and taller and twenty years older than Bob Valdez, said, "Why don't you find out?"

"I was thinking," Valdez said, "if he was dead we could stand here a long time."

R. L. Davis adjusted his hat, which he did often, grabbing the funneled brim, loosening it on his head and pulling it down close to his eyes again and shifting from one cocked hip to the other. "This constable here's got better things to do," R. L. Davis said. "He's busy."

"No," Bob Valdez said. "I was thinking of the man, Rincon. He's dead or he's alive. He's alive maybe he wants to give himself up. In there he has time to think, uh? Maybe—" He stopped. Not one of them was listening. Not even R. L. Davis.

Mr. Malsom was looking at the whiskey wagon; it was on the road above them and over a little ways with men standing by it, being served off the tailgate. "I think we could use something," Mr. Malsom said. His gaze went to Diego Luz the horsebreaker, and Diego straightened up; not much, but a little. He was heavy and very dark and his shirt was tight across the thickness of his body. They said that Diego Luz hit green horses on the muzzle with his fist and they minded him. He had the hands for it; they hung at his sides, not touching or fooling with anything. They turned open, gestured, when Mr. Malsom told him to get the whiskey and as he moved off, climbing the slope, one hand held his holstered revolver to his leg.

Mr. Malsom looked up at the sky, squinting and taking his hat off and putting it on again. He took off his coat and held it hooked over his shoulder by one finger, said something, gestured, and he and Mr.

Beaudry and Mr. Tanner moved a few yards down the slope to a hollow where there was good shade. It was about two or two-thirty then, hot, fairly still and quiet considering the number of people there. Only some of them in the pines and down in the scrub could be seen from where Bob Valdez stood wondering whether he should follow the three men down to the hollow. Or wait for Diego Luz, who was at the whiskey wagon now, where most of the sounds that carried came from: a voice, a word or two that was suddenly clear, or laughter, and people would look up to see what was going on. Some of them by the whiskey wagon had lost interest in the line shack. Others were still watching, though: those farther along the road sitting in wagons and buggies. This was a day, a date, uh? that people would remember and talk about. Sure, I was there, the man in the buggy would be saying a year from now in a saloon over in Benson or St. David or somewhere. The day they got that army deserter, he had a Big-Fifty Sharps and an old Walker and I'll tell you it was ticklish business.

Down in that worn-out pasture, dusty and spotted with desert growth, prickly pear and brittlebush, there was just the sun. It showed the ground cleanly all the way to just in front of the line shack where now, toward the midafternoon, there was shadow coming out from the trees and from the mound the hut was set against.

Somebody in the scrub must have seen the door open. The shout came from there, and Bob Valdez and everybody on the slope was looking by the time the Lipan Apache woman had reached the edge of the shade. She walked out from the hut toward the willow trees carrying a bucket, not hurrying or even looking toward the slope.

Nobody fired at her; though this was not so strange. Putting the front sight on a sod hut and on a person are two different things. The men in the scrub and in the pines didn't know this woman. They weren't after her. She had just appeared. There she was; and no one was sure what to do about her.

She was in the trees a while by the creek, then she was in the open again, walking back toward the hut with the bucket and not hurrying at all: a small figure way across the pasture almost without shape or color, with only the long skirt reaching to the ground to tell it was the woman.

So he's alive, Bob Valdez thought. And he wants to stay alive and he's not giving himself up.

He thought about the woman's nerve and whether Orlando Rincon had sent her out or she had decided this herself. You couldn't tell about an Indian woman. Maybe this was expected of her. The woman didn't count; the man did. You could lose the woman and get another one.

Mr. Tanner didn't look at R. L. Davis. His gaze held on the Lipan Apache woman, inched along with her toward the hut; but must have known R. L. Davis was right next to him.

"She's saying she don't give a goddamn about you and your rifle," Mr. Tanner said.

R. L. Davis looked at him funny. Then he said, "Shoot her?" Like he hoped that's what Mr. Tanner meant.

"Well, you could make her jump some," Mr. Tanner said.

Now R. L. Davis was onstage and he knew it and Bob Valdez could tell he knew it by the way he levered the Winchester, raised it, and fired all in one motion, and as the dust kicked behind the Indian woman, who kept walking and didn't look up, R. L. Davis fired and fired and fired as fast as he could lever and half aim and with everybody watching him, hurrying him, he put four good ones right behind the woman. His last bullet socked into the door just as she reached it and now she did pause and look up at the slope, staring up like she was waiting for him to fire again and giving him a good target if he wanted it.

Mr. Malsom laughed out loud. "She still don't give a goddamn about your rifle."

It stung R. L. Davis, which it was intended to do. "I wasn't aiming at her!"

"But she doesn't know that." Mr. Malsom was grinning, turning then and reaching out a hand as Diego Luz approached them with the whiskey.

"Hell, I wanted to hit her she'd be laying there, you know it."

"Well, now, you go tell her that," Mr. Malsom said, working the cork loose, "and she'll know it." He took a drink from the bottle and passed it to Mr. Beaudry, who drank and handed the bottle to Mr. Tanner. Mr. Tanner did not drink; he passed the bottle to R. L. Davis, who was standing, staring at Mr. Malsom. Finally R. L. Davis jerked the bottle up, took a long swallow, and that part was over.

Mr. Malsom said to Mr. Tanner, "You don't want any?"

"Not today," Mr. Tanner answered. He continued to stare out across the pasture.

Mr. Malsom watched him. "You feel strongly about this army deserter."

"I told you," Mr. Tanner said, "he killed a man was a friend of mine."

"No, I don't believe you did."

"James C. Baxter of Fort Huachuca," Mr. Tanner said. "He come across a *tulapai* still this nigger soldier was working with some Indians. The nigger thought Baxter would tell the army people, so he shot him and ran off with a woman."

"And you saw him this morning."

"I had come in last night and stopped off, going to Tucson," Mr. Tanner said. "This morning I was getting ready to leave when I saw him; him and the woman."

"I was right there," R. L. Davis said. "Right, Mr. Tanner? Him and I were on the porch by the Republic and Rincon goes by in the wagon. Mr. Tanner said, 'You know that man?' I said, 'Only that he's lived up north of town a few months. Him and the woman.' 'Well, I know him,' Mr. Tanner said. 'That man's an army deserter wanted for murder.' I said, 'Well, let's go get him.' He had a start on us and that's how he got to the hut before we could grab on to him. He's been holed up ever since."

Mr. Malsom said, "Then you didn't talk to him."

"Listen," Mr. Tanner said, "I've kept that man's face before my eyes this past year."

Bob Valdez, somewhat behind Mr. Tanner and to the side, moved in a little closer. "You know this is the same man, uh?"

Mr. Tanner looked around. He stared at Valdez. That's all he did— just stared.

"I mean, we have to be sure," Bob Valdez said. "It's a serious thing."

Now Mr. Malsom and Mr. Beaudry were looking up at him. "We," Mr. Beaudry said. "I'll tell you what, Roberto. We need help we'll call you. All right?"

"You hired me," Bob Valdez said, standing alone above them. He was serious but he shrugged and smiled a little to take the edge off the words. "What did you hire me for?"

"Well," Mr. Beaudry said, acting it out, looking past Bob Valdez and along the road both ways, "I was to see some drunk Mexicans I'd point them out."

A person can be in two different places and he will be two different people. Maybe if you think of some more places the person will be more people, but don't take it too far. This is Bob Valdez standing by himself with the shotgun and having only the shotgun to hold on to. This is one Bob Valdez. About twenty years old. Mr. Beaudry and others could try and think of a time when Bob Valdez might have drunk too much or swaggered or had a certain smart look on his face, but they would never recall such a time. This Bob Valdez was all right.

Another Bob Valdez inside the Bob Valdez at the pasture that day worked for the army one time and was a guide when Crook chased Chato and Chihuahua down into the Madres. He was seventeen then, with a Springfield and Apache moccasins that came up to his knees. He would sit at night with the Apache scouts from San Carlos, eating with them and talking some as he learned Chiricahua. He would keep up with them all day and shoot the Springfield one hell of a lot better than any of them could shoot. He came home with a scalp but never showed it to anyone and had thrown it away by the time he went to work for Maricopa. Shortly after that he was named town constable at twenty-five dollars a month, getting the job because he got along with people: the Mexicans in town who drank too much on Saturday night liked him and that was the main thing.

The men with the whiskey bottle had forgotten Valdez. They stayed in the hollow where the shade was cool watching the line shack and waiting for the army deserter to realize it was all up with him. He would realize it and open the door and be cut down as he came outside. It was a matter of time only.

Bob Valdez stayed on the open part of the slope that was turning to shade, sitting now like an Apache and every once in a while making a cigarette and smoking it slowly as he thought about himself and Mr. Tanner and the others, then thinking about the army deserter.

Diego Luz came and squatted next to him, his arms on his knees and his big hands that he used for breaking horses hanging in front of him.

"Stay near if they want you for something," Valdez said. He was watching Beaudry tilt the bottle up. Diego Luz said nothing.

"One of them bends over," Bob Valdez said then, "you kiss it, uh?"

Diego Luz looked at him, patient about it. Not mad or even stirred up. "Why don't you go home?"

"He says Get me a bottle, you run."

"I get it. I don't run."

"Smile and hold your hat, uh?"

"And don't talk so much."

"Not unless they talk to you first."

"You better go home," Diego said.

Bob Valdez said, "That's why you hit the horses."

"Listen," Diego Luz said, scowling a bit now. "They pay me to break horses. They pay you to talk to drunks on Saturday night and keep them from killing somebody. They don't pay you for what you think or how you feel, so if you take their money, keep your mouth shut. All right?"

Diego Luz got up and walked away, down toward the hollow. The hell with this kid, he was thinking. He'll learn or he won't learn, but the hell with him. He was also thinking that maybe he could get a drink from that bottle. Maybe there'd be a half inch left nobody wanted and Mr. Malsom would tell him to kill it.

But it was already finished. R. L. Davis was playing with the bottle, holding it by the neck and flipping it up and catching it as it came down. Beaudry was saying, "What about after dark?" Looking at Mr. Tanner, who was thinking about something else and didn't notice. R L. Davis stopped flipping the bottle. He said, "Put some men on the rise right above the hut; he comes out, bust him."

"Well, they should get the men over there," Mr. Beaudry said, looking at the sky. "It won't be long till dark."

"Where's he going?" Mr. Malsom said.

The others looked up, stopped in whatever they were doing or thinking by the suddenness of Mr. Malsom's voice.

"Hey, Valdez!" R. L. Davis yelled out. "Where do you think you're going?"

Bob Valdez had circled them and was already below them on the slope, leaving the pines now and entering the scrub brush. He didn't stop or look back.

"Valdez!"

Mr. Tanner raised one hand to silence R. L. Davis, all the time watching Bob Valdez getting smaller, going straight through the scrub, not just walking or passing the time but going right out to the pasture.

"Look at him," Mr. Malsom said. There was some admiration in the voice.

"He's dumber than he looks," R. L. Davis said. Then jumped a little as Mr. Tanner touched his arm.

"Come on," Mr. Tanner said. "With a rifle." And started down the slope, hurrying and not seeming to care if he might stumble on the loose gravel.

Bob Valdez was now halfway across the pasture, the shotgun pointed down at his side, his eyes not leaving the door of the line shack. The door was probably already open enough for a rifle barrel to poke through. He guessed the army deserter was covering him, letting him get as close as he wanted; the closer he came, the easier to hit him.

Now he could see all the bullet marks in the door and the clean inner wood where the door was splintered. Two people in that little bake-oven of a place. He saw the door move.

He saw the rag doll on the ground. It was a strange thing, the woman having a doll. Valdez hardly glanced at it but was aware of the button eyes looking up and the discomforted twist of the red wool mouth. Then, just past the doll, when he was wondering if he would go right up to the door and knock on it and wouldn't that be a crazy thing, like visiting somebody, the door opened and the Negro was in the doorway, filling it, standing there in pants and boots but without a shirt in that hot place and holding a long-barreled Walker that was already cocked.

They stood ten feet apart looking at each other, close enough so that no one could fire from the slope.

"I can kill you first," the Negro said, "if you raise that."

With his free hand, the left one, Bob Valdez motioned back over his shoulder. "There's a man there said you killed somebody a year ago."

"What man?"

"Said his name is Tanner."

The Negro shook his head, once each way.

"Said your name is Johnson."

"You know my name."

"I'm telling you what he said."

"Where'd I kill this man?"

"Huachuca."

The Negro hesitated. "That was some time ago I was in the Tenth. More than a year."

"You a deserter?"

"I served it out."

"Then you got something that says so."

"In the wagon, there's a bag there my things are in."

"Will you talk to this man Tanner?"

"If I can hold from hitting him one."

"Listen, why did you run this morning?"

"They come chasing. I don't know what they want." He lowered the gun a little, his brown-stained-looking tired eyes staring intently at Bob Valdez. "What would you do? They came on the run. Next thing I know they a-firing at us. So I pop in this place."

"Will you come with me and talk to him?"

The Negro hesitated again. Then shook his head. "I don't know him."

"Then he won't know you, uh?"

"He didn't know me this morning."

"All right," Bob Valdez said. "I'll get your paper says you were discharged. Then we'll show it to this man, uh?"

The Negro thought it over before he nodded, very slowly, as if still thinking. "All right. Bring him here, I'll say a few words to him."

Bob Valdez smiled a little. "You can point that gun some other way."

"Well . . ." the Negro said, "if everybody's friends." He lowered the Walker to his side.

The wagon was in the willow trees by the creek. Off to the right. But Bob Valdez did not turn right away in that direction. He backed away, watching Orlando Rincon for no reason that he knew of. Maybe because the man was holding a gun and that was reason enough.

He had backed off six or seven feet when Orlando Rincon shoved the Walker down into his belt. Bob Valdez turned and started for the trees.

This was when he looked across the pasture. He saw Mr. Tanner and R. L. Davis at the edge of the scrub trees but wasn't sure it was them. Something tried to tell him it was them, but he did not accept it until he was off to the right, out of the line of fire, and by then the time to yell at them or run toward them was past, for R. L. Davis had the Winchester up and was firing.

They say R. L. Davis was drunk or he would have pinned him square. As it was the bullet shaved Rincon and plowed past him into the hut.

Bob Valdez saw him half turn, either to go inside or look inside, and as he came around again saw the man's eyes on him and his hand pulling the Walker from his belt.

"They weren't supposed to," Bob Valdez said, holding one hand out as if to stop Rincon. "Listen, they weren't supposed to do that!"

The Walker was out of Rincon's belt and he was cocking it. "Don't!" Bob Valdez yelled. "Don't!" Looking right in the man's eyes and seeing it was no use and suddenly hurrying, jerking the shotgun up and pulling both triggers so that the explosions came out in one big blast and Orlando Rincon was spun and thrown back inside.

They came out across the pasture to have a look at the carcass, some going inside where they found the woman also dead, killed by a rifle bullet. They noticed she would have had a child in a few months. Those by the doorway made room as Mr. Tanner and R. L. Davis approached.

Diego Luz came over by Bob Valdez, who had not moved. Valdez stood watching them and he saw Mr. Tanner look down at Rincon and after a moment shake his head.

"It looked like him," Mr. Tanner said. "It sure looked like him."

He saw R. L. Davis squint at Mr. Tanner. "It ain't the one you said?"

Mr. Tanner shook his head again. "I've seen him before, though. Know I've seen him somewheres."

Valdez saw R. L. Davis shrug. "You ask me, they all look alike." He was yawning then, fooling with his hat, and then his eyes swiveled over at Bob Valdez standing with the empty shotgun.

"Constable," R. L. Davis said, "you went and killed the wrong coon."

Bob Valdez started for him, raising the shotgun to swing it like a club, but Diego Luz drew his revolver and came down with it and Valdez dropped to the ground.

Some three years later there was a piece in the paper about a Robert Eladio Valdez who had been hanged for murder in Tularosa, New Mexico. He had shot a man coming out of the Regent Hotel, called him an unprintable name, and shot him four times. This Valdez had previously killed a man in Contention and two in Sands during a bank holdup, had been caught once, escaped from the jail in Mesilla before trial, and identified another time during a holdup near Lordsburg.

"If it is the same Bob Valdez used to live here," Mr. Beaudry said, "it's good we got rid of him."

"Well, it could be," Mr. Malsom said. "But I guess there are Bob Valdezes all over."

"You wonder what gets into them," Mr. Beaudry said.

29

The Tonto Woman

Roundup, Garden City, Doubleday, 1982
(*Western Writers of America Anthology*)

A TIME WOULD COME, within a few years, when Ruben Vega would go to the church in Benson, kneel in the confessional, and say to the priest, "Bless me, Father, for I have sinned. It has been thirty-seven years since my last confession. . . . Since then I have fornicated with many women, maybe eight hundred. No, not that many, considering my work. Maybe six hundred only." And the priest would say, "Do you mean bad women or good women?" And Ruben Vega would say, "They are all good, Father." He would tell the priest he had stolen, in that time, about twenty thousand head of cattle but only maybe fifteen horses. The priest would ask him if he had committed murder. Ruben Vega would say no. "All that stealing you've done," the priest would say, "you've never killed anyone?" And Ruben Vega would say, "Yes, of course, but it was not to commit murder. You understand the distinction? Not to *kill* someone to take a life, but only to save my own."

Even in this time to come, concerned with dying in a state of sin, he would be confident. Ruben Vega knew himself, when he was right, when he was wrong.

NOW, IN A TIME before, with no thought of dying, but with the same confidence and caution that kept him alive, he watched a woman bathe. Watched from a mesquite thicket on the high bank of a wash.

She bathed at the pump that stood in the yard of the adobe, the woman pumping and then stooping to scoop the water from the basin of the irrigation ditch that led off to a vegetable patch of corn and beans. Her dark hair was pinned up in a swirl, piled on top of her head. She was bare to her gray skirt, her upper body pale white, glistening wet in the late afternoon sunlight. Her arms were very thin, her breasts small, but there they were with the rosy blossoms on the tips and Ruben Vega watched them as she bathed, as she raised one arm and her hand rubbed soap under the arm and down over her ribs. Ruben Vega could almost feel those ribs, she was so thin. He felt sorry for her, for all the women like her, stick women drying up in the desert, waiting for a husband to ride in smelling of horse and sweat and leather, lice living in his hair.

There was a stock tank and rickety windmill off in the pasture, but it was empty graze, all dust and scrub. So the man of the house had moved his cows to grass somewhere and would be coming home soon, maybe with his sons. The woman appeared old enough to have young sons. Maybe there was a little girl in the house. The chimney appeared cold. Animals stood in a mesquite-pole corral off to one side of the house, a cow and a calf and a dun-colored horse, that was all. There were a few chickens. No buckboard or wagon. No clothes drying on the line. A lone woman here at day's end.

From fifty yards he watched her. She stood looking this way now, into the red sun, her face raised. There was something strange about her face. Like shadow marks on it, though there was nothing near enough to her to cast shadows.

He waited until she finished bathing and returned to the house before he mounted his bay and came down the wash to the pasture.

Now as he crossed the yard, walking his horse, she would watch him from the darkness of the house and make a judgment about him. When she appeared again it might be with a rifle, depending on how she saw him.

Ruben Vega said to himself, Look, I'm a kind person. I'm not going to hurt nobody.

She would see a bearded man in a cracked straw hat with the brim bent to his eyes. Black beard, with a revolver on his hip and another beneath the leather vest. But look at my eyes, Ruben Vega thought. Let me get close enough so you can see my eyes.

Stepping down from the bay he ignored the house, let the horse drink from the basin of the irrigation ditch as he pumped water and knelt to the wooden platform and put his mouth to the rusted pump spout. Yes, she was watching him. Looking up now at the doorway he could see part of her: a coarse shirt with sleeves too long and the gray skirt. He could see strands of dark hair against the whiteness of the shirt, but could not see her face.

As he rose, straightening, wiping his mouth, he said, "May we use some of your water, please?"

The woman didn't answer him.

He moved away from the pump to the hardpack, hearing the ching of his spurs, removed his hat and gave her a little bow. "Ruben Vega, at your service. Do you know Diego Luz, the horsebreaker?" He pointed off toward a haze of foothills. "He lives up there with his family and delivers horses to the big ranch, the Circle-Eye. Ask Diego Luz, he'll tell you I'm a person of trust." He waited a moment. "May I ask how you're called?" Again he waited.

"You watched me," the woman said.

Ruben Vega stood with his hat in his hand facing the woman, who was half in shadow in the doorway. He said, "I waited. I didn't want to frighten you."

"You watched me," she said again.

"No, I respect your privacy."

She said, "The others look. They come and watch."

He wasn't sure who she meant. Maybe anyone passing by. He said, "You see them watching?"

She said, "What difference does it make?" She said then, "You come from Mexico, don't you?"

"Yes, I was there. I'm here and there, working as a drover." Ruben Vega shrugged. "What else is there to do, uh?" Showing her he was resigned to his station in life.

"You'd better leave," she said.

When he didn't move, the woman came out of the doorway into light and he saw her face clearly for the first time. He felt a shock within him and tried to think of something to say, but could only stare at the blue lines tattooed on her face: three straight lines on each cheek that extended from her cheekbones to her jaw, markings that seemed familiar, though he could not in this moment identify them.

He was conscious of himself standing in the open with nothing to say, the woman staring at him with curiosity, as though wondering if he would hold her gaze and look at her. Like there was nothing unusual about her countenance. Like it was common to see a woman with her face tattooed and you might be expected to comment, if you said anything at all, "Oh, that's a nice design you have there. Where did you have it done?" That would be one way—if you couldn't say something interesting about the weather or about the price of cows in Benson.

Ruben Vega, his mind empty of pleasantries, certain he would never see the woman again, said, "Who did that to you?"

She cocked her head in an easy manner, studying him as he studied her, and said, "Do you know, you're the first person who's come right out and asked."

"Mojave," Ruben Vega said, "but there's something different. Mojaves tattoo their chins only, I believe."

"And look like they were eating berries," the woman said. "I told them if you're going to do it, do it all the way. Not like a blue dribble."

It was in her eyes and in the tone of her voice, a glimpse of the rage she must have felt. No trace of fear in the memory, only cold anger. He could hear her telling the Indians—this skinny woman, probably a girl then—until they did it her way and marked her good for all time. Imprisoned her behind the blue marks on her face.

"How old were you?"

"You've seen me and had your water," the woman said, "now leave."

IT WAS THE SAME type of adobe house as the woman's but with a great difference. There was life here, the warmth of family: children sleeping now, Diego Luz's wife and her mother cleaning up after the meal as the two men sat outside in horsehide chairs and smoked and looked at the night. At one time they had both worked for a man named Sundeen and packed running irons to vent the brands on the cattle they stole. Ruben Vega was still an outlaw, in his fashion, while Diego Luz broke green horses and sold them to cattle companies.

They sat at the edge of the ramada, an awning made of mesquite, and stared at pinpoints of light in the universe. Ruben Vega asked about the extent of graze this season, where the large herds were that belonged to the Maricopa and the Circle-Eye. He had been thinking of cutting out maybe a hundred—he wasn't greedy—and driving them south to sell to the mine companies. He had been scouting the Circle-Eye range, he said, when he came to the strange woman. . . .

The Tonto woman, Diego Luz said. Everyone called her that now.

Yes, she had been living there, married a few years, when she went to visit her family, who lived on the Gila above Painted Rock. Well, some Yavapai came looking for food. They clubbed her parents and two small brothers to death and took the girl north with them. The Yavapai traded her to the Mojave as a slave. . . .

"And they marked her," Ruben Vega said.

"Yes, so when she died the spirits would know she was Mojave and not drag her soul down into a rathole," Diego Luz said.

"Better to go to heaven with your face tattooed," Ruben Vega said, "than not at all. Maybe so."

During a drought the Mojave traded her to a band of Tonto Apaches for two mules and a bag of salt and one day she appeared at Bowie with the Tontos that were brought in to be sent to Oklahoma. Among the desert Indians twelve years and returned home last spring.

"It put age on her," Ruben Vega said. "But what about her husband?"

"Her husband? He banished her," Diego Luz said, "like a leper. Unclean from living among the red niggers. No one speaks of her to him, it isn't allowed."

Ruben Vega frowned. There was something he didn't understand. He said, "Wait a minute—"

And Diego Luz said, "Don't you know who her husband is? Mr. Isham himself, man, of the Circle-Eye. She comes home to find her husband a rich man. He don't live in that hut no more. No, he owns a hundred miles of graze and a house it took them two years to build, the glass and bricks brought in by the Southern Pacific. Sure, the railroad comes and he's a rich cattleman in only a few years."

"He makes her live there alone?"

"She's his wife, he provides for her. But that's all. Once a month his segundo named Bonnet rides out there with supplies and has someone shoe her horse and look at the animals."

"But to live in the desert," Ruben Vega said, still frowning, thoughtful, "with a rusty pump . . ."

"Look at her," Diego Luz said. "What choice does she have?"

It was hot down in this scrub pasture, a place to wither and die. Ruben Vega loosened the new willow-root straw that did not yet conform to his head, though he had shaped the brim to curve down on one side and rise slightly on the other so that the brim slanted across the vision of his left eye. He held on his lap a nearly flat cardboard box that bore the name *L. S. Weiss Mercantile Store.*

The woman gazed up at him, shading her eyes with one hand. Finally she said, "You look different."

"The beard began to itch," Ruben Vega said, making no mention of the patches of gray he had studied in the hotel-room mirror. "So I shaved it off." He rubbed a hand over his jaw and smoothed down the tips of his mustache that was still full and seemed to cover his mouth. When he stepped down from the bay and approached the woman standing by the stick-fence corral, she looked off into the distance and back again.

She said, "You shouldn't be here."

Ruben Vega said, "Your husband doesn't want nobody to look at you. Is that it?" He held the store box, waiting for her to answer. "He has a big house with trees and the San Pedro River in his yard. Why doesn't he hide you there?"

She looked off again and said, "If they find you here, they'll shoot you."

"They," Ruben Vega said. "The ones who watch you bathe? Work for your husband and keep more than a close eye on you, and you'd like to hit them with something, wipe the grins from their faces."

"You better leave," the woman said.

The blue lines on her face were like claw marks, though not as wide as fingers: indelible lines of dye etched into her flesh with a cactus needle, the color worn and faded but still vivid against her skin, the blue matching her eyes.

He stepped close to her, raised his hand to her face, and touched the markings gently with the tips of his fingers, feeling nothing. He raised his eyes to hers. She was staring at him. He said, "You're in there, aren't you? Behind these little bars. They don't seem like much. Not enough to hold you."

She said nothing, but seemed to be waiting.

He said to her, "You should brush your hair. Brush it every day. . . ."

"Why?" the woman said.

"To feel good. You need to wear a dress. A little parasol to match."

"I'm asking you to leave," the woman said. But didn't move from his hand, with its yellowed, stained nails, that was like a fist made of old leather.

"I'll tell you something if I can," Ruben Vega said. "I know women all my life, all kinds of women in the way they look and dress, the way they adorn themselves according to custom. Women are always a wonder to me. When I'm not with a woman I think of them as all the same because I'm thinking of one thing. You understand?"

"Put a sack over their head," the woman said.

"Well, I'm not thinking of what she looks like then, when I'm out in the mountains or somewhere," Ruben Vega said. "That part of her doesn't matter. But when I'm *with* the woman, ah, then I realize how they are all different. You say, of course. This isn't a revelation to you. But maybe it is when you think about it some more."

The woman's eyes changed, turned cold. "You want to go to bed with me? Is that what you're saying, why you bring a gift?"

He looked at her with disappointment, an expression of weariness. But then he dropped the store box and took her to him gently, placing his hands on her shoulders, feeling her small bones in his grasp as he brought her in against him and his arms went around her.

He said, "You're gonna die here. Dry up and blow away."

She said, "Please . . ." Her voice hushed against him.

"They wanted only to mark your chin," Ruben Vega said, "in the custom of those people. But you wanted your own marks, didn't you? *Your* marks, not like anyone else. . . . Well, you got them." After a moment he said to her, very quietly, "Tell me what you want."

The hushed voice close to him said, "I don't know."

He said, "Think about it and remember something. There is no one else in the world like you."

★ ★ ★

HE REINED THE BAY to move out and saw the dust trail rising out of the old pasture, three riders coming, and heard the woman say, "I told you. Now it's too late."

A man on a claybank and two young riders eating his dust, finally separating to come in abreast, reined to a walk as they reached the pump and the irrigation ditch. The woman, walking from the corral to the house, said to them, "What do you want? I don't need anything, Mr. Bonnet."

So this would be the Circle-Eye foreman on the claybank. The man ignored her, his gaze holding on Ruben Vega with a solemn expression, showing he was going to be dead serious. A chew formed a lump in his jaw. He wore army suspenders and sleeve garters, his shirt buttoned up at the neck. As old as you are, Ruben Vega thought, a man who likes a tight feel of security and is serious about his business.

Bonnet said to him finally, "You made a mistake."

"I don't know the rules," Ruben Vega said.

"She told you to leave her be. That's the only rule there is. But you bought yourself a dandy new hat and come back here."

"That's some hat," one of the young riders said. This one held a single-shot Springfield across his pommel. The foreman, Bonnet, turned in his saddle and said something to the other rider, who un-hitched his rope and began shaking out a loop, hanging it nearly to the ground.

It's a show, Ruben Vega thought. He said to Bonnet, "I was leaving."

Bonnet said, "Yes, indeed, you are. On the off end of a rope. We're gonna drag you so you'll know the ground and never cross this land again."

The rider with the Springfield said, "Gimme your hat, mister, so's you don't get it dirty."

At this point Ruben Vega nudged his bay and began moving in on the foreman, who straightened, looking over at the roper, and said, "Well, tie on to him."

But Ruben Vega was close to the foreman now, the bay taller than the claybank, and would move the claybank if the man on his back told him to. Ruben Vega watched the foreman's eyes moving and knew the roper was coming around behind him. Now the foreman turned his head to spit and let go a stream that spattered the hard-pack close to the bay's forelegs.

"Stand still," Bonnet said, "and we'll get her done easy. Or you can run and get snubbed out of your chair. Either way."

Ruben Vega was thinking that he could drink with this ramrod and they'd tell each other stories until they were drunk. The man had thought it would be easy: chase off a Mexican gunnysacker who'd come sniffing the boss's wife. A kid who was good with a rope and another one who could shoot cans off the fence with an old Springfield should be enough.

Ruben Vega said to Bonnet, "Do you know who I am?"

"Tell us," Bonnet said, "so we'll know what the cat drug in and we drug out."

And Ruben Vega said, because he had no choice, "I hear the rope in the air, the one with the rifle is dead. Then you. Then the roper."

His words drew silence because there was nothing more to be said. In the moments that Ruben Vega and the one named Bonnet stared at each other, the woman came out to them holding a revolver, an old Navy Colt, which she raised and laid the barrel against the muzzle of the foreman's claybank.

She said, "Leave now, Mr. Bonnet, or you'll walk nine miles to shade."

There was no argument, little discussion, a few grumbling words. The Tonto woman was still Mrs. Isham. Bonnet rode away with his young hands and a new silence came over the yard.

Ruben Vega said, "He believes you'd shoot his horse." The woman said, "He believes I'd cut steaks, and eat it too. It's how I'm seen after twelve years of that other life."

Ruben Vega began to smile. The woman looked at him and in a few moments she began to smile with him. She shook her head then, but continued to smile. He said to her, "You could have a good time if you want to."

She said, "How, scaring people?"

He said, "If you feel like it." He said, "Get the present I brought you and open it."

✷ ✷ ✷

HE CAME BACK for her the next day in a Concord buggy, wearing his new willow-root straw and a cutaway coat over his revolvers, the coat he'd rented at a funeral parlor. Mrs. Isham wore the pale blue-and-white lace-trimmed dress he'd bought at Weiss's store, sat primly on the bustle, and held the parasol against the afternoon sun all the way to Benson, ten miles, and up the main street to the Charles Crooker Hotel where the drummers and cattlemen and railroad men sitting in their front-porch rockers stared and stared.

They walked past the manager and into the dining room before Ruben Vega removed his hat and pointed to the table he liked, one against the wall between two windows. The waitress in her starched uniform was wide-eyed taking them over and getting them seated. It was early and the dining room was not half filled.

"The place for a quiet dinner," Ruben Vega said. "You see how quiet it is?"

"Everybody's looking at me," Sarah Isham said to the menu in front of her.

Ruben Vega said, "I thought they were looking at me. All right, soon they'll be used to it."

She glanced up and said, "People are leaving."

He said, "That's what you do when you finish eating, you leave."

She looked at him, staring, and said, "Who are you?"

"I told you."

"Only your name."

"You want me to tell you the truth, why I came here?"

"Please."

"To steal some of your husband's cattle."

She began to smile and he smiled. She began to laugh and he laughed, looking openly at the people looking at them, but not bothered by them. Of course they'd look. How could they help it? A Mexican rider and a woman with blue stripes on her face sitting at a table in the hotel dining room, laughing. He said, "Do you like fish? I know your Indian brothers didn't serve you none. It's against their religion. Some things are for religion, as you know, and some things are against it. We spend all our lives learning customs. Then they change them. I'll tell you something else if you promise not to be angry or point your pistol at me. Something else I could do the rest of my life. I could look at you and touch you and love you."

Her hand moved across the linen tablecloth to his with the cracked, yellowed nails and took hold of it, clutched it.

She said, "You're going to leave."

He said, "When it's time."

She said, "I know you. I don't know anyone else."

He said, "You're the loveliest woman I've ever met. And the strongest. Are you ready? I think the man coming now is your husband."

It seemed strange to Ruben Vega that the man stood looking at him and not at his wife. The man seemed not too old for her, as he had expected, but too self-important. A man with a very serious demeanor, as though his business had failed or someone in his family had passed away. The man's wife was still clutching the hand with the gnarled fingers. Maybe that was it. Ruben Vega was going to lift her hand from his, but then thought, Why? He said as pleasantly as he was able, "Yes, can I help you?"

Mr. Isham said, "You have one minute to mount up and ride out of town."

"Why don't you sit down," Ruben Vega said, "have a glass of wine with us?" He paused and said, "I'll introduce you to your wife."

Sarah Isham laughed; not loud but with a warmth to it and Ruben Vega had to look at her and smile. It seemed all right to release her hand now. As he did he said, "Do you know this gentleman?"

"I'm not sure I've had the pleasure," Sarah Isham said. "Why does he stand there?"

"I don't know," Ruben Vega said. "He seems worried about something."

"I've warned you," Mr. Isham said. "You can walk out or be dragged out."

Ruben Vega said, "He has something about wanting to drag people.

Why is that?" And again heard Sarah's laugh, a giggle now that she covered with her hand. Then she looked up at her husband, her face with its blue tribal lines raised to the soft light of the dining room.

She said, "John, look at me. . . . Won't you please sit with us?"

Now it was as if the man had to make a moral decision, first consult his conscience, then consider the manner in which he would pull the chair out—the center of attention. When finally he was seated, upright on the chair and somewhat away from the table, Ruben Vega thought, All that to sit down. He felt sorry for the man now, because the man was not the kind who could say what he felt.

Sarah said, "John, can you look at me?"

He said, "Of course I can."

"Then do it. I'm right here."

"We'll talk later," her husband said.

She said, "When? Is there a visitor's day?"

"You'll be coming to the house, soon."

"You mean to see it?"

"To live there."

She looked at Ruben Vega with just the trace of a smile, a sad one. Then said to her husband, "I don't know if I want to. I don't know you. So I don't know if I want to be married to you. Can you understand that?"

Ruben Vega was nodding as she spoke. He could understand it. He heard the man say, "But we *are* married. I have an obligation to you and I respect it. Don't I provide for you?"

Sarah said, "Oh, my God—" and looked at Ruben Vega. "Did you hear that? He provides for me." She smiled again, not able to hide it, while her husband began to frown, confused.

"He's a generous man," Ruben Vega said, pushing up from the table. He saw her smile fade, though something warm remained in her eyes. "I'm sorry. I have to leave. I'm going on a trip tonight, south, and first I have to pick up a few things." He moved around the table to take one of her hands in his, not caring what the husband thought. He said, "You'll do all right, whatever you decide. Just keep in mind there's no one else in the world like you."

She said, "I can always charge admission. Do you think ten cents a look is too high?"

"At least that," Ruben Vega said. "But you'll think of something better."

He left her there in the dining room of the Charles Crooker Hotel in Benson, Arizona—maybe to see her again sometime, maybe not—and went out with a good conscience to take some of her husband's cattle.

30

"Hurrah for Captain Early!"

New Trails, New York, Doubleday, 1994
(*Western Writers of America Anthology*)

THE SECOND BANNER said HERO OF SAN JUAN HILL. Both were tied to the upstairs balcony of the Congress Hotel and looked down on La Salle Street in Sweetmary, a town named for a coppermine. The banners read across the building as a single statement. This day that Captain Early was expected home from the war in Cuba, over now these two months, was October 10, 1898.

The manager of the hotel and one of his desk clerks were the first to observe the colored man who entered the lobby and dropped his bedroll on the red velvet settee where it seemed he was about to sit down. Bold as brass. A tall, well-built colored man wearing a suit of clothes that looked new and appeared to fit him as though it might possibly be his own and not one handed down to him. He wore the suit, a stiff collar, and a necktie. With the manager nearby but not yet aware of the intruder, the young desk clerk spoke up, raised his voice to tell the person, "You can't sit down there."

The colored man turned his attention to the desk, taking a moment before he said, "Why is that?"

His quiet tone caused the desk clerk to hesitate and look over at the manager, who stood holding the day's mail, letters that had arrived on the El Paso & Southwestern morning run along with several guests now registered at the hotel and, apparently, this colored person. It was hard to tell his age, other than to say he was no longer a young man. He did seem clean and his bedroll was done up in bleached canvas.

"A hotel lobby," the desk clerk said, "is not a public place anyone can make theirself at home in. What is it you want here?"

At least he was uncovered, standing there now hat in hand. But then he said, "I'm waiting on Bren Early."

"*Bren* is it," the desk clerk said. "Captain Early's an acquaintance of yours?"

"We go way back a ways."

"You worked for him?"

"Some."

At this point the manager said, "We're all waiting for Captain Early. Why don't you go out front and watch for him?" Ending the conversation.

The desk clerk—his name was Monty—followed the colored man to the front entrance and stepped out on the porch to watch him, bedroll over his shoulder, walking south on La Salle the two short blocks to Fourth Street. Monty returned to the desk, where he said to the manager, "He walked right in the Gold Dollar."

The manager didn't look up from his mail.

TWO RIDERS FROM the Circle-Eye, a spread on the San Pedro that delivered beef to the mine company, were at a table with their glasses of beer: a rider named Macon and a rider named Wayman, young men who wore sweat-stained hats down on their eyes as they stared at the Negro. Right there, the bartender speaking to him as he poured a whiskey, still speaking as the colored man drank it and the bartender poured him another one. Macon asked Wayman if he had ever seen a nigger wearing a suit of clothes and a necktie. Wayman said he couldn't recall. When they finished drinking their beer and walked up to the bar, the colored man gone now, Macon asked the bartender who in the hell that smoke thought he was coming in here. "You would think," Macon said, "he'd go to one of the places where the miners drink."

The bartender appeared to smile, for some reason finding humor in Macon's remark. He said, "Boys, that was Bo Catlett. I imagine Bo drinks just about wherever he feels like drinking."

"Why?" Macon asked it, surprised. "He suppose to be somebody?"

"Bo lives up at White Tanks," the bartender told him, "at the Indin agency. Went to war and now he's home."

Macon squinted beneath the hat brim funneled low on his eyes. He said, "Nobody told me they was niggers in the war." Sounding as though it was the bartender's fault he hadn't been informed. When the bartender didn't add anything to help him out, Macon said, "Wayman's brother Wyatt was in the war, with Teddy Roosevelt's Rough Riders. Only, Wyatt didn't come home like the nigger."

Wayman, about eighteen years old, was nodding his head now.

Because nothing about this made sense to Macon, it was becoming an irritation. Again he said to Wayman, "You ever see a smoke wearing a suit of clothes like that?" He said, "Je-sus Christ."

BO CATLETT WALKED up La Salle Street favoring his left leg some, though the limp, caused by a Mauser bullet or by the regiment surgeon who cut it out of his hip, was barely noticeable. He stared at the sight of the mine works against the sky, ugly, but something monumental about it: straight ahead up the grade, the main shaft scaffolding and company buildings, the crushing mill lower down, ore tailings that humped this way in ridges on down the slope to run out at the edge of town. A sorry place, dark and forlorn; men walked up the grade from boardinghouses on Mill Street to spend half their life underneath the ground, buried before they were dead. Three whiskeys in him, Catlett returned to the hotel on the corner of Second Street, looked up at the sign that said HURRAH FOR CAPTAIN EARLY!, and had to grin. THE HERO OF SAN JUAN HILL my ass.

Catlett mounted the steps to the porch, where he dropped his bedroll and took one of the rocking chairs all in a row, the porch empty, close on noon but nobody sitting out here, no drummers calling on La Salle Mining of New Jersey, the company still digging and scraping but running low on payload copper, operating only the day shift now. The rocking chairs, all dark green, needed painting. Man, but made of cane and comfortable with that nice squeak back and forth, back and forth. . . . Bo Catlett watched two riders coming this way up the street, couple of cowboys . . . Catlett wondering how many times he had sat down in a real chair since April twenty-fifth when war was declared and he left Arizona to go looking for his old regiment, trailed them to Fort Assinniboine in the Department of the Dakotas, then clear across the country to Camp Chickamauga in Georgia and on down to Tampa where he caught up with them and Lt. John Pershing looked at his twenty-four years of service and put him up for squadron sergeant major. It didn't seem like any twenty-four years. . . .

Going back to when he joined the First Kansas Colored Volunteers in '63, age fifteen. Wounded at Honey Springs the same year. Guarded Rebel prisoners at Rock Island, took part in the occupation of Galveston. Then after the war got sent out here to join the all-Negro Tenth Cavalry on frontier station, Arizona Territory, and deal with hostile Apaches. In '87 went to Mexico with Lieutenant Brendan Early out of Fort Huachuca—Bren and a contract guide named Dana Moon, now the agent at the White Tanks reservation—brought back a one-eyed Mimbreño named Loco, brought back a white woman the renegade Apache had run off with—and Dana Moon later married—and they all got their pictures in some newspapers. Mustered out that same year, '87 . . . Drove a wagon for Capt. Early Hunting Expeditions Incorporated before going to work for Dana at White Tanks. He'd be sitting on Dana's porch this evening with a glass of mescal and Dana would say, "Well, now you've seen the elephant I don't imagine you'll want to stay around here." He'd tell Dana he saw the elephant a long time ago and wasn't too impressed. Just then another voice, not Dana's, said out loud to him:

"So you was in the war, huh?"

It was one of the cowboys. He sat his mount, a little claybank quarter horse, close to the porch rail, sat leaning on the pommel to show he was at ease, his hat low on his eyes, staring directly at Catlett in his rocking chair. The other one sat his mount, a bay, more out in the street, maybe holding back. This boy was not at ease but fidgety. Catlett remembered them in the Gold Dollar.

Now the one close said, "What was it you did over there in Cuba?"

Meaning a colored man. What did a colored man do. Like most people the boy not knowing anything about Negro soldiers in the war. This one squinting at him had size and maybe got his way enough he believed he could say whatever he pleased, or use a tone of voice that would irritate the person addressed. As he did just now.

"What did I do over there?" Catlett said. "What everybody did, I was in the war."

"You wrangle stock for the Rough Riders?"

"Where'd you get that idea?"

"I asked you a question. Is that what you did, tend their stock?"

Once Catlett decided to remain civil and maybe this boy would go away, he said, "There wasn't no stock. The Rough Riders, *even* the Rough Riders, were afoot. The only people had horses were artillery, pulling caissons with their Hotchkiss guns and the coffee grinders, what they called the Gatling guns. Lemme see," Catlett said, "they had some mules, too, but I didn't tend anybody's stock."

"His brother was a Rough Rider," Macon said, raising one hand to hook his thumb at Wayman. "Served with Colonel Teddy Roosevelt and got killed in an ambush—the only way greasers know how to fight. I like to hear what you people were doing while his brother Wyatt was getting killed."

You people. Look at him trying to start a fight.

"You believe it was my fault he got killed?"

"I asked you what you were doing."

It wasn't even this kid's business. Catlett thinking, Well, see if you can educate him, and said, "Las Guásimas. You ever hear of it?"

The kid stared with his eyes half shut. Suspicious, or letting you know he's serious, Catlett thought. Keen eyed and mean; you're not gonna put anything past him.

"What's it, a place over there?"

"That's right, Las Guásimas, the place where it happened. On the way to Santiago de Coo-ba. Sixteen men killed that day, mostly by rifle fire, and something like fifty wounded. Except it wasn't what you said, the dons pulling an ambush. It was more the Rough Riders walking along not looking where they was going."

The cowboy, Macon, said, "Je-sus Christ, you saying the Rough Riders didn't know what they were *do*ing?" Like this was something impossible to believe.

"They mighta had an idea *what* they was doing," Catlett said, "only thing it wasn't what they *shoulda* been doing." He said, "You understand the difference?" And thought, What're you explaining it to him for? The boy giving him that mean look again, ready to defend the Rough Riders. All right, he was so proud of Teddy's people, why hadn't he been over there with them?

"Look," Catlett said, using a quiet tone now, "the way it was, the dons had sharpshooters in these trees, a thicket of mangoes and palm trees growing wild you couldn't see into. You understand? Had men hidden in there were expert with the rifle, these Mausers they used with smokeless powder. Teddy's people come along a ridge was all covered with these trees and run into the dons, see, the dons letting some of the Rough Riders pass and then closing on 'em. So, yeah, it was an ambush in a way." Catlett paused. "We was down on the road, once we caught up, moving in the same direction." He paused again, remembering something the cowboy said that bothered him. "There's nothing wrong with an ambush—like say you think it ain't *fair*? If you can set it up and keep your people behind cover, do it. There was a captain with the Rough Riders said he believed an officer should never take cover, should stand out there and be an example to his men. The captain said, 'There ain't a Spanish bullet made that can kill me.' Stepped out in the open and got shot in the head."

A couple of cowboys looking like the two who were mounted had come out of the Chinaman's picking their teeth and now stood by to see what was going on. Some people who had come out of the hotel were standing along the steps.

Catlett took all this in as he paused again, getting the words straight in his mind to tell how they left the road, some companies of the Tenth and the First, all regular Army, went up the slope laying down fire and run off the dons before the Rough Riders got cut to pieces, the Rough Riders volunteers and not experienced in all kind of situations—the reason they didn't know shit about advancing through hostile country or, get right down to it, what they were doing in Cuba, these people that come looking for glory and got served sharpshooters with Mausers and mosquitoes carrying yellow fever. Tell these cowboys the true story. General Wheeler, "Fightin' Joe" from the Confederate side in the Civil

War now thirty-three years later an old man with a white beard; sees the Spanish pulling back at Las Guásimas and says, "Boys, we got the Yankees on the run." Man like that directing a battle. . . .

Tell the *whole* story if you gonna tell it, go back to sitting in the hold of the ship in Port Tampa a month, not allowed to go ashore for fear of causing incidents with white people who didn't want the men of the Tenth coming in their stores and cafés, running off their customers. Tell them—so we land in Cuba at a place called Daiquirí . . . saying in his mind then, Listen to me now. Was the Tenth at Daiquirí, the Ninth at Siboney. Experienced cavalry regiments that come off frontier station after thirty years dealing with hostile renegades, cutthroat horse thieves, reservation jumpers, land in Cuba and they put us to work unloading the ships while Teddy's people march off to meet the enemy and win some medals, yeah, and would've been wiped out at El Caney and on San Juan Hill if the colored boys hadn't come along and saved Colonel Teddy's ass and all his Rough Rider asses, showed them how to go up a hill and take a blockhouse. Saved them so the Rough Riders could become America's heroes.

All this in Bo Catlett's head and the banners welcoming Capt. Early hanging over him.

One of the cowboys from the Chinaman's must've asked what was going on, because now the smart-aleck one brought his claybank around and began talking to them, glancing back at the porch now and again with his mean look. The two from the Chinaman's stood with their thumbs in their belts, while the mounted cowboy had his hooked around his suspenders now. None of them wore a gun belt or appeared to be armed. Now the two riders stepped down from their mounts and followed the other two along the street to a place called the Belle Alliance, a miners' saloon, and went inside.

Bo Catlett was used to mean dirty looks and looks of indifference, a man staring at him as though he wasn't even there. Now, the thing with white people, they had a hard time believing colored men fought in the war. You never saw a colored man on a U.S. Army recruiting poster or a picture of colored soldiers in newspapers. White people believed colored people could not be relied on in war. But why? There were some colored people that went out and killed wild animals, even lions, with a spear. No gun, a spear. And made hats out of the manes. See a colored man standing there in front of a lion coming at him fast as a train running down grade, stands there with his spear, doesn't move, and they say colored men can't be relied on?

There was a story in newspapers how when Teddy Roosevelt was at the Hill, strutting around in the open, he saw colored troopers going back to the rear and he drew his revolver and threatened to shoot them—till he found out they were going after ammunition. His own Rough Riders were pinned down in the guinea grass, the Spanish sharpshooters picking at them from up in the blockhouses. So the Tenth showed the white boys how to go up the hill angry, firing and yelling, making noise, set on driving the garlics clean from the hill. . . .

Found Bren Early and his company lying in the weeds, the scrub— that's all it was up that hill, scrub and sand, hard to get a footing in places; nobody ran all the way up, it was get up a ways and stop to fire, covering each other. Found Bren Early with a whistle in his mouth. He got up and started blowing it and waving his sword—come on, boys, to glory—and a Mauser bullet smacked him in the butt, on account of the way he was turned to his people, and Bren Early grunted, dropped his sword, and went down in the scrub to lay there cursing his luck, no doubt mortified to look like he got shot going the wrong way. Bo Catlett didn't believe Bren saw him pick up the sword. Picked it up, waved it at the Rough Riders and his Tenth Cav troopers, and they all went up that hill together, his troopers yelling, some of them singing, actually singing "They'll Be a Hot Time in the Old Town Tonight." Singing and shooting, honest to God, scaring the dons right out of their blockhouse. It was up on the crest Catlett got shot in his right hip and was taken to the Third Cav dressing station. It was set up on the Aguadores River at a place called "bloody ford," being it was under fire till the Hill was captured. Catlett remembered holding on to the sword, tight, while the regimental surgeon dug the bullet out of him and he tried hard not to scream, biting his mouth till it bled. After, he was sent home and spent a month at Camp Wikoff, near Montauk out on Long Island, with a touch of yellow fever. Saw President McKinley when he came by September third and made a speech, the President saying what they did over there in Cuba "commanded the unstinted praise of all your countrymen." Till he walked away from Montauk and came back into the world, Sergeant Major Catlett actually did believe he and the other members of the Tenth would be recognized as war heroes.

He wished Bren would hurry up and get here. He'd ask the hero of San Juan Hill how his heinie was and if he was getting much unstinted praise. If Bren didn't come pretty soon, Catlett decided he'd see him another time. Get a horse out of the livery and ride it up to White Tanks.

THE FOUR CIRCLE-EYE riders sat at a front table in the Belle Alliance with a bottle of Green River whiskey, Macon staring out the window. The hotel was across the street and up the block a ways, but Macon could see it, the colored man in the suit of clothes still sitting on the porch, if he tilted his chair back and held on to the windowsill. He said, "No, sir, nobody told me they was niggers in the war."

Wayman said to the other two Circle-Eye riders, "Macon can't get over it."

Macon's gaze came away from the window. "It was *your* brother got killed."

Wayman said, "I know he did."

Macon said, "You don't care?"

The Circle-Eye riders watched him let his chair come down to hit the floor hard. They watched him get up without another word and walk out.

"I never thought much of coloreds," one of the Circle-Eye riders said, "but you never hear me take on about 'em like Macon. What's his trouble?"

"I guess he wants to shoot somebody," Wayman said. "The time he shot that chili picker in Nogales? Macon worked hisself up to it the same way."

CATLETT WATCHED the one that was looking for a fight come through the doors and go to the claybank, the reins looped once around the tie rail. He didn't touch the reins, though. What he did was reach into a saddlebag and bring out what Catlett judged to be a Colt .44 pistol. Right then he heard:

"Only guests of the hotel are allowed to sit out here."

Catlett watched the cowboy checking his loads now, turning the cylinder of his six-shooter, the metal catching a glint of light from the sun, though the look of the pistol was dull and it appeared to be an old model.

Monty the desk clerk, standing there looking at Catlett without getting too close, said, "You'll have to leave . . . right now."

The cowboy was looking this way.

Making up his mind, Catlett believed. All right, now, yeah, he's made it up.

"Did you hear what I said?"

Catlett took time to look at Monty and then pointed off down the street. He said, "You see that young fella coming this way with the pistol? He think he like to shoot me. Say you don't allow people to sit here aren't staying at the ho-tel. How about, you allow them to get shot if they not a guest?"

He watched the desk clerk, who didn't seem to know whether to shit or go blind, eyes wide open, turn and run back in the lobby.

The cowboy, Macon, stood in the middle of the street now holding the six-shooter against his leg.

★　★　★

CATLETT, STILL seated in the rocker, said, "You a mean rascal, ain't you? Don't take no sass, huh?"

The cowboy said something agreeing that Catlett didn't catch, the cowboy looking over to see his friends coming up the street now from the barroom. When he looked at the hotel porch again, Catlett was standing at the railing, his bedroll upright next to him leaning against it.

"I can be a mean rascal too," Catlett said, unbuttoning his suit coat. "I want you to know that before you take this too far. You understand?"

"You insulted Colonel Roosevelt and his Rough Riders," the cowboy said, "and you insulted Wayman's brother, killed in action over there in Cuba."

"How come," Catlett said, "you weren't there?"

"I was ready, don't worry, when the war ended. But we're talking about *you.* I say you're a dirty lying nigger and have no respect for people better'n you are. I want you to apologize to the colonel and his men and to Wayman's dead brother. . . ."

"Or what?" Catlett said.

"Answer to me," the cowboy said. "Are you armed? You aren't, you better get yourself a pistol."

"You want to shoot me," Catlett said, " 'cause I went to Cuba and you didn't."

The cowboy was shaking his head. " 'Cause you lied. Have you got a pistol or not?"

Catlett said, "You calling me out, huh? You want us to fight a duel?"

"Less you apologize. Else get a pistol."

"But if I'm the one being called out, I have my choice of weapons, don't I? That's how I seen it work, twenty-four years in the U.S. Army in two wars. You hear what I'm saying?"

The cowboy was frowning now beneath his hat brim, squinting up at Bo Catlett. He said, "Pistols, it's what you use."

Catlett nodded. "If I say so."

"Well, what else is there?"

Confused and getting a mean look.

Catlett slipped his hand into the upright end of his bedroll and began to tug at something inside—the cowboy watching, the Circle-Eye riders in the street watching, the desk clerk and manager in the doorway and several hotel guests near them who had come out to the porch, all watching as Catlett drew a sword from the bedroll, a cavalry saber, the curved blade flashing as it caught the sunlight. He came past the people watching and down off the porch toward the cowboy in his hat and boots fixed with spurs that chinged as he turned to face Catlett, shorter than Catlett, appearing confused again holding the six-shooter at his side.

"If I choose to use sabers," Catlett said, "is that agreeable with you?"

"I don't have no *saber.*"

Meanness showing now in his eyes.

"Well, you best get one."

"I never even had a sword in my hand."

Irritated. Drunk, too, his eyes not focusing as they should. Now he was looking over his shoulder at the Circle-Eye riders, maybe wanting them to tell him what to do.

One of them, not Wayman but one of the others, called out, "You got your .44 in your hand, ain't you? What're you waiting on?"

Catlett raised the saber to lay the tip against Macon's breastbone, saying to him, "You use your pistol and I use steel? All right, if that's how you want it. See if you can shoot me 'fore this blade is sticking out your back. You game? . . . Speak up, boy."

★ ★ ★

IN THE HOTEL dining room having a cup of coffee, Catlett heard the noise outside, the cheering that meant Capt. Early had arrived. Catlett waited. He wished one of the waitresses would refill his cup, but they weren't around now, nobody was. A half hour passed before Capt. Early entered the dining room and came over to the table, leaving the people he was with. Catlett rose and they embraced, the hotel people and guests watching. It was while they stood this way that Bren saw, over Catlett's shoulder, the saber lying on the table, the curved steel on white linen. Catlett sat down. Bren looked closely at the saber's hilt. He picked it up and there was applause from the people watching. The captain bowed to them and sat down with the sergeant major.

"You went up the hill with this?"

"Somebody had to."

"I'm being recommended for a medal. 'For courage and pluck in continuing to advance under fire on the Spanish fortified position at the battle of Las Guásimas, Cuba, June twenty-fourth, 1898.'"

Catlett nodded. After a moment he said, "Will you tell me something? What was that war about?"

"You mean why'd we fight the dons?"

"Yeah, tell me."

"To free the oppressed Cuban people. Relieve them of Spanish domination."

"That's what I thought."

"You didn't know why you went to war?"

"I guess I knew," Catlett said. "I just wasn't sure."